JAMES PATTERSON
& EMILY RAYMOND
ILLUSTRATED BY VALERIA WICKER

JIMMY Patterson Books
Little, Brown and Company
New York Boston

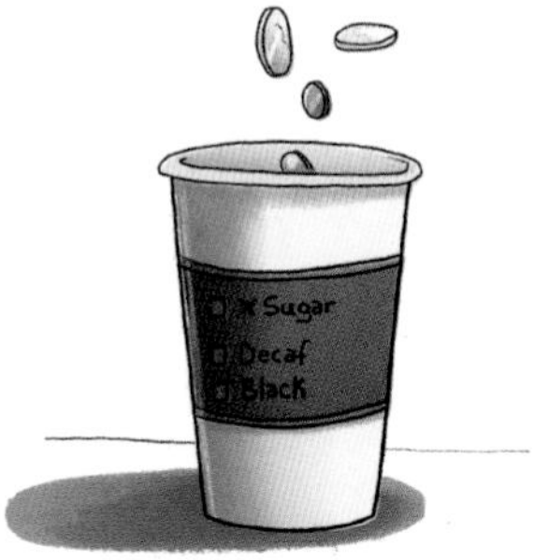
Sugar
Decaf
Black

Illustrations by Valeria Wicker
Colorist: Caitlin Quirk

Cover art by Valeria Wicker. Title lettering by Cassie Gonzales. Cover design by Tracy Shaw.

JIMMY Patterson Books / Little, Brown and Company
Hachette Book Group
1290 Avenue of the Americas, New York, NY 10104
JimmyPatterson.org

First Edition: April 2022

JIMMY Patterson Books is an imprint of Little, Brown and Company, a division of Hachette Book Group, Inc. The Little, Brown name and logo are trademarks of Hachette Book Group, Inc. The JIMMY Patterson Books® name and logo are trademarks of JBP Business, LLC.
The publisher is not responsible for websites (or their content) that are not owned by the publisher.

Library of Congress Cataloging-in-Publication Data
Names: Patterson, James, 1947- author. | Raymond, Emily, author. |
Wicker, Valeria, illustrator.
Title: The runaway's diary / James Patterson & Emily Raymond;
illustrated by Valeria Wicker.
Description: First edition. | New York : JIMMY Patterson Books/Little, Brown and Company, 2022. | Summary: After Eleanor's older sister, Sam, runs away to Seattle, Eleanor goes on adventure looking for her.
Identifiers: LCCN 2021043320 | ISBN 9780316500234 (trade paperback) | ISBN 9780316395427 |
ISBN 9780316500685 (ebook)
Subjects: CYAC: Graphic novels—Fiction. | Sisters—Fiction. | Runaways—Fiction. | Storytelling—Fiction.
| LCGFT: Graphic novels.
Classification: LCC PZ7.7.P279 Run 2022 | DDC [E]—dc23
LC record available at https://lccn.loc.gov/2021043320

ISBNs: 978-0-316-50023-4 (pbk.), 978-0-316-39542-7 (paper over board), 978-0-316-50068-5 (ebook), 978-0-316-39986-9 (ebook), 978-0-316-39997-5 (ebook)
Printed in China
APS

Hardcover: 10 9 8 7 6 5 4 3 2 1
Paperback: 10 9 8 7 6 5 4 3 2 1

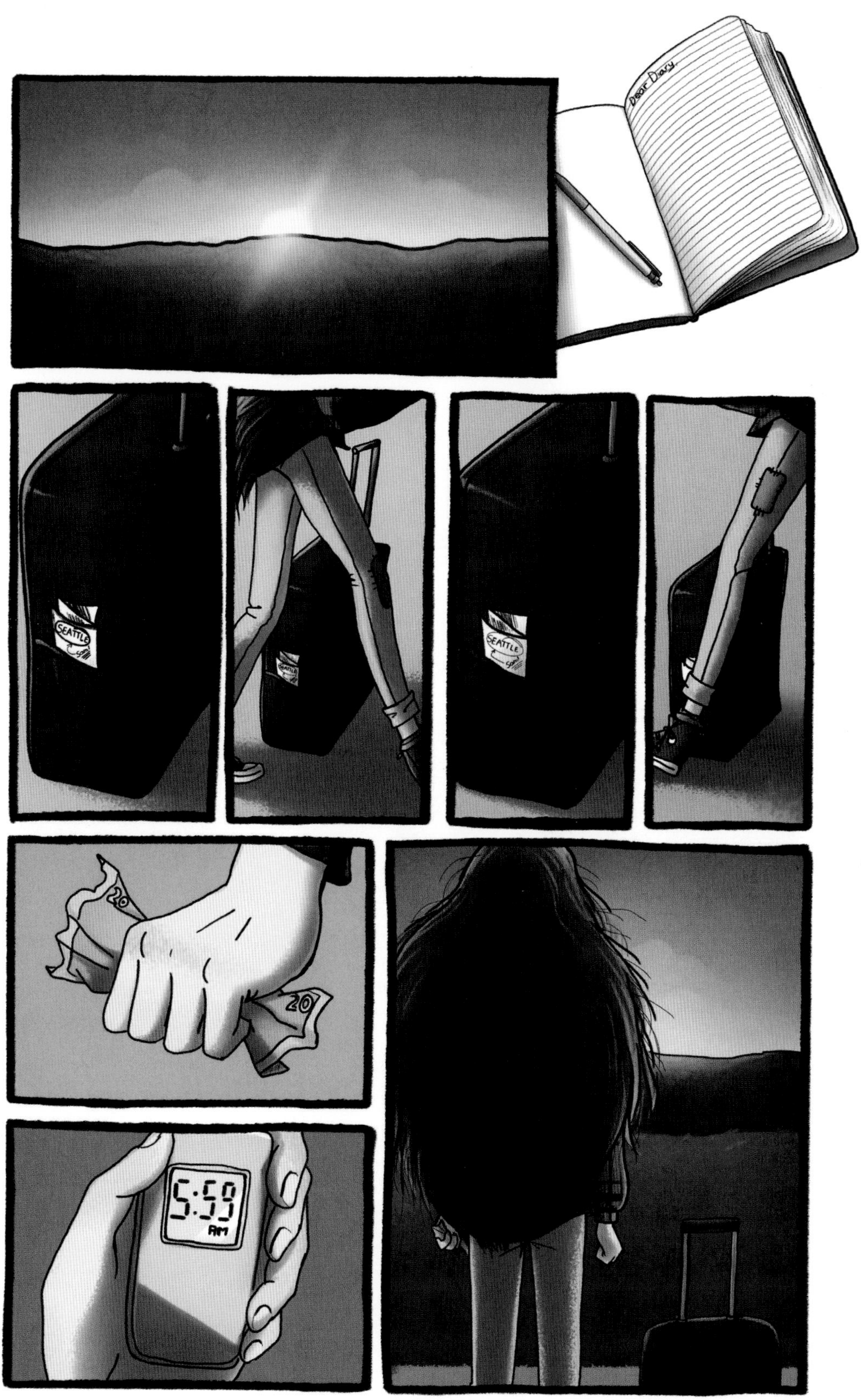
Dear Diary
SEATTLE
SEATTLE
20
20
5:59
AM

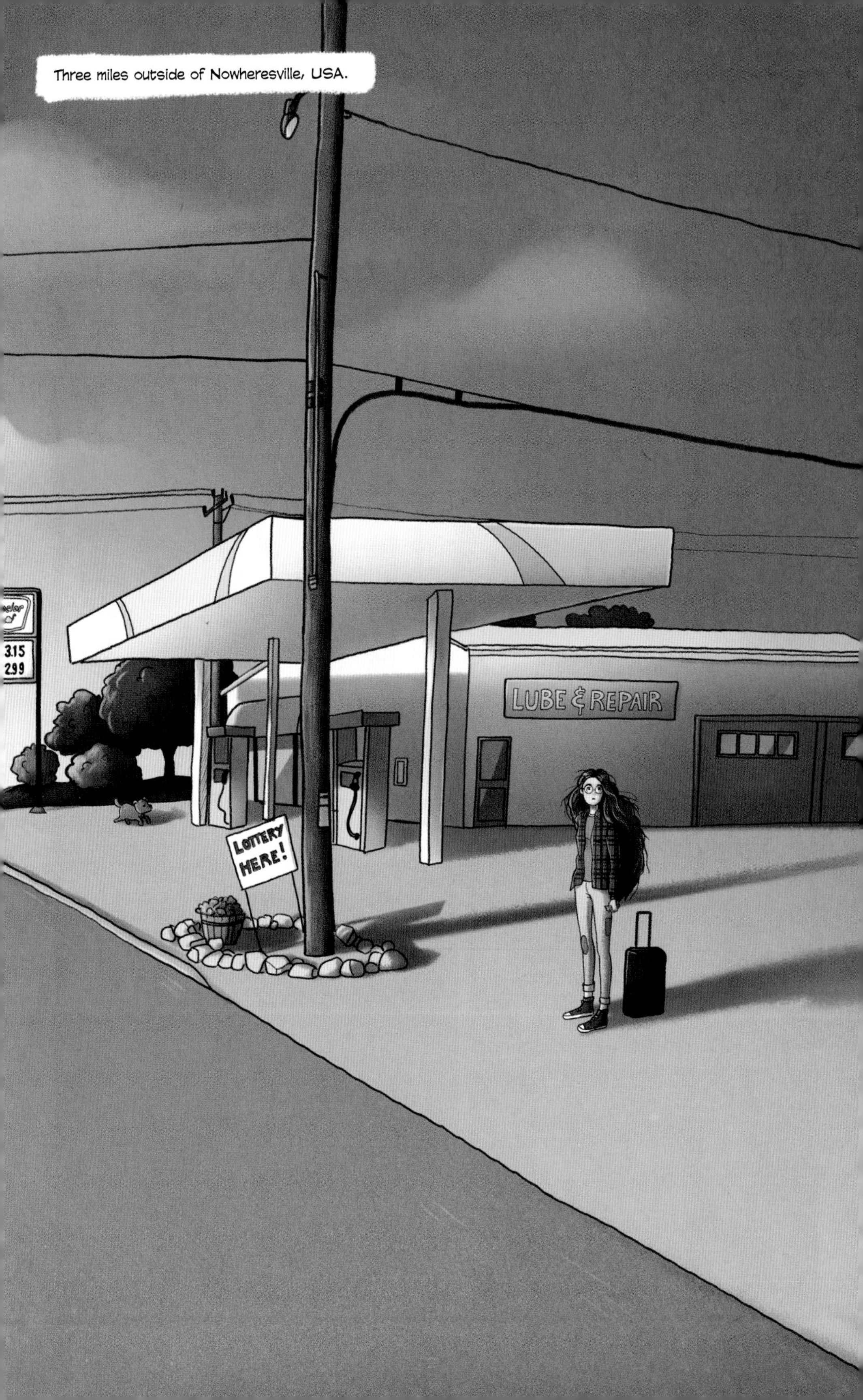
Three miles outside of Nowheresville, USA.
3.15
2.99
LUBE & REPAIR
LOTTERY HERE!

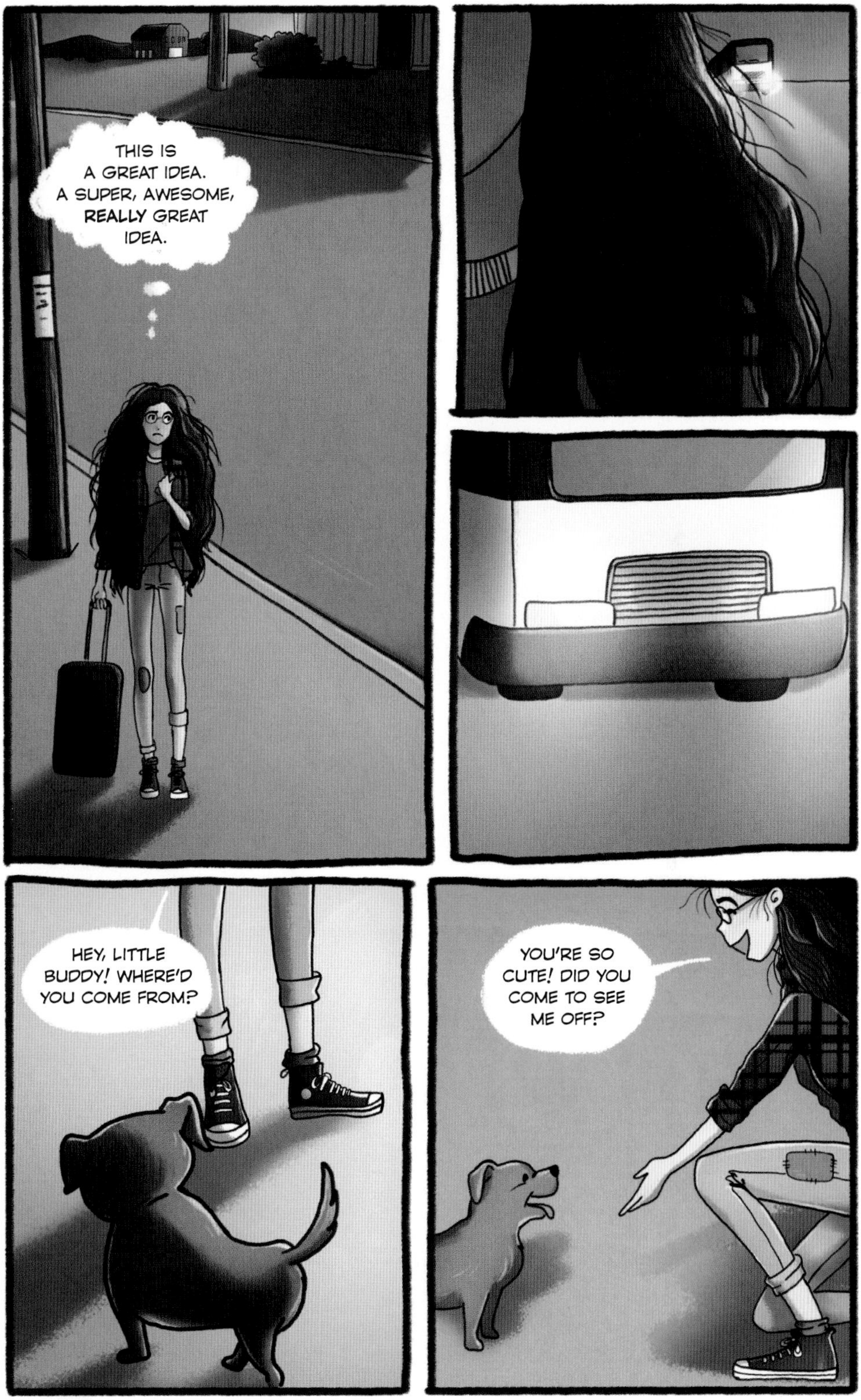
THIS IS A GREAT IDEA. A SUPER, AWESOME, **REALLY** GREAT IDEA.
HEY, LITTLE BUDDY! WHERE'D YOU COME FROM?
YOU'RE SO CUTE! DID YOU COME TO SEE ME OFF?

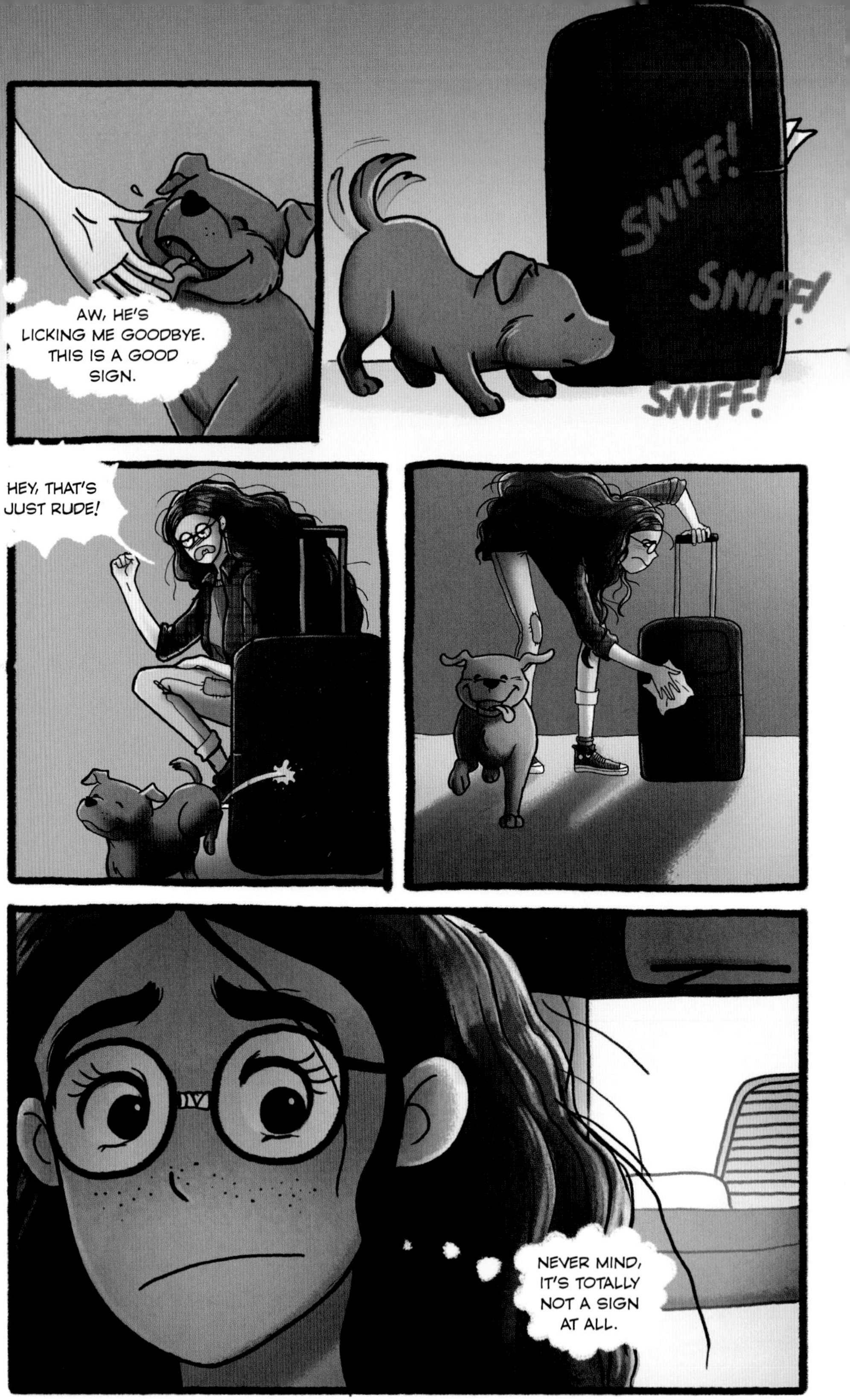
AW, HE'S LICKING ME GOODBYE. THIS IS A GOOD SIGN.
SNIFF!
SNIFF!
SNIFF!
HEY, THAT'S JUST RUDE!
NEVER MIND, IT'S TOTALLY NOT A SIGN AT ALL.

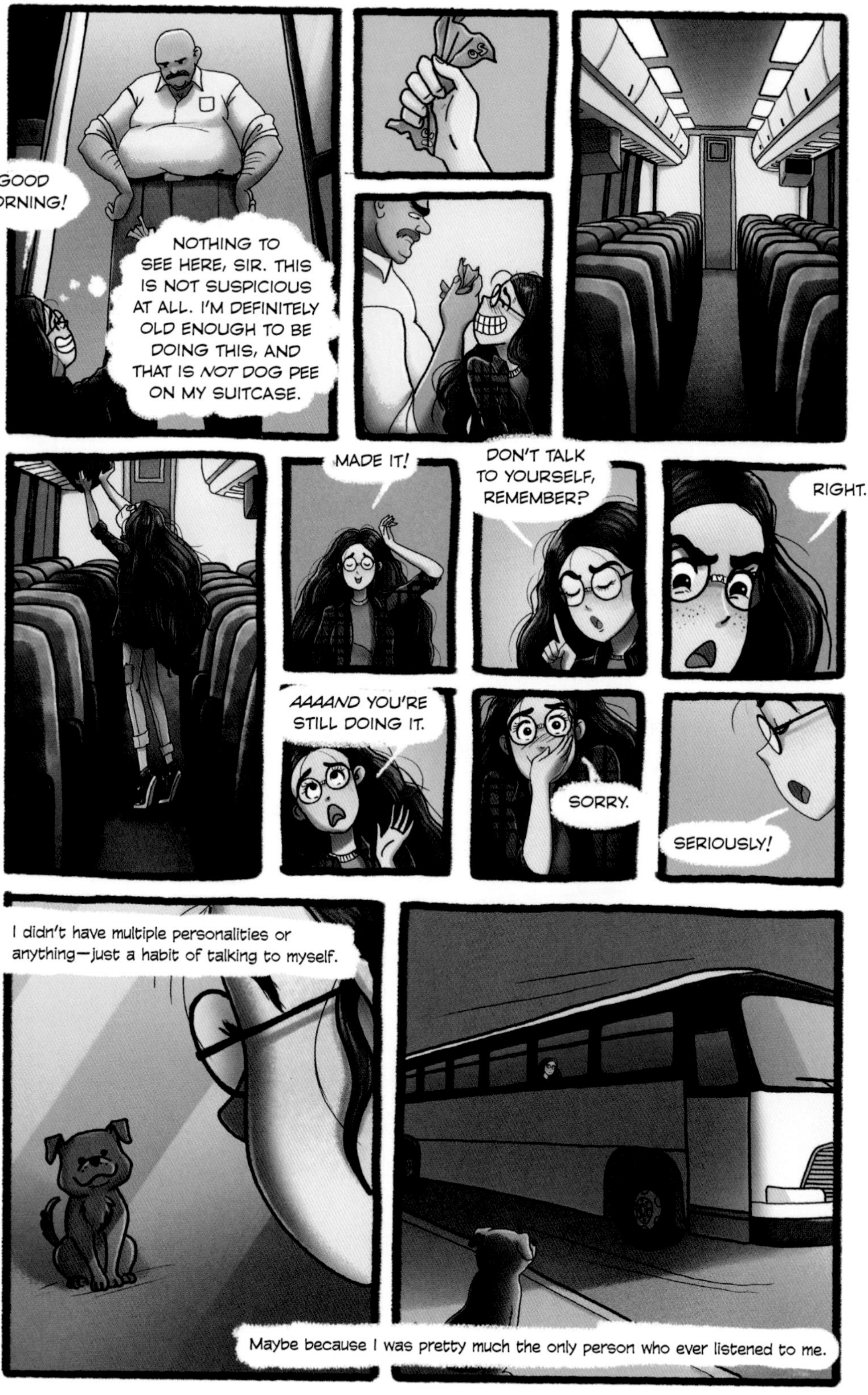
GOOD MORNING!
NOTHING TO SEE HERE, SIR. THIS IS NOT SUSPICIOUS AT ALL. I'M DEFINITELY OLD ENOUGH TO BE DOING THIS, AND THAT IS *NOT* DOG PEE ON MY SUITCASE.
MADE IT!
DON'T TALK TO YOURSELF, REMEMBER?
RIGHT.
AAAAND YOU'RE STILL DOING IT.
SORRY.
SERIOUSLY!
I didn't have multiple personalities or anything—just a habit of talking to myself.
Maybe because I was pretty much the only person who ever listened to me.

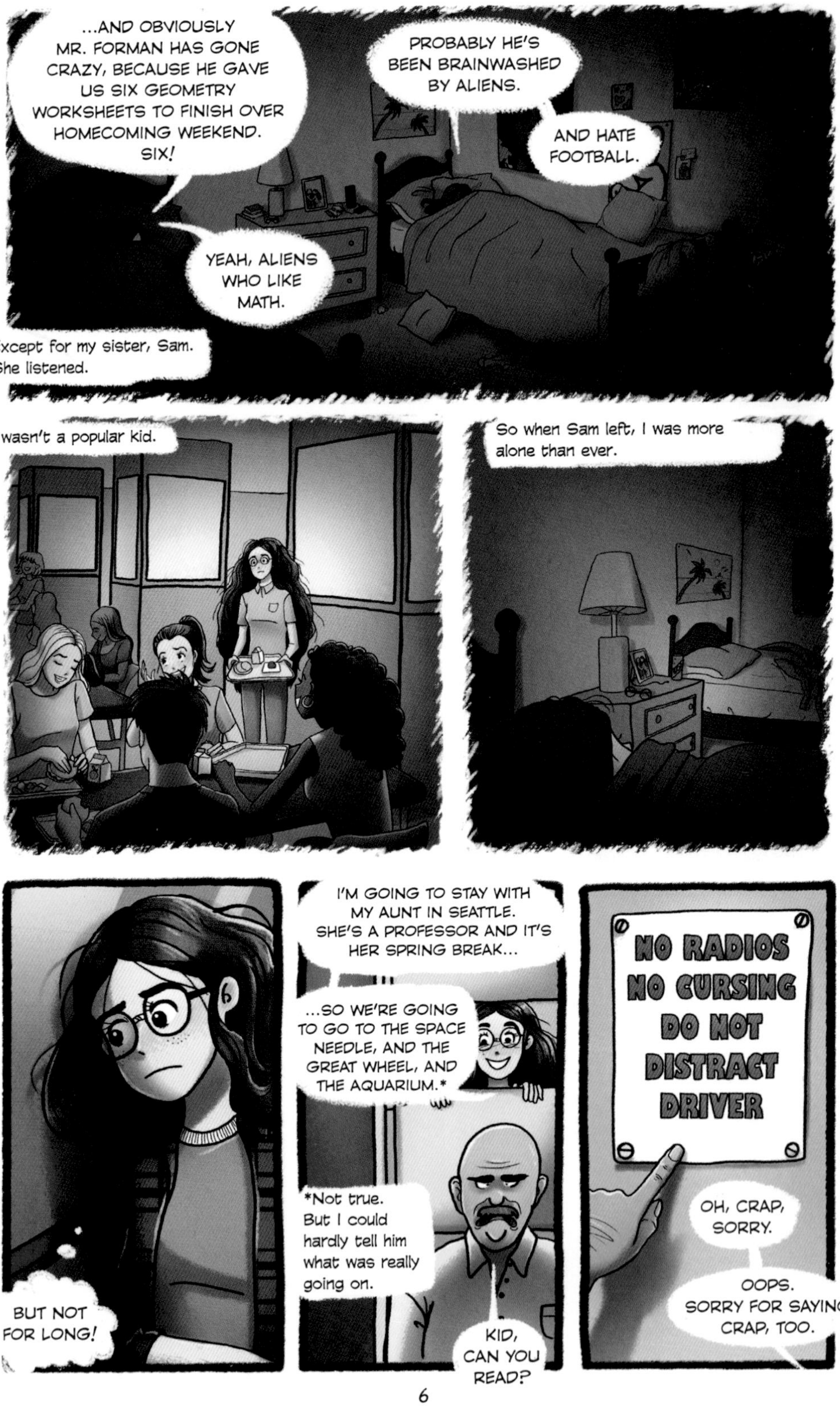
...AND OBVIOUSLY MR. FORMAN HAS GONE CRAZY, BECAUSE HE GAVE US SIX GEOMETRY WORKSHEETS TO FINISH OVER HOMECOMING WEEKEND. SIX!
PROBABLY HE'S BEEN BRAINWASHED BY ALIENS.
AND HATE FOOTBALL.
YEAH, ALIENS WHO LIKE MATH.
Except for my sister, Sam. She listened.
I wasn't a popular kid.
So when Sam left, I was more alone than ever.
BUT NOT FOR LONG!
I'M GOING TO STAY WITH MY AUNT IN SEATTLE. SHE'S A PROFESSOR AND IT'S HER SPRING BREAK...
...SO WE'RE GOING TO GO TO THE SPACE NEEDLE, AND THE GREAT WHEEL, AND THE AQUARIUM.*
*Not true. But I could hardly tell him what was really going on.
KID, CAN YOU READ?
NO RADIOS
NO CURSING
DO NOT DISTRACT DRIVER
OH, CRAP, SORRY.
OOPS. SORRY FOR SAYING CRAP, TOO.

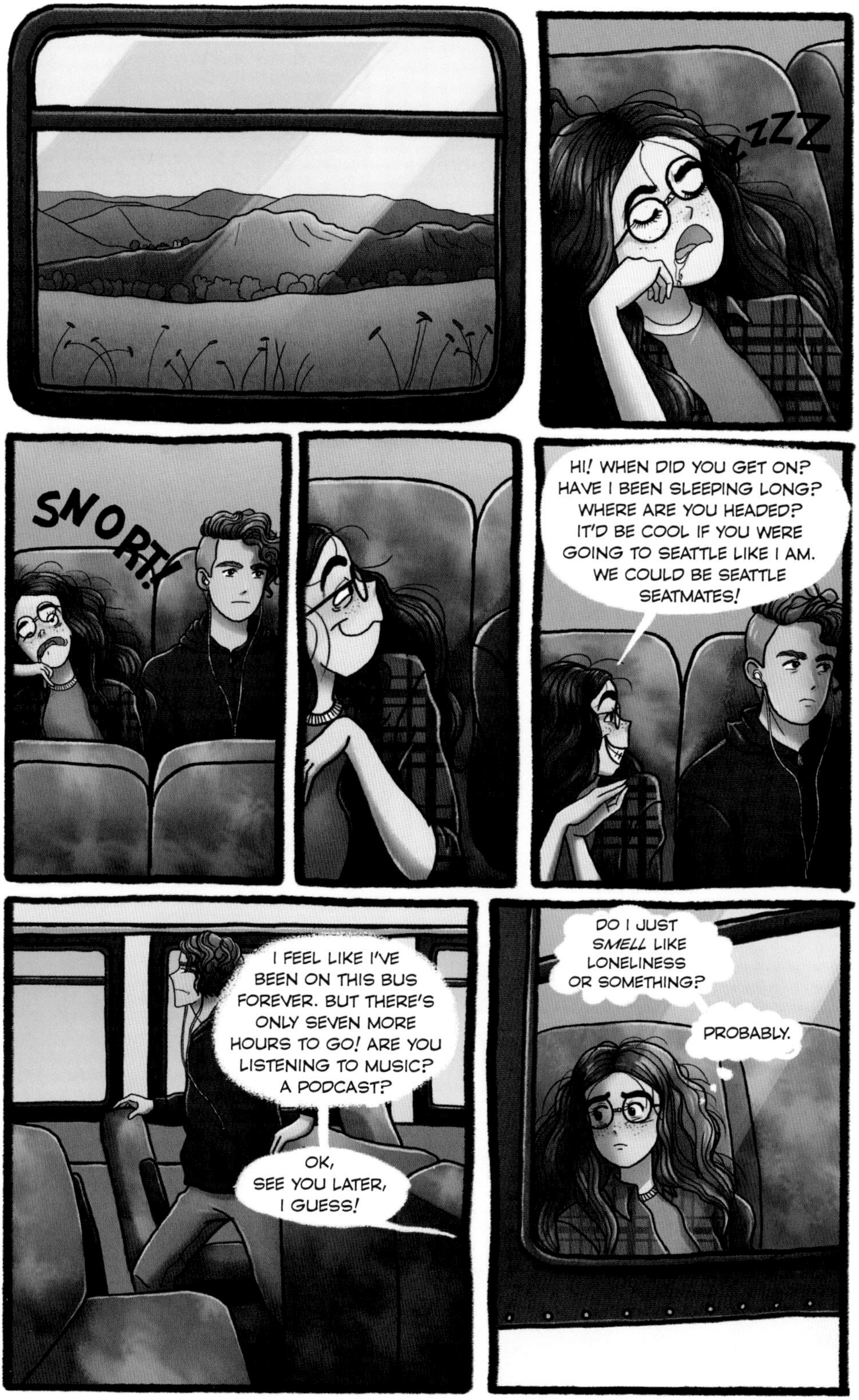
ZZZZ
SNORT!
HI! WHEN DID YOU GET ON? HAVE I BEEN SLEEPING LONG? WHERE ARE YOU HEADED? IT'D BE COOL IF YOU WERE GOING TO SEATTLE LIKE I AM. WE COULD BE SEATTLE SEATMATES!
I FEEL LIKE I'VE BEEN ON THIS BUS FOREVER. BUT THERE'S ONLY SEVEN MORE HOURS TO GO! ARE YOU LISTENING TO MUSIC? A PODCAST?
OK, SEE YOU LATER, I GUESS!
DO I JUST SMELL LIKE LONELINESS OR SOMETHING?
PROBABLY.

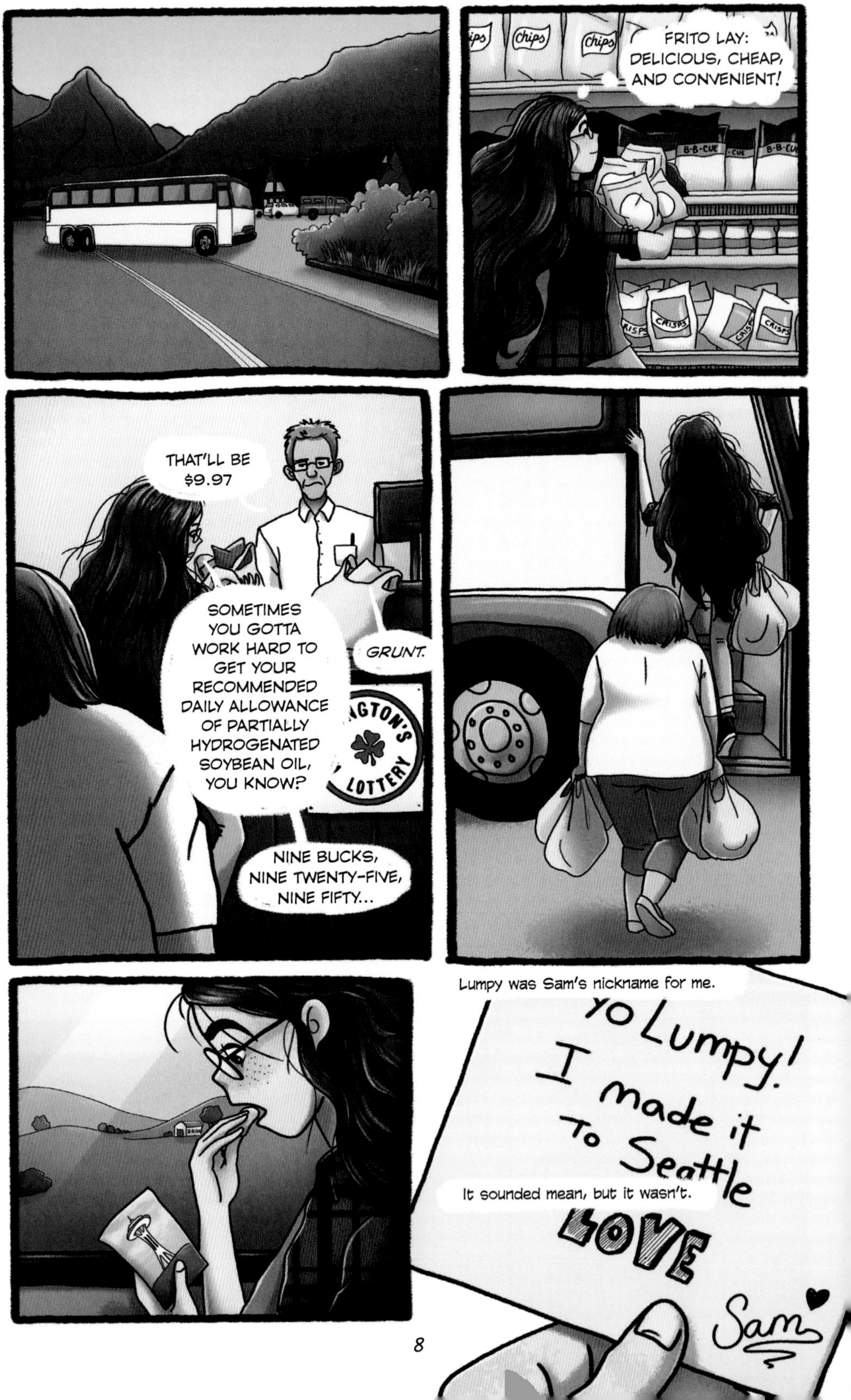
Chips
FRITO LAY: DELICIOUS, CHEAP, AND CONVENIENT!
B-B-CUE
CRISPS
THAT'LL BE $9.97
SOMETIMES YOU GOTTA WORK HARD TO GET YOUR RECOMMENDED DAILY ALLOWANCE OF PARTIALLY HYDROGENATED SOYBEAN OIL, YOU KNOW?
GRUNT.
LOTTERY
NINE BUCKS, NINE TWENTY-FIVE, NINE FIFTY...
Lumpy was Sam's nickname for me.
Yo Lumpy! I made it To Seattle
It sounded mean, but it wasn't.
LOVE
Sam

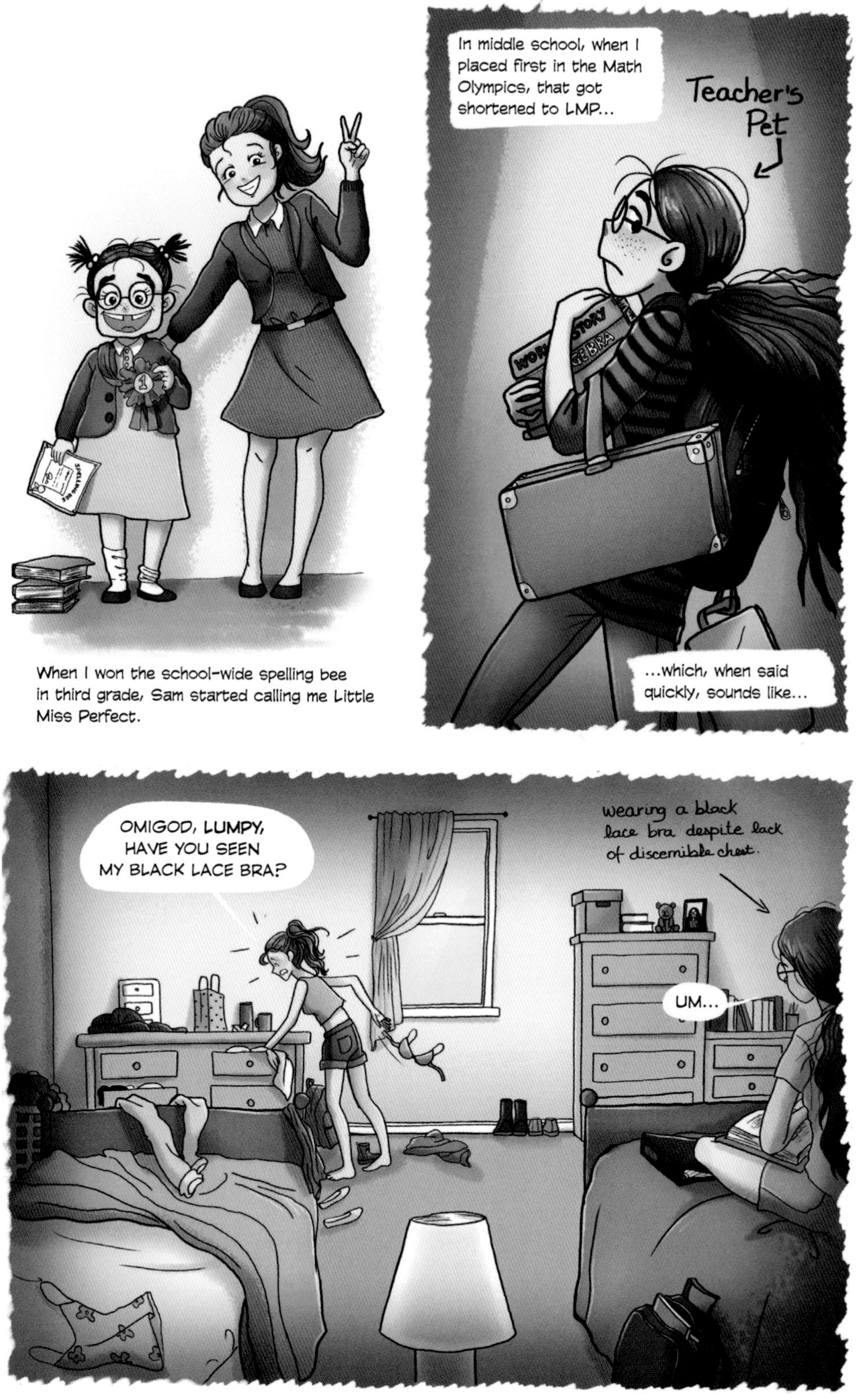
When I won the school-wide spelling bee in third grade, Sam started calling me Little Miss Perfect.
SPELLING BEE
In middle school, when I placed first in the Math Olympics, that got shortened to LMP...
Teacher's Pet
...which, when said quickly, sounds like...
OMIGOD, LUMPY, HAVE YOU SEEN MY BLACK LACE BRA?
wearing a black lace bra despite lack of discernible chest.
UM...

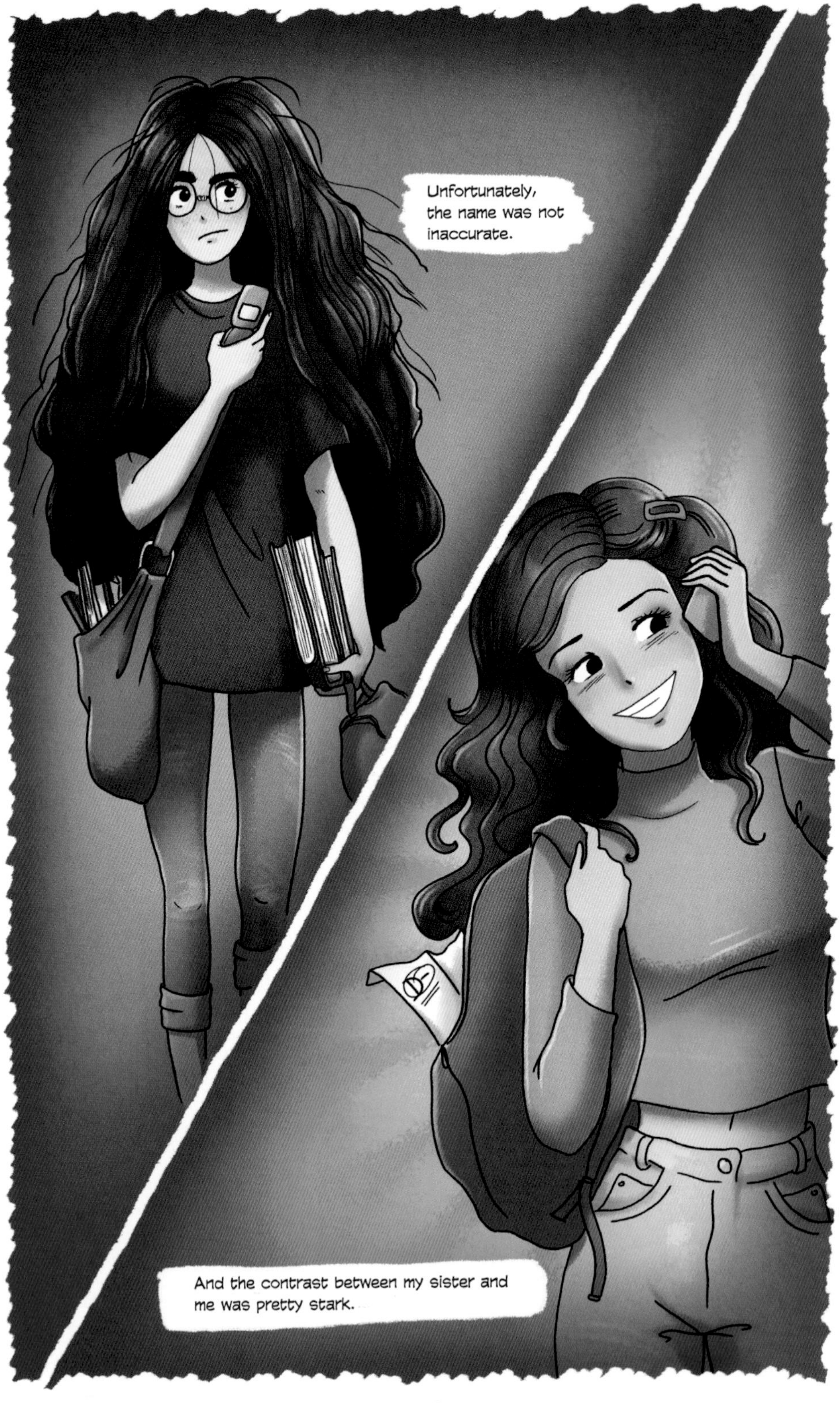
Unfortunately, the name was not inaccurate.
And the contrast between my sister and me was pretty stark.

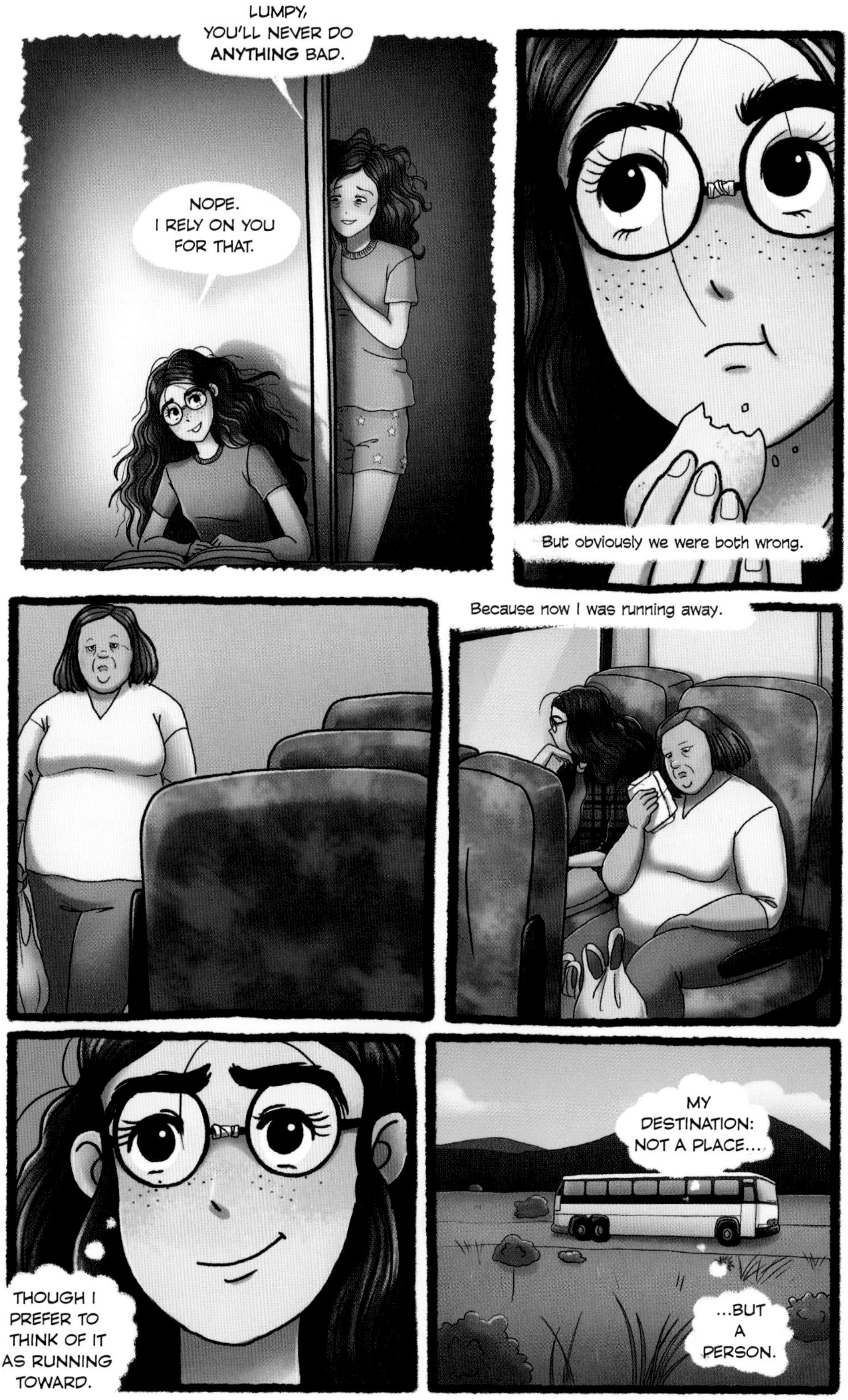
LUMPY, YOU'LL NEVER DO ANYTHING BAD.
NOPE. I RELY ON YOU FOR THAT.
But obviously we were both wrong.
Because now I was running away.
THOUGH I PREFER TO THINK OF IT AS RUNNING TOWARD.
MY DESTINATION: NOT A PLACE...
...BUT A PERSON.

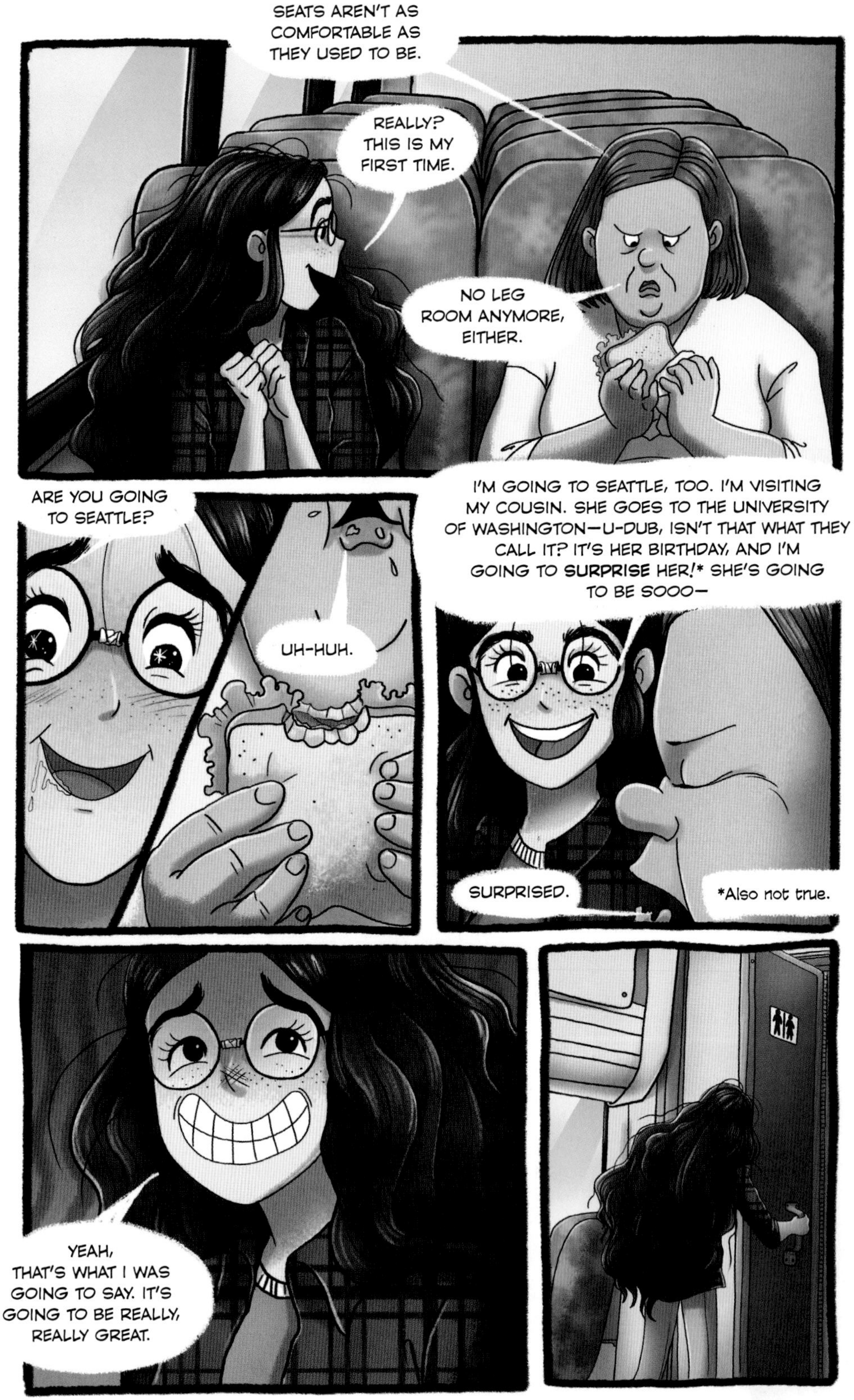
SEATS AREN'T AS COMFORTABLE AS THEY USED TO BE.
REALLY? THIS IS MY FIRST TIME.
NO LEG ROOM ANYMORE, EITHER.
ARE YOU GOING TO SEATTLE?
UH-HUH.
I'M GOING TO SEATTLE, TOO. I'M VISITING MY COUSIN. SHE GOES TO THE UNIVERSITY OF WASHINGTON—U-DUB, ISN'T THAT WHAT THEY CALL IT? IT'S HER BIRTHDAY, AND I'M GOING TO SURPRISE HER!* SHE'S GOING TO BE SOOO—
SURPRISED.
*Also not true.
YEAH, THAT'S WHAT I WAS GOING TO SAY. IT'S GOING TO BE REALLY, REALLY GREAT.

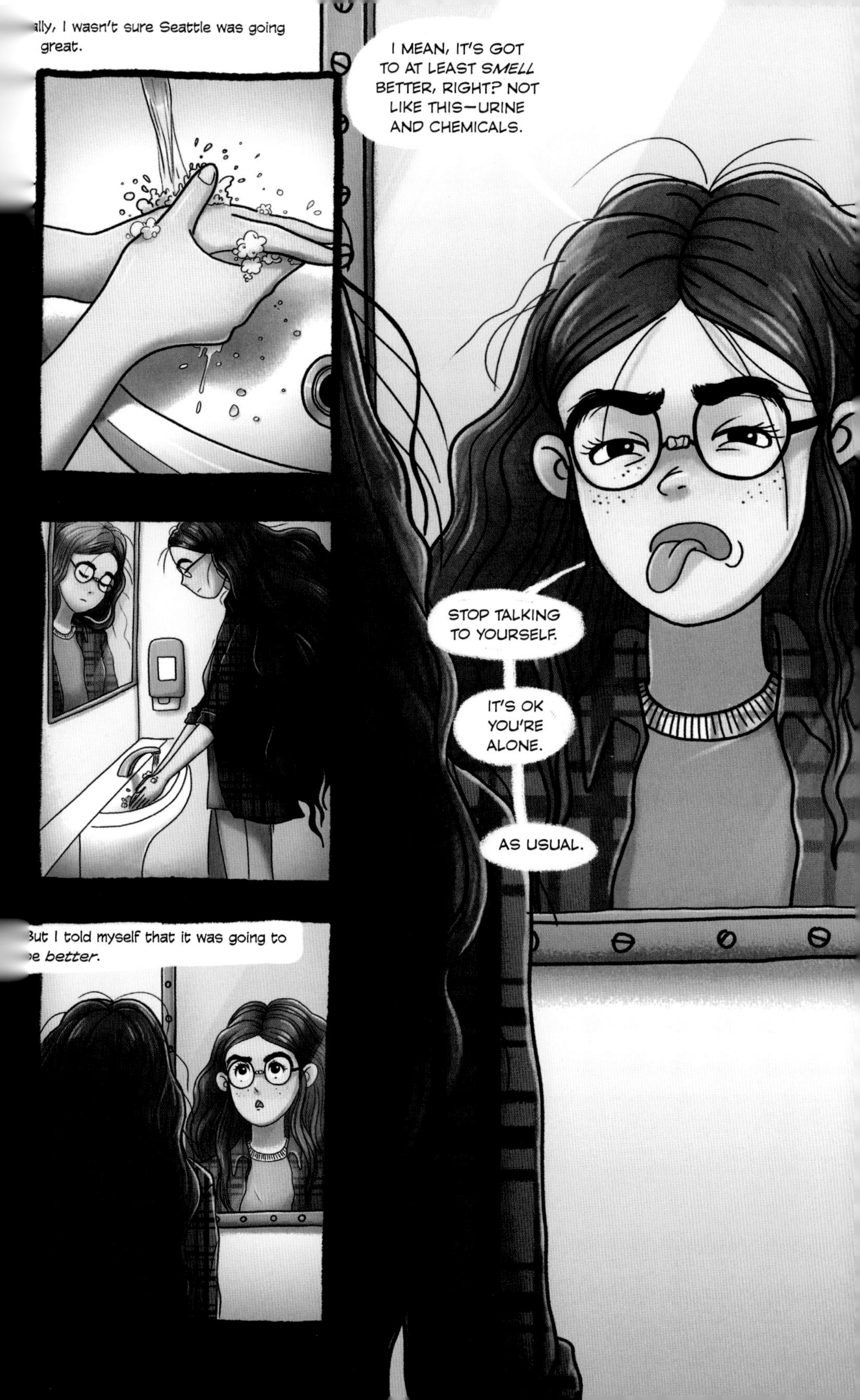
ally, I wasn't sure Seattle was going
great.
ut I told myself that it was going to
e better.
I MEAN, IT'S GOT TO AT LEAST SMELL BETTER, RIGHT? NOT LIKE THIS—URINE AND CHEMICALS.
STOP TALKING TO YOURSELF.
IT'S OK YOU'RE ALONE.
AS USUAL.

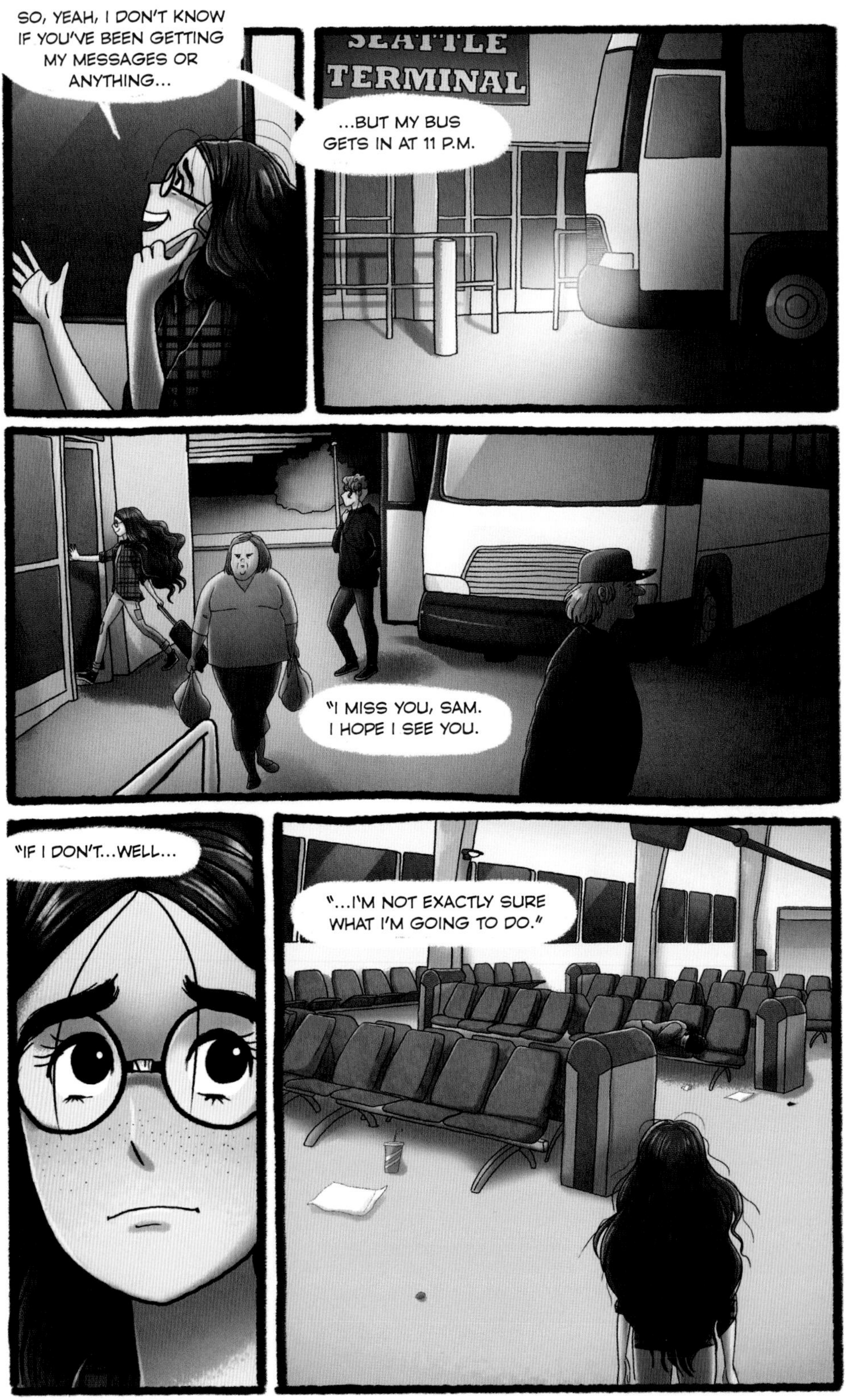
SO, YEAH, I DON'T KNOW IF YOU'VE BEEN GETTING MY MESSAGES OR ANYTHING...
SEATTLE TERMINAL
...BUT MY BUS GETS IN AT 11 P.M.
"I MISS YOU, SAM. I HOPE I SEE YOU.
"IF I DON'T...WELL...
"...I'M NOT EXACTLY SURE WHAT I'M GOING TO DO."

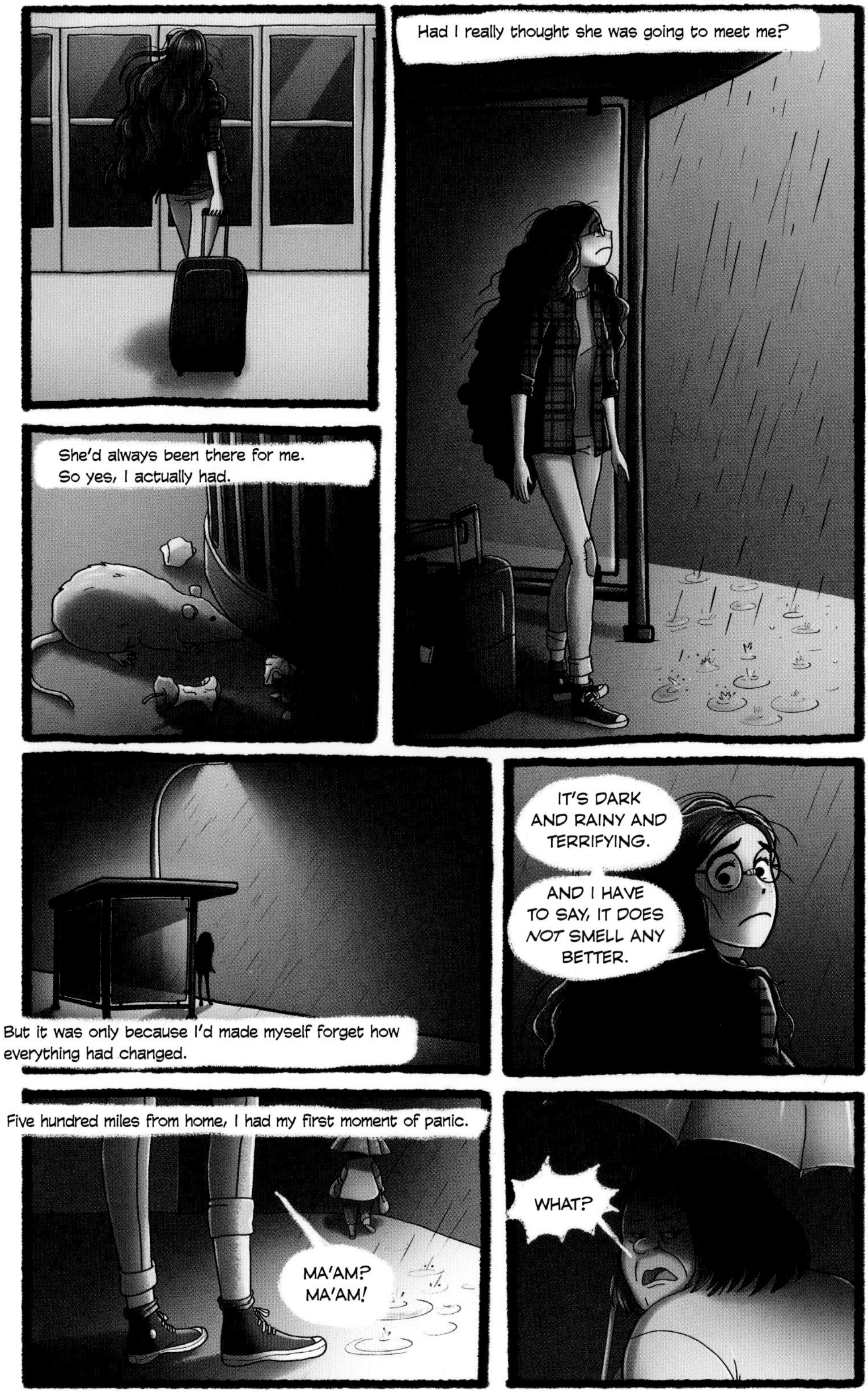
Had I really thought she was going to meet me?
She'd always been there for me.
So yes, I actually had.
But it was only because I'd made myself forget how everything had changed.
IT'S DARK AND RAINY AND TERRIFYING.
AND I HAVE TO SAY, IT DOES *NOT* SMELL ANY BETTER.
Five hundred miles from home, I had my first moment of panic.
MA'AM? MA'AM!
WHAT?

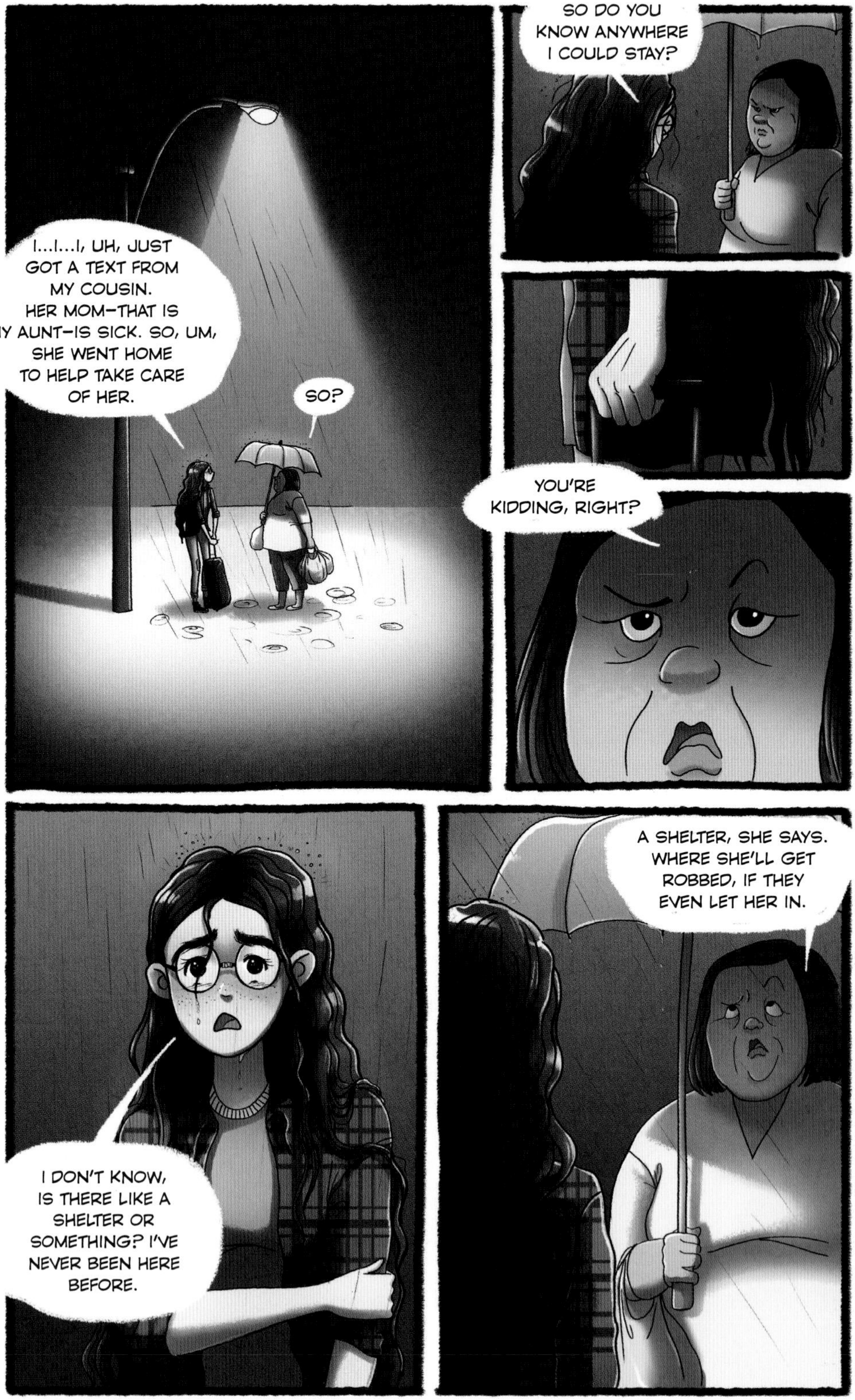
I...I...I, UH, JUST GOT A TEXT FROM MY COUSIN. HER MOM—THAT IS MY AUNT—IS SICK. SO, UM, SHE WENT HOME TO HELP TAKE CARE OF HER.
SO?
SO DO YOU KNOW ANYWHERE I COULD STAY?
YOU'RE KIDDING, RIGHT?
I DON'T KNOW, IS THERE LIKE A SHELTER OR SOMETHING? I'VE NEVER BEEN HERE BEFORE.
A SHELTER, SHE SAYS. WHERE SHE'LL GET ROBBED, IF THEY EVEN LET HER IN.

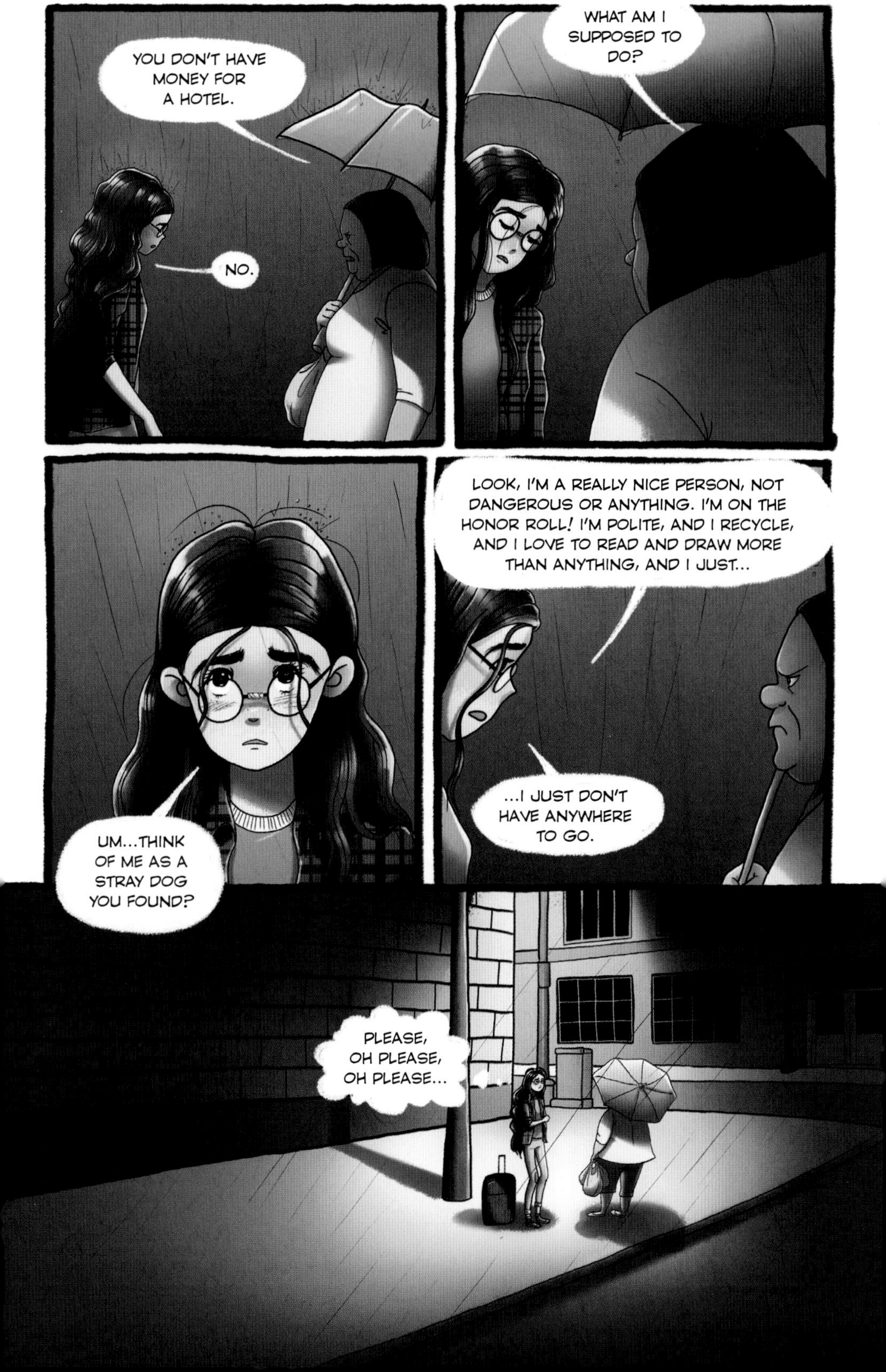
YOU DON'T HAVE MONEY FOR A HOTEL.
NO.
WHAT AM I SUPPOSED TO DO?
UM...THINK OF ME AS A STRAY DOG YOU FOUND?
LOOK, I'M A REALLY NICE PERSON, NOT DANGEROUS OR ANYTHING. I'M ON THE HONOR ROLL! I'M POLITE, AND I RECYCLE, AND I LOVE TO READ AND DRAW MORE THAN ANYTHING, AND I JUST...
...I JUST DON'T HAVE ANYWHERE TO GO.
PLEASE, OH PLEASE, OH PLEASE...

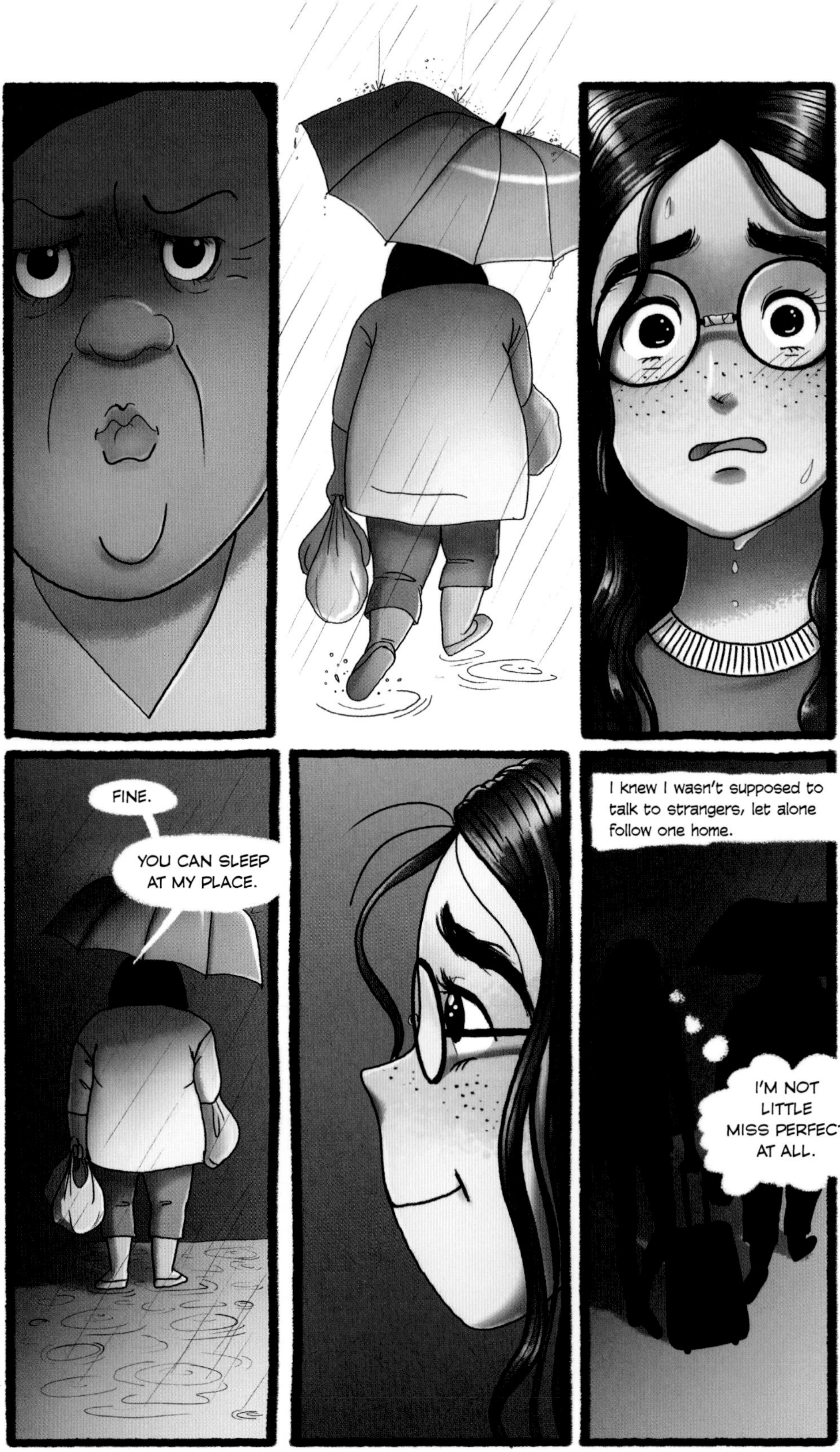
FINE.
YOU CAN SLEEP AT MY PLACE.
I knew I wasn't supposed to talk to strangers, let alone follow one home.
I'M NOT LITTLE MISS PERFECT AT ALL.

But I wasn't supposed to do a lot of things that I ended up doing.

I REALLY, REALLY APPRECIATE YOU LETTING ME STAY WITH YOU. I PROMISE NOT TO BE ANY TROUBLE. WOW, CAN YOU REALLY SEE THE BAY FROM HERE?

HARDLY.

I'M ELEANOR,* BY THE WAY. WHAT'S YOUR NAME?

LEO.

OH, THAT'S COOL, LIKE THE ZODIAC SIGN!

HELP DESK

NO, LIKE TOLSTOY. YOU'VE PROBABLY NEVER HEARD OF HIM.

*Not the name I was born with. The name I chose.

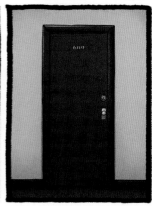

HERE WE ARE, HOME, SHIT HOME.

WHAT?

JUST KIDDING. THIS PLACE IS THE BEE'S KNEES. I'LL SHOW YOU WHERE YOU CAN SLEEP.

Leo's spare room was smaller than a jail cell.
But it was **my** jail cell.

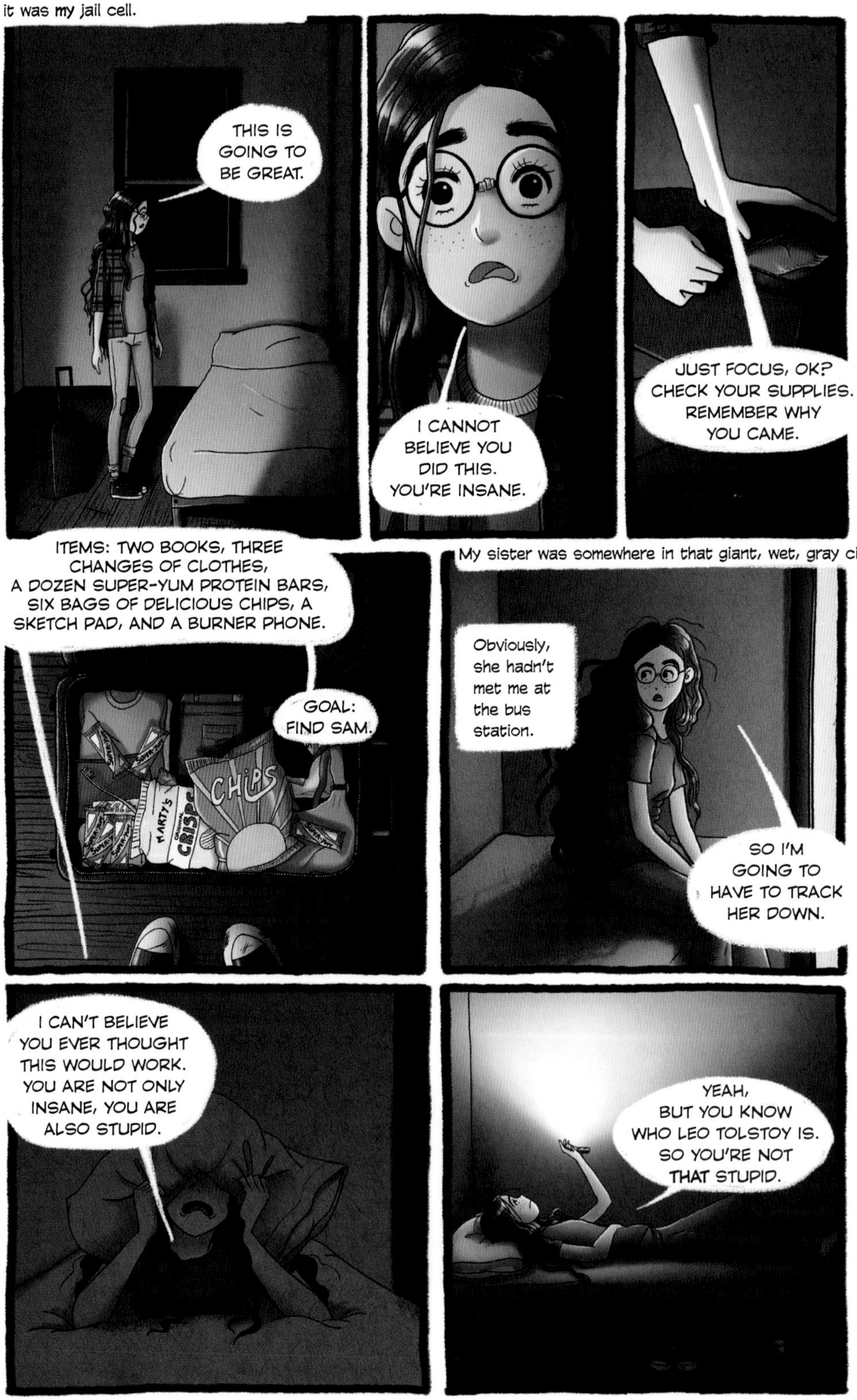
THIS IS GOING TO BE GREAT.
I CANNOT BELIEVE YOU DID THIS. YOU'RE INSANE.
JUST FOCUS, OK? CHECK YOUR SUPPLIES. REMEMBER WHY YOU CAME.
ITEMS: TWO BOOKS, THREE CHANGES OF CLOTHES, A DOZEN SUPER-YUM PROTEIN BARS, SIX BAGS OF DELICIOUS CHIPS, A SKETCH PAD, AND A BURNER PHONE.
GOAL: FIND SAM.
CHIPS
MARTY'S ORIGINAL CRISPS
My sister was somewhere in that giant, wet, gray city.
Obviously, she hadn't met me at the bus station.
SO I'M GOING TO HAVE TO TRACK HER DOWN.
I CAN'T BELIEVE YOU EVER THOUGHT THIS WOULD WORK. YOU ARE NOT ONLY INSANE, YOU ARE ALSO STUPID.
YEAH, BUT YOU KNOW WHO LEO TOLSTOY IS. SO YOU'RE NOT **THAT** STUPID.

In the morning, I told Leo that I didn't actually know when my cousin was coming back.

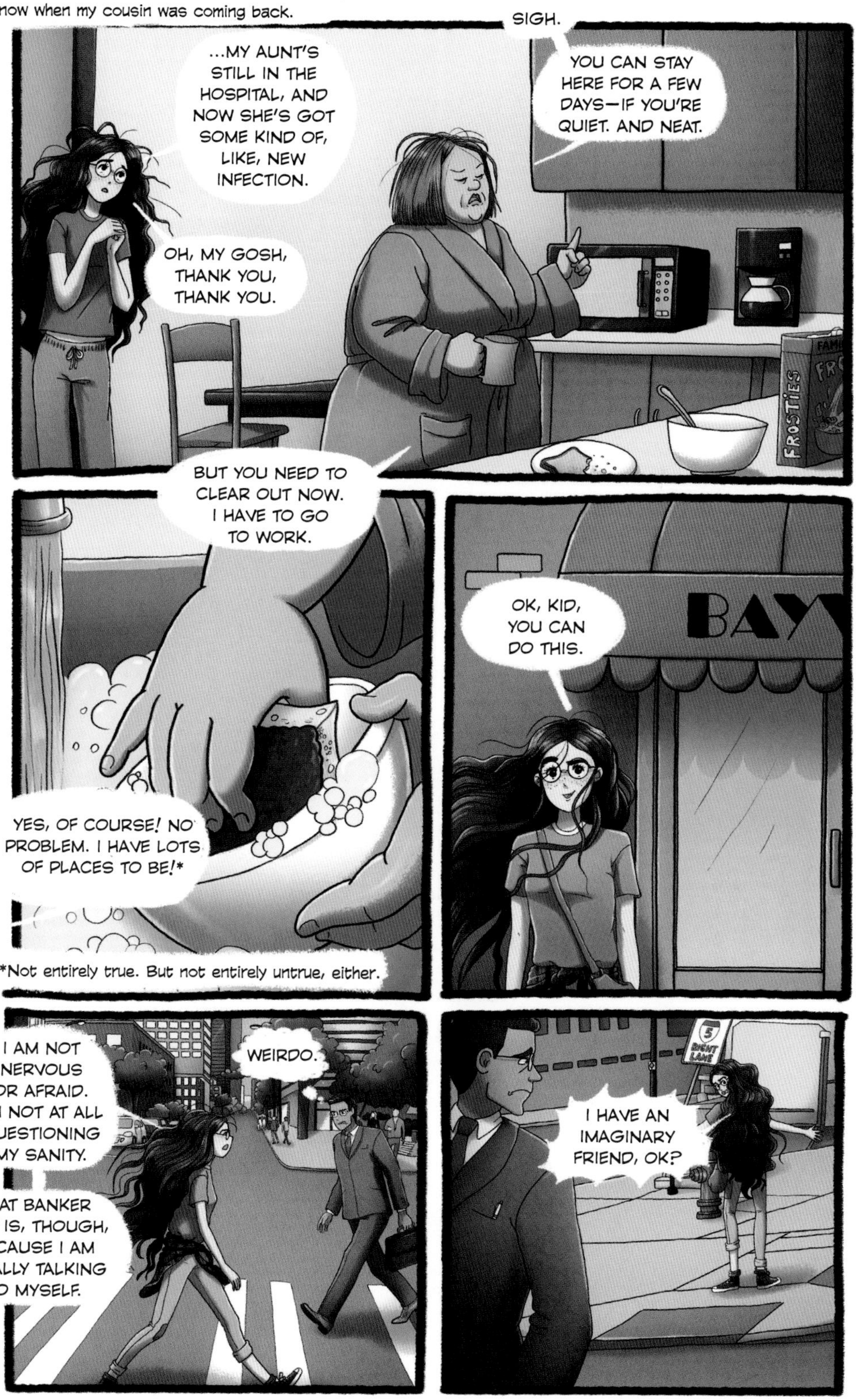
...MY AUNT'S STILL IN THE HOSPITAL, AND NOW SHE'S GOT SOME KIND OF, LIKE, NEW INFECTION.
SIGH.
YOU CAN STAY HERE FOR A FEW DAYS—IF YOU'RE QUIET. AND NEAT.
OH, MY GOSH, THANK YOU, THANK YOU.
FROSTIES
BUT YOU NEED TO CLEAR OUT NOW. I HAVE TO GO TO WORK.
YES, OF COURSE! NO PROBLEM. I HAVE LOTS OF PLACES TO BE!*
*Not entirely true. But not entirely untrue, either.
OK, KID, YOU CAN DO THIS.
BAY
I AM NOT NERVOUS OR AFRAID. I'M NOT AT ALL QUESTIONING MY SANITY.
WEIRDO.
THAT BANKER GUY IS, THOUGH, BECAUSE I AM TOTALLY TALKING TO MYSELF.
I HAVE AN IMAGINARY FRIEND, OK?

I HOPE THIS IS THE RIGHT DIRECTION.

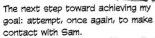

The next step toward achieving my goal: attempt, once again, to make contact with Sam.

OOF!

THUMP!

SORRY!

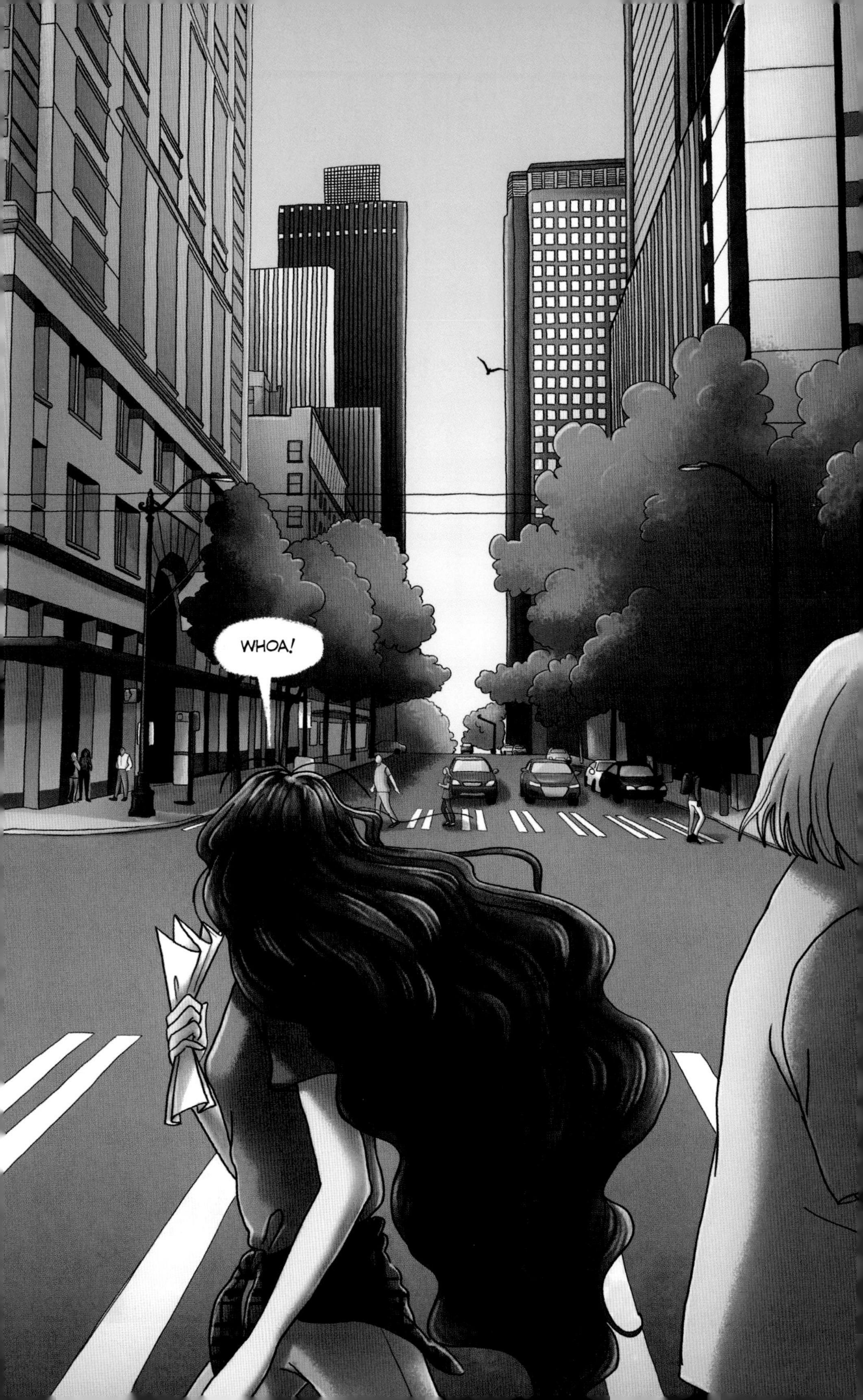
WHOA!

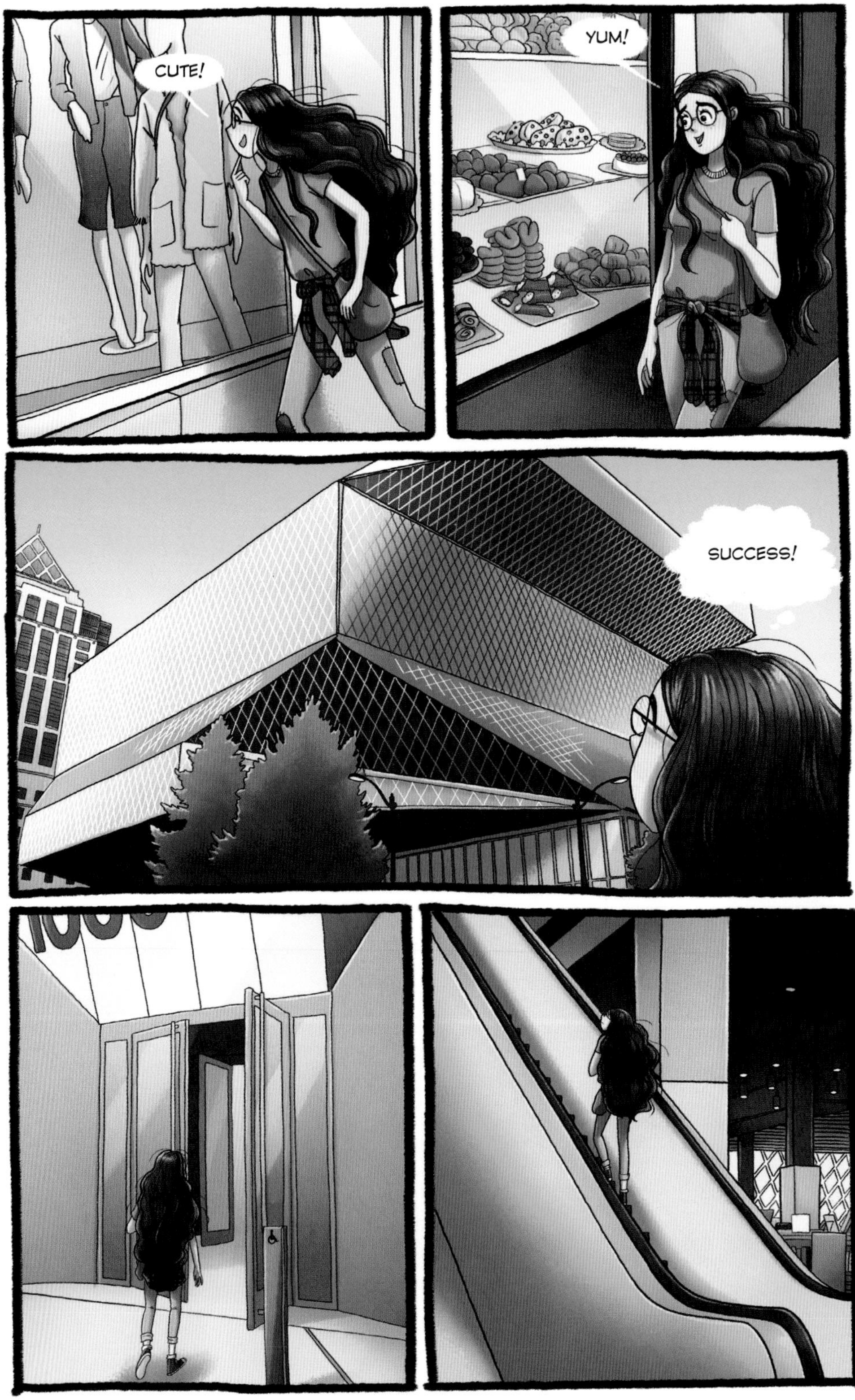
CUTE!
YUM!
SUCCESS!

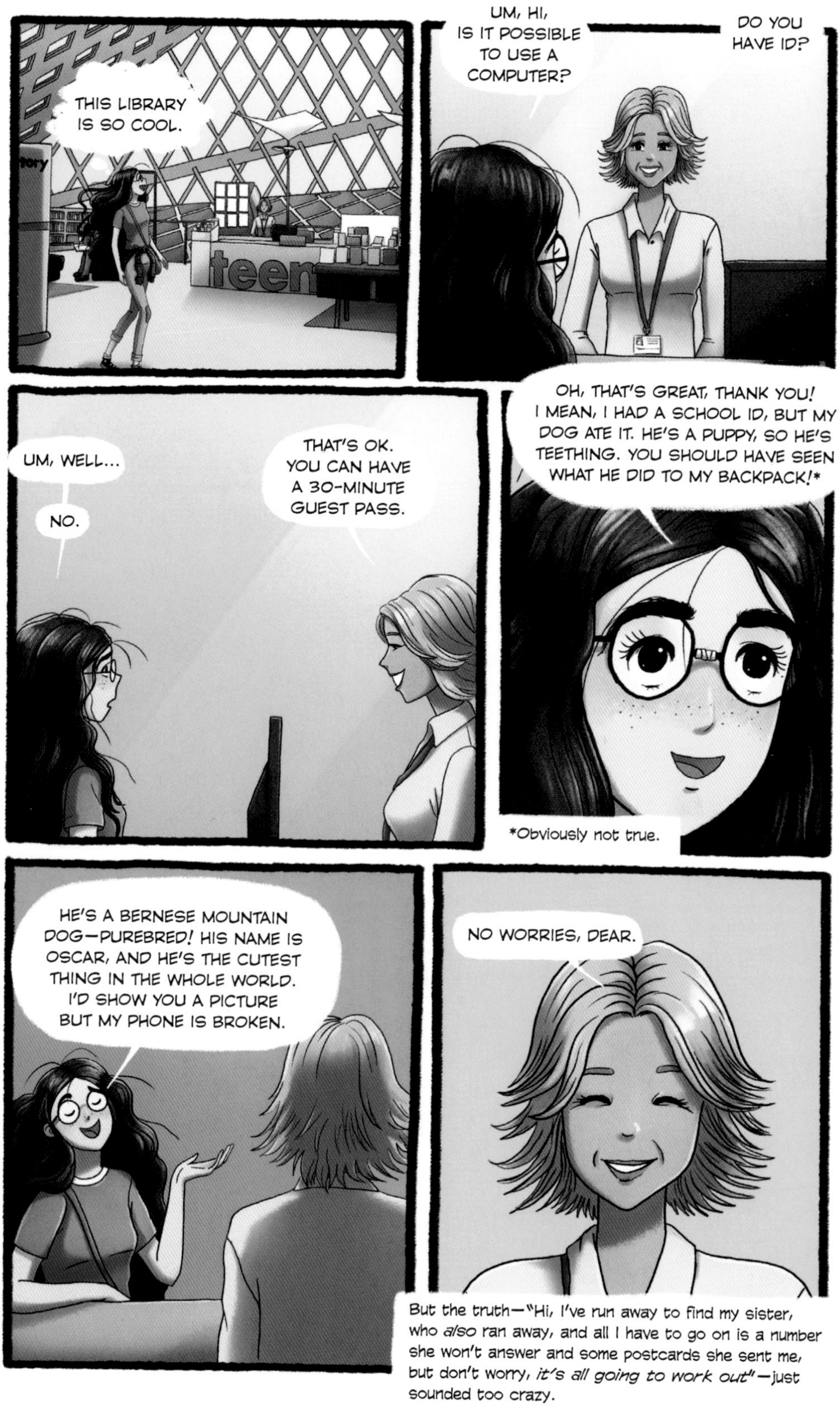
THIS LIBRARY IS SO COOL.
teen
UM, HI, IS IT POSSIBLE TO USE A COMPUTER?
DO YOU HAVE ID?
UM, WELL...
NO.
THAT'S OK. YOU CAN HAVE A 30-MINUTE GUEST PASS.
OH, THAT'S GREAT, THANK YOU! I MEAN, I HAD A SCHOOL ID, BUT MY DOG ATE IT. HE'S A PUPPY, SO HE'S TEETHING. YOU SHOULD HAVE SEEN WHAT HE DID TO MY BACKPACK!*
*Obviously not true.
HE'S A BERNESE MOUNTAIN DOG—PUREBRED! HIS NAME IS OSCAR, AND HE'S THE CUTEST THING IN THE WHOLE WORLD. I'D SHOW YOU A PICTURE BUT MY PHONE IS BROKEN.
NO WORRIES, DEAR.
But the truth—"Hi, I've run away to find my sister, who *also* ran away, and all I have to go on is a number she won't answer and some postcards she sent me, but don't worry, *it's all going to work out*"—just sounded too crazy.

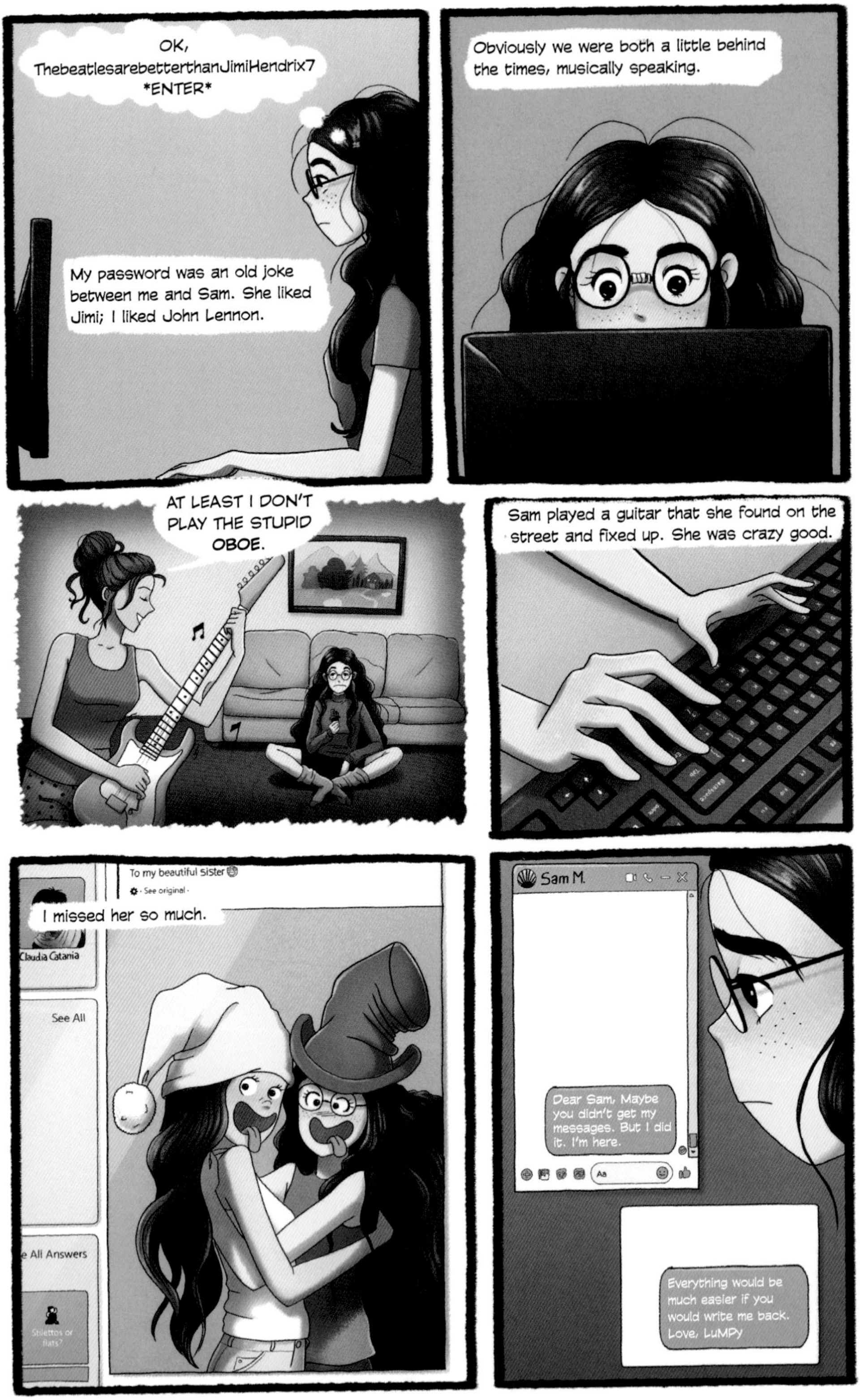
OK, ThebeatlesarebetterthanJimiHendrix7 *ENTER*
My password was an old joke between me and Sam. She liked Jimi; I liked John Lennon.
Obviously we were both a little behind the times, musically speaking.
AT LEAST I DON'T PLAY THE STUPID OBOE.
Sam played a guitar that she found on the street and fixed up. She was crazy good.
To my beautiful sister
See original
I missed her so much.
Claudia Catania
See All
e All Answers
Sam M.
Dear Sam, Maybe you didn't get my messages. But I did it. I'm here.
Aa
Everything would be much easier if you would write me back. Love, LuMPy

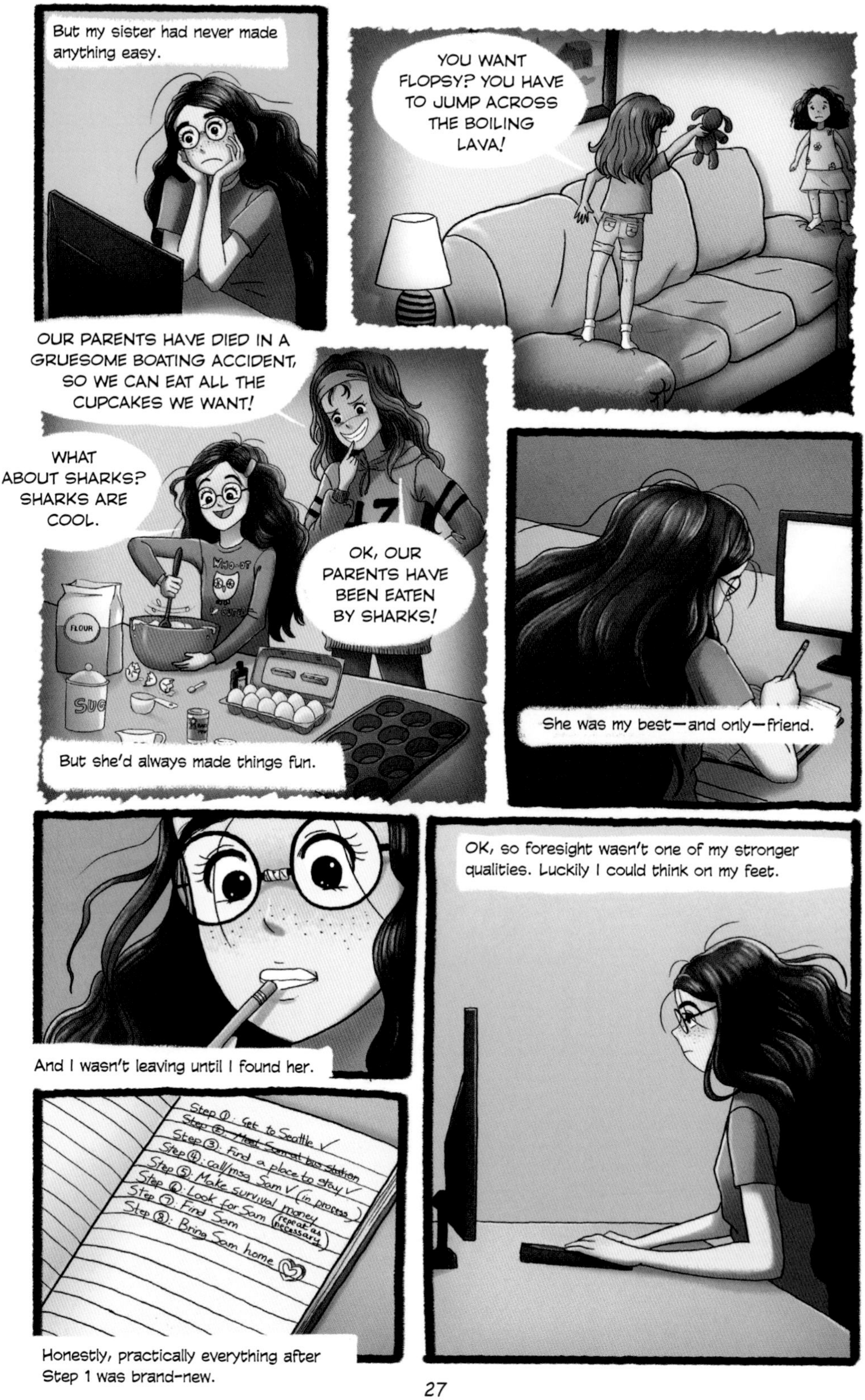
But my sister had never made anything easy.
YOU WANT FLOPSY? YOU HAVE TO JUMP ACROSS THE BOILING LAVA!
OUR PARENTS HAVE DIED IN A GRUESOME BOATING ACCIDENT, SO WE CAN EAT ALL THE CUPCAKES WE WANT!
WHAT ABOUT SHARKS? SHARKS ARE COOL.
OK, OUR PARENTS HAVE BEEN EATEN BY SHARKS!
FLOUR
SUG
But she'd always made things fun.
She was my best—and only—friend.
And I wasn't leaving until I found her.
OK, so foresight wasn't one of my stronger qualities. Luckily I could think on my feet.
Step 1: Get to Seattle ✓
Step 2: Meet Sam at bus station
Step 3: Find a place to stay ✓
Step 4: call/msg Sam ✓ (in process)
Step 5: Make survival money
Step 6: Look for Sam (repeat as necessary)
Step 7: Find Sam
Step 8: Bring Sam home ♡
Honestly, practically everything after Step 1 was brand-new.

Seattle
jobs
all
jobs
+ show 31 categories
search titles only
has image
posted today
bundle duplicates
include nearby areas
MILES FROM ZIP
miles
from zip
internship
non-profit
telecommute
employment type
full-time
part-time
contract
employee's choice
reset
update search
search jobs
list
<<
< prev
1 - 120 / 1001
next >
Paying to give foot massage!
Um...
Pirate Ship Crew - UNIQUE opportunity!
Ahoy, matey!
Musician Needs Lyrics
Hiring Asphalt Estimator TODAY!
Want to adopt Human Pet
No thanks!
NEEDED ASAP: EXPERIENCED Piano Mover
Do you sunburn easily? PAID MEDICAL SUNSCREEN STUDY
Casting New Competition Show For You & Your Dog!!
EXPERIENCED HANDYMAN NEEDED ASAP!
WHAT DO YOU THINK A HUMAN PET DOES?
YOU PROBABLY DON'T WANT TO KNOW.
YEAH, MAYBE NOT.
CARPET INSTALLER? EYELASH EXTENSION MODEL?
It turned out there were not many things I was qualified for.
I had five minutes left on my internet pass.
(3) Faceboot
CLICK!
CLICK!
I checked my messages.
Dear Sam,
Maybe you didn't get my messages. But I did it. I'm here.
Everything would be much easier if you would write me back.
Love, LuMPy
NOTHING.
OF COURSE.
Then, with a tiny *ding*, the computer logged me out.
DING!

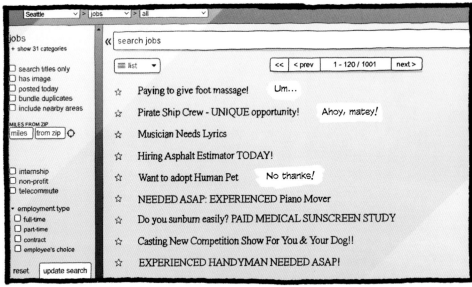

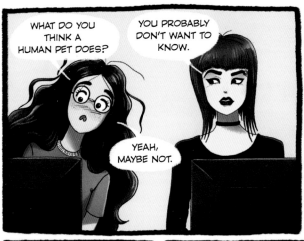

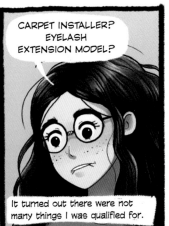

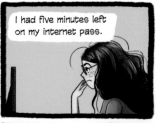

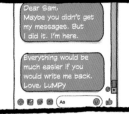

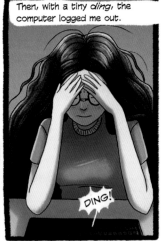

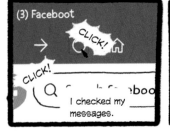

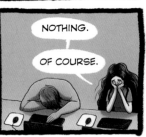

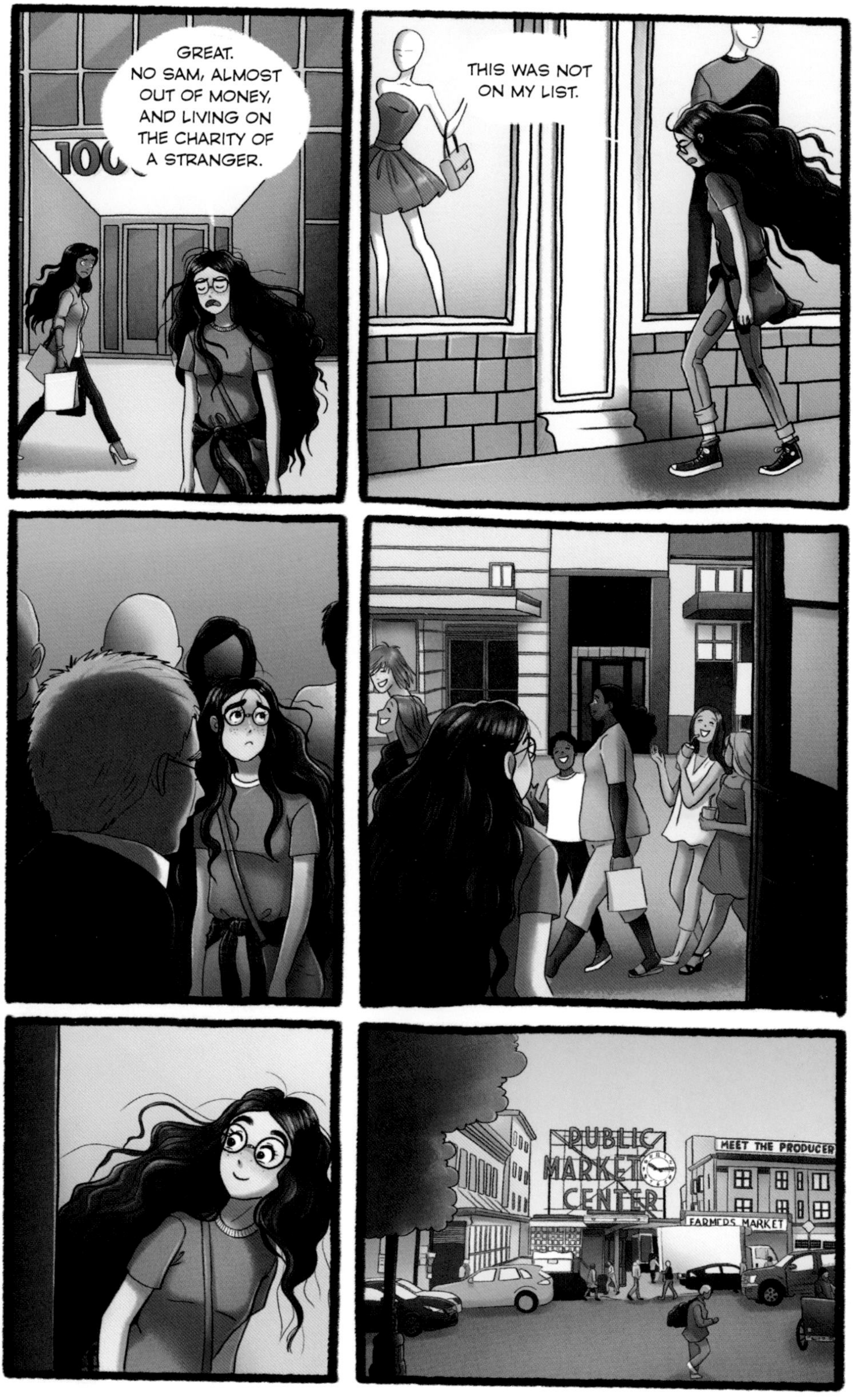
GREAT.
NO SAM, ALMOST OUT OF MONEY, AND LIVING ON THE CHARITY OF A STRANGER.
THIS WAS NOT ON MY LIST.
PUBLIC MARKET CENTER
MEET THE PRODUCER
FARMERS MARKET

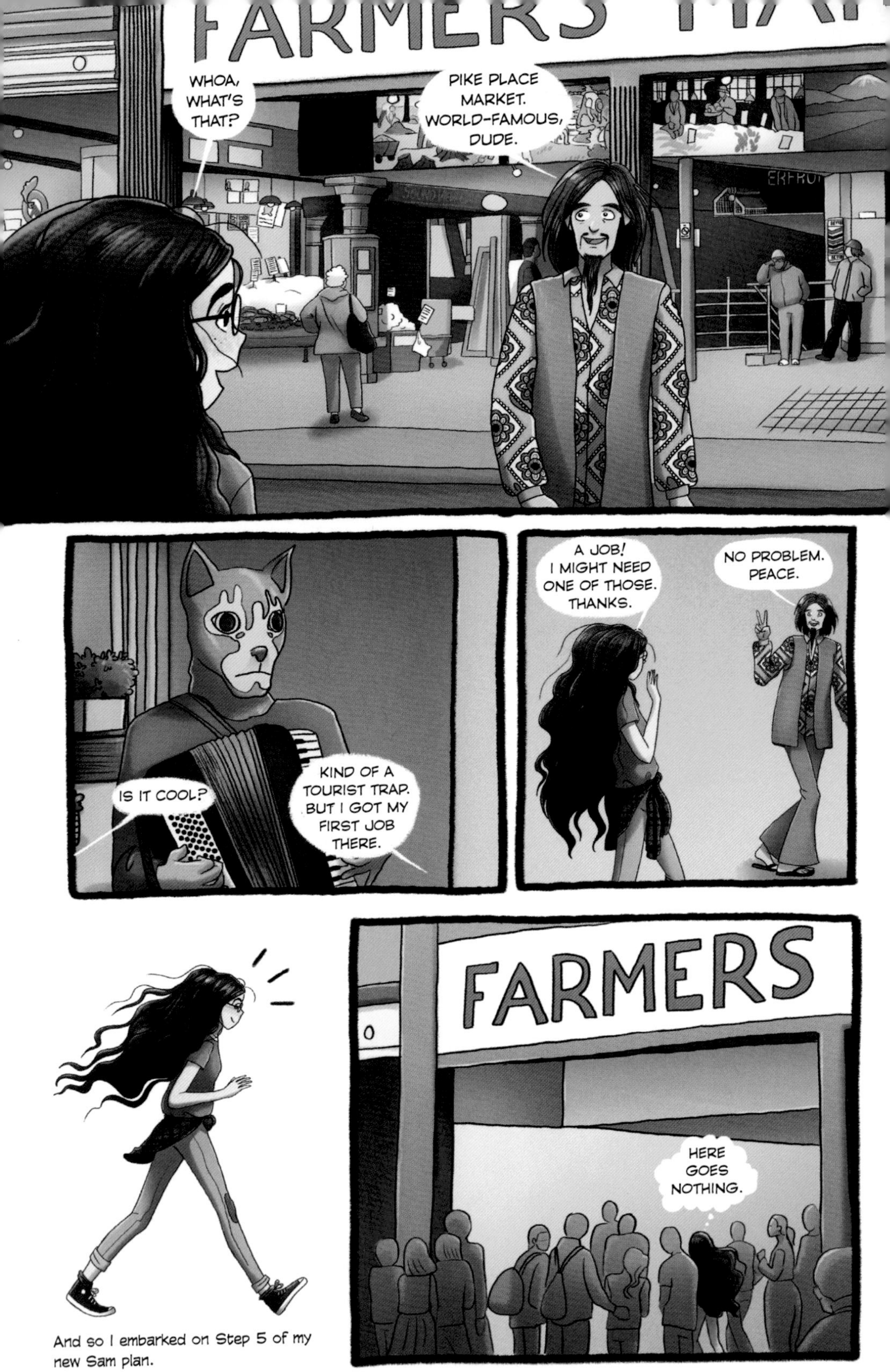
FARMERS
WHOA, WHAT'S THAT?
PIKE PLACE MARKET. WORLD-FAMOUS, DUDE.
IS IT COOL?
KIND OF A TOURIST TRAP. BUT I GOT MY FIRST JOB THERE.
A JOB! I MIGHT NEED ONE OF THOSE. THANKS.
NO PROBLEM. PEACE.
And so I embarked on Step 5 of my new Sam plan.
FARMERS
HERE GOES NOTHING.

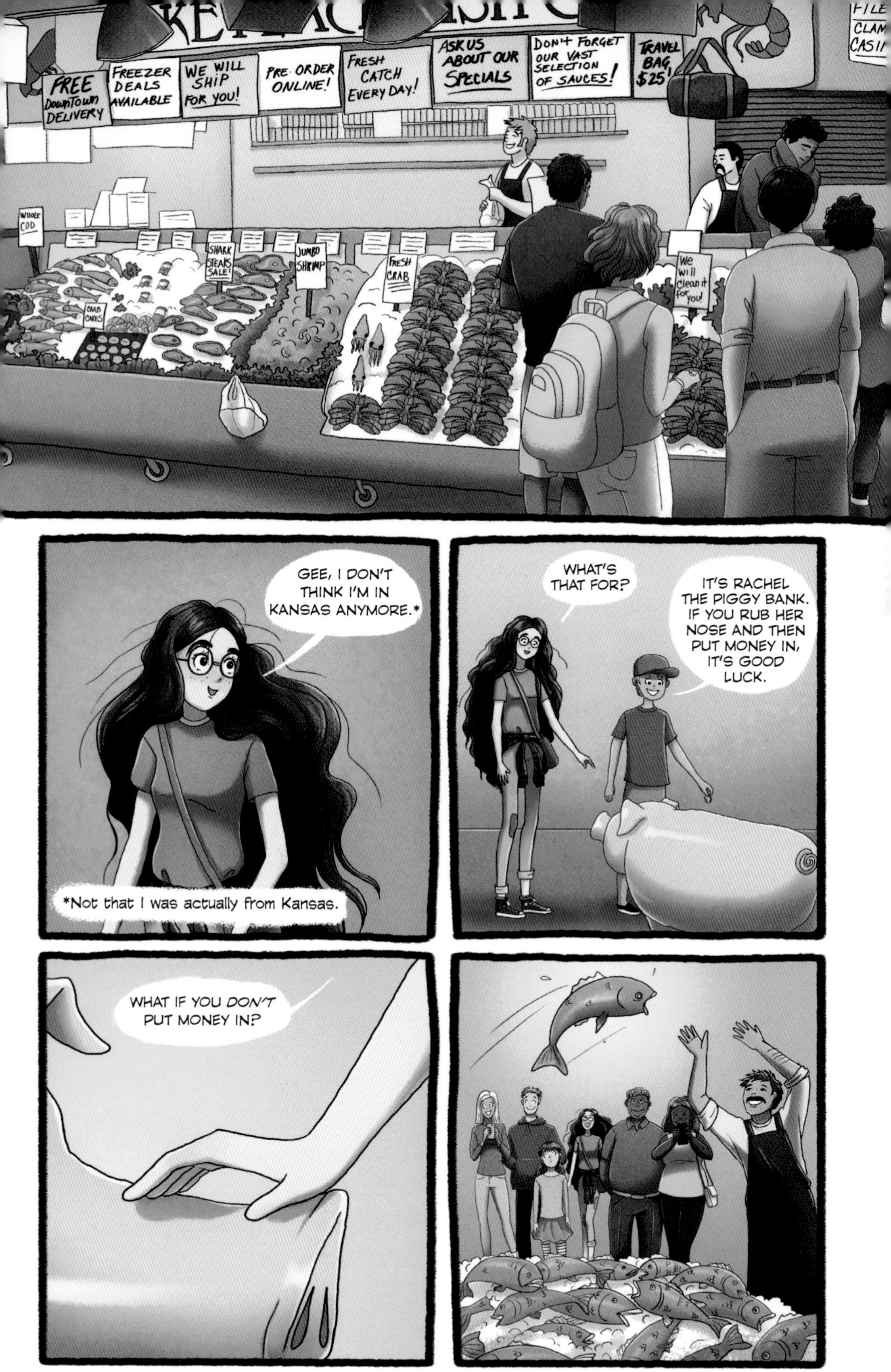
FREE DownTown DELIVERY
FREEZER DEALS AVAILABLE
WE WILL SHIP FOR YOU!
PRE-ORDER ONLINE!
FRESH CATCH EVERY DAY!
ASK US ABOUT OUR SPECIALS
DON'T FORGET OUR VAST SELECTION OF SAUCES!
TRAVEL BAG $25!
WHOLE COD
SHARK STEAKS SALE!
JUMBO SHRIMP
FRESH CRAB
CRAB CAKES
We will clean it for you!
GEE, I DON'T THINK I'M IN KANSAS ANYMORE.*
*Not that I was actually from Kansas.
WHAT'S THAT FOR?
IT'S RACHEL THE PIGGY BANK. IF YOU RUB HER NOSE AND THEN PUT MONEY IN, IT'S GOOD LUCK.
WHAT IF YOU *DON'T* PUT MONEY IN?

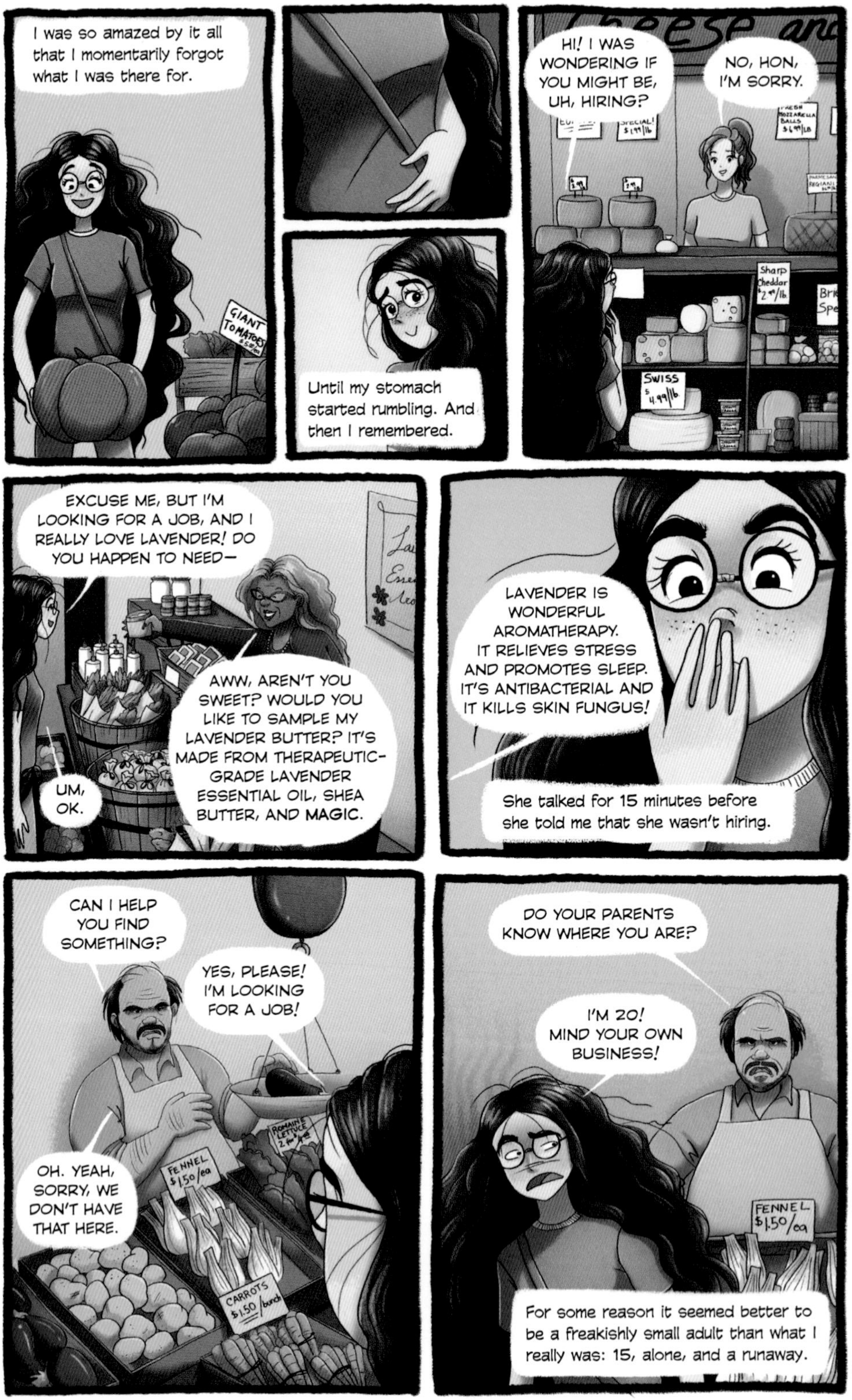
I was so amazed by it all that I momentarily forgot what I was there for.
GIANT TOMATOES
Until my stomach started rumbling. And then I remembered.
HI! I WAS WONDERING IF YOU MIGHT BE, UH, HIRING?
NO, HON, I'M SORRY.
Sharp Cheddar
SWISS $4.99/lb.
EXCUSE ME, BUT I'M LOOKING FOR A JOB, AND I REALLY LOVE LAVENDER! DO YOU HAPPEN TO NEED—
AWW, AREN'T YOU SWEET? WOULD YOU LIKE TO SAMPLE MY LAVENDER BUTTER? IT'S MADE FROM THERAPEUTIC-GRADE LAVENDER ESSENTIAL OIL, SHEA BUTTER, AND MAGIC.
UM, OK.
LAVENDER IS WONDERFUL AROMATHERAPY. IT RELIEVES STRESS AND PROMOTES SLEEP. IT'S ANTIBACTERIAL AND IT KILLS SKIN FUNGUS!
She talked for 15 minutes before she told me that she wasn't hiring.
CAN I HELP YOU FIND SOMETHING?
YES, PLEASE! I'M LOOKING FOR A JOB!
OH. YEAH, SORRY, WE DON'T HAVE THAT HERE.
FENNEL $1.50/ea
CARROTS $1.50/bunch
DO YOUR PARENTS KNOW WHERE YOU ARE?
I'M 20! MIND YOUR OWN BUSINESS!
FENNEL $1.50/ea
For some reason it seemed better to be a freakishly small adult than what I really was: 15, alone, and a runaway.

UM, DO YOU GUYS NEED ANY HELP? BECAUSE I NEED A JOB.

CAN YOU CATCH A SLIPPERY, 20-POUND FISH?

ABSOLUTELY!

FRESH CLAMS

BY THE POUND

TARTAR SAUCE

BABY CLAMS

CRAB LEGS

SALMON

MATT

TUNA

I asked for work at 20 different places before I ended up where I'd begun.

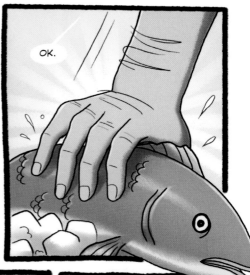

OK.

CATCH!

EEP!

WHACK!

SPLAT!

HOW ABOUT A SECOND CHANCE?

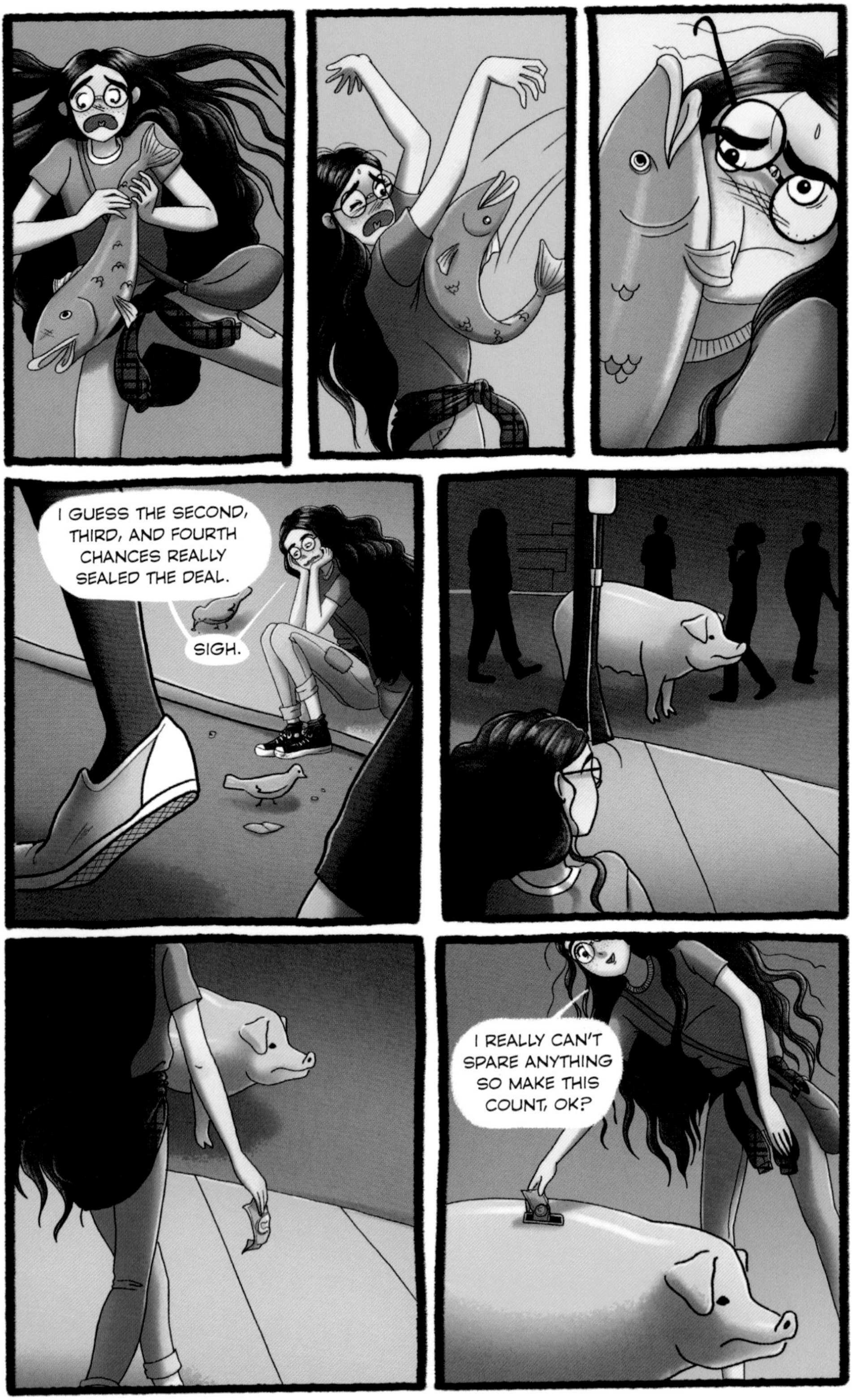
I GUESS THE SECOND, THIRD, AND FOURTH CHANCES REALLY SEALED THE DEAL.
SIGH.
I REALLY CAN'T SPARE ANYTHING SO MAKE THIS COUNT, OK?

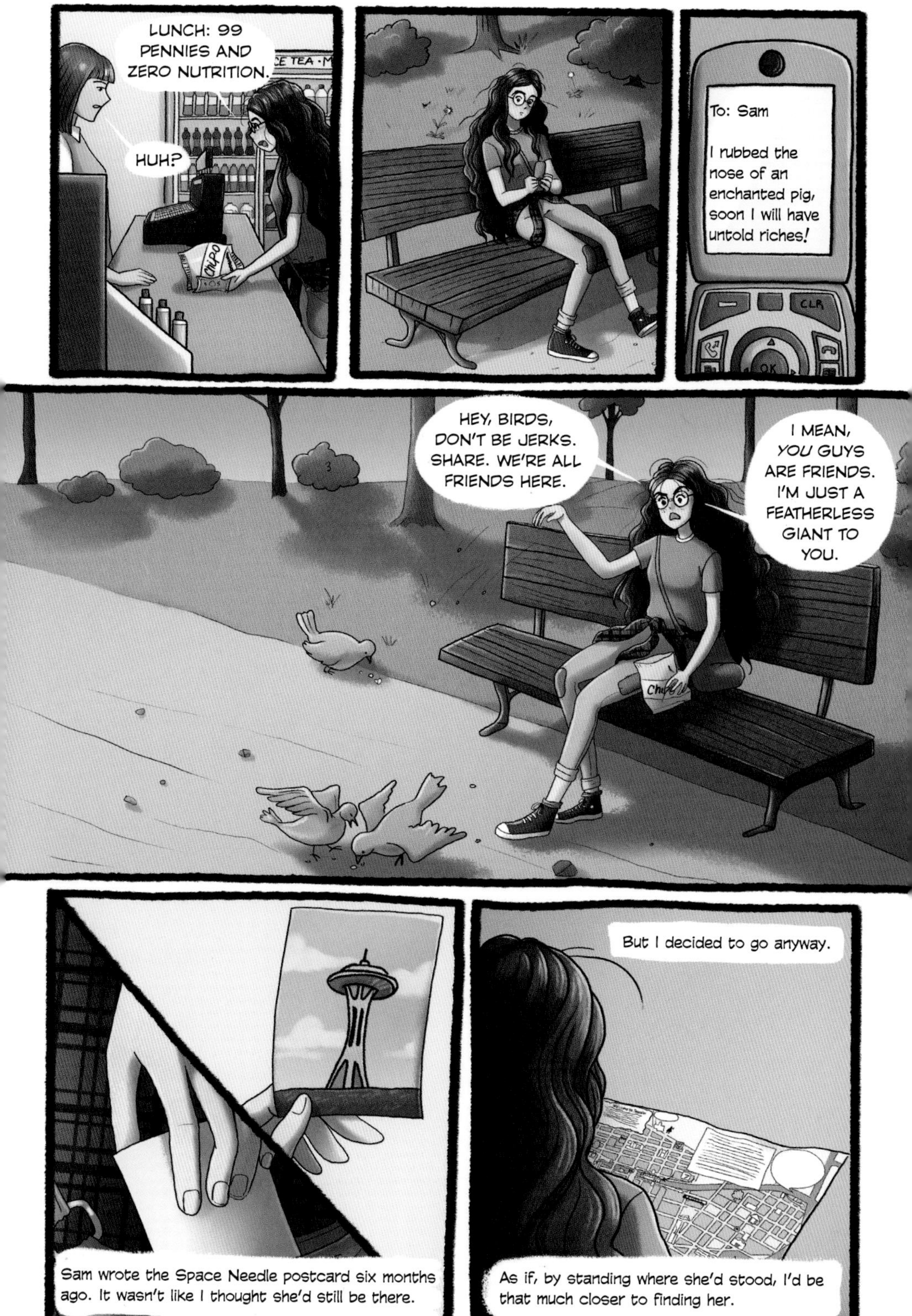

LUNCH: 99 PENNIES AND ZERO NUTRITION.
HUH?
CE TEA
CHIPO
To: Sam
I rubbed the nose of an enchanted pig, soon I will have untold riches!
CLR
OK
HEY, BIRDS, DON'T BE JERKS. SHARE. WE'RE ALL FRIENDS HERE.
I MEAN, YOU GUYS ARE FRIENDS. I'M JUST A FEATHERLESS GIANT TO YOU.
Sam wrote the Space Needle postcard six months ago. It wasn't like I thought she'd still be there.
But I decided to go anyway.
As if, by standing where she'd stood, I'd be that much closer to finding her.

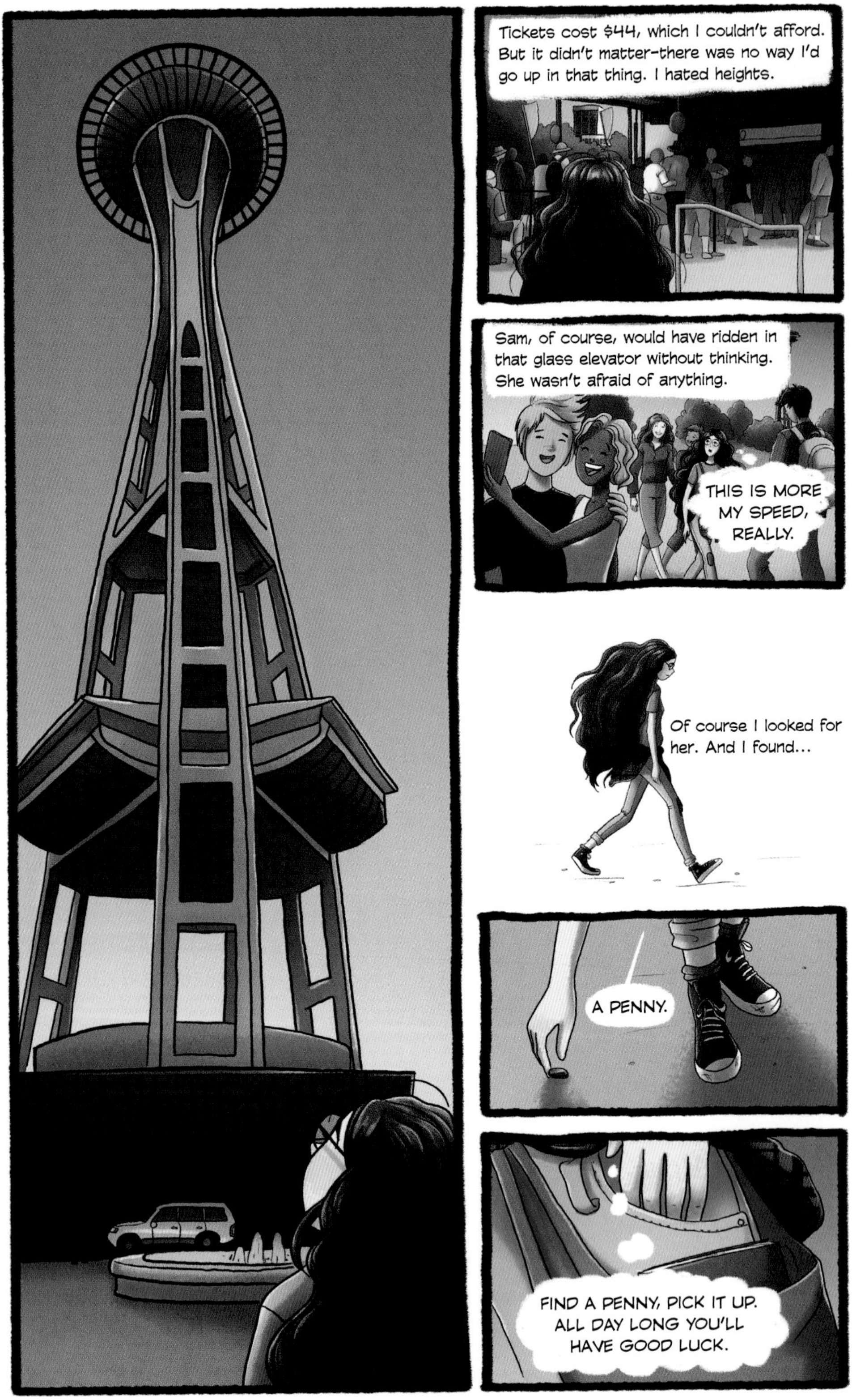
Tickets cost $44, which I couldn't afford. But it didn't matter–there was no way I'd go up in that thing. I hated heights.
Sam, of course, would have ridden in that glass elevator without thinking. She wasn't afraid of anything.
THIS IS MORE MY SPEED, REALLY.
Of course I looked for her. And I found...
A PENNY.
FIND A PENNY, PICK IT UP. ALL DAY LONG YOU'LL HAVE GOOD LUCK.

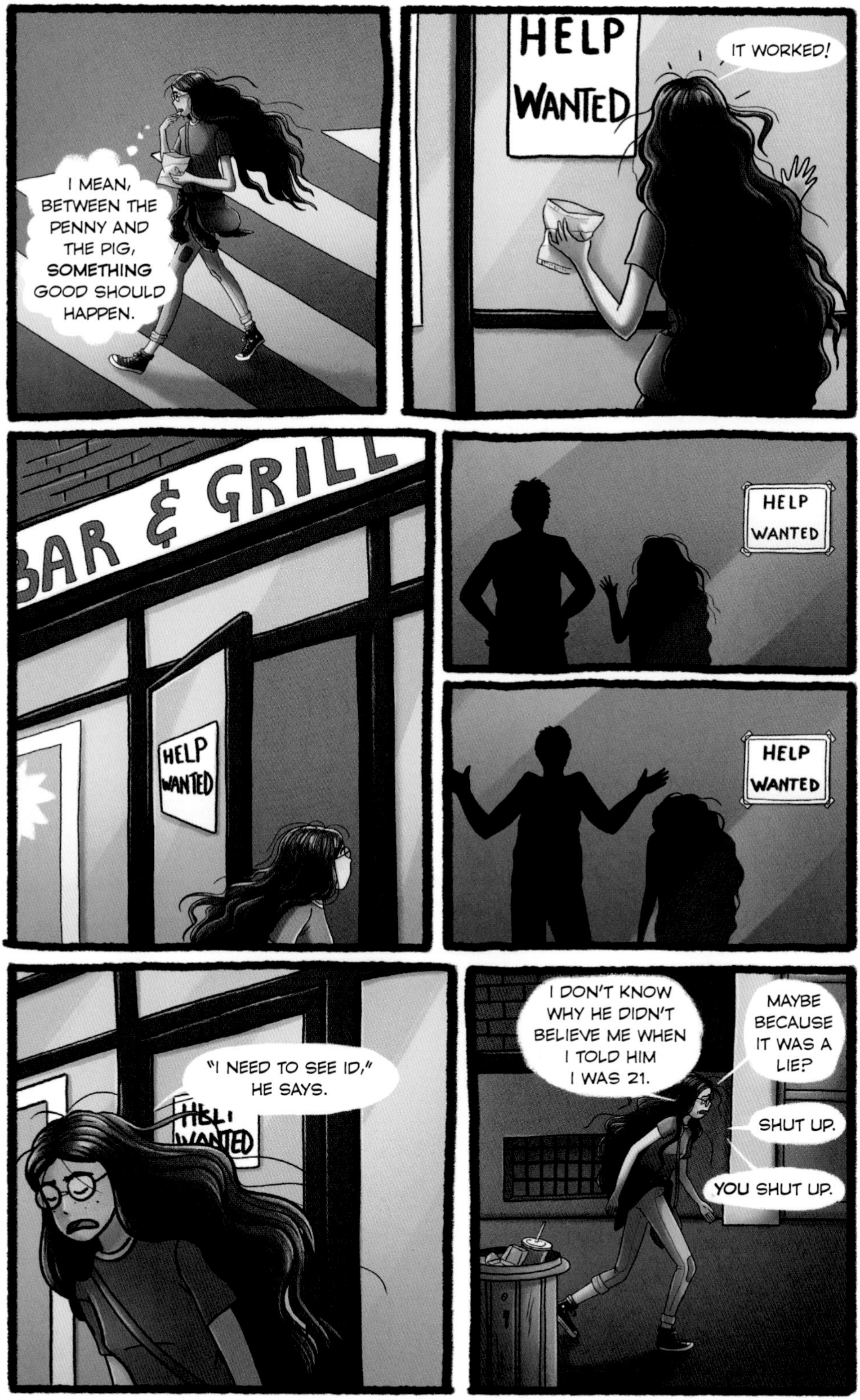
I MEAN, BETWEEN THE PENNY AND THE PIG, SOMETHING GOOD SHOULD HAPPEN.
HELP WANTED
IT WORKED!
BAR & GRILL
HELP WANTED
HELP WANTED
HELP WANTED
"I NEED TO SEE ID," HE SAYS.
I DON'T KNOW WHY HE DIDN'T BELIEVE ME WHEN I TOLD HIM I WAS 21.
MAYBE BECAUSE IT WAS A LIE?
SHUT UP.
YOU SHUT UP.

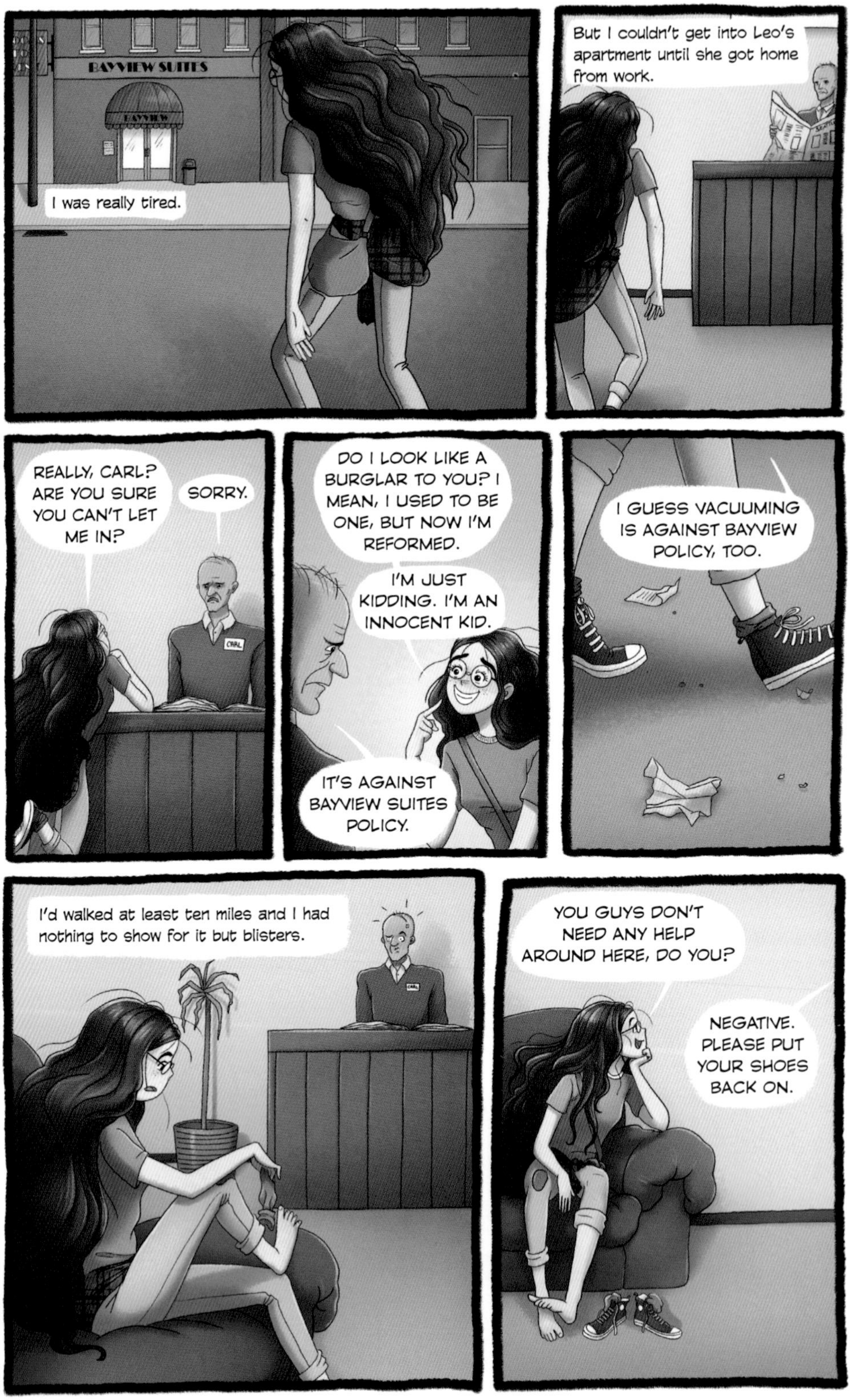
BAYVIEW SUITES
BAYVIEW
I was really tired.
But I couldn't get into Leo's apartment until she got home from work.
REALLY, CARL? ARE YOU SURE YOU CAN'T LET ME IN?
SORRY.
CARL
DO I LOOK LIKE A BURGLAR TO YOU? I MEAN, I USED TO BE ONE, BUT NOW I'M REFORMED.
I'M JUST KIDDING. I'M AN INNOCENT KID.
IT'S AGAINST BAYVIEW SUITES POLICY.
I GUESS VACUUMING IS AGAINST BAYVIEW POLICY, TOO.
I'd walked at least ten miles and I had nothing to show for it but blisters.
YOU GUYS DON'T NEED ANY HELP AROUND HERE, DO YOU?
NEGATIVE. PLEASE PUT YOUR SHOES BACK ON.

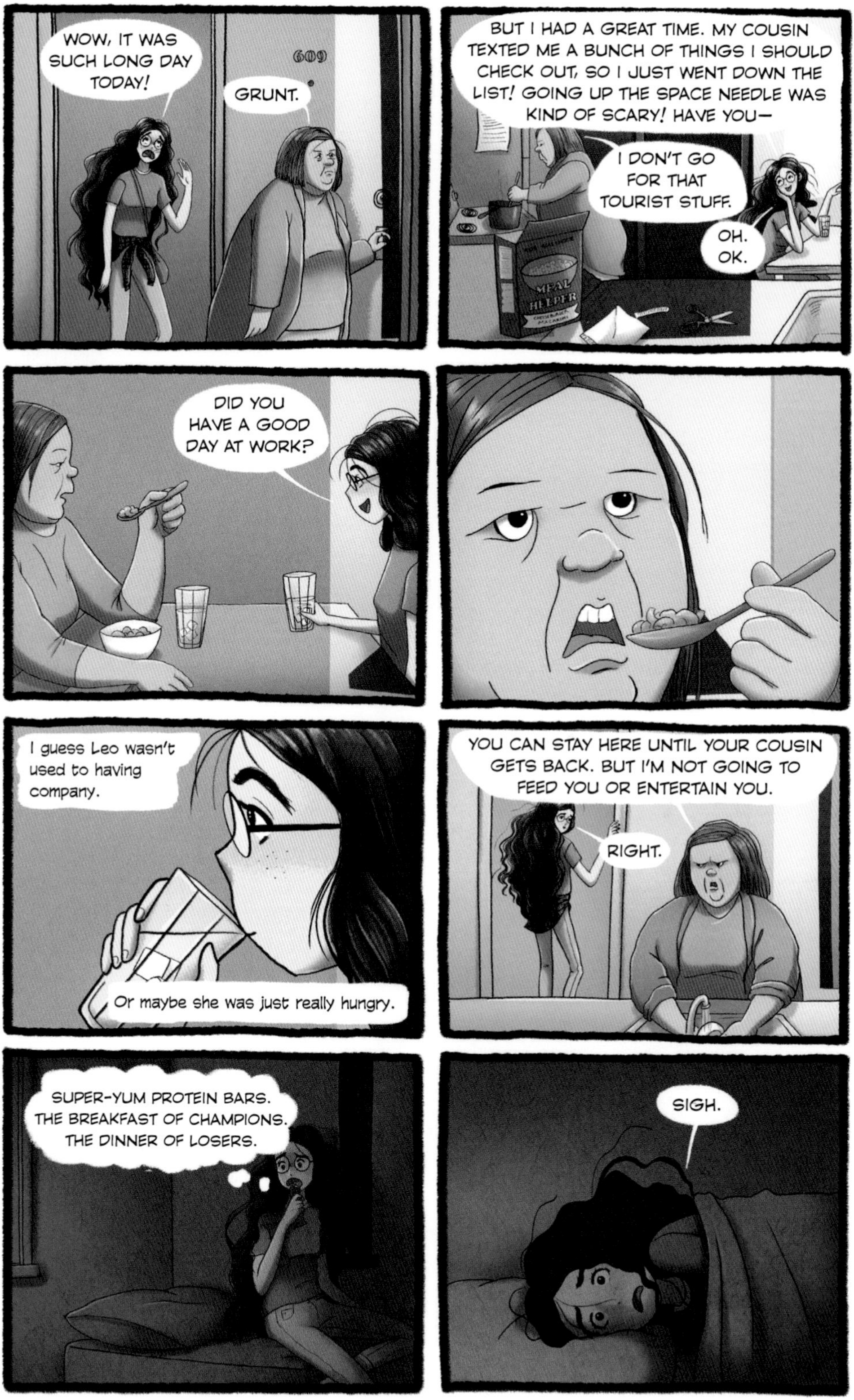
WOW, IT WAS SUCH LONG DAY TODAY!
GRUNT.
BUT I HAD A GREAT TIME. MY COUSIN TEXTED ME A BUNCH OF THINGS I SHOULD CHECK OUT, SO I JUST WENT DOWN THE LIST! GOING UP THE SPACE NEEDLE WAS KIND OF SCARY! HAVE YOU—
I DON'T GO FOR THAT TOURIST STUFF.
OH. OK.
MEAL HELPER
DID YOU HAVE A GOOD DAY AT WORK?
I guess Leo wasn't used to having company.
Or maybe she was just really hungry.
YOU CAN STAY HERE UNTIL YOUR COUSIN GETS BACK. BUT I'M NOT GOING TO FEED YOU OR ENTERTAIN YOU.
RIGHT.
SUPER-YUM PROTEIN BARS. THE BREAKFAST OF CHAMPIONS. THE DINNER OF LOSERS.
SIGH.

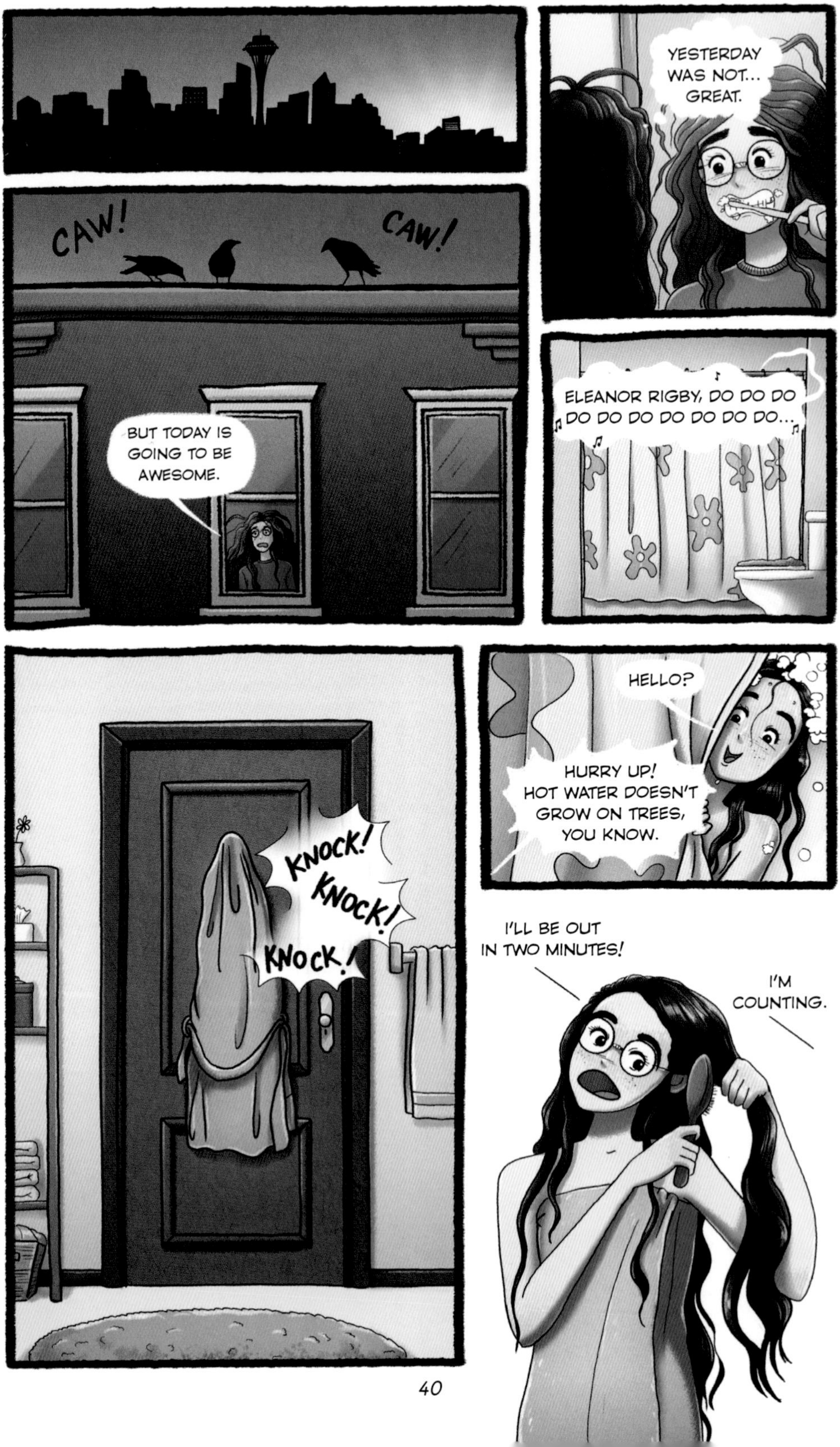
YESTERDAY WAS NOT... GREAT.
CAW!
CAW!
BUT TODAY IS GOING TO BE AWESOME.
ELEANOR RIGBY, DO DO DO DO DO DO DO DO DO DO...
KNOCK! KNOCK! KNOCK!
HELLO?
HURRY UP! HOT WATER DOESN'T GROW ON TREES, YOU KNOW.
I'LL BE OUT IN TWO MINUTES!
I'M COUNTING.

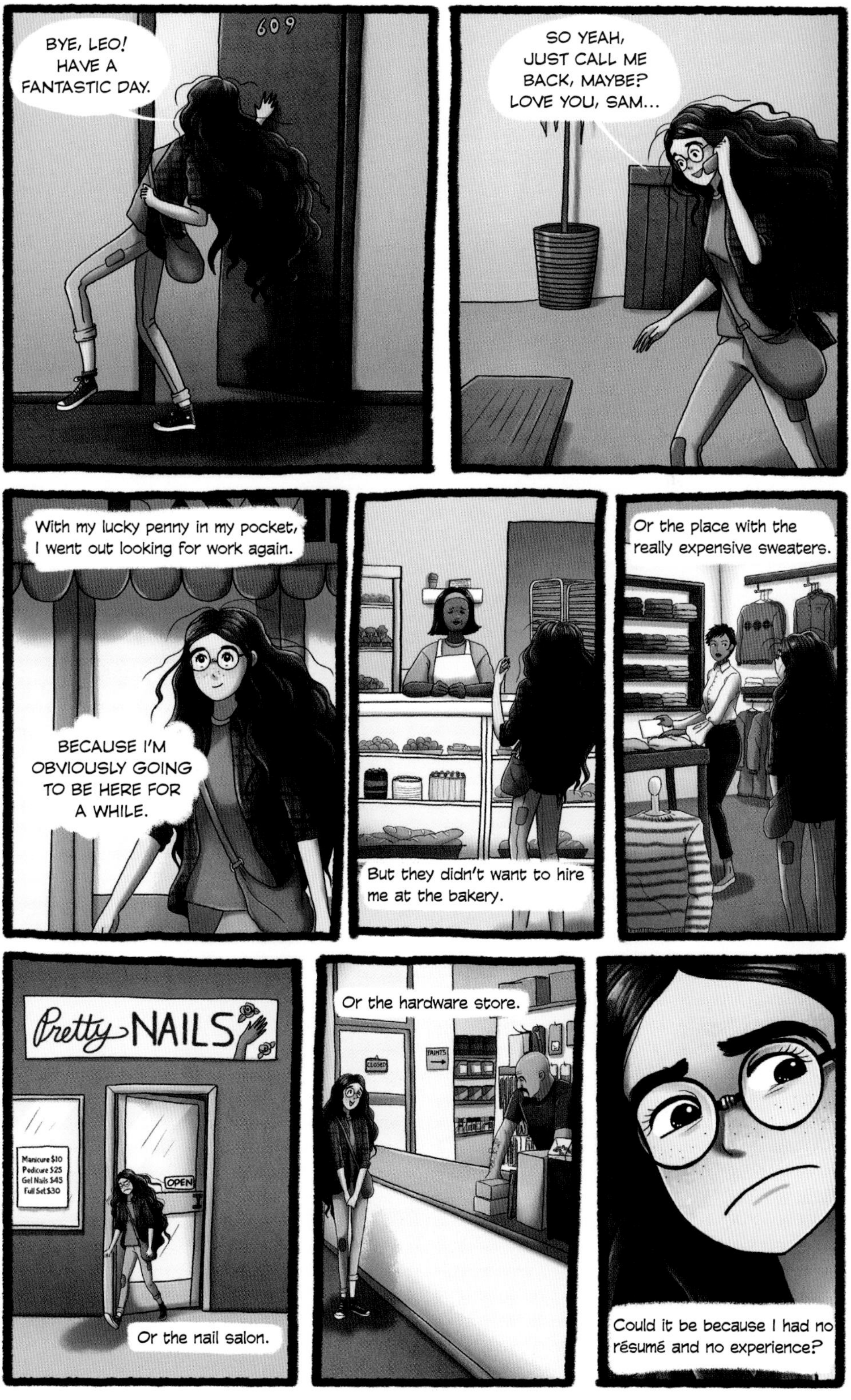
BYE, LEO! HAVE A FANTASTIC DAY.
609
SO YEAH, JUST CALL ME BACK, MAYBE? LOVE YOU, SAM...
With my lucky penny in my pocket, I went out looking for work again.
BECAUSE I'M OBVIOUSLY GOING TO BE HERE FOR A WHILE.
But they didn't want to hire me at the bakery.
Or the place with the really expensive sweaters.
Pretty NAILS
Manicure $10
Pedicure $25
Gel Nails $45
Full Set $30
OPEN
Or the nail salon.
Or the hardware store.
CLOSED
PAINTS
Could it be because I had no résumé and no experience?

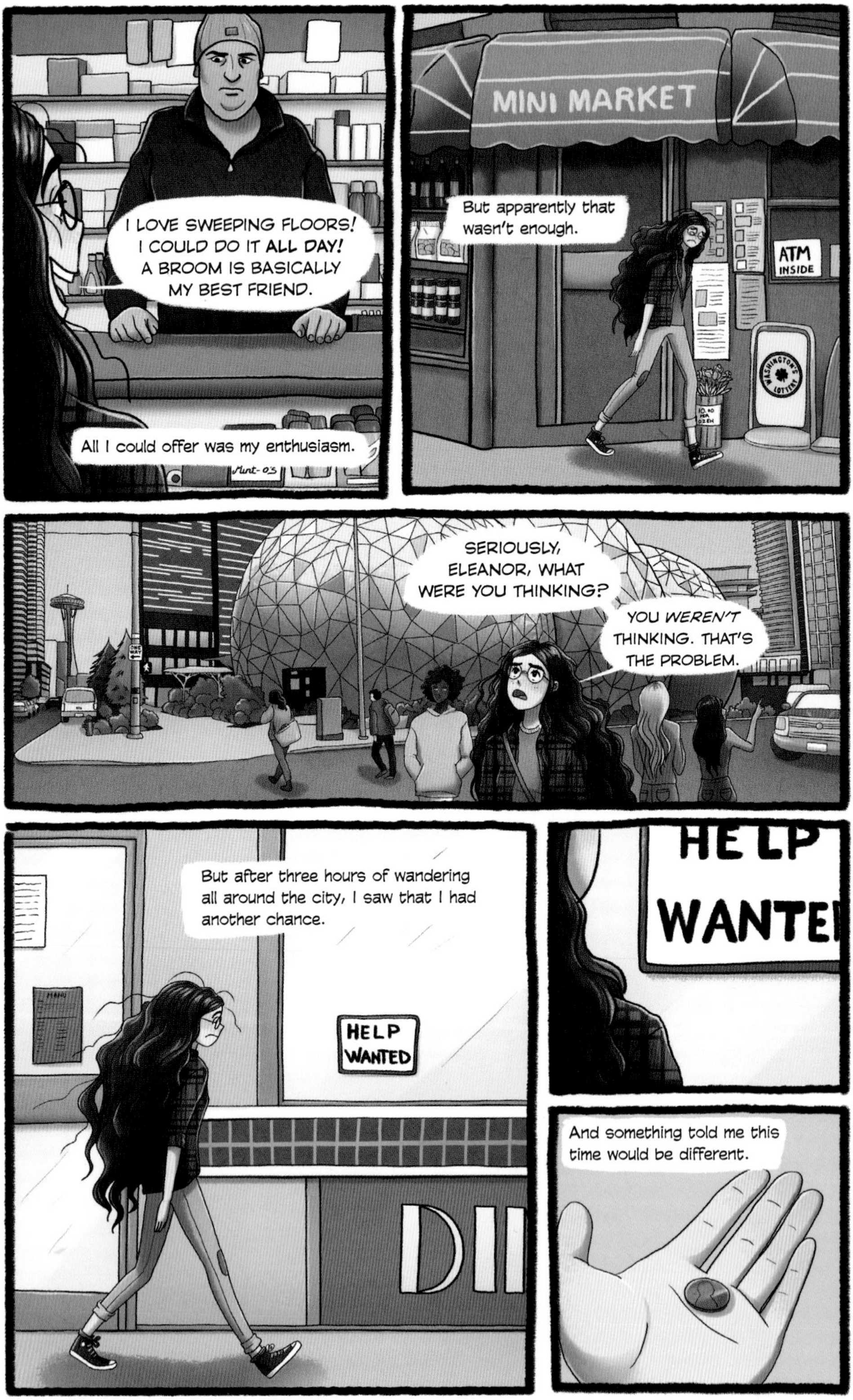
I LOVE SWEEPING FLOORS! I COULD DO IT **ALL DAY!** A BROOM IS BASICALLY MY BEST FRIEND.
All I could offer was my enthusiasm.
MINI MARKET
But apparently that wasn't enough.
ATM INSIDE
SERIOUSLY, ELEANOR, WHAT WERE YOU THINKING?
YOU *WEREN'T* THINKING. THAT'S THE PROBLEM.
But after three hours of wandering all around the city, I saw that I had another chance.
HELP WANTED
And something told me this time would be different.

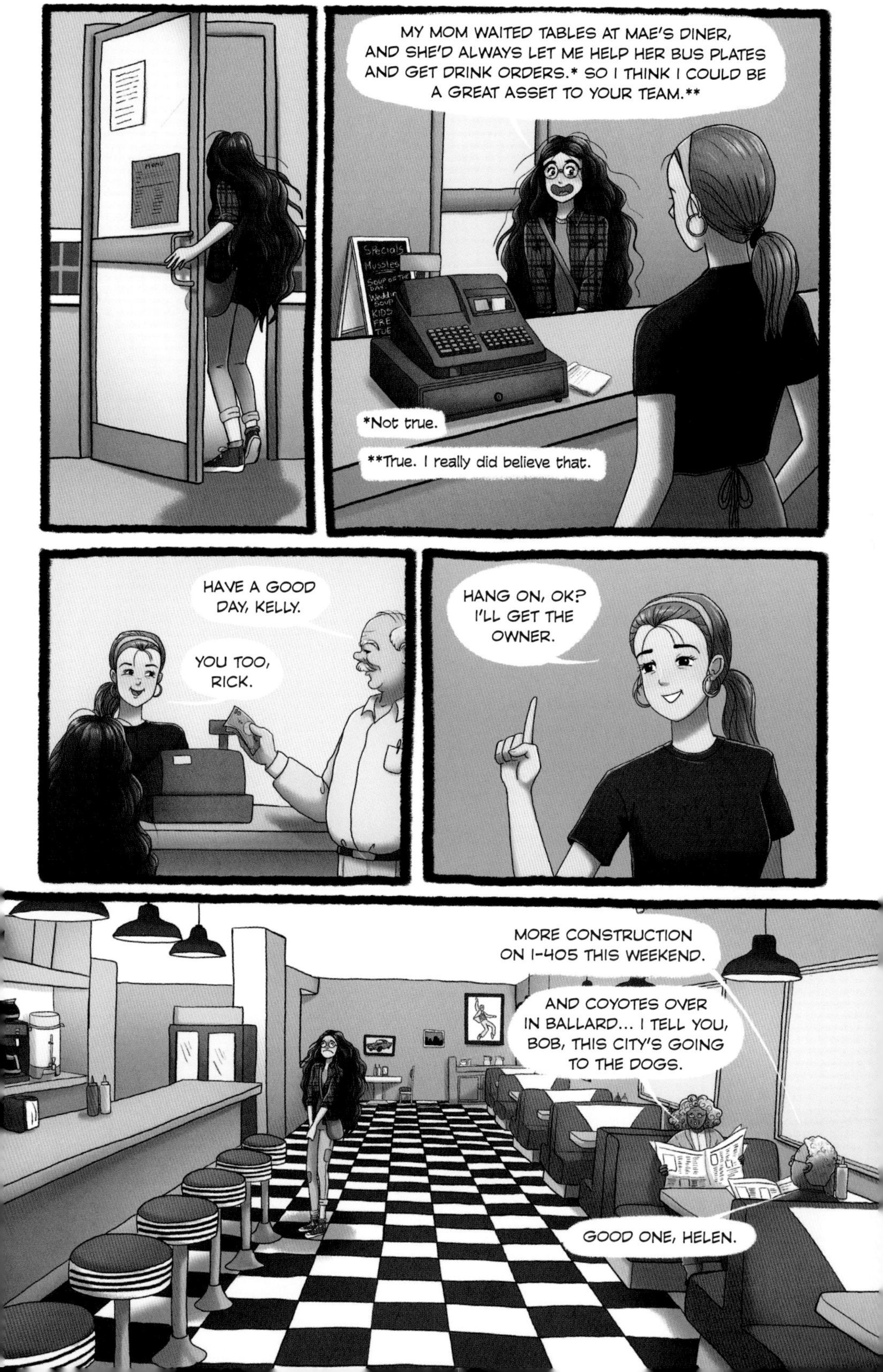
MY MOM WAITED TABLES AT MAE'S DINER, AND SHE'D ALWAYS LET ME HELP HER BUS PLATES AND GET DRINK ORDERS.* SO I THINK I COULD BE A GREAT ASSET TO YOUR TEAM.**
Specials
Mussles
Soup of the day.
Wedding soup
Kids free Tue
*Not true.
**True. I really did believe that.
HAVE A GOOD DAY, KELLY.
YOU TOO, RICK.
HANG ON, OK? I'LL GET THE OWNER.
MORE CONSTRUCTION ON I-405 THIS WEEKEND.
AND COYOTES OVER IN BALLARD... I TELL YOU, BOB, THIS CITY'S GOING TO THE DOGS.
GOOD ONE, HELEN.

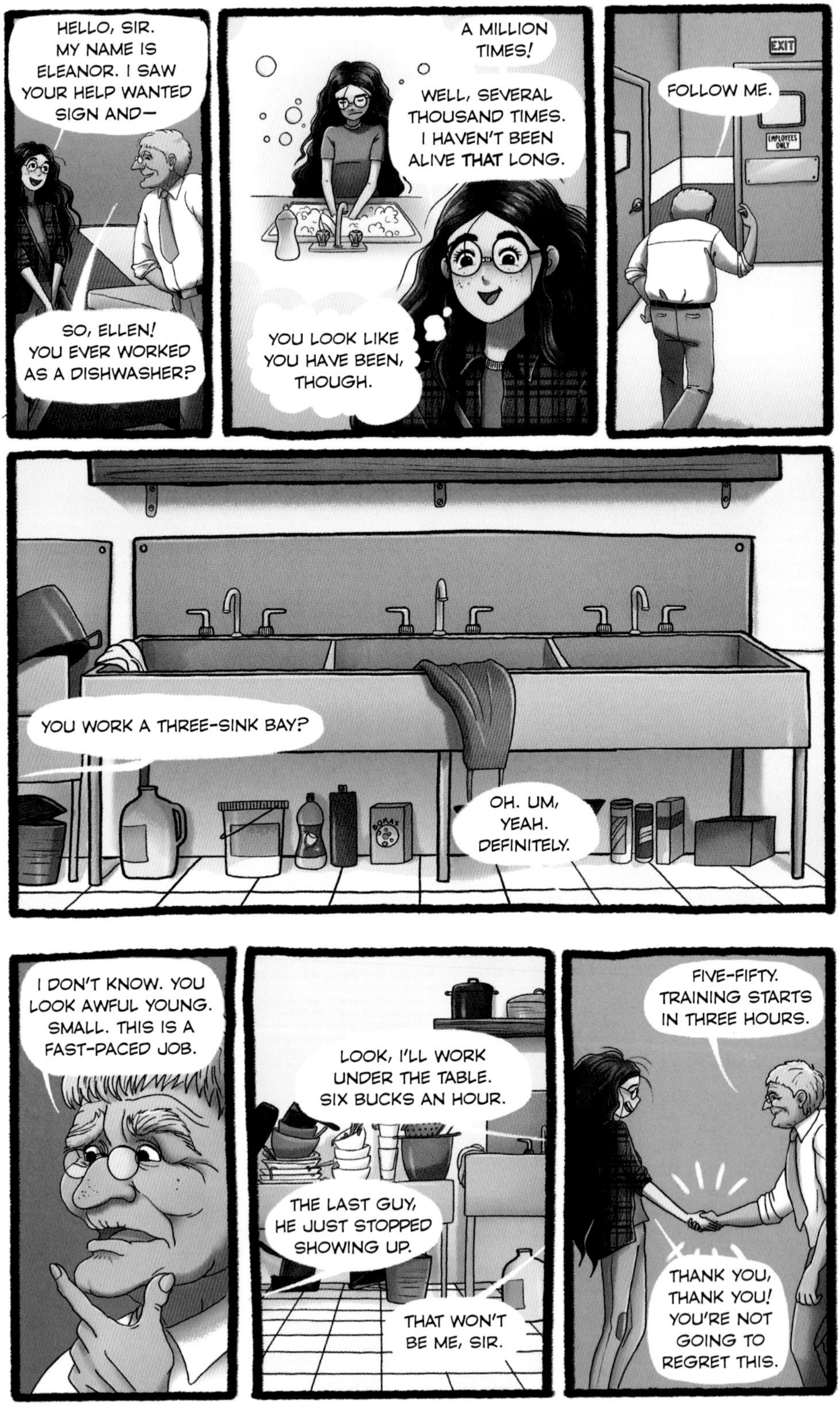
HELLO, SIR. MY NAME IS ELEANOR. I SAW YOUR HELP WANTED SIGN AND—
SO, ELLEN! YOU EVER WORKED AS A DISHWASHER?
A MILLION TIMES!
WELL, SEVERAL THOUSAND TIMES. I HAVEN'T BEEN ALIVE THAT LONG.
YOU LOOK LIKE YOU HAVE BEEN, THOUGH.
EXIT
FOLLOW ME.
EMPLOYEES ONLY
YOU WORK A THREE-SINK BAY?
BORAX
OH. UM, YEAH. DEFINITELY.
I DON'T KNOW. YOU LOOK AWFUL YOUNG. SMALL. THIS IS A FAST-PACED JOB.
LOOK, I'LL WORK UNDER THE TABLE. SIX BUCKS AN HOUR.
THE LAST GUY, HE JUST STOPPED SHOWING UP.
THAT WON'T BE ME, SIR.
FIVE-FIFTY. TRAINING STARTS IN THREE HOURS.
THANK YOU, THANK YOU! YOU'RE NOT GOING TO REGRET THIS.

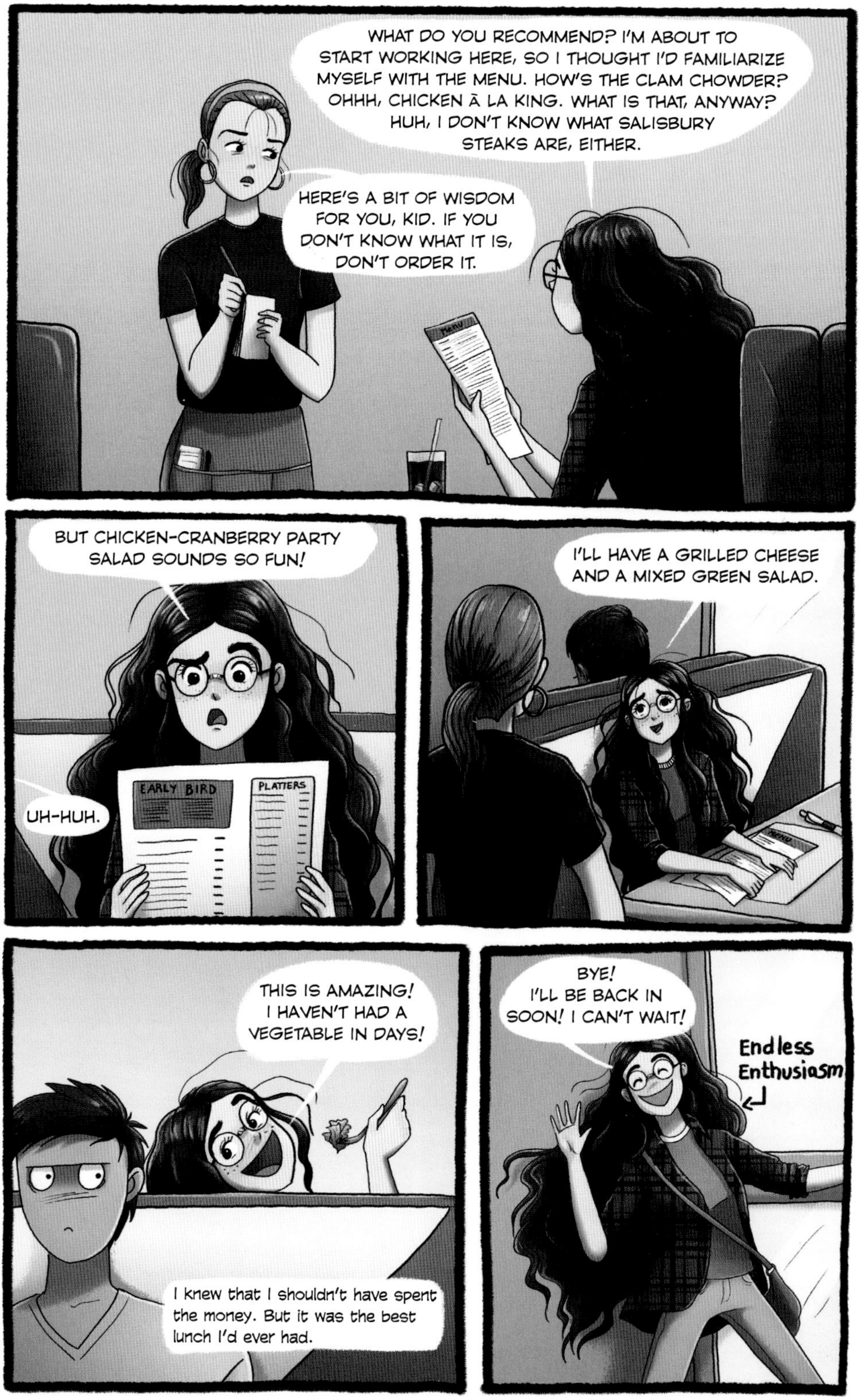
WHAT DO YOU RECOMMEND? I'M ABOUT TO START WORKING HERE, SO I THOUGHT I'D FAMILIARIZE MYSELF WITH THE MENU. HOW'S THE CLAM CHOWDER? OHHH, CHICKEN Ā LA KING. WHAT IS THAT, ANYWAY? HUH, I DON'T KNOW WHAT SALISBURY STEAKS ARE, EITHER.
HERE'S A BIT OF WISDOM FOR YOU, KID. IF YOU DON'T KNOW WHAT IT IS, DON'T ORDER IT.
MENU
BUT CHICKEN-CRANBERRY PARTY SALAD SOUNDS SO FUN!
UH-HUH.
EARLY BIRD
PLATTERS
I'LL HAVE A GRILLED CHEESE AND A MIXED GREEN SALAD.
MENU
THIS IS AMAZING! I HAVEN'T HAD A VEGETABLE IN DAYS!
I knew that I shouldn't have spent the money. But it was the best lunch I'd ever had.
BYE! I'LL BE BACK IN SOON! I CAN'T WAIT!
Endless Enthusiasm

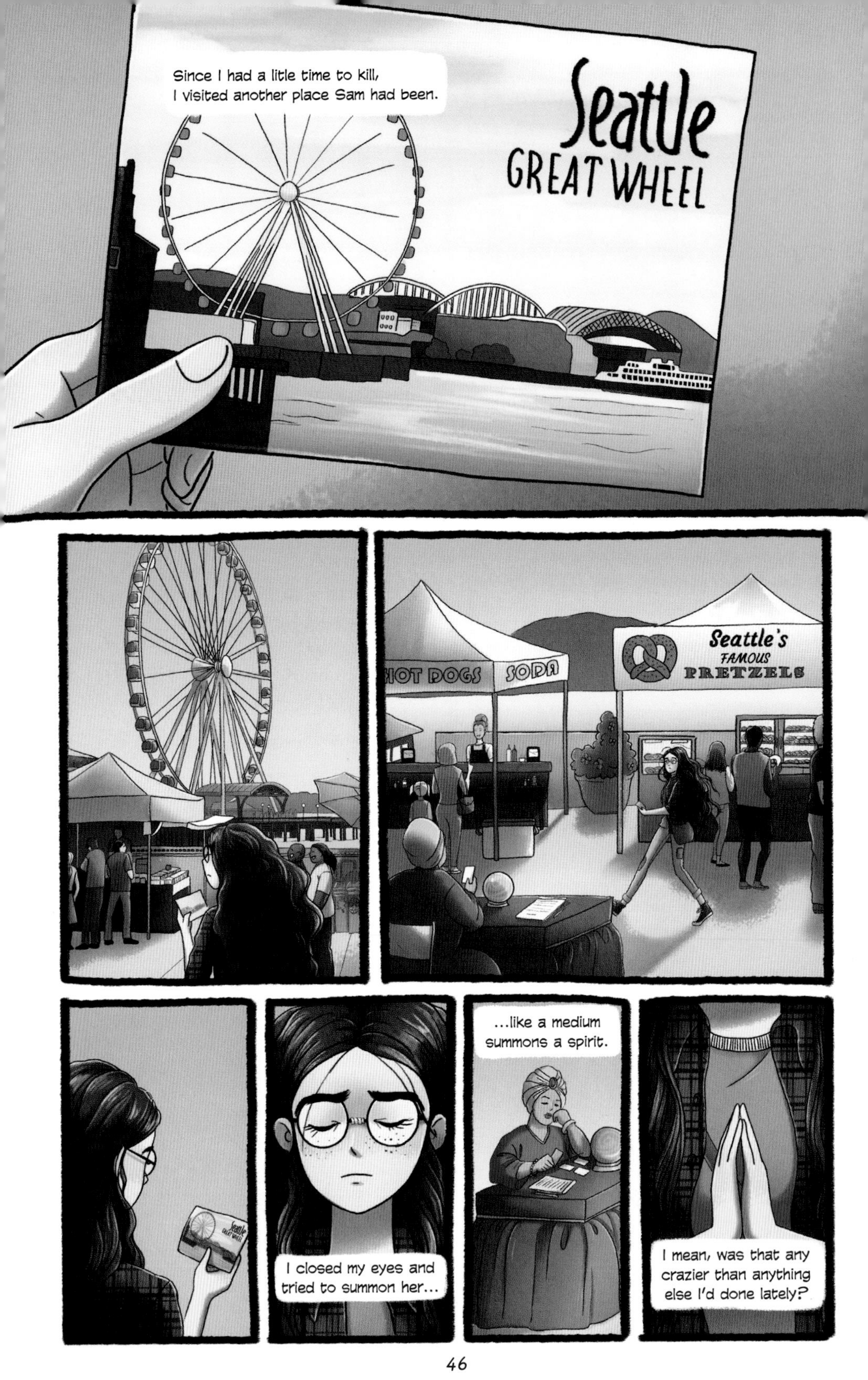
Since I had a little time to kill,
I visited another place Sam had been.
Seattle
GREAT WHEEL
HOT DOGS
SODA
Seattle's
FAMOUS
PRETZELS
Seattle
GREAT WHEEL
I closed my eyes and
tried to summon her...
...like a medium
summons a spirit.
I mean, was that any
crazier than anything
else I'd done lately?

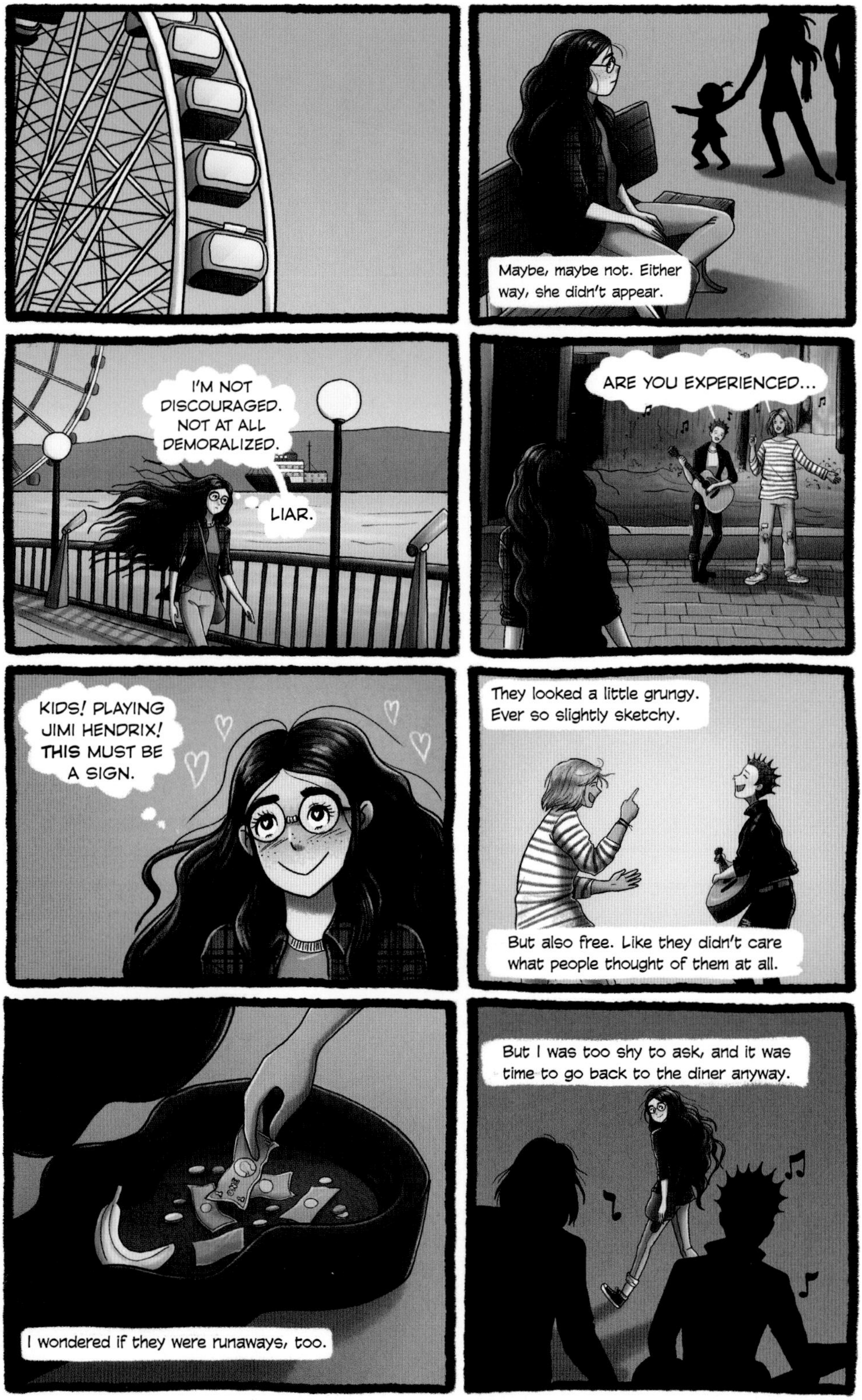
Maybe, maybe not. Either way, she didn't appear.
I'M NOT DISCOURAGED. NOT AT ALL DEMORALIZED.
LIAR.
ARE YOU EXPERIENCED...
KIDS! PLAYING JIMI HENDRIX! THIS MUST BE A SIGN.
They looked a little grungy. Ever so slightly sketchy.
But also free. Like they didn't care what people thought of them at all.
I wondered if they were runaways, too.
But I was too shy to ask, and it was time to go back to the diner anyway.

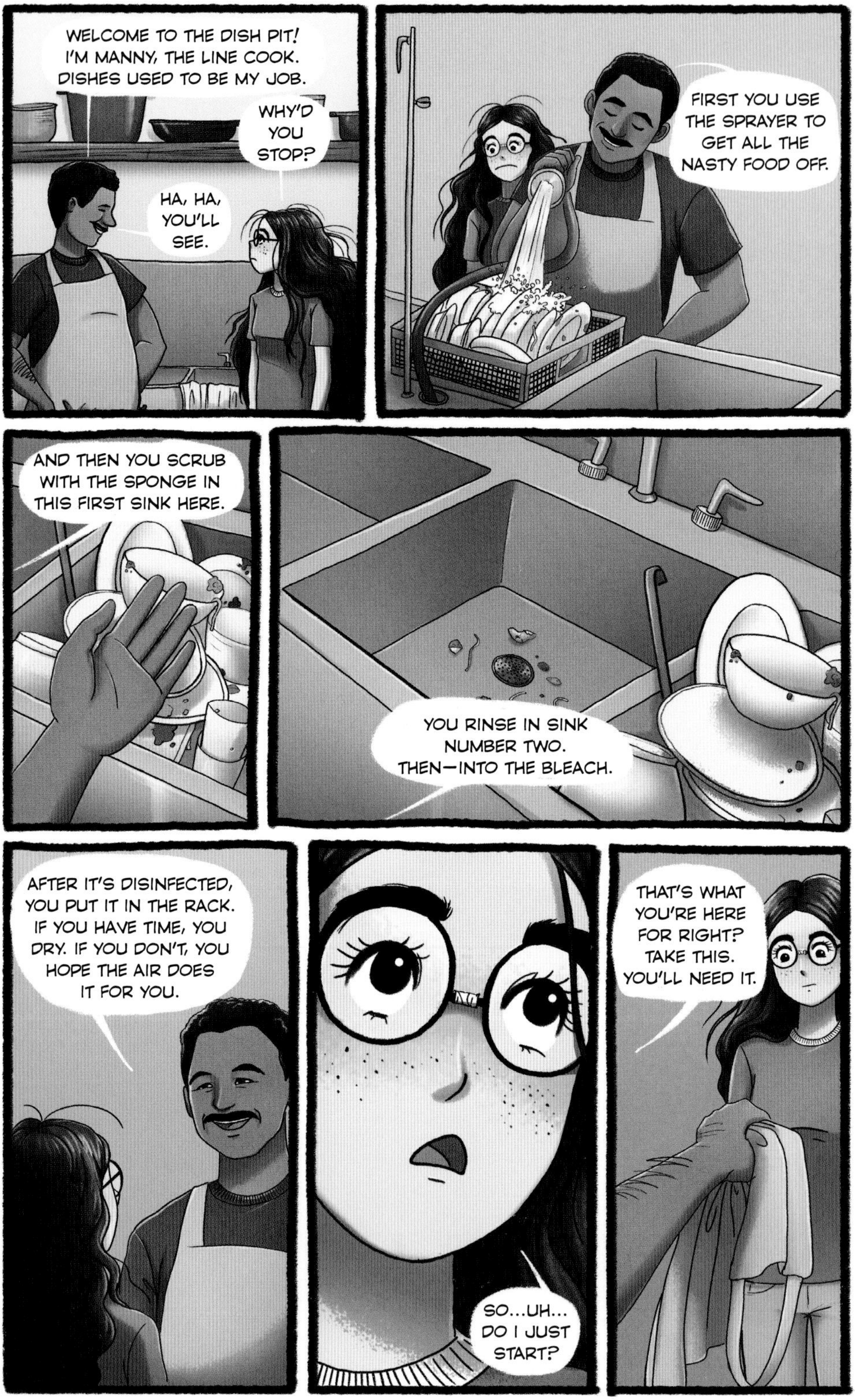
WELCOME TO THE DISH PIT! I'M MANNY, THE LINE COOK. DISHES USED TO BE MY JOB.
WHY'D YOU STOP?
HA, HA, YOU'LL SEE.
FIRST YOU USE THE SPRAYER TO GET ALL THE NASTY FOOD OFF.
AND THEN YOU SCRUB WITH THE SPONGE IN THIS FIRST SINK HERE.
YOU RINSE IN SINK NUMBER TWO. THEN—INTO THE BLEACH.
AFTER IT'S DISINFECTED, YOU PUT IT IN THE RACK. IF YOU HAVE TIME, YOU DRY. IF YOU DON'T, YOU HOPE THE AIR DOES IT FOR YOU.
SO...UH... DO I JUST START?
THAT'S WHAT YOU'RE HERE FOR RIGHT? TAKE THIS. YOU'LL NEED IT.

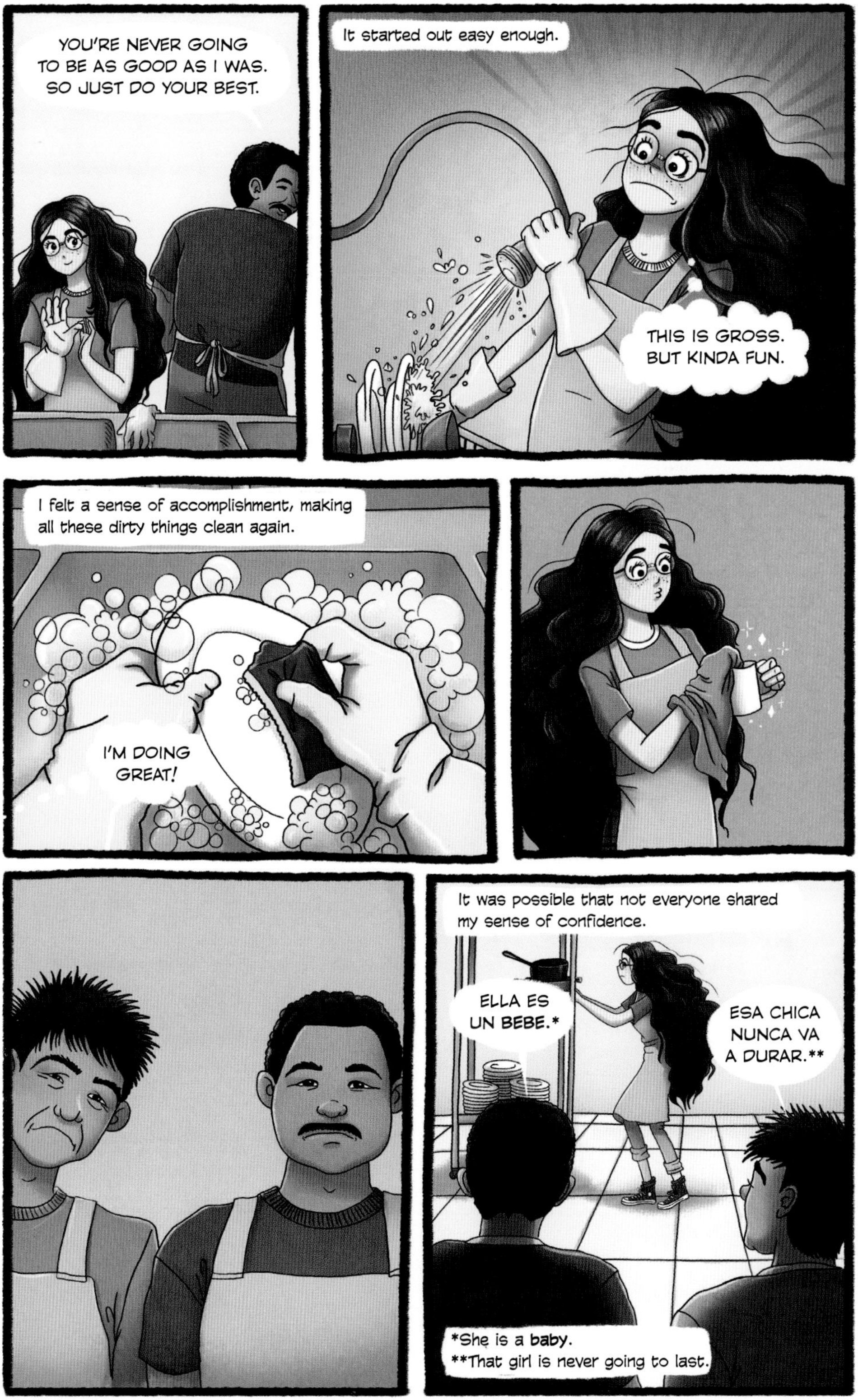
YOU'RE NEVER GOING TO BE AS GOOD AS I WAS. SO JUST DO YOUR BEST.
It started out easy enough.
THIS IS GROSS. BUT KINDA FUN.
I felt a sense of accomplishment, making all these dirty things clean again.
I'M DOING GREAT!
It was possible that not everyone shared my sense of confidence.
ELLA ES UN BEBE.*
ESA CHICA NUNCA VA A DURAR.**
*She is a **baby**.
**That girl is never going to last.

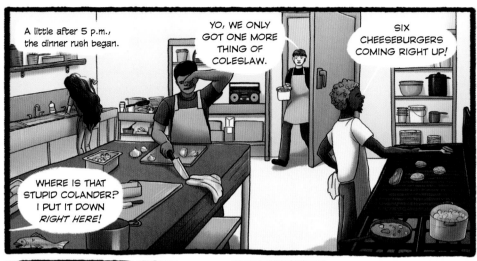

A little after 5 p.m., the dinner rush began.

YO, WE ONLY GOT ONE MORE THING OF COLESLAW.

SIX CHEESEBURGERS COMING RIGHT UP!

WHERE IS THAT STUPID COLANDER? I PUT IT DOWN *RIGHT HERE!*

BILL, CAN YOU GRAB THE MOP? TABLE 18 SPILLED SOUP.

HOW 'BOUT I GIVE 'EM A RAG AND THEY CLEAN IT UP THEIR DANG SELVES?

BRAD, I WROTE **NO KETCHUP** ON THE TICKET. I NEED ANOTHER KIDDIE BURGER BEFORE THAT LITTLE BRAT **SCREAMS** HIS HEAD OFF.

It must have been 90 degrees in that kitchen.

And about 120 decibels.

HURRY UP WITH THE CARROTS, BRO!

♪ ANOTHER ONE BITES THE DUST...

DOES THIS BACON SMELL FUNNY?

TABLE 7 ORDERED THE MUSSELS.

I HOPE THEY HAVE WILLS.

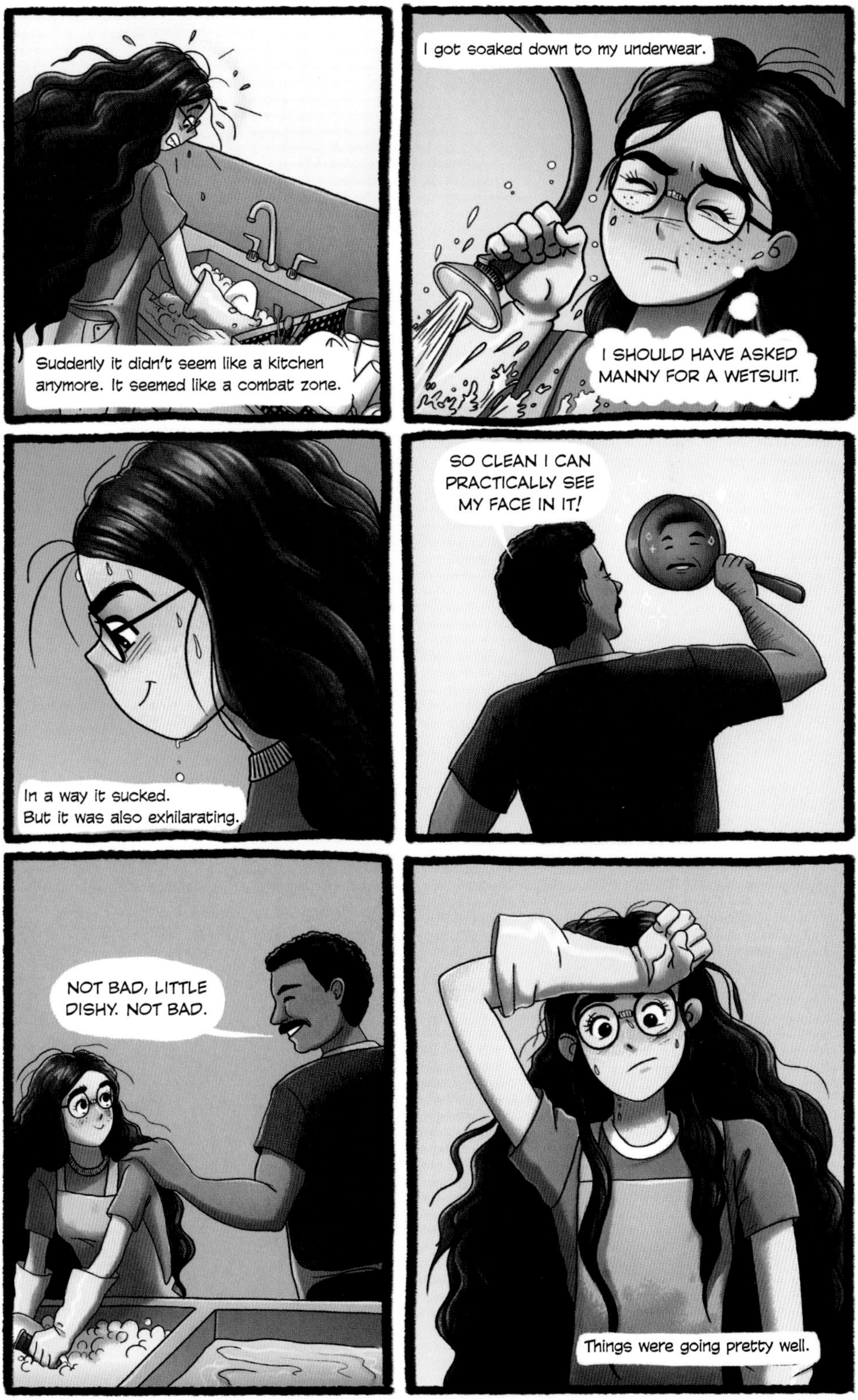
Suddenly it didn't seem like a kitchen anymore. It seemed like a combat zone.
I got soaked down to my underwear.
I SHOULD HAVE ASKED MANNY FOR A WETSUIT.
In a way it sucked. But it was also exhilarating.
SO CLEAN I CAN PRACTICALLY SEE MY FACE IN IT!
NOT BAD, LITTLE DISHY. NOT BAD.
Things were going pretty well.

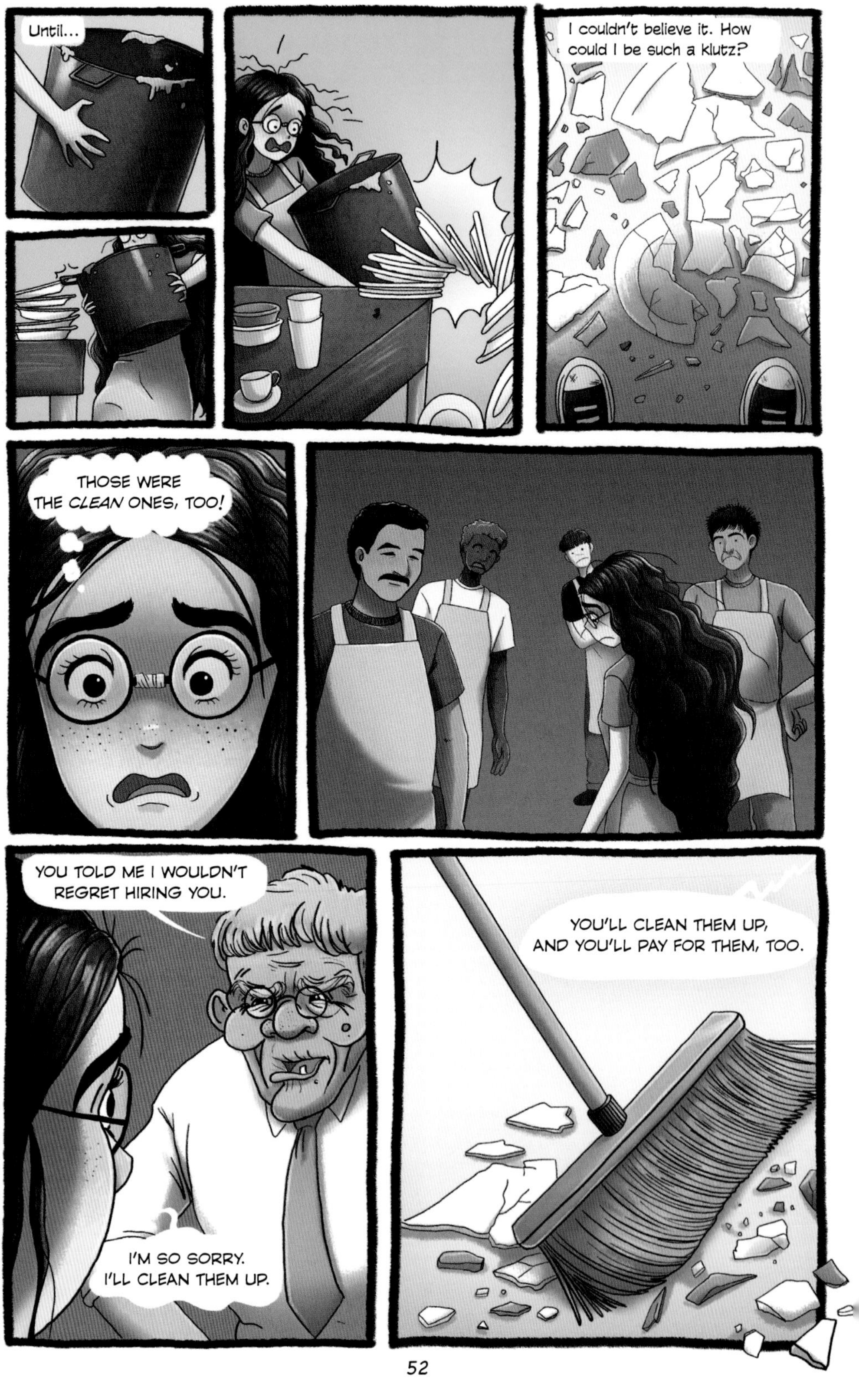
Until...
I couldn't believe it. How could I be such a klutz?
THOSE WERE THE *CLEAN* ONES, TOO!
YOU TOLD ME I WOULDN'T REGRET HIRING YOU.
I'M SO SORRY. I'LL CLEAN THEM UP.
YOU'LL CLEAN THEM UP, AND YOU'LL PAY FOR THEM, TOO.

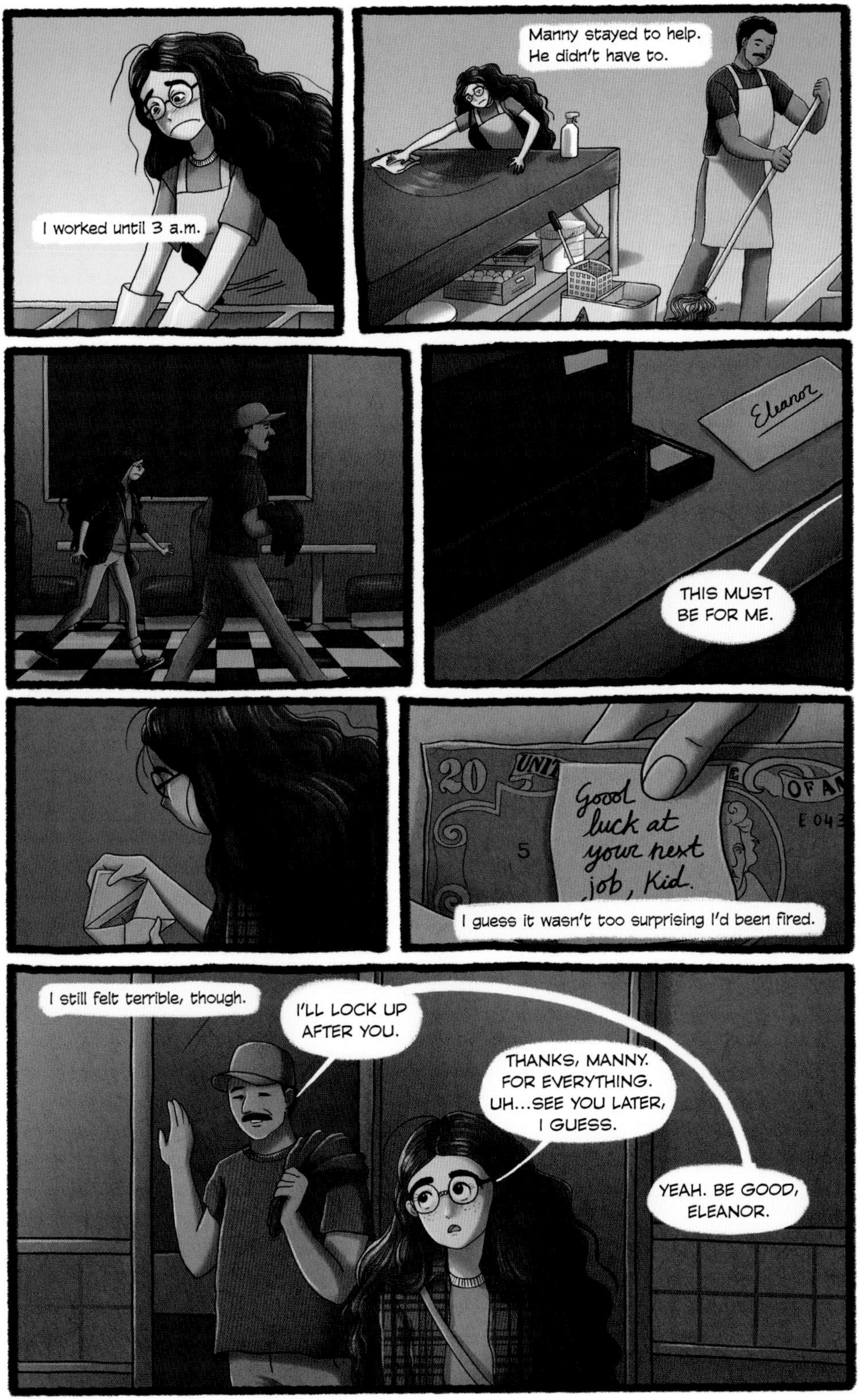
I worked until 3 a.m.
Manny stayed to help. He didn't have to.
Eleanor
THIS MUST BE FOR ME.
Good luck at your next job, Kid.
I guess it wasn't too surprising I'd been fired.
I still felt terrible, though.
I'LL LOCK UP AFTER YOU.
THANKS, MANNY. FOR EVERYTHING. UH...SEE YOU LATER, I GUESS.
YEAH. BE GOOD, ELEANOR.

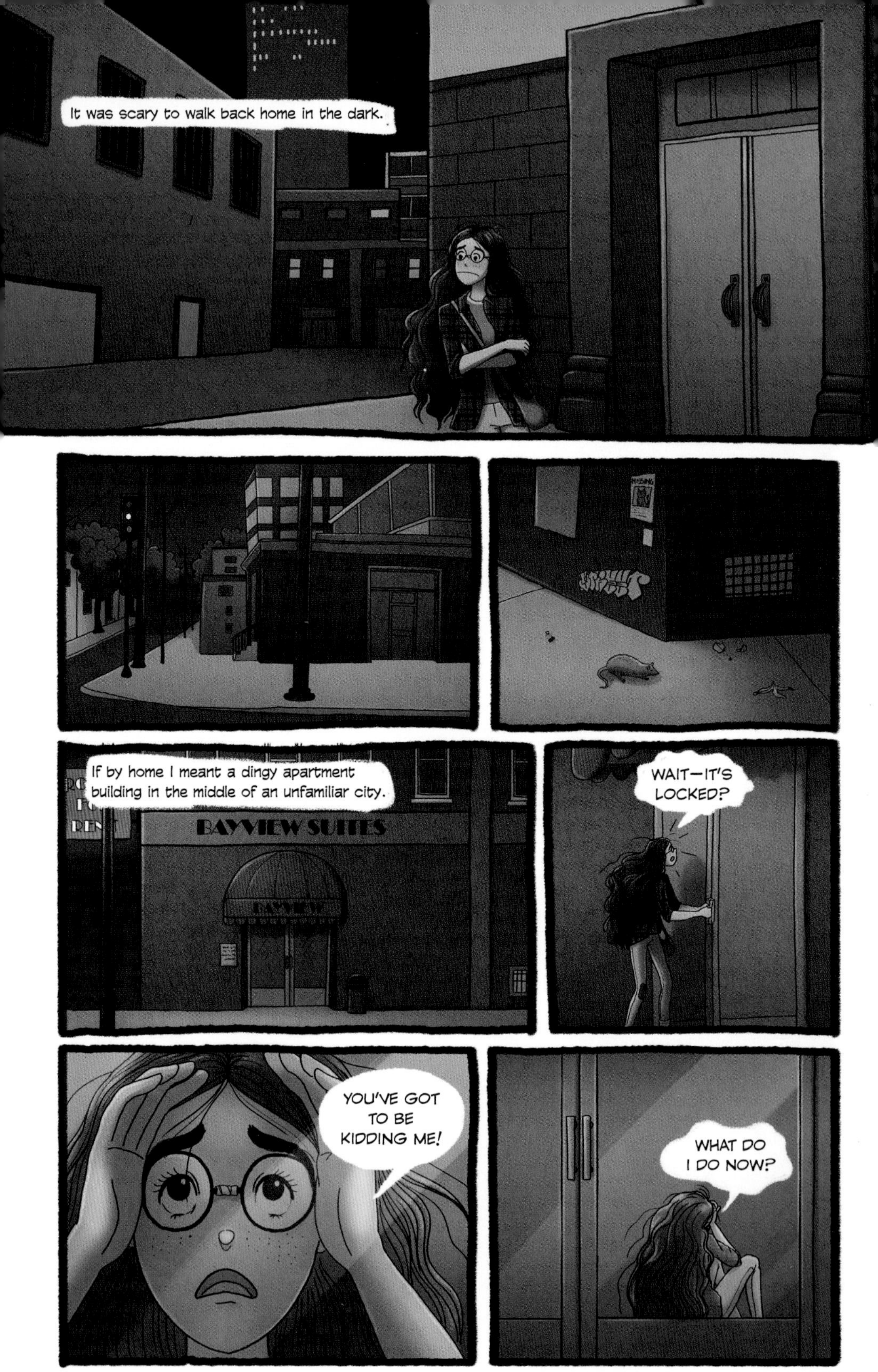
It was scary to walk back home in the dark.
If by home I meant a dingy apartment building in the middle of an unfamiliar city.
BAYVIEW SUITES
WAIT—IT'S LOCKED?
YOU'VE GOT TO BE KIDDING ME!
WHAT DO I DO NOW?

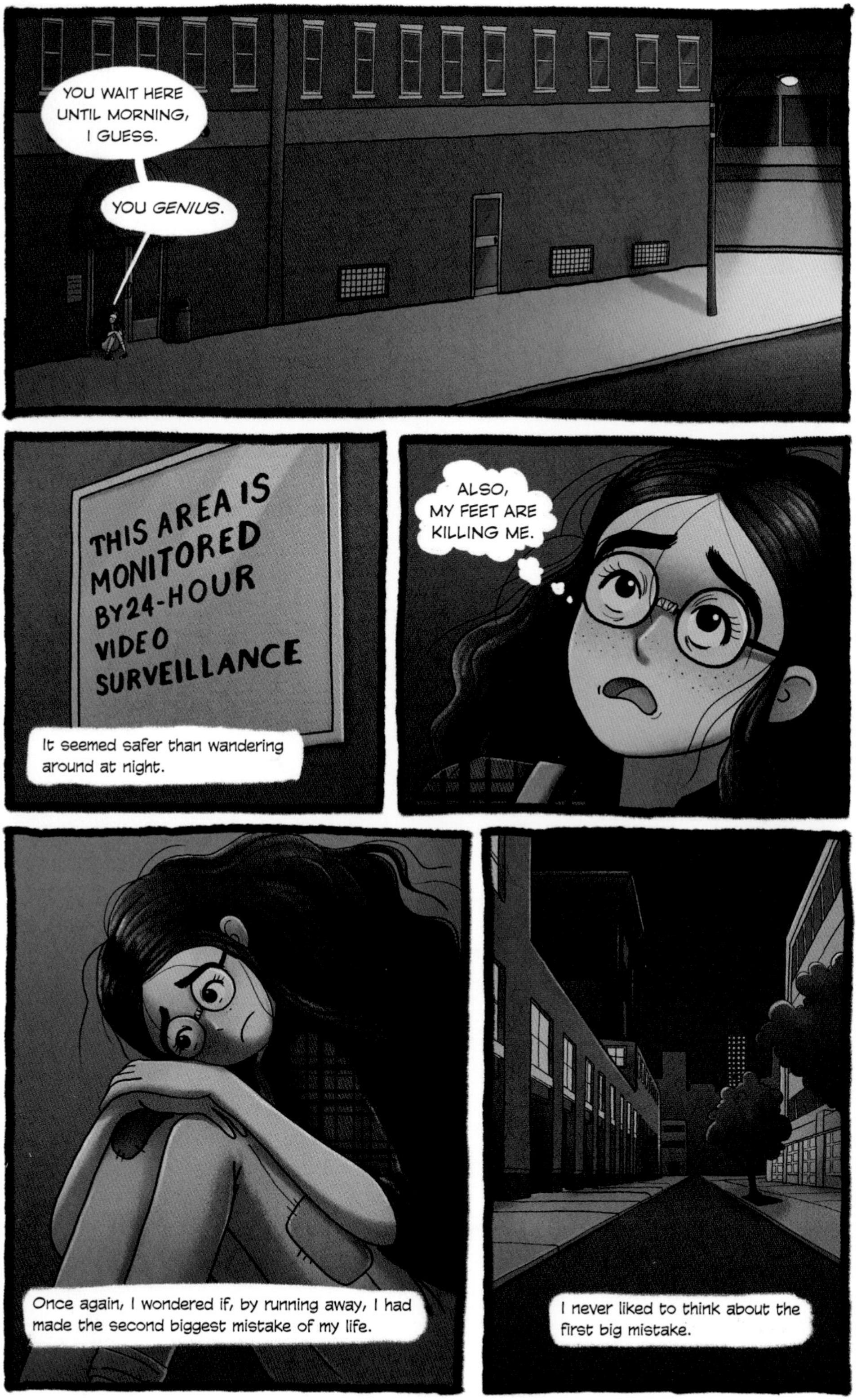
YOU WAIT HERE UNTIL MORNING, I GUESS.
YOU GENIUS.
THIS AREA IS MONITORED BY24-HOUR VIDEO SURVEILLANCE
It seemed safer than wandering around at night.
ALSO, MY FEET ARE KILLING ME.
Once again, I wondered if, by running away, I had made the second biggest mistake of my life.
I never liked to think about the first big mistake.

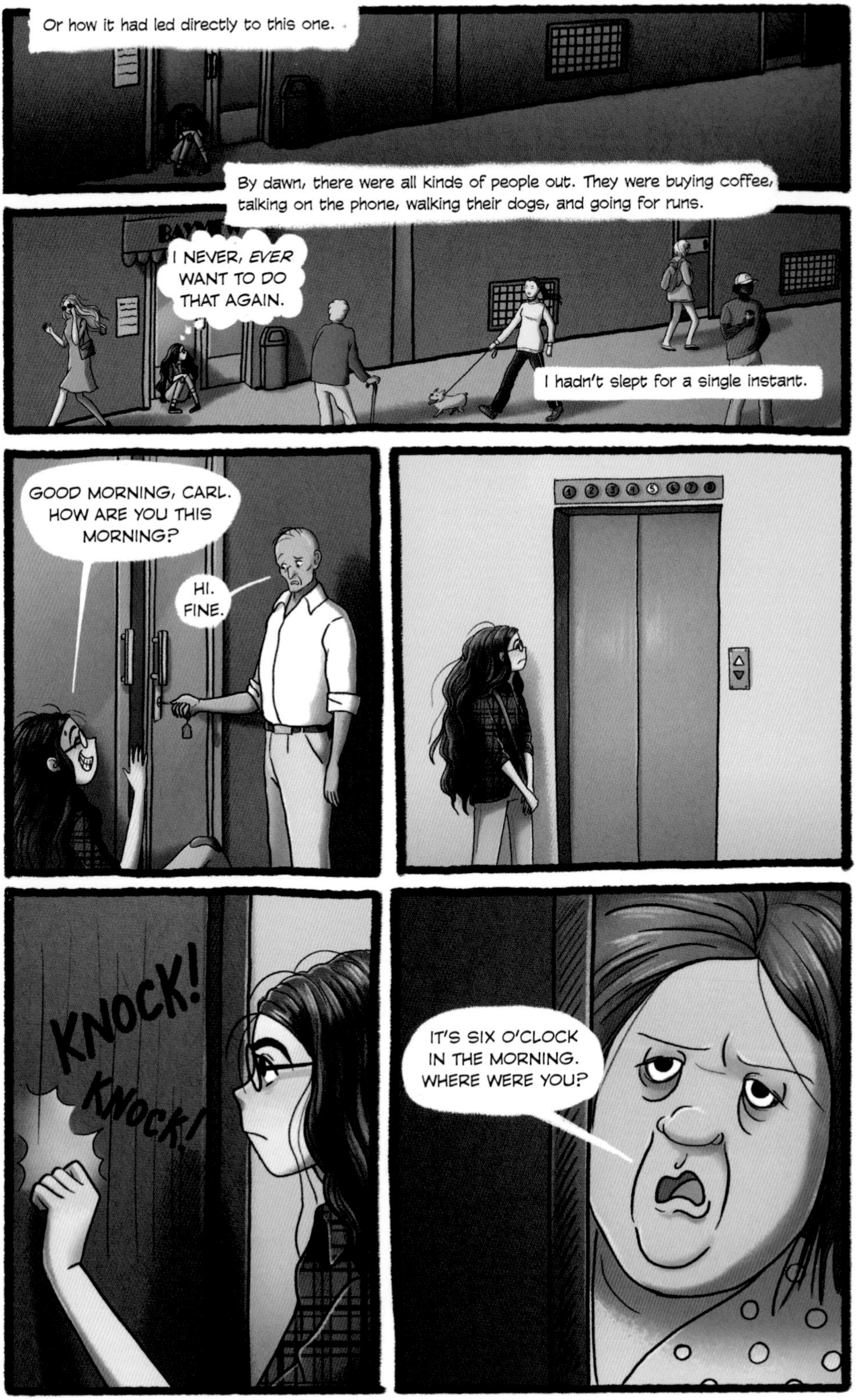
Or how it had led directly to this one.
By dawn, there were all kinds of people out. They were buying coffee, talking on the phone, walking their dogs, and going for runs.
I NEVER, EVER WANT TO DO THAT AGAIN.
I hadn't slept for a single instant.
GOOD MORNING, CARL. HOW ARE YOU THIS MORNING?
HI. FINE.
KNOCK! KNOCK!
IT'S SIX O'CLOCK IN THE MORNING. WHERE WERE YOU?

I'M SORRY. I WORKED REALLY LATE LAST NIGHT, AND WHEN I GOT BACK HERE THE DOORS WERE LOCKED.

YOU WERE WORKING? LIKE A JOB? I THOUGHT YOU WERE HERE TO VISIT YOUR COUSIN.

...

WHAT ARE YOU DOING HERE? ARE YOU REALLY IN COLLEGE? DO YOU EVEN *HAVE* A COUSIN?

Leo wasn't exactly *nice*, but she was letting me stay with her.

I felt like I owed her the truth.

YOU NEVER LEARN, DO YOU, LEO? YOU TRUST PEOPLE AND THEY ALWAYS TAKE ADVANTAGE. YOU'RE JUST TOO SOFT.

SORRY I HAVEN'T, UM, BEEN COMPLETELY HONEST. I DON'T HAVE A COUSIN. I MEAN, I DO, BUT SHE DOESN'T LIVE HERE.

SHE'S AN X-RAY TECHNICIAN IN MONTANA. SHE DID GO TO U-DUB, THOUGH. I DIDN'T MAKE THAT PART UP. SHE'S REALLY NICE.

SORRY, I'M BEING KIND OF RANDOM, AREN'T I? YOU WANT TO KNOW WHAT I'M DOING IN SEATTLE. WELL, I CAME HERE BECAUSE... I'M LOOKING FOR SOMEONE.

I DON'T KNOW HOW I'M GOING TO FIND HER, THOUGH...SHE'S...WELL... IT'S BEEN A WHILE SINCE I'VE SEEN HER. AND I'M NOT SURE SHE WANTS TO BE FOUND.

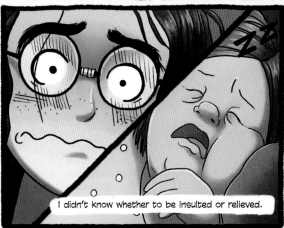

ZZZZzz...

I didn't know whether to be insulted or relieved.

I'M SORRY I MADE YOU WORRY.

I went straight to bed, and sleep until noon.

WHAT?

—SNORT!—

WHERE AM I?

OH, RIGHT.

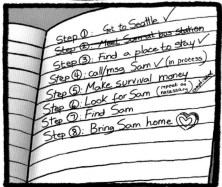

Step ① : Get to Seattle ✓
Step ② : Meet Sam at bus station ✓
Step ③ : Find a place to stay ✓
Step ④ : call/msg Sam ✓ (in process)
Step ⑤ : Make survival money
Step ⑥ : Look for Sam (repeat as necessary) continued
Step ⑦ : Find Sam
Step ⑧ : Bring Sam home ♡

Seeing those kids at the fountain had given me an idea.

An idea I frankly should've had already.

Sam used to skip school to hang out at Sonic Boom, the music store two towns over.

Making friends was easy for her.

EFFORTLESSLY COOL

So was blowing off homework, chores, and my parents' attempts to ground her.

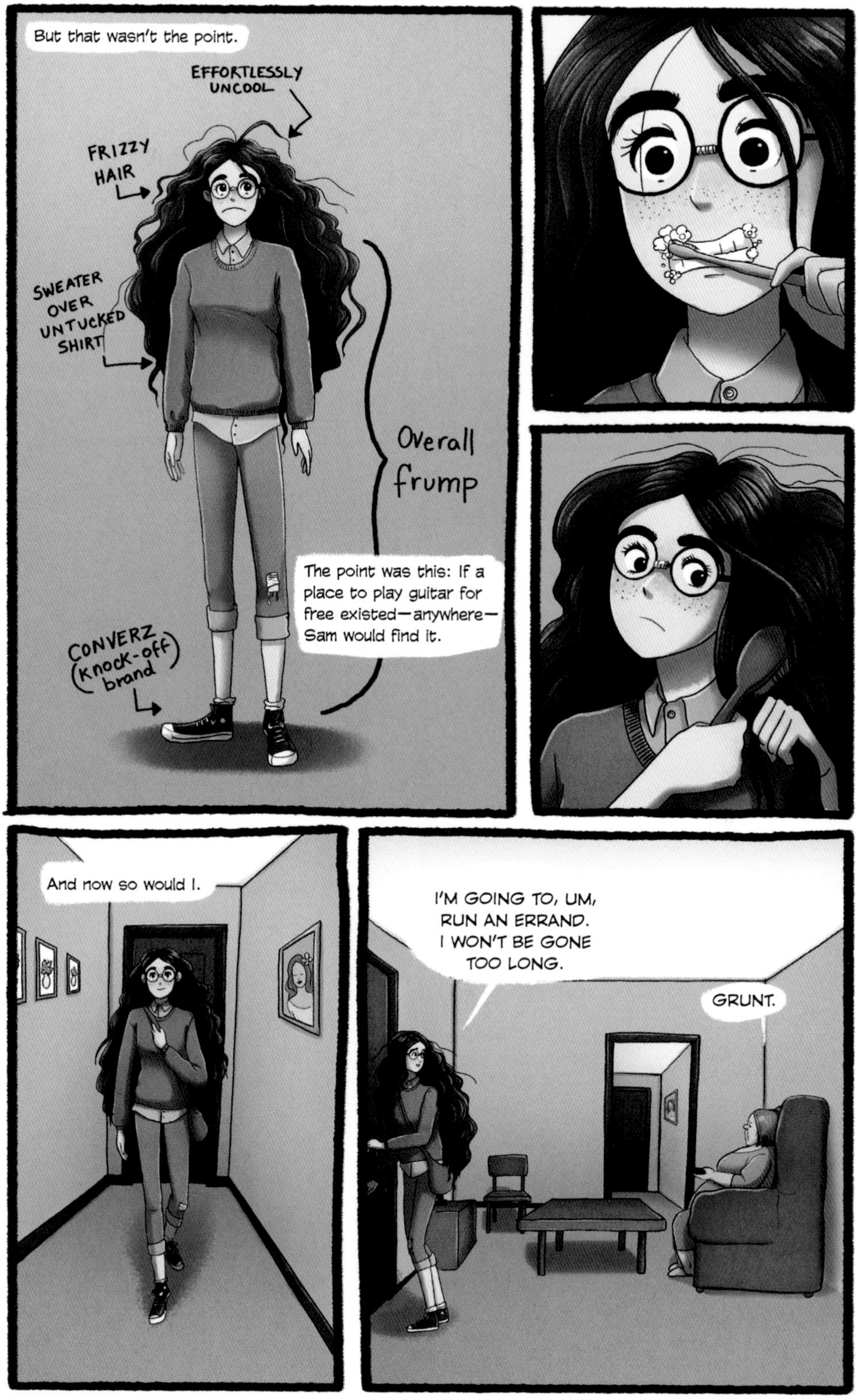
But that wasn't the point.
EFFORTLESSLY UNCOOL
FRIZZY HAIR
SWEATER OVER UNTUCKED SHIRT
Overall frump
The point was this: If a place to play guitar for free existed—anywhere—Sam would find it.
CONVERZ (knock-off brand)
And now so would I.
I'M GOING TO, UM, RUN AN ERRAND. I WON'T BE GONE TOO LONG.
GRUNT.

EMERALD CITY GUITARS, HERE I COME.

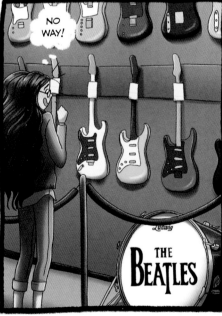

NO WAY!

THE BEATLES

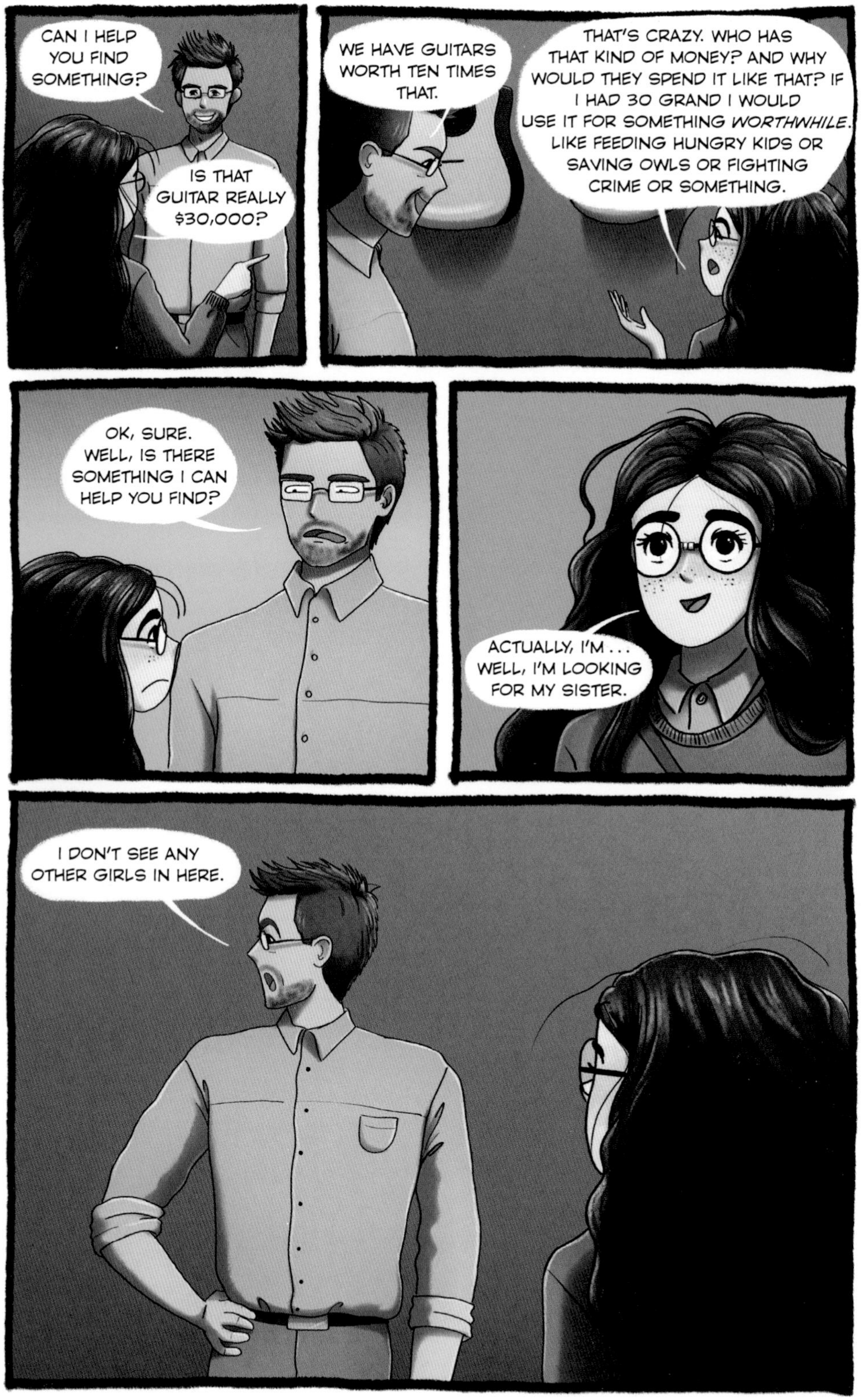
CAN I HELP YOU FIND SOMETHING?
IS THAT GUITAR REALLY $30,000?
WE HAVE GUITARS WORTH TEN TIMES THAT.
THAT'S CRAZY. WHO HAS THAT KIND OF MONEY? AND WHY WOULD THEY SPEND IT LIKE THAT? IF I HAD 30 GRAND I WOULD USE IT FOR SOMETHING *WORTHWHILE*. LIKE FEEDING HUNGRY KIDS OR SAVING OWLS OR FIGHTING CRIME OR SOMETHING.
OK, SURE. WELL, IS THERE SOMETHING I CAN HELP YOU FIND?
ACTUALLY, I'M . . . WELL, I'M LOOKING FOR MY SISTER.
I DON'T SEE ANY OTHER GIRLS IN HERE.

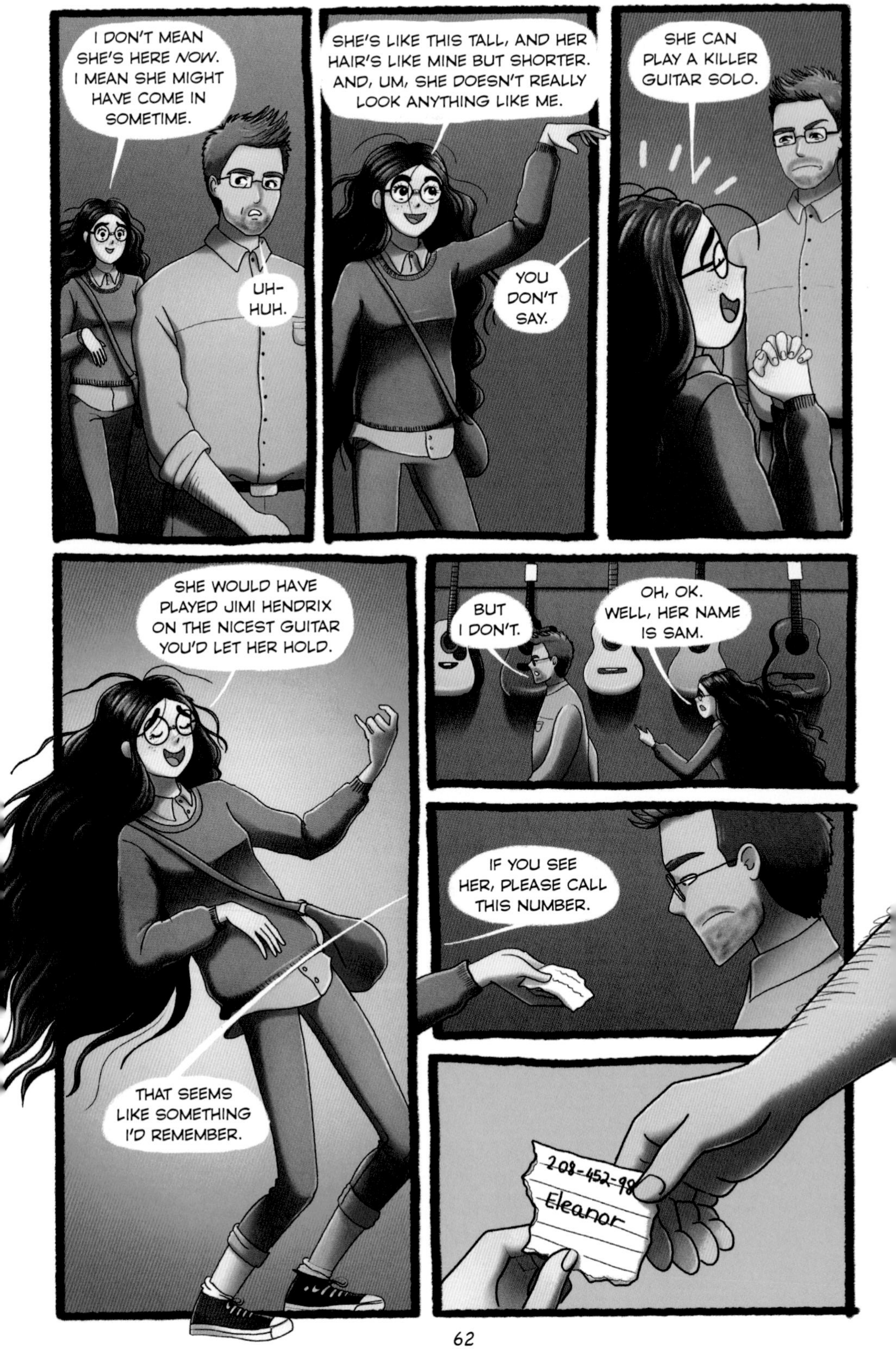
I DON'T MEAN SHE'S HERE *NOW*. I MEAN SHE MIGHT HAVE COME IN SOMETIME.
UH-HUH.
SHE'S LIKE THIS TALL, AND HER HAIR'S LIKE MINE BUT SHORTER. AND, UM, SHE DOESN'T REALLY LOOK ANYTHING LIKE ME.
YOU DON'T SAY.
SHE CAN PLAY A KILLER GUITAR SOLO.
SHE WOULD HAVE PLAYED JIMI HENDRIX ON THE NICEST GUITAR YOU'D LET HER HOLD.
THAT SEEMS LIKE SOMETHING I'D REMEMBER.
OH, OK. WELL, HER NAME IS SAM.
BUT I DON'T.
IF YOU SEE HER, PLEASE CALL THIS NUMBER.
208-452-98
Eleanor

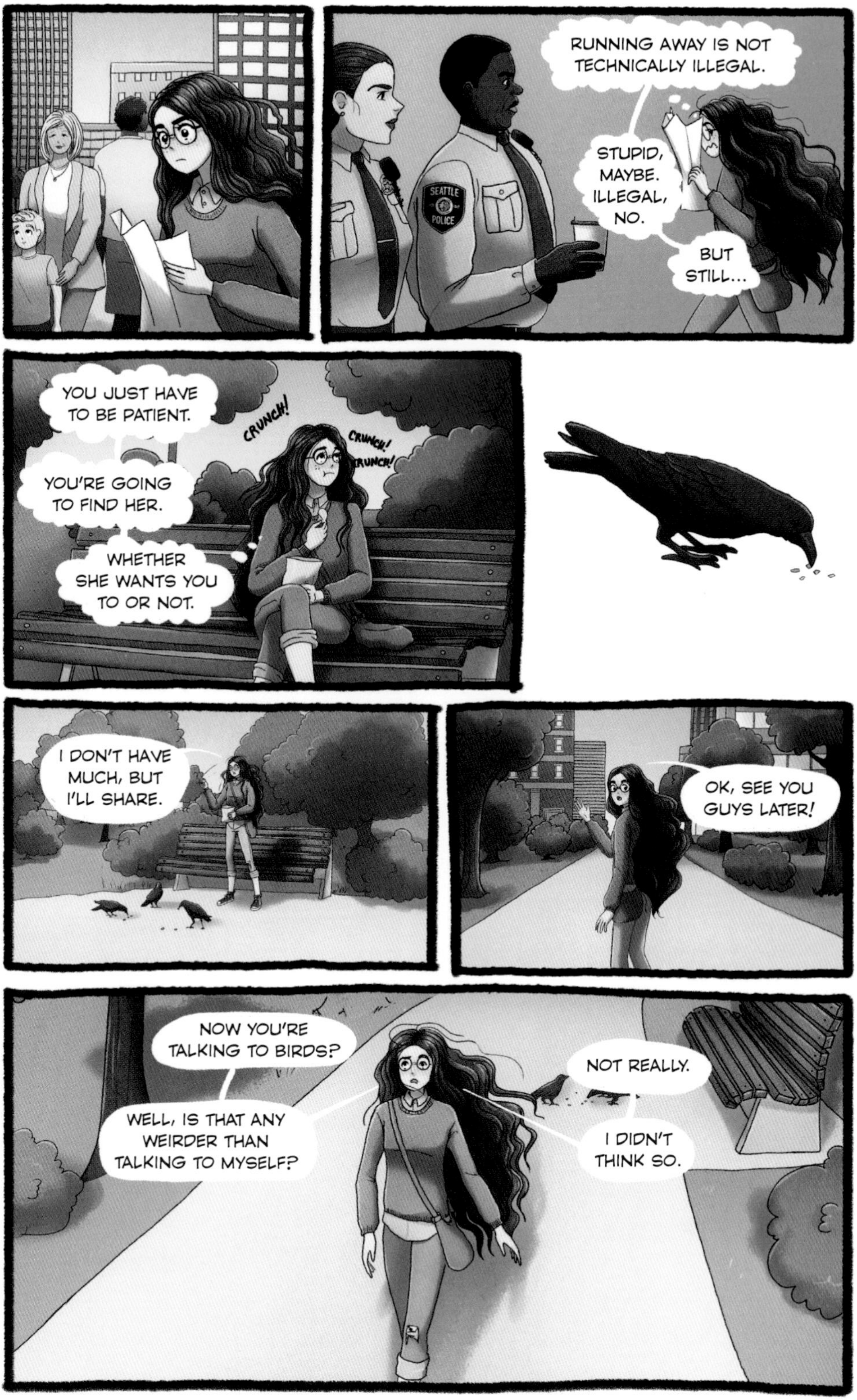
RUNNING AWAY IS NOT TECHNICALLY ILLEGAL.
STUPID, MAYBE. ILLEGAL, NO.
BUT STILL...
YOU JUST HAVE TO BE PATIENT.
CRUNCH!
CRUNCH!
CRUNCH!
YOU'RE GOING TO FIND HER.
WHETHER SHE WANTS YOU TO OR NOT.
SEATTLE POLICE
I DON'T HAVE MUCH, BUT I'LL SHARE.
OK, SEE YOU GUYS LATER!
NOW YOU'RE TALKING TO BIRDS?
WELL, IS THAT ANY WEIRDER THAN TALKING TO MYSELF?
NOT REALLY.
I DIDN'T THINK SO.

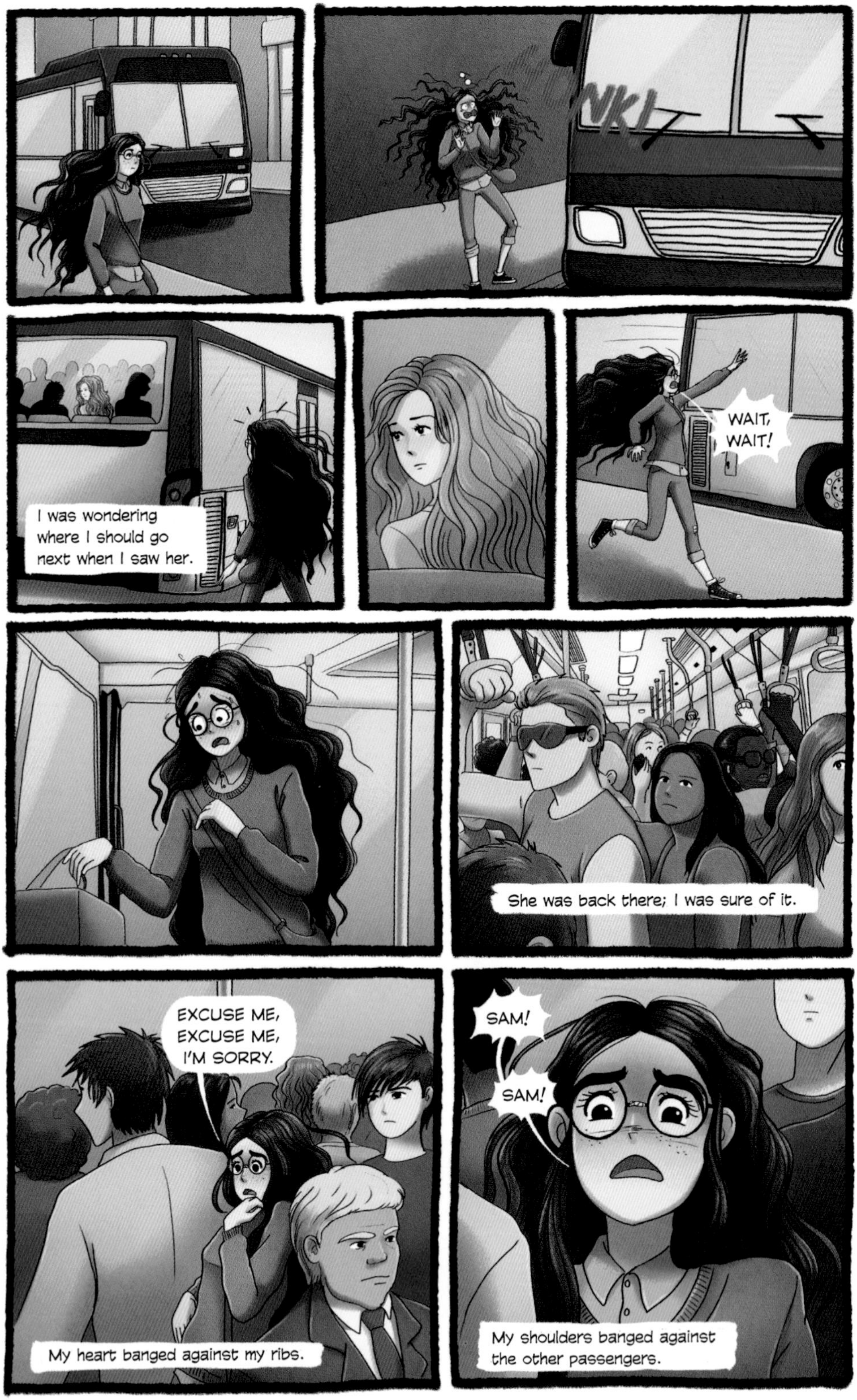
NK!
I was wondering where I should go next when I saw her.
WAIT, WAIT!
She was back there; I was sure of it.
EXCUSE ME, EXCUSE ME, I'M SORRY.
My heart banged against my ribs.
SAM!
SAM!
My shoulders banged against the other passengers.

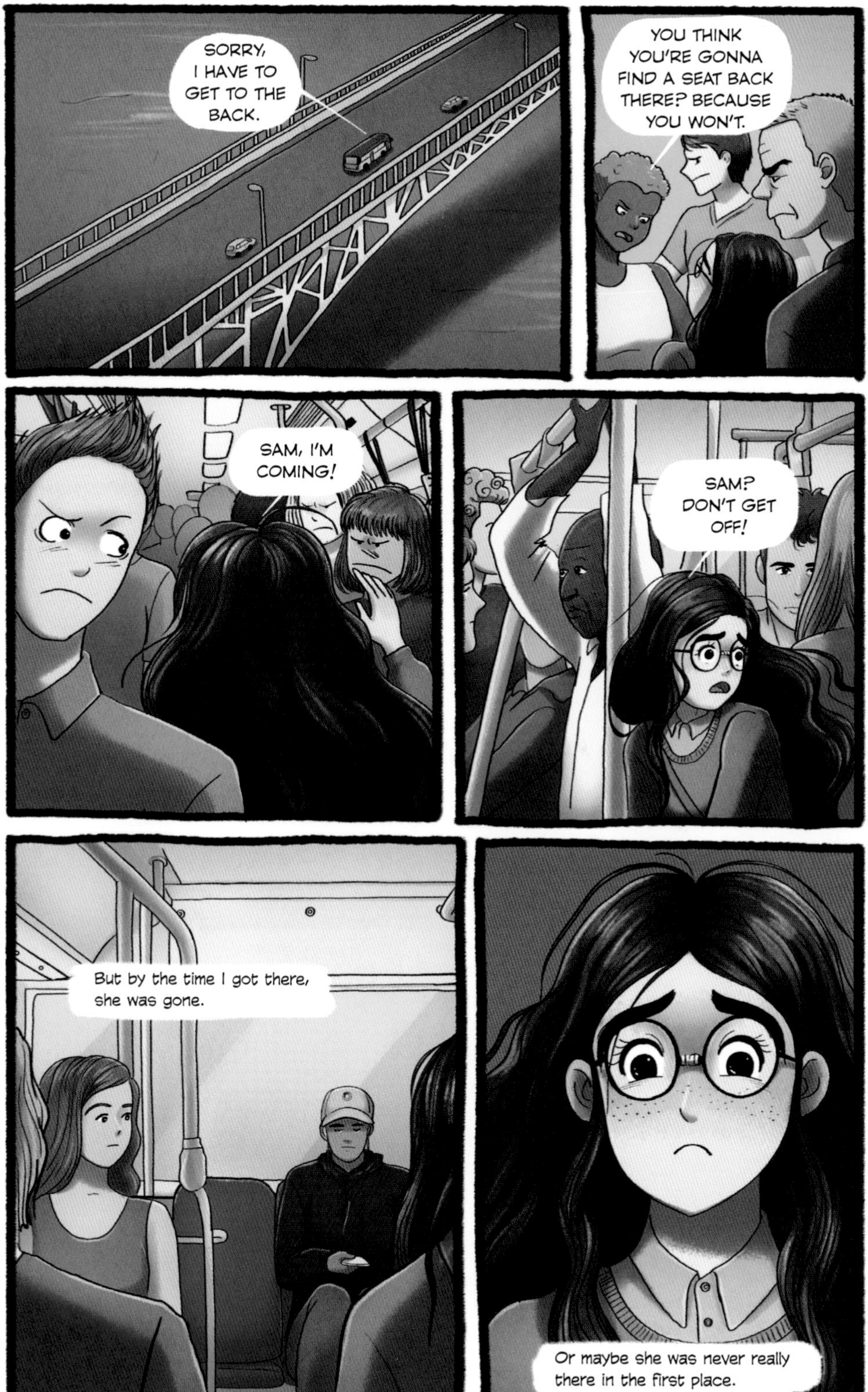
SORRY, I HAVE TO GET TO THE BACK.
YOU THINK YOU'RE GONNA FIND A SEAT BACK THERE? BECAUSE YOU WON'T.
SAM, I'M COMING!
SAM? DON'T GET OFF!
But by the time I got there, she was gone.
Or maybe she was never really there in the first place.

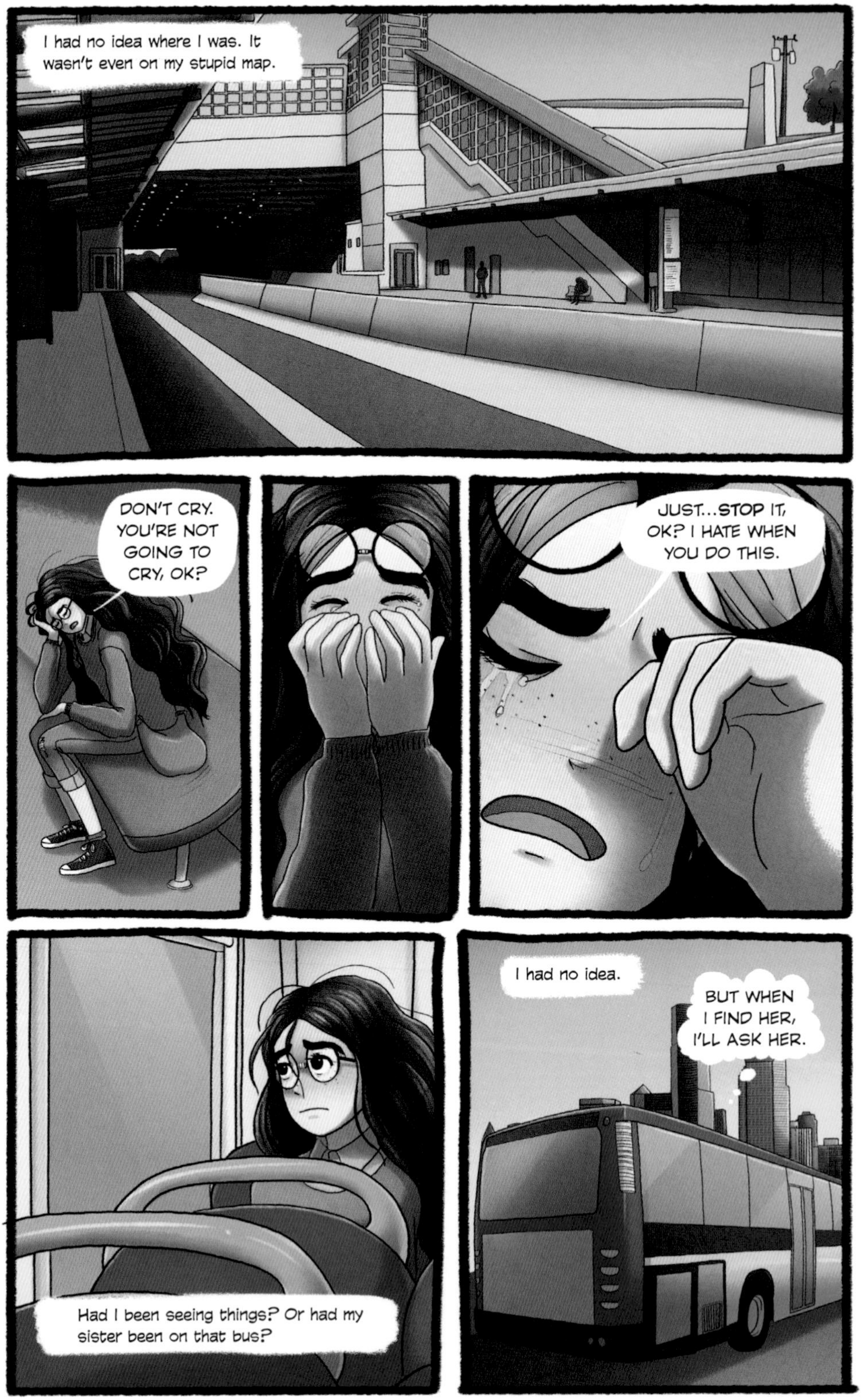

I had no idea where I was. It wasn't even on my stupid map.
DON'T CRY. YOU'RE NOT GOING TO CRY, OK?
JUST...STOP IT, OK? I HATE WHEN YOU DO THIS.
Had I been seeing things? Or had my sister been on that bus?
I had no idea.
BUT WHEN I FIND HER, I'LL ASK HER.

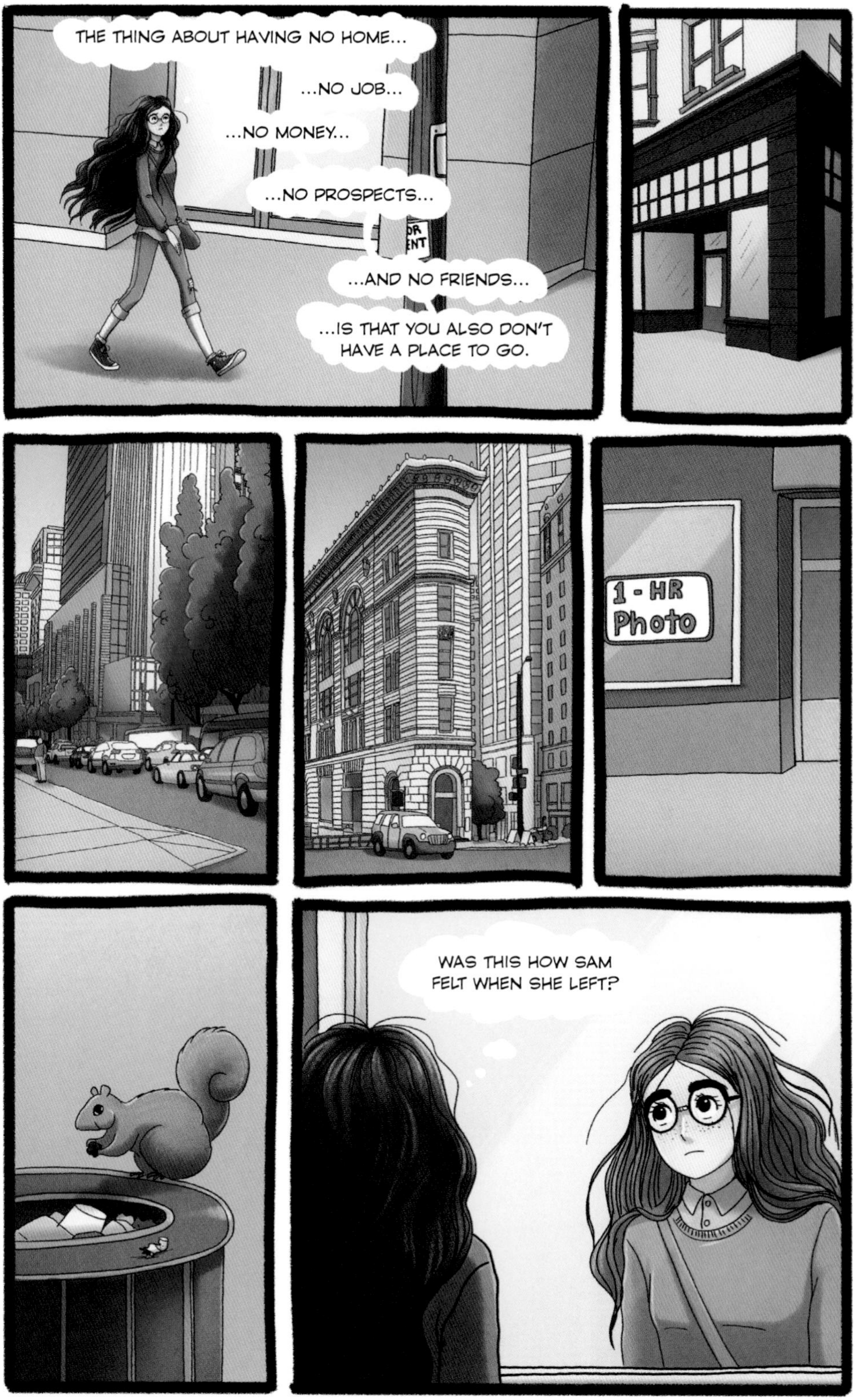
THE THING ABOUT HAVING NO HOME...
...NO JOB...
...NO MONEY...
...NO PROSPECTS...
...AND NO FRIENDS...
...IS THAT YOU ALSO DON'T HAVE A PLACE TO GO.
1-HR Photo
WAS THIS HOW SAM FELT WHEN SHE LEFT?

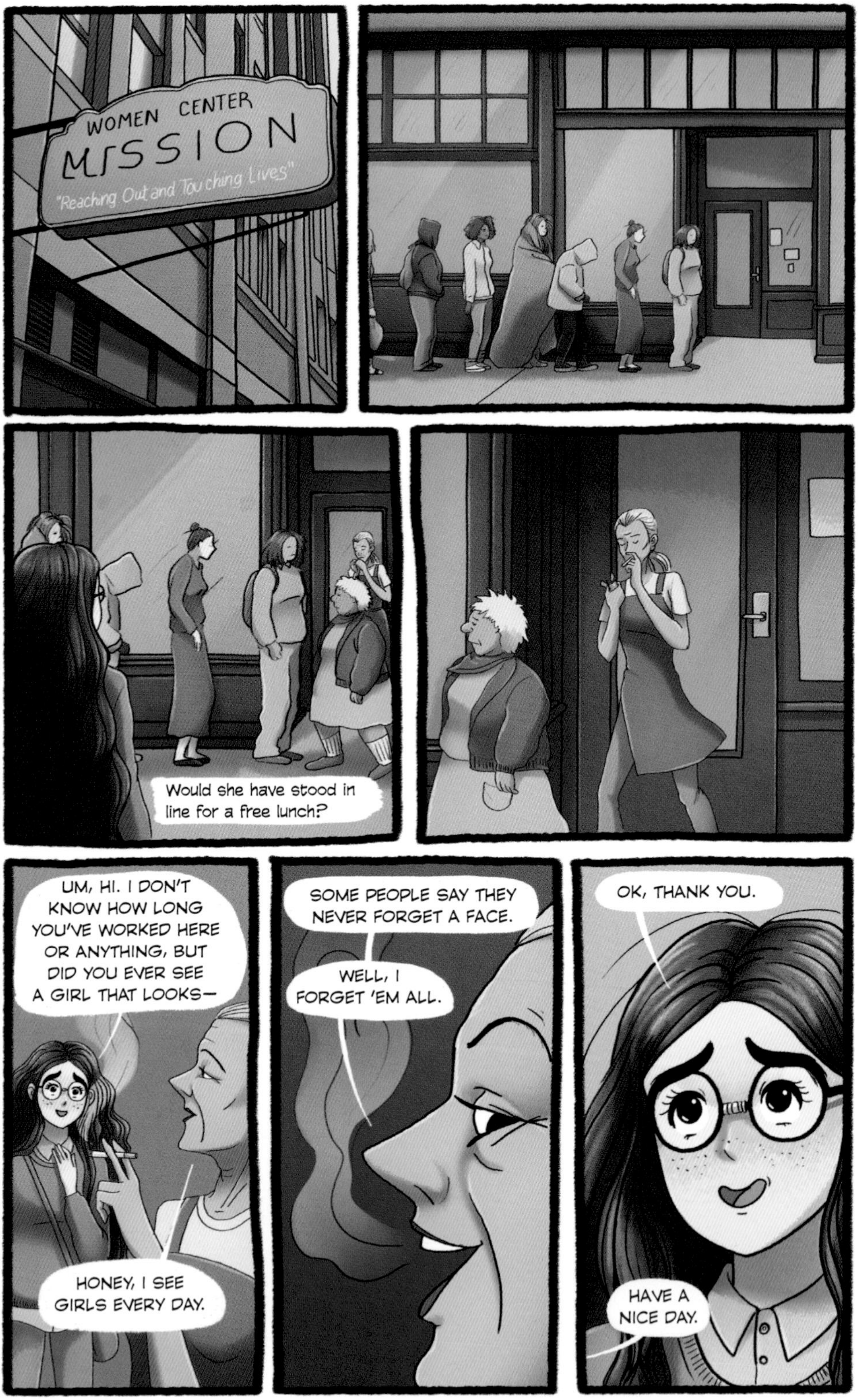
WOMEN CENTER
MISSION
"Reaching Out and Touching Lives"
Would she have stood in line for a free lunch?
UM, HI. I DON'T KNOW HOW LONG YOU'VE WORKED HERE OR ANYTHING, BUT DID YOU EVER SEE A GIRL THAT LOOKS—
HONEY, I SEE GIRLS EVERY DAY.
SOME PEOPLE SAY THEY NEVER FORGET A FACE.
WELL, I FORGET 'EM ALL.
OK, THANK YOU.
HAVE A NICE DAY.

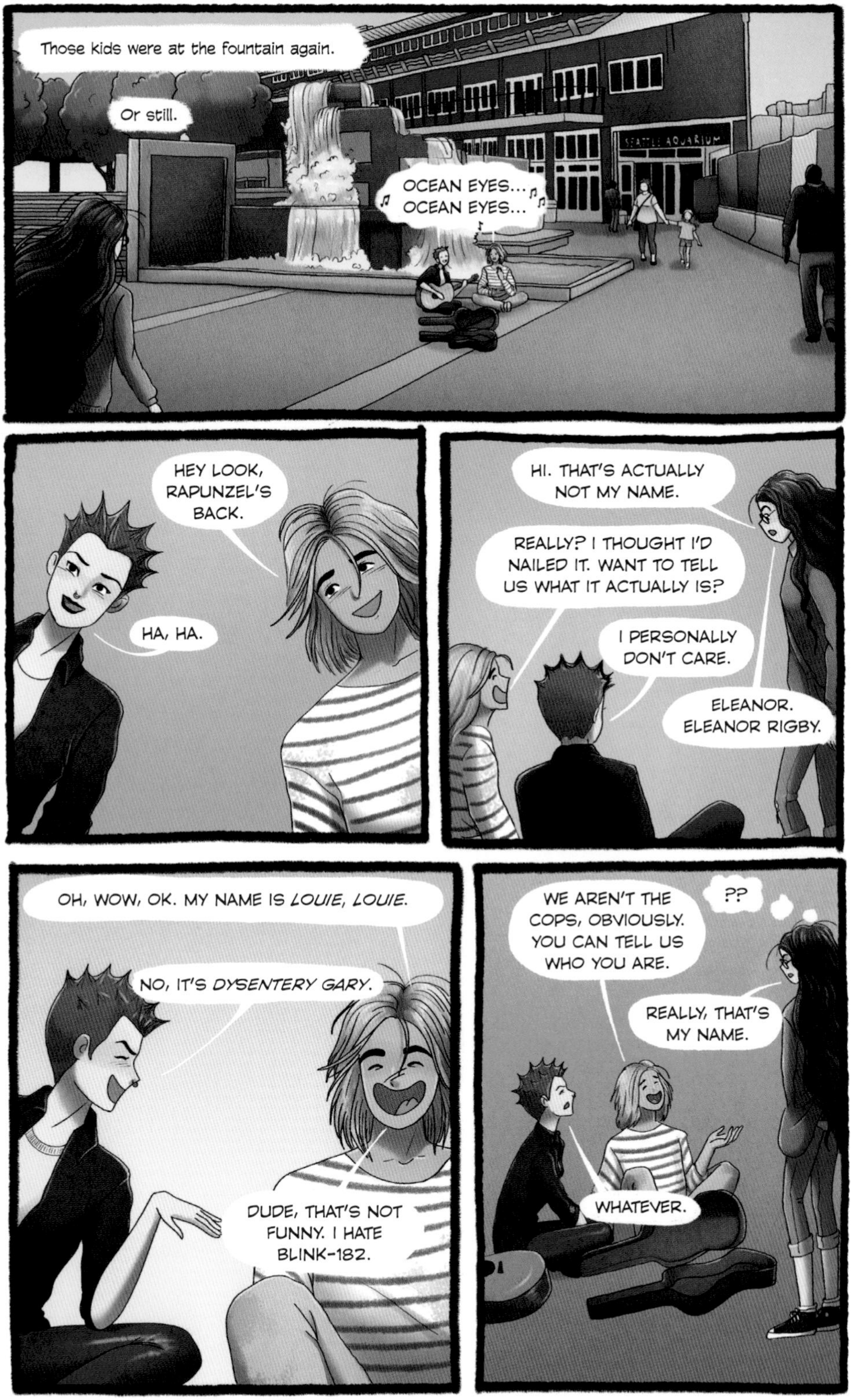
Those kids were at the fountain again.
Or still.
SEATTLE AQUARIUM
OCEAN EYES... OCEAN EYES...
HEY LOOK, RAPUNZEL'S BACK.
HA, HA.
HI. THAT'S ACTUALLY NOT MY NAME.
REALLY? I THOUGHT I'D NAILED IT. WANT TO TELL US WHAT IT ACTUALLY IS?
I PERSONALLY DON'T CARE.
ELEANOR. ELEANOR RIGBY.
OH, WOW, OK. MY NAME IS *LOUIE, LOUIE.*
NO, IT'S *DYSENTERY GARY.*
DUDE, THAT'S NOT FUNNY. I HATE BLINK-182.
WE AREN'T THE COPS, OBVIOUSLY. YOU CAN TELL US WHO YOU ARE.
??
REALLY, THAT'S MY NAME.
WHATEVER.

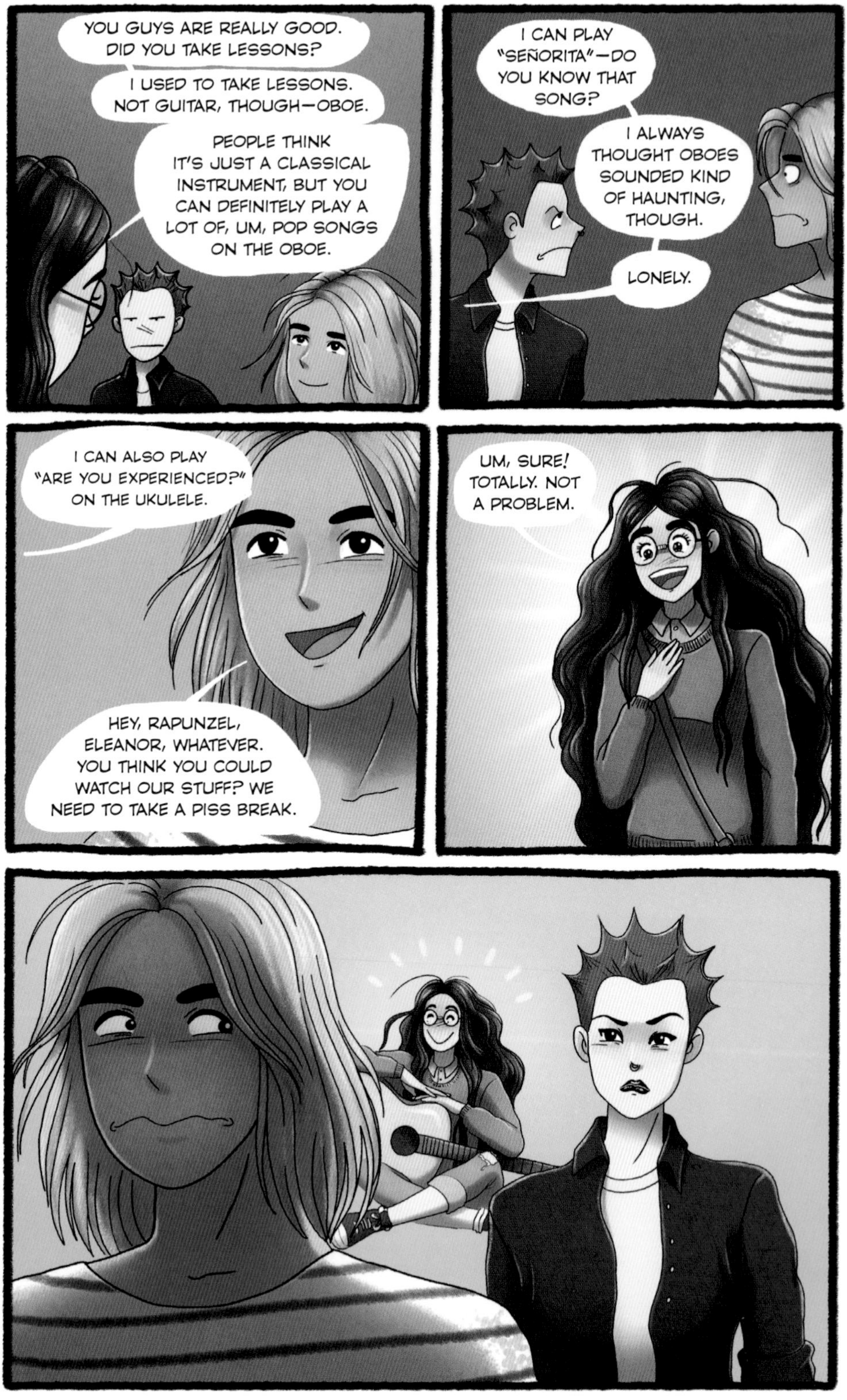
YOU GUYS ARE REALLY GOOD. DID YOU TAKE LESSONS?
I USED TO TAKE LESSONS. NOT GUITAR, THOUGH—OBOE.
PEOPLE THINK IT'S JUST A CLASSICAL INSTRUMENT, BUT YOU CAN DEFINITELY PLAY A LOT OF, UM, POP SONGS ON THE OBOE.
I CAN PLAY "SEÑORITA"—DO YOU KNOW THAT SONG?
I ALWAYS THOUGHT OBOES SOUNDED KIND OF HAUNTING, THOUGH.
LONELY.
I CAN ALSO PLAY "ARE YOU EXPERIENCED?" ON THE UKULELE.
HEY, RAPUNZEL, ELEANOR, WHATEVER. YOU THINK YOU COULD WATCH OUR STUFF? WE NEED TO TAKE A PISS BREAK.
UM, SURE! TOTALLY. NOT A PROBLEM.

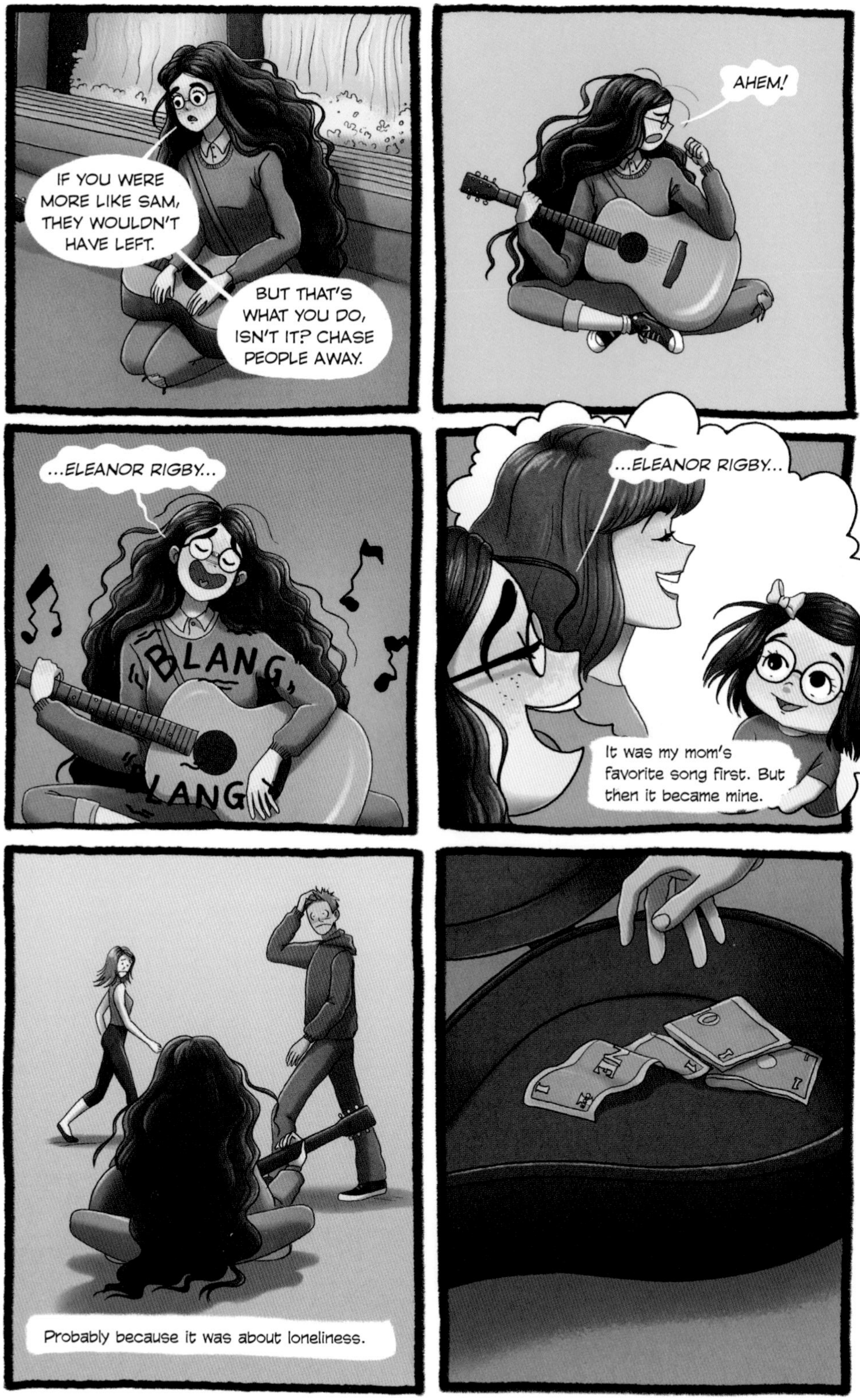
IF YOU WERE MORE LIKE SAM, THEY WOULDN'T HAVE LEFT.
BUT THAT'S WHAT YOU DO, ISN'T IT? CHASE PEOPLE AWAY.
AHEM!
...ELEANOR RIGBY...
BLANG
BLANG
...ELEANOR RIGBY...
It was my mom's favorite song first. But then it became mine.
Probably because it was about loneliness.

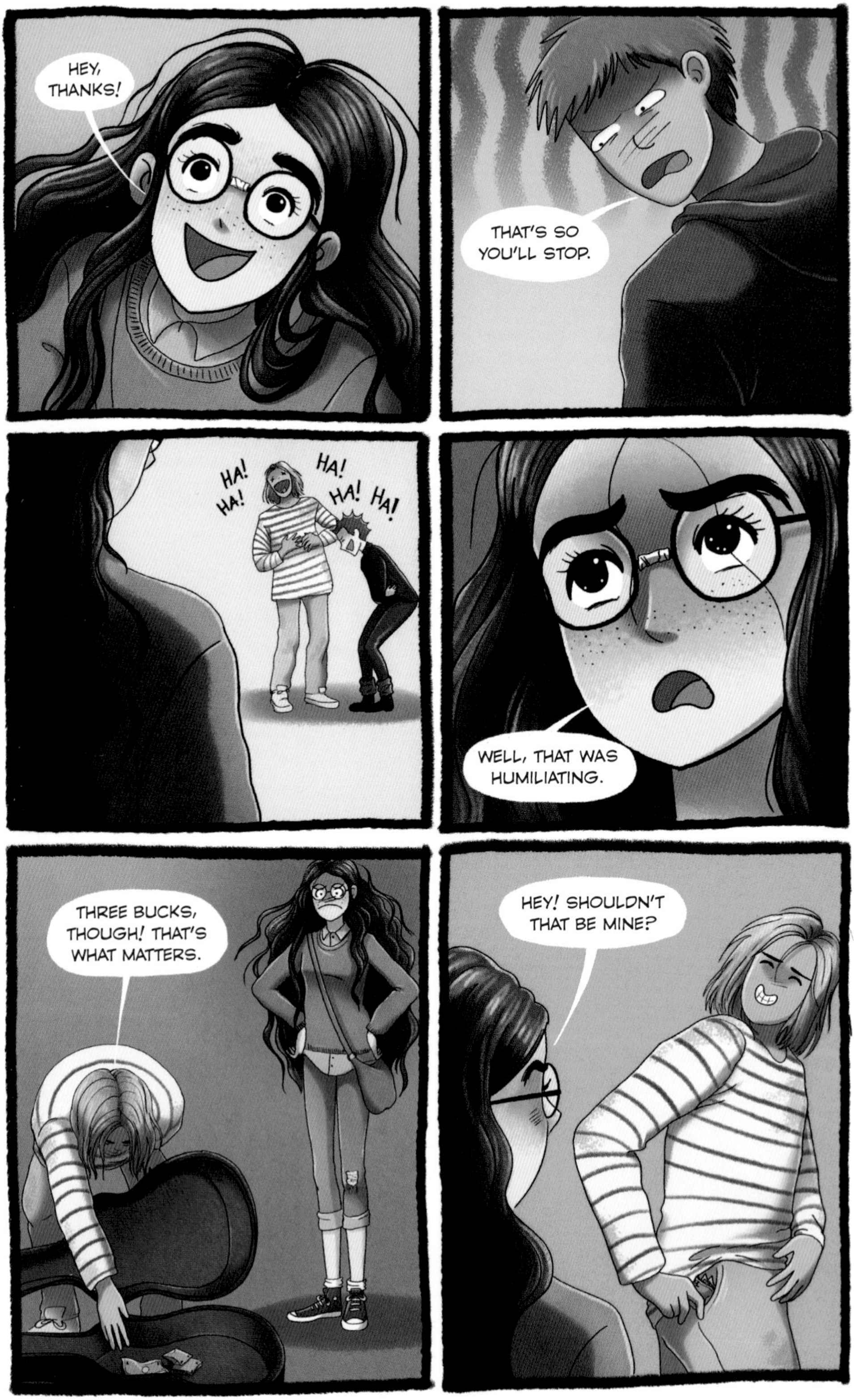
HEY, THANKS!
THAT'S SO YOU'LL STOP.
HA! HA!
HA!
HA! HA!
WELL, THAT WAS HUMILIATING.
THREE BUCKS, THOUGH! THAT'S WHAT MATTERS.
HEY! SHOULDN'T THAT BE MINE?

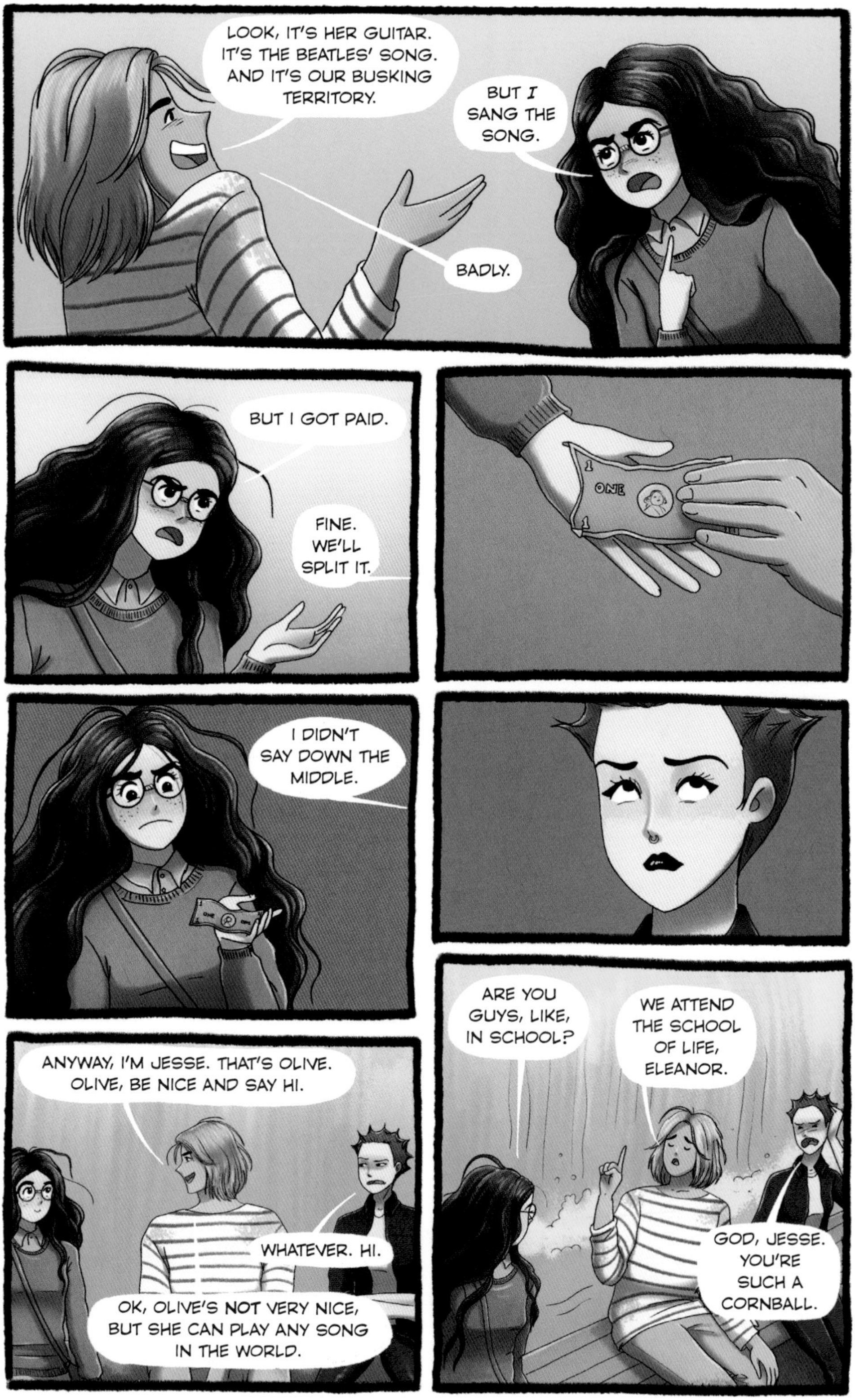
LOOK, IT'S HER GUITAR. IT'S THE BEATLES' SONG. AND IT'S OUR BUSKING TERRITORY.
BUT *I* SANG THE SONG.
BADLY.
BUT I GOT PAID.
FINE. WE'LL SPLIT IT.
ONE
I DIDN'T SAY DOWN THE MIDDLE.
ANYWAY, I'M JESSE. THAT'S OLIVE. OLIVE, BE NICE AND SAY HI.
WHATEVER. HI.
OK, OLIVE'S **NOT** VERY NICE, BUT SHE CAN PLAY ANY SONG IN THE WORLD.
ARE YOU GUYS, LIKE, IN SCHOOL?
WE ATTEND THE SCHOOL OF LIFE, ELEANOR.
GOD, JESSE. YOU'RE SUCH A CORNBALL.

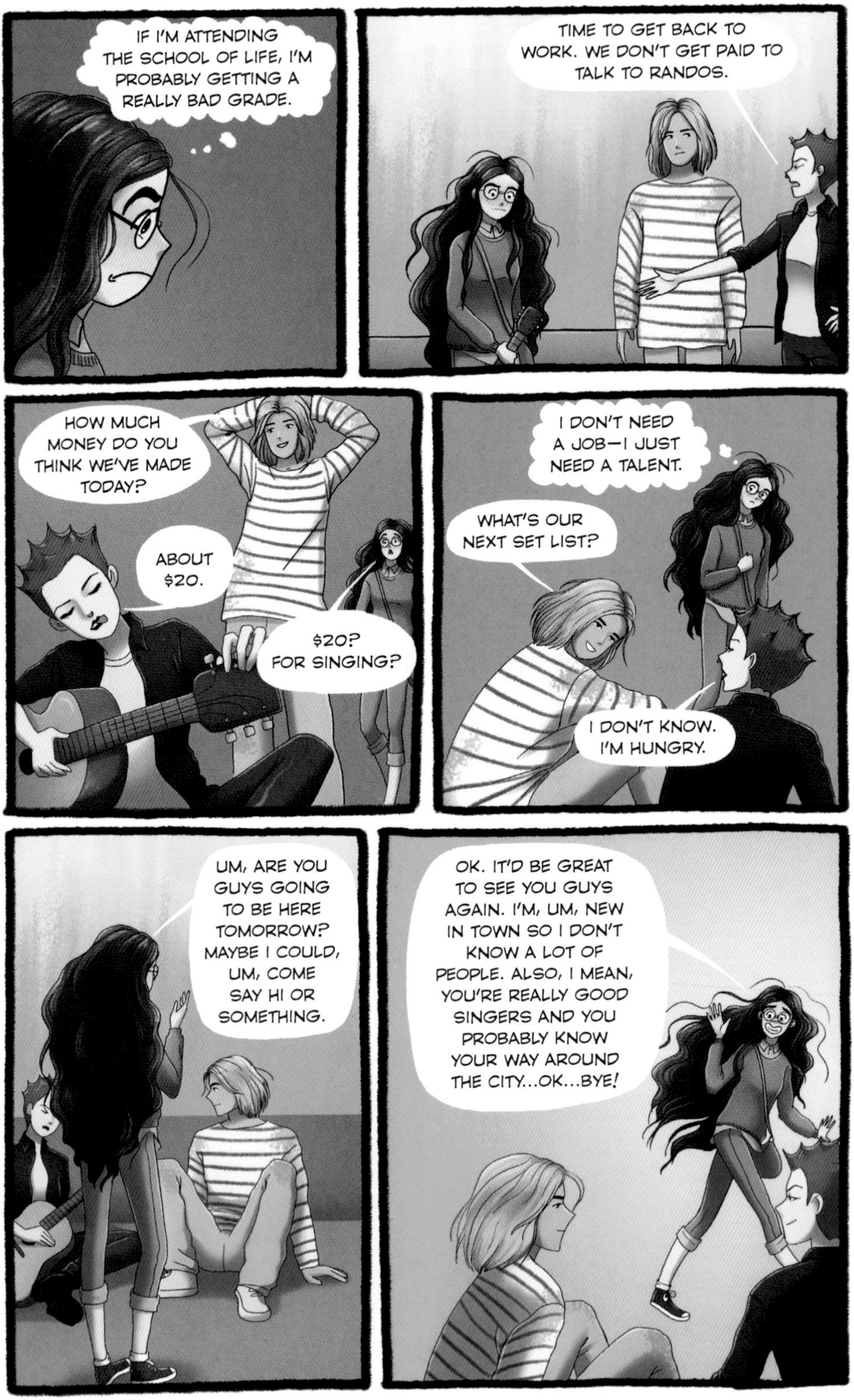
IF I'M ATTENDING THE SCHOOL OF LIFE, I'M PROBABLY GETTING A REALLY BAD GRADE.
TIME TO GET BACK TO WORK. WE DON'T GET PAID TO TALK TO RANDOS.
HOW MUCH MONEY DO YOU THINK WE'VE MADE TODAY?
ABOUT $20.
$20? FOR SINGING?
I DON'T NEED A JOB—I JUST NEED A TALENT.
WHAT'S OUR NEXT SET LIST?
I DON'T KNOW. I'M HUNGRY.
UM, ARE YOU GUYS GOING TO BE HERE TOMORROW? MAYBE I COULD, UM, COME SAY HI OR SOMETHING.
OK. IT'D BE GREAT TO SEE YOU GUYS AGAIN. I'M, UM, NEW IN TOWN SO I DON'T KNOW A LOT OF PEOPLE. ALSO, I MEAN, YOU'RE REALLY GOOD SINGERS AND YOU PROBABLY KNOW YOUR WAY AROUND THE CITY...OK...BYE!

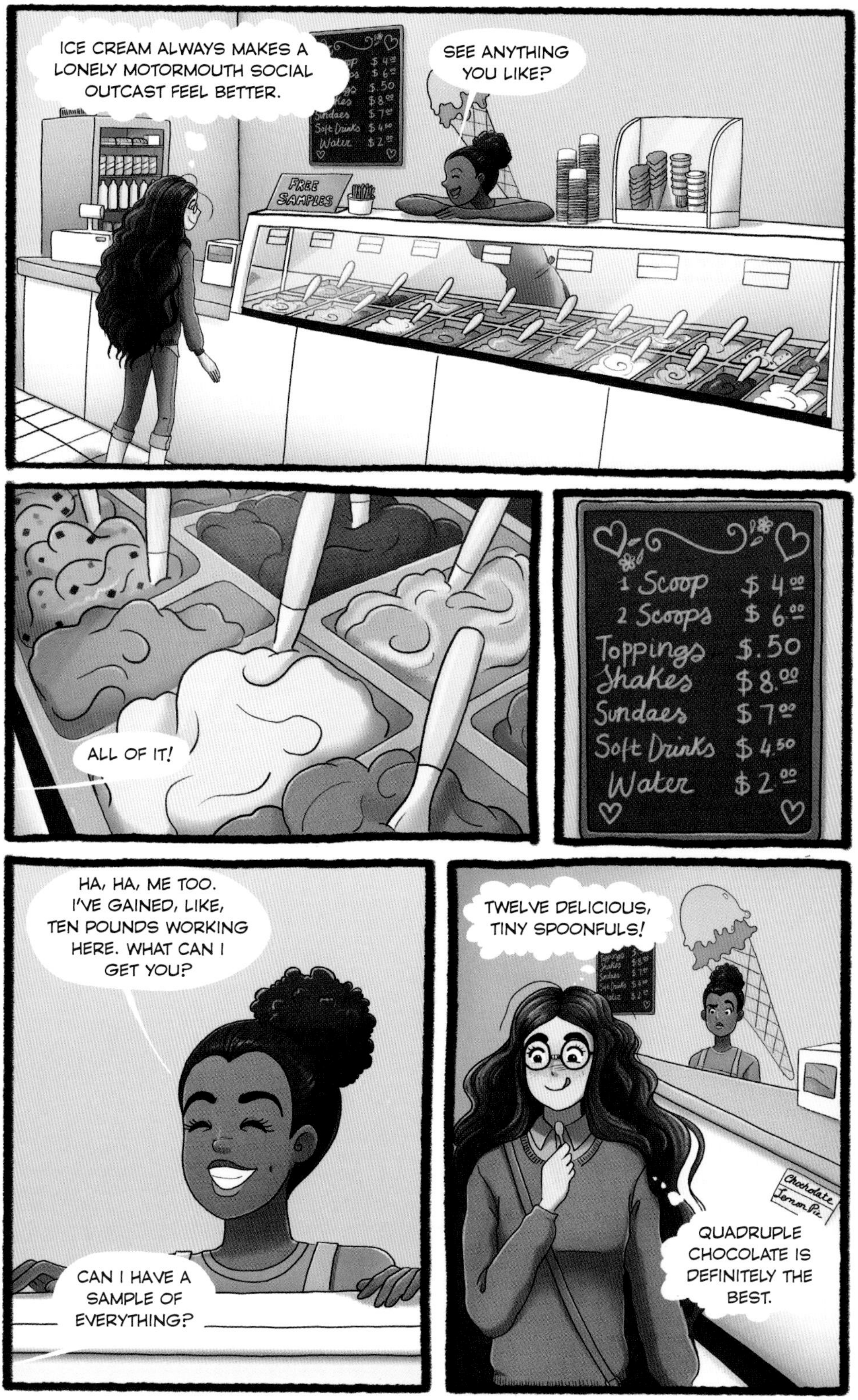
ICE CREAM ALWAYS MAKES A LONELY MOTORMOUTH SOCIAL OUTCAST FEEL BETTER.
SEE ANYTHING YOU LIKE?
FREE SAMPLES
ALL OF IT!
1 Scoop $4.00
2 Scoops $6.00
Toppings $.50
Shakes $8.00
Sundaes $7.00
Soft Drinks $4.50
Water $2.00
HA, HA, ME TOO. I'VE GAINED, LIKE, TEN POUNDS WORKING HERE. WHAT CAN I GET YOU?
CAN I HAVE A SAMPLE OF EVERYTHING?
TWELVE DELICIOUS, TINY SPOONFULS!
Chocolate
Lemon Pie
QUADRUPLE CHOCOLATE IS DEFINITELY THE BEST.

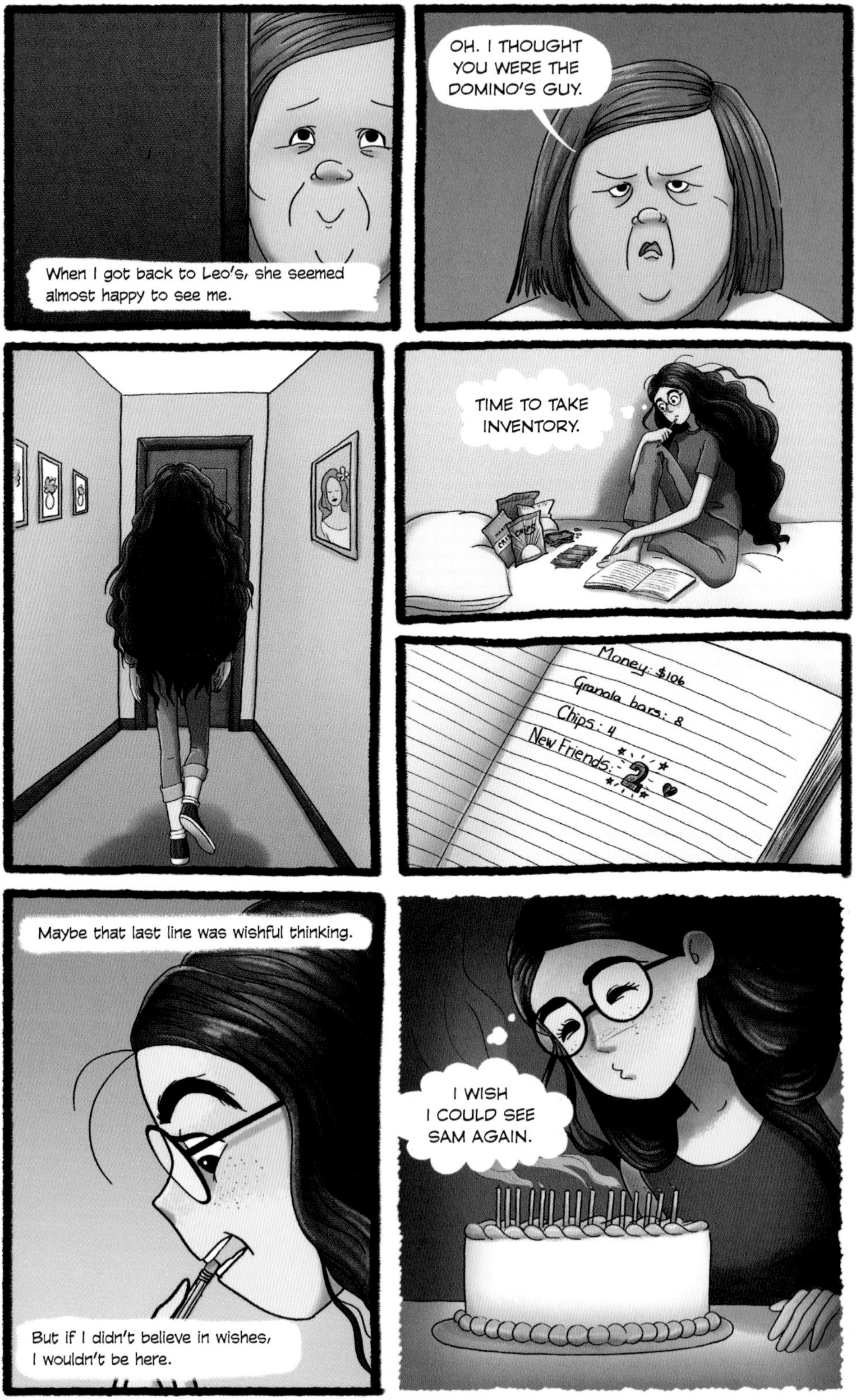
When I got back to Leo's, she seemed almost happy to see me.
OH. I THOUGHT YOU WERE THE DOMINO'S GUY.
TIME TO TAKE INVENTORY.
Money: $106
Granola bars: 8
Chips: 4
New Friends: 2
Maybe that last line was wishful thinking.
But if I didn't believe in wishes, I wouldn't be here.
I WISH I COULD SEE SAM AGAIN.

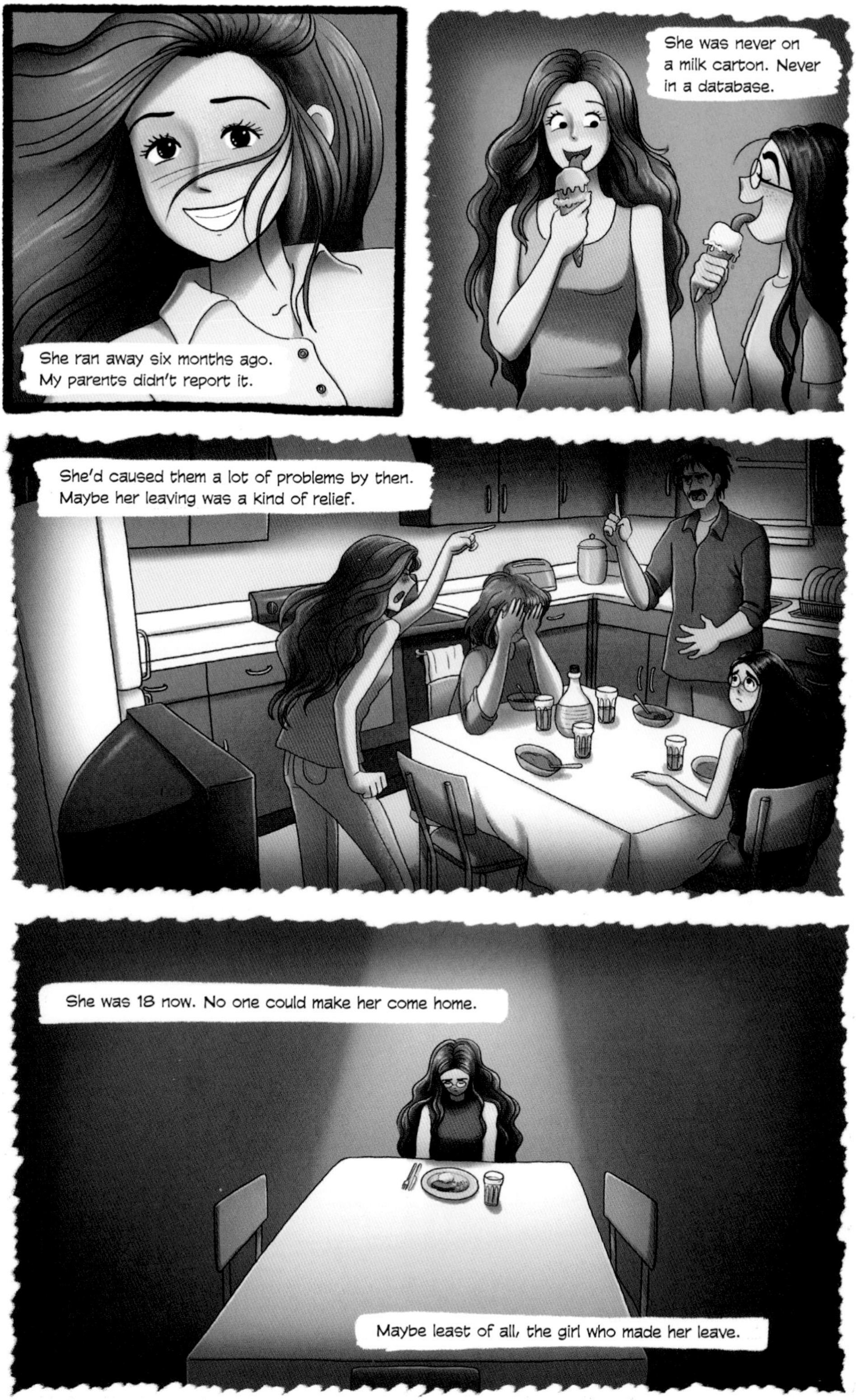
She ran away six months ago. My parents didn't report it.
She was never on a milk carton. Never in a database.
She'd caused them a lot of problems by then. Maybe her leaving was a kind of relief.
She was 18 now. No one could make her come home.
Maybe least of all, the girl who made her leave.

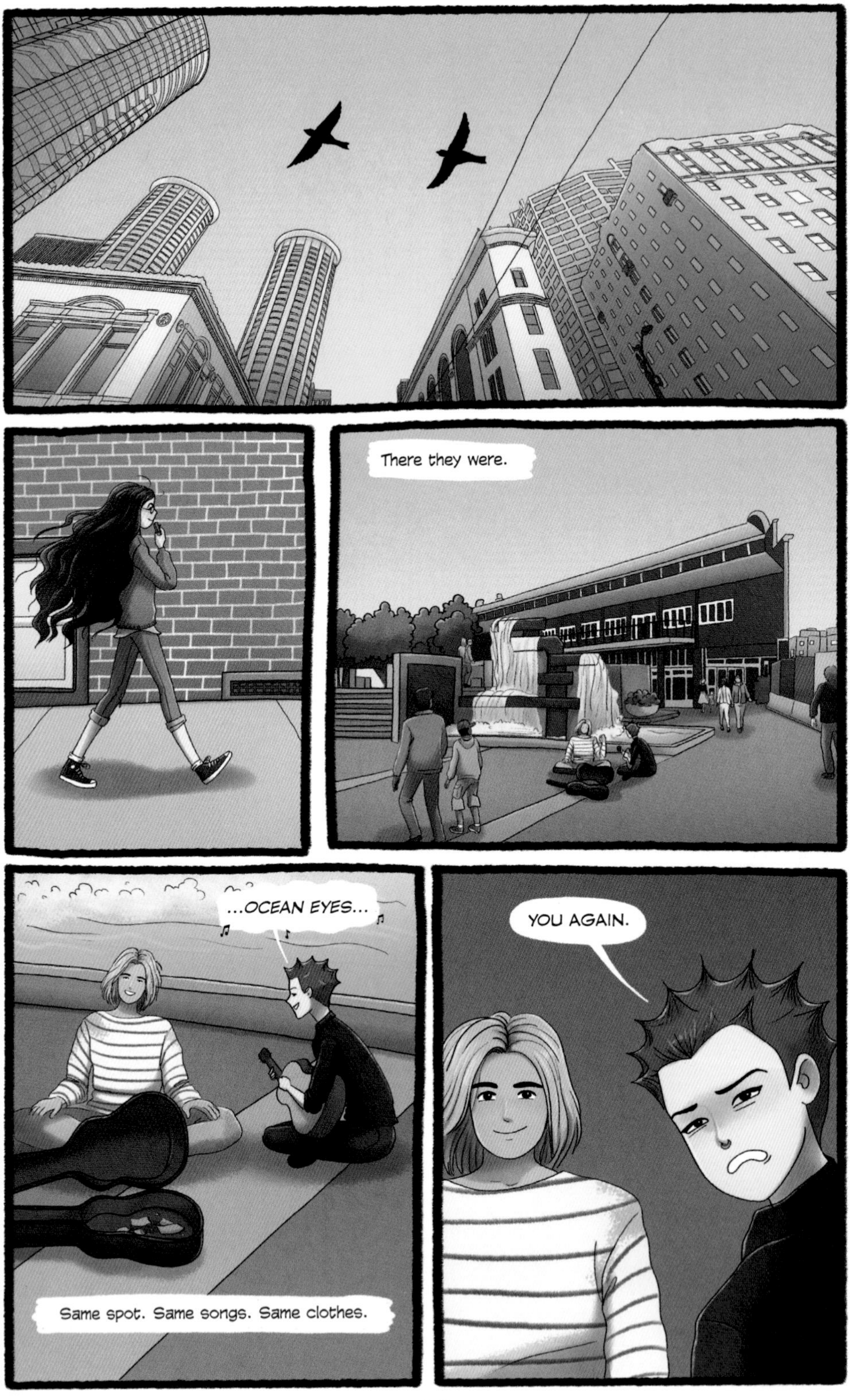
There they were.
...OCEAN EYES...
Same spot. Same songs. Same clothes.
YOU AGAIN.

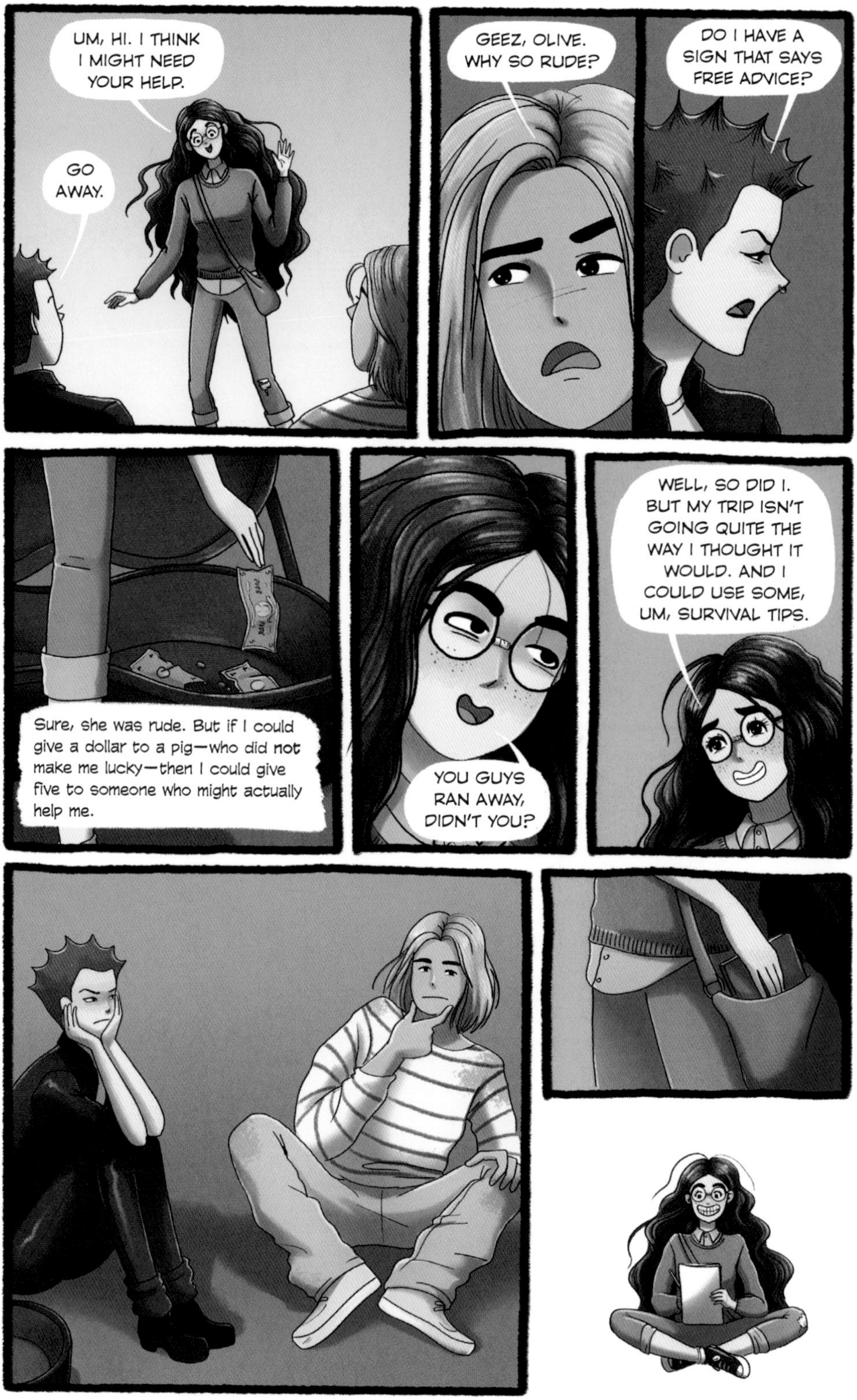
UM, HI. I THINK I MIGHT NEED YOUR HELP.
GO AWAY.
GEEZ, OLIVE. WHY SO RUDE?
DO I HAVE A SIGN THAT SAYS FREE ADVICE?
Sure, she was rude. But if I could give a dollar to a pig—who did **not** make me lucky—then I could give five to someone who might actually help me.
YOU GUYS RAN AWAY, DIDN'T YOU?
WELL, SO DID I. BUT MY TRIP ISN'T GOING QUITE THE WAY I THOUGHT IT WOULD. AND I COULD USE SOME, UM, SURVIVAL TIPS.

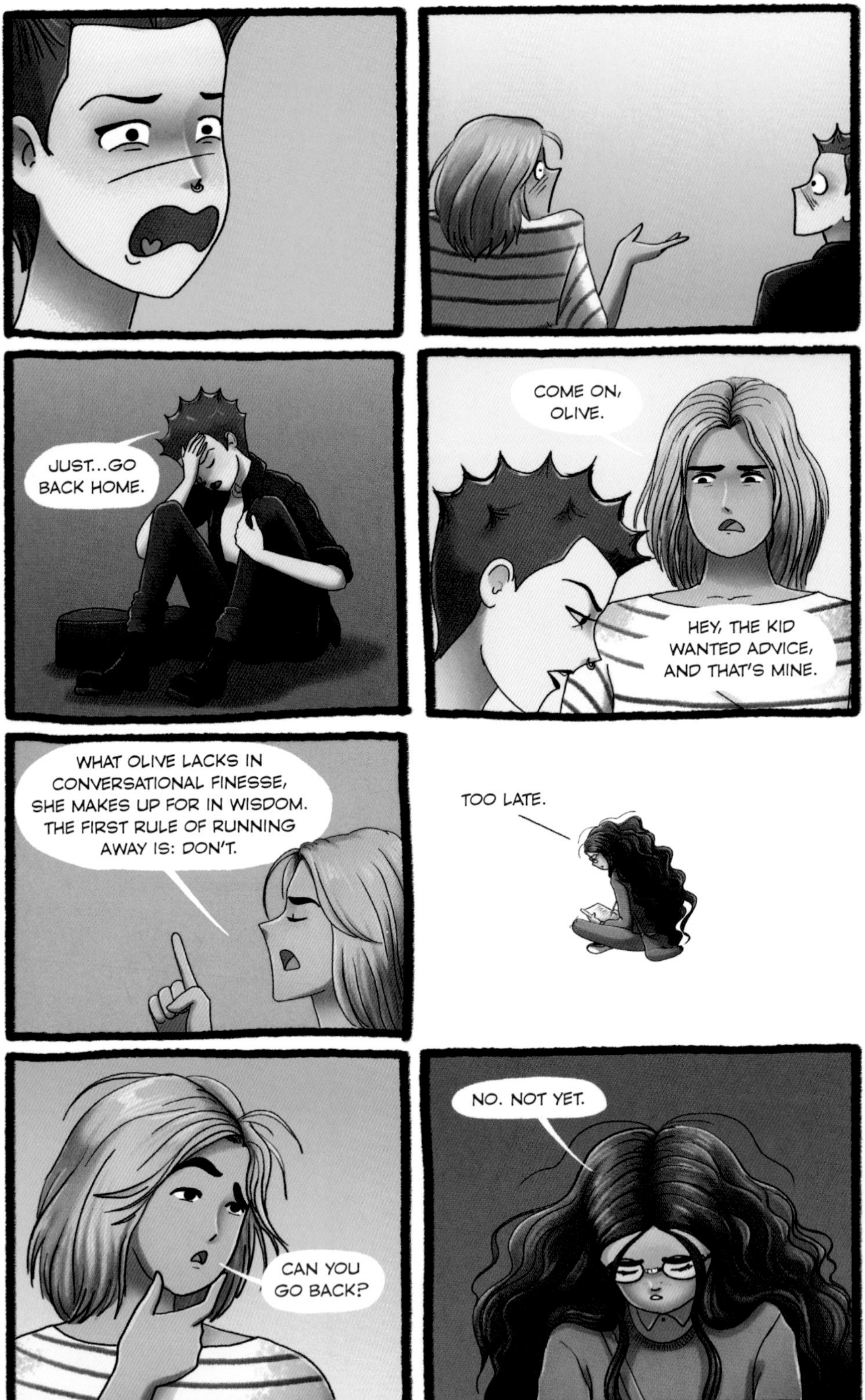
JUST...GO BACK HOME.
COME ON, OLIVE.
HEY, THE KID WANTED ADVICE, AND THAT'S MINE.
WHAT OLIVE LACKS IN CONVERSATIONAL FINESSE, SHE MAKES UP FOR IN WISDOM. THE FIRST RULE OF RUNNING AWAY IS: DON'T.
TOO LATE.
CAN YOU GO BACK?
NO. NOT YET.

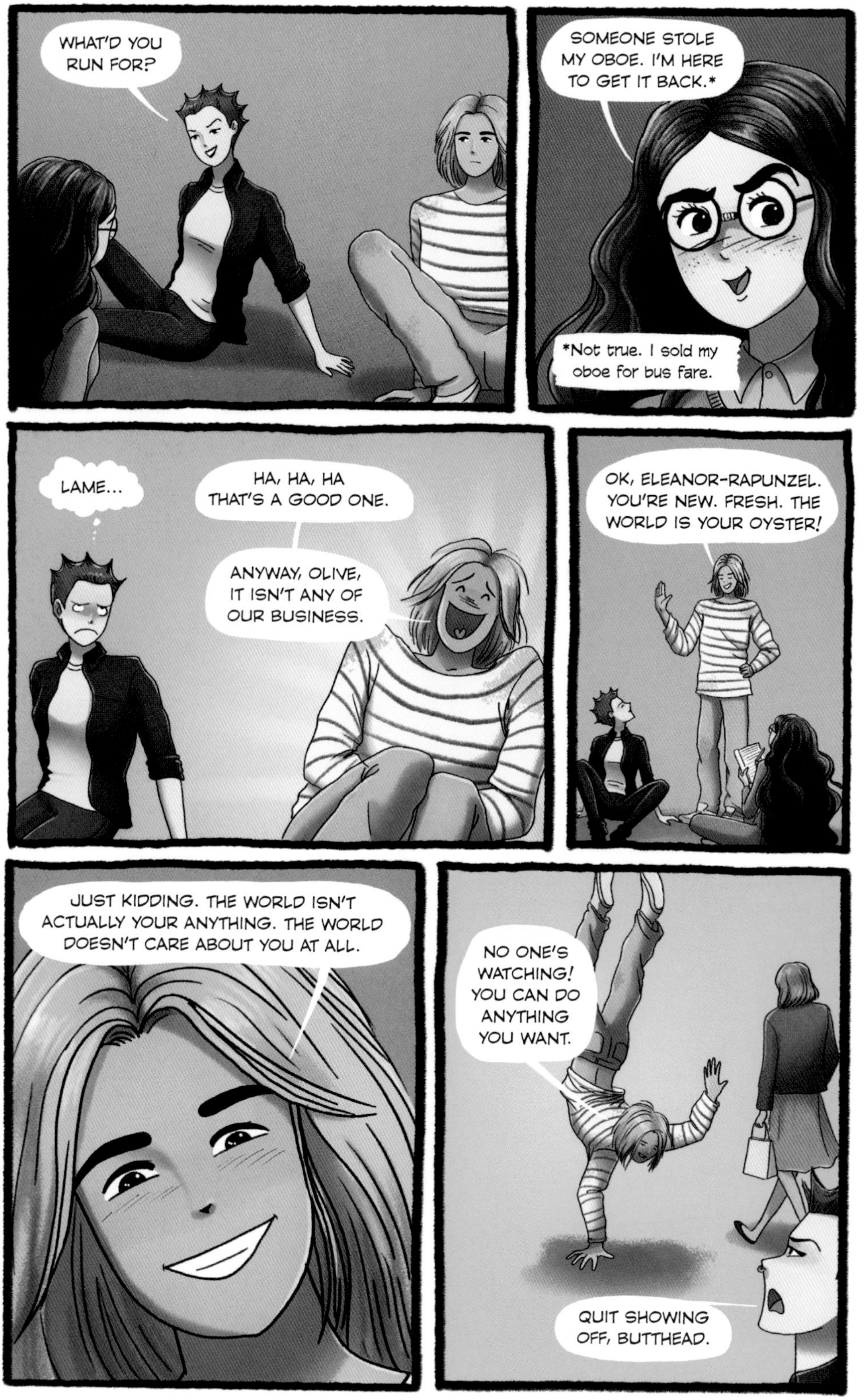
WHAT'D YOU RUN FOR?
SOMEONE STOLE MY OBOE. I'M HERE TO GET IT BACK.*
*Not true. I sold my oboe for bus fare.
LAME...
HA, HA, HA THAT'S A GOOD ONE.
ANYWAY, OLIVE, IT ISN'T ANY OF OUR BUSINESS.
OK, ELEANOR-RAPUNZEL. YOU'RE NEW. FRESH. THE WORLD IS YOUR OYSTER!
JUST KIDDING. THE WORLD ISN'T ACTUALLY YOUR ANYTHING. THE WORLD DOESN'T CARE ABOUT YOU AT ALL.
NO ONE'S WATCHING! YOU CAN DO ANYTHING YOU WANT.
QUIT SHOWING OFF, BUTTHEAD.

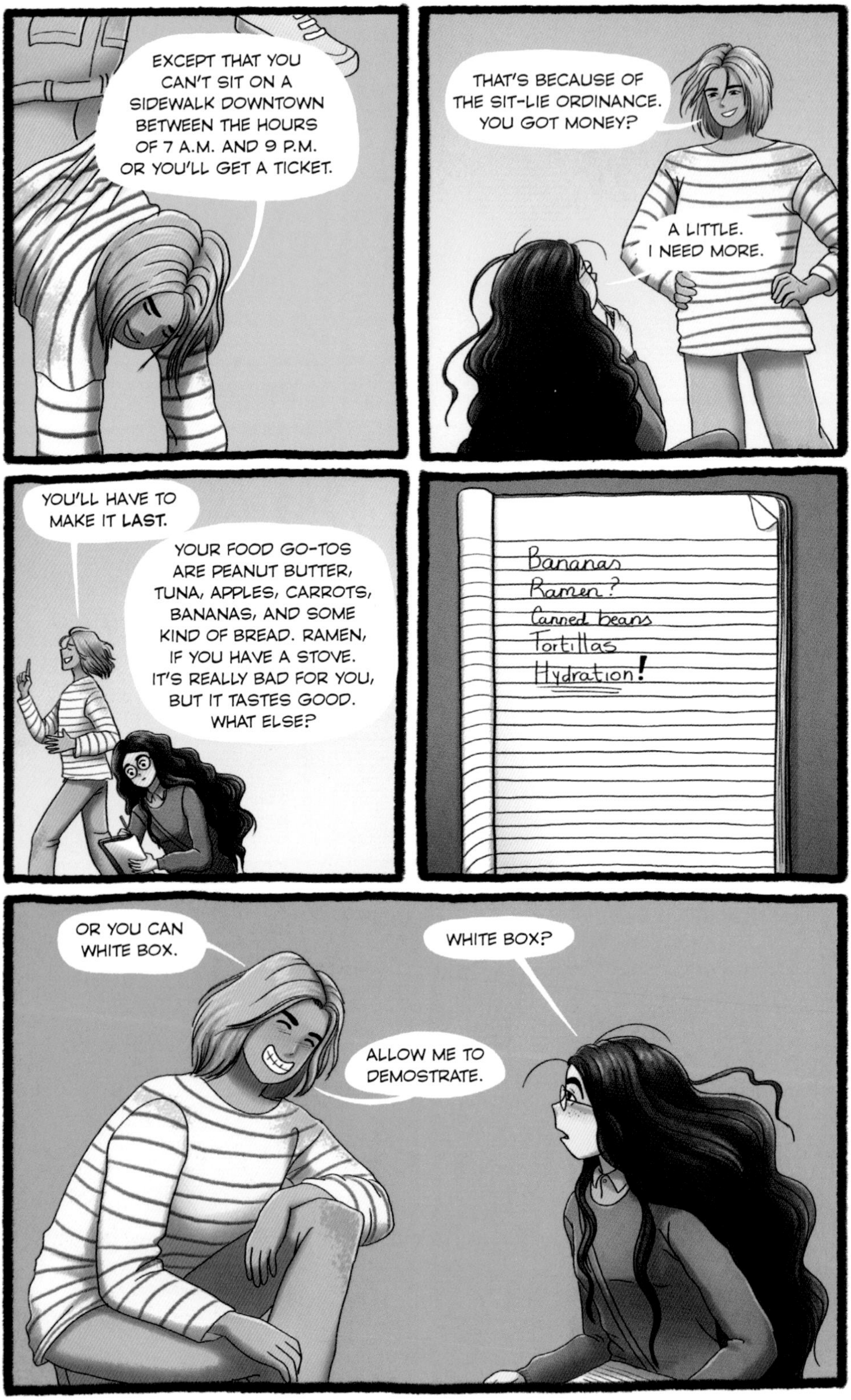
EXCEPT THAT YOU CAN'T SIT ON A SIDEWALK DOWNTOWN BETWEEN THE HOURS OF 7 A.M. AND 9 P.M. OR YOU'LL GET A TICKET.
THAT'S BECAUSE OF THE SIT-LIE ORDINANCE. YOU GOT MONEY?
A LITTLE. I NEED MORE.
YOU'LL HAVE TO MAKE IT **LAST**.
YOUR FOOD GO-TOS ARE PEANUT BUTTER, TUNA, APPLES, CARROTS, BANANAS, AND SOME KIND OF BREAD. RAMEN, IF YOU HAVE A STOVE. IT'S REALLY BAD FOR YOU, BUT IT TASTES GOOD. WHAT ELSE?
Bananas
Ramen?
Canned beans
Tortillas
Hydration!
OR YOU CAN WHITE BOX.
WHITE BOX?
ALLOW ME TO DEMOSTRATE.

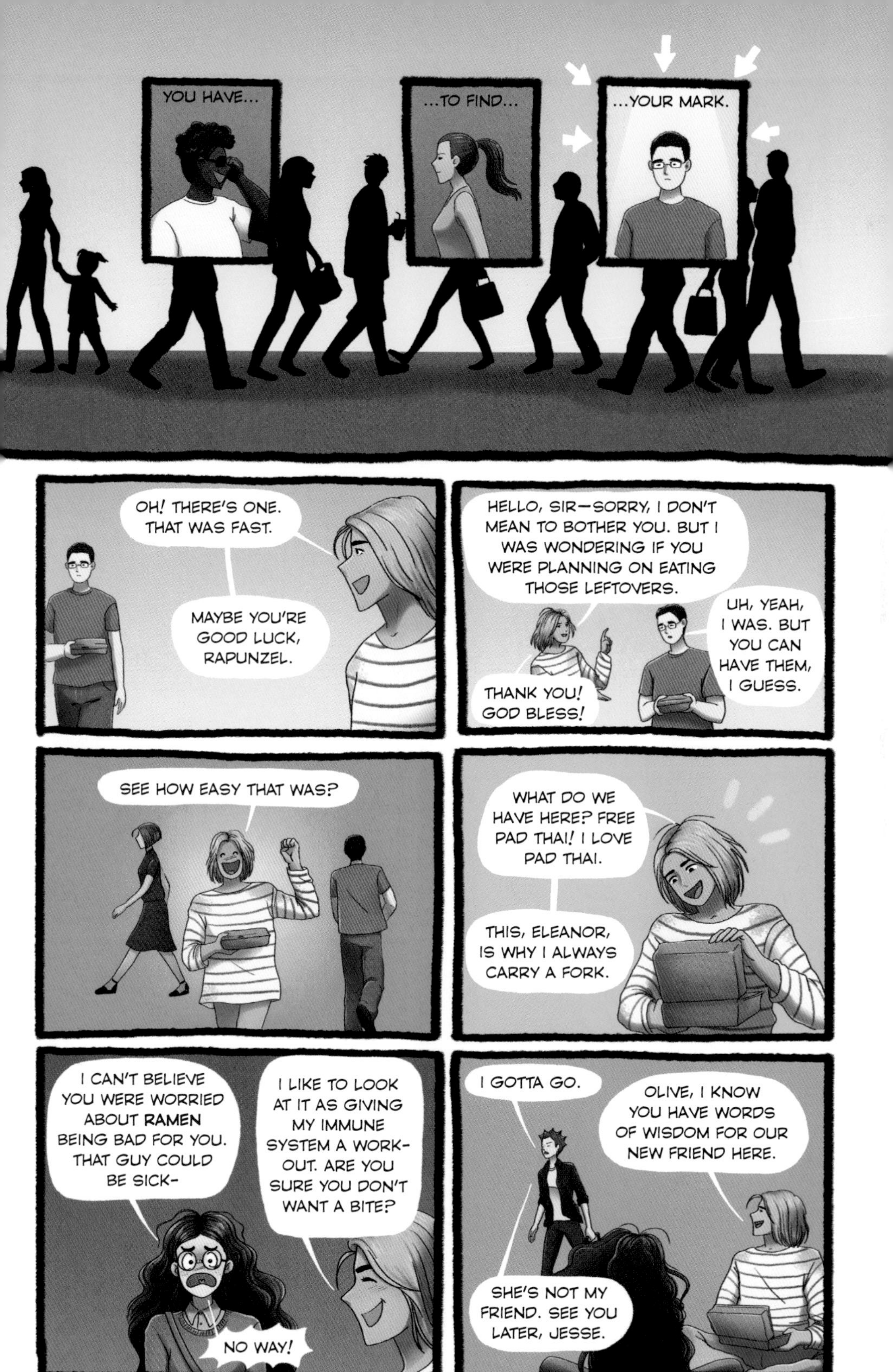
YOU HAVE...
...TO FIND...
...YOUR MARK.
OH! THERE'S ONE. THAT WAS FAST.
MAYBE YOU'RE GOOD LUCK, RAPUNZEL.
HELLO, SIR—SORRY, I DON'T MEAN TO BOTHER YOU. BUT I WAS WONDERING IF YOU WERE PLANNING ON EATING THOSE LEFTOVERS.
UH, YEAH, I WAS. BUT YOU CAN HAVE THEM, I GUESS.
THANK YOU! GOD BLESS!
SEE HOW EASY THAT WAS?
WHAT DO WE HAVE HERE? FREE PAD THAI! I LOVE PAD THAI.
THIS, ELEANOR, IS WHY I ALWAYS CARRY A FORK.
I CAN'T BELIEVE YOU WERE WORRIED ABOUT **RAMEN** BEING BAD FOR YOU. THAT GUY COULD BE SICK-
I LIKE TO LOOK AT IT AS GIVING MY IMMUNE SYSTEM A WORK-OUT. ARE YOU SURE YOU DON'T WANT A BITE?
NO WAY!
I GOTTA GO.
OLIVE, I KNOW YOU HAVE WORDS OF WISDOM FOR OUR NEW FRIEND HERE.
SHE'S NOT MY FRIEND. SEE YOU LATER, JESSE.

I'M SORRY. I FEEL LIKE I CHASED HER AWAY.

SHE JUST DOESN'T LIKE PEOPLE THAT MUCH. DON'T TAKE IT PERSONALLY.

BUT SHE LIKES YOU.

WELL, IT'S HARD NOT TO. DON'T YOU THINK?

He was sort of right.

Not that I would admit it to him.

SO WHAT'S THE SECOND RULE OF RUNNING AWAY?

WELL, I WOULD HAVE SAID "DON'T DO IT ALONE." BUT I DON'T WANT YOU TO FEEL LIKE YOU'RE DOING EVERYTHING WRONG.

EVEN THOUGH I AM?

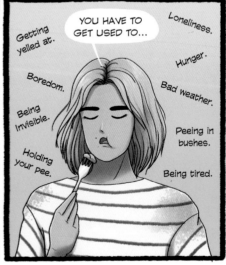

YOU HAVE TO GET USED TO...

Getting yelled at.

Loneliness.

Boredom.

Hunger.

Being Invisible.

Bad weather.

Holding your pee.

Peeing in bushes.

Being tired.

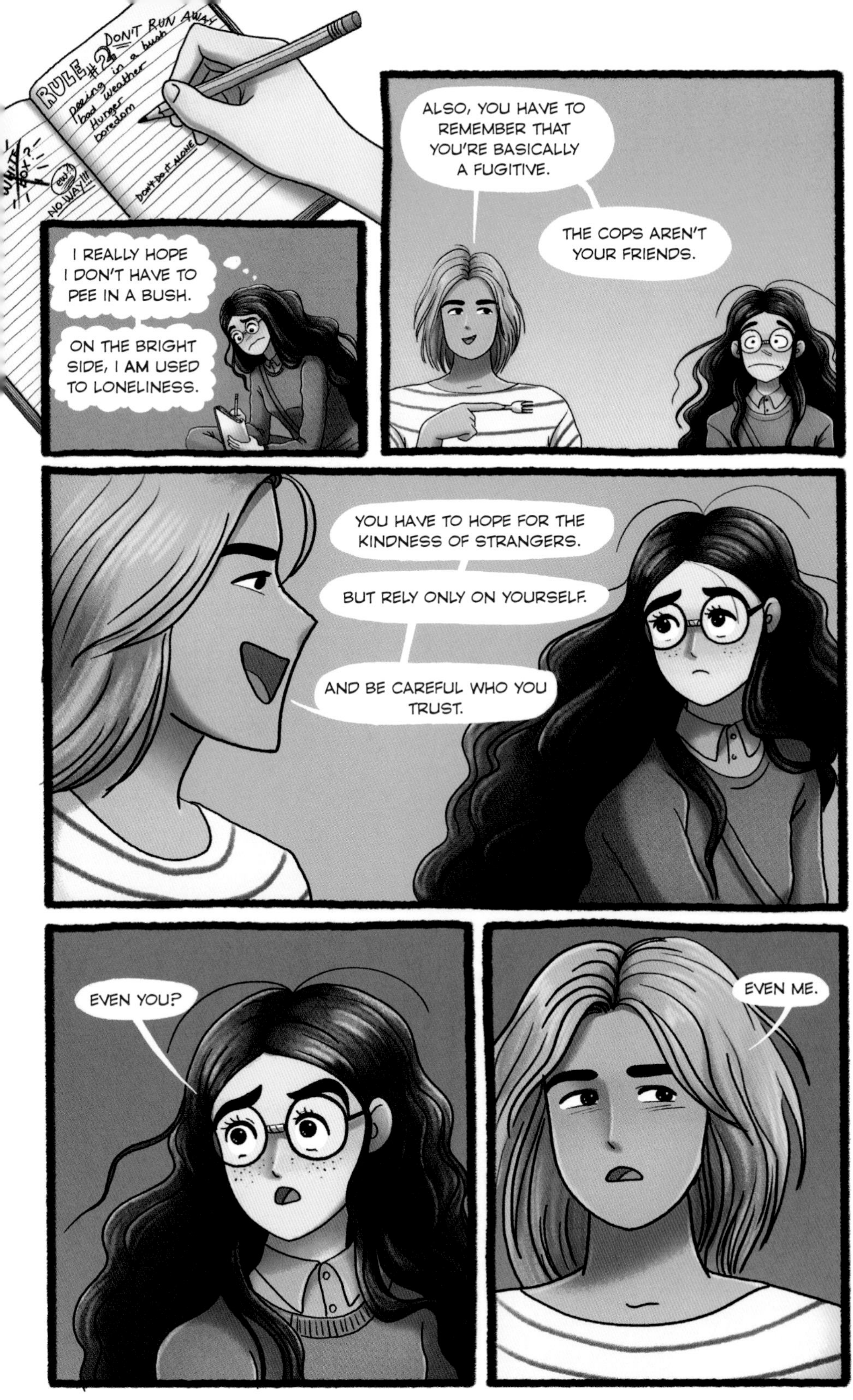
RULE #2 DON'T RUN AWAY
peeing in a bush
bad weather
Hunger
boredom
DON'T DO IT ALONE
NO WAY!!!
I REALLY HOPE I DON'T HAVE TO PEE IN A BUSH.
ON THE BRIGHT SIDE, I AM USED TO LONELINESS.
ALSO, YOU HAVE TO REMEMBER THAT YOU'RE BASICALLY A FUGITIVE.
THE COPS AREN'T YOUR FRIENDS.
YOU HAVE TO HOPE FOR THE KINDNESS OF STRANGERS.
BUT RELY ONLY ON YOURSELF.
AND BE CAREFUL WHO YOU TRUST.
EVEN YOU?
EVEN ME.

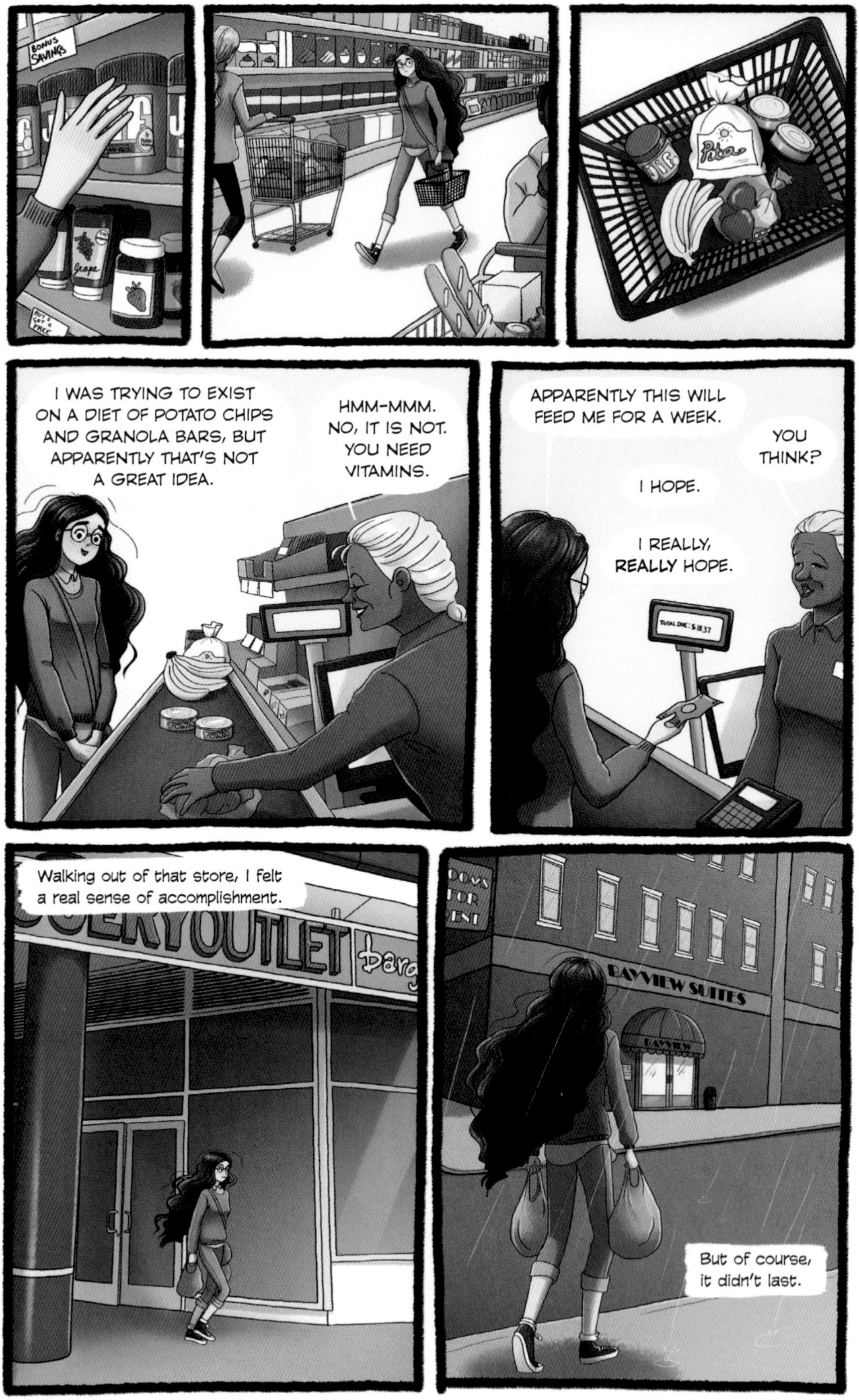
BONUS SAVINGS
Grape
Pita
I WAS TRYING TO EXIST ON A DIET OF POTATO CHIPS AND GRANOLA BARS, BUT APPARENTLY THAT'S NOT A GREAT IDEA.
HMM-MMM. NO, IT IS NOT. YOU NEED VITAMINS.
TUNA
APPARENTLY THIS WILL FEED ME FOR A WEEK.
YOU THINK?
I HOPE.
I REALLY, **REALLY** HOPE.
TOTAL DUE: $18.37
Walking out of that store, I felt a real sense of accomplishment.
OUTLET
BAYVIEW SUITES
BAYVIEW
But of course, it didn't last.

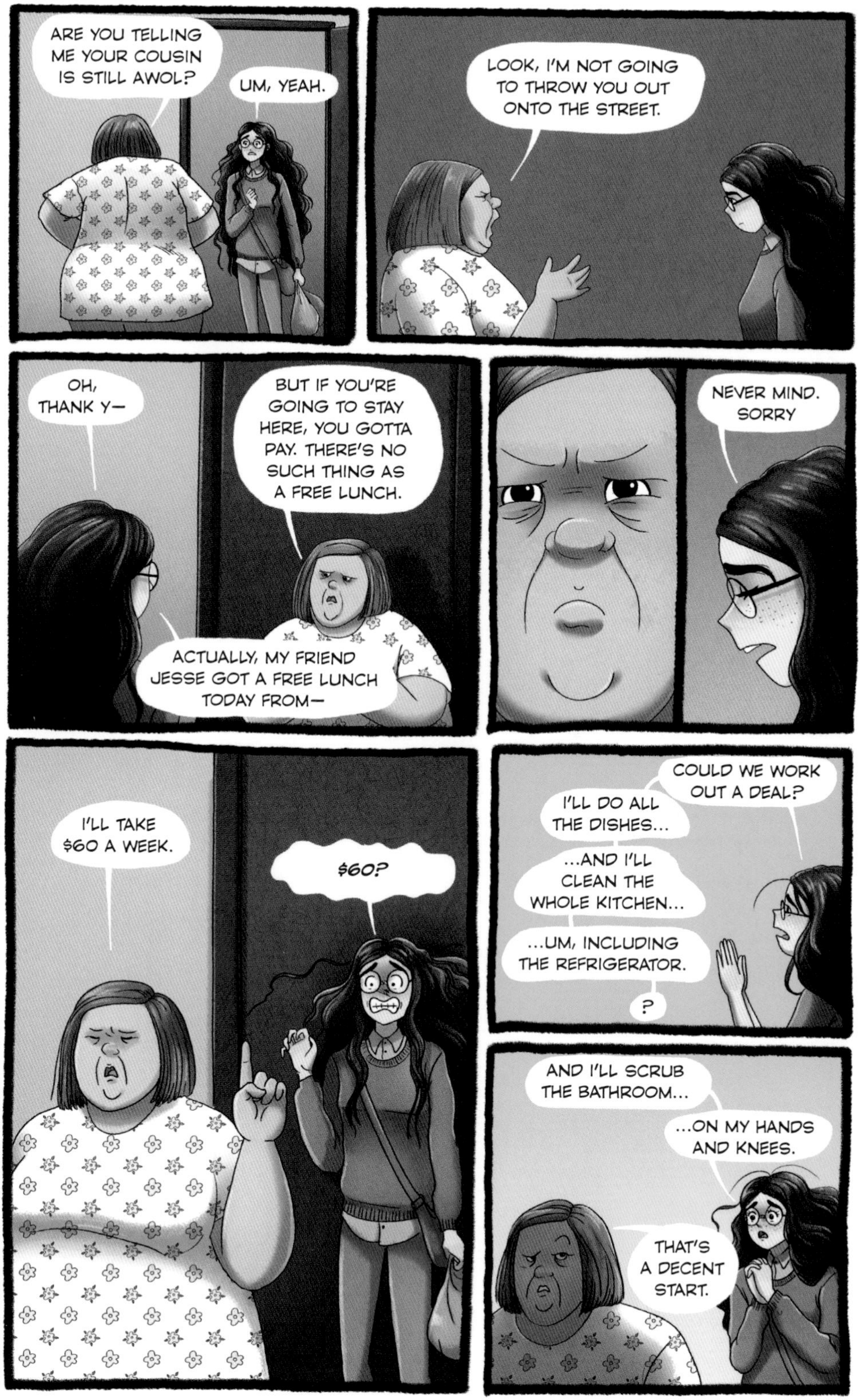
ARE YOU TELLING ME YOUR COUSIN IS STILL AWOL?
UM, YEAH.
LOOK, I'M NOT GOING TO THROW YOU OUT ONTO THE STREET.
OH, THANK Y—
BUT IF YOU'RE GOING TO STAY HERE, YOU GOTTA PAY. THERE'S NO SUCH THING AS A FREE LUNCH.
ACTUALLY, MY FRIEND JESSE GOT A FREE LUNCH TODAY FROM—
NEVER MIND. SORRY
I'LL TAKE $60 A WEEK.
$60?
COULD WE WORK OUT A DEAL?
I'LL DO ALL THE DISHES...
...AND I'LL CLEAN THE WHOLE KITCHEN...
...UM, INCLUDING THE REFRIGERATOR.
?
AND I'LL SCRUB THE BATHROOM...
...ON MY HANDS AND KNEES.
THAT'S A DECENT START.

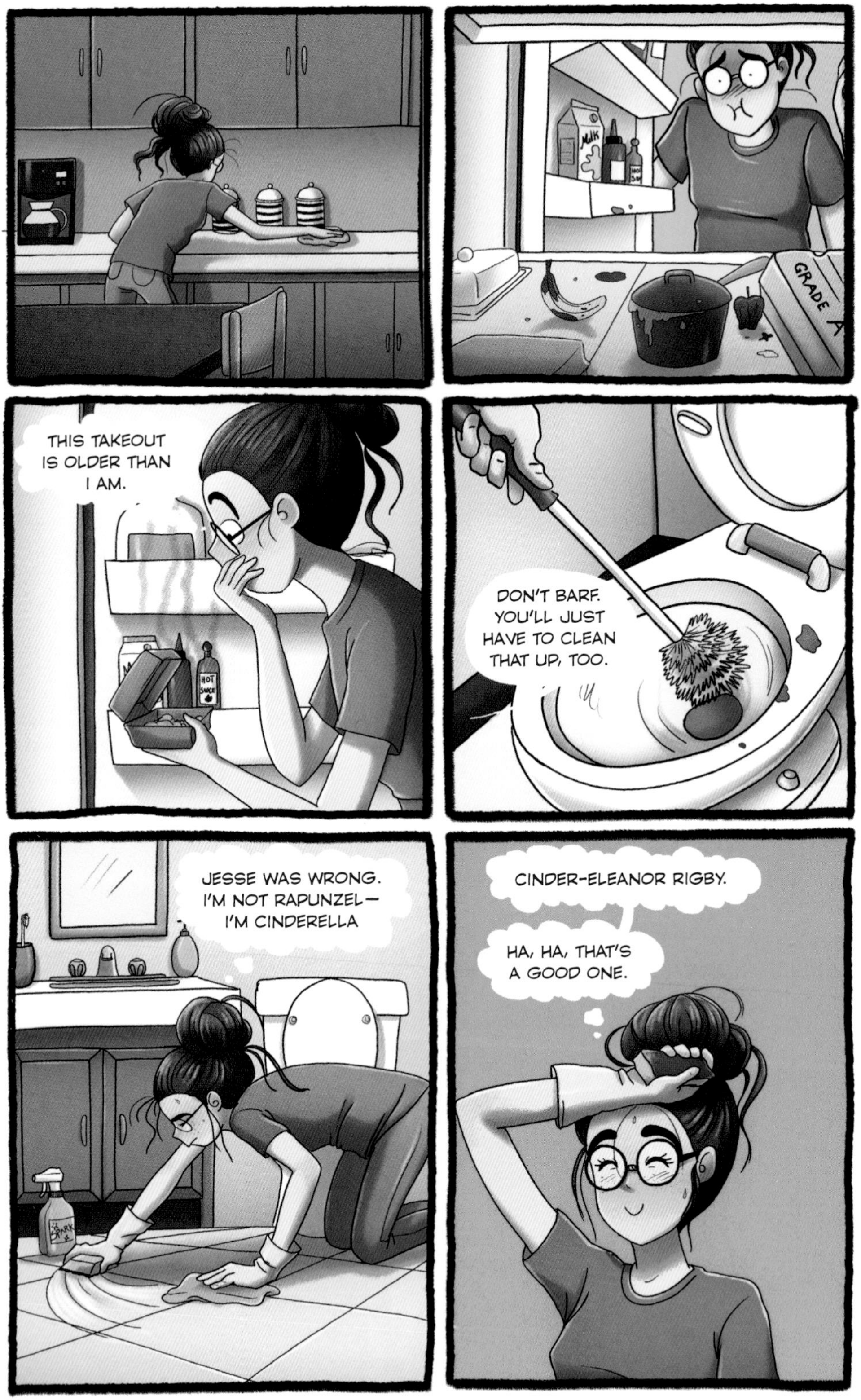

MILK
HOT SAUCE
GRADE A
THIS TAKEOUT IS OLDER THAN I AM.
HOT SAUCE
DON'T BARF. YOU'LL JUST HAVE TO CLEAN THAT UP, TOO.
JESSE WAS WRONG. I'M NOT RAPUNZEL— I'M CINDERELLA
CINDER-ELEANOR RIGBY.
HA, HA, THAT'S A GOOD ONE.

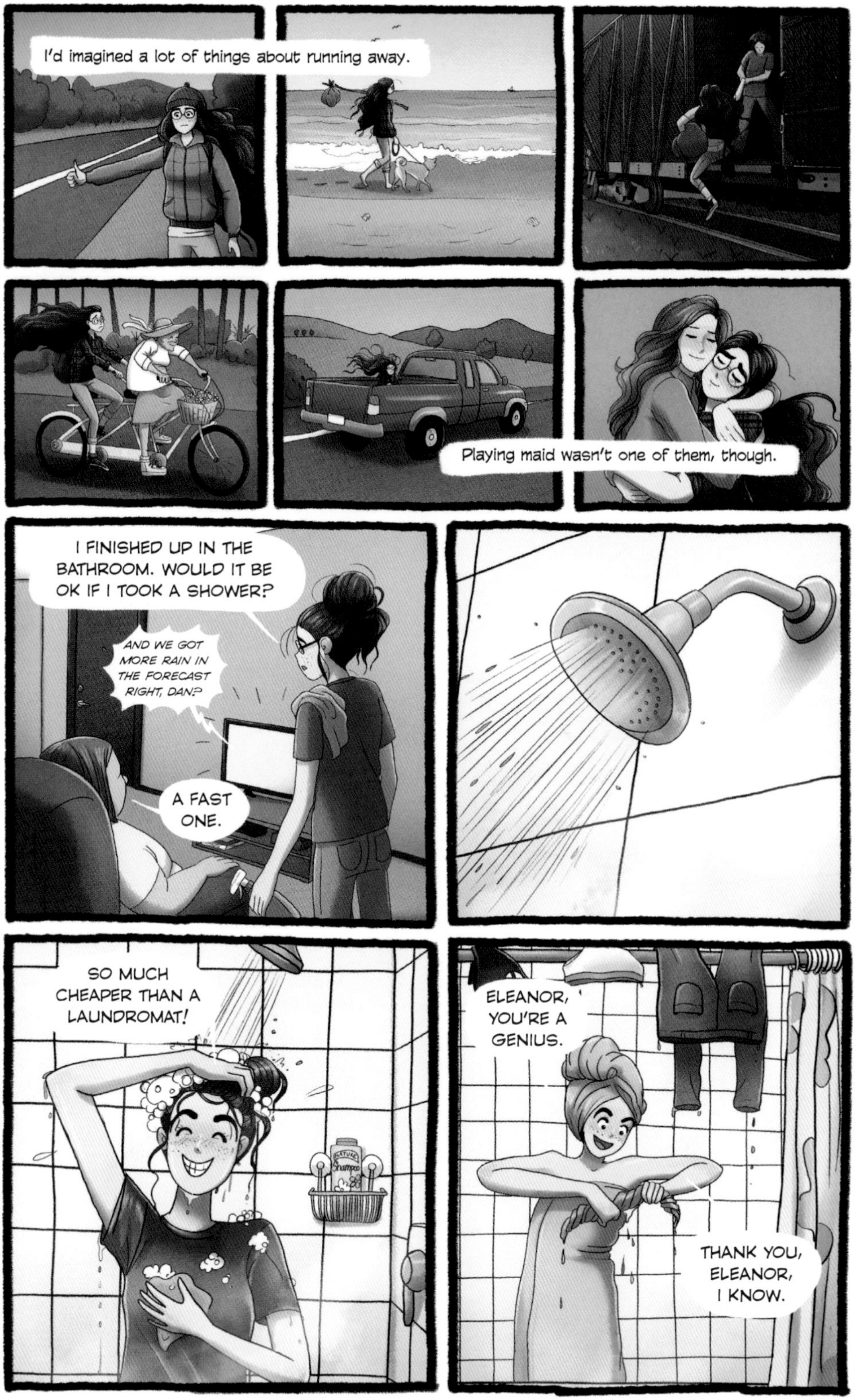
I'd imagined a lot of things about running away.
Playing maid wasn't one of them, though.
I FINISHED UP IN THE BATHROOM. WOULD IT BE OK IF I TOOK A SHOWER?
AND WE GOT MORE RAIN IN THE FORECAST RIGHT, DAN?
A FAST ONE.
SO MUCH CHEAPER THAN A LAUNDROMAT!
ELEANOR, YOU'RE A GENIUS.
THANK YOU, ELEANOR, I KNOW.

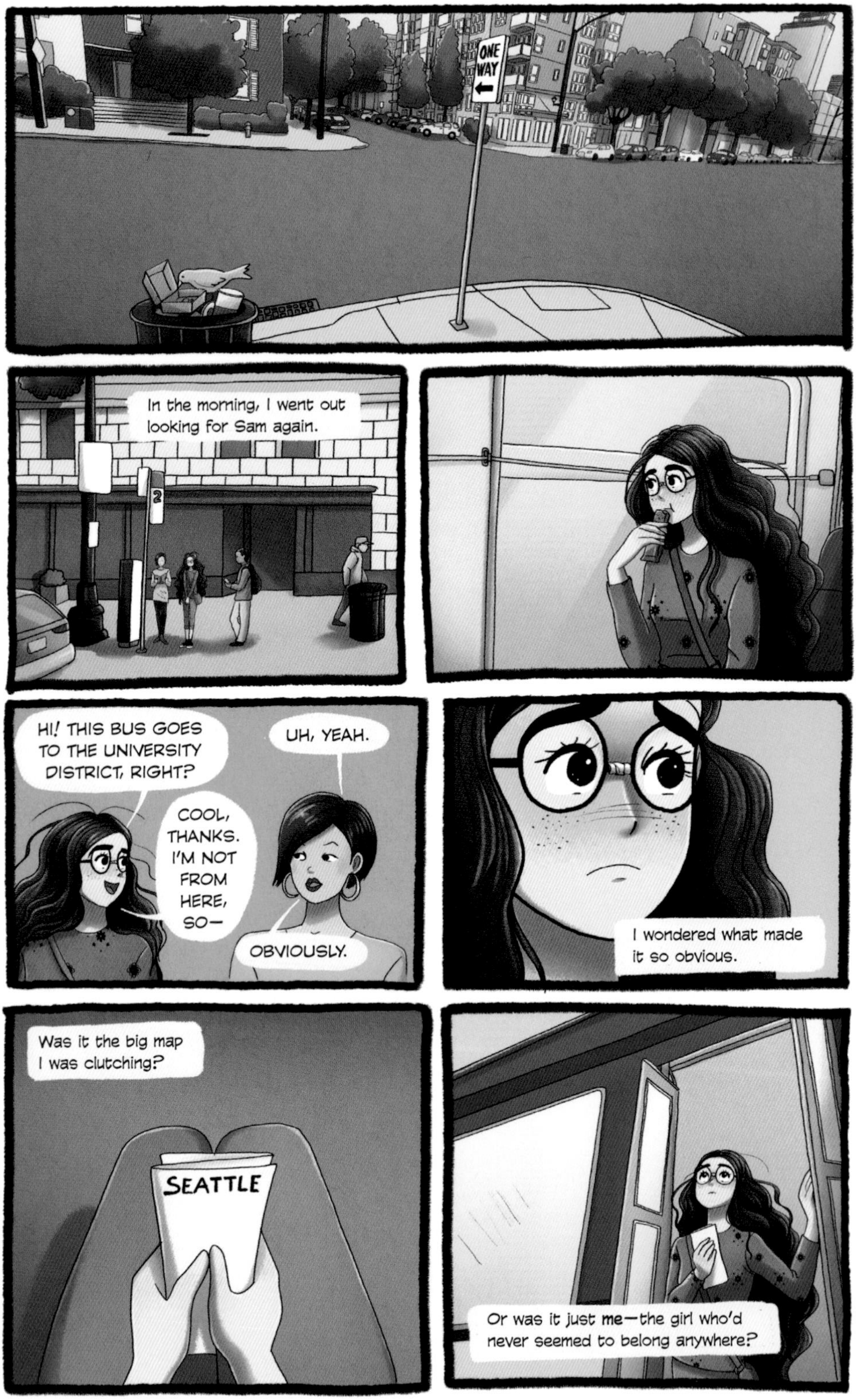
ONE WAY
In the morning, I went out looking for Sam again.
2
HI! THIS BUS GOES TO THE UNIVERSITY DISTRICT, RIGHT?
UH, YEAH.
COOL, THANKS. I'M NOT FROM HERE, SO—
OBVIOUSLY.
I wondered what made it so obvious.
Was it the big map I was clutching?
SEATTLE
Or was it just **me**—the girl who'd never seemed to belong anywhere?

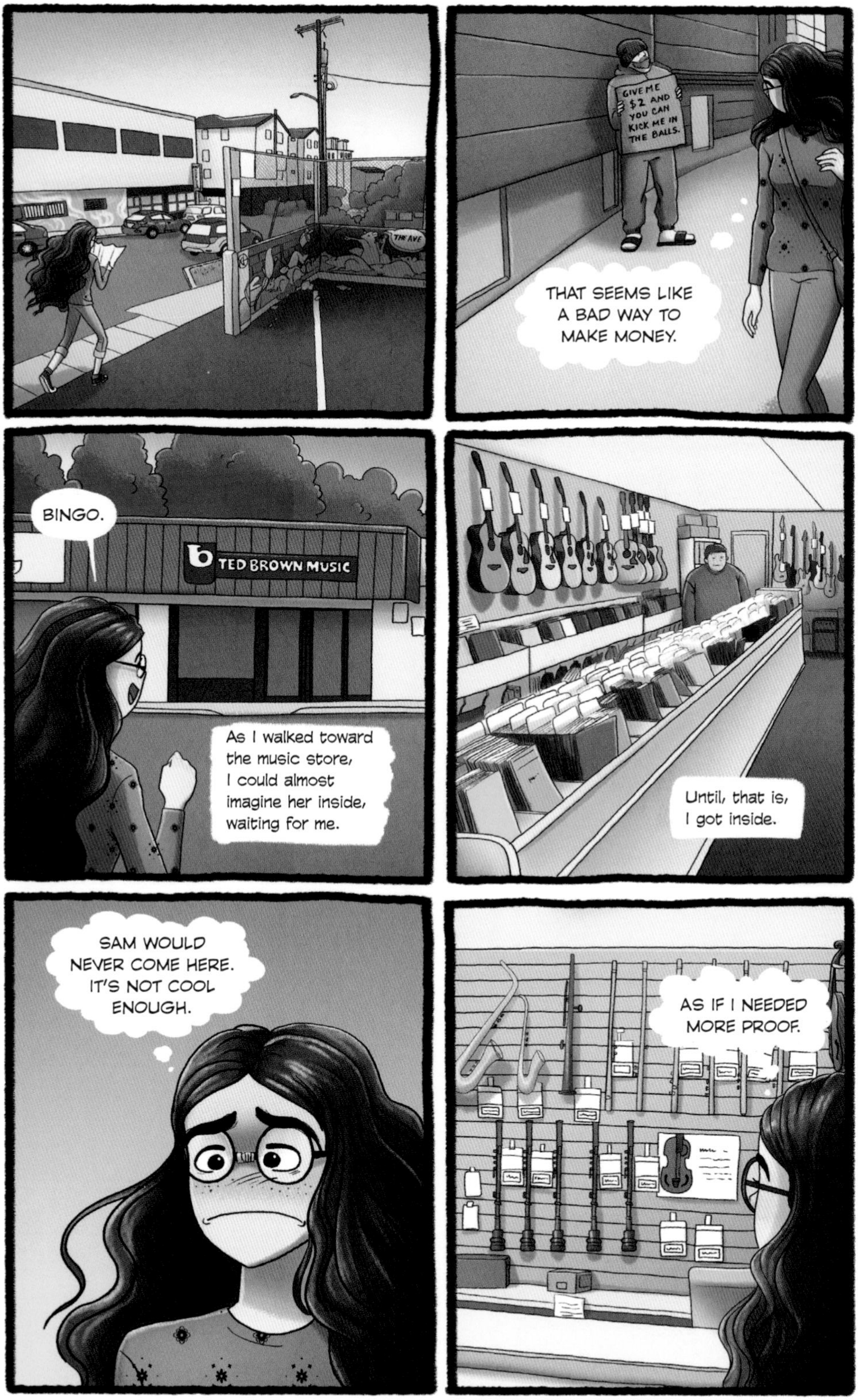
THE AVE
GIVE ME $2 AND YOU CAN KICK ME IN THE BALLS.
THAT SEEMS LIKE A BAD WAY TO MAKE MONEY.
BINGO.
TED BROWN MUSIC
As I walked toward the music store, I could almost imagine her inside, waiting for me.
Until, that is, I got inside.
SAM WOULD NEVER COME HERE. IT'S NOT COOL ENOUGH.
AS IF I NEEDED MORE PROOF.

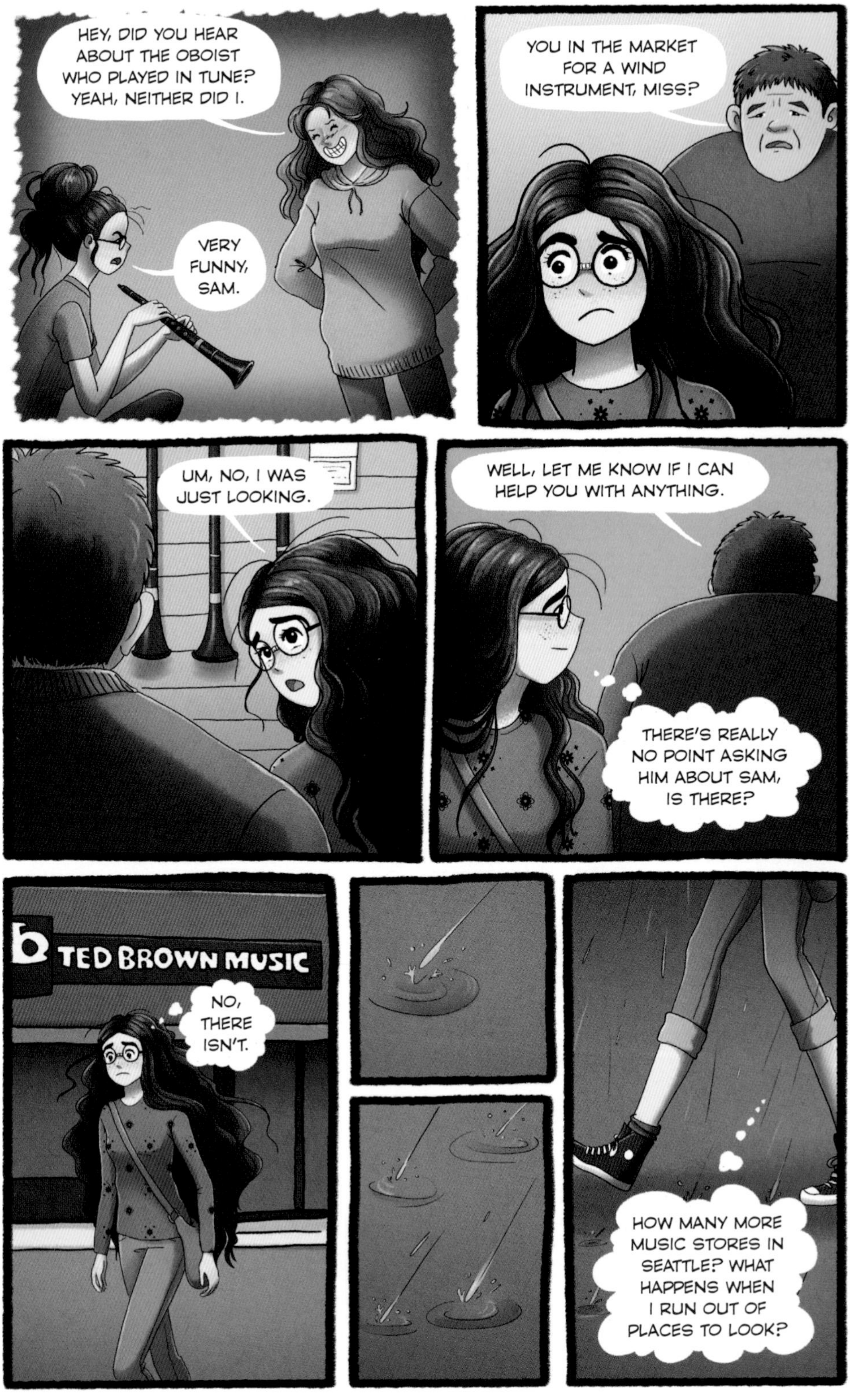
HEY, DID YOU HEAR ABOUT THE OBOIST WHO PLAYED IN TUNE? YEAH, NEITHER DID I.
VERY FUNNY, SAM.
YOU IN THE MARKET FOR A WIND INSTRUMENT, MISS?
UM, NO, I WAS JUST LOOKING.
WELL, LET ME KNOW IF I CAN HELP YOU WITH ANYTHING.
THERE'S REALLY NO POINT ASKING HIM ABOUT SAM, IS THERE?
TED BROWN MUSIC
NO, THERE ISN'T.
HOW MANY MORE MUSIC STORES IN SEATTLE? WHAT HAPPENS WHEN I RUN OUT OF PLACES TO LOOK?

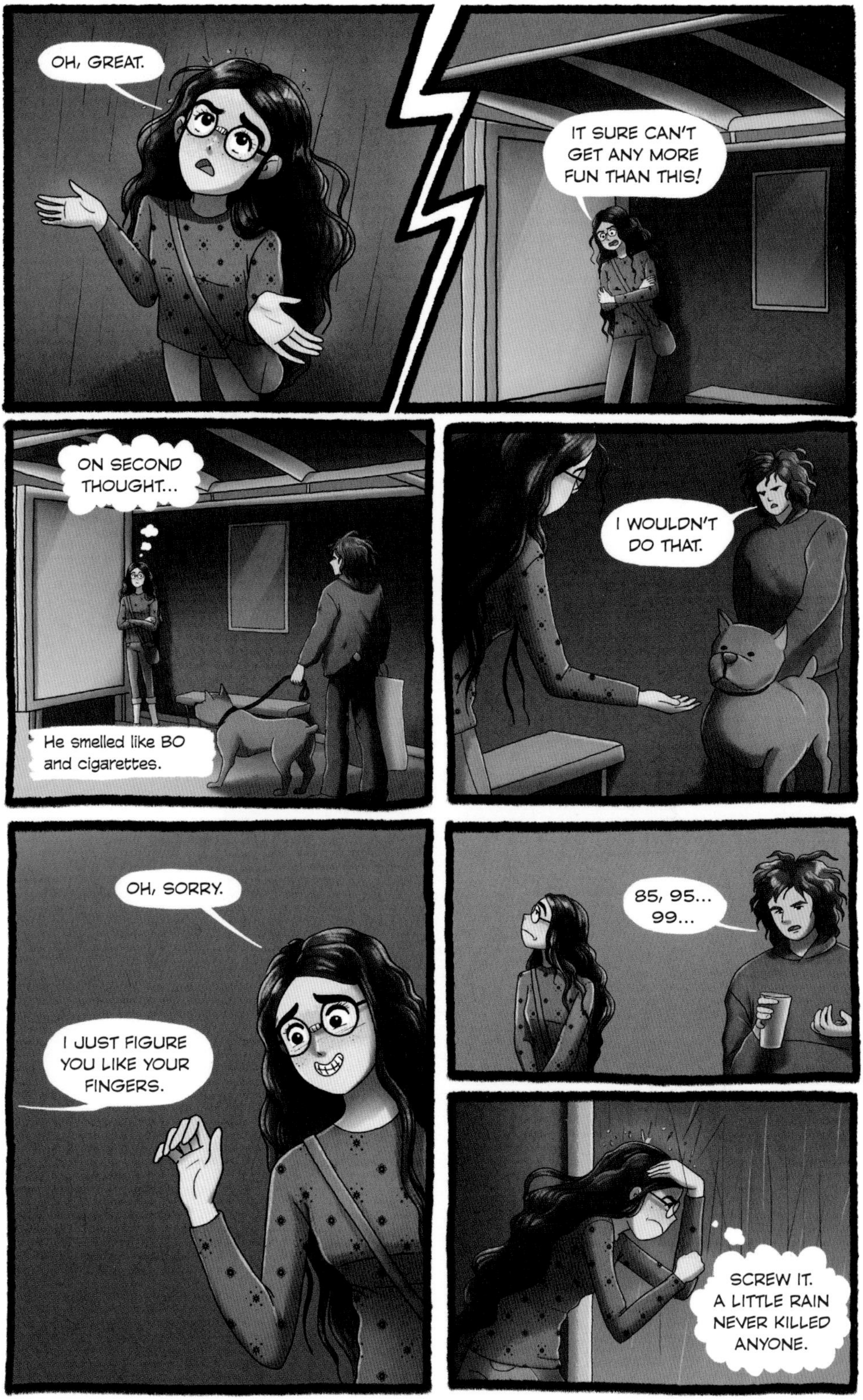
OH, GREAT.
IT SURE CAN'T GET ANY MORE FUN THAN THIS!
ON SECOND THOUGHT...
He smelled like BO and cigarettes.
I WOULDN'T DO THAT.
OH, SORRY.
I JUST FIGURE YOU LIKE YOUR FINGERS.
85, 95... 99...
SCREW IT. A LITTLE RAIN NEVER KILLED ANYONE.

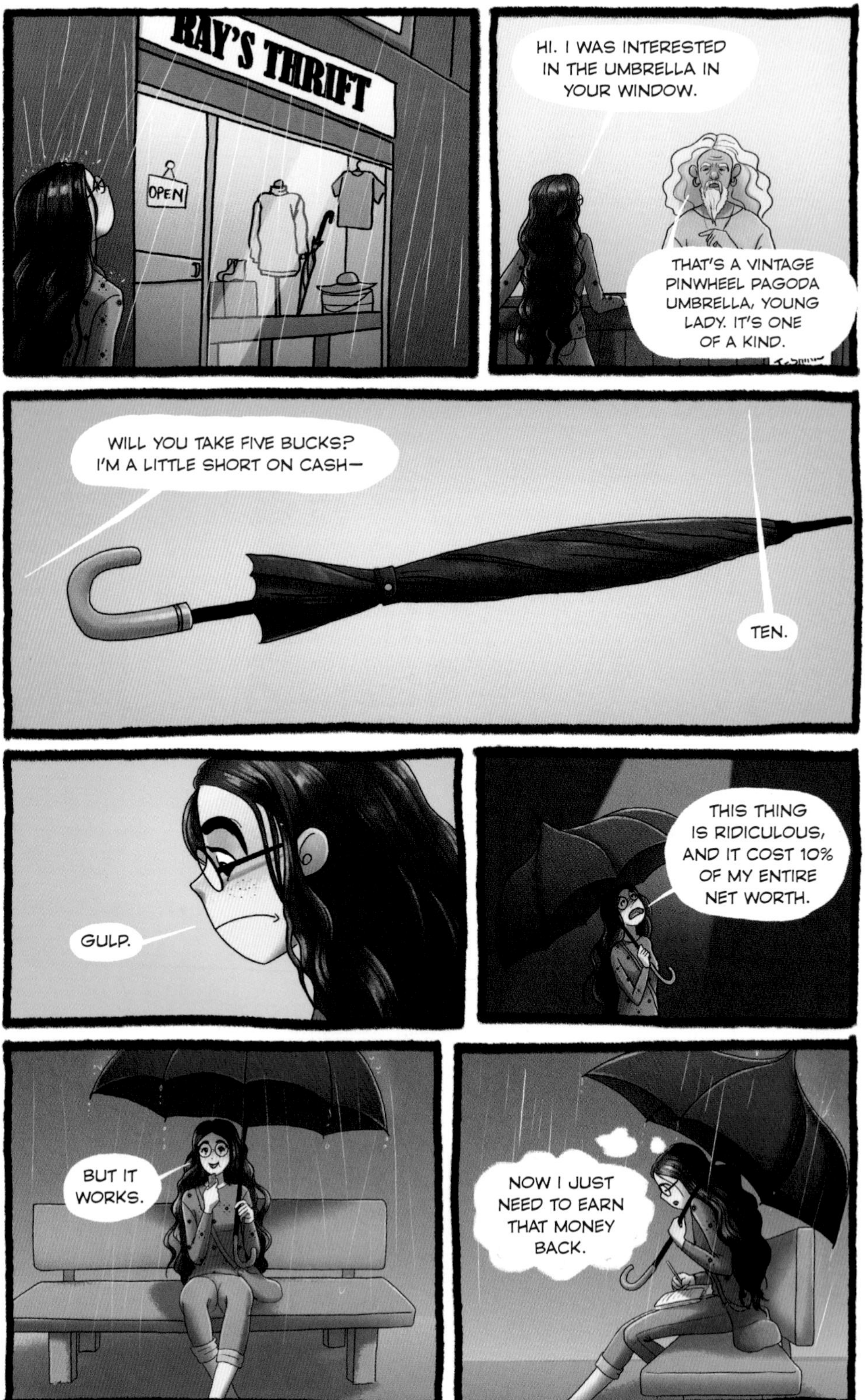
RAY'S THRIFT
OPEN
HI. I WAS INTERESTED IN THE UMBRELLA IN YOUR WINDOW.
THAT'S A VINTAGE PINWHEEL PAGODA UMBRELLA, YOUNG LADY. IT'S ONE OF A KIND.
WILL YOU TAKE FIVE BUCKS? I'M A LITTLE SHORT ON CASH—
TEN.
GULP.
THIS THING IS RIDICULOUS, AND IT COST 10% OF MY ENTIRE NET WORTH.
BUT IT WORKS.
NOW I JUST NEED TO EARN THAT MONEY BACK.

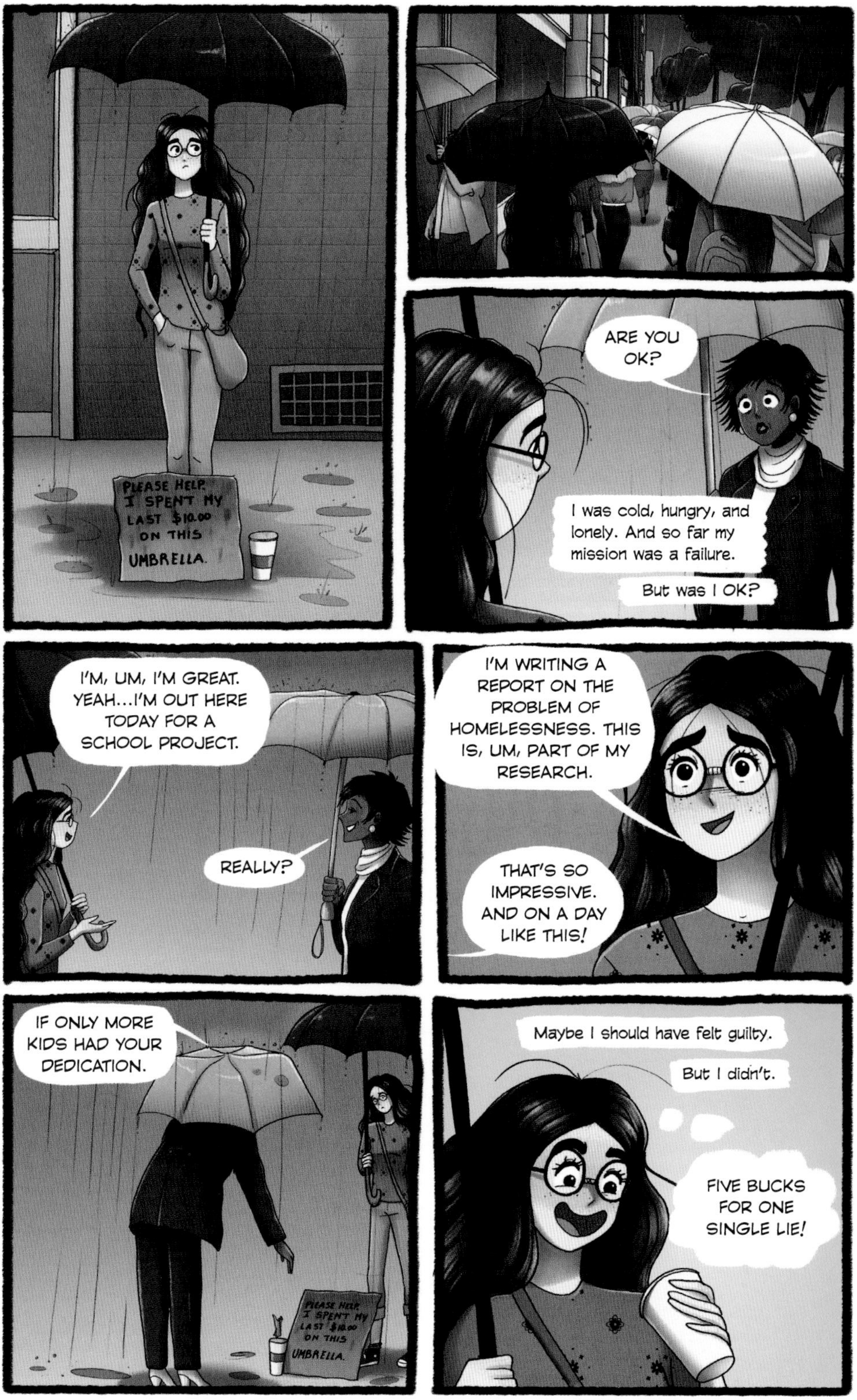
PLEASE HELP. I SPENT MY LAST $10.00 ON THIS UMBRELLA.
ARE YOU OK?
I was cold, hungry, and lonely. And so far my mission was a failure.
But was I OK?
I'M, UM, I'M GREAT. YEAH...I'M OUT HERE TODAY FOR A SCHOOL PROJECT.
REALLY?
I'M WRITING A REPORT ON THE PROBLEM OF HOMELESSNESS. THIS IS, UM, PART OF MY RESEARCH.
THAT'S SO IMPRESSIVE. AND ON A DAY LIKE THIS!
IF ONLY MORE KIDS HAD YOUR DEDICATION.
PLEASE HELP. I SPENT MY LAST $10.00 ON THIS UMBRELLA.
Maybe I should have felt guilty.
But I didn't.
FIVE BUCKS FOR ONE SINGLE LIE!

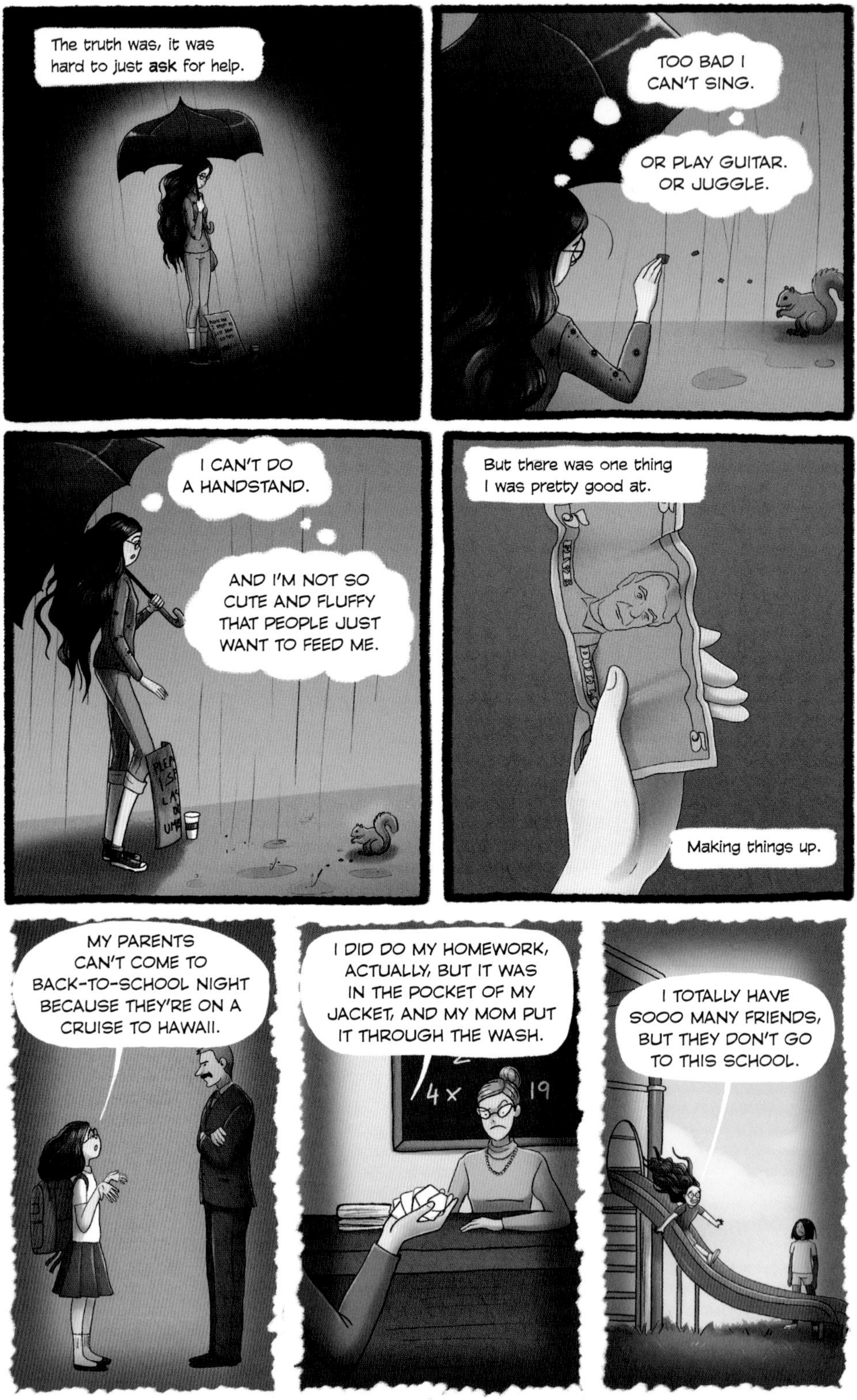
The truth was, it was hard to just **ask** for help.
TOO BAD I CAN'T SING.
OR PLAY GUITAR. OR JUGGLE.
I CAN'T DO A HANDSTAND.
AND I'M NOT SO CUTE AND FLUFFY THAT PEOPLE JUST WANT TO FEED ME.
But there was one thing I was pretty good at.
Making things up.
MY PARENTS CAN'T COME TO BACK-TO-SCHOOL NIGHT BECAUSE THEY'RE ON A CRUISE TO HAWAII.
I DID DO MY HOMEWORK, ACTUALLY, BUT IT WAS IN THE POCKET OF MY JACKET, AND MY MOM PUT IT THROUGH THE WASH.
I TOTALLY HAVE SOOO MANY FRIENDS, BUT THEY DON'T GO TO THIS SCHOOL.

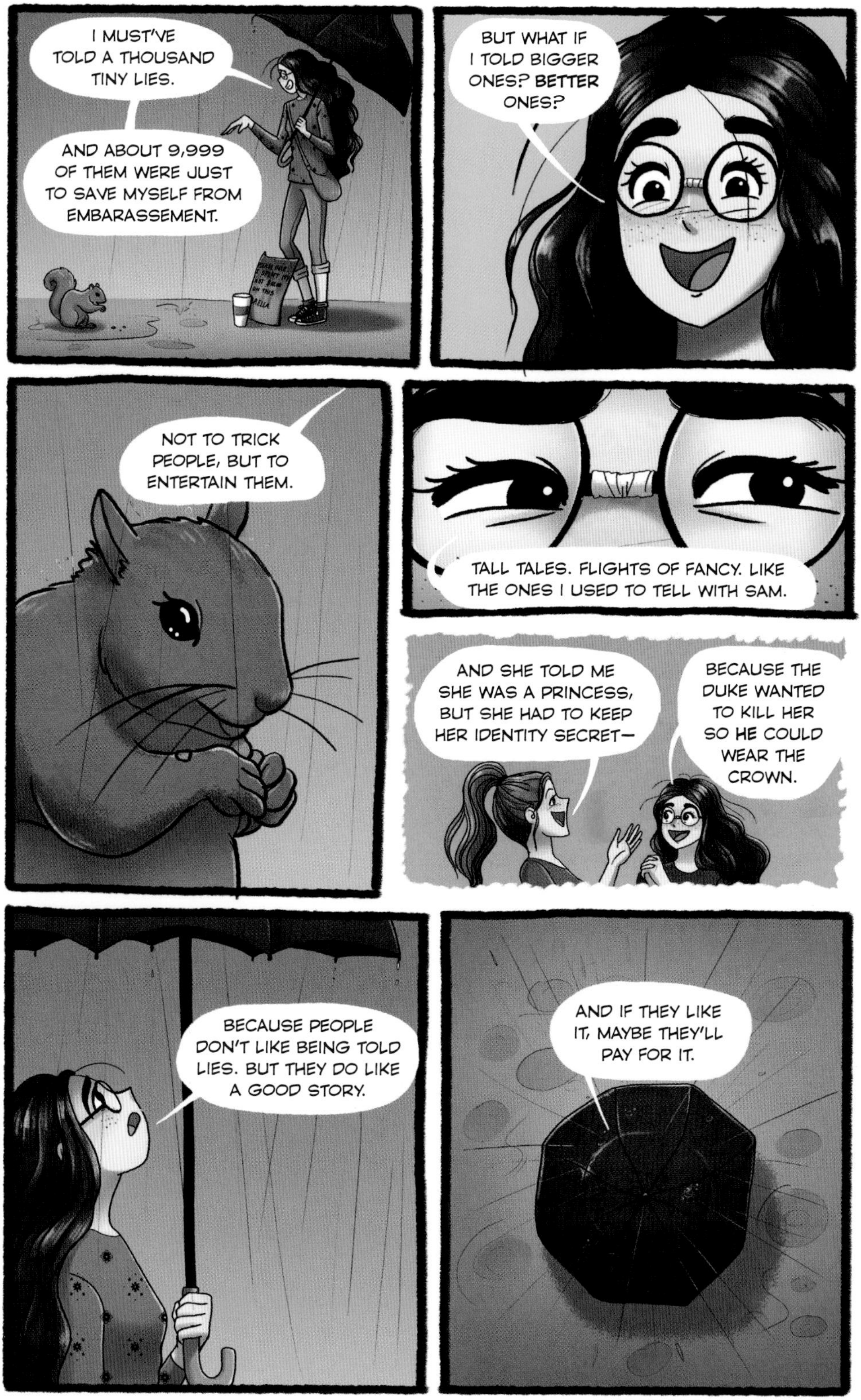
I MUST'VE TOLD A THOUSAND TINY LIES.
AND ABOUT 9,999 OF THEM WERE JUST TO SAVE MYSELF FROM EMBARASSEMENT.
BUT WHAT IF I TOLD BIGGER ONES? BETTER ONES?
NOT TO TRICK PEOPLE, BUT TO ENTERTAIN THEM.
TALL TALES. FLIGHTS OF FANCY. LIKE THE ONES I USED TO TELL WITH SAM.
AND SHE TOLD ME SHE WAS A PRINCESS, BUT SHE HAD TO KEEP HER IDENTITY SECRET—
BECAUSE THE DUKE WANTED TO KILL HER SO HE COULD WEAR THE CROWN.
BECAUSE PEOPLE DON'T LIKE BEING TOLD LIES. BUT THEY DO LIKE A GOOD STORY.
AND IF THEY LIKE IT, MAYBE THEY'LL PAY FOR IT.

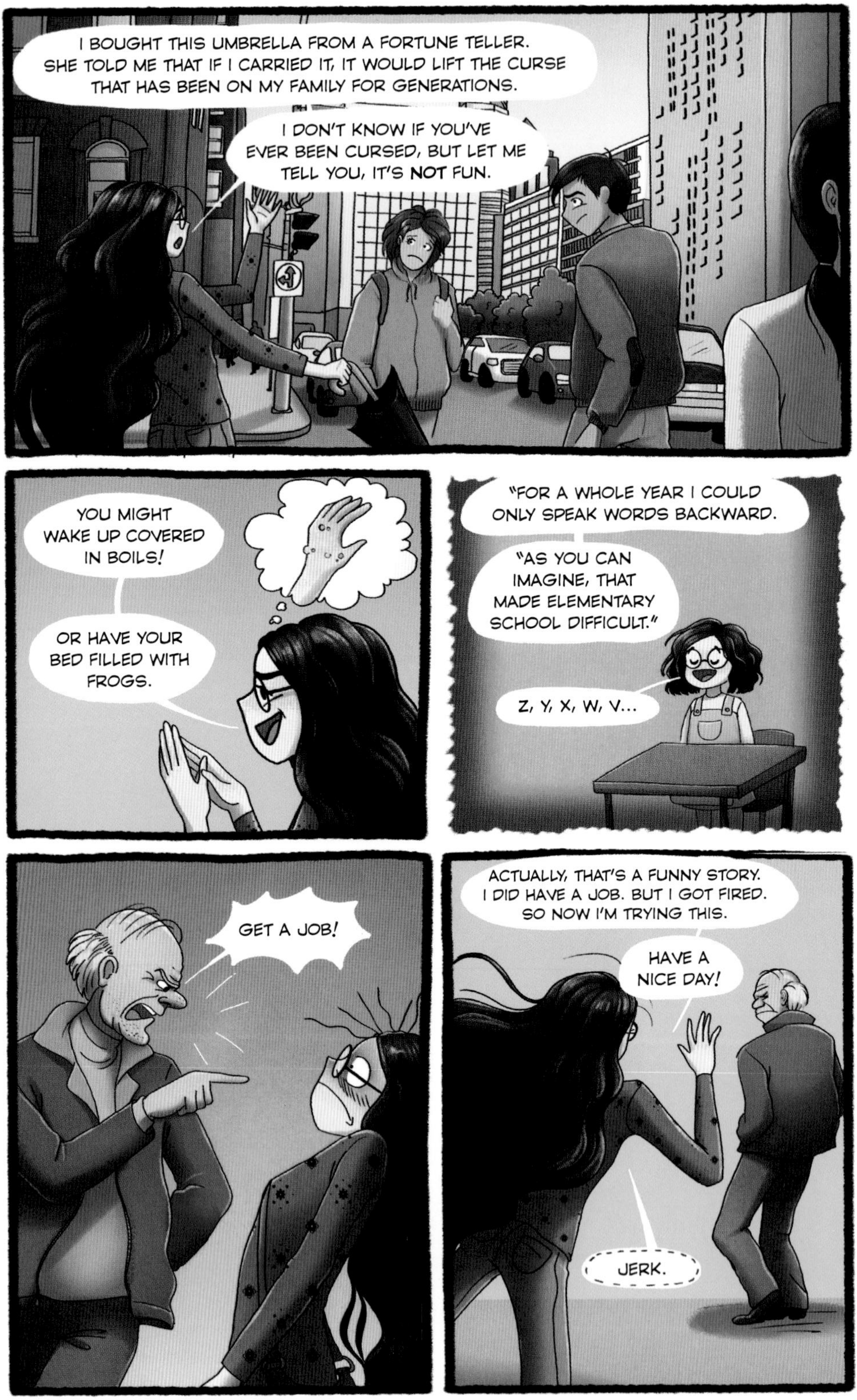
I BOUGHT THIS UMBRELLA FROM A FORTUNE TELLER. SHE TOLD ME THAT IF I CARRIED IT, IT WOULD LIFT THE CURSE THAT HAS BEEN ON MY FAMILY FOR GENERATIONS.
I DON'T KNOW IF YOU'VE EVER BEEN CURSED, BUT LET ME TELL YOU, IT'S **NOT** FUN.
YOU MIGHT WAKE UP COVERED IN BOILS!
OR HAVE YOUR BED FILLED WITH FROGS.
"FOR A WHOLE YEAR I COULD ONLY SPEAK WORDS BACKWARD.
"AS YOU CAN IMAGINE, THAT MADE ELEMENTARY SCHOOL DIFFICULT."
Z, Y, X, W, V...
GET A JOB!
ACTUALLY, THAT'S A FUNNY STORY. I DID HAVE A JOB. BUT I GOT FIRED. SO NOW I'M TRYING THIS.
HAVE A NICE DAY!
JERK.

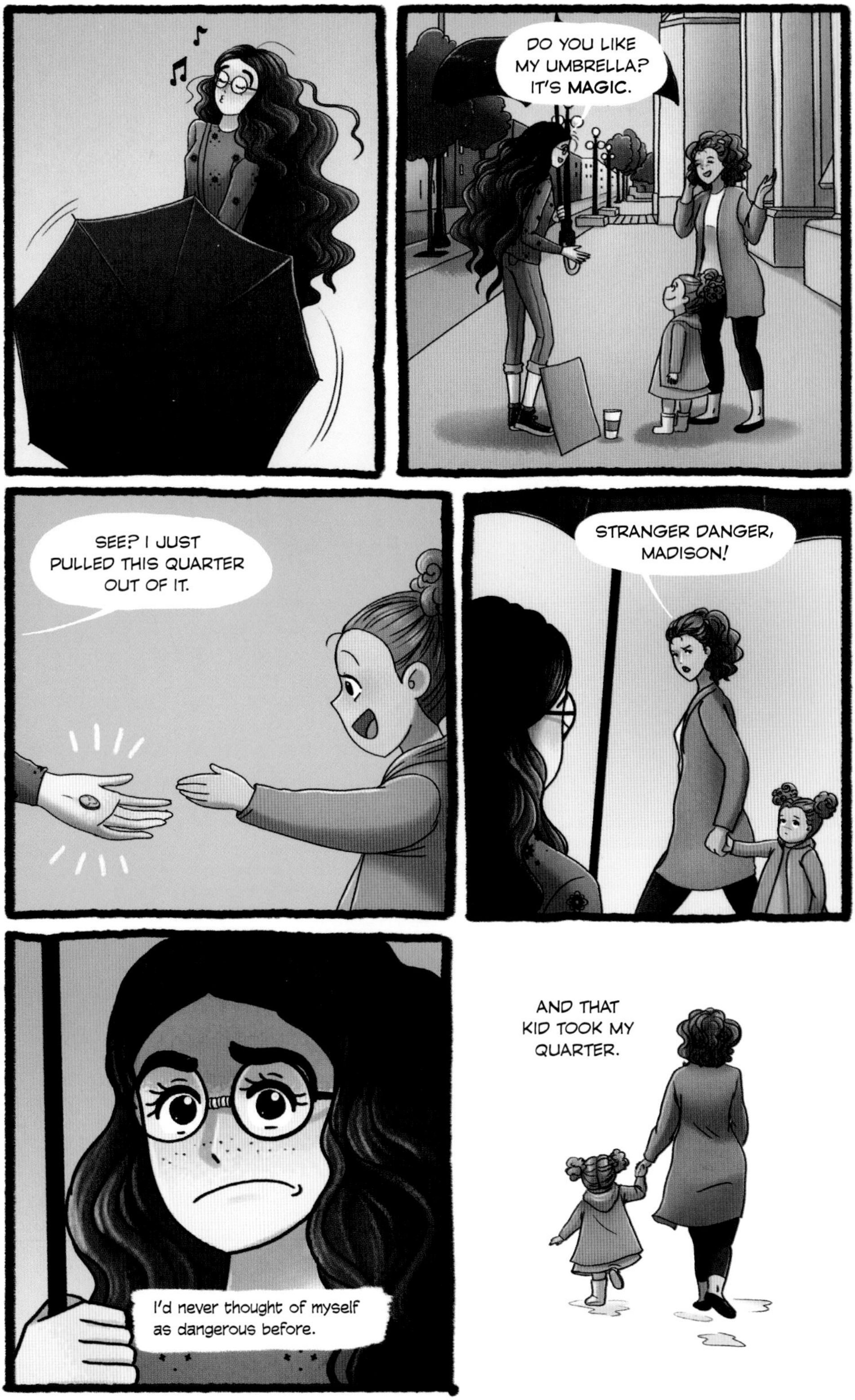
DO YOU LIKE MY UMBRELLA? IT'S **MAGIC**.
SEE? I JUST PULLED THIS QUARTER OUT OF IT.
STRANGER DANGER, MADISON!
I'd never thought of myself as dangerous before.
AND THAT KID TOOK MY QUARTER.

It was not what I call a great start.

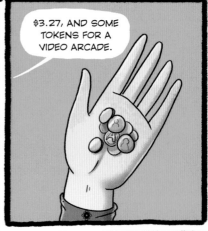

$3.27, AND SOME TOKENS FOR A VIDEO ARCADE.

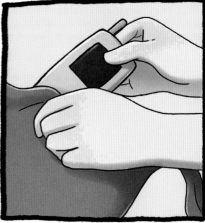

HEY, IT'S ME AGAIN. CALL ME BACK BEFORE I GET EATEN BY A SHARK WHO ATE OUR PARENTS. REMEMBER THAT STORY, SAM? THAT WAS FUNNY... OK...UM...BYE.

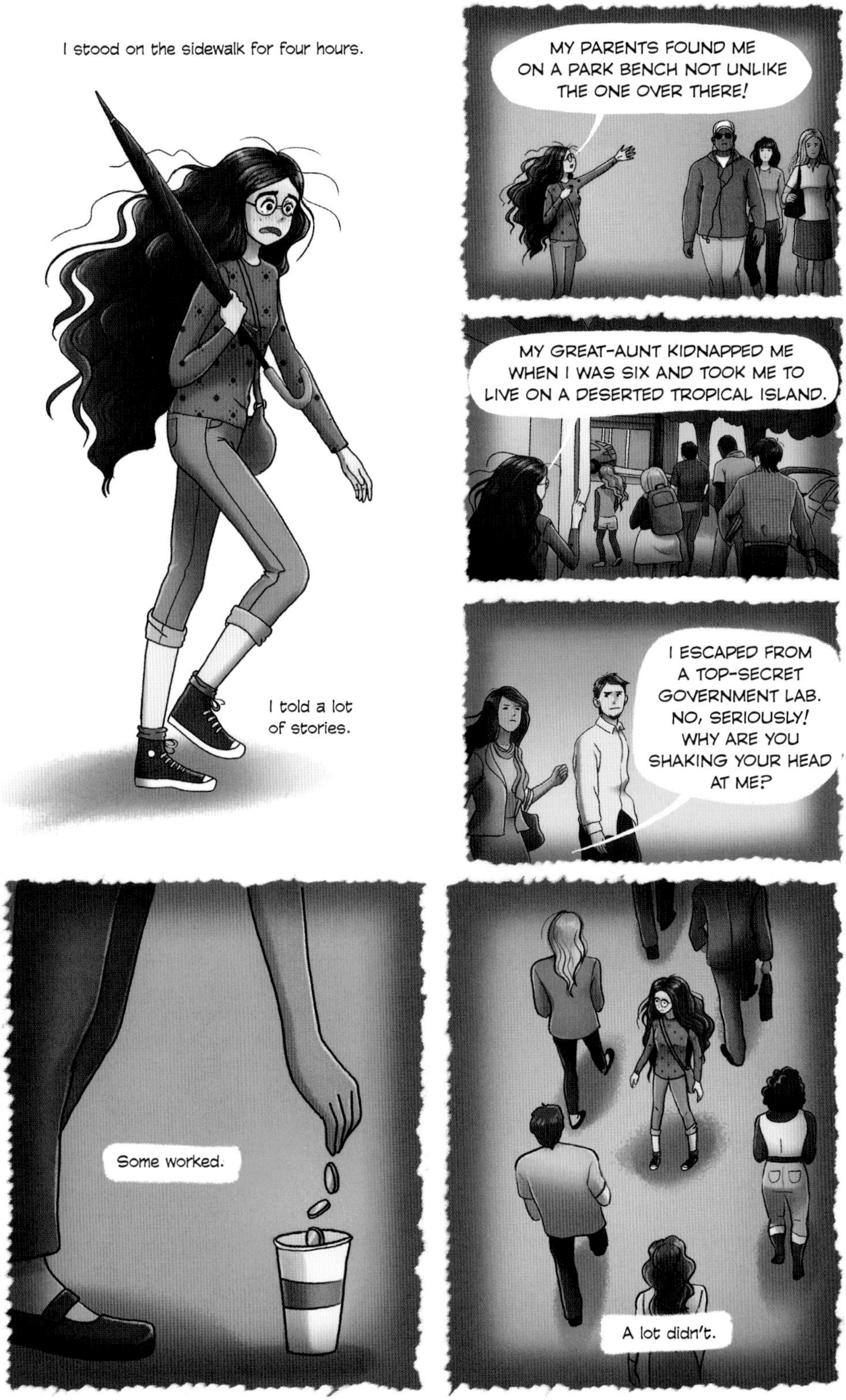
I stood on the sidewalk for four hours.
I told a lot of stories.
MY PARENTS FOUND ME ON A PARK BENCH NOT UNLIKE THE ONE OVER THERE!
MY GREAT-AUNT KIDNAPPED ME WHEN I WAS SIX AND TOOK ME TO LIVE ON A DESERTED TROPICAL ISLAND.
I ESCAPED FROM A TOP-SECRET GOVERNMENT LAB. NO, SERIOUSLY! WHY ARE YOU SHAKING YOUR HEAD AT ME?
Some worked.
A lot didn't.

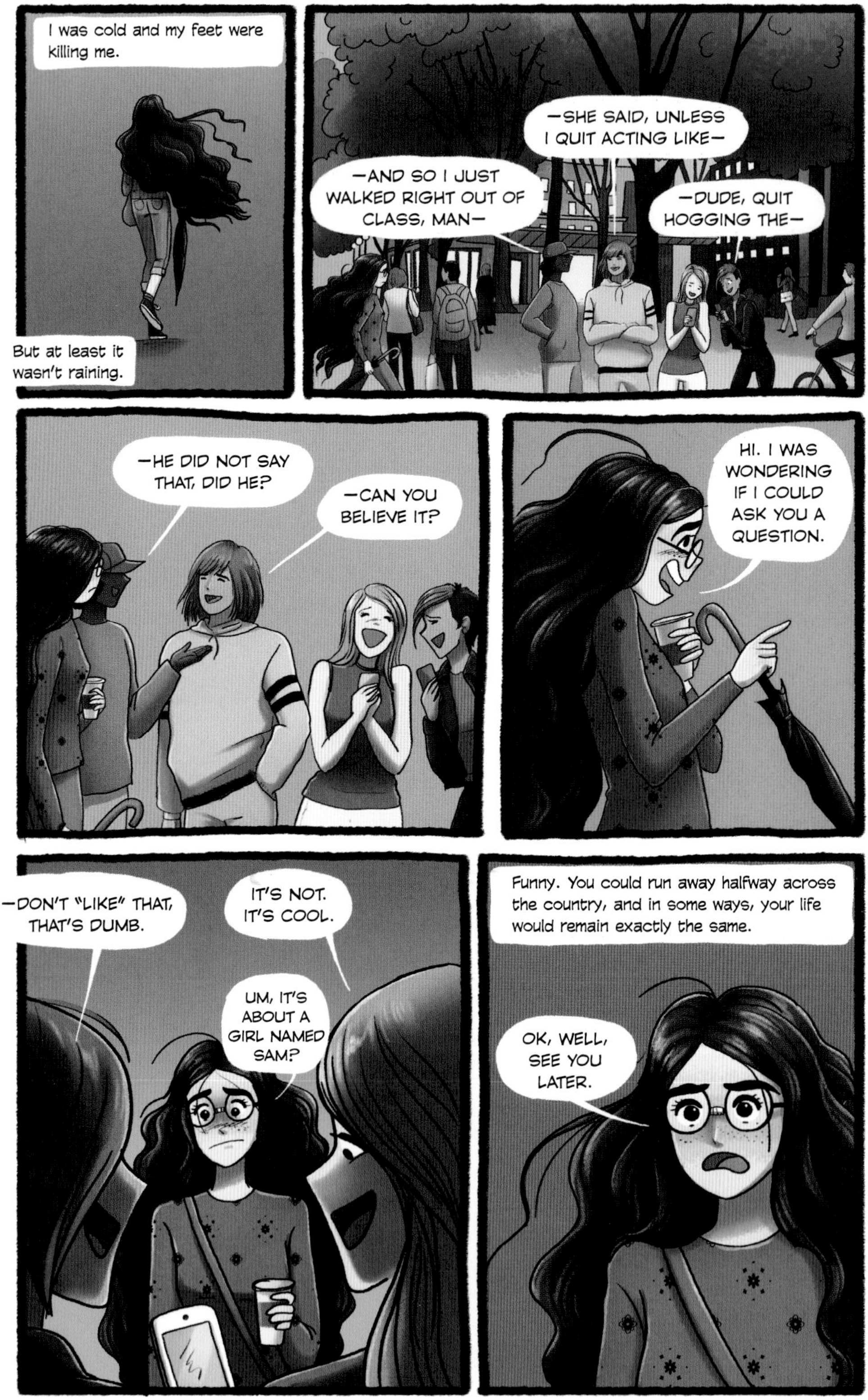
I was cold and my feet were killing me.
But at least it wasn't raining.
—SHE SAID, UNLESS I QUIT ACTING LIKE—
—AND SO I JUST WALKED RIGHT OUT OF CLASS, MAN—
—DUDE, QUIT HOGGING THE—
—HE DID NOT SAY THAT, DID HE?
—CAN YOU BELIEVE IT?
HI. I WAS WONDERING IF I COULD ASK YOU A QUESTION.
—DON'T "LIKE" THAT, THAT'S DUMB.
IT'S NOT. IT'S COOL.
UM, IT'S ABOUT A GIRL NAMED SAM?
Funny. You could run away halfway across the country, and in some ways, your life would remain exactly the same.
OK, WELL, SEE YOU LATER.

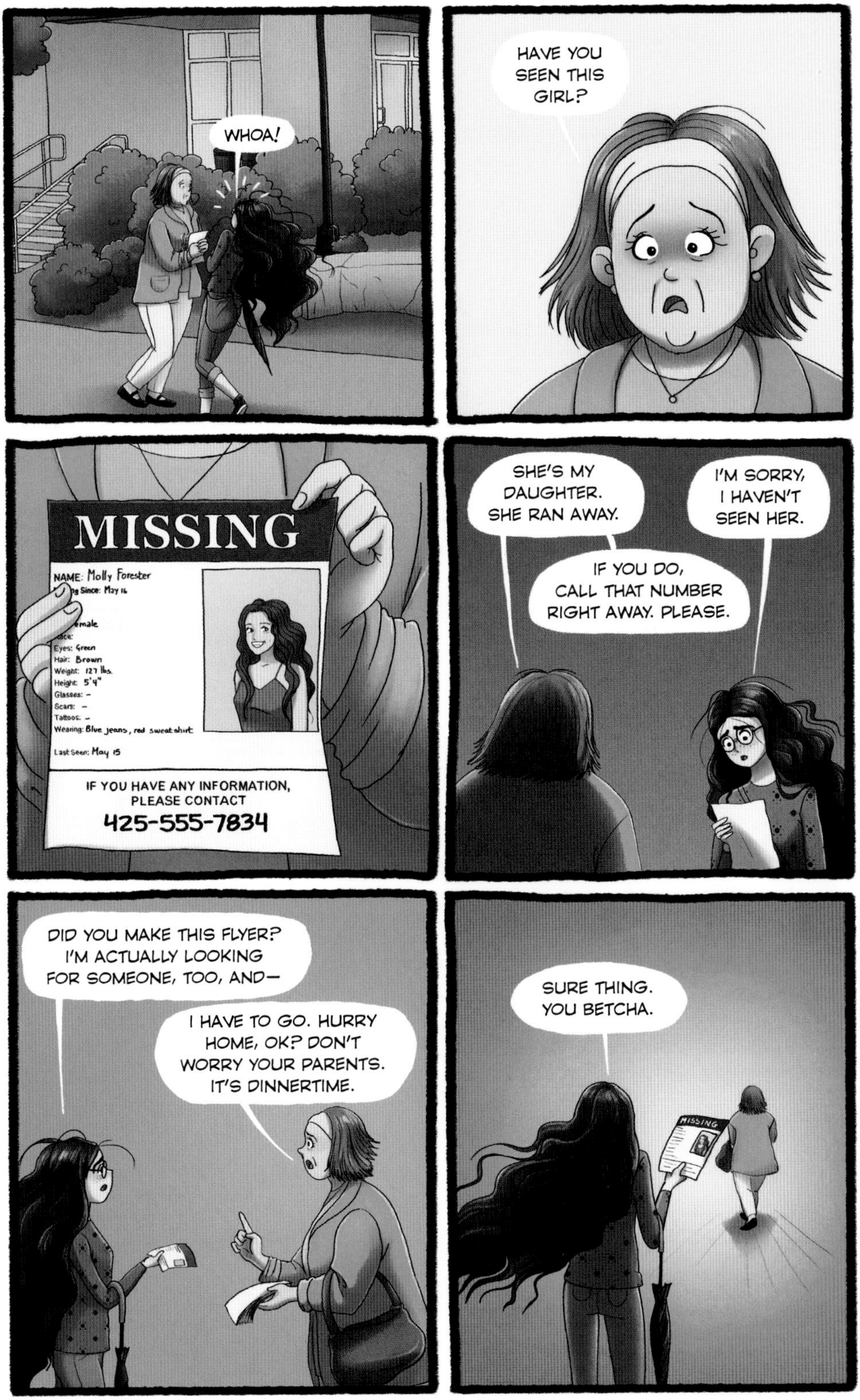
WHOA!
HAVE YOU SEEN THIS GIRL?
MISSING
NAME: Molly Forester
ng Since: May 16
emale
Eyes: Green
Hair: Brown
Weight: 127 lbs.
Height: 5'4"
Glasses: –
Scars: –
Tattoos: –
Wearing: Blue jeans, red sweatshirt
Last Seen: May 15
IF YOU HAVE ANY INFORMATION, PLEASE CONTACT
425-555-7834
SHE'S MY DAUGHTER. SHE RAN AWAY.
I'M SORRY, I HAVEN'T SEEN HER.
IF YOU DO, CALL THAT NUMBER RIGHT AWAY. PLEASE.
DID YOU MAKE THIS FLYER? I'M ACTUALLY LOOKING FOR SOMEONE, TOO, AND—
I HAVE TO GO. HURRY HOME, OK? DON'T WORRY YOUR PARENTS. IT'S DINNERTIME.
SURE THING. YOU BETCHA.
MISSING

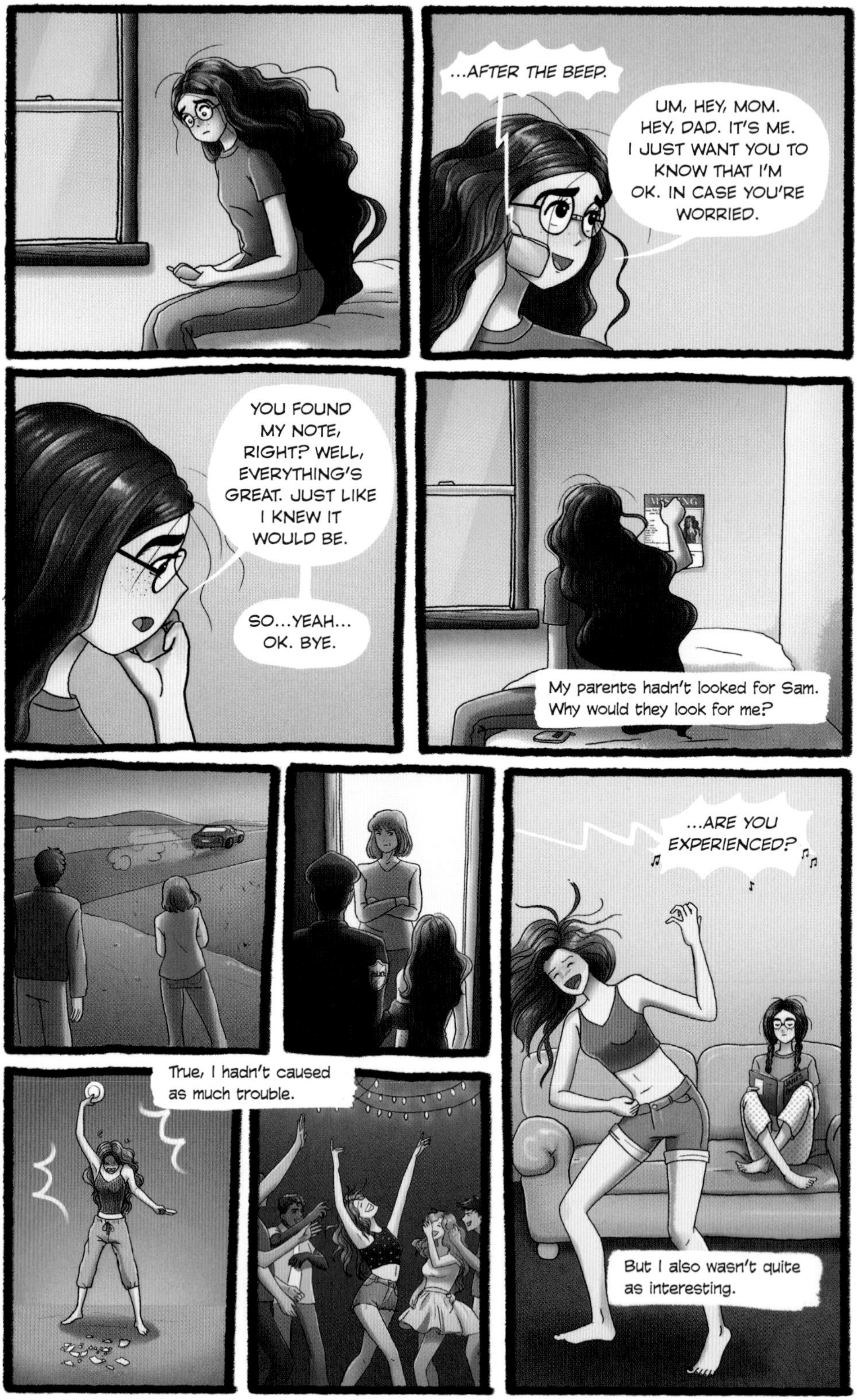
...AFTER THE BEEP.
UM, HEY, MOM. HEY, DAD. IT'S ME. I JUST WANT YOU TO KNOW THAT I'M OK. IN CASE YOU'RE WORRIED.
YOU FOUND MY NOTE, RIGHT? WELL, EVERYTHING'S GREAT. JUST LIKE I KNEW IT WOULD BE.
SO...YEAH... OK. BYE.
My parents hadn't looked for Sam. Why would they look for me?
...ARE YOU EXPERIENCED?
True, I hadn't caused as much trouble.
But I also wasn't quite as interesting.

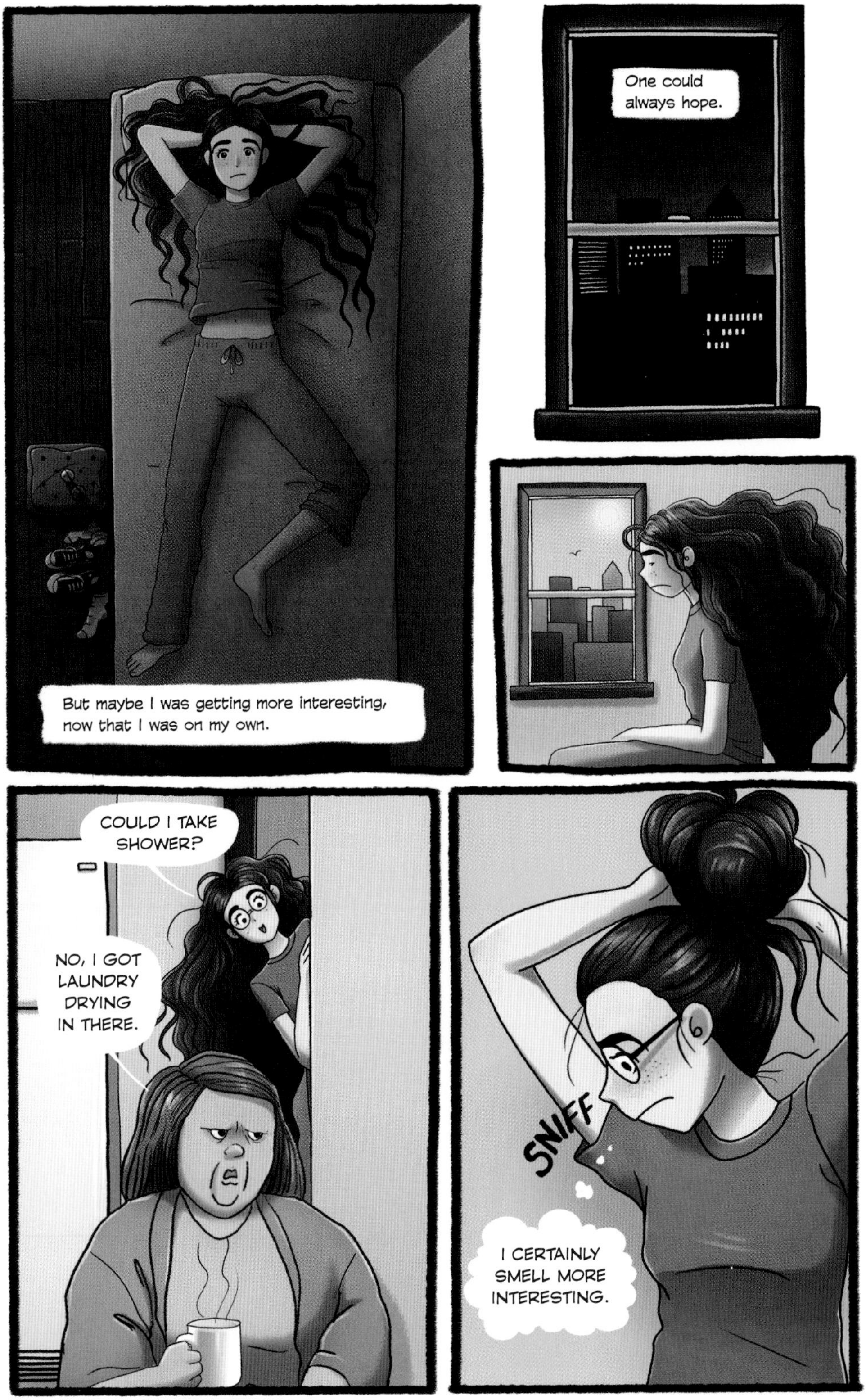
But maybe I was getting more interesting, now that I was on my own.
One could always hope.
COULD I TAKE SHOWER?
NO, I GOT LAUNDRY DRYING IN THERE.
SNIFF
I CERTAINLY SMELL MORE INTERESTING.

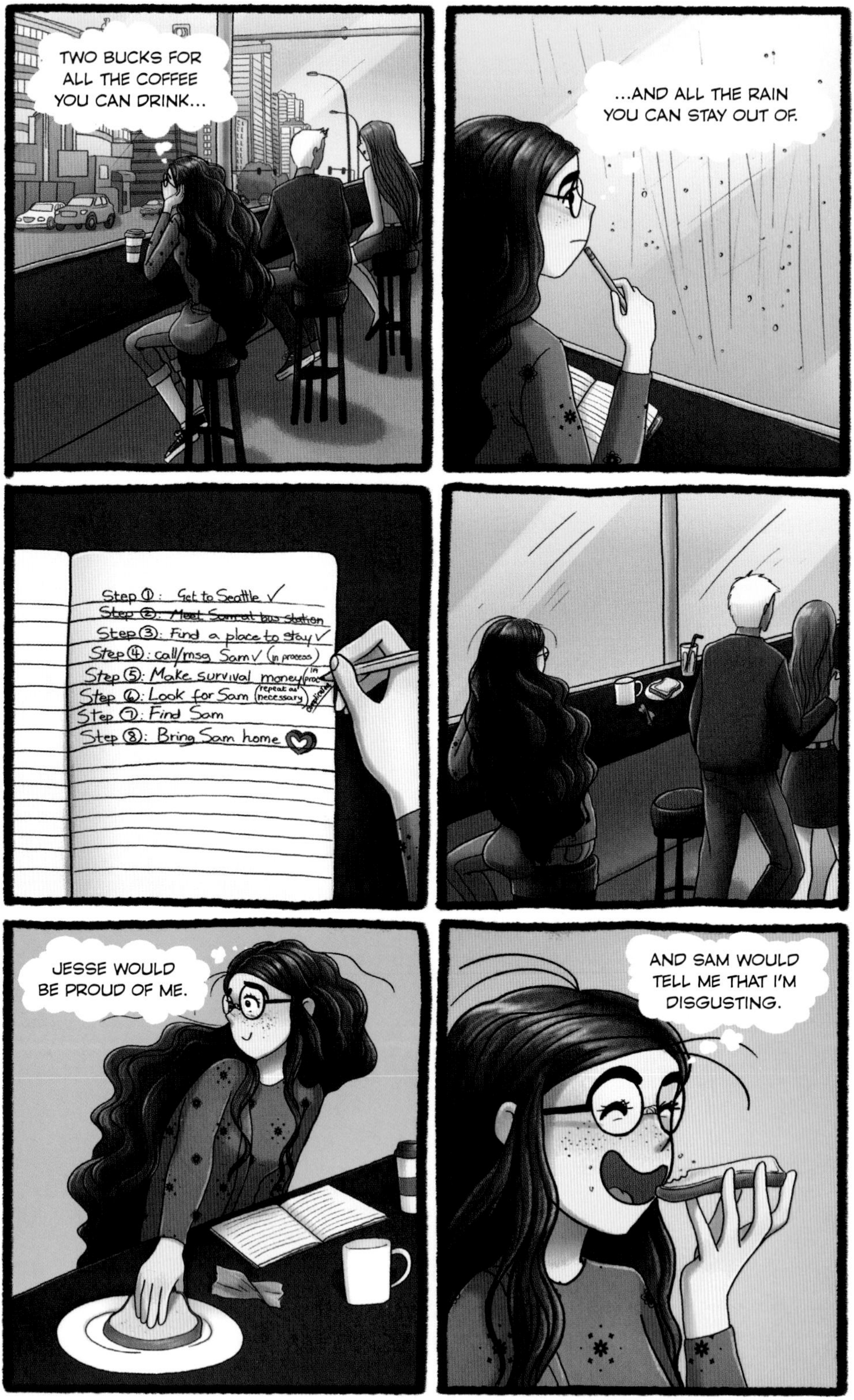
TWO BUCKS FOR ALL THE COFFEE YOU CAN DRINK...
...AND ALL THE RAIN YOU CAN STAY OUT OF.
Step ①: Get to Seattle ✓
~~Step ②: Meet Sam at bus station~~
Step ③: Find a place to stay ✓
Step ④: call/msg Sam ✓ (in process)
Step ⑤: Make survival money (in proc
Step ⑥: Look for Sam (repeat as necessary)
Step ⑦: Find Sam
Step ⑧: Bring Sam home
JESSE WOULD BE PROUD OF ME.
AND SAM WOULD TELL ME THAT I'M DISGUSTING.

It was time for Step 4. Again.

I checked—for the millionth time—to see if she'd written me back.

But of course she hadn't.

Find people, contact background checks

Trusted by over 35 million people

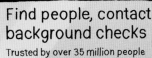

PEOPLE SEARCH   REVERSE PHONE   REVERSE ADD

Samantha   ×   City, State

SO THIS IS A FRIEND YOU'RE LOOKING FOR? SOMEONE FROM CAMP?

YEAH.

The nice librarian tried to help. She had some special database she could check.

But it was as if my sister had simply vanished.

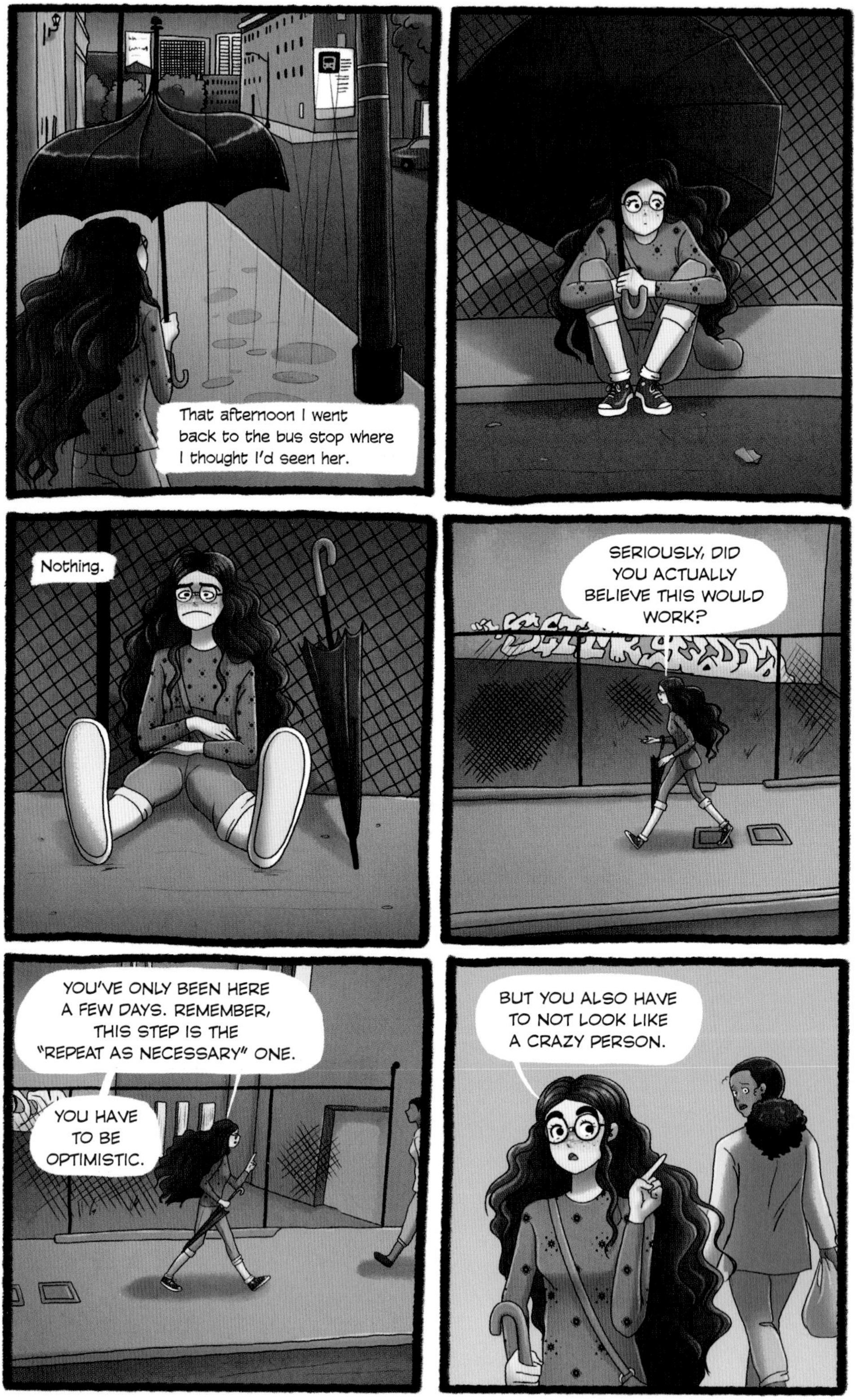
That afternoon I went back to the bus stop where I thought I'd seen her.
Nothing.
SERIOUSLY, DID YOU ACTUALLY BELIEVE THIS WOULD WORK?
YOU'VE ONLY BEEN HERE A FEW DAYS. REMEMBER, THIS STEP IS THE "REPEAT AS NECESSARY" ONE.
YOU HAVE TO BE OPTIMISTIC.
BUT YOU ALSO HAVE TO NOT LOOK LIKE A CRAZY PERSON.

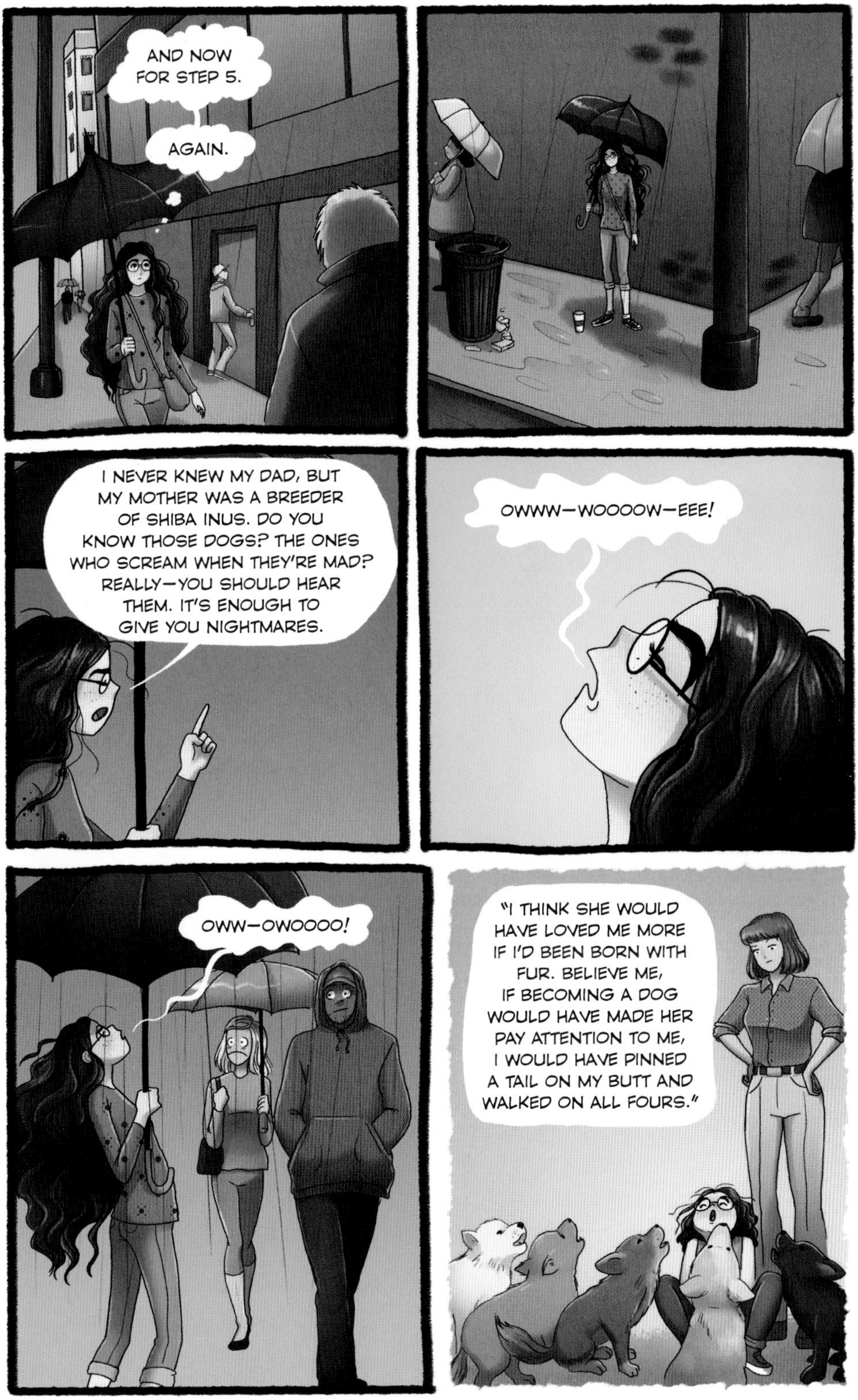
AND NOW FOR STEP 5.
AGAIN.
I NEVER KNEW MY DAD, BUT MY MOTHER WAS A BREEDER OF SHIBA INUS. DO YOU KNOW THOSE DOGS? THE ONES WHO SCREAM WHEN THEY'RE MAD? REALLY—YOU SHOULD HEAR THEM. IT'S ENOUGH TO GIVE YOU NIGHTMARES.
OWWW—WOOOOW—EEE!
OWW—OWOOOO!
"I THINK SHE WOULD HAVE LOVED ME MORE IF I'D BEEN BORN WITH FUR. BELIEVE ME, IF BECOMING A DOG WOULD HAVE MADE HER PAY ATTENTION TO ME, I WOULD HAVE PINNED A TAIL ON MY BUTT AND WALKED ON ALL FOURS."

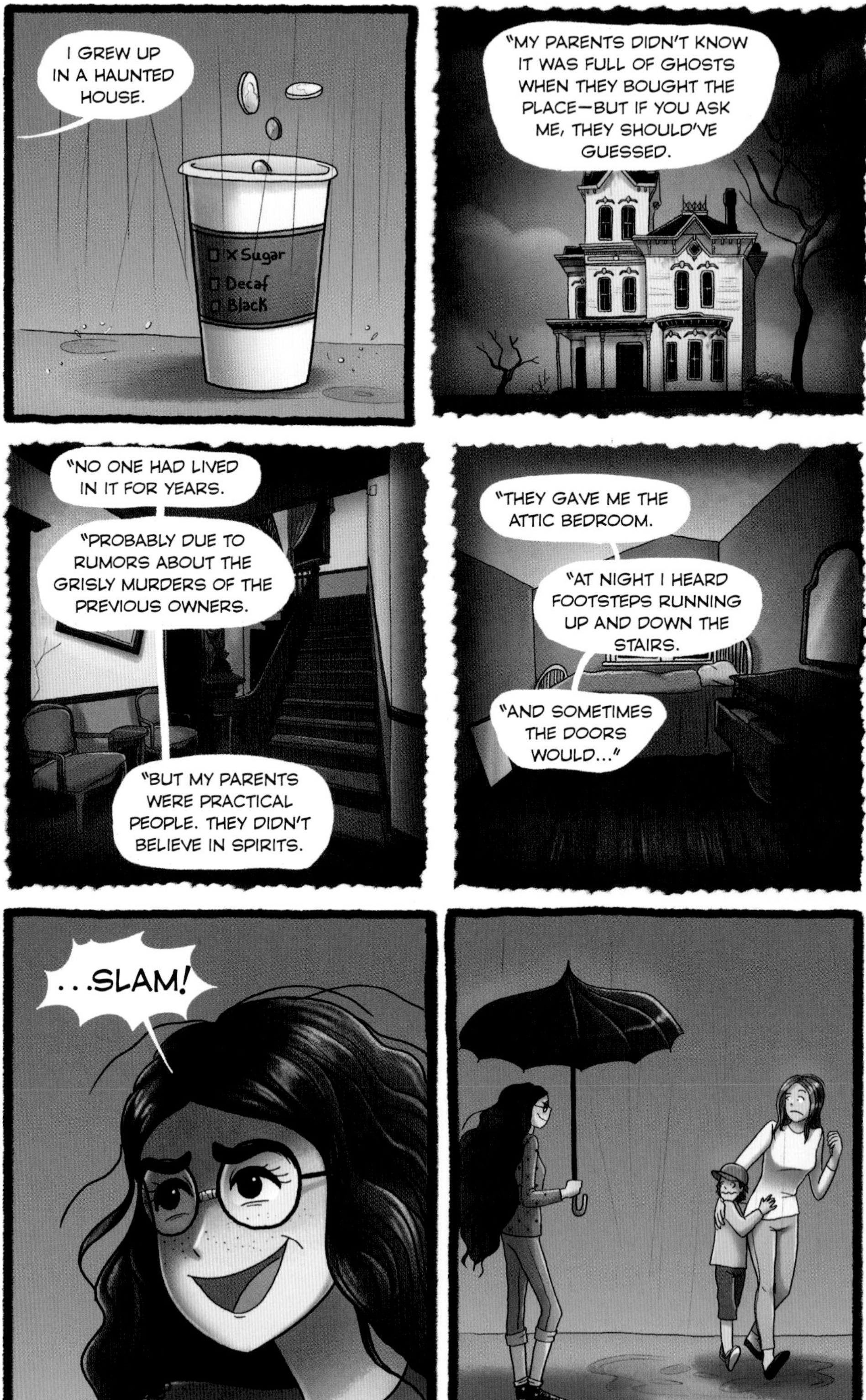
I GREW UP IN A HAUNTED HOUSE.
☐ X Sugar
☐ Decaf
☐ Black
"MY PARENTS DIDN'T KNOW IT WAS FULL OF GHOSTS WHEN THEY BOUGHT THE PLACE—BUT IF YOU ASK ME, THEY SHOULD'VE GUESSED.
"NO ONE HAD LIVED IN IT FOR YEARS.
"PROBABLY DUE TO RUMORS ABOUT THE GRISLY MURDERS OF THE PREVIOUS OWNERS.
"BUT MY PARENTS WERE PRACTICAL PEOPLE. THEY DIDN'T BELIEVE IN SPIRITS.
"THEY GAVE ME THE ATTIC BEDROOM.
"AT NIGHT I HEARD FOOTSTEPS RUNNING UP AND DOWN THE STAIRS.
"AND SOMETIMES THE DOORS WOULD..."
...SLAM!

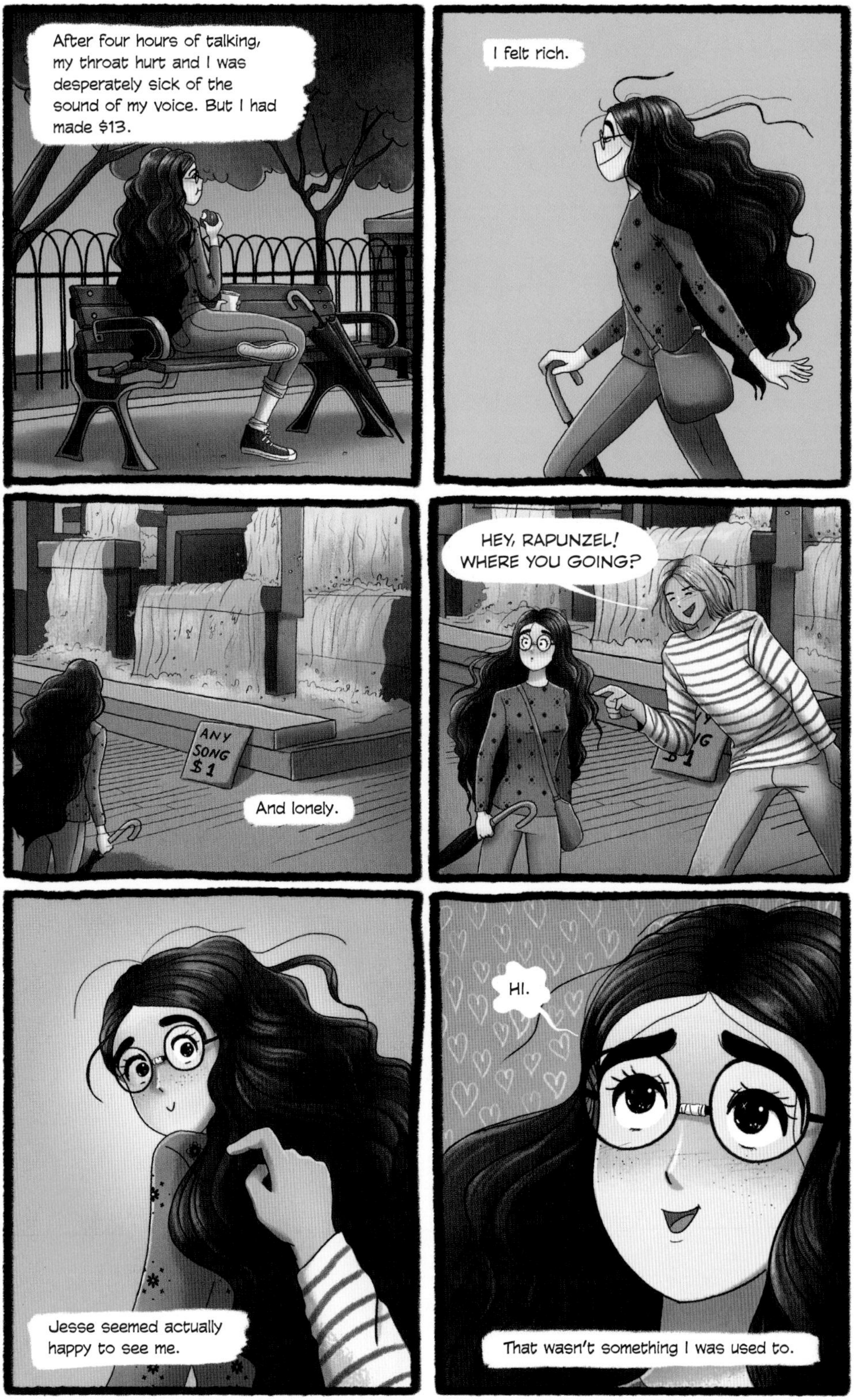
After four hours of talking, my throat hurt and I was desperately sick of the sound of my voice. But I had made $13.
I felt rich.
ANY SONG $1
And lonely.
HEY, RAPUNZEL! WHERE YOU GOING?
HI.
Jesse seemed actually happy to see me.
That wasn't something I was used to.

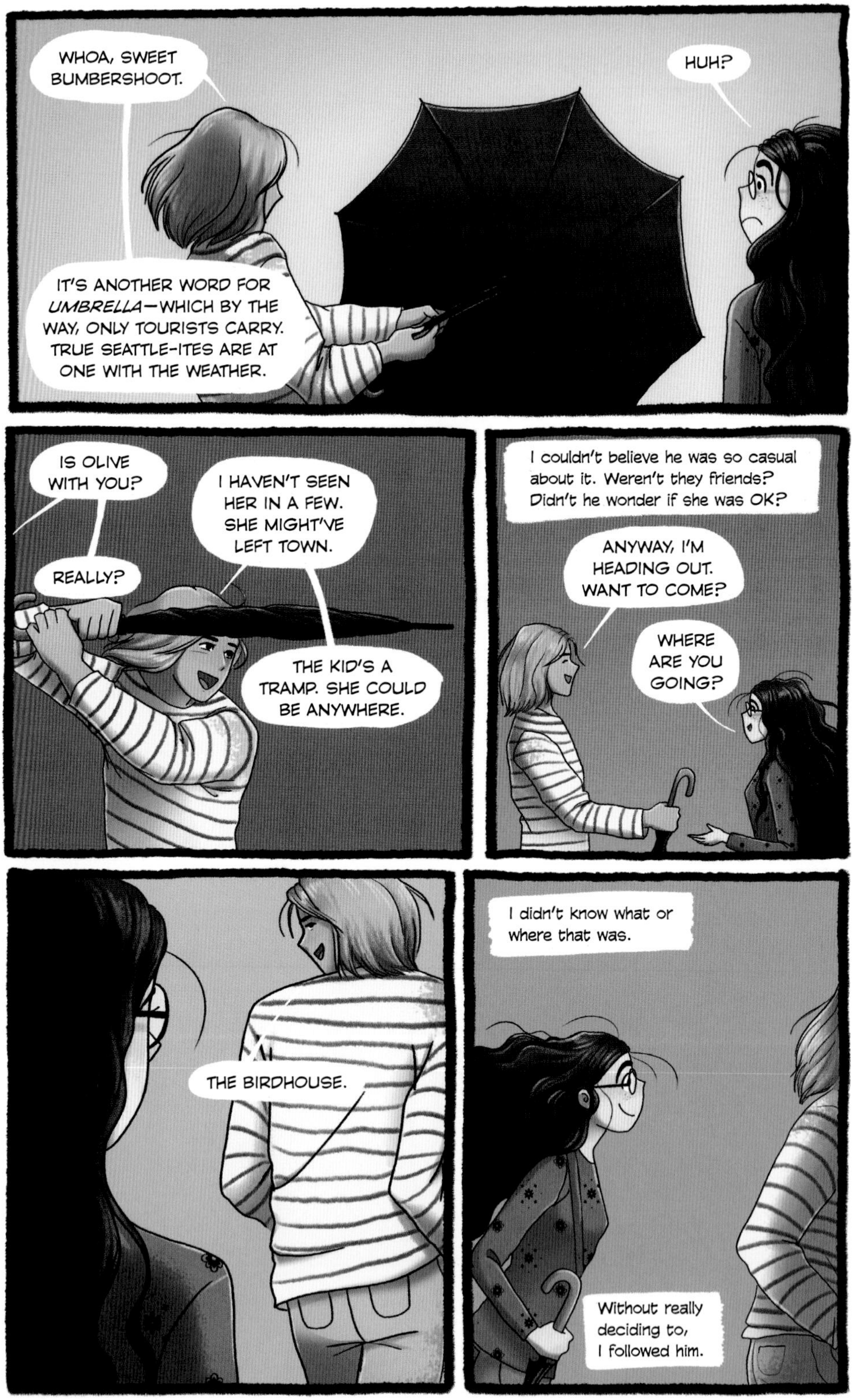
WHOA, SWEET BUMBERSHOOT.
HUH?
IT'S ANOTHER WORD FOR *UMBRELLA*—WHICH BY THE WAY, ONLY TOURISTS CARRY. TRUE SEATTLE-ITES ARE AT ONE WITH THE WEATHER.
IS OLIVE WITH YOU?
I HAVEN'T SEEN HER IN A FEW. SHE MIGHT'VE LEFT TOWN.
REALLY?
THE KID'S A TRAMP. SHE COULD BE ANYWHERE.
I couldn't believe he was so casual about it. Weren't they friends? Didn't he wonder if she was OK?
ANYWAY, I'M HEADING OUT. WANT TO COME?
WHERE ARE YOU GOING?
THE BIRDHOUSE.
I didn't know what or where that was.
Without really deciding to, I followed him.

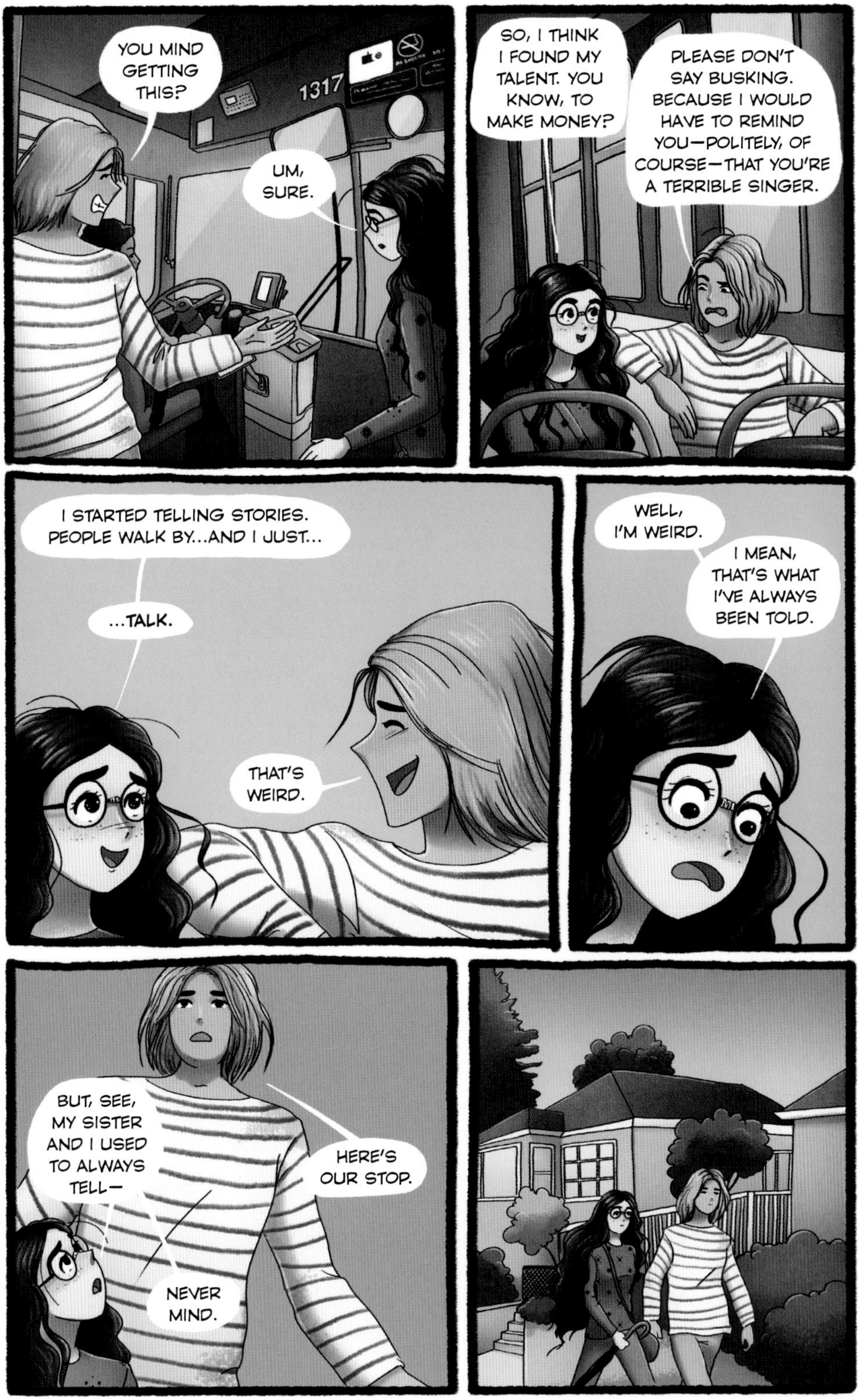
YOU MIND GETTING THIS?
1317
UM, SURE.
SO, I THINK I FOUND MY TALENT. YOU KNOW, TO MAKE MONEY?
PLEASE DON'T SAY BUSKING. BECAUSE I WOULD HAVE TO REMIND YOU—POLITELY, OF COURSE—THAT YOU'RE A TERRIBLE SINGER.
I STARTED TELLING STORIES. PEOPLE WALK BY...AND I JUST...
...TALK.
THAT'S WEIRD.
WELL, I'M WEIRD.
I MEAN, THAT'S WHAT I'VE ALWAYS BEEN TOLD.
BUT, SEE, MY SISTER AND I USED TO ALWAYS TELL—
HERE'S OUR STOP.
NEVER MIND.

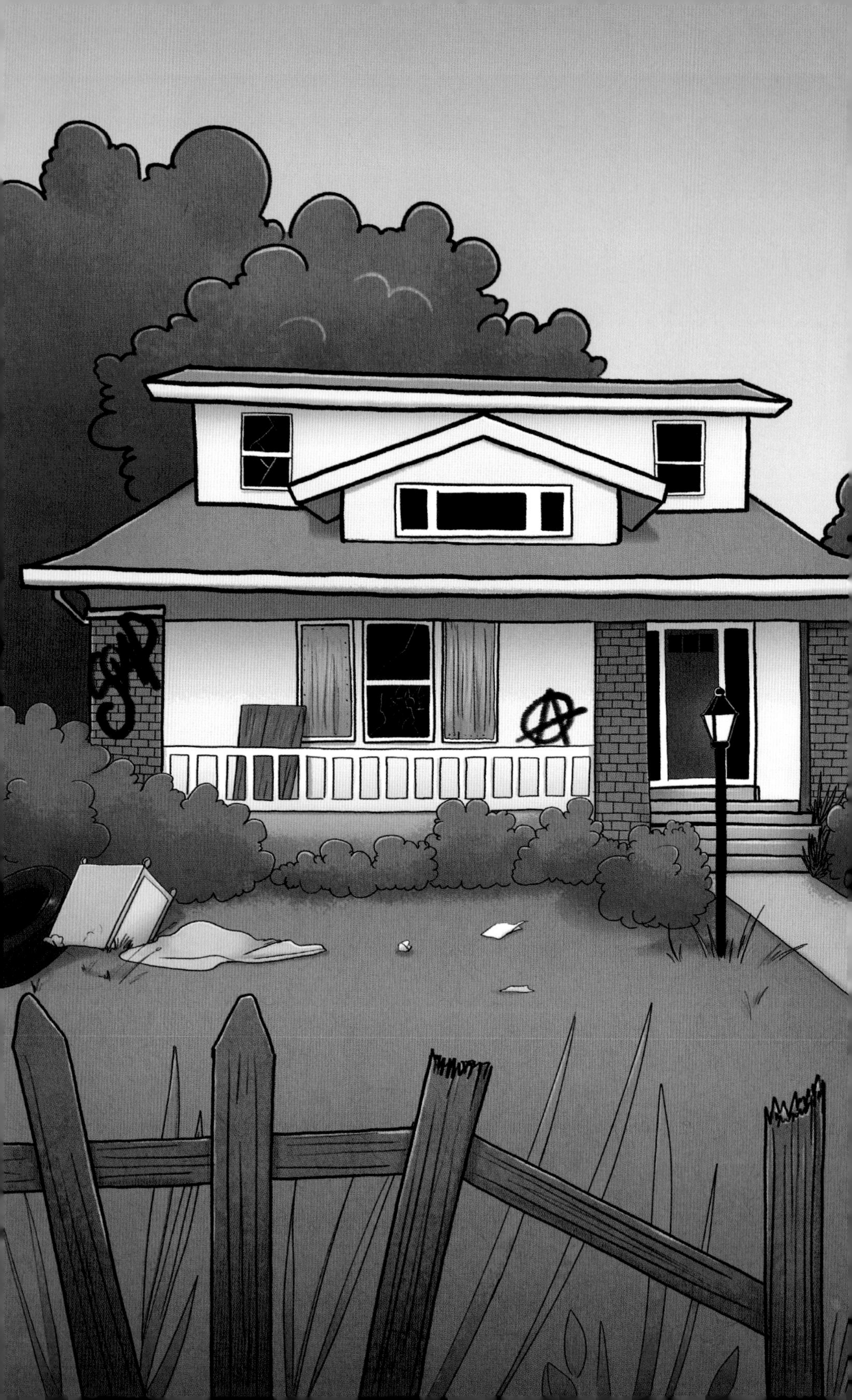

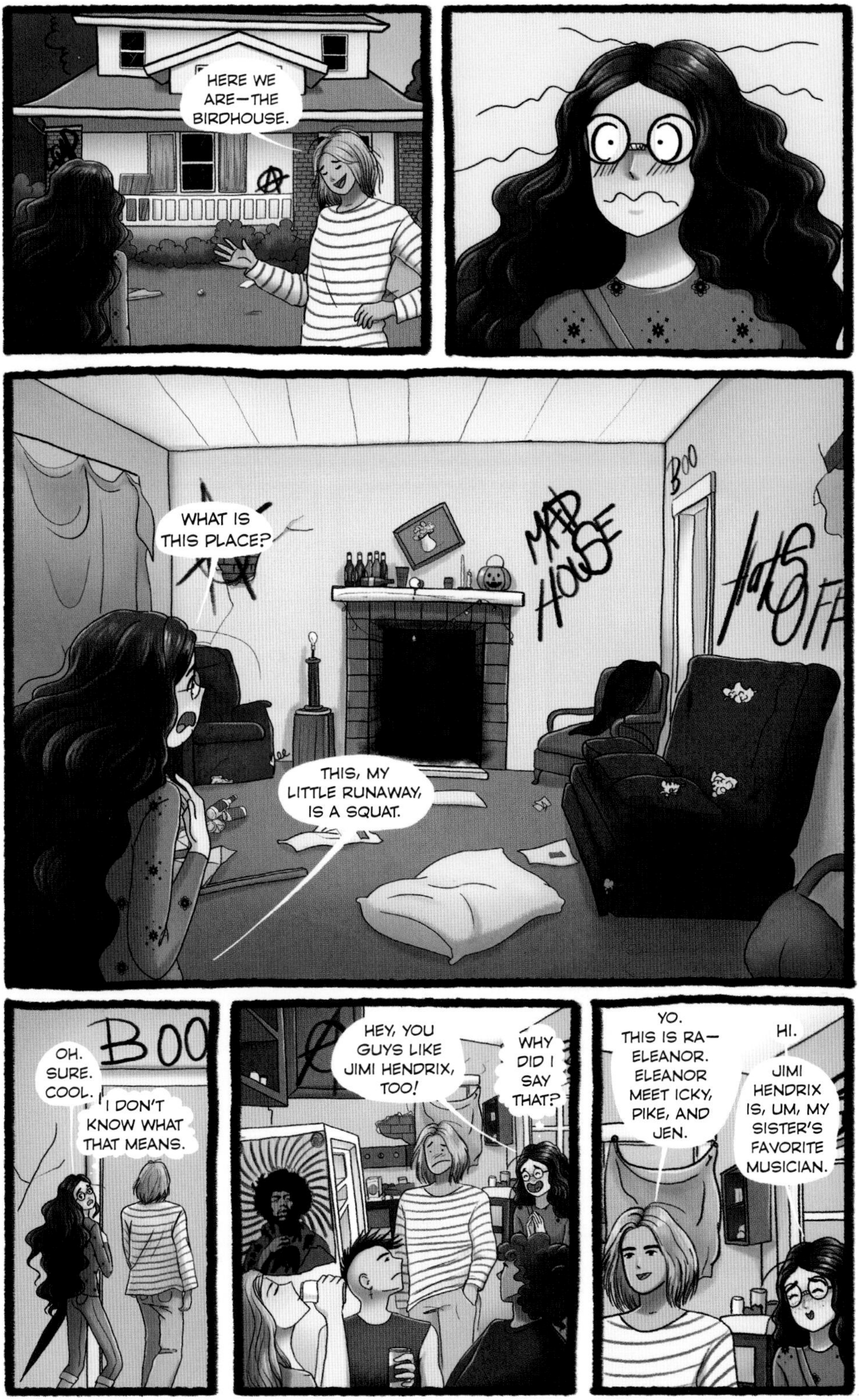
HERE WE ARE—THE BIRDHOUSE.
WHAT IS THIS PLACE?
BOO
MAD HOUSE
THIS, MY LITTLE RUNAWAY, IS A SQUAT.
BOO
OH. SURE. COOL.
I DON'T KNOW WHAT THAT MEANS.
HEY, YOU GUYS LIKE JIMI HENDRIX, TOO!
WHY DID I SAY THAT?
YO. THIS IS RA— ELEANOR. ELEANOR MEET ICKY, PIKE, AND JEN.
HI.
JIMI HENDRIX IS, UM, MY SISTER'S FAVORITE MUSICIAN.

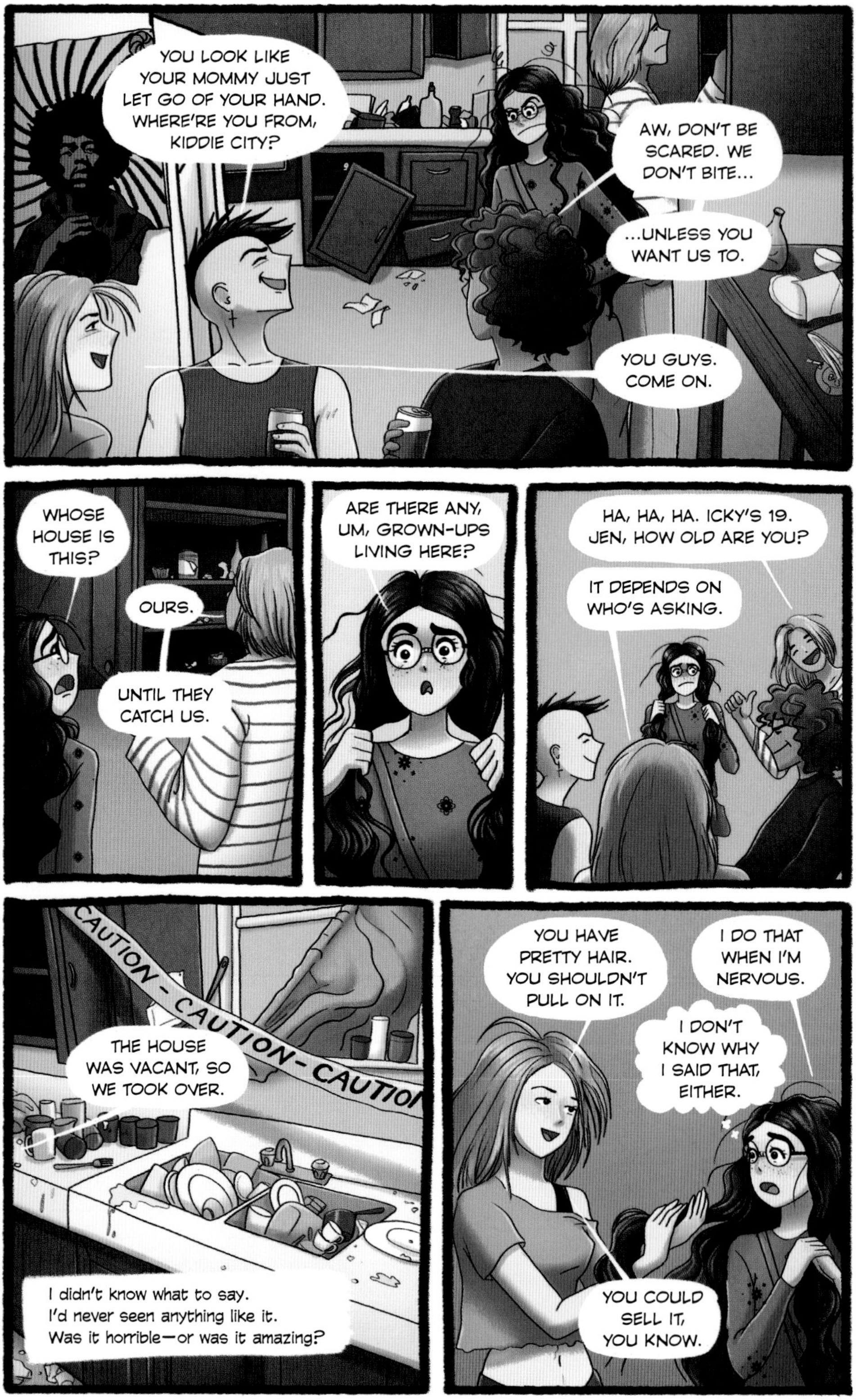
YOU LOOK LIKE YOUR MOMMY JUST LET GO OF YOUR HAND. WHERE'RE YOU FROM, KIDDIE CITY?
AW, DON'T BE SCARED. WE DON'T BITE...
...UNLESS YOU WANT US TO.
YOU GUYS. COME ON.
WHOSE HOUSE IS THIS?
OURS.
UNTIL THEY CATCH US.
ARE THERE ANY, UM, GROWN-UPS LIVING HERE?
HA, HA, HA. ICKY'S 19. JEN, HOW OLD ARE YOU?
IT DEPENDS ON WHO'S ASKING.
CAUTION - CAUTION - CAUTION - CAUTION
THE HOUSE WAS VACANT, SO WE TOOK OVER.
I didn't know what to say.
I'd never seen anything like it.
Was it horrible—or was it amazing?
YOU HAVE PRETTY HAIR. YOU SHOULDN'T PULL ON IT.
I DO THAT WHEN I'M NERVOUS.
I DON'T KNOW WHY I SAID THAT, EITHER.
YOU COULD SELL IT, YOU KNOW.

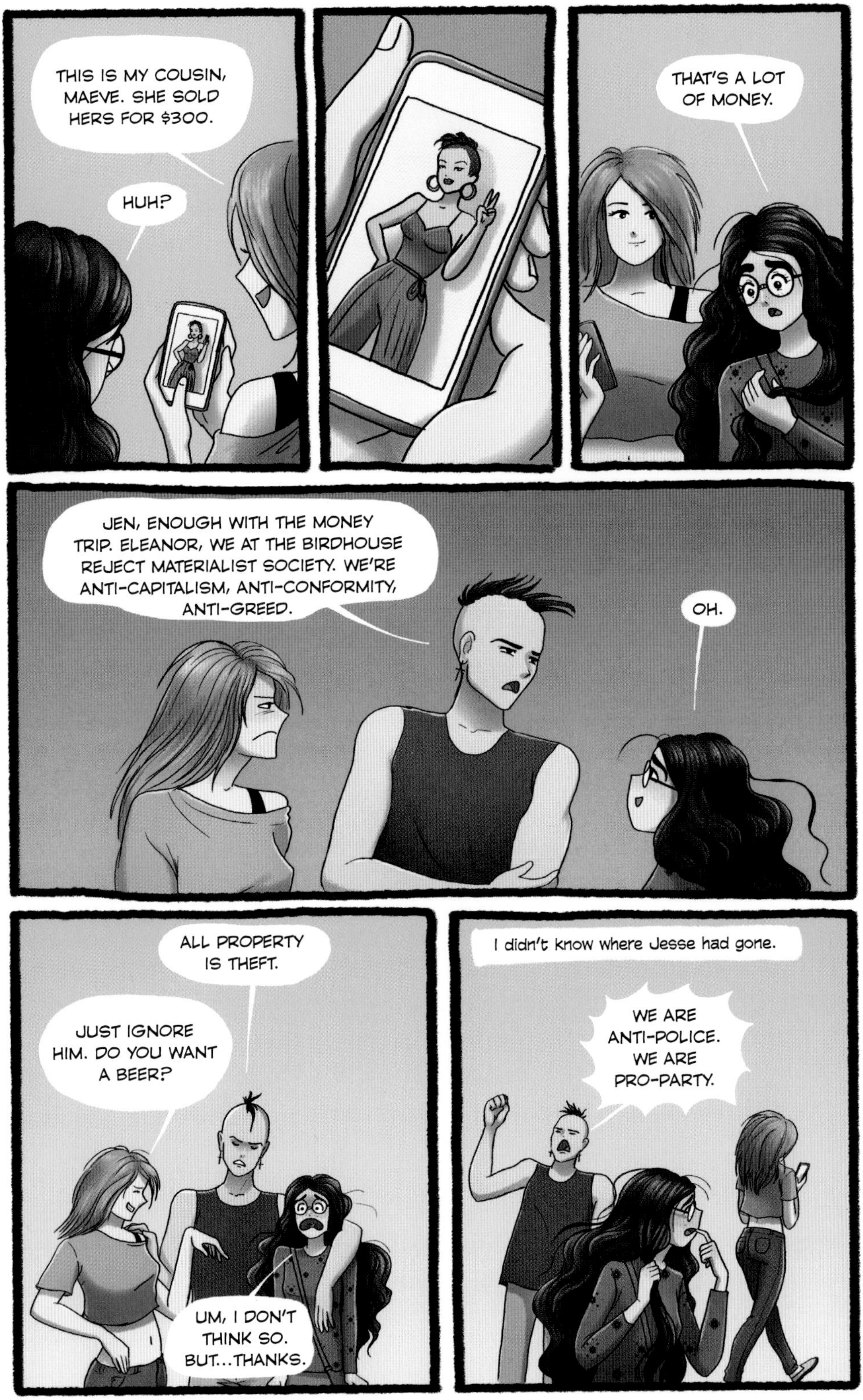
THIS IS MY COUSIN, MAEVE. SHE SOLD HERS FOR $300.
HUH?
THAT'S A LOT OF MONEY.
JEN, ENOUGH WITH THE MONEY TRIP. ELEANOR, WE AT THE BIRDHOUSE REJECT MATERIALIST SOCIETY. WE'RE ANTI-CAPITALISM, ANTI-CONFORMITY, ANTI-GREED.
OH.
ALL PROPERTY IS THEFT.
JUST IGNORE HIM. DO YOU WANT A BEER?
UM, I DON'T THINK SO. BUT...THANKS.
I didn't know where Jesse had gone.
WE ARE ANTI-POLICE. WE ARE PRO-PARTY.

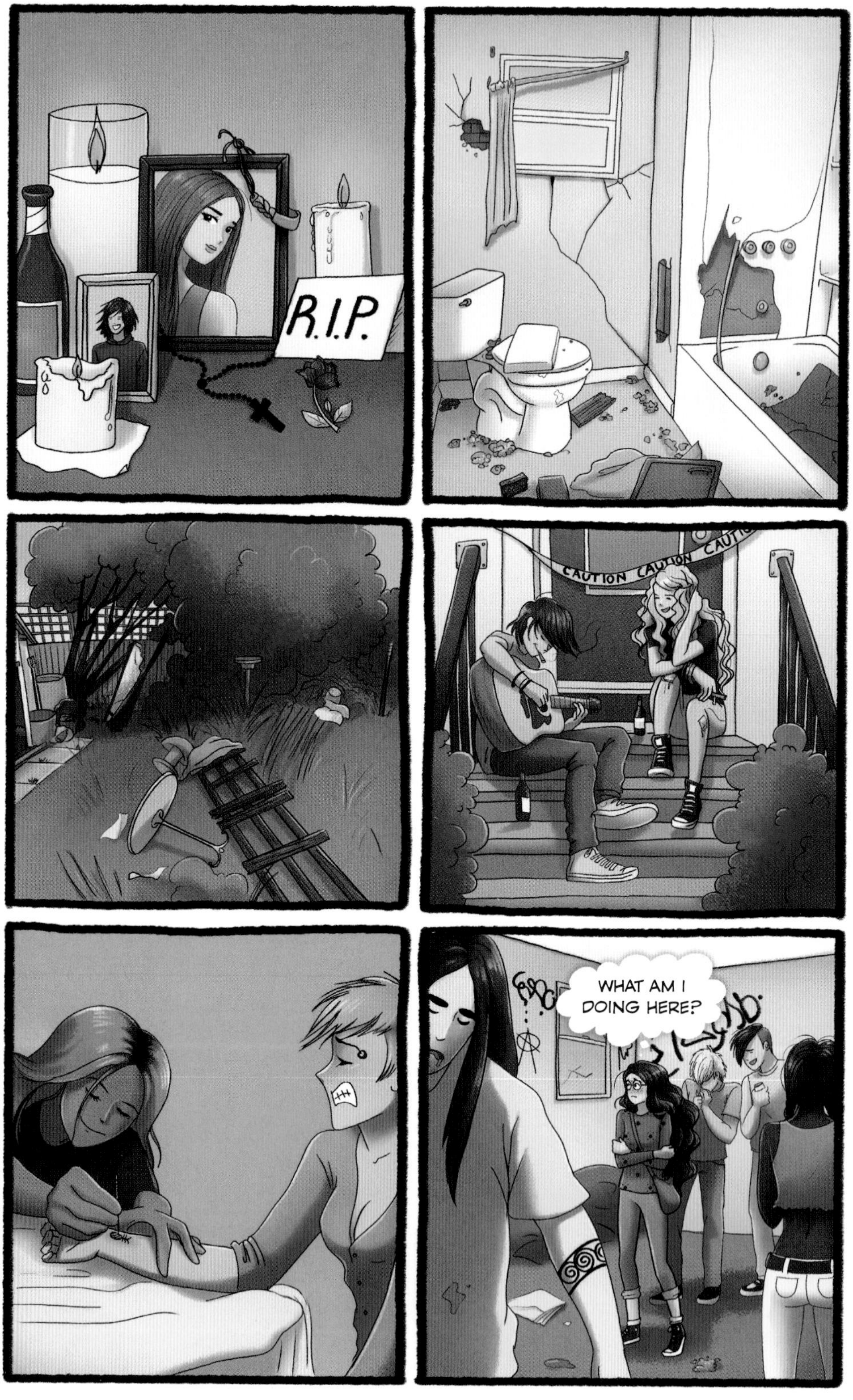
R.I.P.
CAUTION CAUTION CAUTION CAUTIO
WHAT AM I DOING HERE?

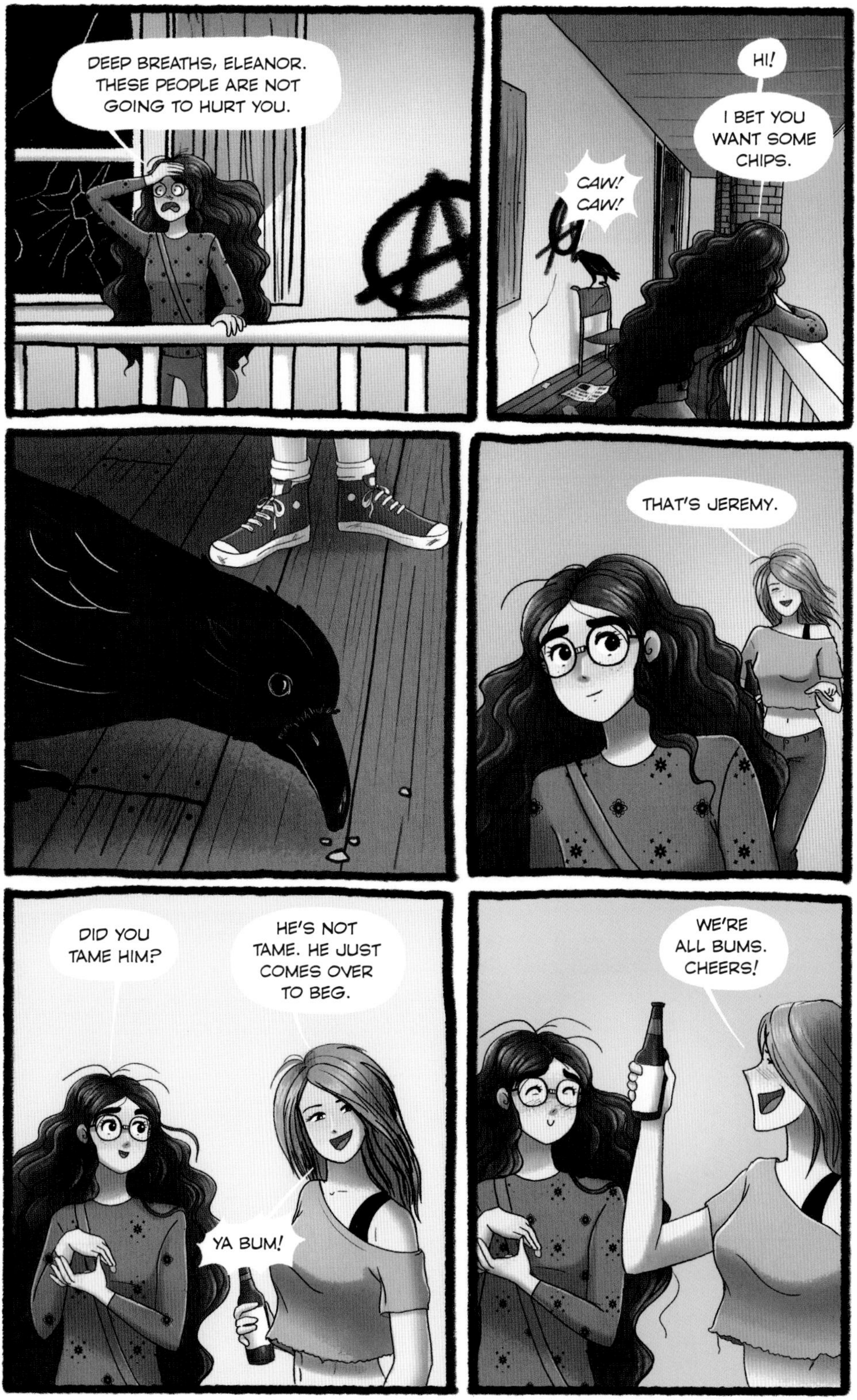
DEEP BREATHS, ELEANOR. THESE PEOPLE ARE NOT GOING TO HURT YOU.
HI!
I BET YOU WANT SOME CHIPS.
CAW! CAW!
THAT'S JEREMY.
DID YOU TAME HIM?
HE'S NOT TAME. HE JUST COMES OVER TO BEG.
YA BUM!
WE'RE ALL BUMS. CHEERS!

YOU REMIND ME OF SOMEONE.

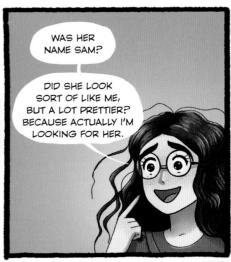

WAS HER NAME SAM?

DID SHE LOOK SORT OF LIKE ME, BUT A LOT PRETTIER? BECAUSE ACTUALLY I'M LOOKING FOR HER.

BUT IT'S ALMOST LIKE SHE'S HIDING FROM ME

I DON'T THINK SO. NO, IT'S SOMEONE ELSE.

HMMM. I DON'T KNOW.

IT'LL COME TO ME.

OK. I HOPE SO.

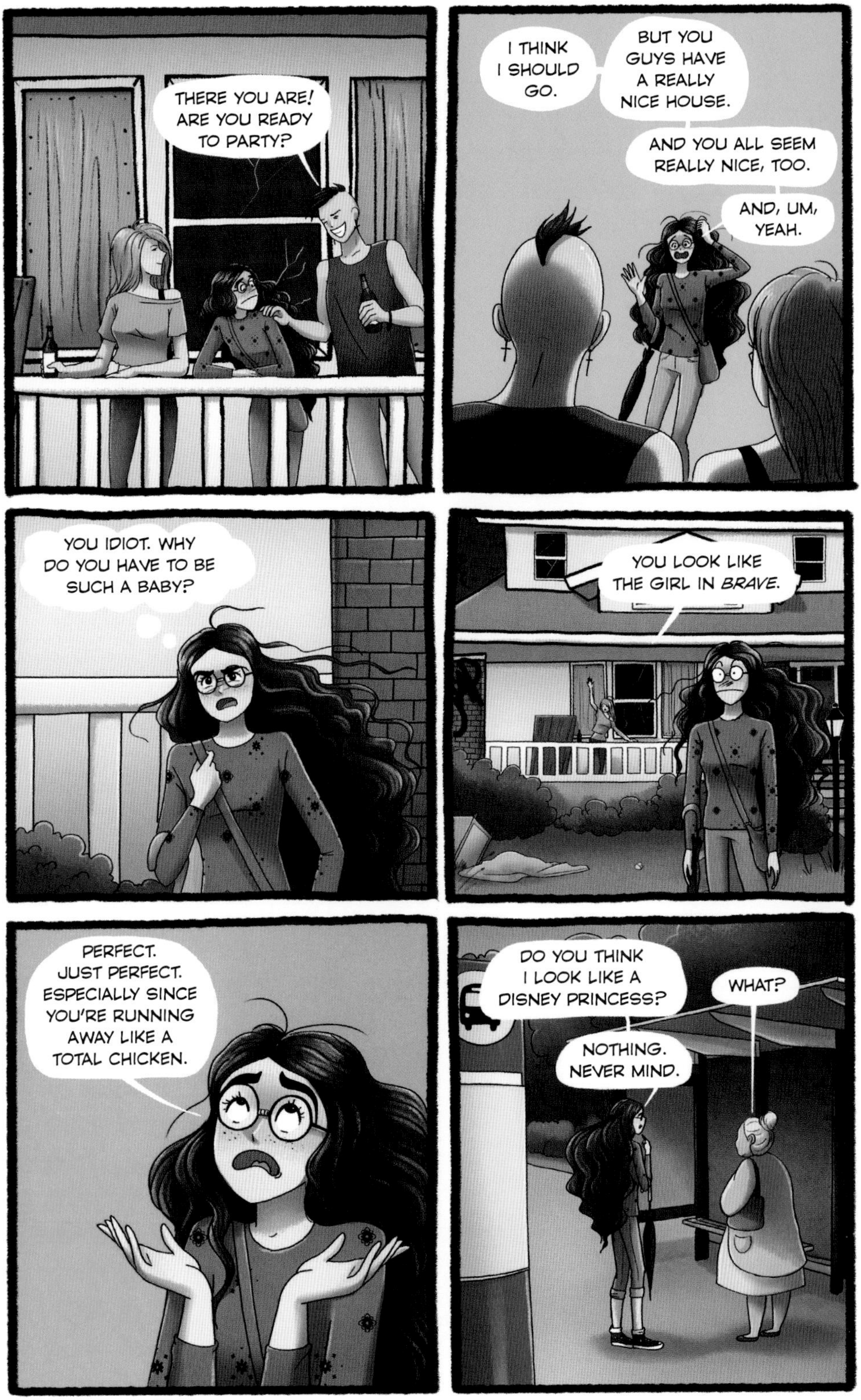
THERE YOU ARE! ARE YOU READY TO PARTY?
I THINK I SHOULD GO.
BUT YOU GUYS HAVE A REALLY NICE HOUSE.
AND YOU ALL SEEM REALLY NICE, TOO.
AND, UM, YEAH.
YOU IDIOT. WHY DO YOU HAVE TO BE SUCH A BABY?
YOU LOOK LIKE THE GIRL IN *BRAVE*.
PERFECT. JUST PERFECT. ESPECIALLY SINCE YOU'RE RUNNING AWAY LIKE A TOTAL CHICKEN.
DO YOU THINK I LOOK LIKE A DISNEY PRINCESS?
WHAT?
NOTHING. NEVER MIND.

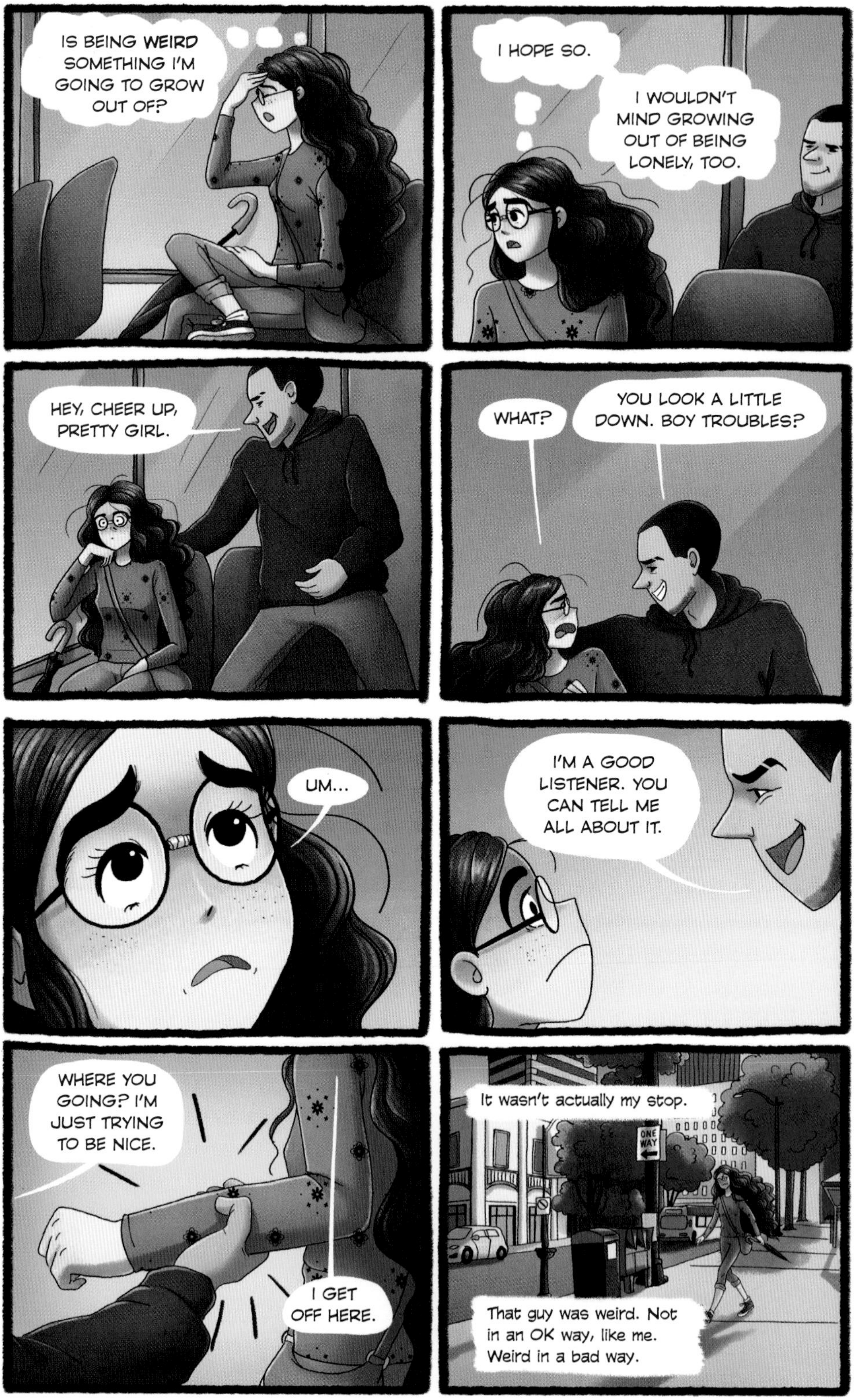
IS BEING WEIRD SOMETHING I'M GOING TO GROW OUT OF?
I HOPE SO.
I WOULDN'T MIND GROWING OUT OF BEING LONELY, TOO.
HEY, CHEER UP, PRETTY GIRL.
WHAT?
YOU LOOK A LITTLE DOWN. BOY TROUBLES?
UM...
I'M A GOOD LISTENER. YOU CAN TELL ME ALL ABOUT IT.
WHERE YOU GOING? I'M JUST TRYING TO BE NICE.
I GET OFF HERE.
It wasn't actually my stop.
ONE WAY
That guy was weird. Not in an OK way, like me. Weird in a bad way.

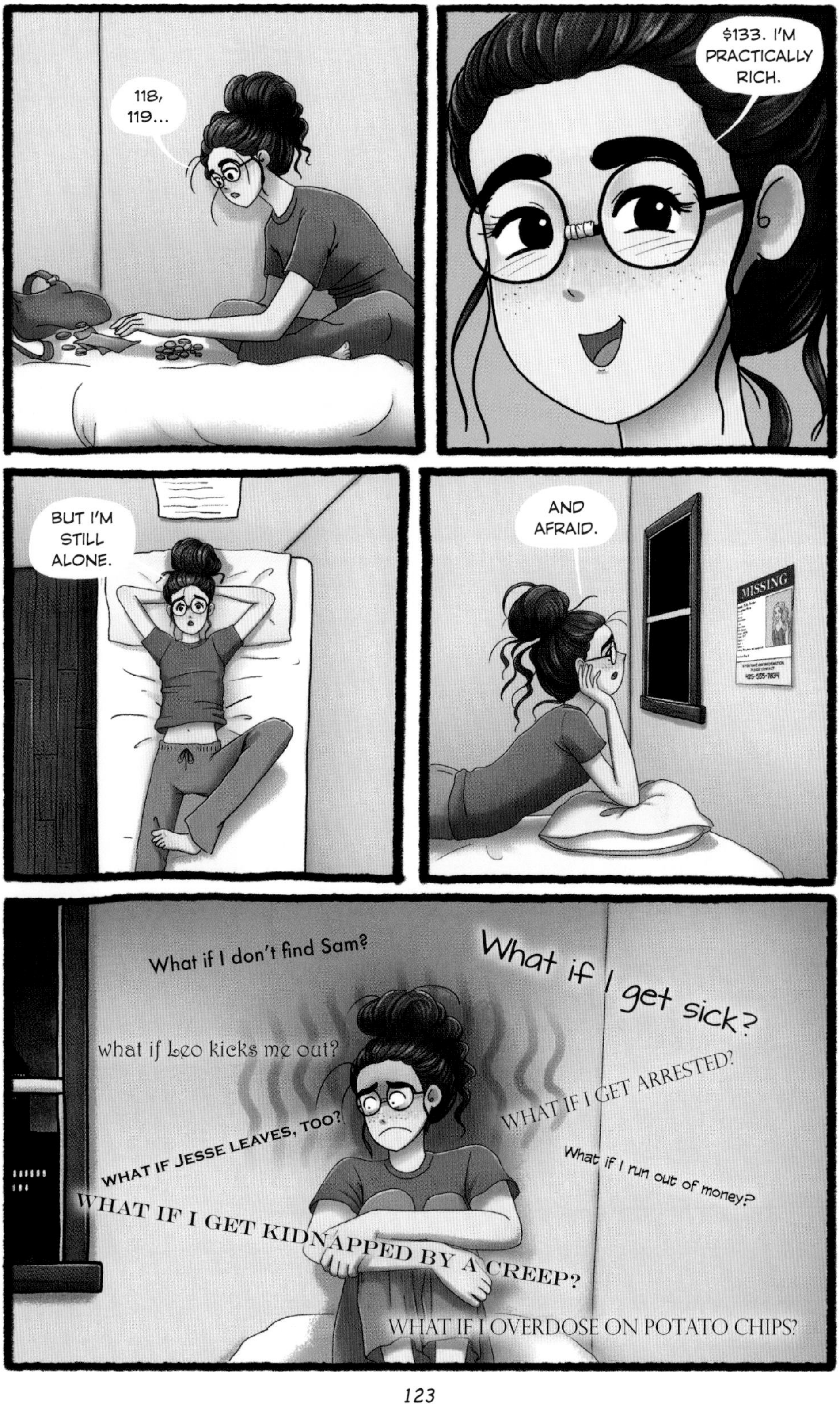

118, 119...
$133. I'M PRACTICALLY RICH.
BUT I'M STILL ALONE.
AND AFRAID.
What if I don't find Sam?
What if I get sick?
what if Leo kicks me out?
WHAT IF I GET ARRESTED?
WHAT IF JESSE LEAVES, TOO?
What if I run out of money?
WHAT IF I GET KIDNAPPED BY A CREEP?
WHAT IF I OVERDOSE ON POTATO CHIPS?

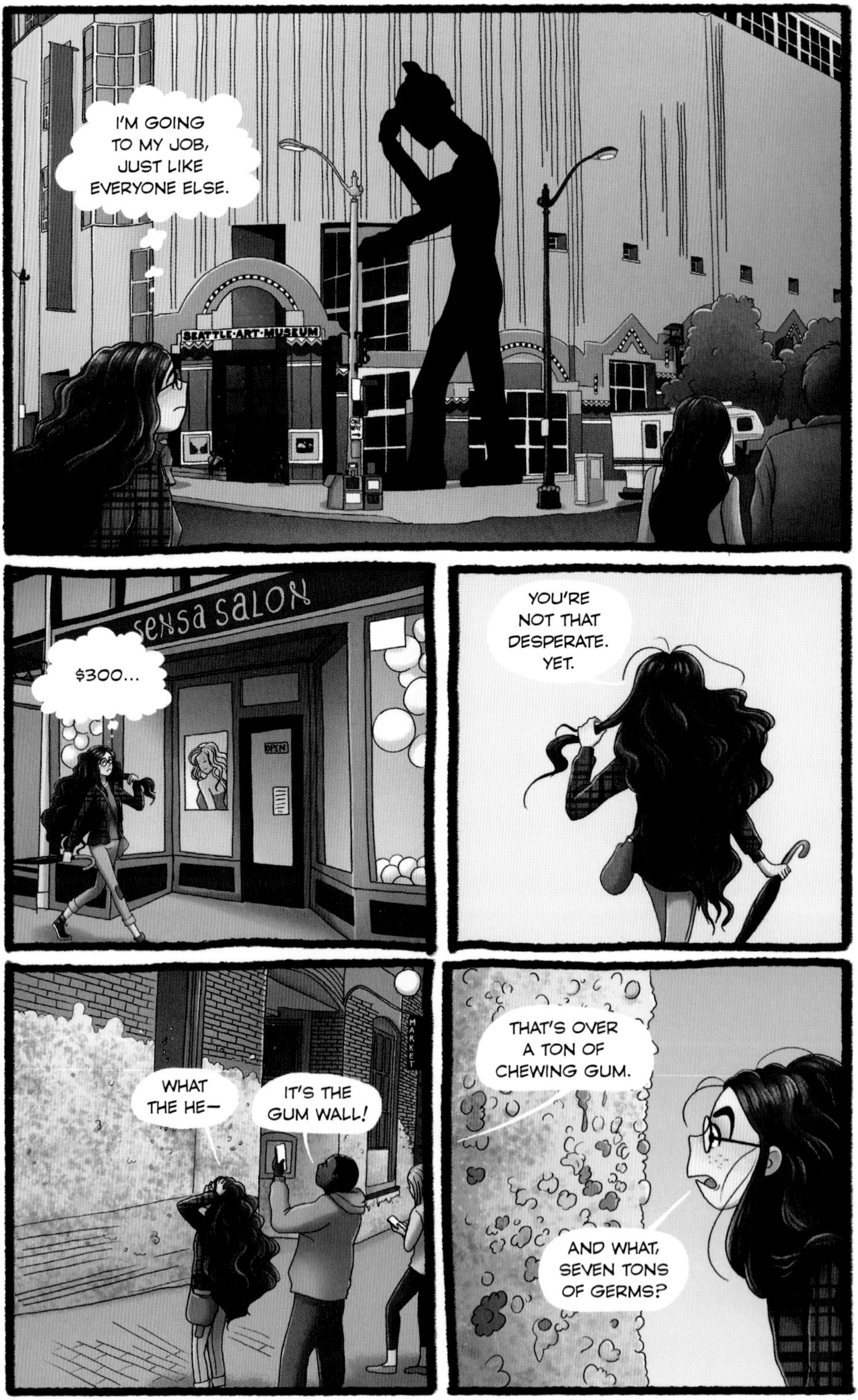
I'M GOING TO MY JOB, JUST LIKE EVERYONE ELSE.
SEATTLE·ART·MUSEUM
SENSA SALON
$300...
OPEN
YOU'RE NOT THAT DESPERATE. YET.
MARKET
WHAT THE HE—
IT'S THE GUM WALL!
THAT'S OVER A TON OF CHEWING GUM.
AND WHAT, SEVEN TONS OF GERMS?

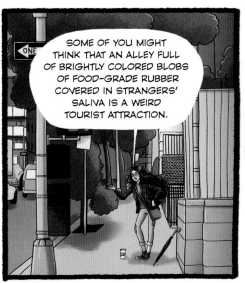

SOME OF YOU MIGHT THINK THAT AN ALLEY FULL OF BRIGHTLY COLORED BLOBS OF FOOD-GRADE RUBBER COVERED IN STRANGERS' SALIVA IS A WEIRD TOURIST ATTRACTION.

BECAUSE IT IS.

BUT IF YOU REALLY WANT TO SEE WEIRD, YOU SHOULD COME TO MY HOUSE, BECAUSE MY PARENTS ARE WORLD-FAMOUS TAXIDERMERMISTS.

"WE'VE GOT EAGLES, OWLS, FOXES, BEAVERS, WOLVES, BOBCATS, AND A BEAR...

"...AND THAT'S JUST IN THE LIVING ROOM.

"TRY DRIVING TO A MOVIE WITH YOUR FRIENDS AND HAVING YOUR MOM STOP, HALFWAY TO THE THEATER, TO SCRAPE A DEAD RACCON OFF THE ROAD."

THAT WILL **NOT** MAKE YOU POPULAR.

HEY.

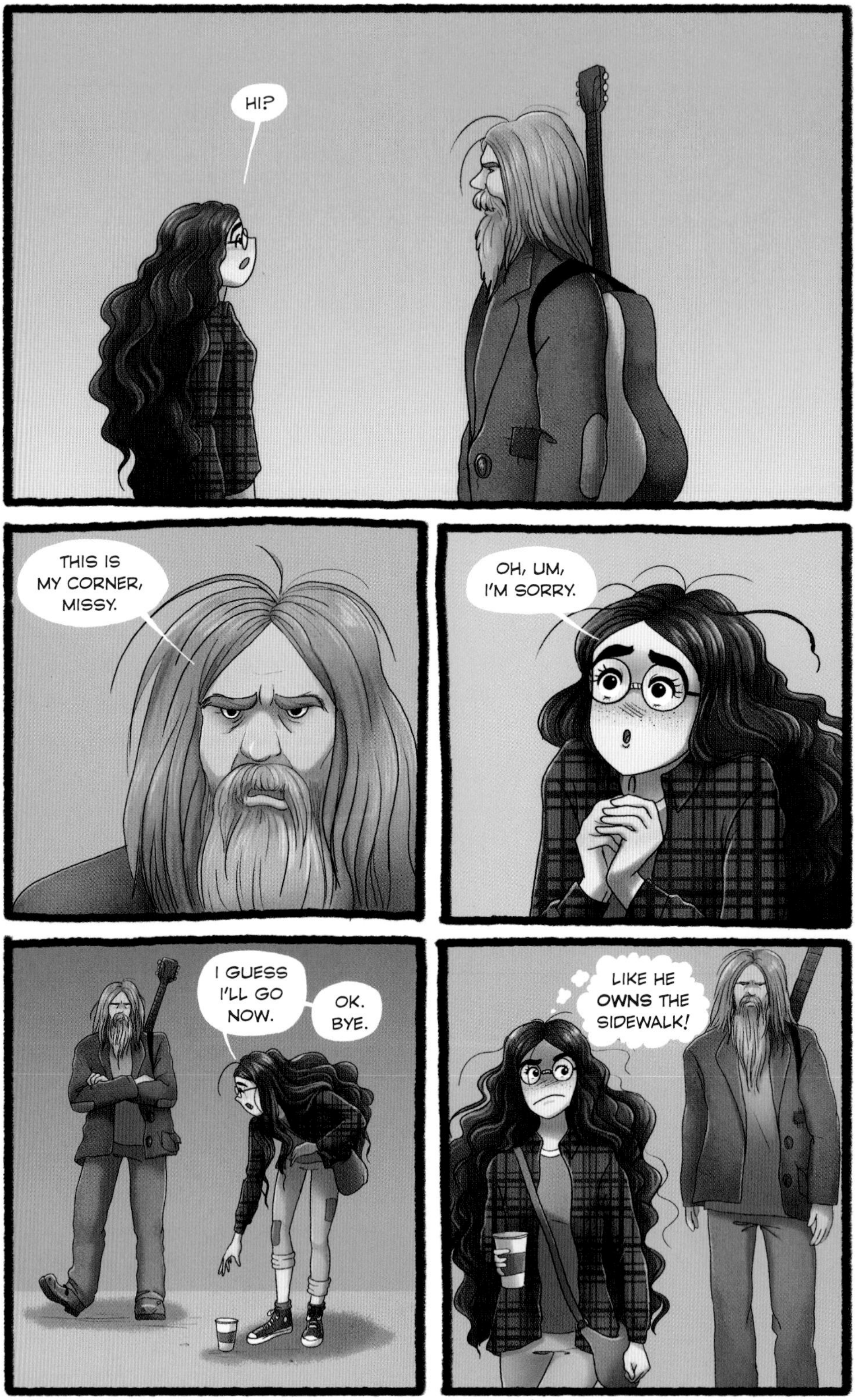
HI?
THIS IS MY CORNER, MISSY.
OH, UM, I'M SORRY.
I GUESS I'LL GO NOW.
OK. BYE.
LIKE HE OWNS THE SIDEWALK!

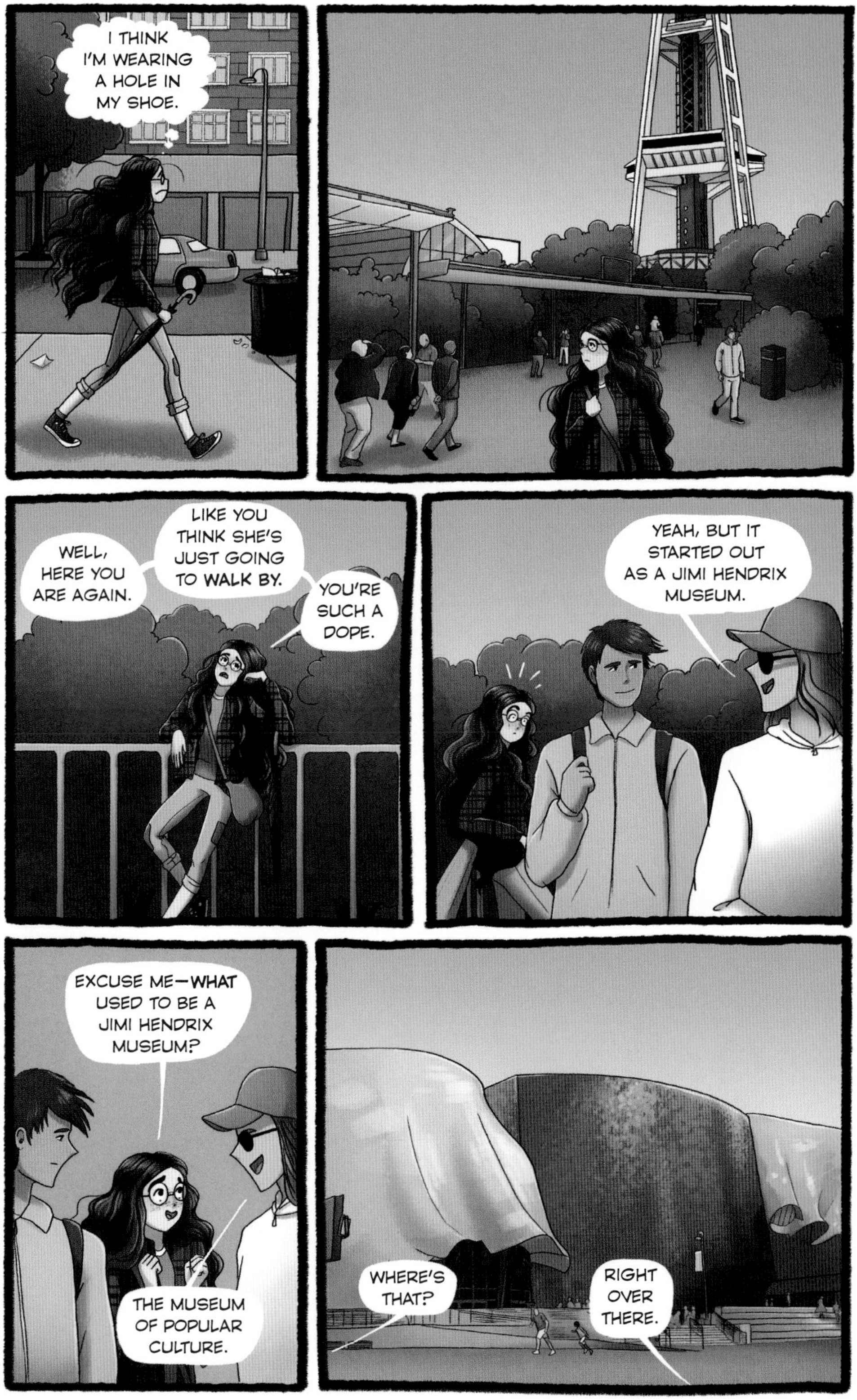
I THINK I'M WEARING A HOLE IN MY SHOE.
WELL, HERE YOU ARE AGAIN.
LIKE YOU THINK SHE'S JUST GOING TO WALK BY.
YOU'RE SUCH A DOPE.
YEAH, BUT IT STARTED OUT AS A JIMI HENDRIX MUSEUM.
EXCUSE ME—WHAT USED TO BE A JIMI HENDRIX MUSEUM?
THE MUSEUM OF POPULAR CULTURE.
WHERE'S THAT?
RIGHT OVER THERE.

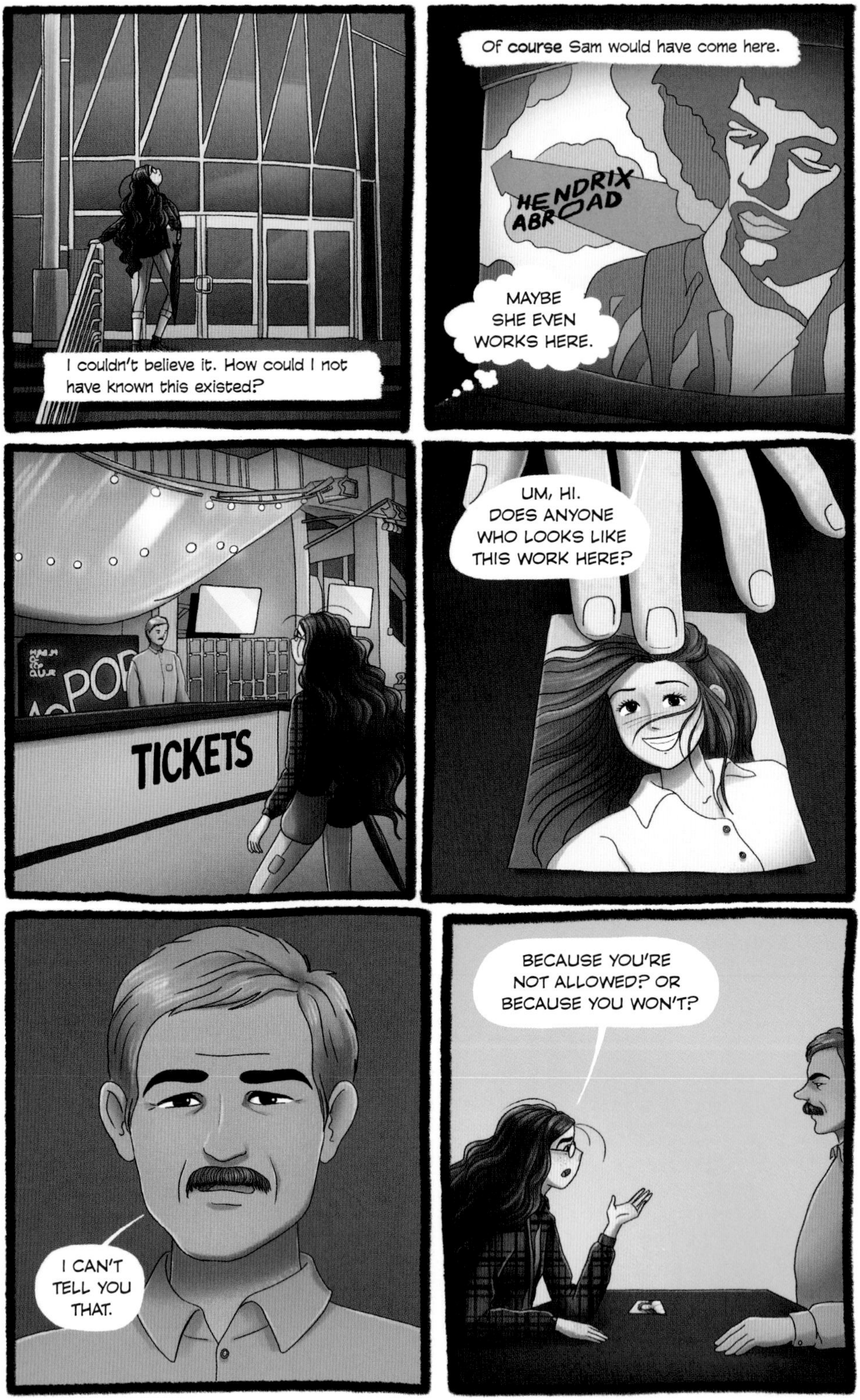
I couldn't believe it. How could I not have known this existed?
Of course Sam would have come here.
HENDRIX ABROAD
MAYBE SHE EVEN WORKS HERE.
TICKETS
UM, HI. DOES ANYONE WHO LOOKS LIKE THIS WORK HERE?
I CAN'T TELL YOU THAT.
BECAUSE YOU'RE NOT ALLOWED? OR BECAUSE YOU WON'T?

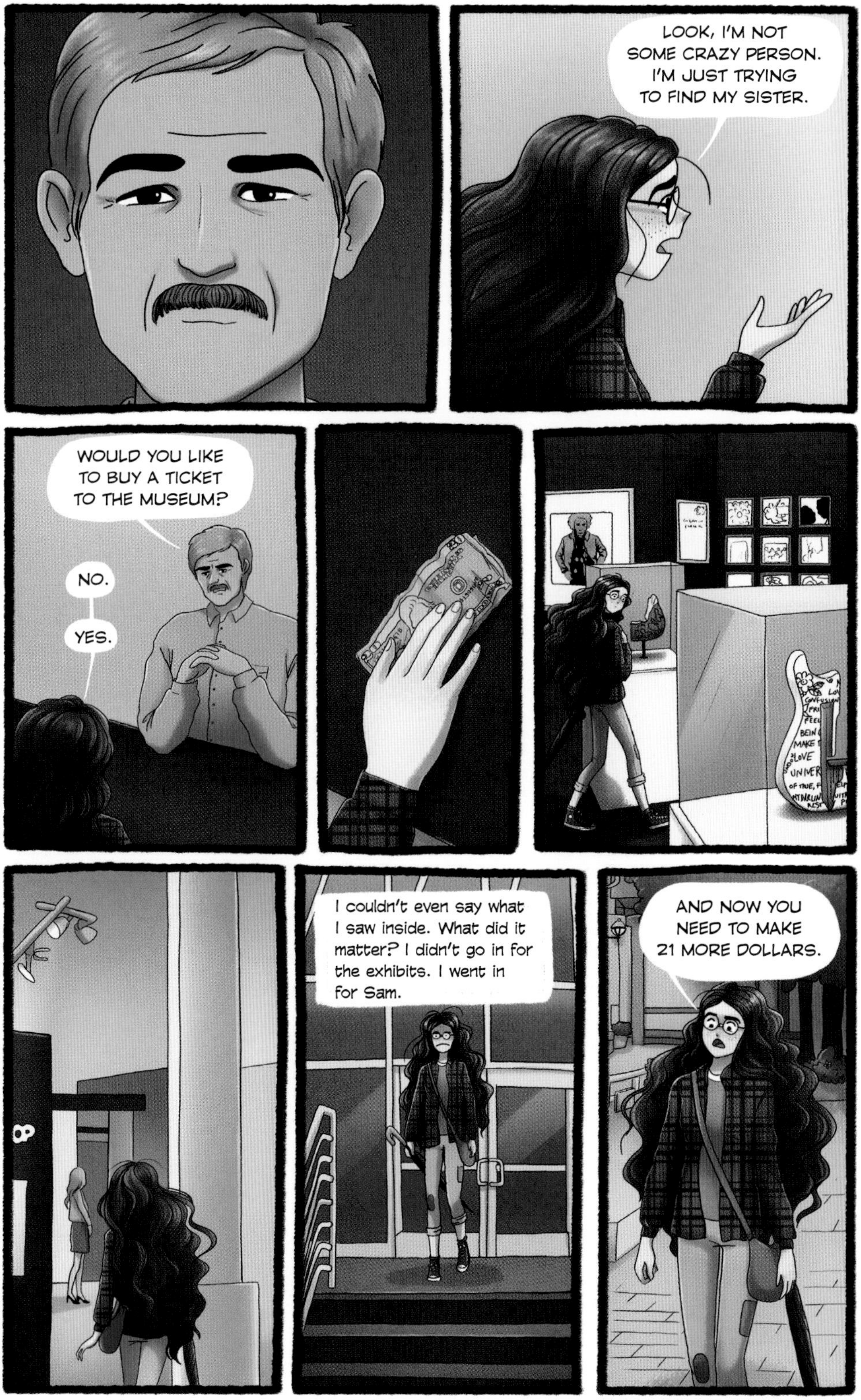
LOOK, I'M NOT SOME CRAZY PERSON. I'M JUST TRYING TO FIND MY SISTER.
WOULD YOU LIKE TO BUY A TICKET TO THE MUSEUM?
NO.
YES.
I couldn't even say what I saw inside. What did it matter? I didn't go in for the exhibits. I went in for Sam.
AND NOW YOU NEED TO MAKE 21 MORE DOLLARS.

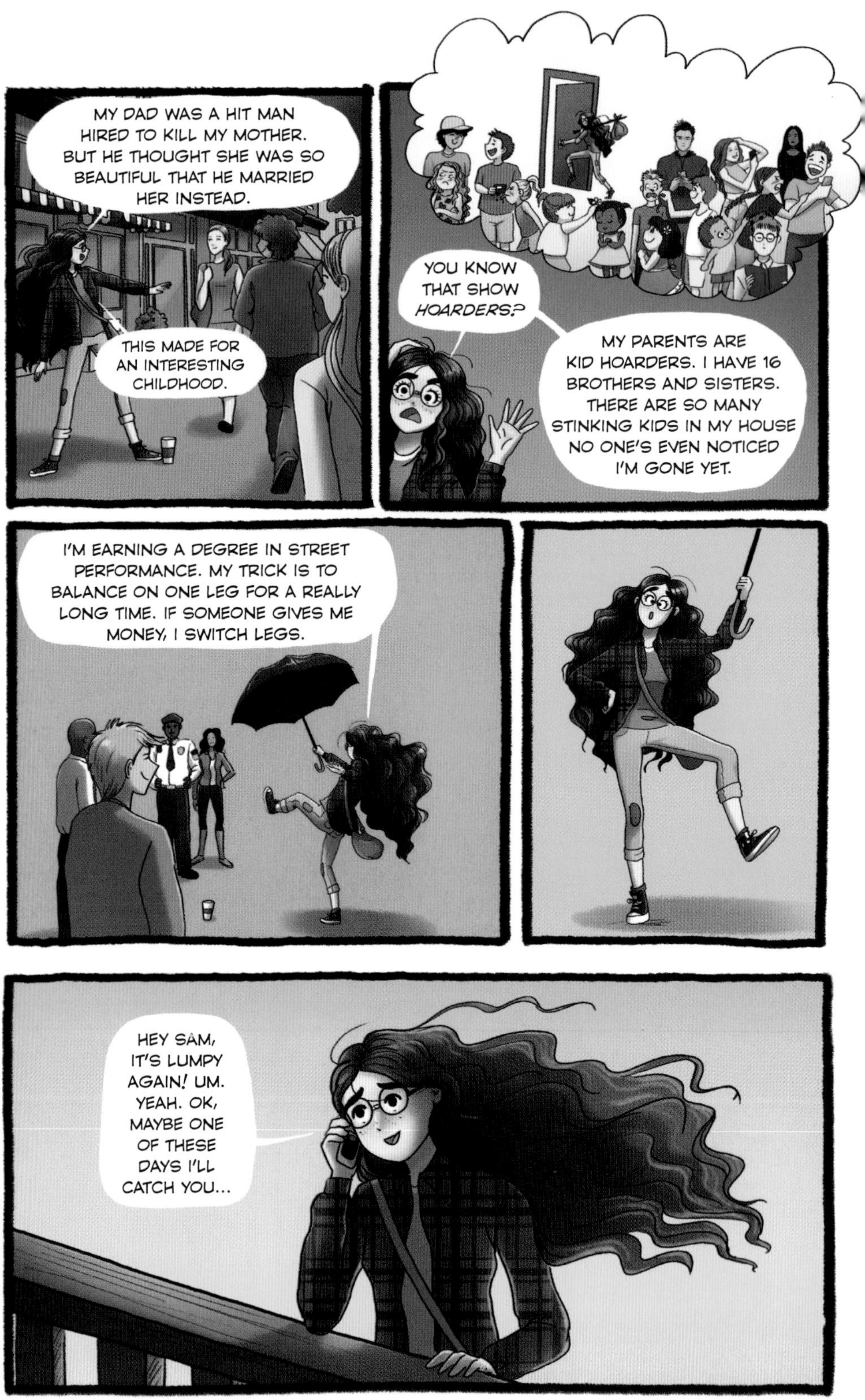
MY DAD WAS A HIT MAN HIRED TO KILL MY MOTHER. BUT HE THOUGHT SHE WAS SO BEAUTIFUL THAT HE MARRIED HER INSTEAD.
THIS MADE FOR AN INTERESTING CHILDHOOD.
YOU KNOW THAT SHOW *HOARDERS?*
MY PARENTS ARE KID HOARDERS. I HAVE 16 BROTHERS AND SISTERS. THERE ARE SO MANY STINKING KIDS IN MY HOUSE NO ONE'S EVEN NOTICED I'M GONE YET.
I'M EARNING A DEGREE IN STREET PERFORMANCE. MY TRICK IS TO BALANCE ON ONE LEG FOR A REALLY LONG TIME. IF SOMEONE GIVES ME MONEY, I SWITCH LEGS.
HEY SAM, IT'S LUMPY AGAIN! UM. YEAH. OK, MAYBE ONE OF THESE DAYS I'LL CATCH YOU...

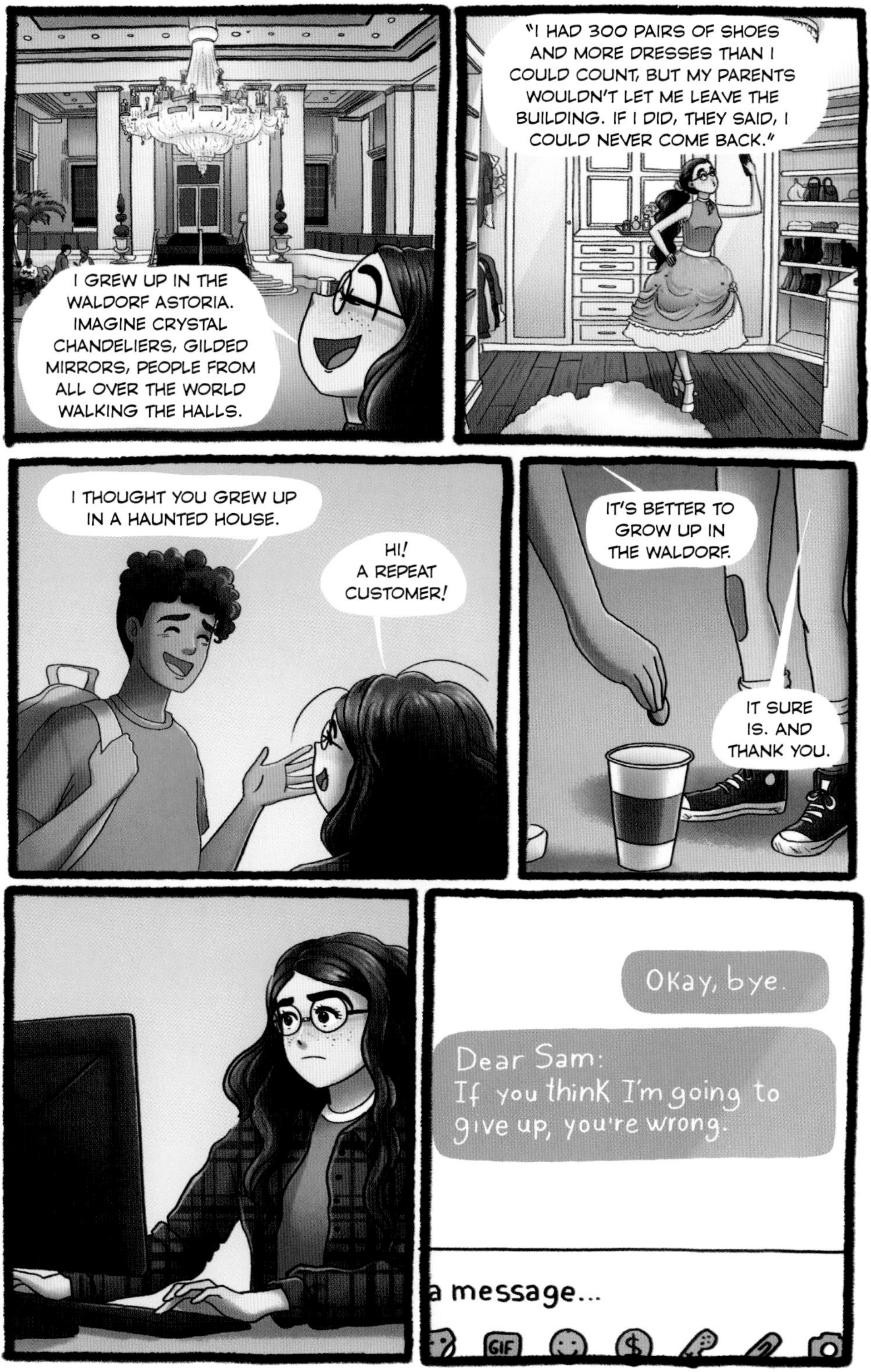
I GREW UP IN THE WALDORF ASTORIA. IMAGINE CRYSTAL CHANDELIERS, GILDED MIRRORS, PEOPLE FROM ALL OVER THE WORLD WALKING THE HALLS.
"I HAD 300 PAIRS OF SHOES AND MORE DRESSES THAN I COULD COUNT, BUT MY PARENTS WOULDN'T LET ME LEAVE THE BUILDING. IF I DID, THEY SAID, I COULD NEVER COME BACK."
I THOUGHT YOU GREW UP IN A HAUNTED HOUSE.
HI! A REPEAT CUSTOMER!
IT'S BETTER TO GROW UP IN THE WALDORF.
IT SURE IS. AND THANK YOU.
Okay, bye.
Dear Sam:
If you think I'm going to give up, you're wrong.
a message...
GIF

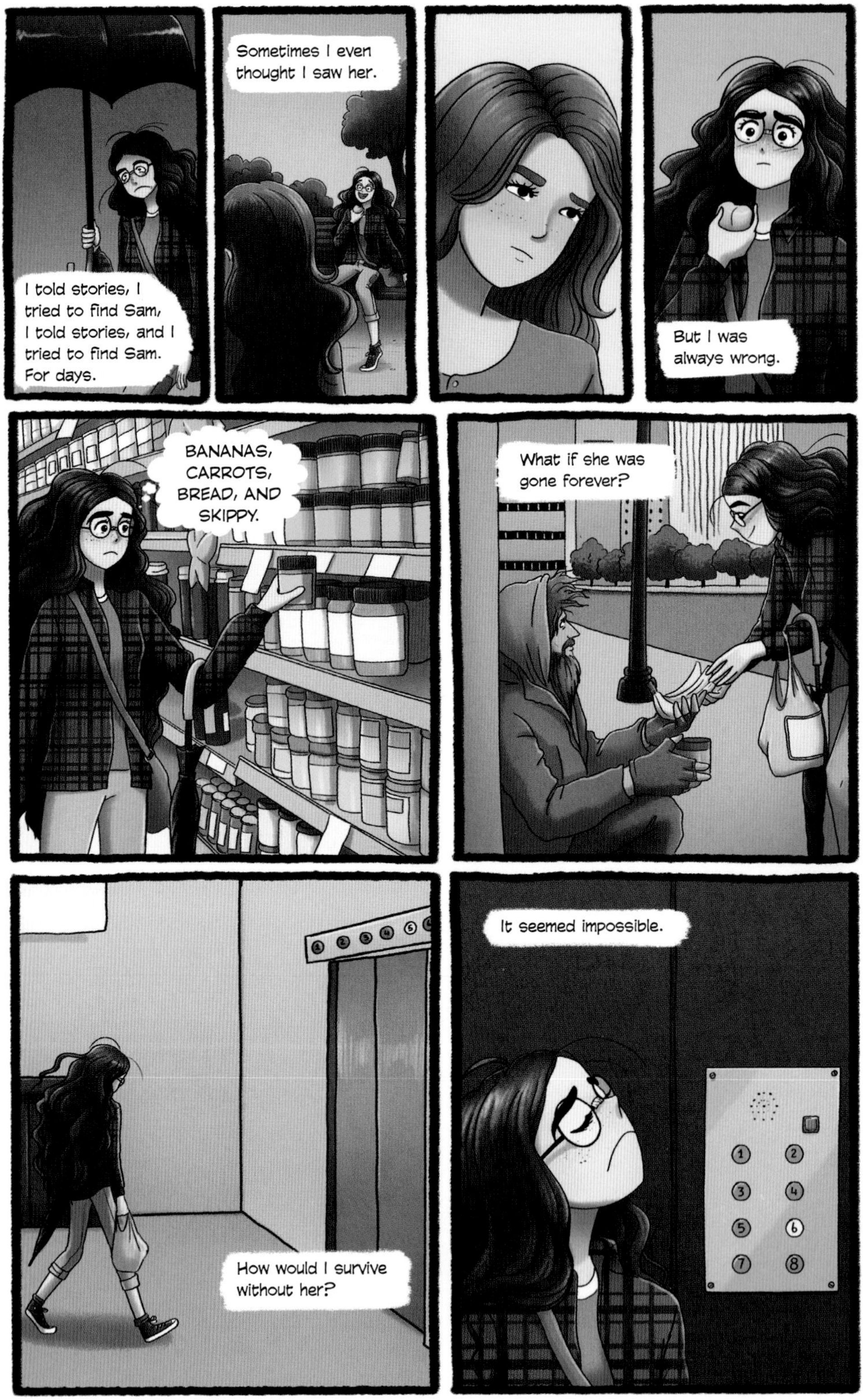
I told stories, I tried to find Sam, I told stories, and I tried to find Sam. For days.
Sometimes I even thought I saw her.
But I was always wrong.
BANANAS, CARROTS, BREAD, AND SKIPPY.
What if she was gone forever?
How would I survive without her?
It seemed impossible.

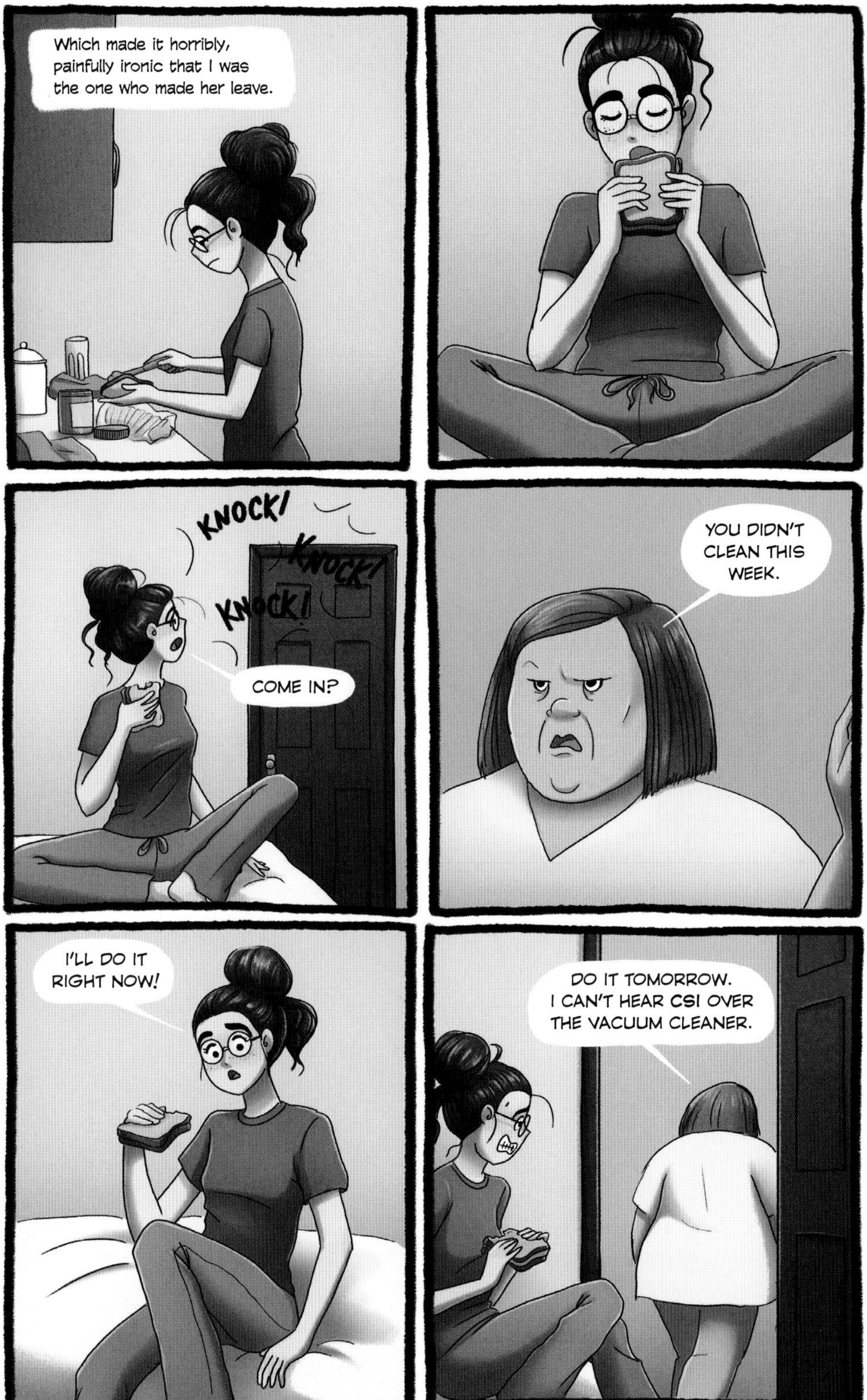
Which made it horribly, painfully ironic that I was the one who made her leave.
KNOCK!
KNOCK!
KNOCK!
COME IN?
YOU DIDN'T CLEAN THIS WEEK.
I'LL DO IT RIGHT NOW!
DO IT TOMORROW. I CAN'T HEAR CSI OVER THE VACUUM CLEANER.

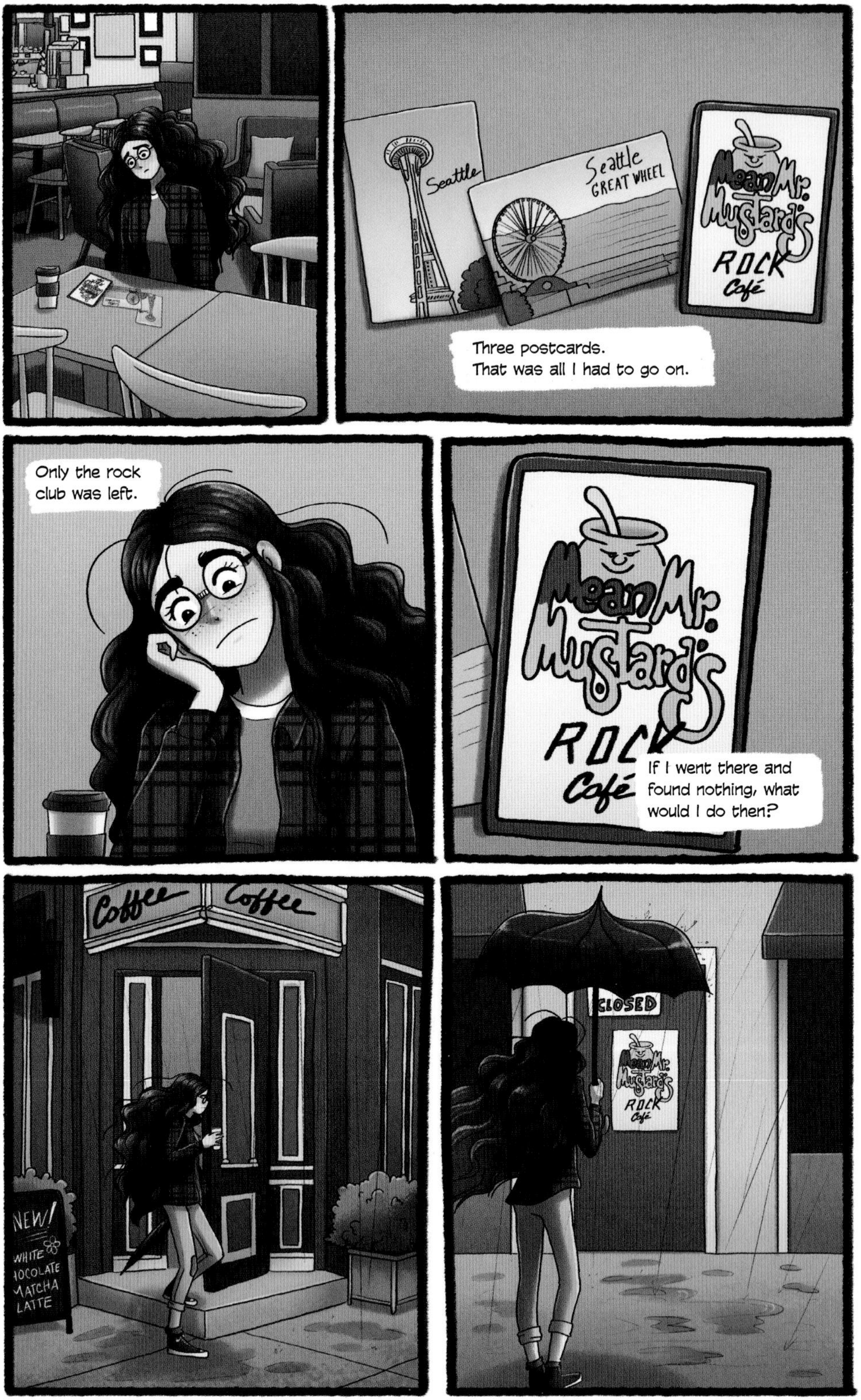
Seattle
Seattle
GREAT WHEEL
Mean Mr. Mustard's
ROCK
Café
Three postcards.
That was all I had to go on.
Only the rock club was left.
Mean Mr. Mustard's
ROCK
Café
If I went there and found nothing, what would I do then?
Coffee
Coffee
NEW!
WHITE
HOCOLATE
MATCHA
LATTE
CLOSED
Mean Mr. Mustard's
ROCK
Café

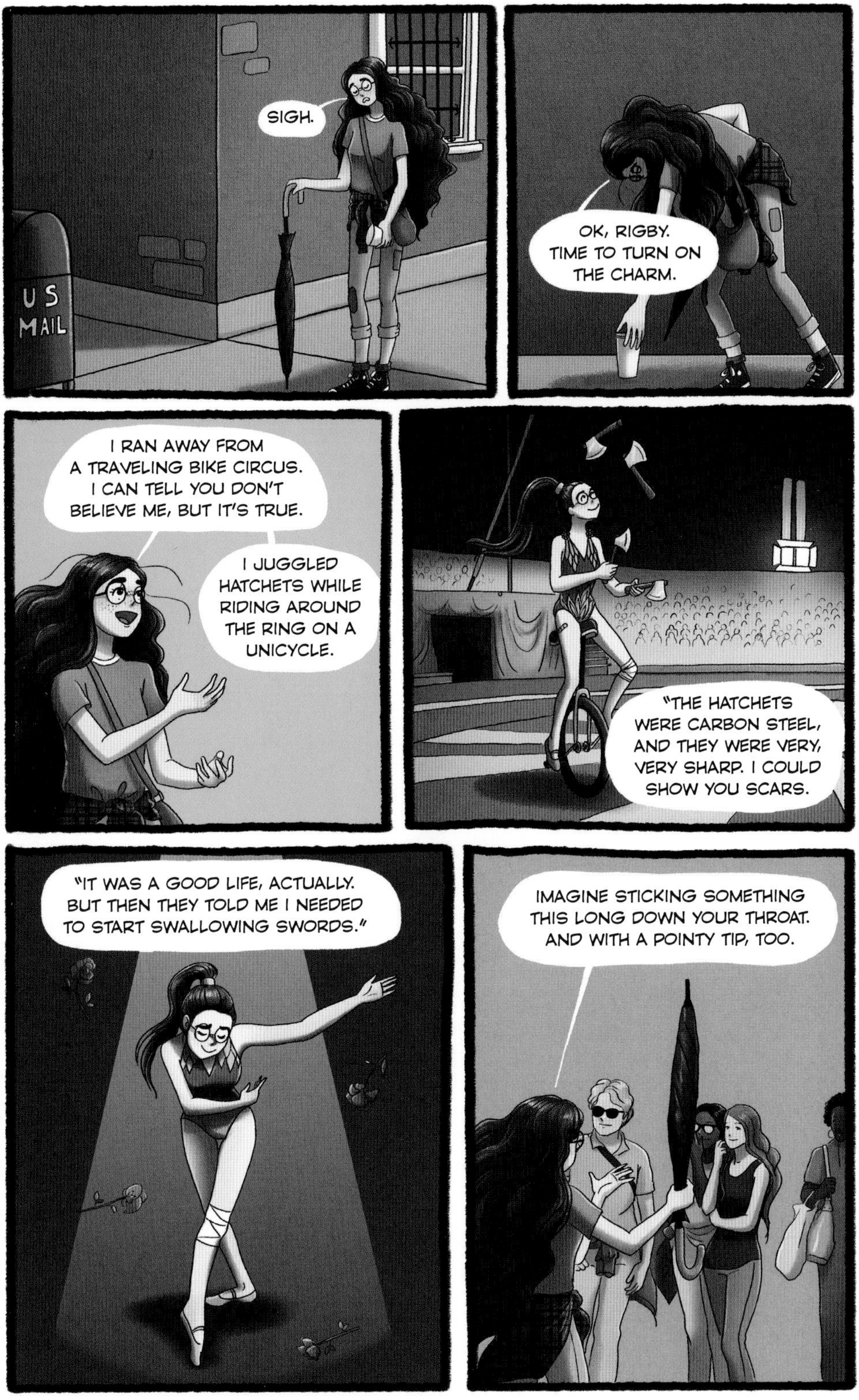
US MAIL
SIGH.
OK, RIGBY.
TIME TO TURN ON
THE CHARM.
I RAN AWAY FROM A TRAVELING BIKE CIRCUS. I CAN TELL YOU DON'T BELIEVE ME, BUT IT'S TRUE.
I JUGGLED HATCHETS WHILE RIDING AROUND THE RING ON A UNICYCLE.
"THE HATCHETS WERE CARBON STEEL, AND THEY WERE VERY, VERY SHARP. I COULD SHOW YOU SCARS.
"IT WAS A GOOD LIFE, ACTUALLY. BUT THEN THEY TOLD ME I NEEDED TO START SWALLOWING SWORDS."
IMAGINE STICKING SOMETHING THIS LONG DOWN YOUR THROAT. AND WITH A POINTY TIP, TOO.

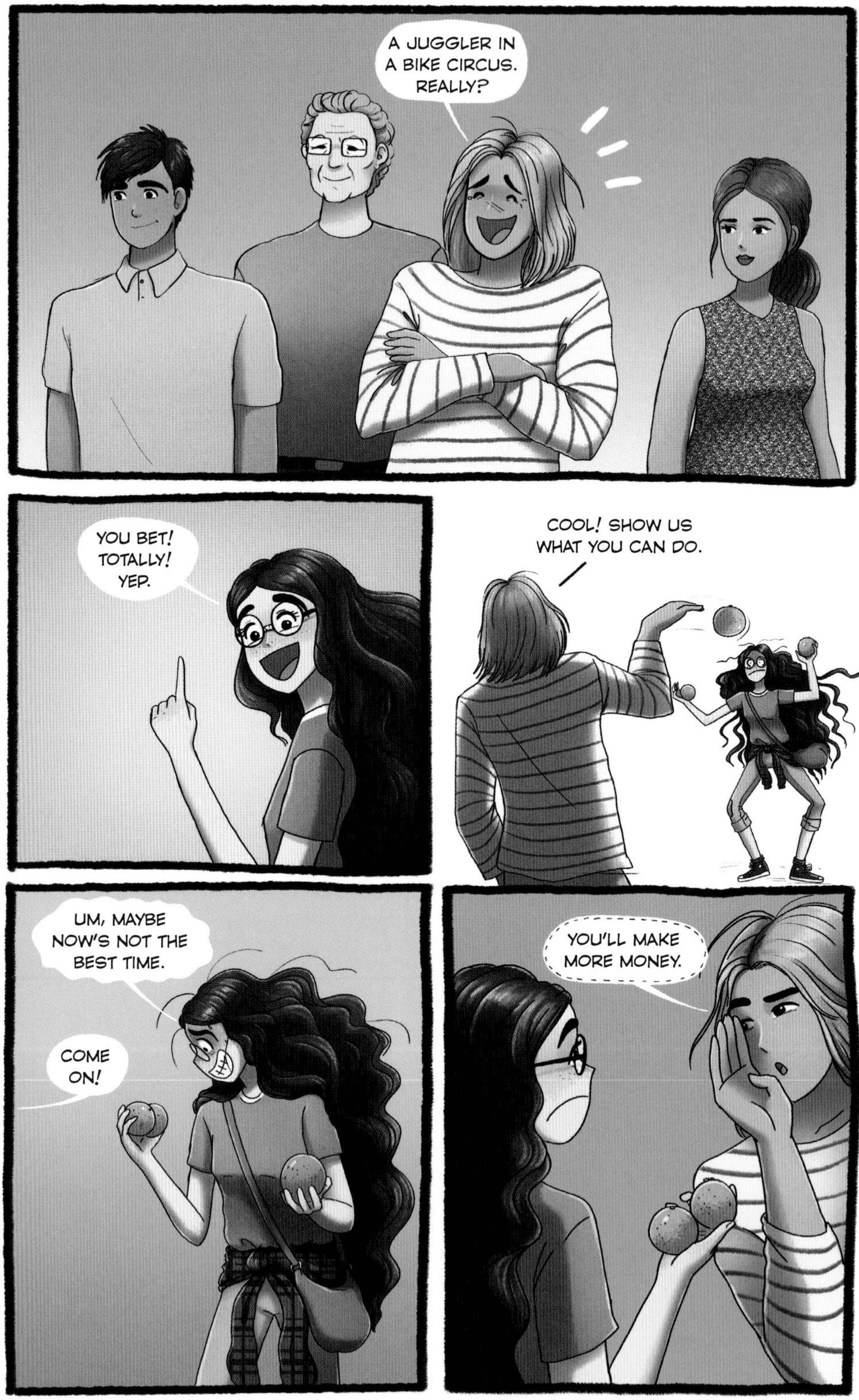

A JUGGLER IN A BIKE CIRCUS. REALLY?
YOU BET! TOTALLY! YEP.
COOL! SHOW US WHAT YOU CAN DO.
UM, MAYBE NOW'S NOT THE BEST TIME.
COME ON!
YOU'LL MAKE MORE MONEY.

I HURT MY WRIST A LITTLE, SEE...

COME ON, ORANGES AREN'T EVEN SHARP.

DO IT!

HERE GOES NOTHING.

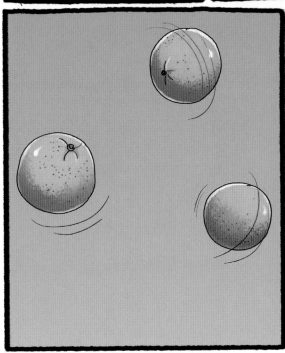

UM. I GUESS I'M A LITTLE RUSTY.

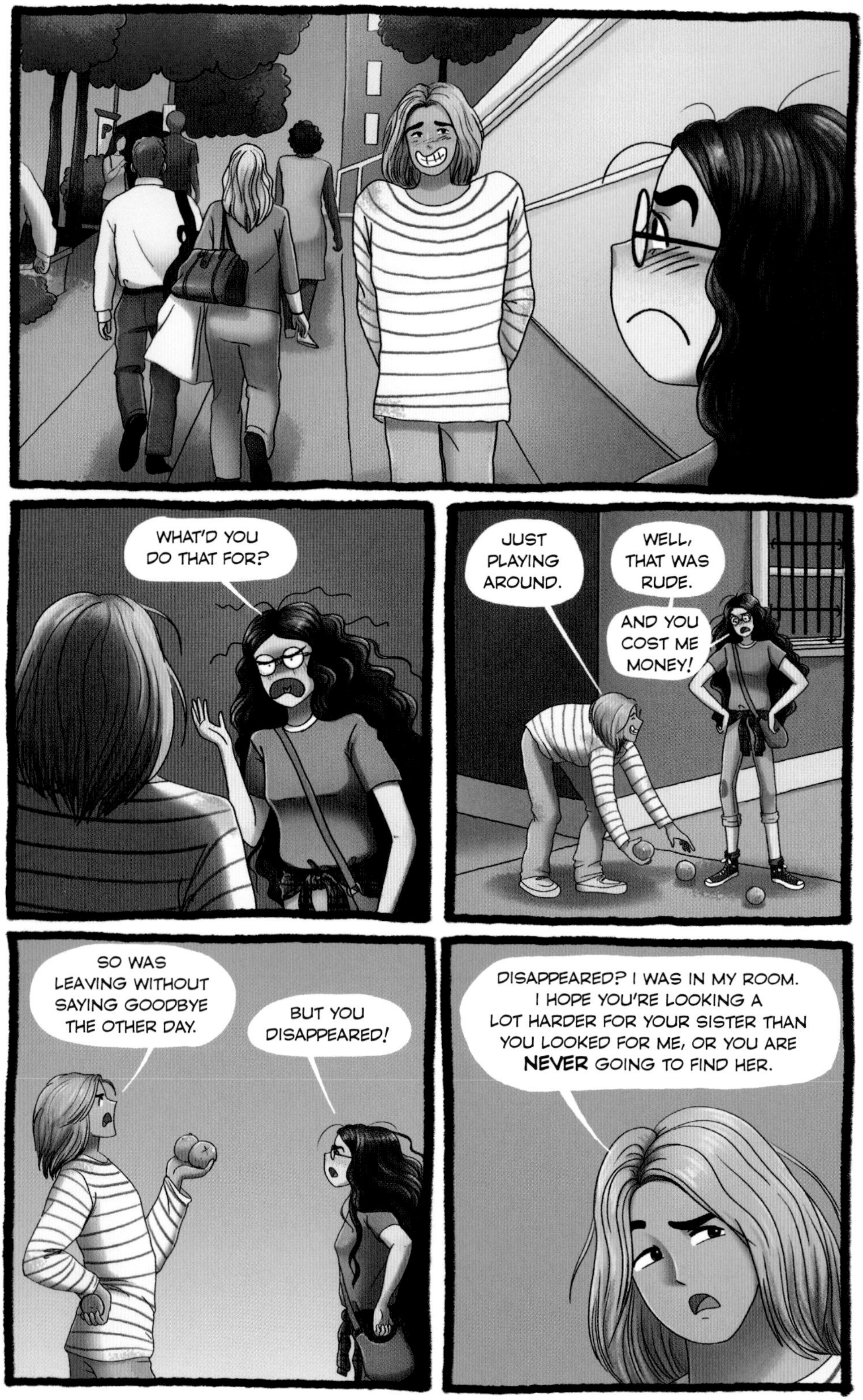
WHAT'D YOU DO THAT FOR?
JUST PLAYING AROUND.
WELL, THAT WAS RUDE.
AND YOU COST ME MONEY!
SO WAS LEAVING WITHOUT SAYING GOODBYE THE OTHER DAY.
BUT YOU DISAPPEARED!
DISAPPEARED? I WAS IN MY ROOM. I HOPE YOU'RE LOOKING A LOT HARDER FOR YOUR SISTER THAN YOU LOOKED FOR ME, OR YOU ARE NEVER GOING TO FIND HER.

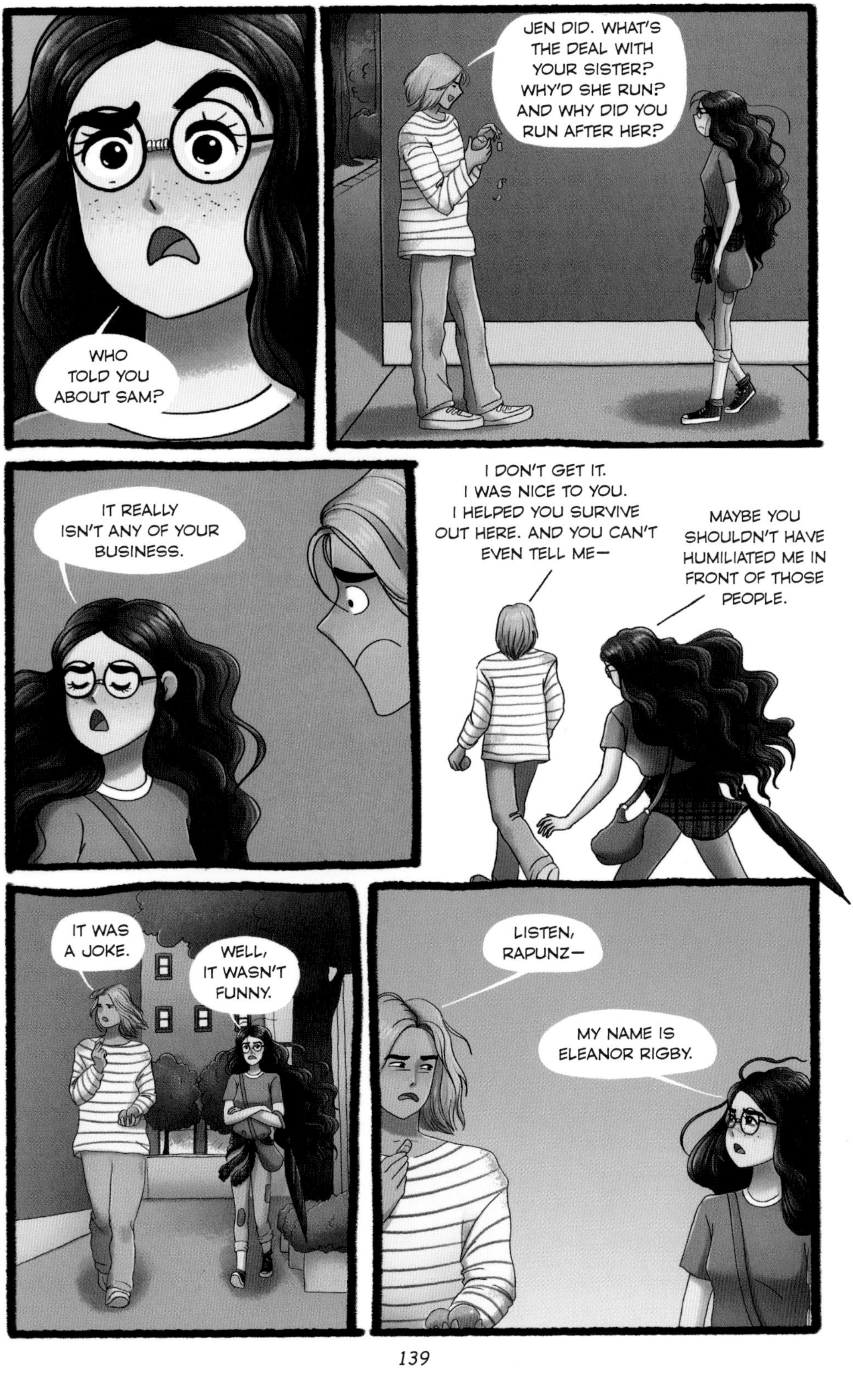
WHO TOLD YOU ABOUT SAM?
JEN DID. WHAT'S THE DEAL WITH YOUR SISTER? WHY'D SHE RUN? AND WHY DID YOU RUN AFTER HER?
IT REALLY ISN'T ANY OF YOUR BUSINESS.
I DON'T GET IT. I WAS NICE TO YOU. I HELPED YOU SURVIVE OUT HERE. AND YOU CAN'T EVEN TELL ME—
MAYBE YOU SHOULDN'T HAVE HUMILIATED ME IN FRONT OF THOSE PEOPLE.
IT WAS A JOKE.
WELL, IT WASN'T FUNNY.
LISTEN, RAPUNZ—
MY NAME IS ELEANOR RIGBY.

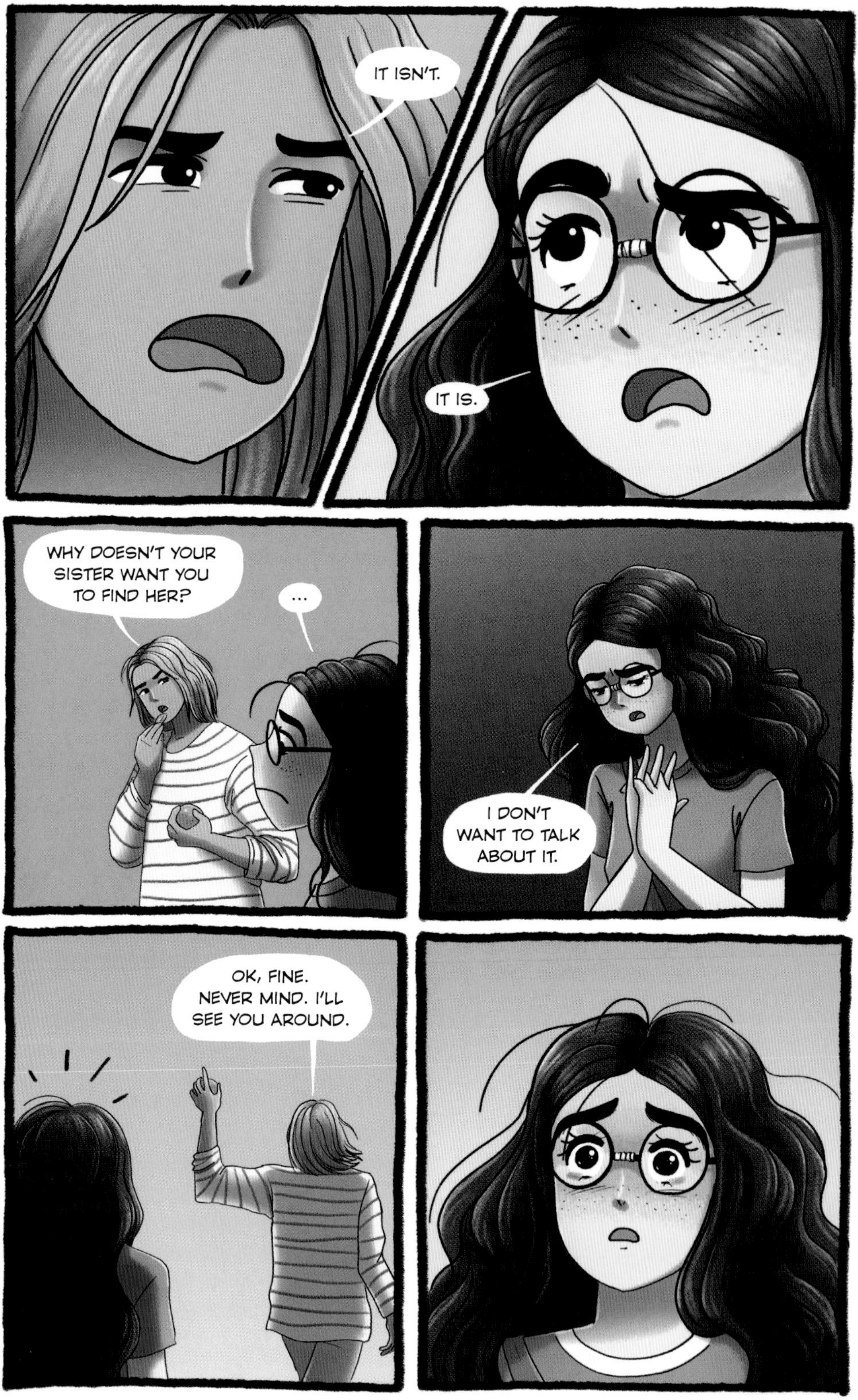
IT ISN'T.
IT IS.
WHY DOESN'T YOUR SISTER WANT YOU TO FIND HER?
...
I DON'T WANT TO TALK ABOUT IT.
OK, FINE. NEVER MIND. I'LL SEE YOU AROUND.

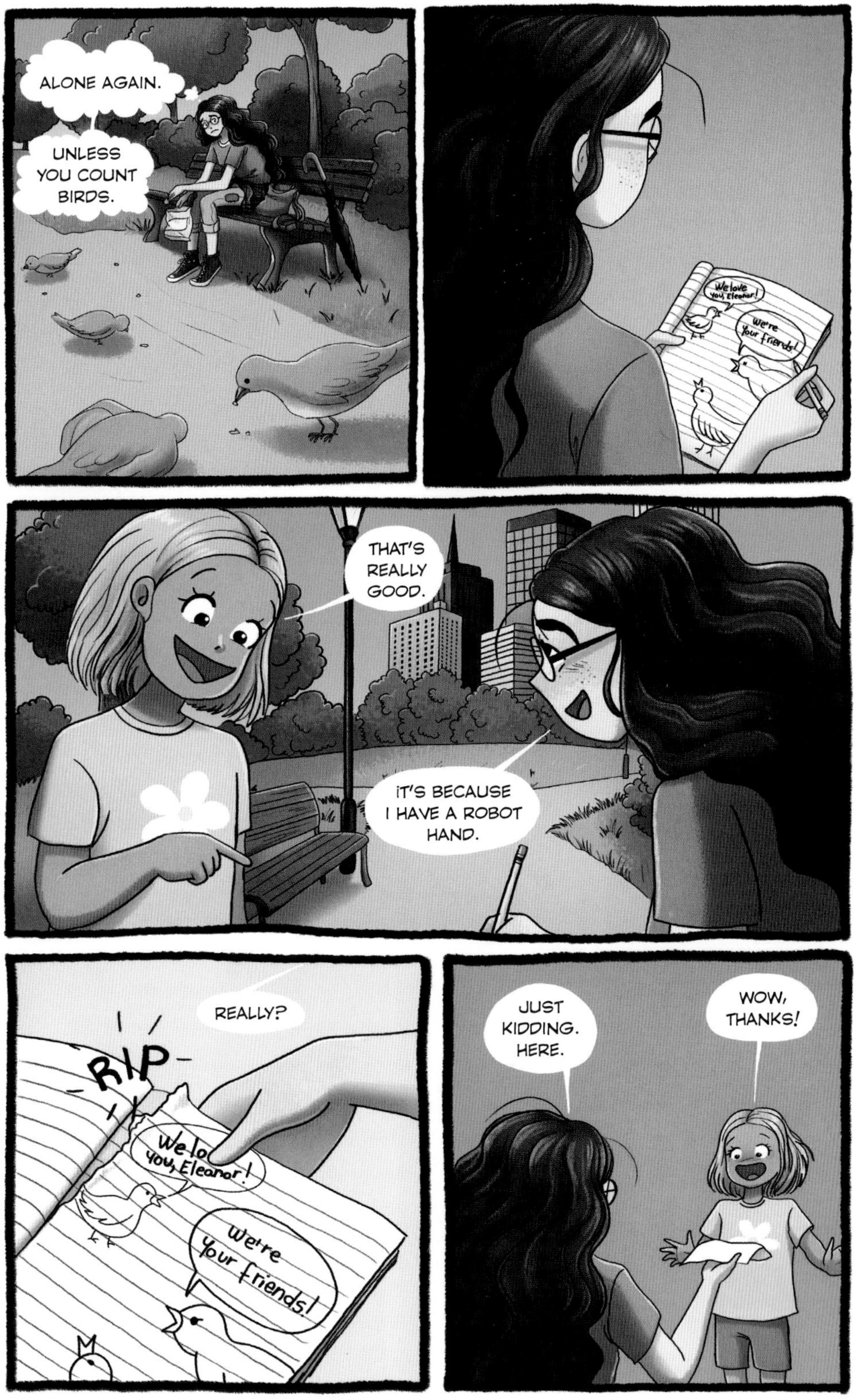
ALONE AGAIN.
UNLESS YOU COUNT BIRDS.
We love you, Eleanor!
We're your friends!
THAT'S REALLY GOOD.
IT'S BECAUSE I HAVE A ROBOT HAND.
REALLY?
RIP
We lo you, Eleanor!
We're your friends!
JUST KIDDING. HERE.
WOW, THANKS!

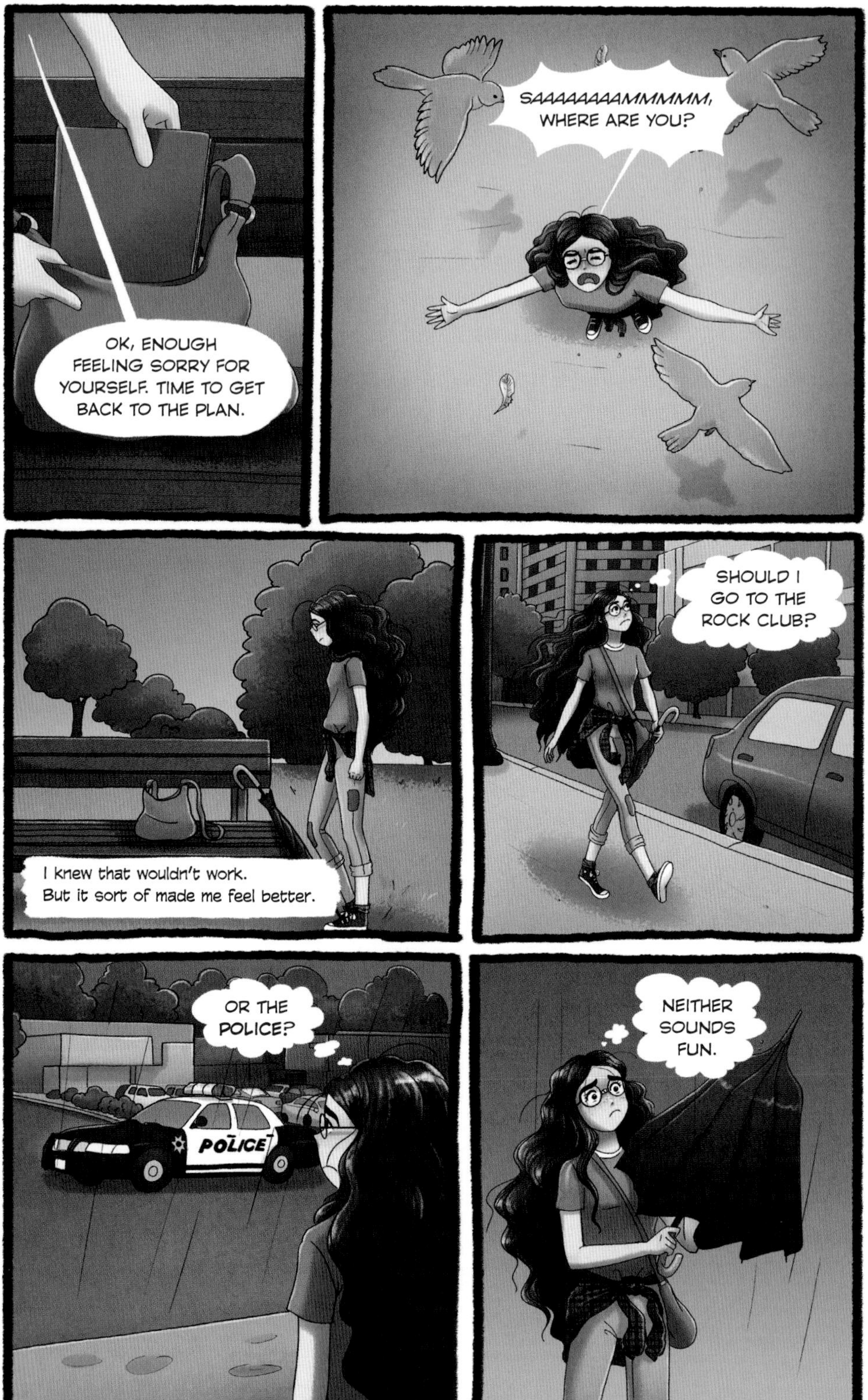
OK, ENOUGH FEELING SORRY FOR YOURSELF. TIME TO GET BACK TO THE PLAN.
SAAAAAAAAMMMMM, WHERE ARE YOU?
I knew that wouldn't work.
But it sort of made me feel better.
SHOULD I GO TO THE ROCK CLUB?
OR THE POLICE?
POLICE
NEITHER SOUNDS FUN.

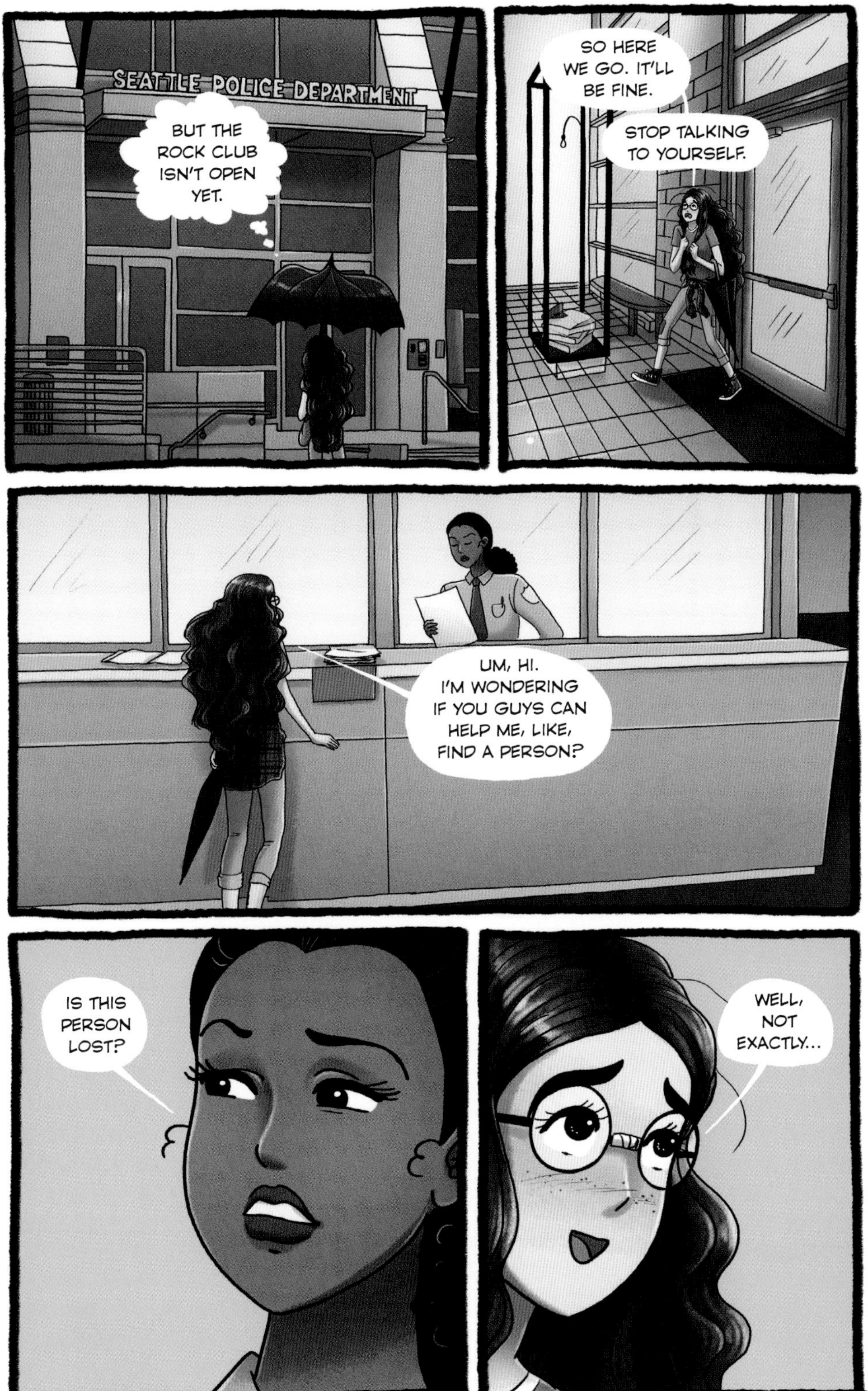
SEATTLE POLICE DEPARTMENT
BUT THE ROCK CLUB ISN'T OPEN YET.
SO HERE WE GO. IT'LL BE FINE.
STOP TALKING TO YOURSELF.
UM, HI. I'M WONDERING IF YOU GUYS CAN HELP ME, LIKE, FIND A PERSON?
IS THIS PERSON LOST?
WELL, NOT EXACTLY...

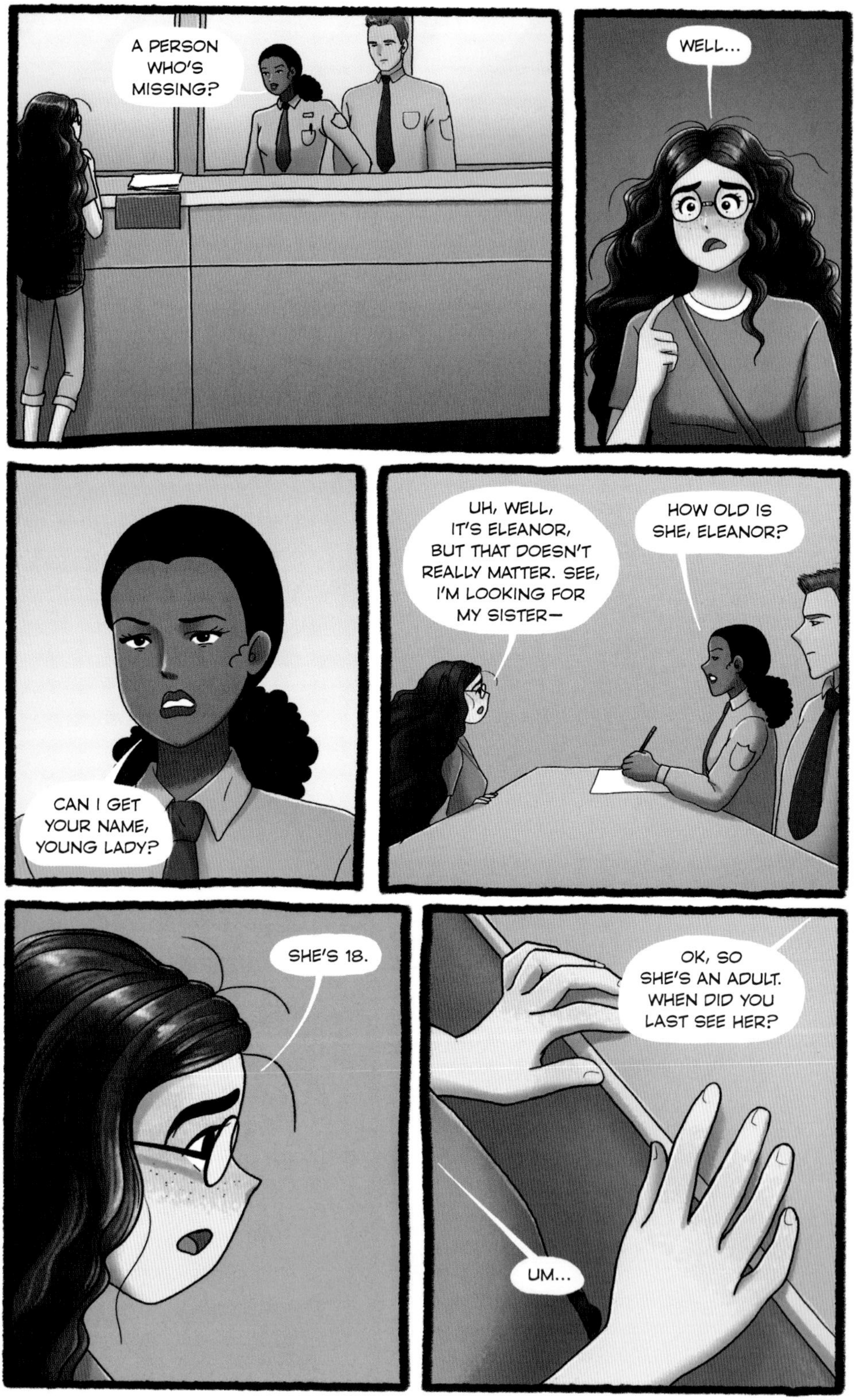
A PERSON WHO'S MISSING?
WELL...
CAN I GET YOUR NAME, YOUNG LADY?
UH, WELL, IT'S ELEANOR, BUT THAT DOESN'T REALLY MATTER. SEE, I'M LOOKING FOR MY SISTER—
HOW OLD IS SHE, ELEANOR?
SHE'S 18.
OK, SO SHE'S AN ADULT. WHEN DID YOU LAST SEE HER?
UM...

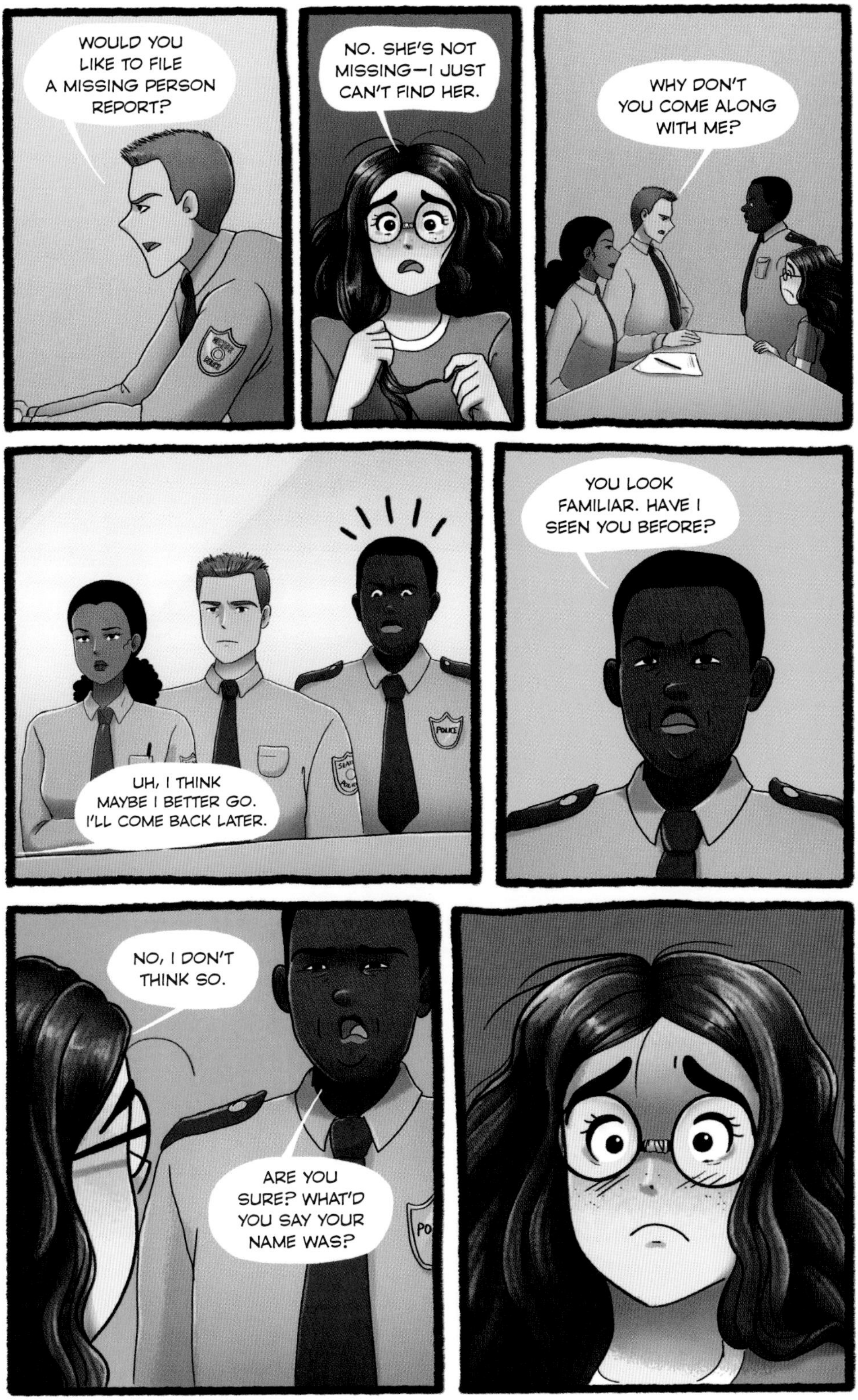
WOULD YOU LIKE TO FILE A MISSING PERSON REPORT?
NO. SHE'S NOT MISSING—I JUST CAN'T FIND HER.
WHY DON'T YOU COME ALONG WITH ME?
UH, I THINK MAYBE I BETTER GO. I'LL COME BACK LATER.
YOU LOOK FAMILIAR. HAVE I SEEN YOU BEFORE?
NO, I DON'T THINK SO.
ARE YOU SURE? WHAT'D YOU SAY YOUR NAME WAS?

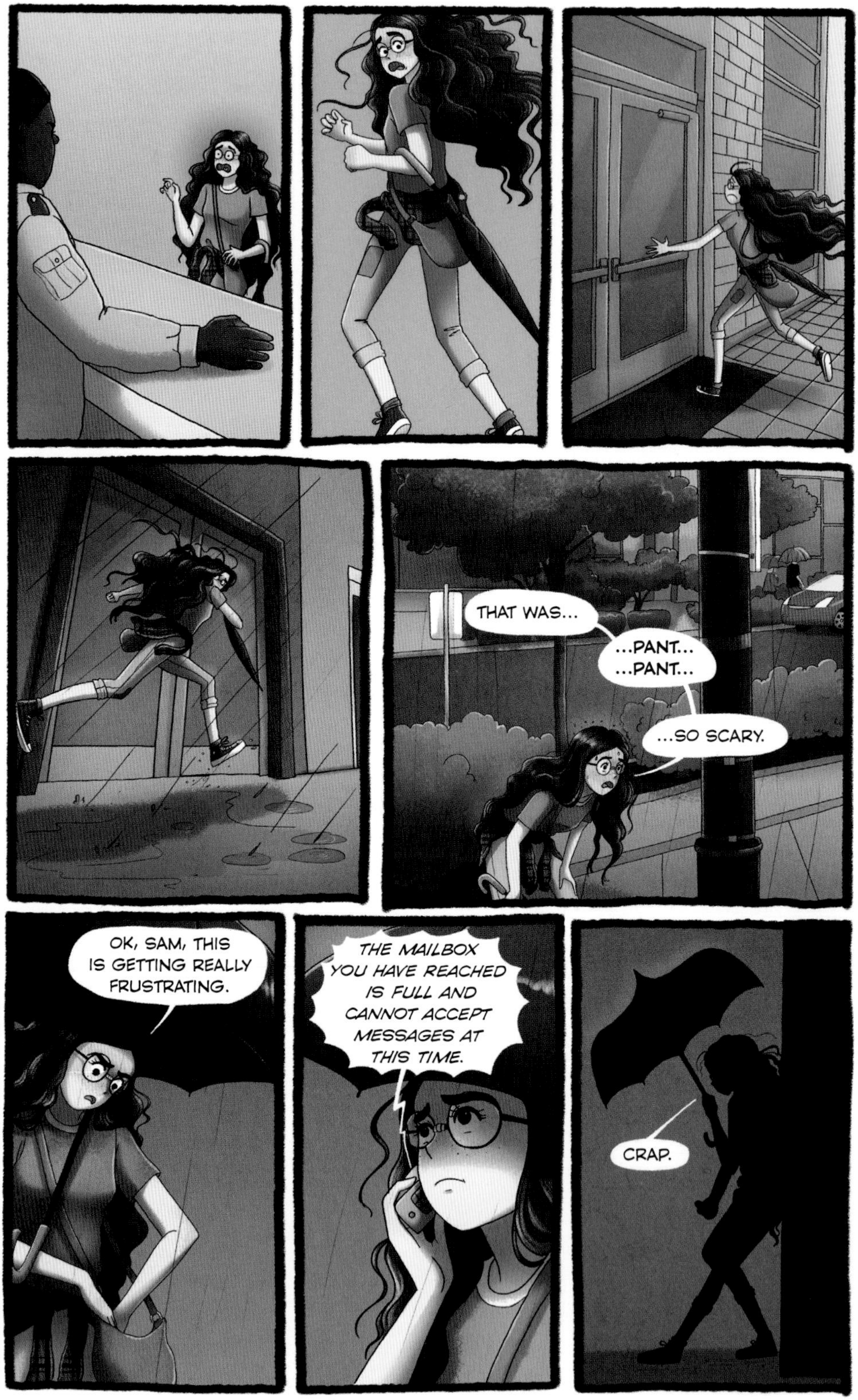
THAT WAS...
...PANT...
...PANT...
...SO SCARY.
OK, SAM, THIS IS GETTING REALLY FRUSTRATING.
THE MAILBOX YOU HAVE REACHED IS FULL AND CANNOT ACCEPT MESSAGES AT THIS TIME.
CRAP.

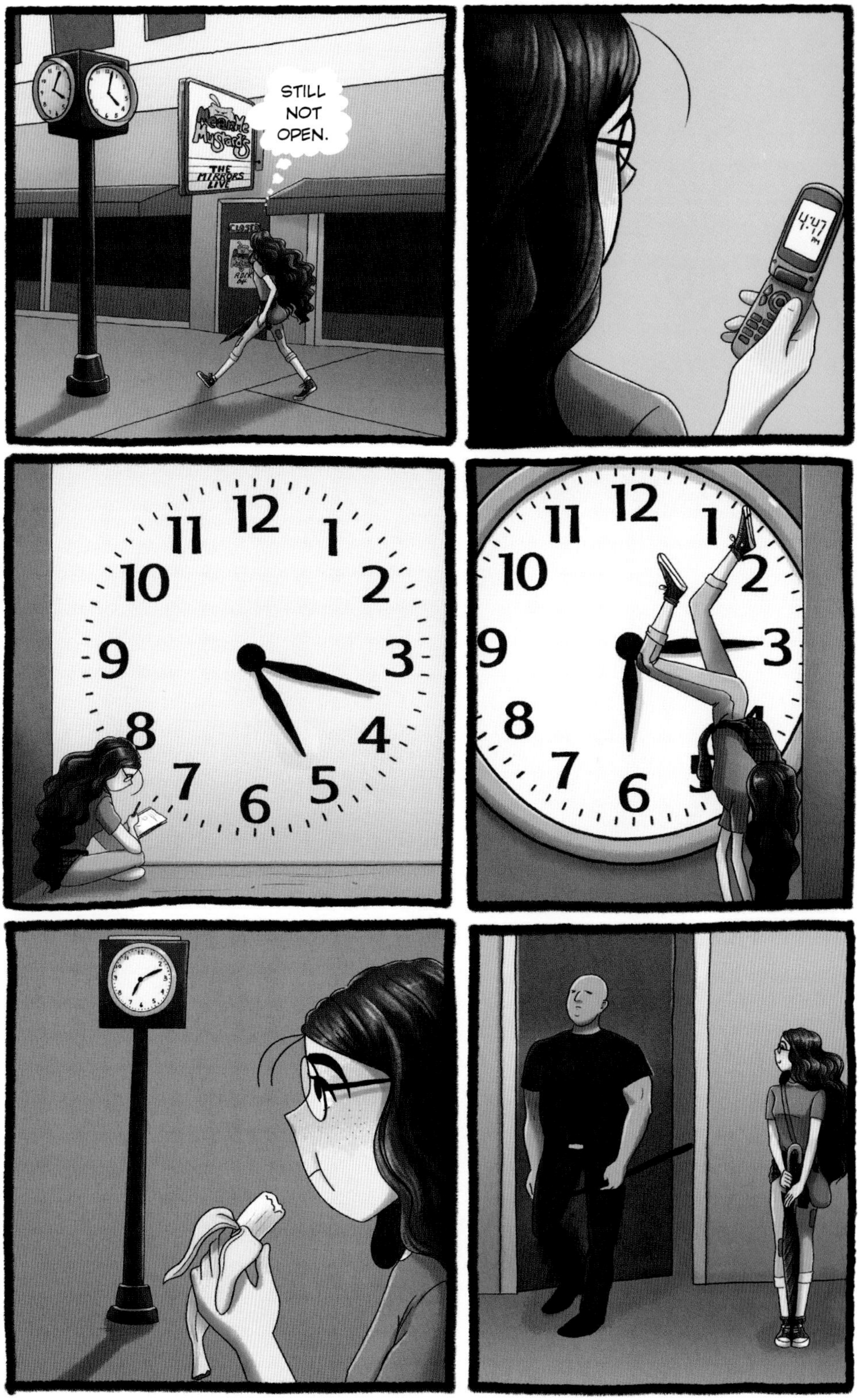
STILL NOT OPEN.
THE MIRRORS LIVE

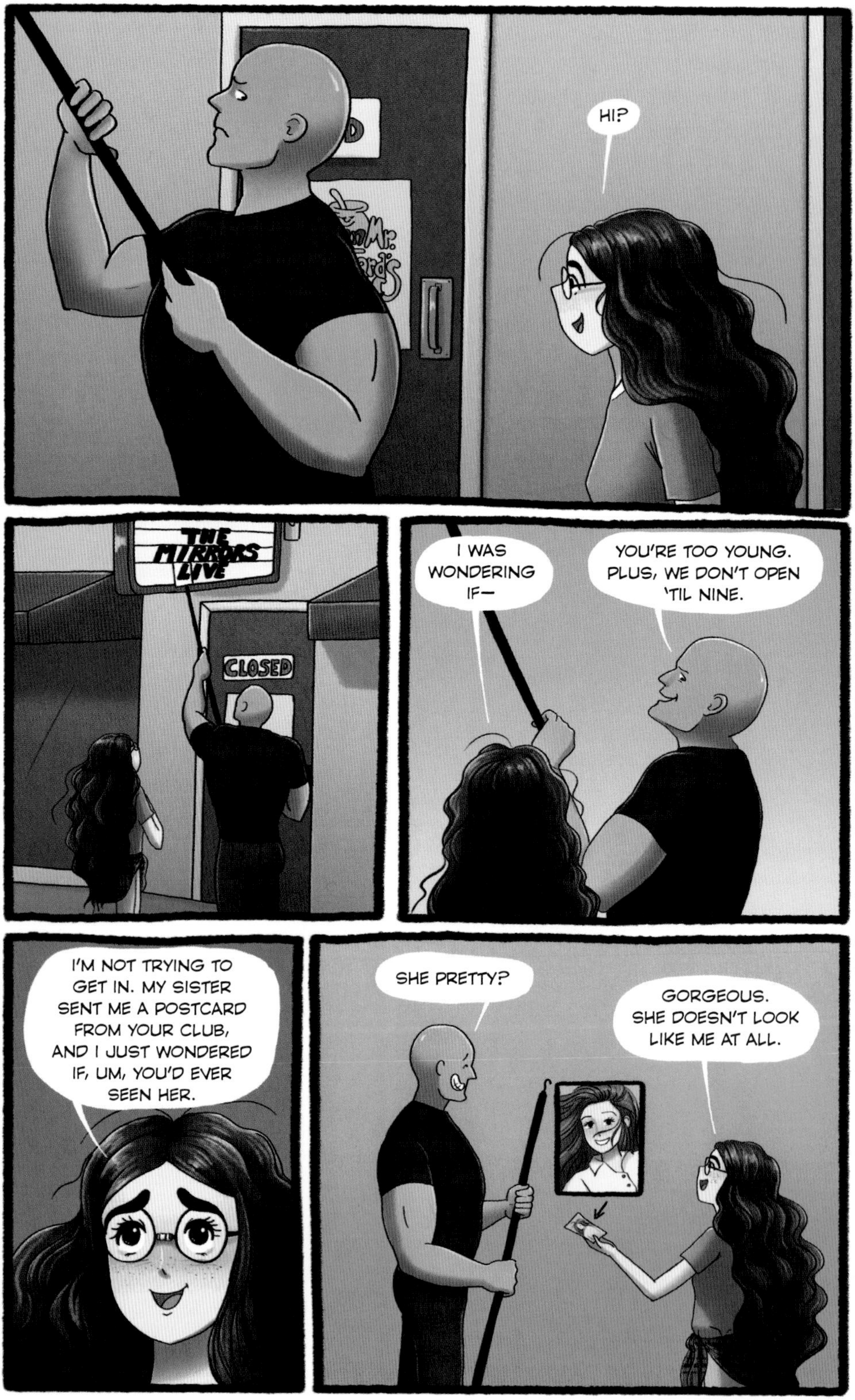
HI?
Mr. Ford's
THE MIRRORS LIVE
CLOSED
I WAS WONDERING IF—
YOU'RE TOO YOUNG. PLUS, WE DON'T OPEN 'TIL NINE.
I'M NOT TRYING TO GET IN. MY SISTER SENT ME A POSTCARD FROM YOUR CLUB, AND I JUST WONDERED IF, UM, YOU'D EVER SEEN HER.
SHE PRETTY?
GORGEOUS. SHE DOESN'T LOOK LIKE ME AT ALL.

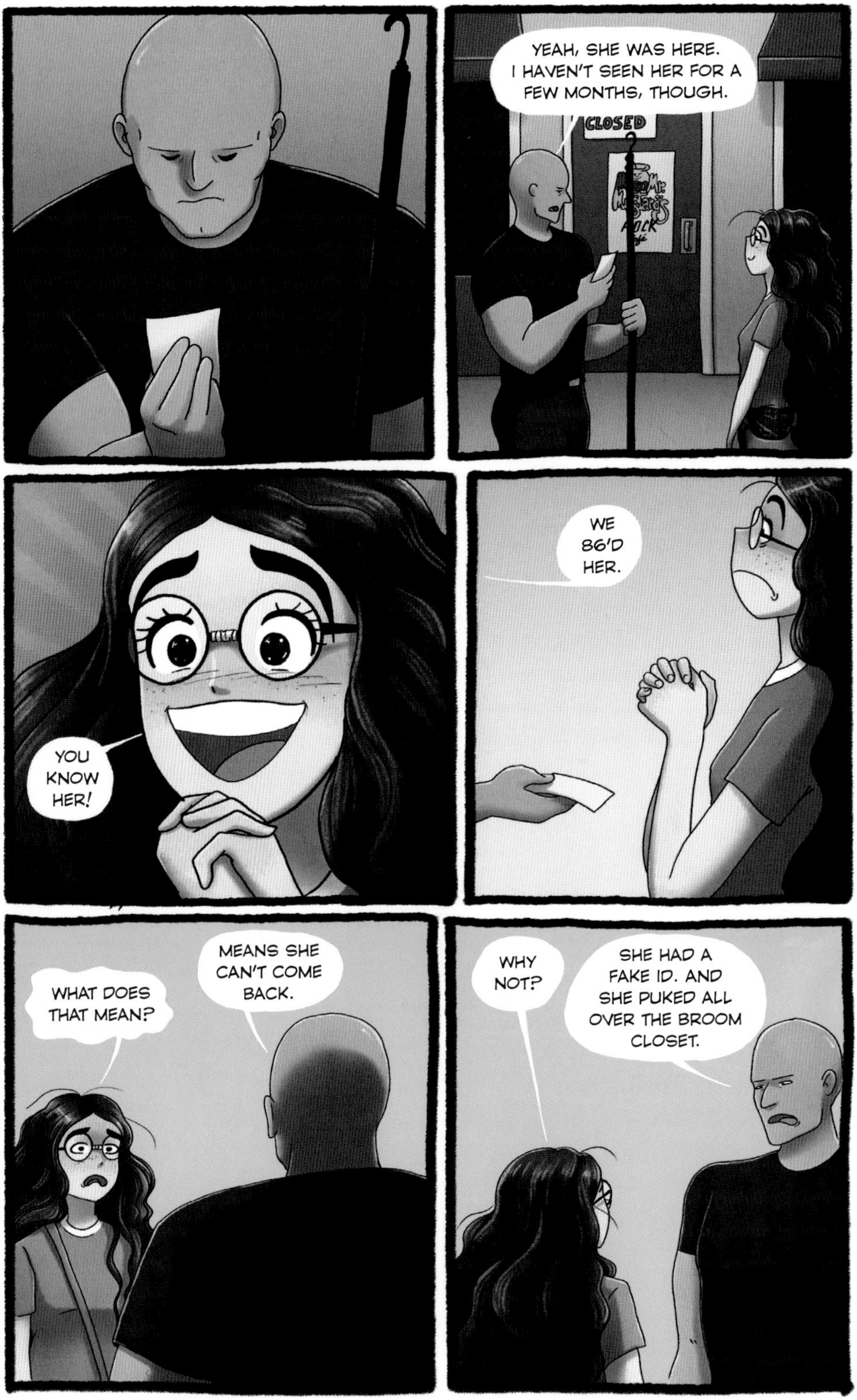
YEAH, SHE WAS HERE. I HAVEN'T SEEN HER FOR A FEW MONTHS, THOUGH.
CLOSED
YOU KNOW HER!
WE 86'D HER.
WHAT DOES THAT MEAN?
MEANS SHE CAN'T COME BACK.
WHY NOT?
SHE HAD A FAKE ID. AND SHE PUKED ALL OVER THE BROOM CLOSET.

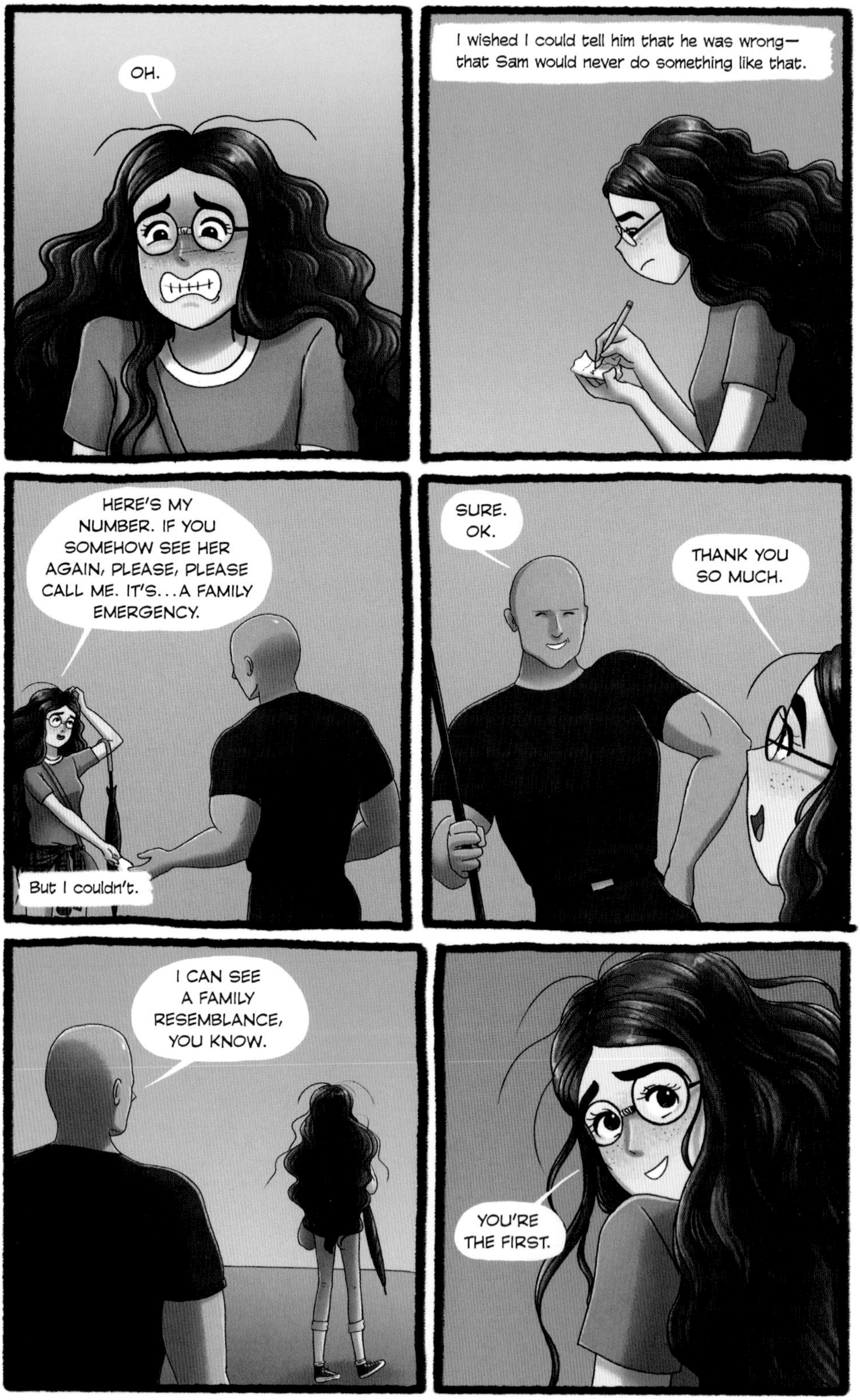
OH.
I wished I could tell him that he was wrong—that Sam would never do something like that.
HERE'S MY NUMBER. IF YOU SOMEHOW SEE HER AGAIN, PLEASE, PLEASE CALL ME. IT'S...A FAMILY EMERGENCY.
But I couldn't.
SURE. OK.
THANK YOU SO MUCH.
I CAN SEE A FAMILY RESEMBLANCE, YOU KNOW.
YOU'RE THE FIRST.

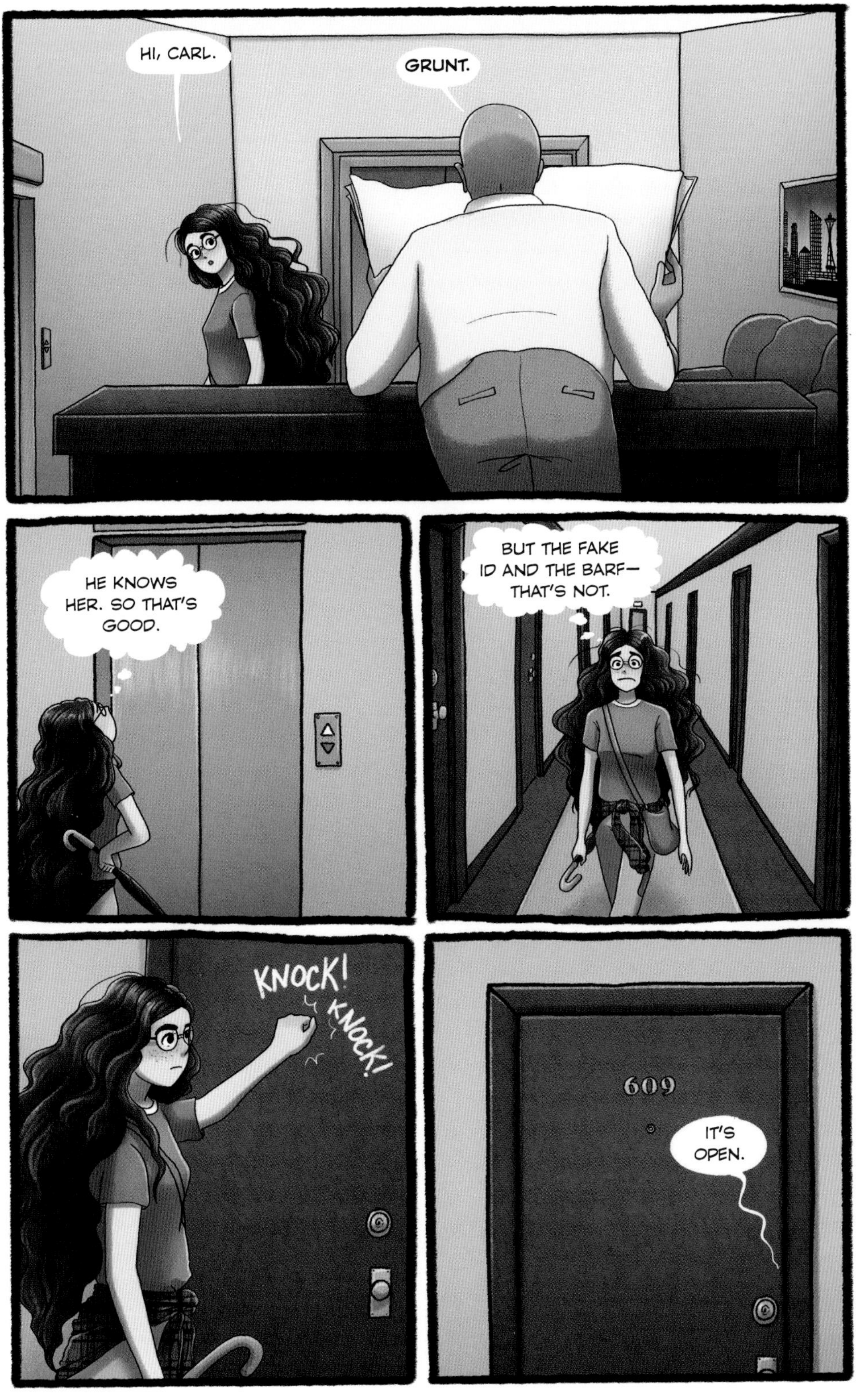
HI, CARL.
GRUNT.
HE KNOWS HER. SO THAT'S GOOD.
BUT THE FAKE ID AND THE BARF— THAT'S NOT.
KNOCK!
KNOCK!
609
IT'S OPEN.

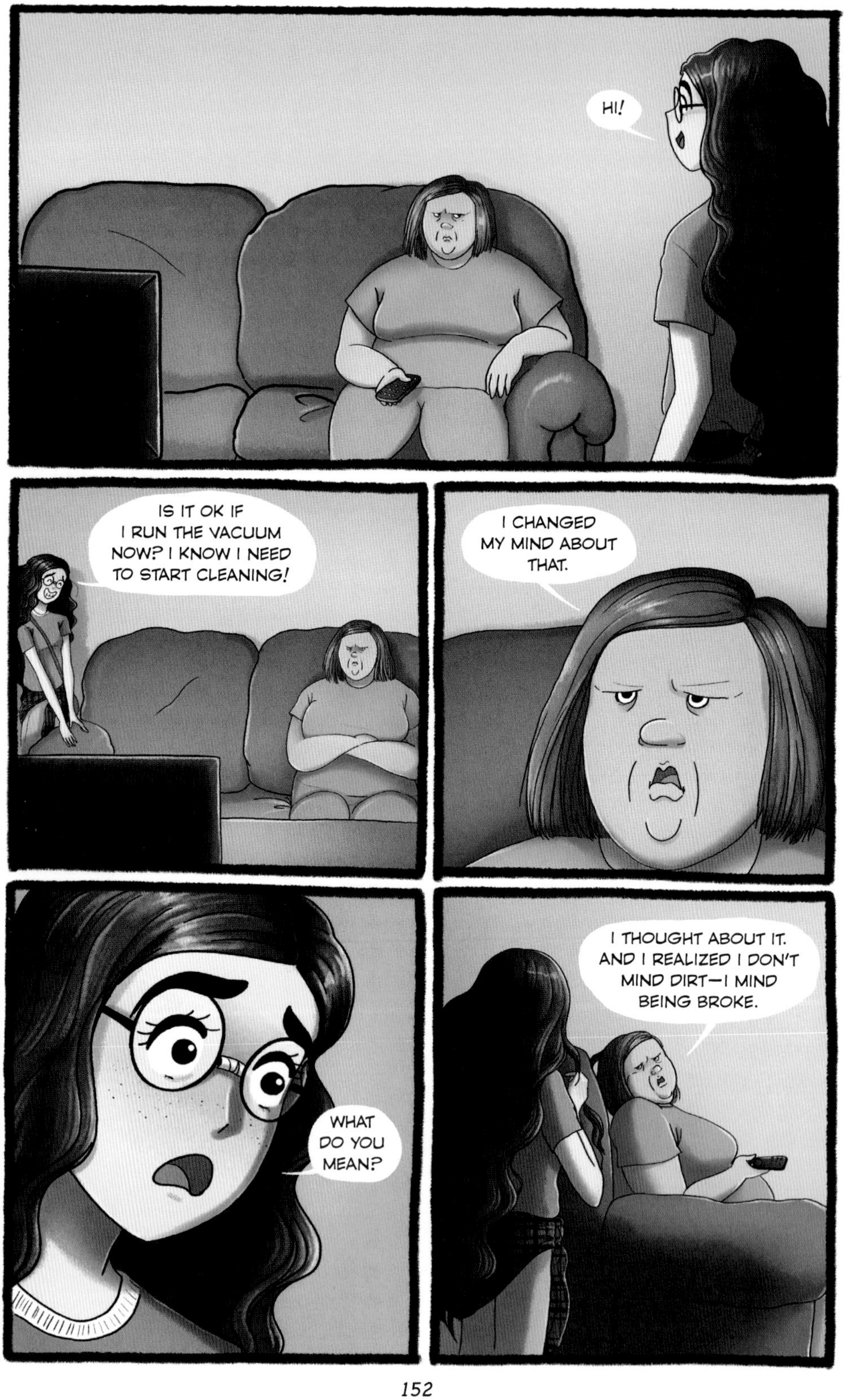
HI!
IS IT OK IF I RUN THE VACUUM NOW? I KNOW I NEED TO START CLEANING!
I CHANGED MY MIND ABOUT THAT.
WHAT DO YOU MEAN?
I THOUGHT ABOUT IT. AND I REALIZED I DON'T MIND DIRT—I MIND BEING BROKE.

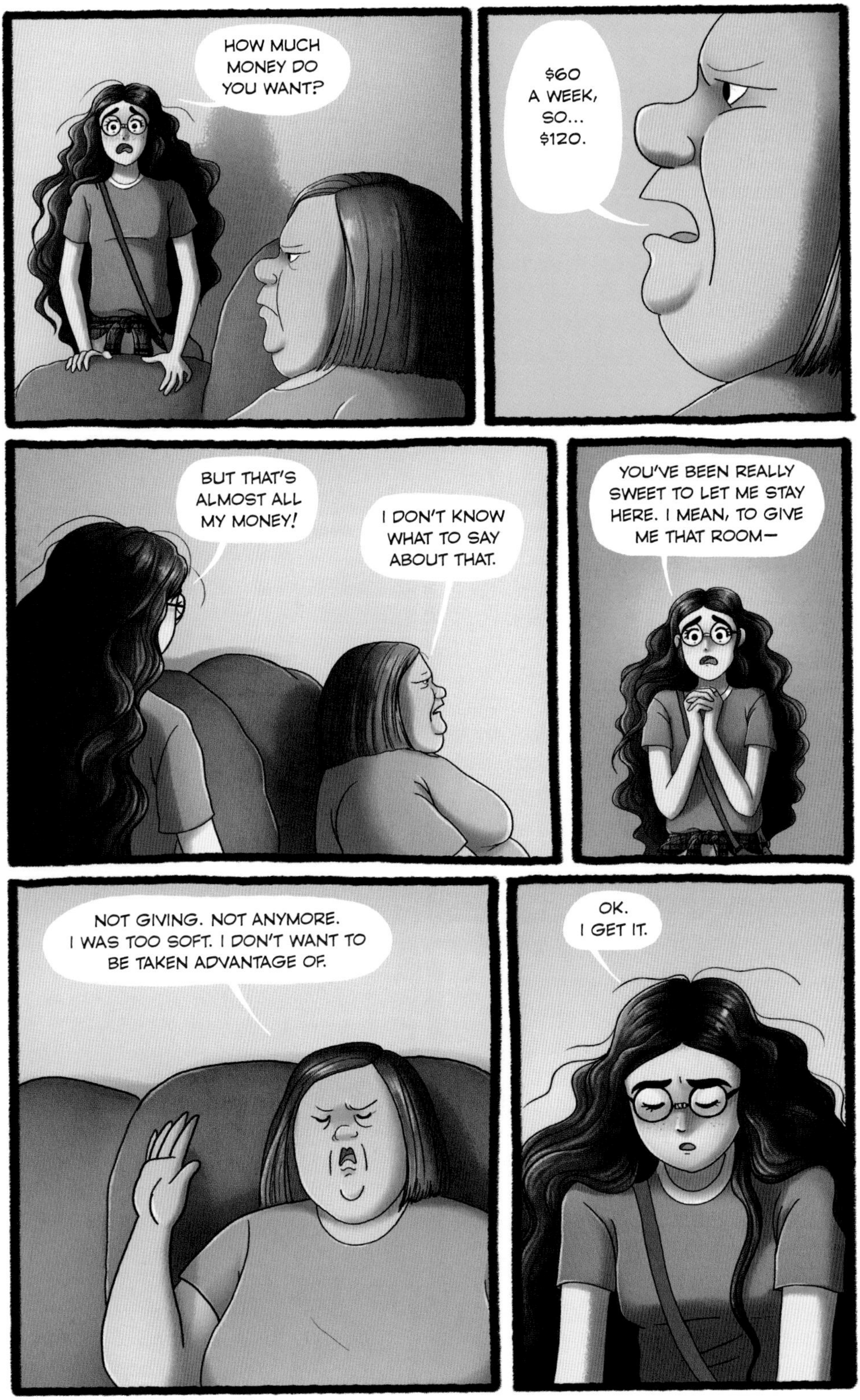
HOW MUCH MONEY DO YOU WANT?
$60 A WEEK, SO... $120.
BUT THAT'S ALMOST ALL MY MONEY!
I DON'T KNOW WHAT TO SAY ABOUT THAT.
YOU'VE BEEN REALLY SWEET TO LET ME STAY HERE. I MEAN, TO GIVE ME THAT ROOM—
NOT GIVING. NOT ANYMORE. I WAS TOO SOFT. I DON'T WANT TO BE TAKEN ADVANTAGE OF.
OK. I GET IT.

RIP!

IS

Forester
16

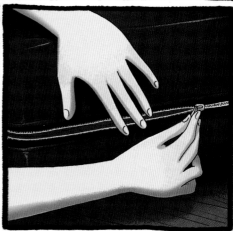

ONE MAN IS
DEAD AND ONE
HAS BEEN ARRESTED
AFTER A FIGHT
OUTSIDE A WEST
SEATTLE BAR.

WE'LL HAVE THAT
STORY AND MORE
COMING UP AFTER
THE BREAK.

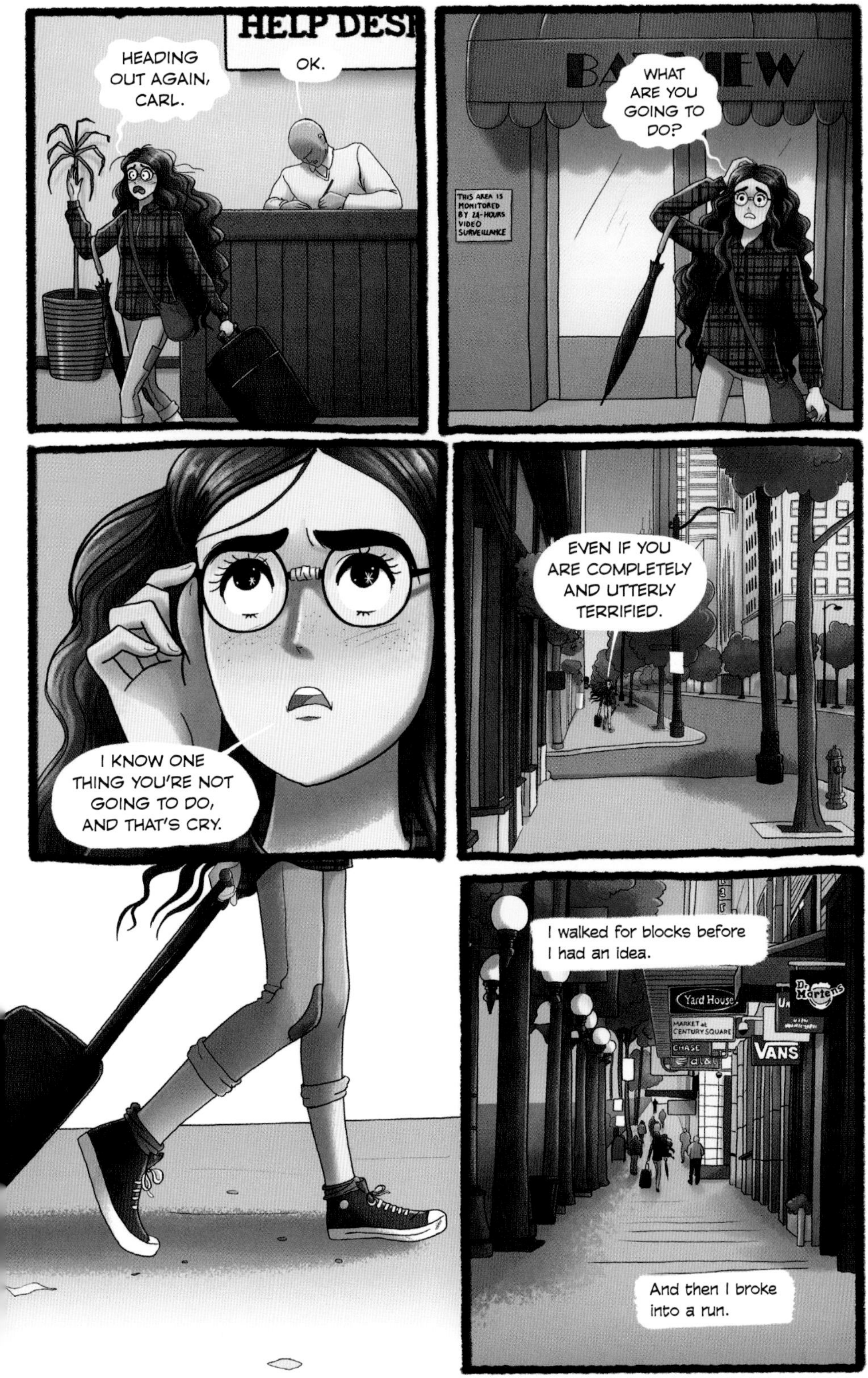
HELP DES
HEADING OUT AGAIN, CARL.
OK.
WHAT ARE YOU GOING TO DO?
THIS AREA IS MONITORED BY 24-HOURS VIDEO SURVEILLANCE
I KNOW ONE THING YOU'RE NOT GOING TO DO, AND THAT'S CRY.
EVEN IF YOU ARE COMPLETELY AND UTTERLY TERRIFIED.
I walked for blocks before I had an idea.
Yard House
MARKET at CENTURY SQUARE
CHASE
VANS
Dr. Martens
And then I broke into a run.

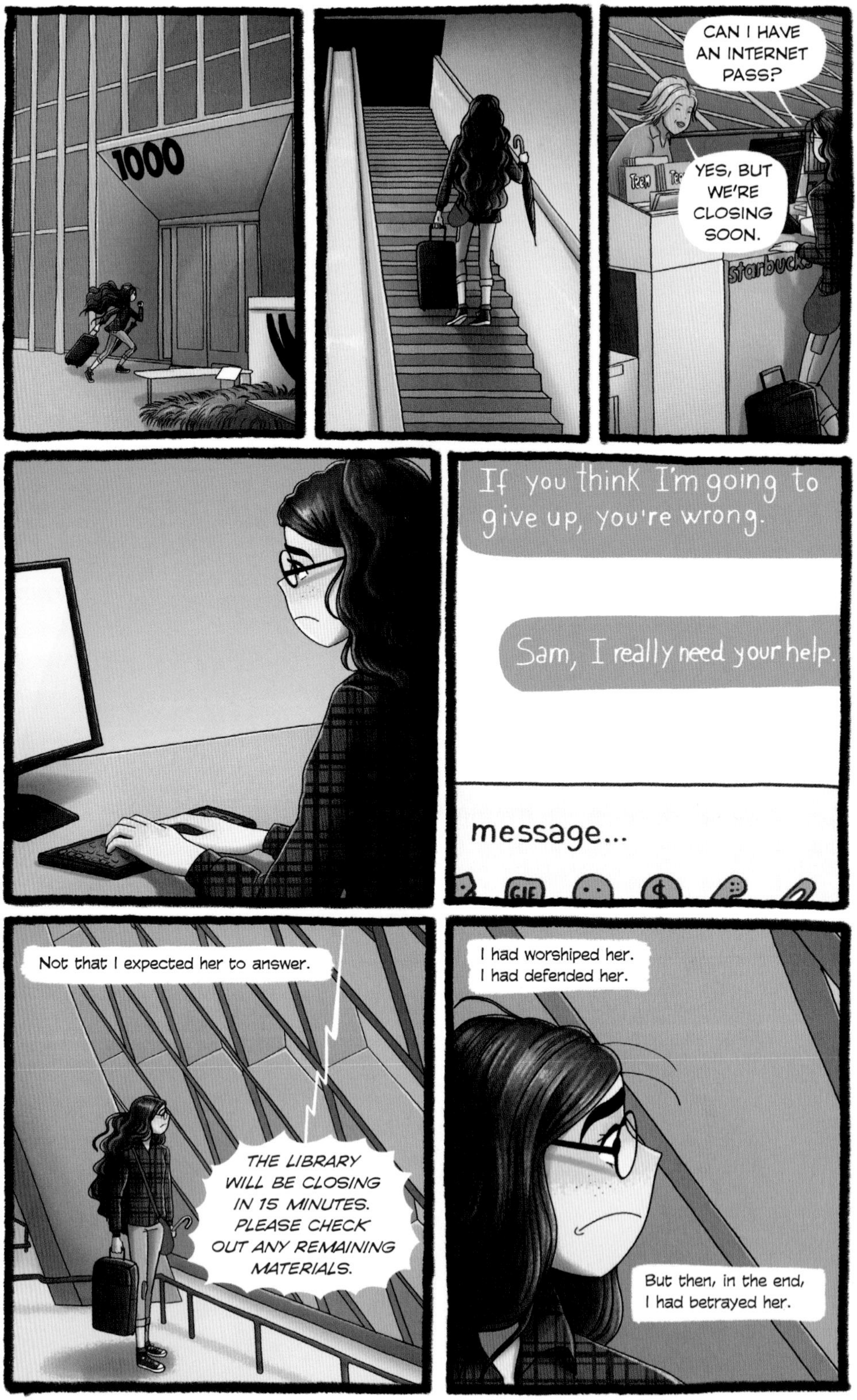
1000
CAN I HAVE AN INTERNET PASS?
YES, BUT WE'RE CLOSING SOON.
If you think I'm going to give up, you're wrong.
Sam, I really need your help.
message...
Not that I expected her to answer.
THE LIBRARY WILL BE CLOSING IN 15 MINUTES. PLEASE CHECK OUT ANY REMAINING MATERIALS.
I had worshiped her.
I had defended her.
But then, in the end, I had betrayed her.

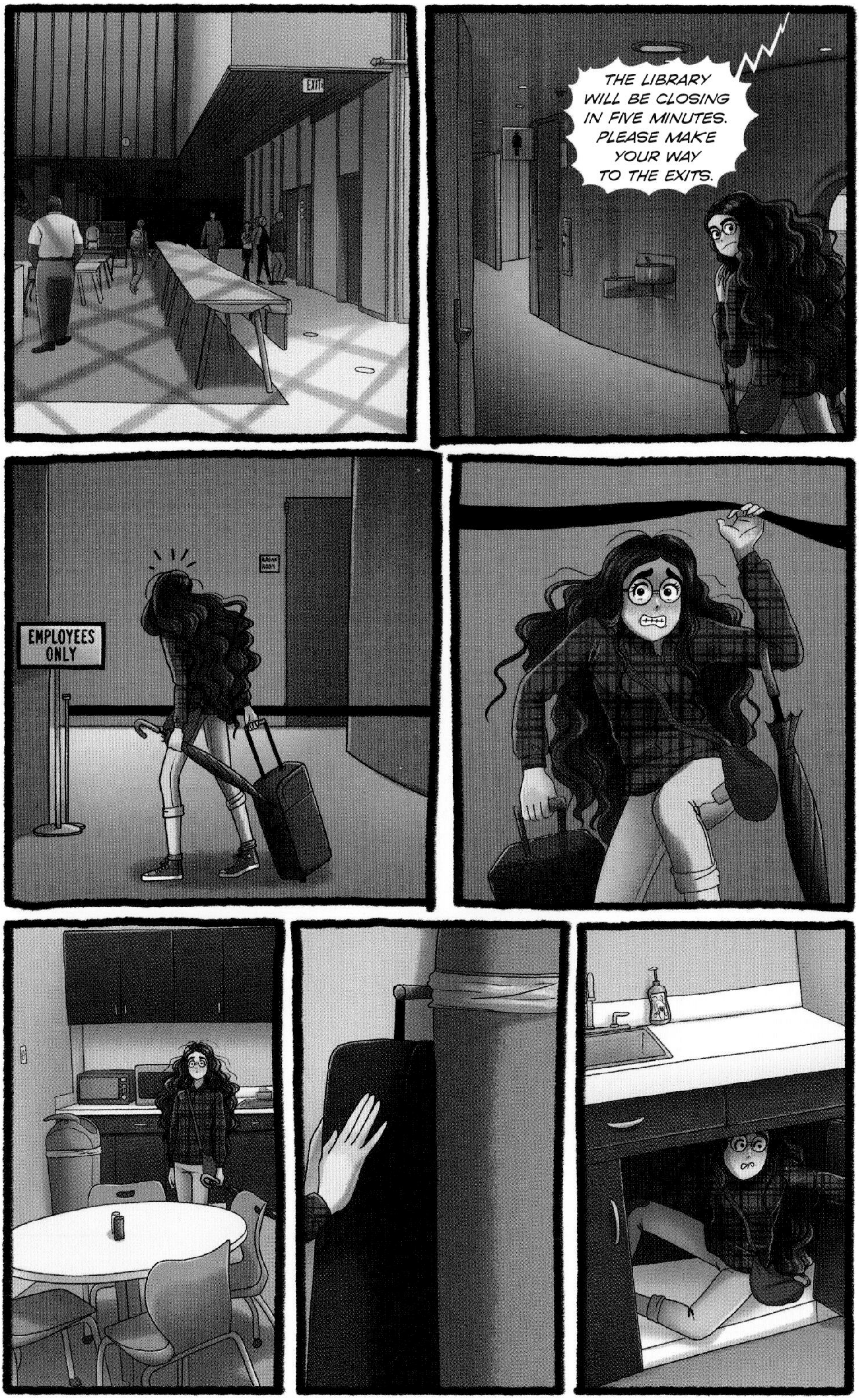
EXIT
THE LIBRARY WILL BE CLOSING IN FIVE MINUTES. PLEASE MAKE YOUR WAY TO THE EXITS.
EMPLOYEES ONLY

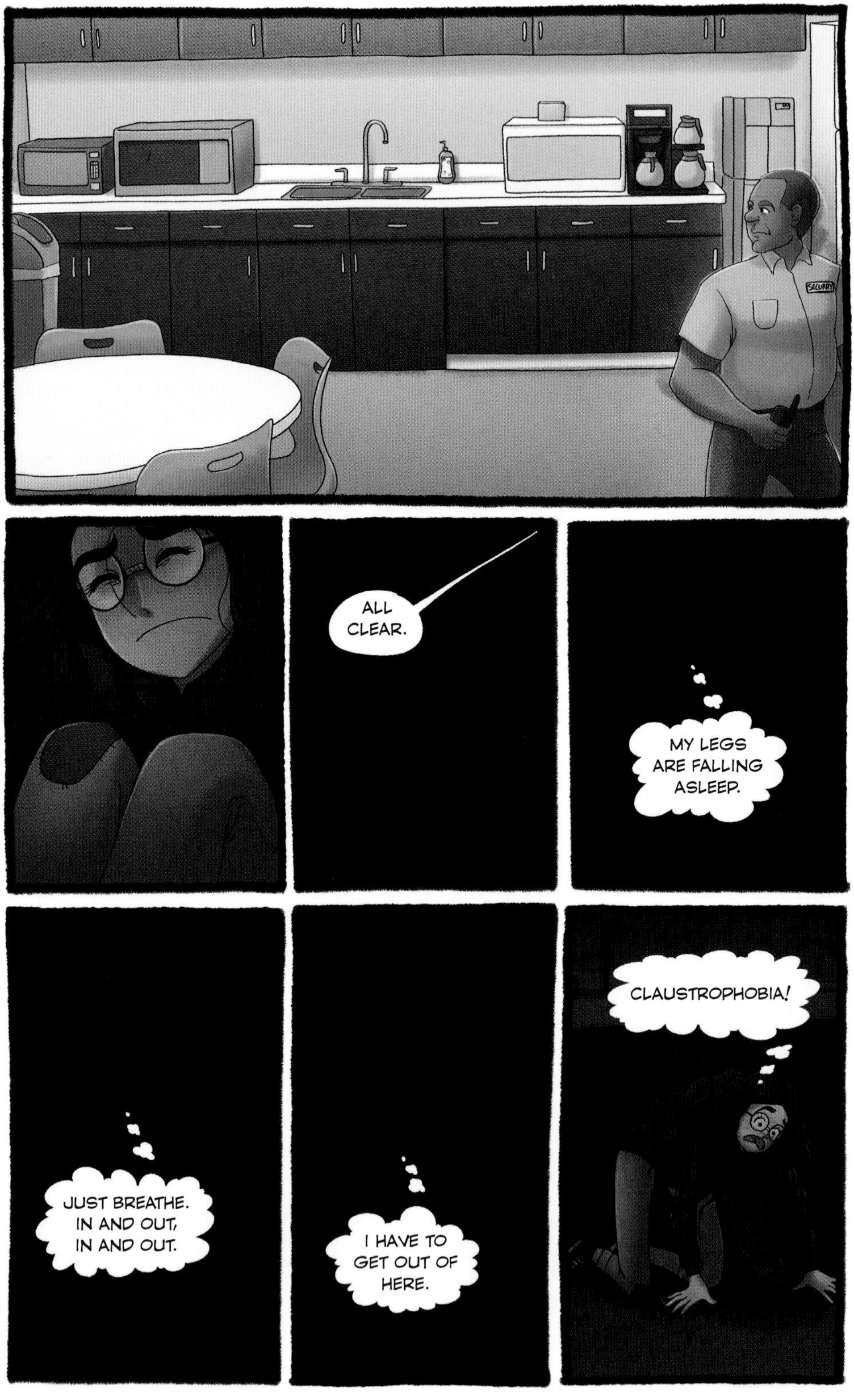
SECURITY
ALL CLEAR.
MY LEGS ARE FALLING ASLEEP.
JUST BREATHE. IN AND OUT, IN AND OUT.
I HAVE TO GET OUT OF HERE.
CLAUSTROPHOBIA!

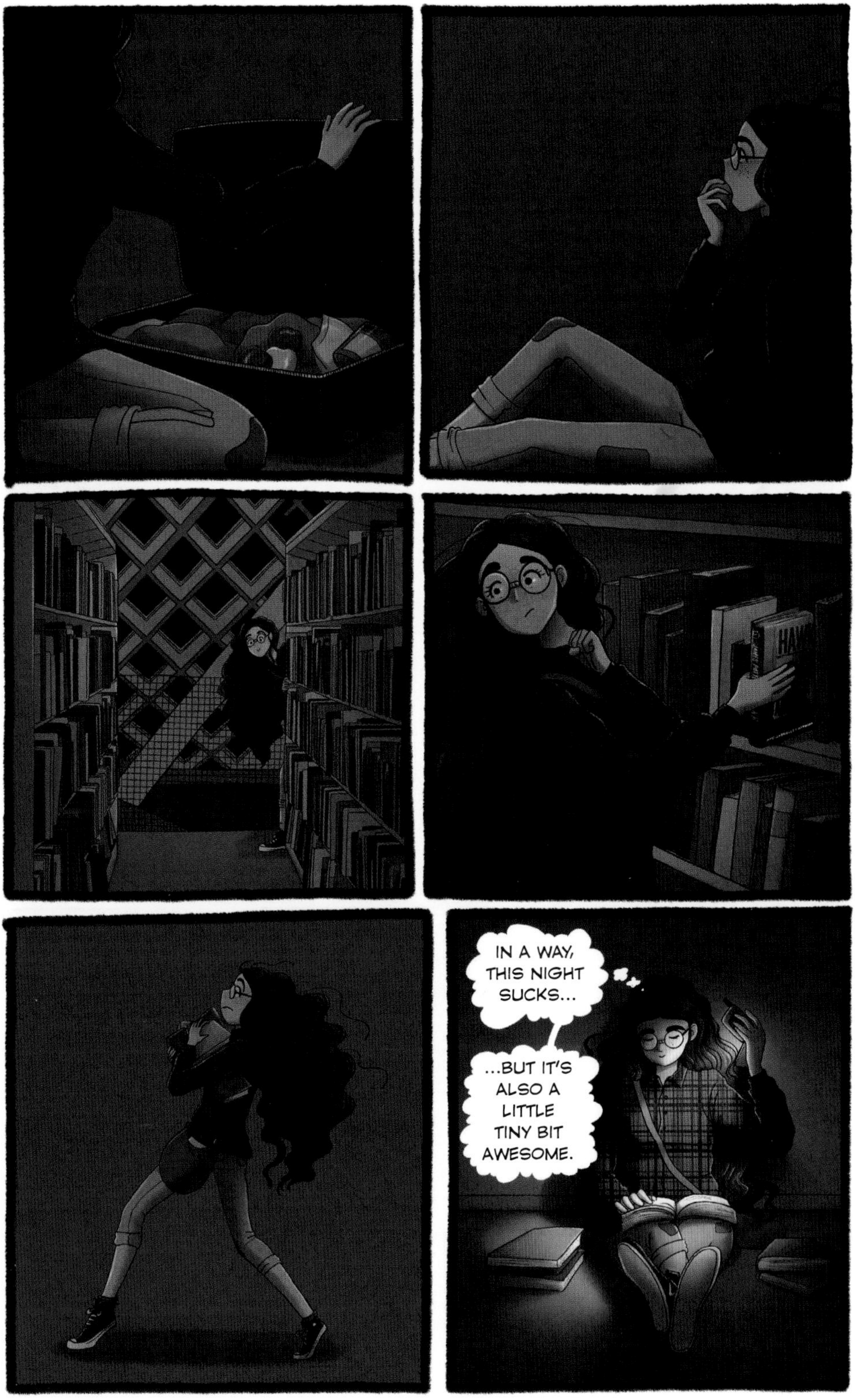
IN A WAY, THIS NIGHT SUCKS...
...BUT IT'S ALSO A LITTLE TINY BIT AWESOME.

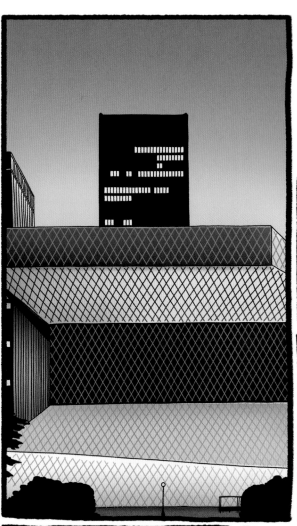

YOU LOOK LIKE YOU DIDN'T SLEEP AT ALL.

BECAUSE YOU BARELY DID.

I hid in a stall until the library opened.

And then I went out to start my day.

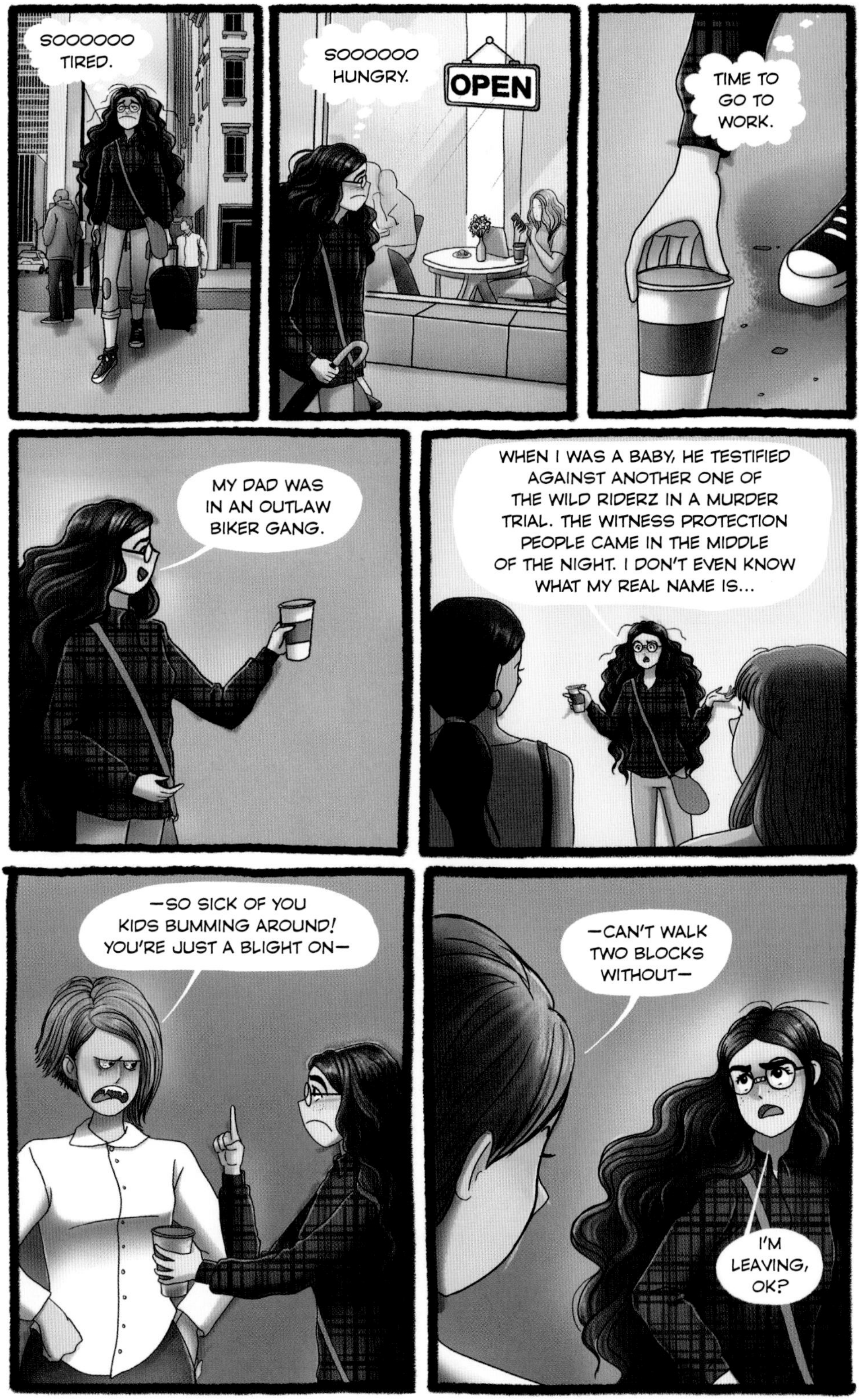
SOOOOOO TIRED.
SOOOOOO HUNGRY.
OPEN
TIME TO GO TO WORK.
MY DAD WAS IN AN OUTLAW BIKER GANG.
WHEN I WAS A BABY, HE TESTIFIED AGAINST ANOTHER ONE OF THE WILD RIDERZ IN A MURDER TRIAL. THE WITNESS PROTECTION PEOPLE CAME IN THE MIDDLE OF THE NIGHT. I DON'T EVEN KNOW WHAT MY REAL NAME IS...
—SO SICK OF YOU KIDS BUMMING AROUND! YOU'RE JUST A BLIGHT ON—
—CAN'T WALK TWO BLOCKS WITHOUT—
I'M LEAVING, OK?

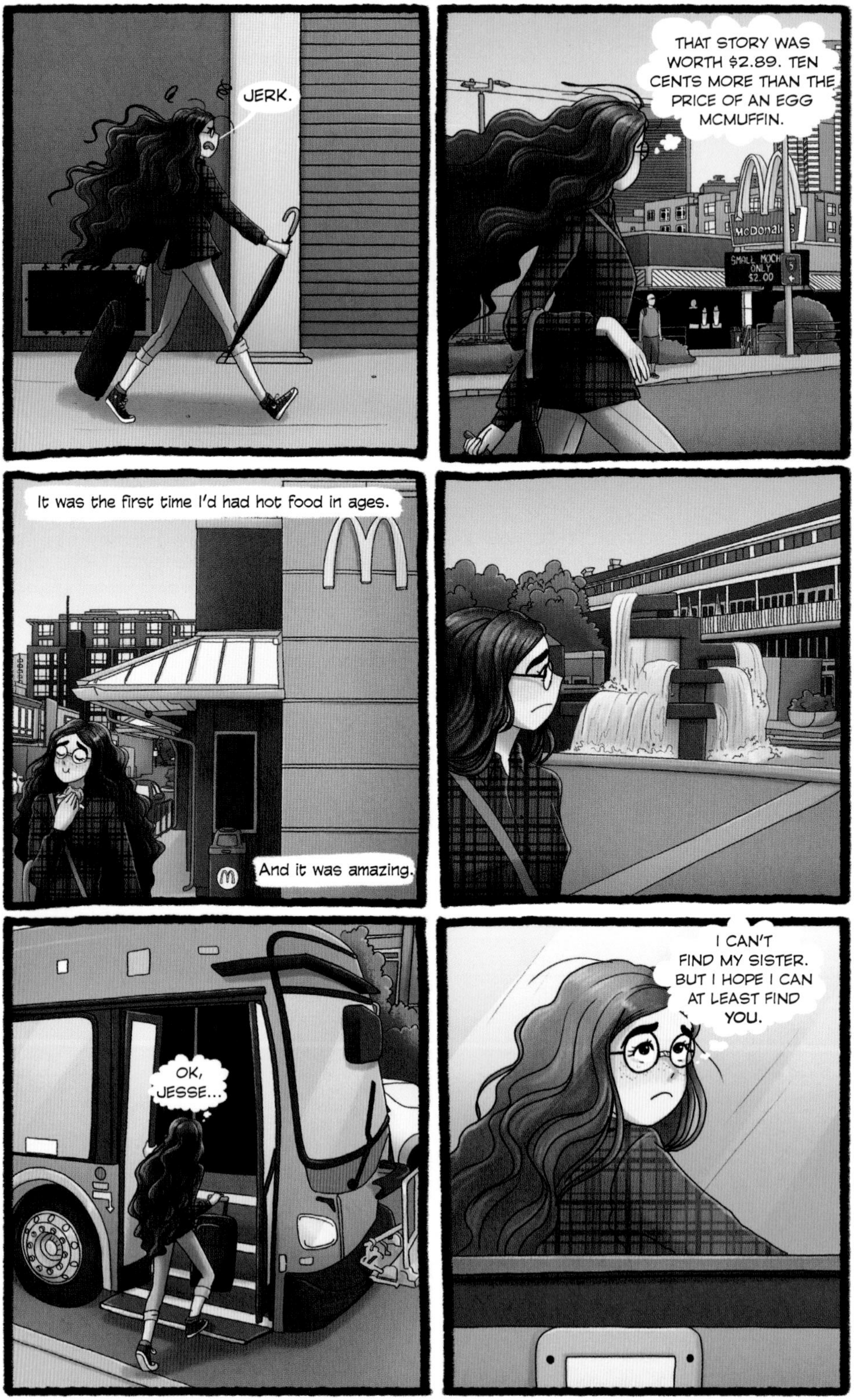
JERK.
THAT STORY WAS WORTH $2.89. TEN CENTS MORE THAN THE PRICE OF AN EGG MCMUFFIN.
McDonald's
SMALL MOCHA ONLY $2.00
It was the first time I'd had hot food in ages.
And it was amazing.
OK, JESSE...
I CAN'T FIND MY SISTER. BUT I HOPE I CAN AT LEAST FIND YOU.

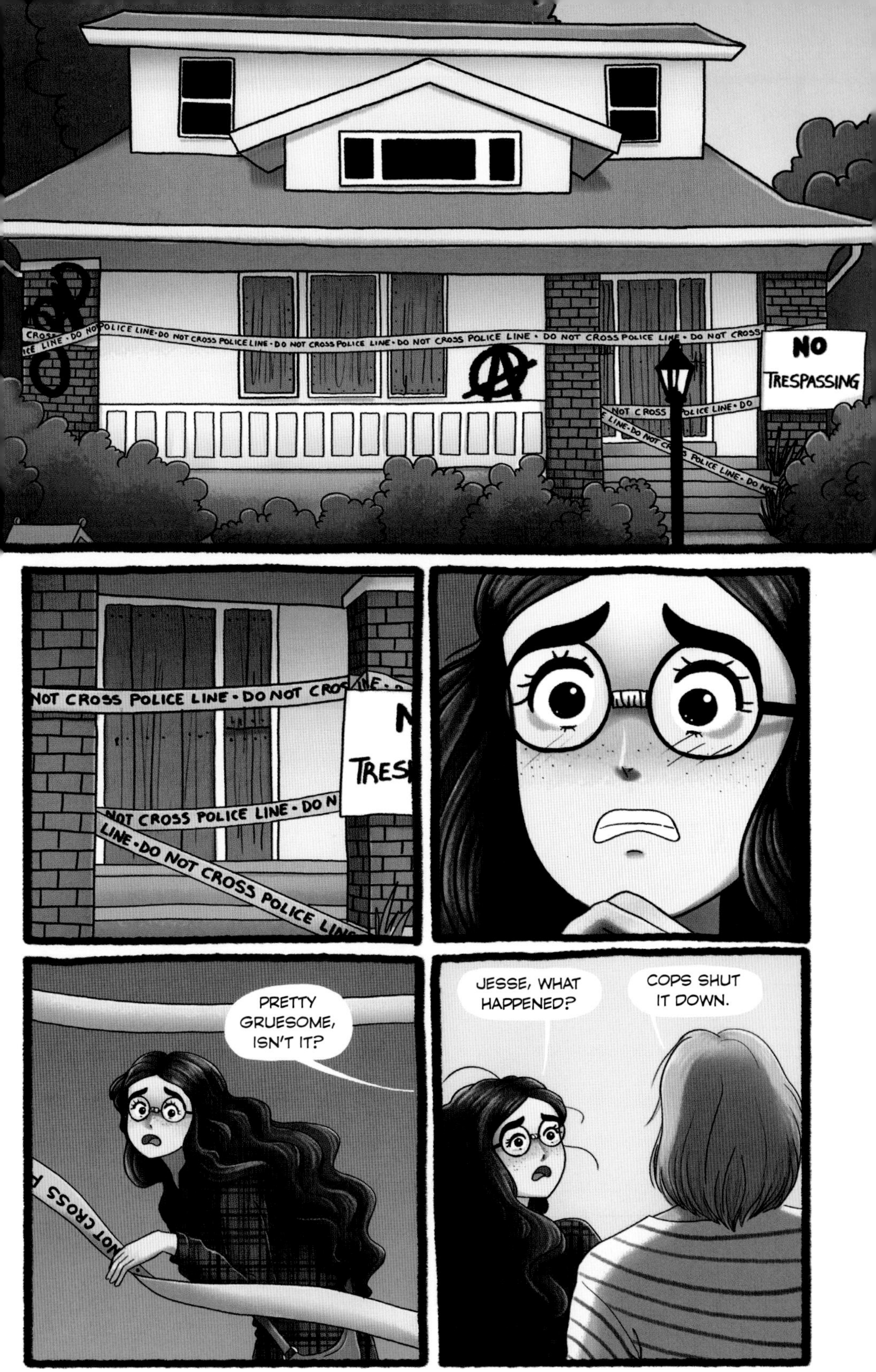

DO NOT CROSS POLICE LINE
NO TRESPASSING
PRETTY GRUESOME, ISN'T IT?
JESSE, WHAT HAPPENED?
COPS SHUT IT DOWN.

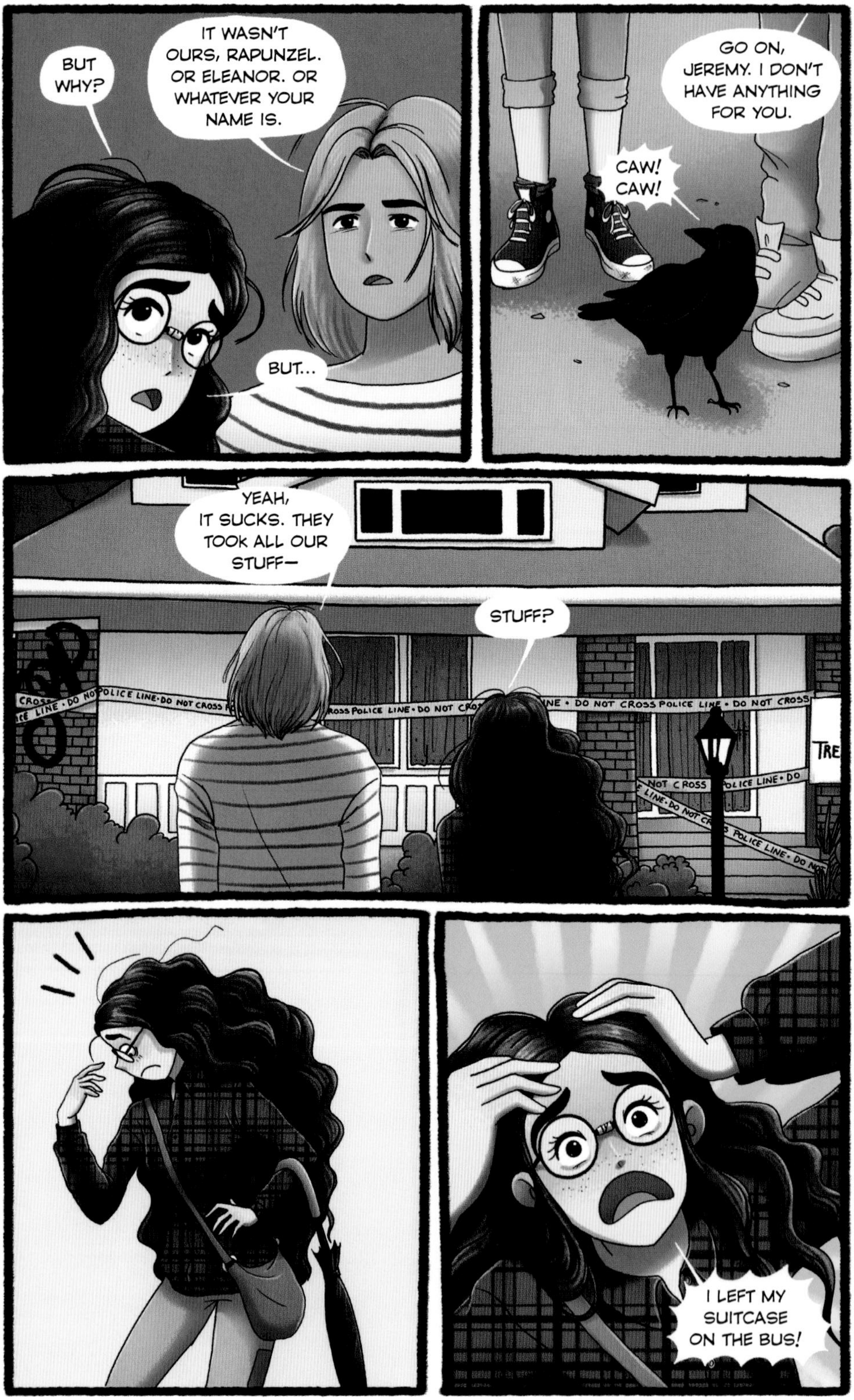
BUT WHY?
IT WASN'T OURS, RAPUNZEL. OR ELEANOR. OR WHATEVER YOUR NAME IS.
BUT...
GO ON, JEREMY. I DON'T HAVE ANYTHING FOR YOU.
CAW! CAW!
YEAH, IT SUCKS. THEY TOOK ALL OUR STUFF—
STUFF?
POLICE LINE • DO NOT CROSS
I LEFT MY SUITCASE ON THE BUS!

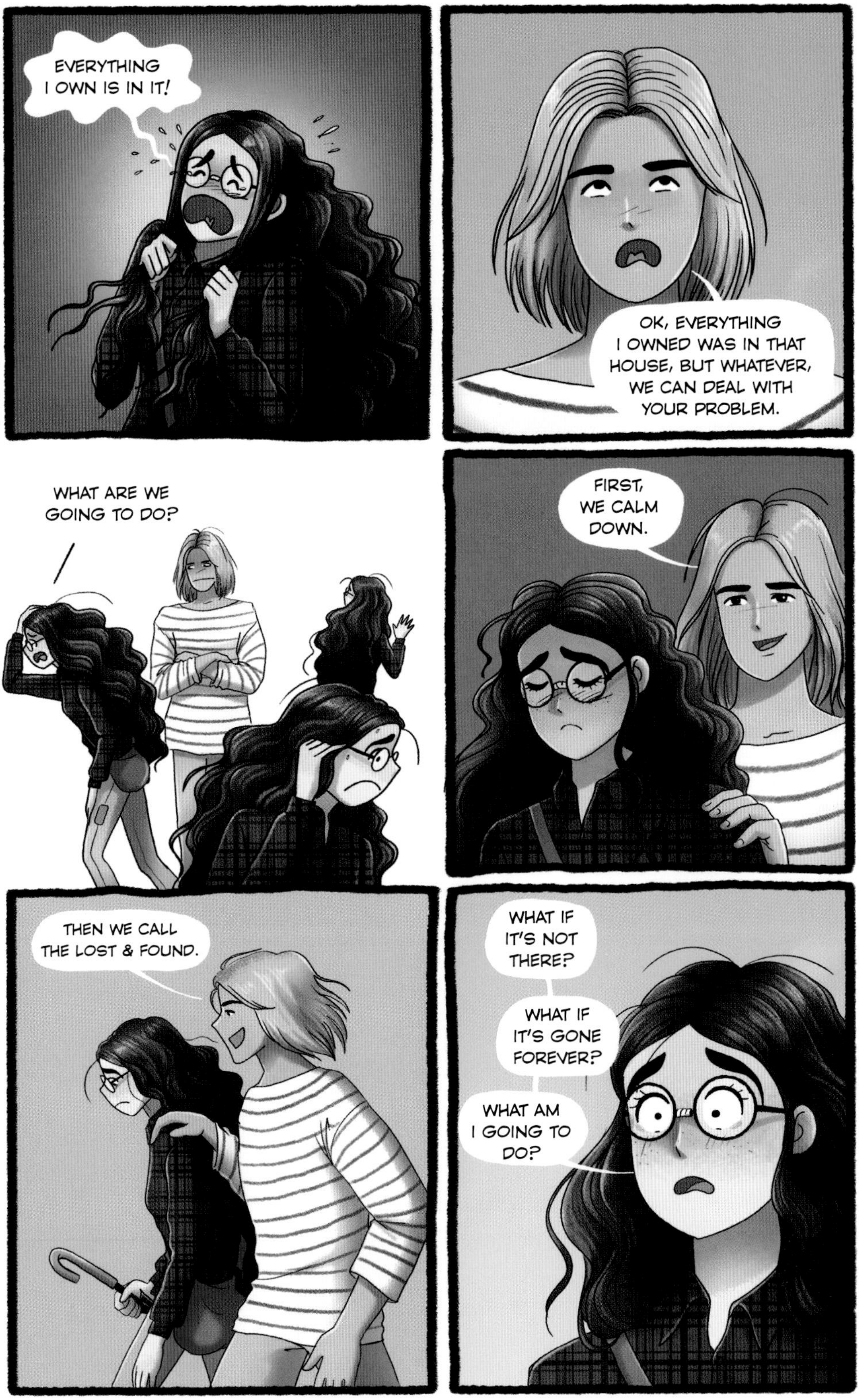
EVERYTHING I OWN IS IN IT!
OK, EVERYTHING I OWNED WAS IN THAT HOUSE, BUT WHATEVER, WE CAN DEAL WITH YOUR PROBLEM.
WHAT ARE WE GOING TO DO?
FIRST, WE CALM DOWN.
THEN WE CALL THE LOST & FOUND.
WHAT IF IT'S NOT THERE?
WHAT IF IT'S GONE FOREVER?
WHAT AM I GOING TO DO?

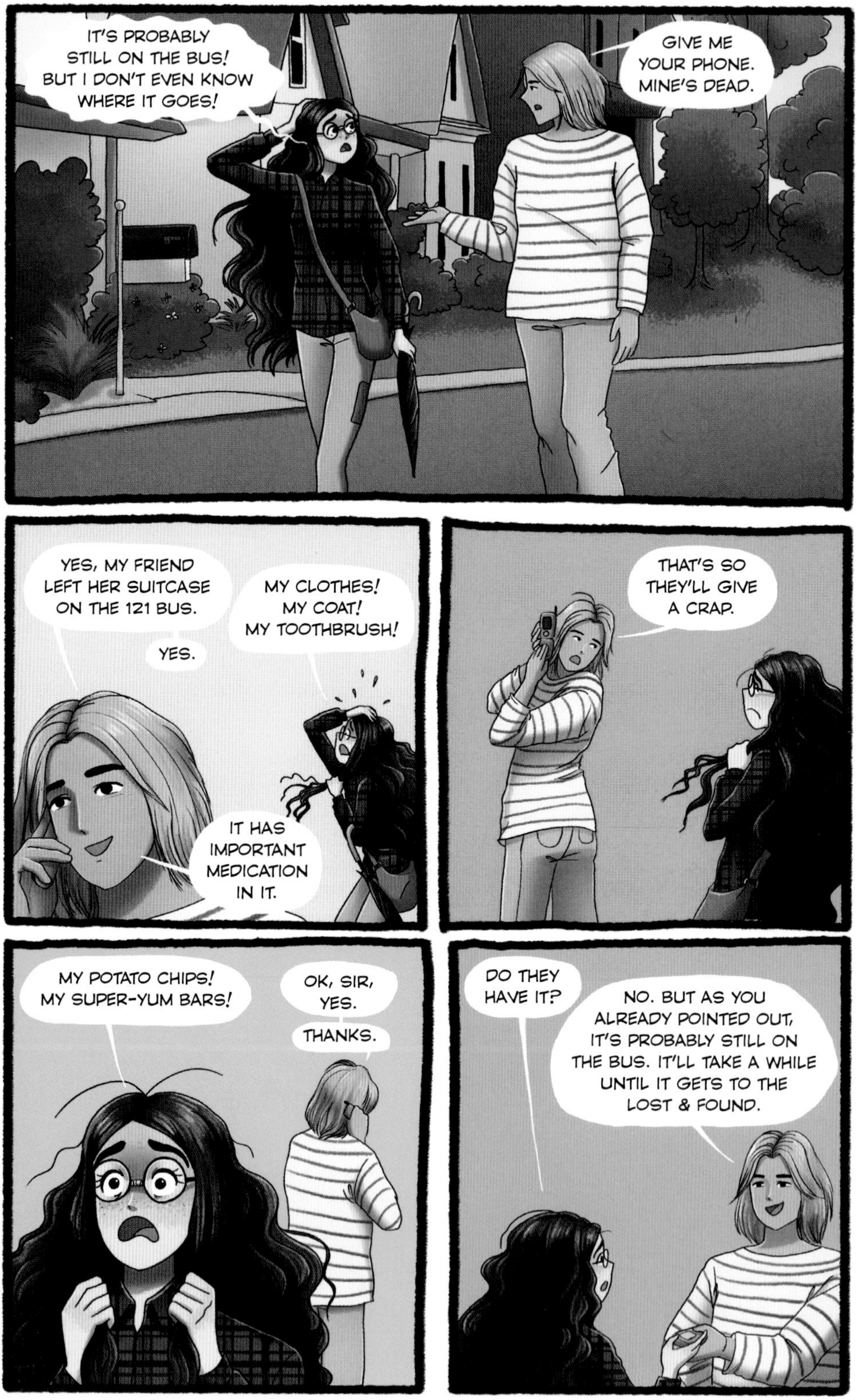
IT'S PROBABLY STILL ON THE BUS! BUT I DON'T EVEN KNOW WHERE IT GOES!
GIVE ME YOUR PHONE. MINE'S DEAD.
YES, MY FRIEND LEFT HER SUITCASE ON THE 121 BUS.
YES.
MY CLOTHES! MY COAT! MY TOOTHBRUSH!
IT HAS IMPORTANT MEDICATION IN IT.
THAT'S SO THEY'LL GIVE A CRAP.
MY POTATO CHIPS! MY SUPER-YUM BARS!
OK, SIR, YES.
THANKS.
DO THEY HAVE IT?
NO. BUT AS YOU ALREADY POINTED OUT, IT'S PROBABLY STILL ON THE BUS. IT'LL TAKE A WHILE UNTIL IT GETS TO THE LOST & FOUND.

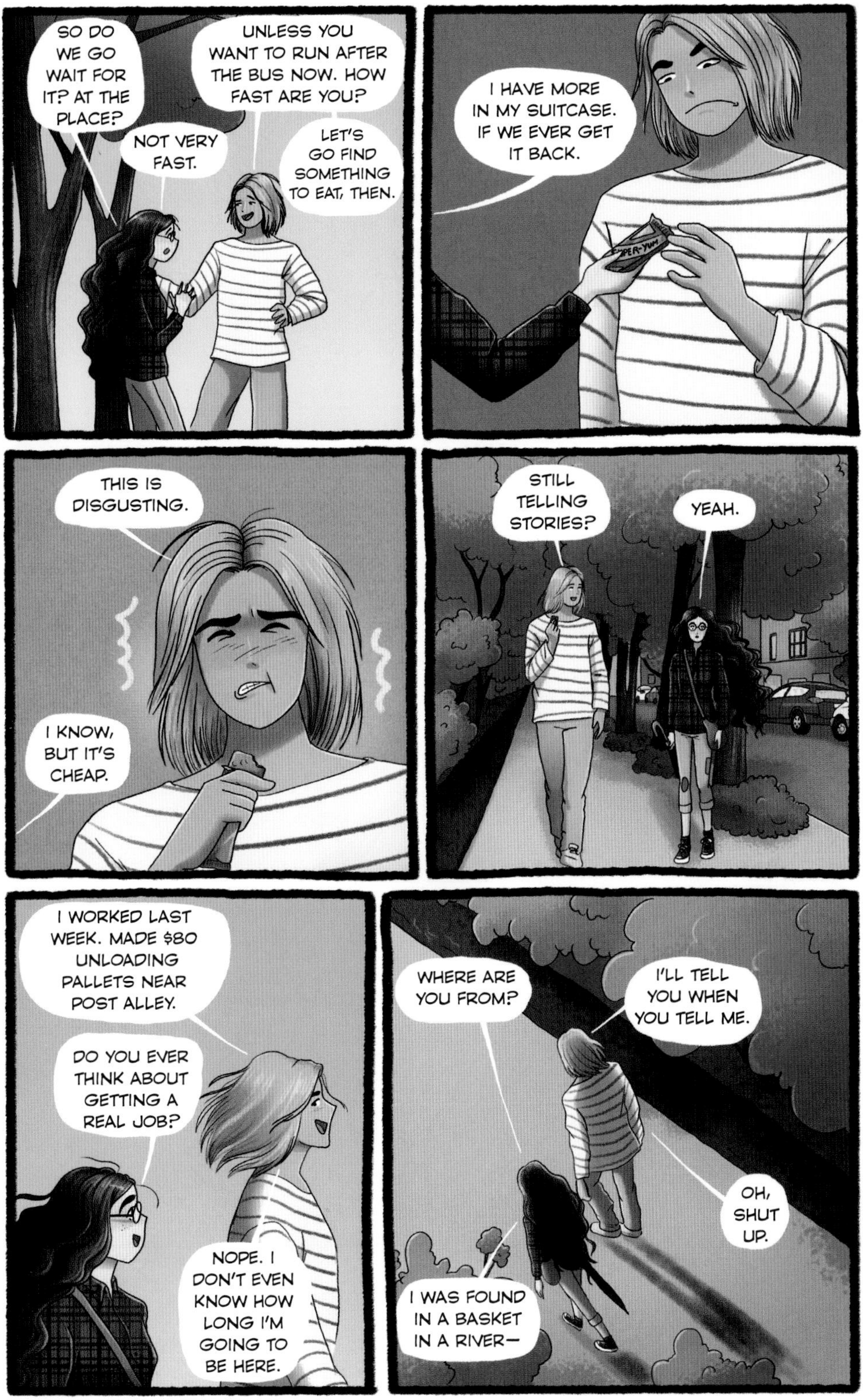
SO DO WE GO WAIT FOR IT? AT THE PLACE?
UNLESS YOU WANT TO RUN AFTER THE BUS NOW. HOW FAST ARE YOU?
NOT VERY FAST.
LET'S GO FIND SOMETHING TO EAT, THEN.
I HAVE MORE IN MY SUITCASE. IF WE EVER GET IT BACK.
THIS IS DISGUSTING.
I KNOW, BUT IT'S CHEAP.
STILL TELLING STORIES?
YEAH.
I WORKED LAST WEEK. MADE $80 UNLOADING PALLETS NEAR POST ALLEY.
DO YOU EVER THINK ABOUT GETTING A REAL JOB?
NOPE. I DON'T EVEN KNOW HOW LONG I'M GOING TO BE HERE.
WHERE ARE YOU FROM?
I'LL TELL YOU WHEN YOU TELL ME.
I WAS FOUND IN A BASKET IN A RIVER—
OH, SHUT UP.

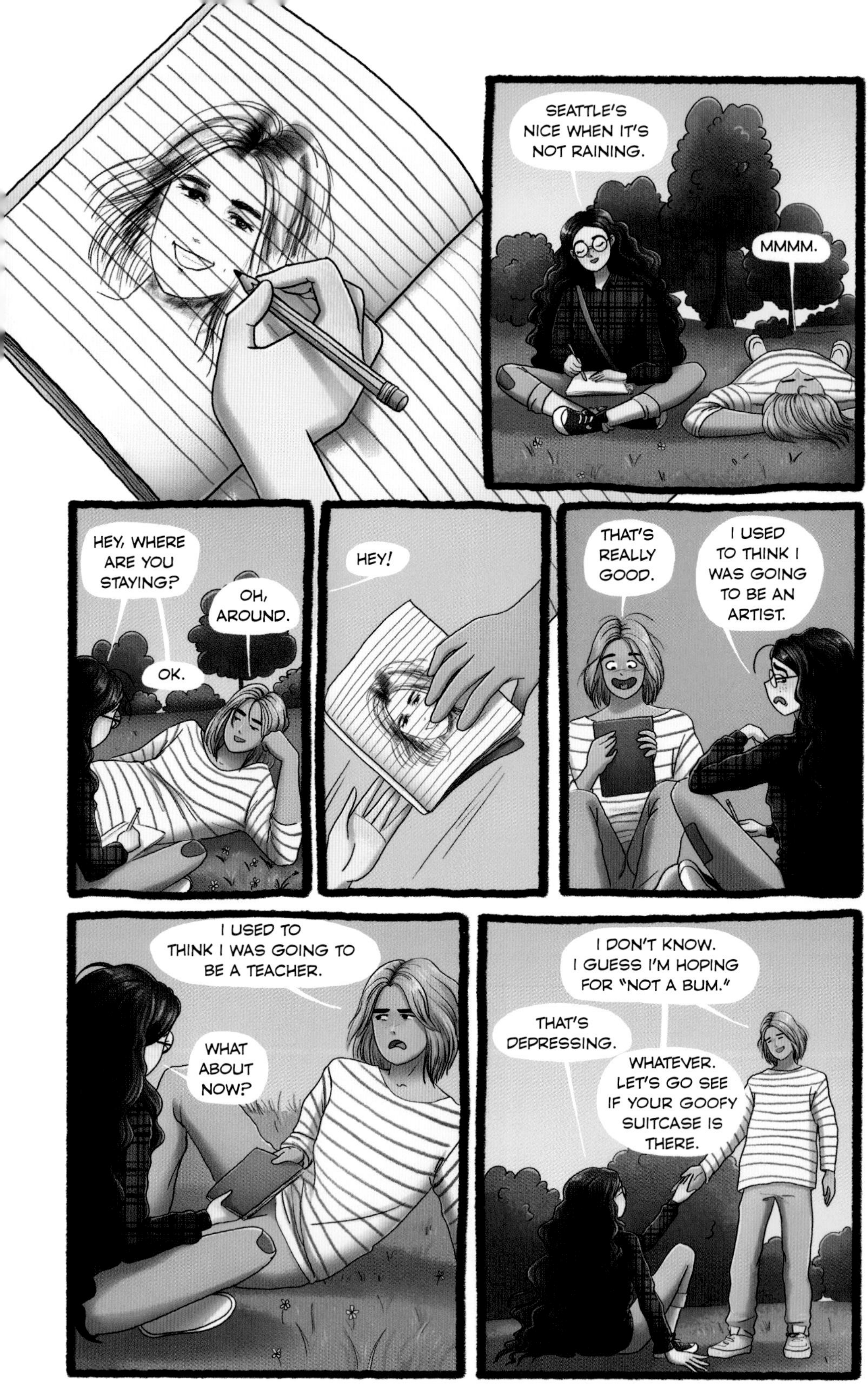
SEATTLE'S NICE WHEN IT'S NOT RAINING.
MMMM.
HEY, WHERE ARE YOU STAYING?
OH, AROUND.
OK.
HEY!
THAT'S REALLY GOOD.
I USED TO THINK I WAS GOING TO BE AN ARTIST.
I USED TO THINK I WAS GOING TO BE A TEACHER.
WHAT ABOUT NOW?
I DON'T KNOW. I GUESS I'M HOPING FOR "NOT A BUM."
THAT'S DEPRESSING.
WHATEVER. LET'S GO SEE IF YOUR GOOFY SUITCASE IS THERE.

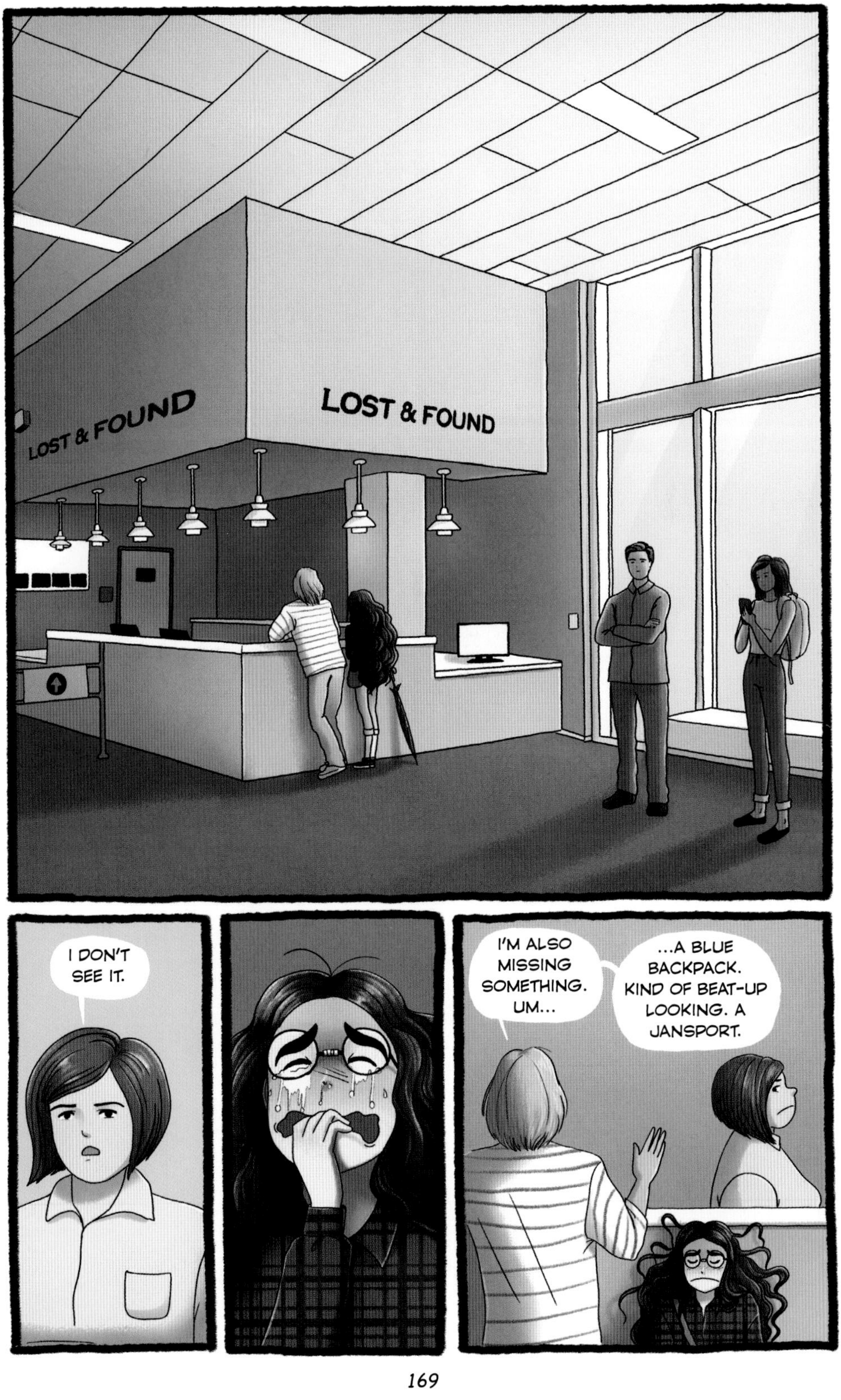
LOST & FOUND
LOST & FOUND
I DON'T SEE IT.
I'M ALSO MISSING SOMETHING. UM...
...A BLUE BACKPACK. KIND OF BEAT-UP LOOKING. A JANSPORT.

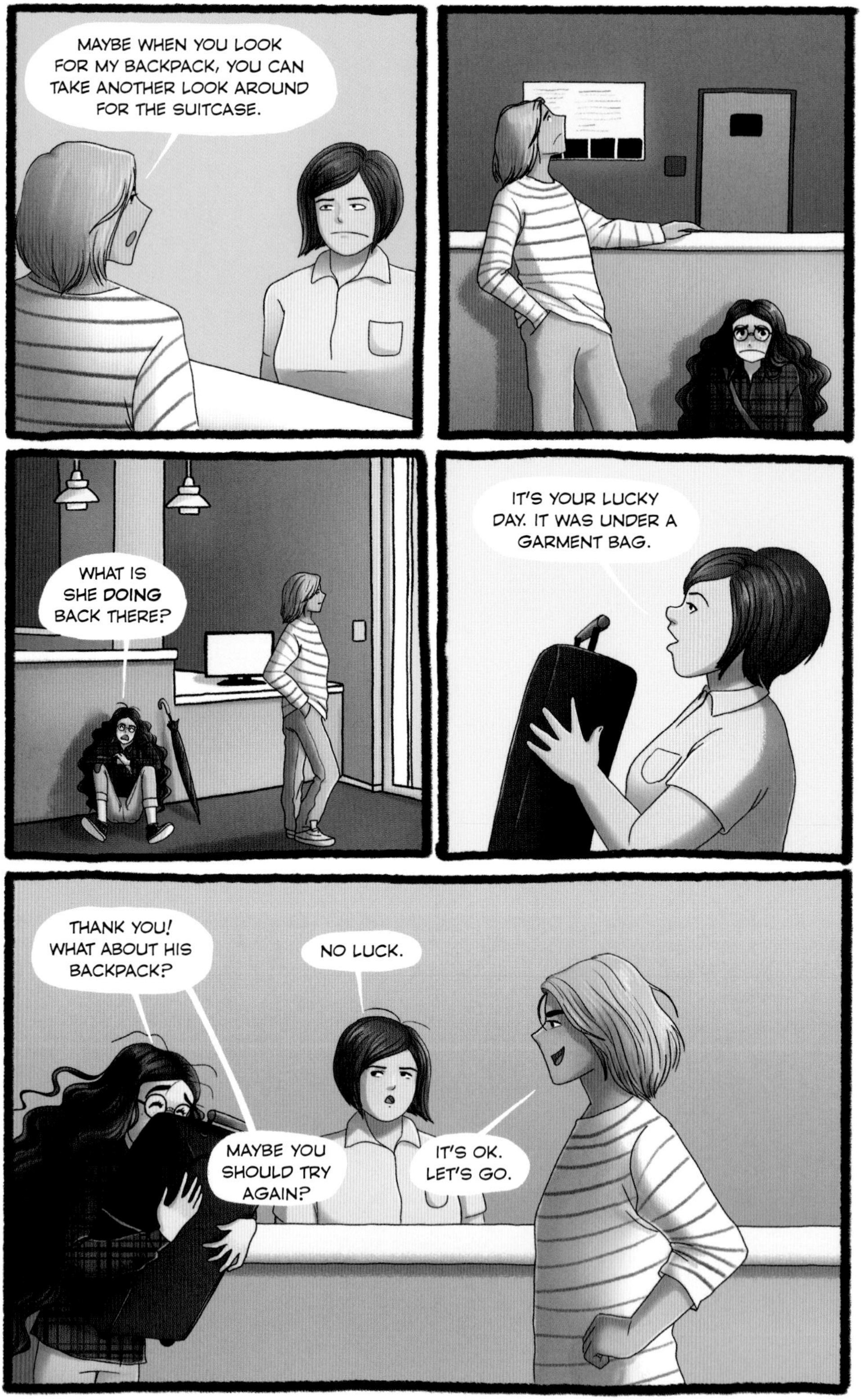
MAYBE WHEN YOU LOOK FOR MY BACKPACK, YOU CAN TAKE ANOTHER LOOK AROUND FOR THE SUITCASE.
WHAT IS SHE DOING BACK THERE?
IT'S YOUR LUCKY DAY. IT WAS UNDER A GARMENT BAG.
THANK YOU! WHAT ABOUT HIS BACKPACK?
NO LUCK.
MAYBE YOU SHOULD TRY AGAIN?
IT'S OK. LET'S GO.

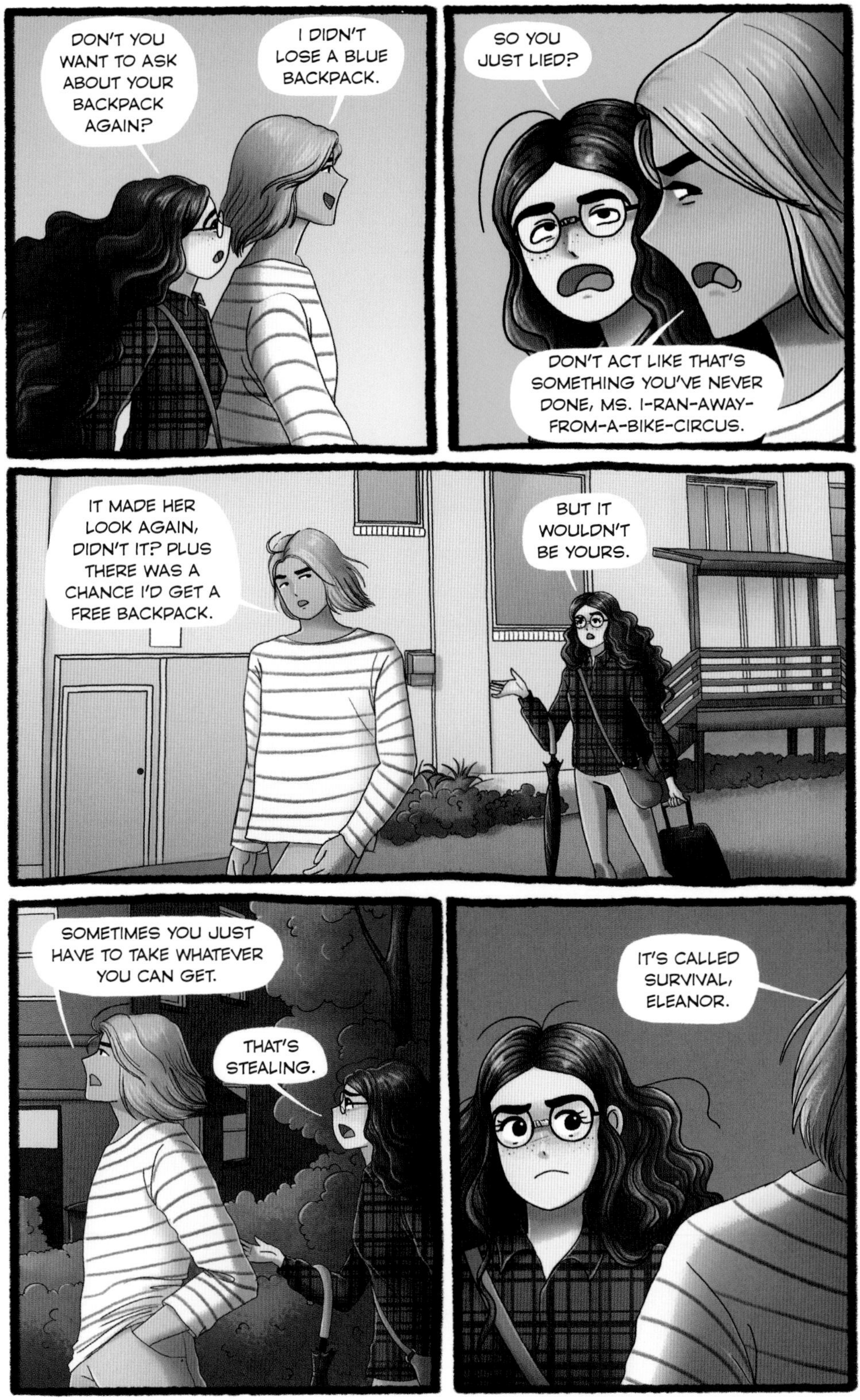
DON'T YOU WANT TO ASK ABOUT YOUR BACKPACK AGAIN?
I DIDN'T LOSE A BLUE BACKPACK.
SO YOU JUST LIED?
DON'T ACT LIKE THAT'S SOMETHING YOU'VE NEVER DONE, MS. I-RAN-AWAY-FROM-A-BIKE-CIRCUS.
IT MADE HER LOOK AGAIN, DIDN'T IT? PLUS THERE WAS A CHANCE I'D GET A FREE BACKPACK.
BUT IT WOULDN'T BE YOURS.
SOMETIMES YOU JUST HAVE TO TAKE WHATEVER YOU CAN GET.
THAT'S STEALING.
IT'S CALLED SURVIVAL, ELEANOR.

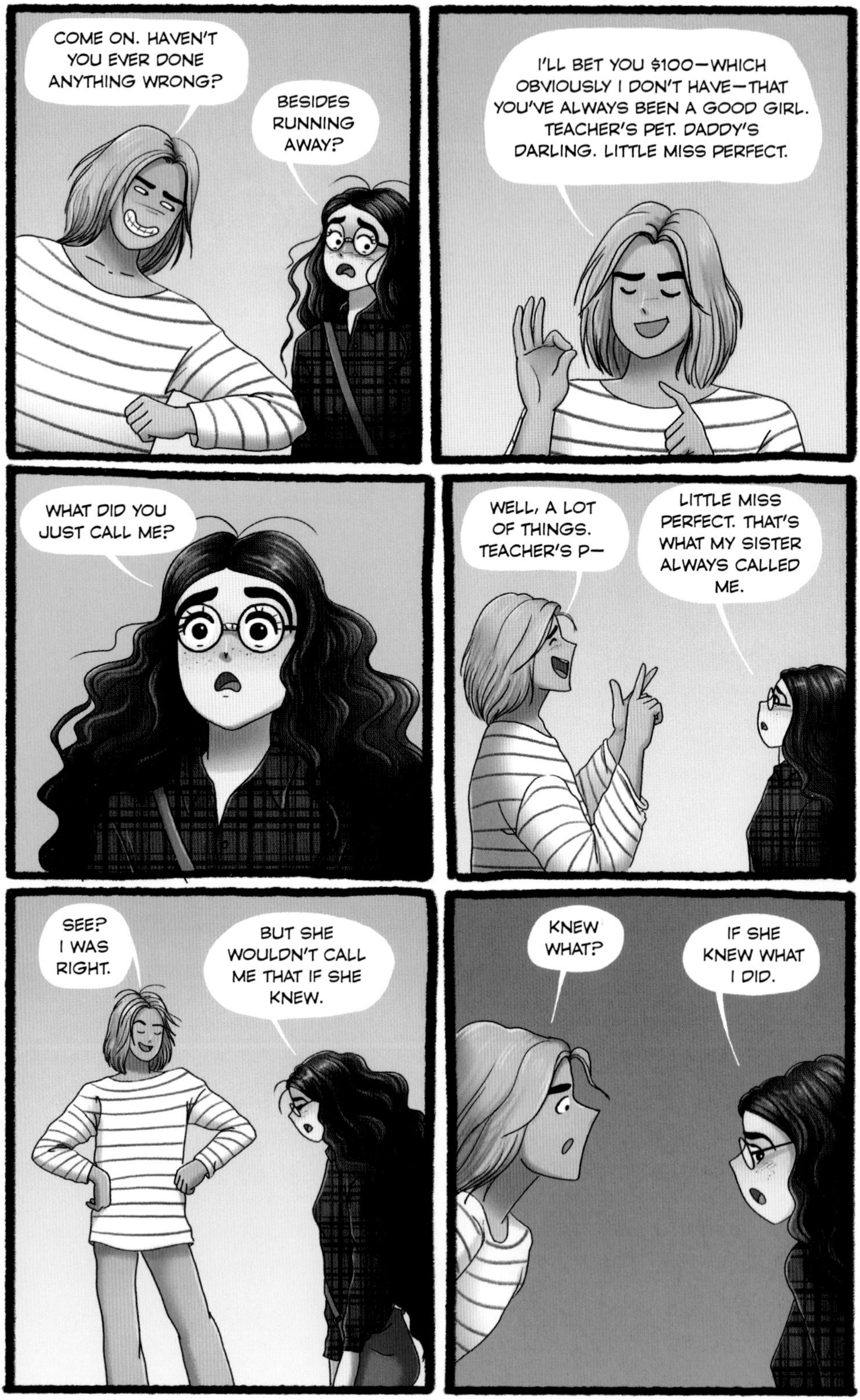
COME ON. HAVEN'T YOU EVER DONE ANYTHING WRONG?
BESIDES RUNNING AWAY?
I'LL BET YOU $100—WHICH OBVIOUSLY I DON'T HAVE—THAT YOU'VE ALWAYS BEEN A GOOD GIRL. TEACHER'S PET. DADDY'S DARLING. LITTLE MISS PERFECT.
WHAT DID YOU JUST CALL ME?
WELL, A LOT OF THINGS. TEACHER'S P—
LITTLE MISS PERFECT. THAT'S WHAT MY SISTER ALWAYS CALLED ME.
SEE? I WAS RIGHT.
BUT SHE WOULDN'T CALL ME THAT IF SHE KNEW.
KNEW WHAT?
IF SHE KNEW WHAT I DID.

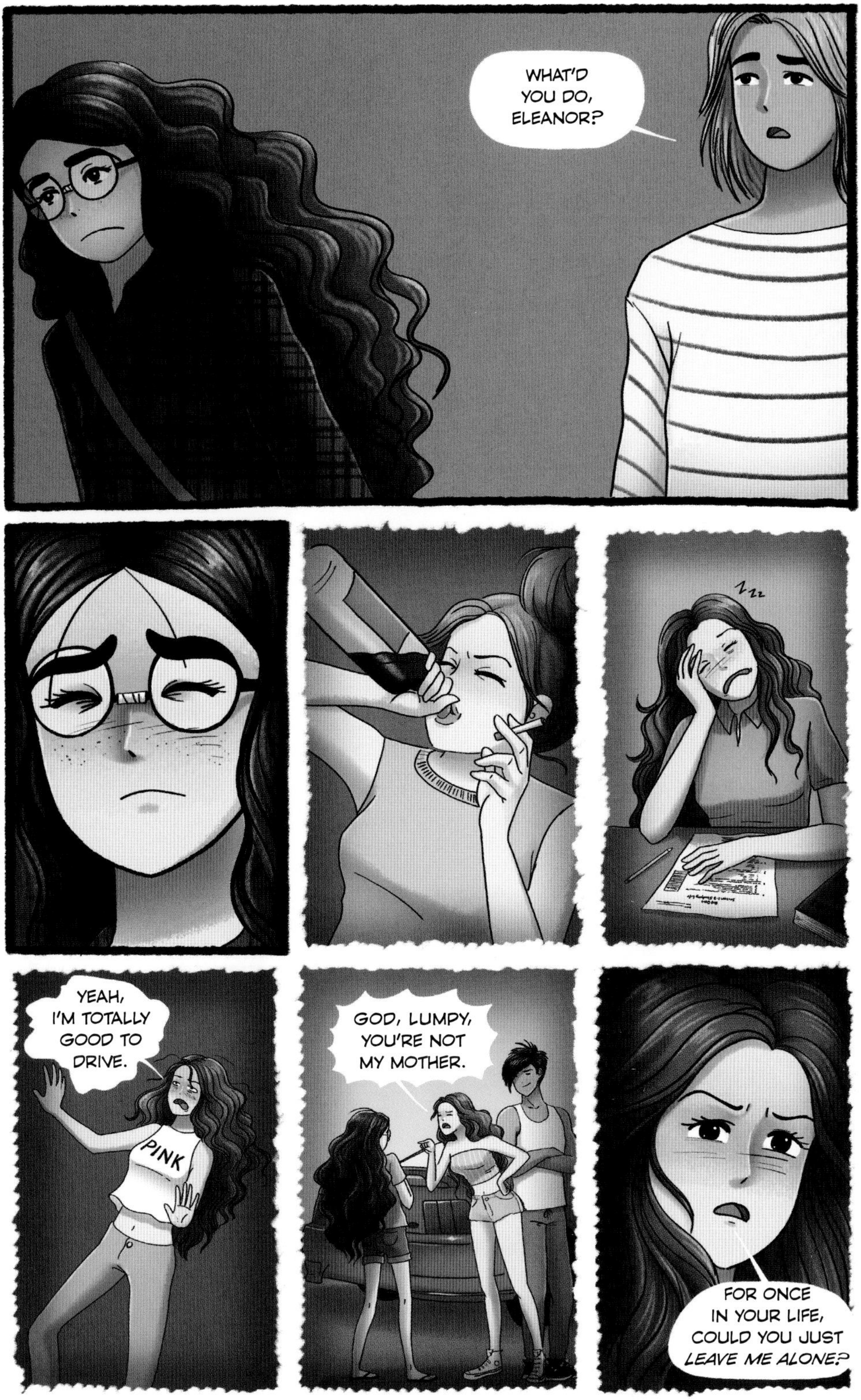
WHAT'D YOU DO, ELEANOR?
ZZZ
YEAH, I'M TOTALLY GOOD TO DRIVE.
PINK
GOD, LUMPY, YOU'RE NOT MY MOTHER.
FOR ONCE IN YOUR LIFE, COULD YOU JUST *LEAVE ME ALONE?*

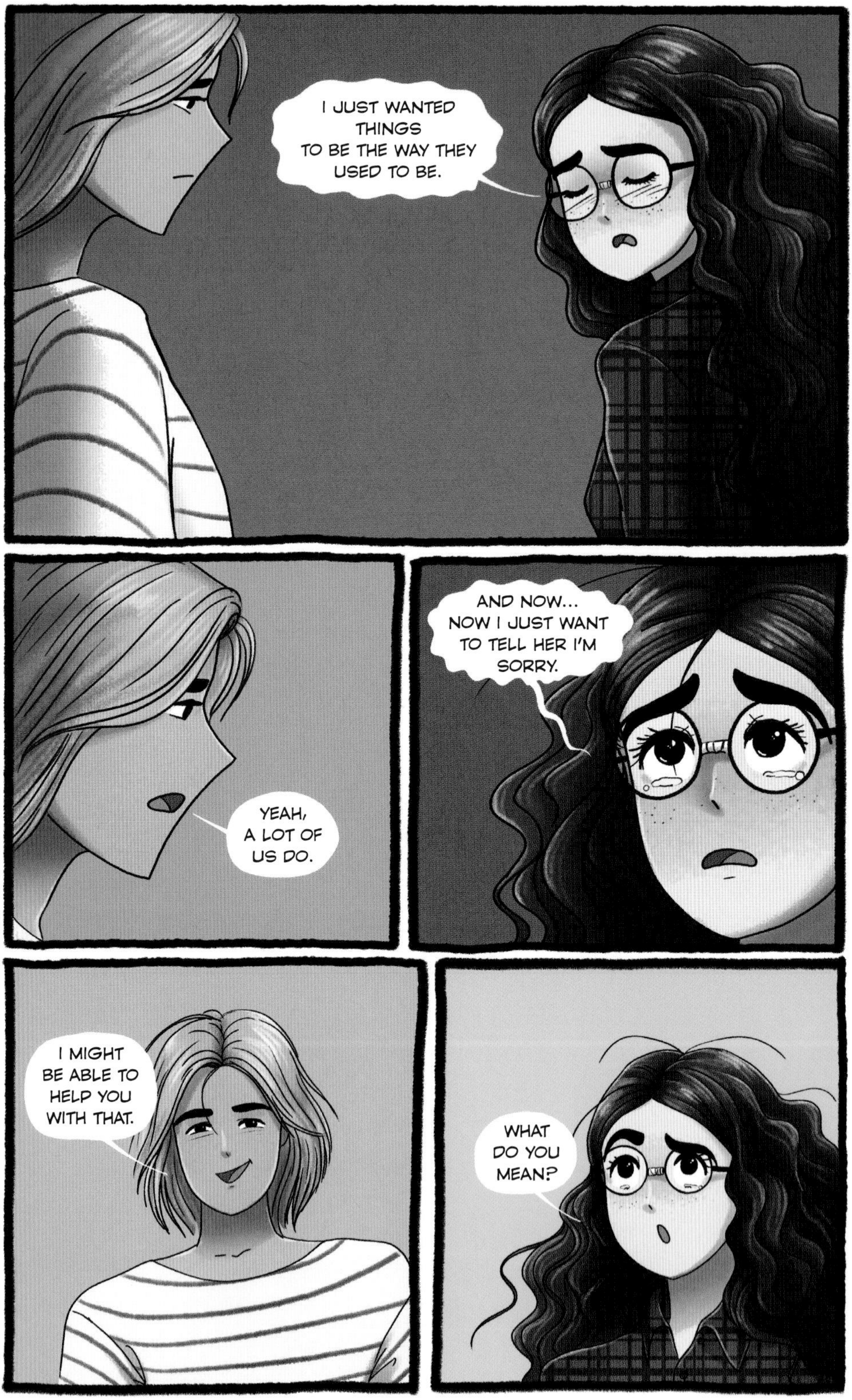
I JUST WANTED THINGS TO BE THE WAY THEY USED TO BE.
YEAH, A LOT OF US DO.
AND NOW... NOW I JUST WANT TO TELL HER I'M SORRY.
I MIGHT BE ABLE TO HELP YOU WITH THAT.
WHAT DO YOU MEAN?

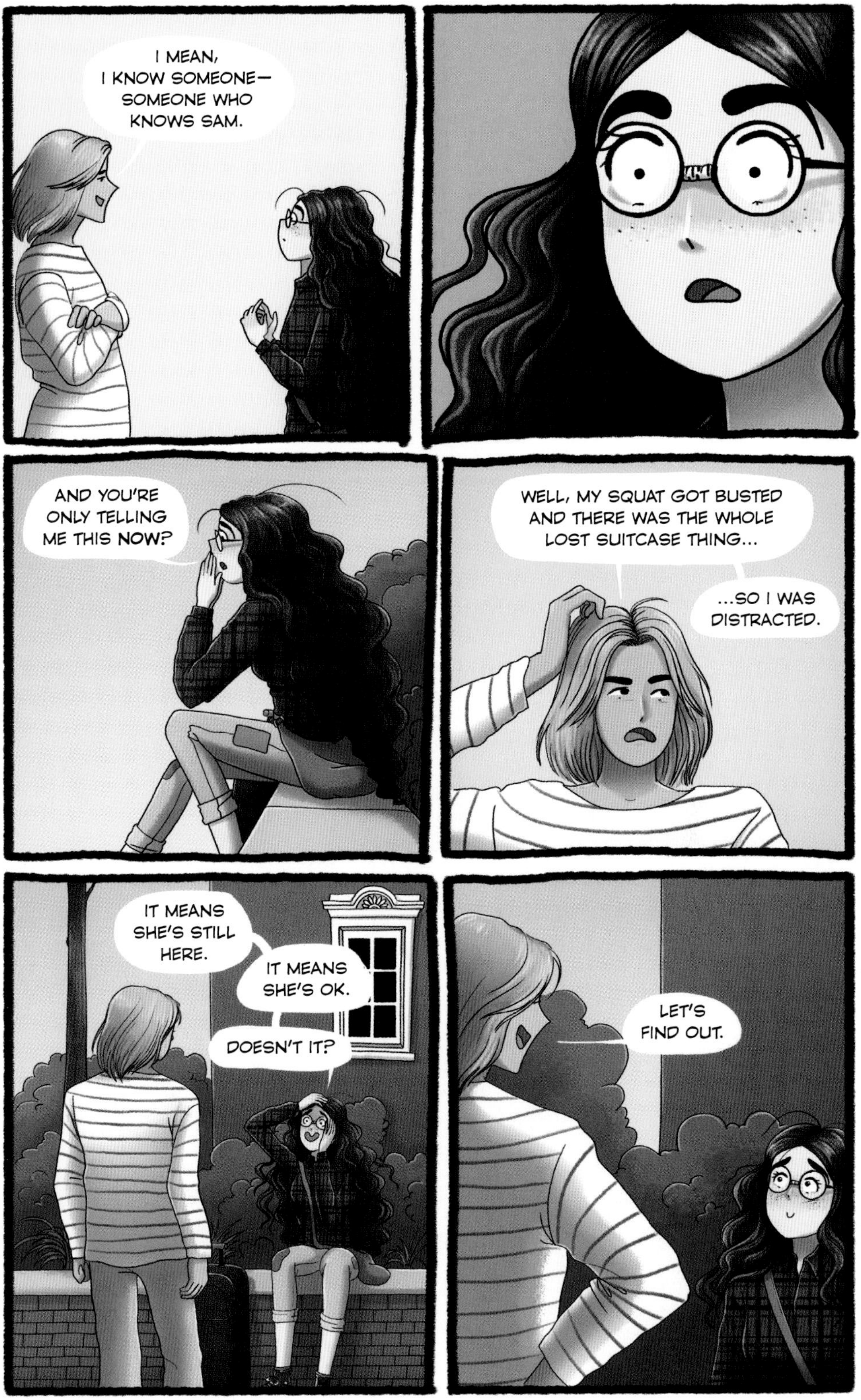
I MEAN,
I KNOW SOMEONE—
SOMEONE WHO
KNOWS SAM.
AND YOU'RE
ONLY TELLING
ME THIS **NOW**?
WELL, MY SQUAT GOT BUSTED
AND THERE WAS THE WHOLE
LOST SUITCASE THING...
...SO I WAS
DISTRACTED.
IT MEANS
SHE'S STILL
HERE.
IT MEANS
SHE'S OK.
DOESN'T IT?
LET'S
FIND OUT.

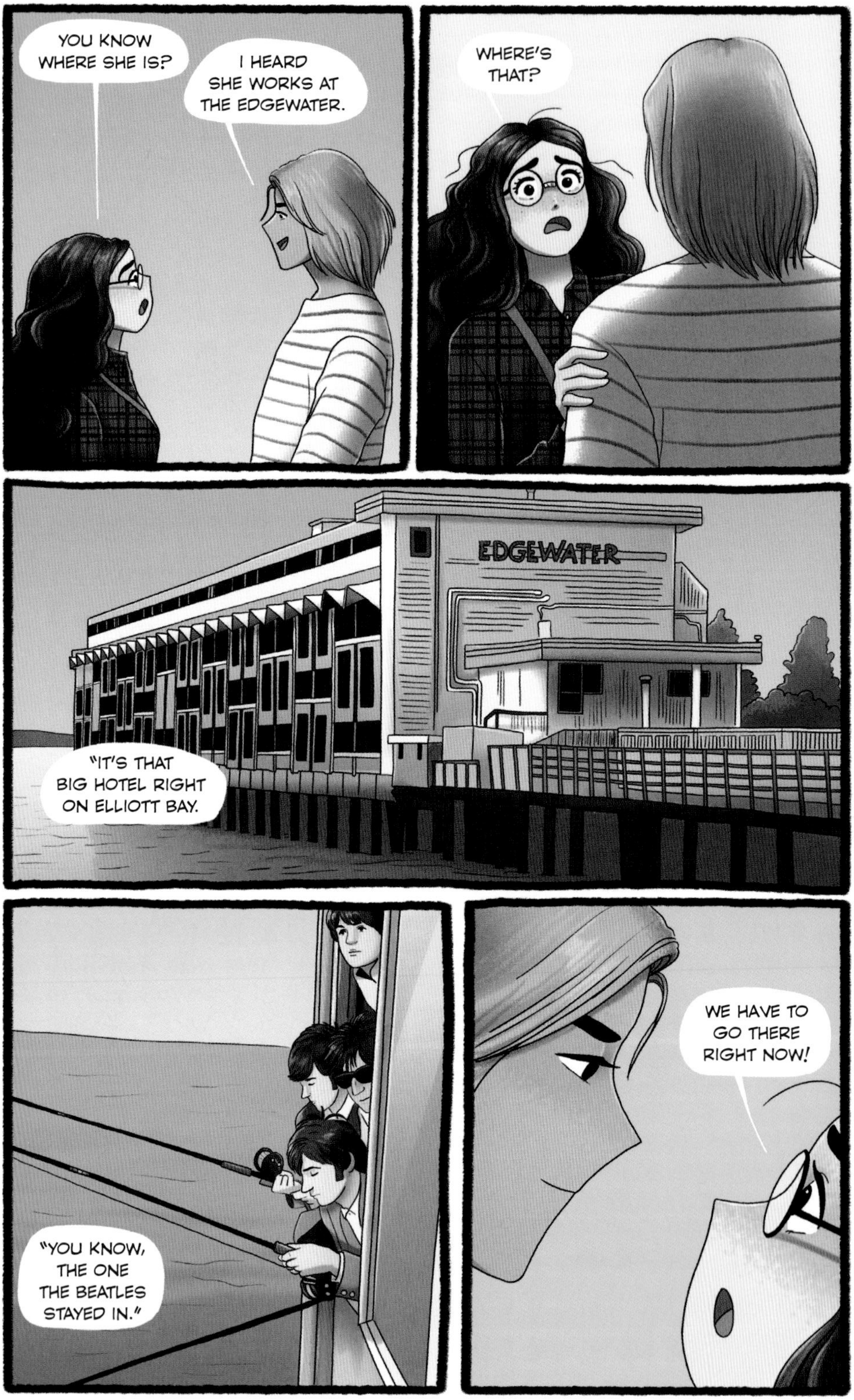
YOU KNOW WHERE SHE IS?
I HEARD SHE WORKS AT THE EDGEWATER.
WHERE'S THAT?
EDGEWATER
"IT'S THAT BIG HOTEL RIGHT ON ELLIOTT BAY.
"YOU KNOW, THE ONE THE BEATLES STAYED IN."
WE HAVE TO GO THERE RIGHT NOW!

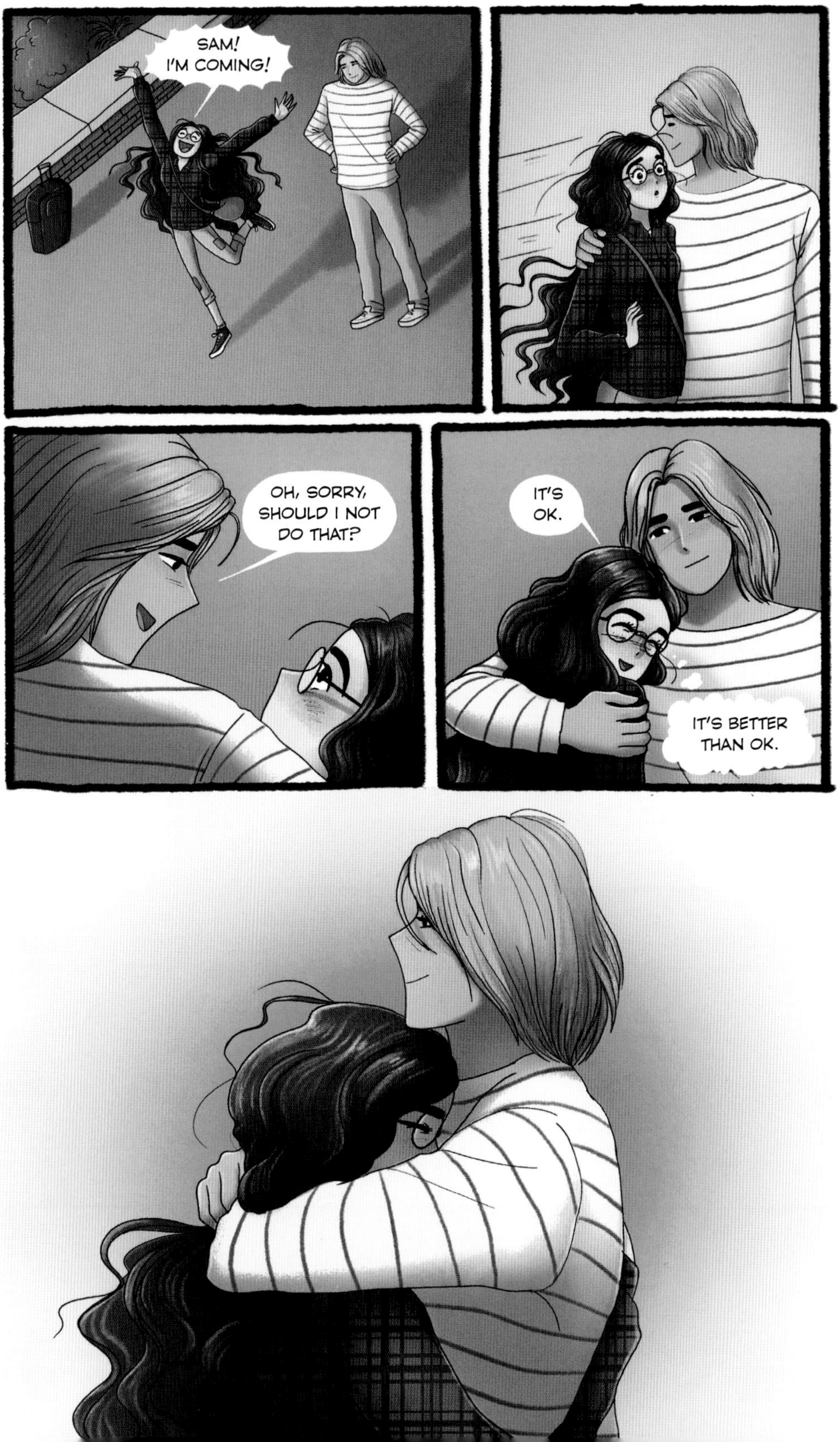
SAM!
I'M COMING!
OH, SORRY, SHOULD I NOT DO THAT?
IT'S OK.
IT'S BETTER THAN OK.

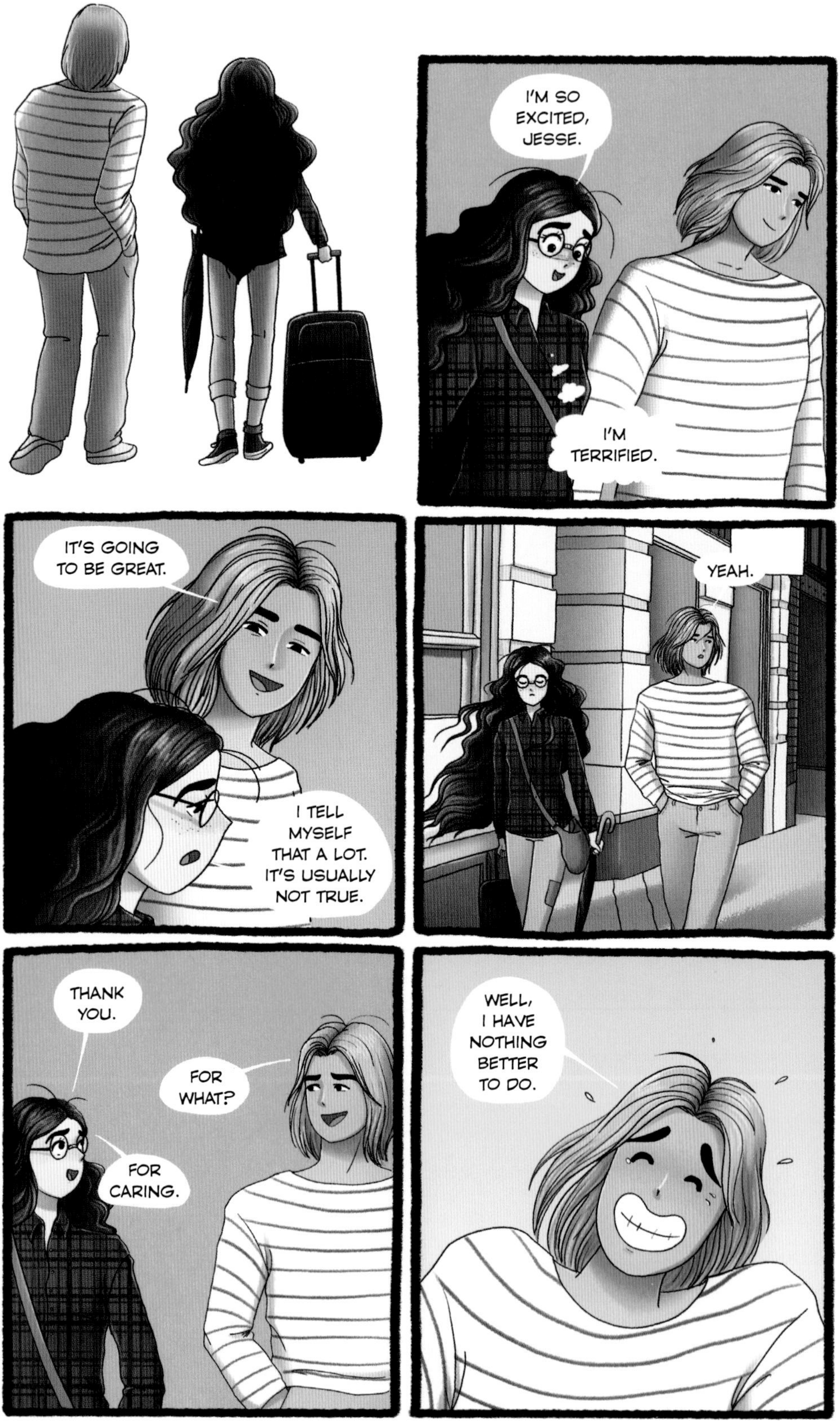
I'M SO EXCITED, JESSE.
I'M TERRIFIED.
IT'S GOING TO BE GREAT.
I TELL MYSELF THAT A LOT. IT'S USUALLY NOT TRUE.
YEAH.
THANK YOU.
FOR WHAT?
FOR CARING.
WELL, I HAVE NOTHING BETTER TO DO.

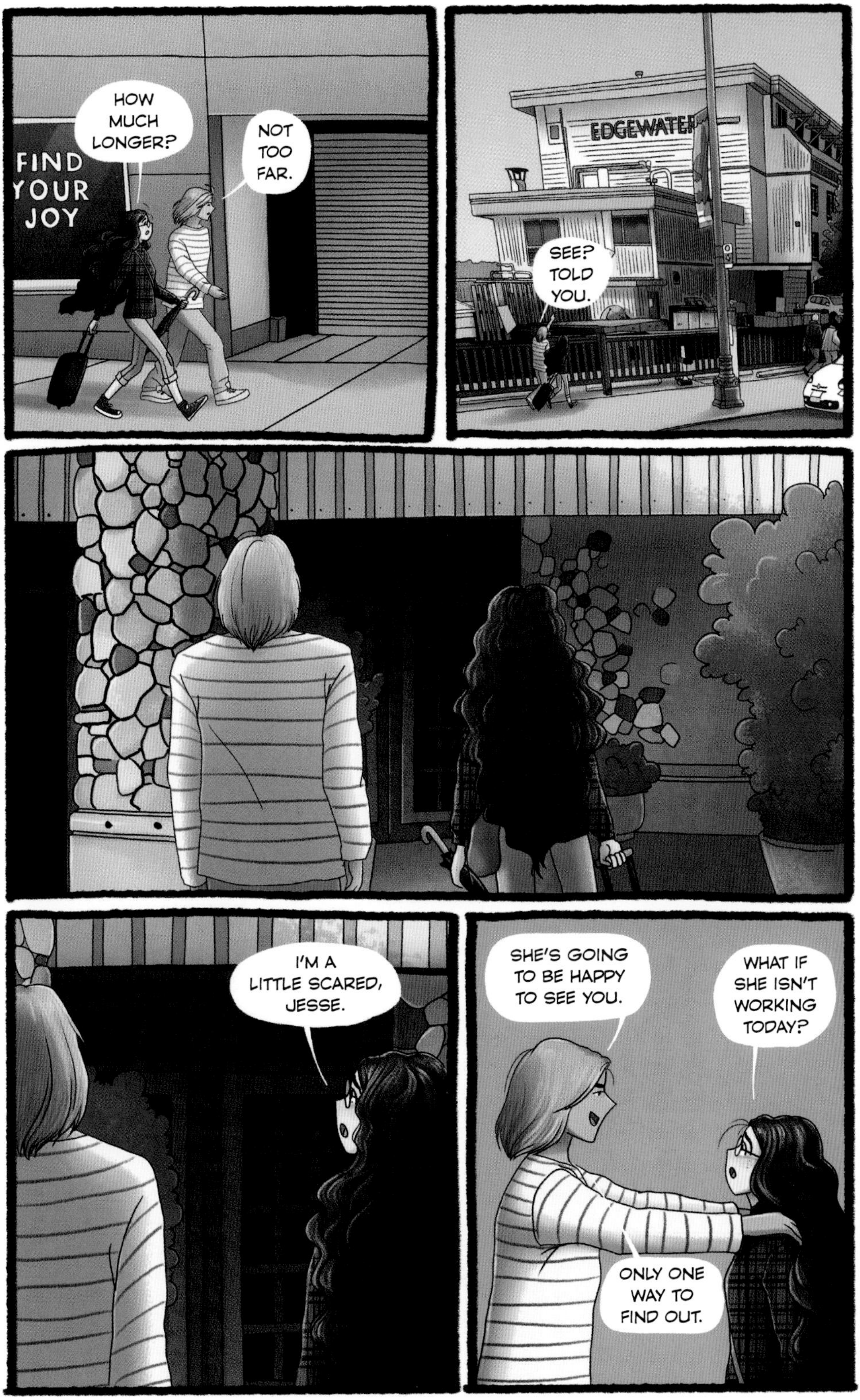
FIND YOUR JOY
HOW MUCH LONGER?
NOT TOO FAR.
EDGEWATER
SEE? TOLD YOU.
I'M A LITTLE SCARED, JESSE.
SHE'S GOING TO BE HAPPY TO SEE YOU.
WHAT IF SHE ISN'T WORKING TODAY?
ONLY ONE WAY TO FIND OUT.

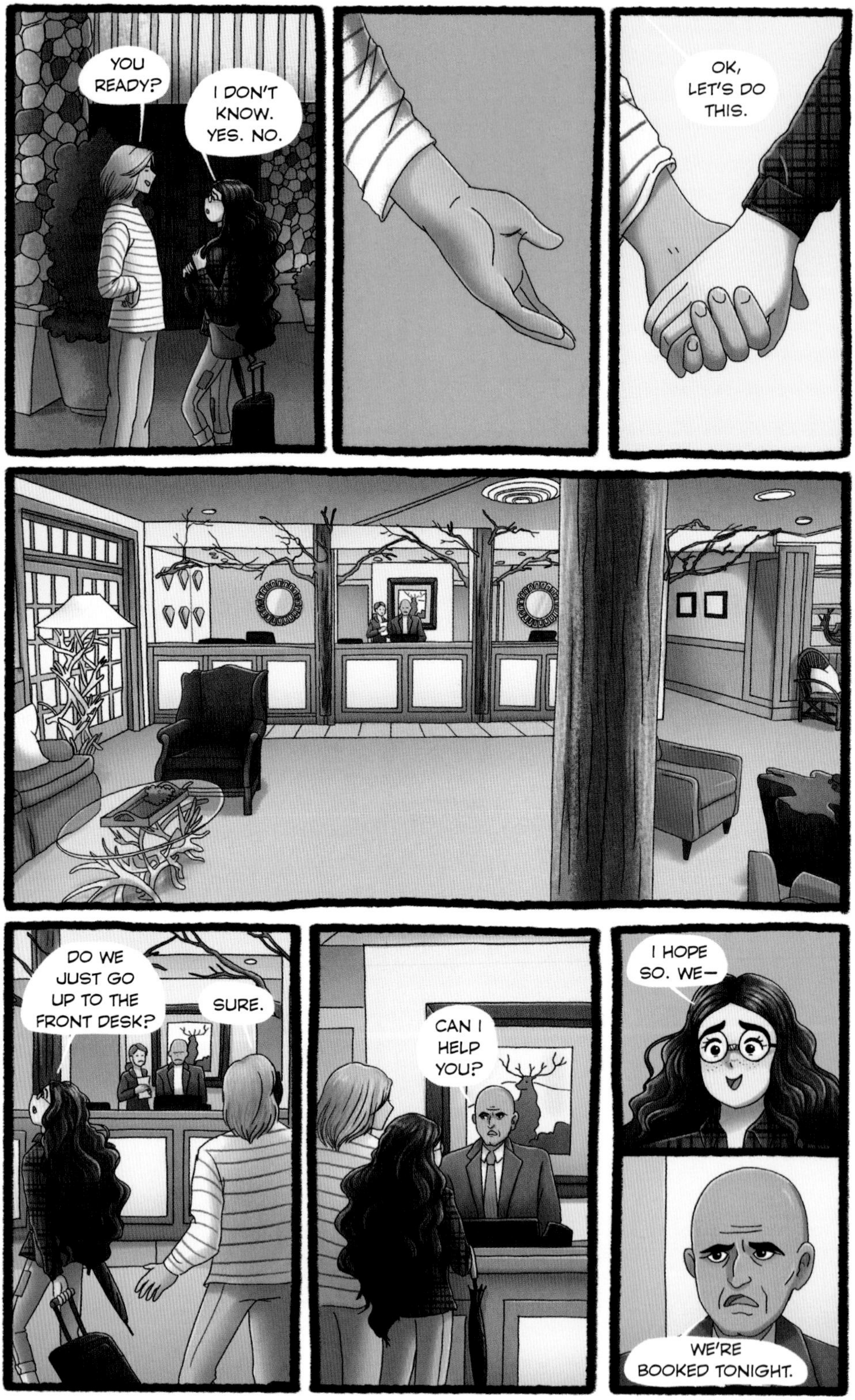
YOU READY?
I DON'T KNOW. YES. NO.
OK, LET'S DO THIS.
DO WE JUST GO UP TO THE FRONT DESK?
SURE.
CAN I HELP YOU?
I HOPE SO. WE—
WE'RE BOOKED TONIGHT.

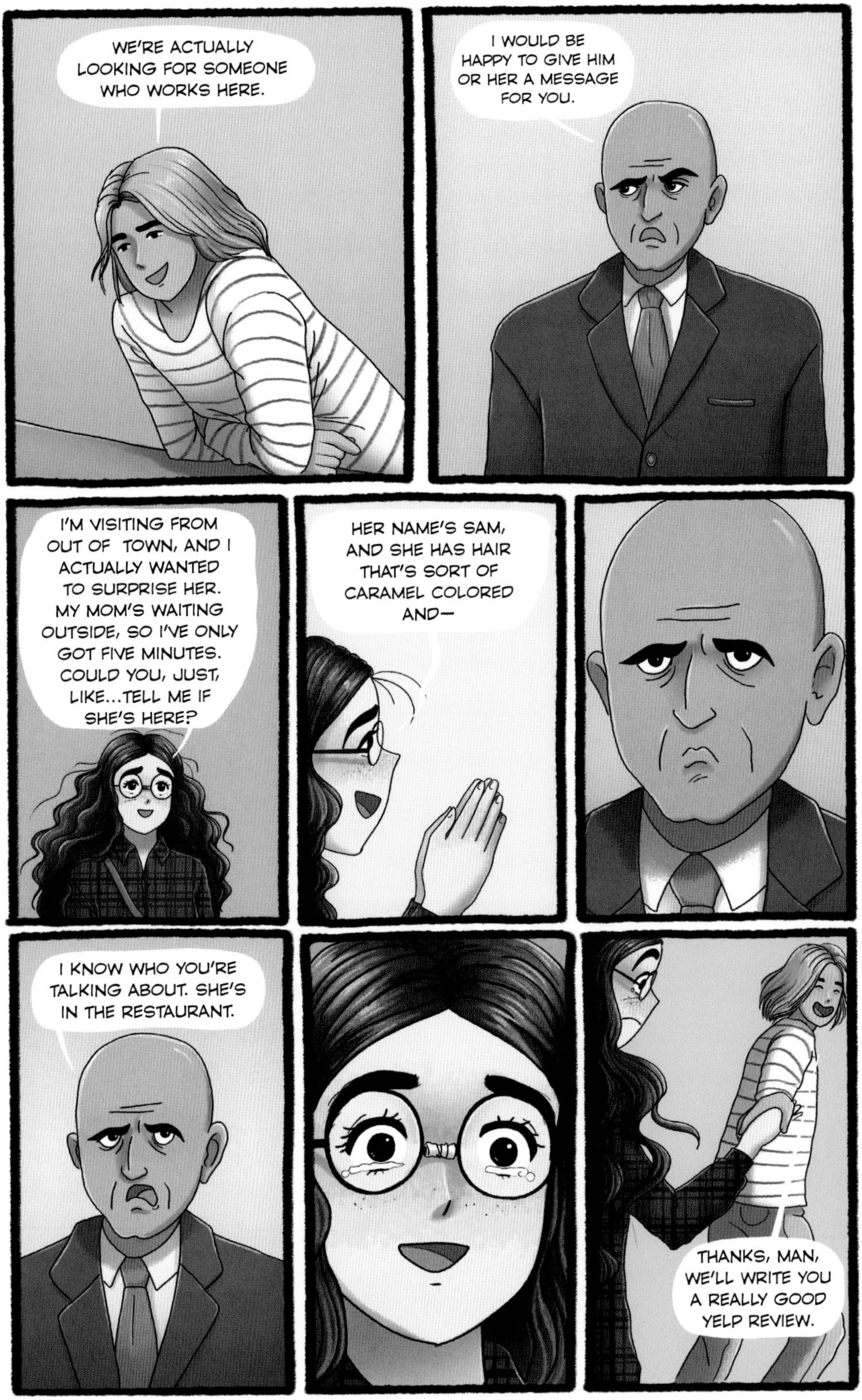
WE'RE ACTUALLY LOOKING FOR SOMEONE WHO WORKS HERE.
I WOULD BE HAPPY TO GIVE HIM OR HER A MESSAGE FOR YOU.
I'M VISITING FROM OUT OF TOWN, AND I ACTUALLY WANTED TO SURPRISE HER. MY MOM'S WAITING OUTSIDE, SO I'VE ONLY GOT FIVE MINUTES. COULD YOU, JUST, LIKE...TELL ME IF SHE'S HERE?
HER NAME'S SAM, AND SHE HAS HAIR THAT'S SORT OF CARAMEL COLORED AND—
I KNOW WHO YOU'RE TALKING ABOUT. SHE'S IN THE RESTAURANT.
THANKS, MAN, WE'LL WRITE YOU A REALLY GOOD YELP REVIEW.

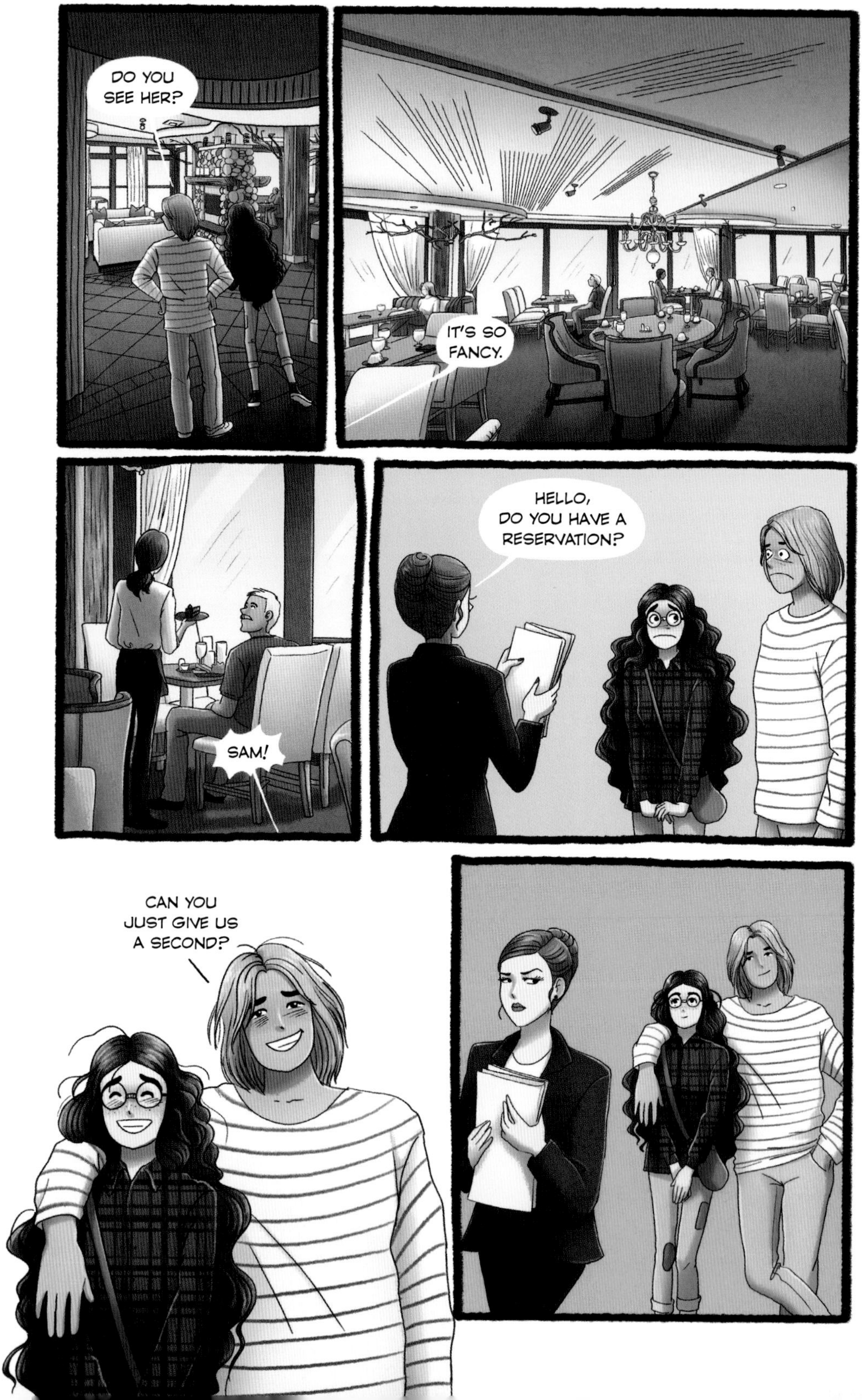
DO YOU SEE HER?
IT'S SO FANCY.
SAM!
HELLO, DO YOU HAVE A RESERVATION?
CAN YOU JUST GIVE US A SECOND?

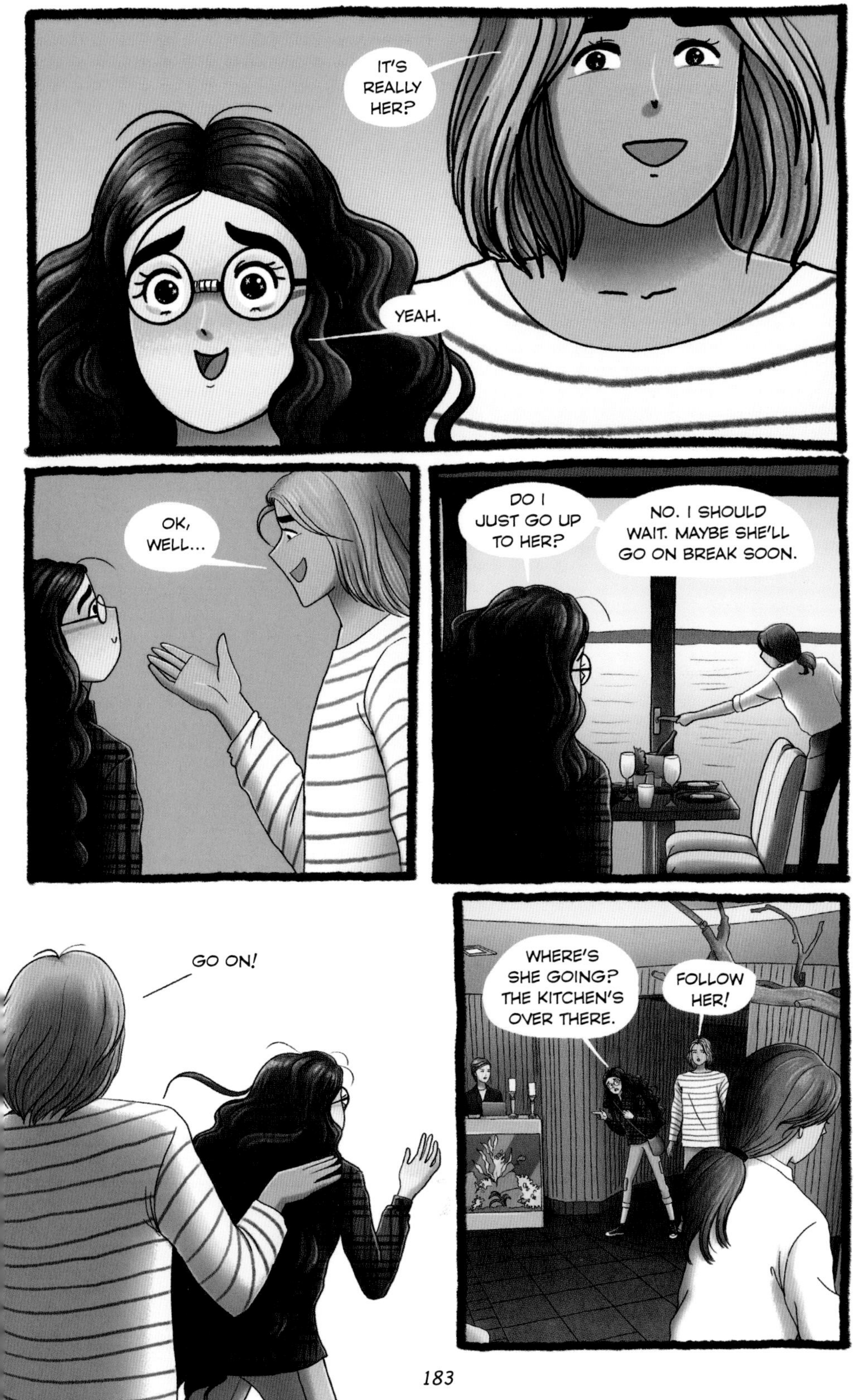
IT'S REALLY HER?
YEAH.
OK, WELL...
DO I JUST GO UP TO HER?
NO. I SHOULD WAIT. MAYBE SHE'LL GO ON BREAK SOON.
GO ON!
WHERE'S SHE GOING? THE KITCHEN'S OVER THERE.
FOLLOW HER!

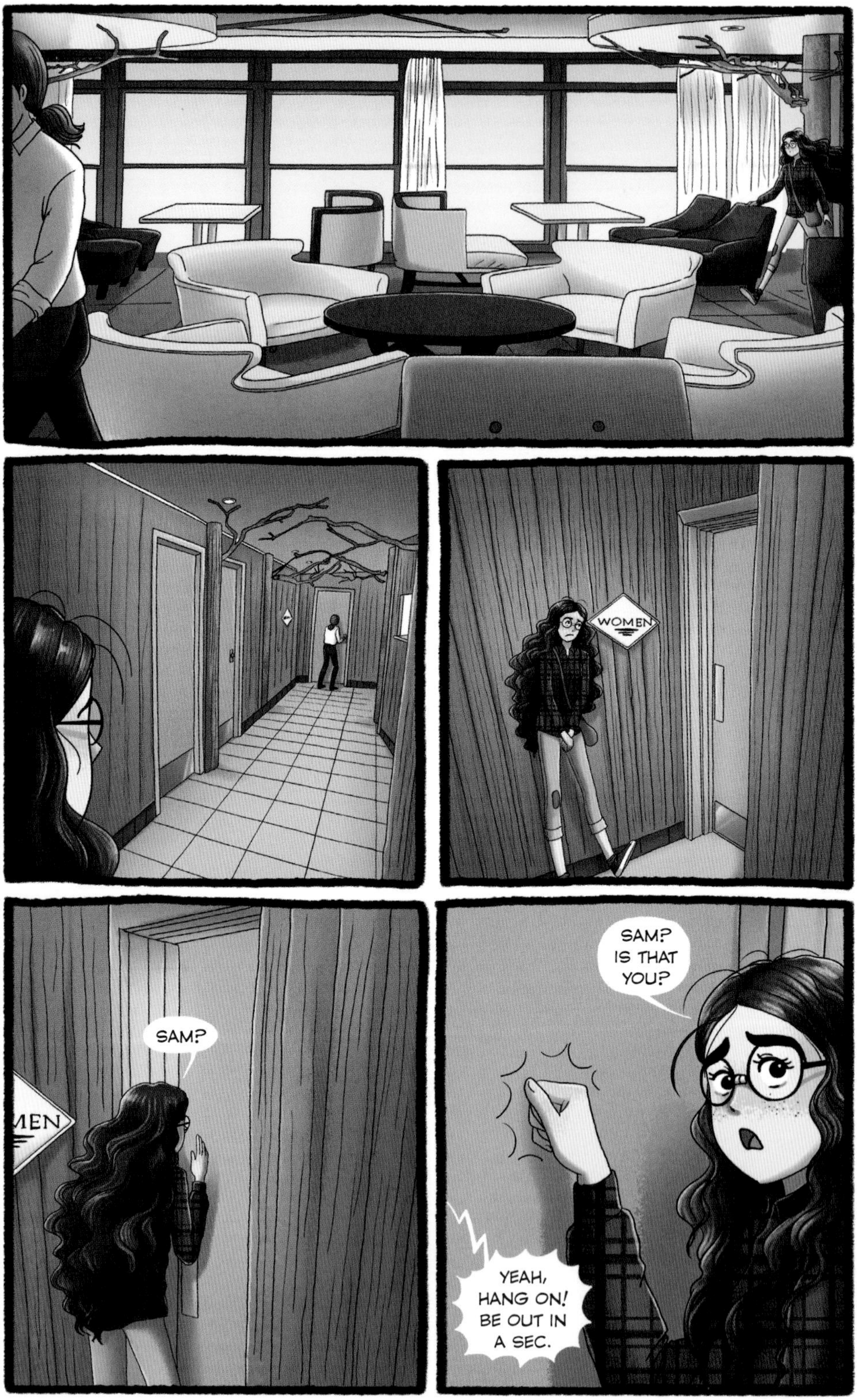
WOMEN
SAM?
SAM? IS THAT YOU?
YEAH, HANG ON! BE OUT IN A SEC.

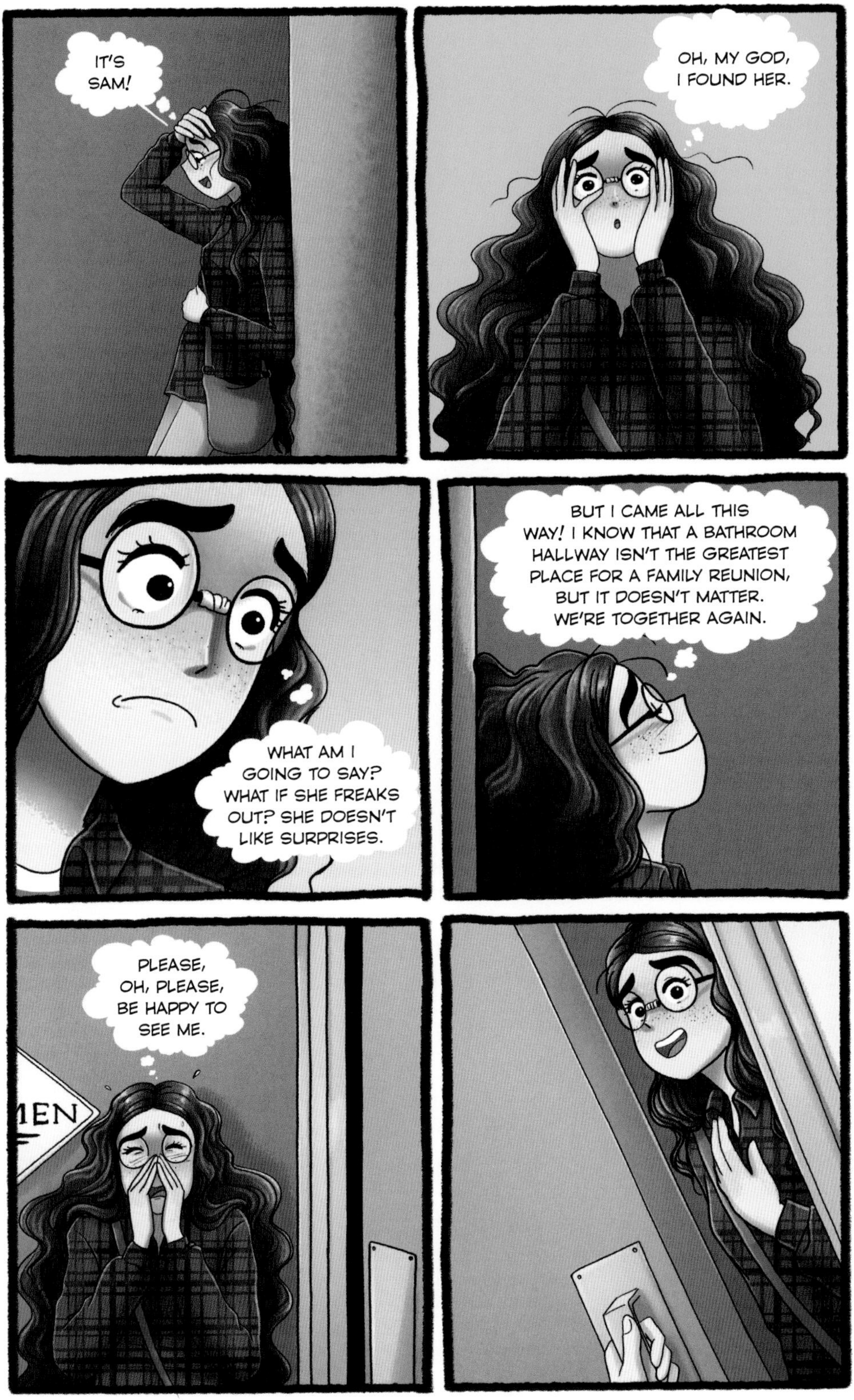
IT'S SAM!
OH, MY GOD, I FOUND HER.
WHAT AM I GOING TO SAY? WHAT IF SHE FREAKS OUT? SHE DOESN'T LIKE SURPRISES.
BUT I CAME ALL THIS WAY! I KNOW THAT A BATHROOM HALLWAY ISN'T THE GREATEST PLACE FOR A FAMILY REUNION, BUT IT DOESN'T MATTER. WE'RE TOGETHER AGAIN.
PLEASE, OH, PLEASE, BE HAPPY TO SEE ME.
MEN

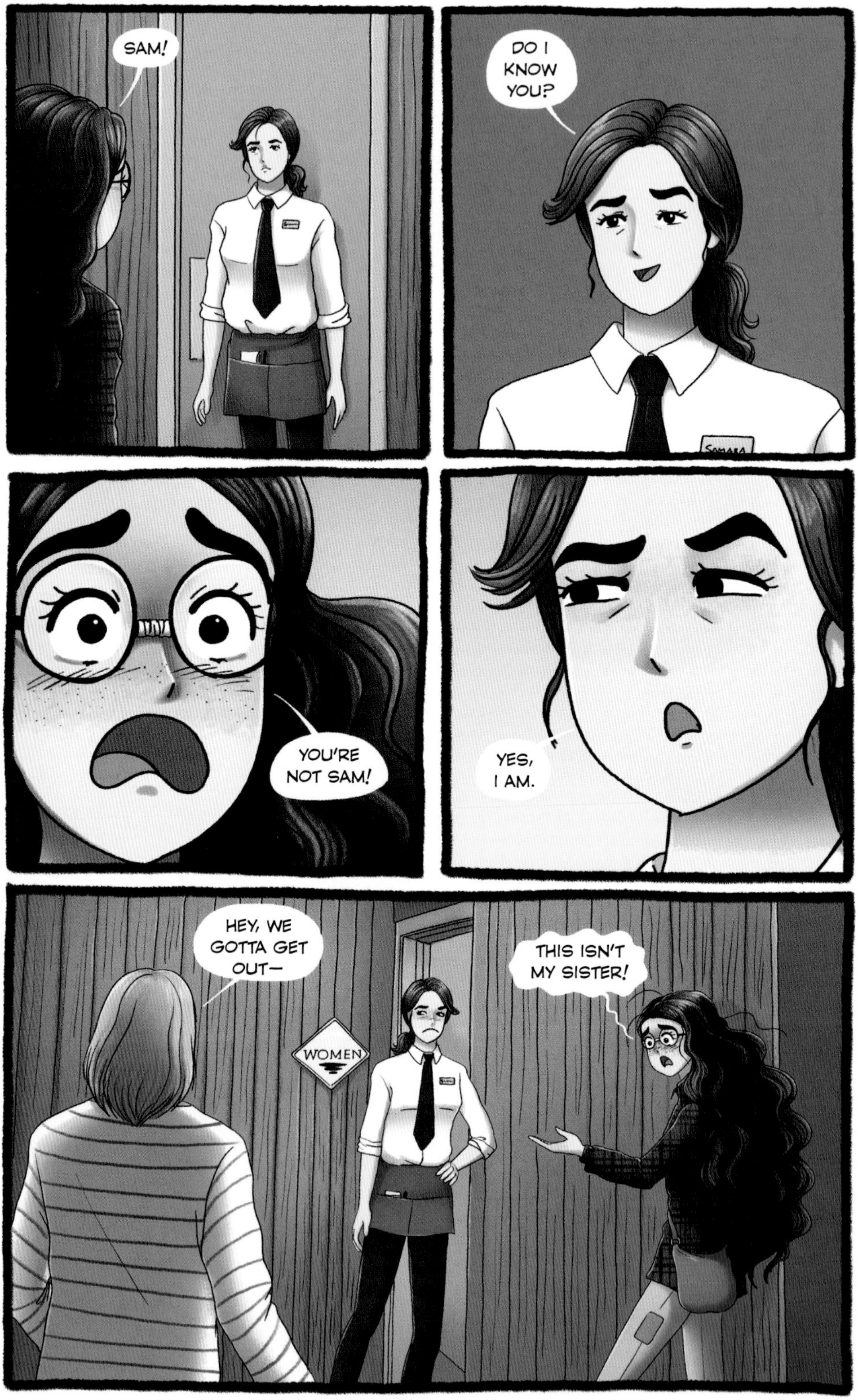
SAM!
DO I KNOW YOU?
YOU'RE NOT SAM!
YES, I AM.
HEY, WE GOTTA GET OUT—
WOMEN
THIS ISN'T MY SISTER!

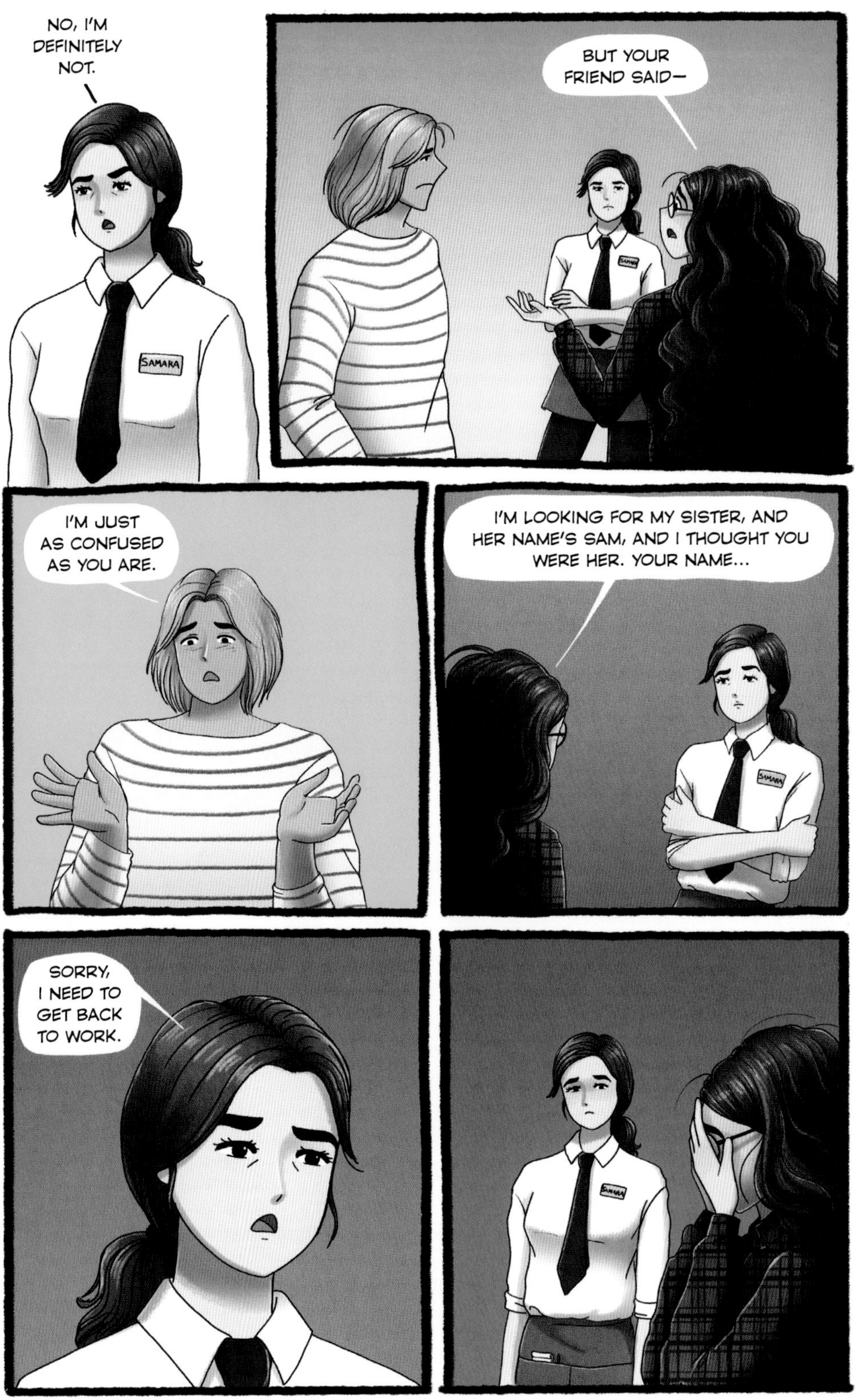
NO, I'M DEFINITELY NOT.
BUT YOUR FRIEND SAID—
SAMARA
I'M JUST AS CONFUSED AS YOU ARE.
I'M LOOKING FOR MY SISTER, AND HER NAME'S SAM, AND I THOUGHT YOU WERE HER. YOUR NAME...
SORRY, I NEED TO GET BACK TO WORK.

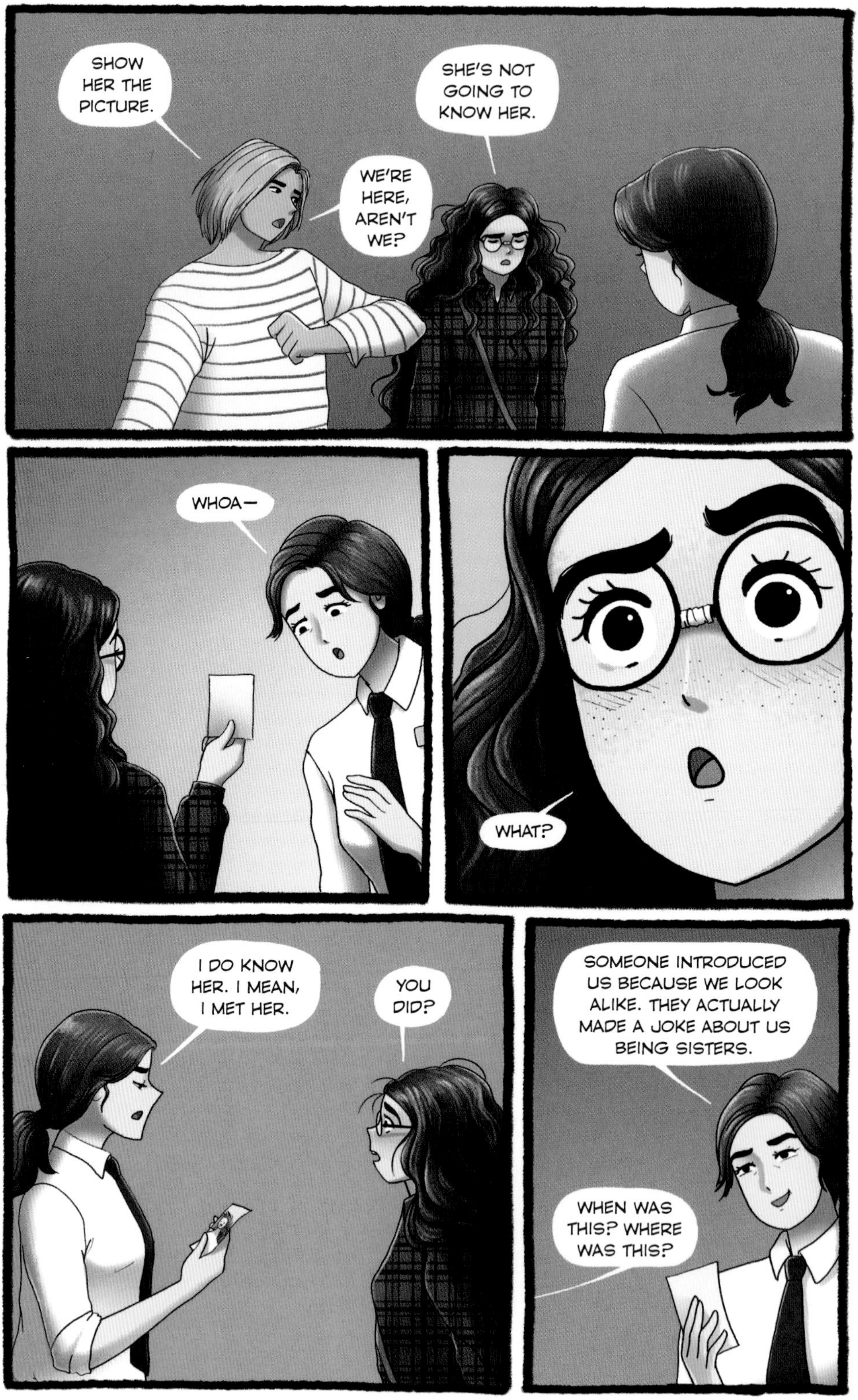
SHOW HER THE PICTURE.
SHE'S NOT GOING TO KNOW HER.
WE'RE HERE, AREN'T WE?
WHOA—
WHAT?
I DO KNOW HER. I MEAN, I MET HER.
YOU DID?
SOMEONE INTRODUCED US BECAUSE WE LOOK ALIKE. THEY ACTUALLY MADE A JOKE ABOUT US BEING SISTERS.
WHEN WAS THIS? WHERE WAS THIS?

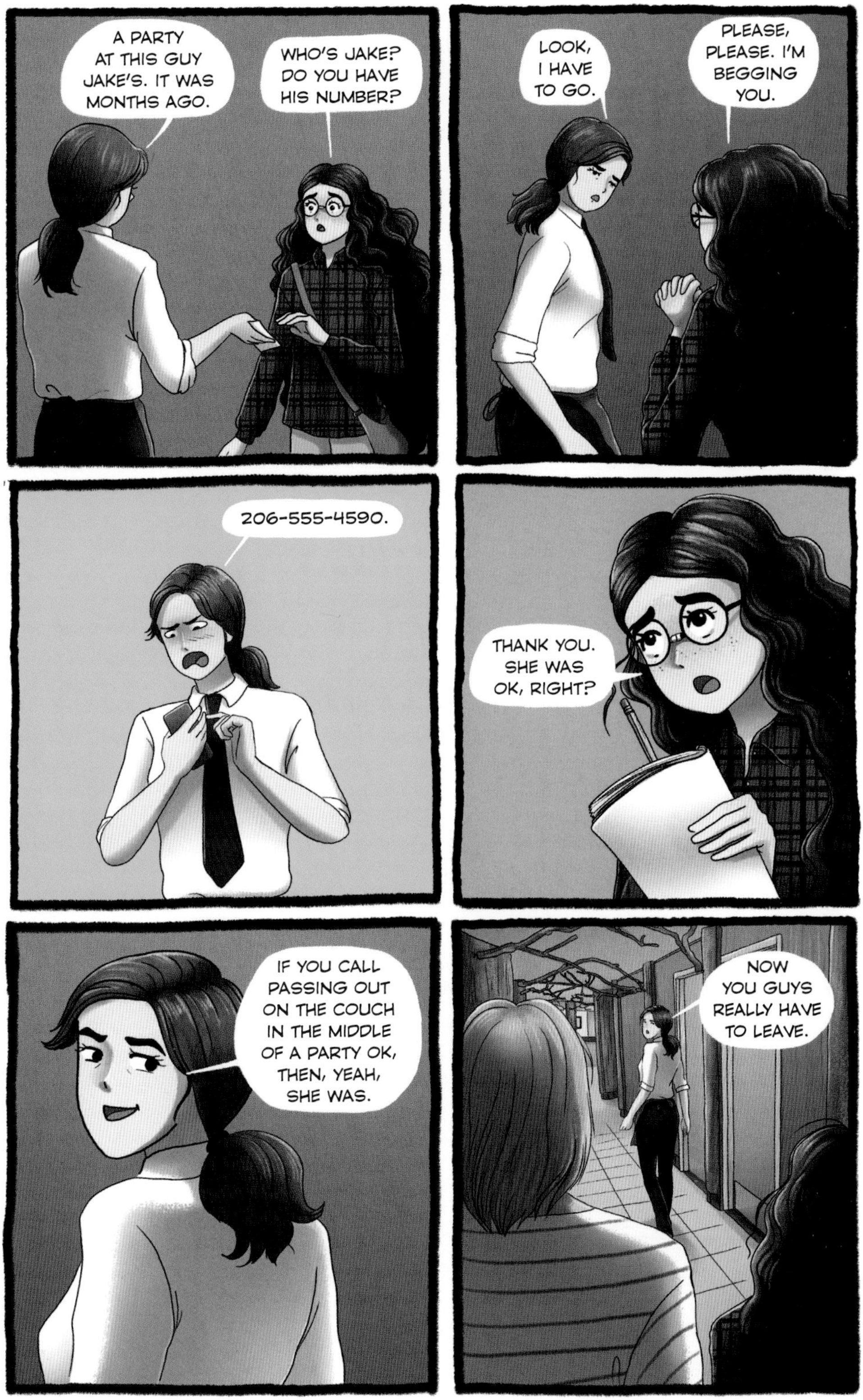
A PARTY AT THIS GUY JAKE'S. IT WAS MONTHS AGO.
WHO'S JAKE? DO YOU HAVE HIS NUMBER?
LOOK, I HAVE TO GO.
PLEASE, PLEASE. I'M BEGGING YOU.
206-555-4590.
THANK YOU. SHE WAS OK, RIGHT?
IF YOU CALL PASSING OUT ON THE COUCH IN THE MIDDLE OF A PARTY OK, THEN, YEAH, SHE WAS.
NOW YOU GUYS REALLY HAVE TO LEAVE.

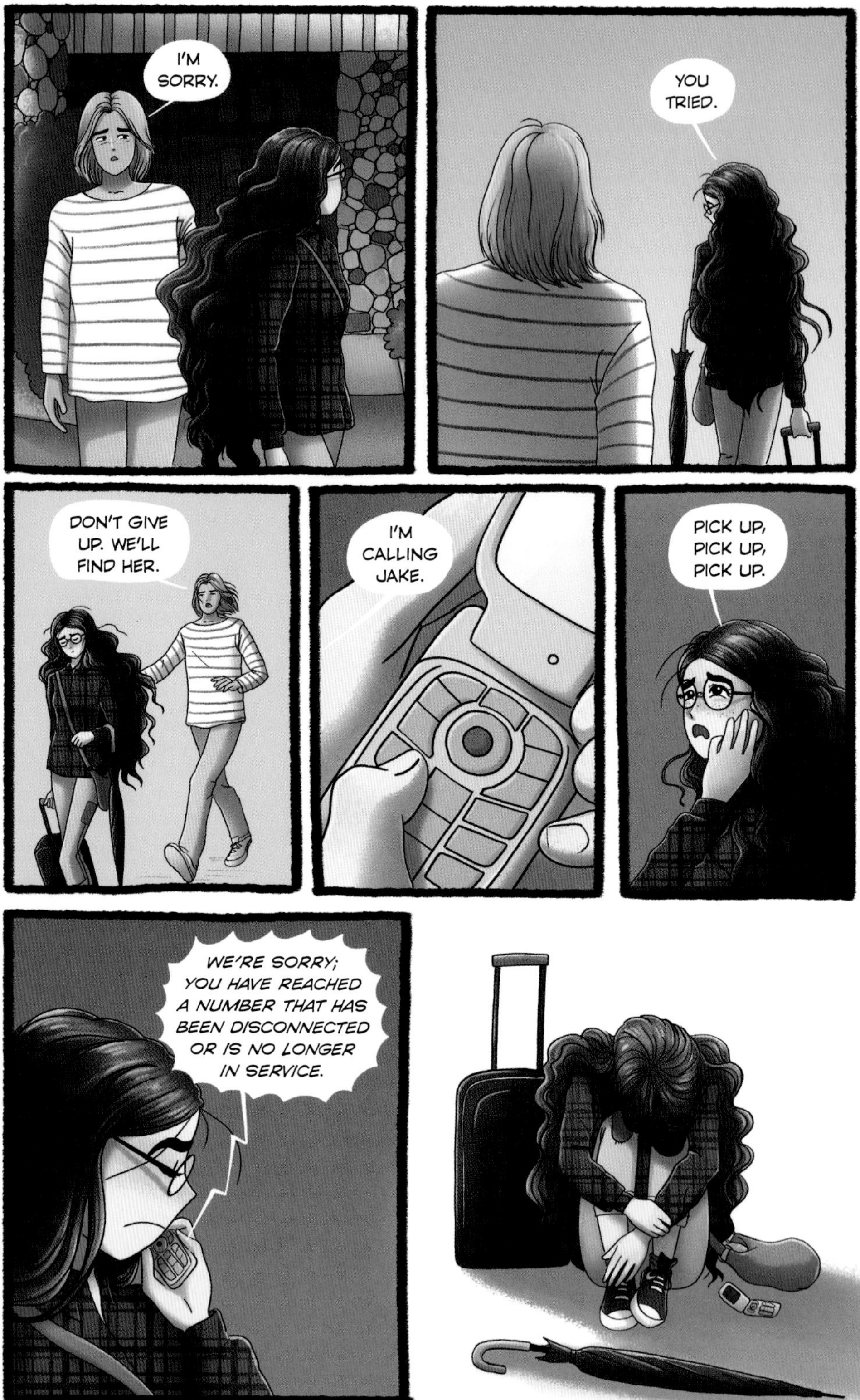
I'M SORRY.
YOU TRIED.
DON'T GIVE UP. WE'LL FIND HER.
I'M CALLING JAKE.
PICK UP, PICK UP, PICK UP.
WE'RE SORRY; YOU HAVE REACHED A NUMBER THAT HAS BEEN DISCONNECTED OR IS NO LONGER IN SERVICE.

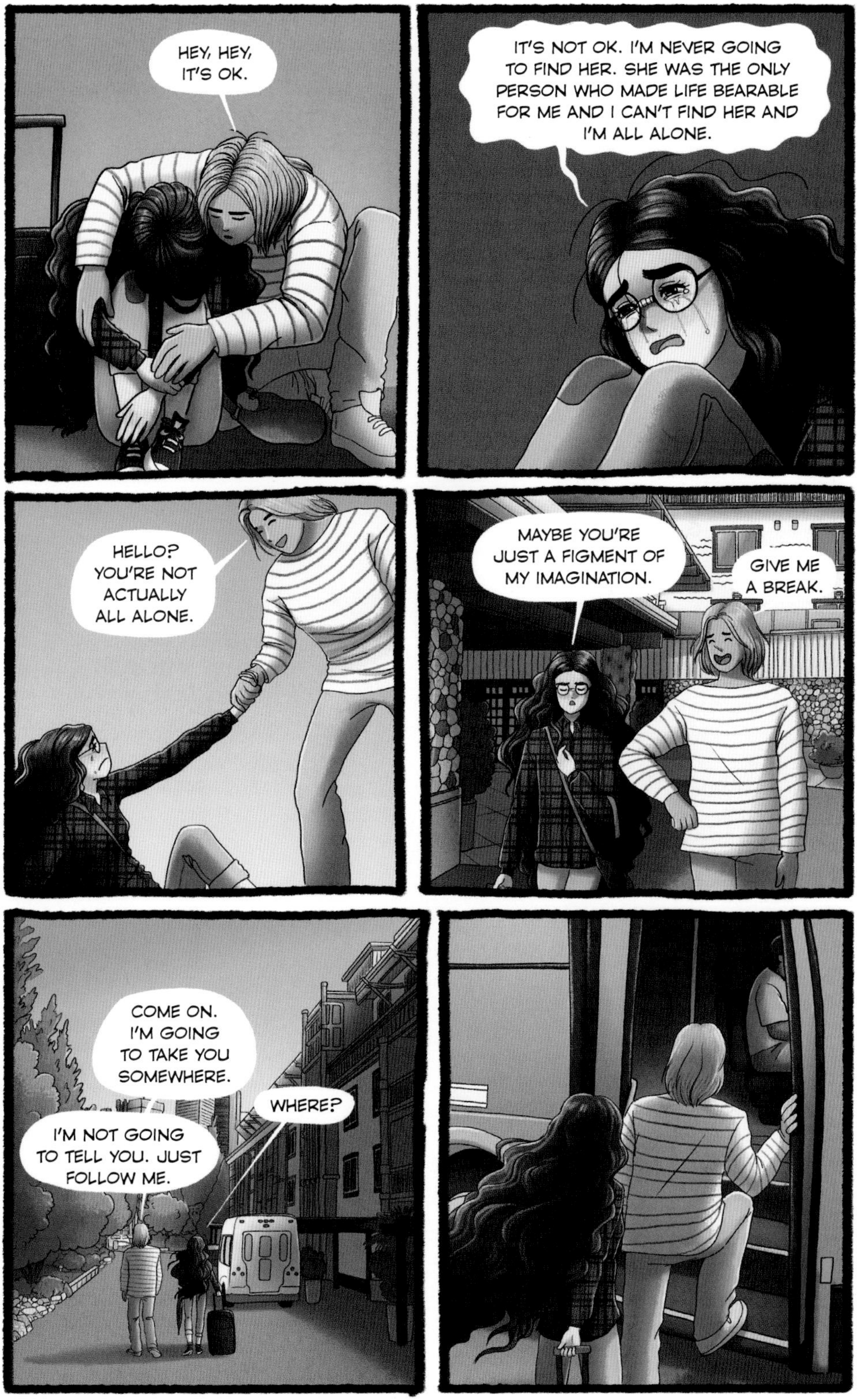
HEY, HEY, IT'S OK.
IT'S NOT OK. I'M NEVER GOING TO FIND HER. SHE WAS THE ONLY PERSON WHO MADE LIFE BEARABLE FOR ME AND I CAN'T FIND HER AND I'M ALL ALONE.
HELLO? YOU'RE NOT ACTUALLY ALL ALONE.
MAYBE YOU'RE JUST A FIGMENT OF MY IMAGINATION.
GIVE ME A BREAK.
COME ON. I'M GOING TO TAKE YOU SOMEWHERE.
WHERE?
I'M NOT GOING TO TELL YOU. JUST FOLLOW ME.

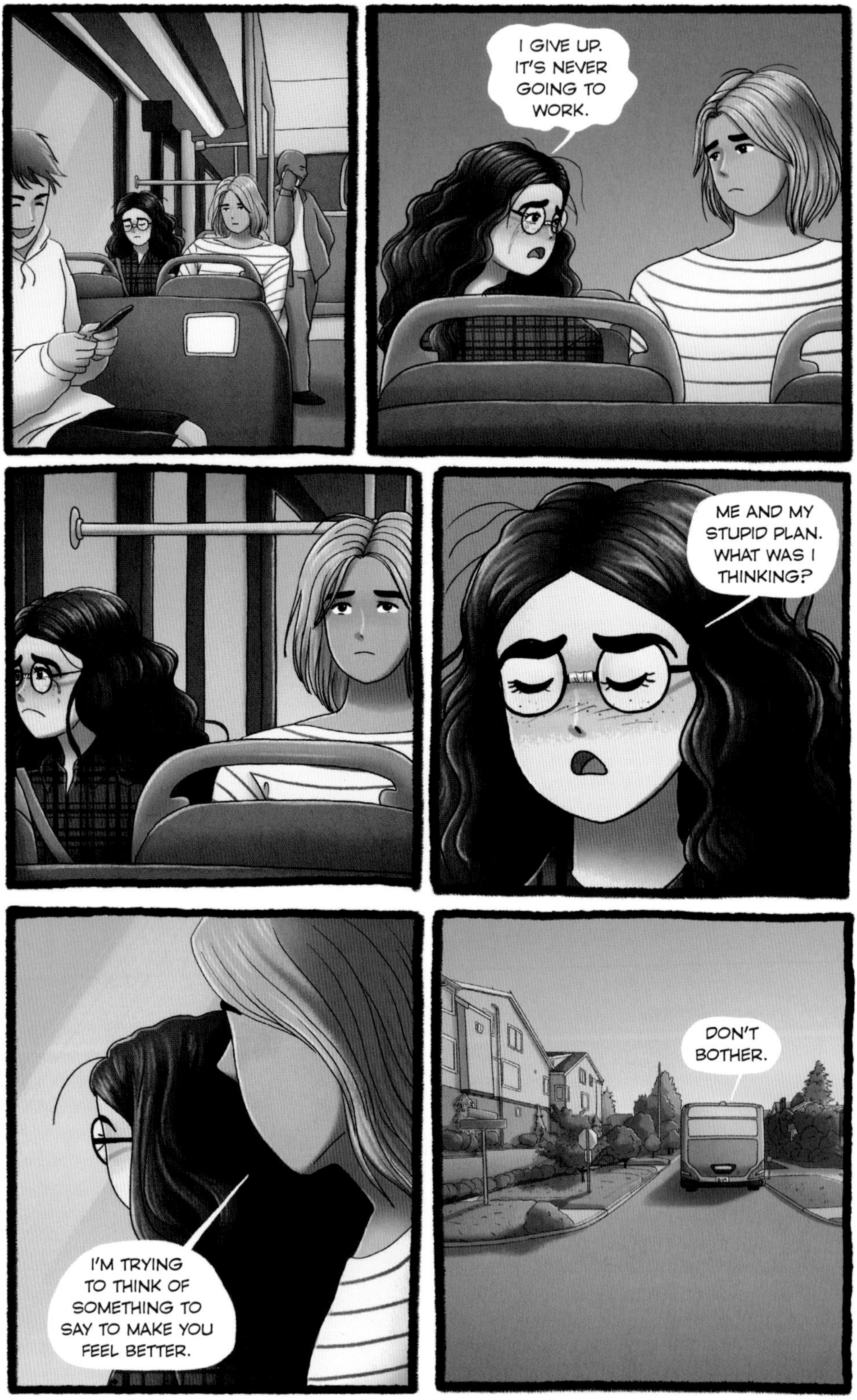
I GIVE UP. IT'S NEVER GOING TO WORK.
ME AND MY STUPID PLAN. WHAT WAS I THINKING?
I'M TRYING TO THINK OF SOMETHING TO SAY TO MAKE YOU FEEL BETTER.
DON'T BOTHER.

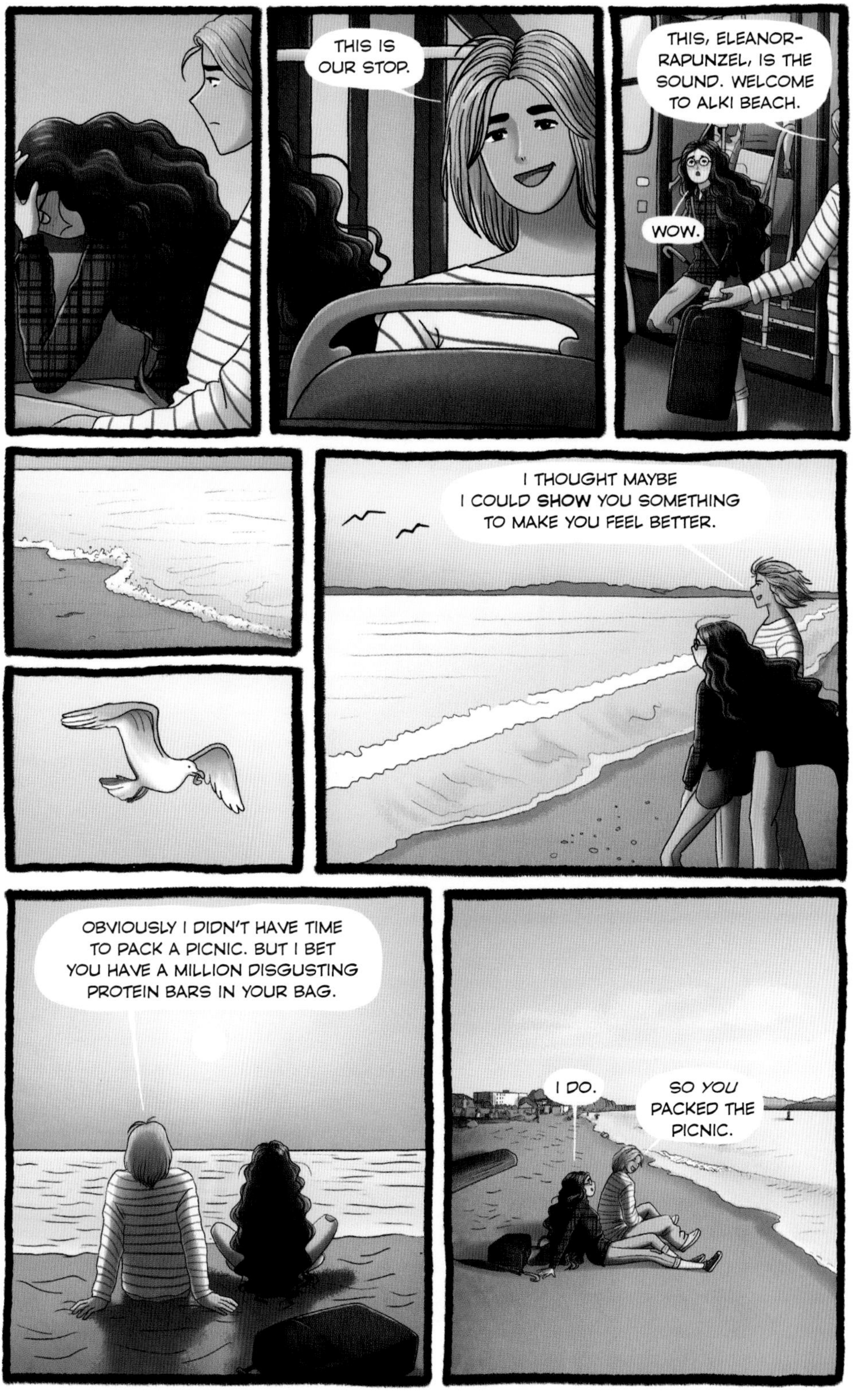
THIS IS OUR STOP.
THIS, ELEANOR-RAPUNZEL, IS THE SOUND. WELCOME TO ALKI BEACH.
WOW.
I THOUGHT MAYBE I COULD SHOW YOU SOMETHING TO MAKE YOU FEEL BETTER.
OBVIOUSLY I DIDN'T HAVE TIME TO PACK A PICNIC. BUT I BET YOU HAVE A MILLION DISGUSTING PROTEIN BARS IN YOUR BAG.
I DO.
SO YOU PACKED THE PICNIC.

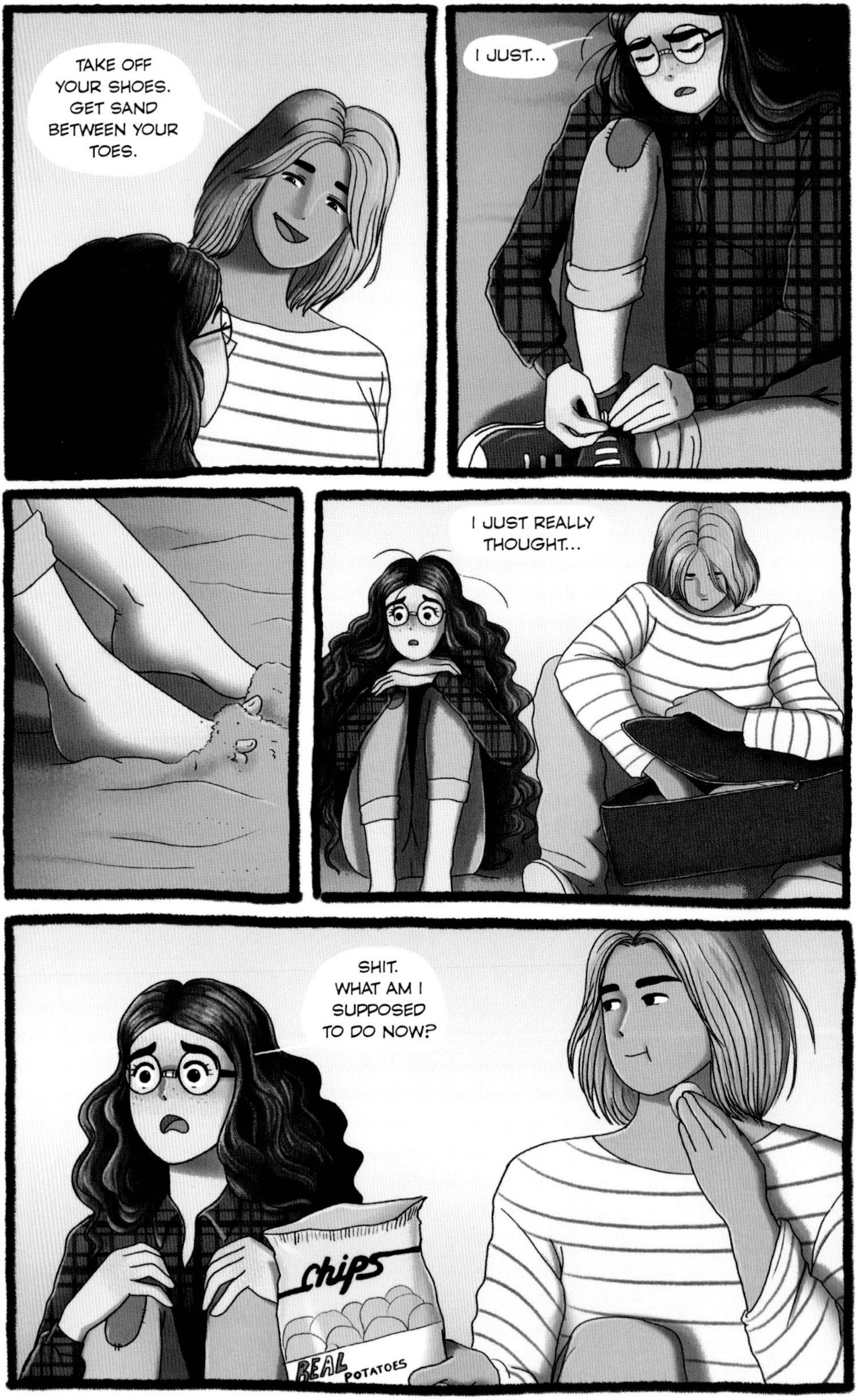
TAKE OFF YOUR SHOES. GET SAND BETWEEN YOUR TOES.
I JUST...
I JUST REALLY THOUGHT...
SHIT. WHAT AM I SUPPOSED TO DO NOW?
chips
REAL POTATOES

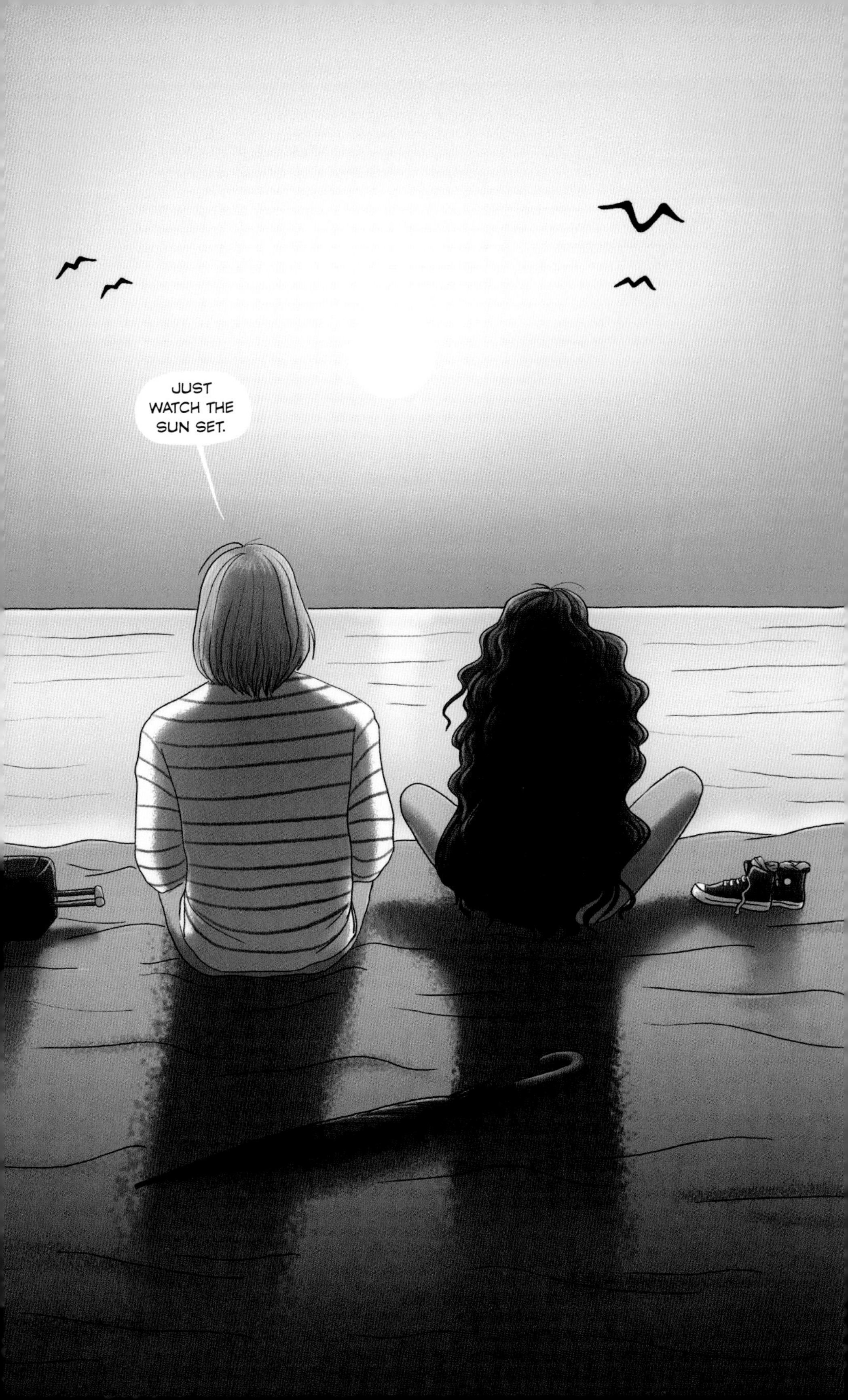
JUST WATCH THE SUN SET.

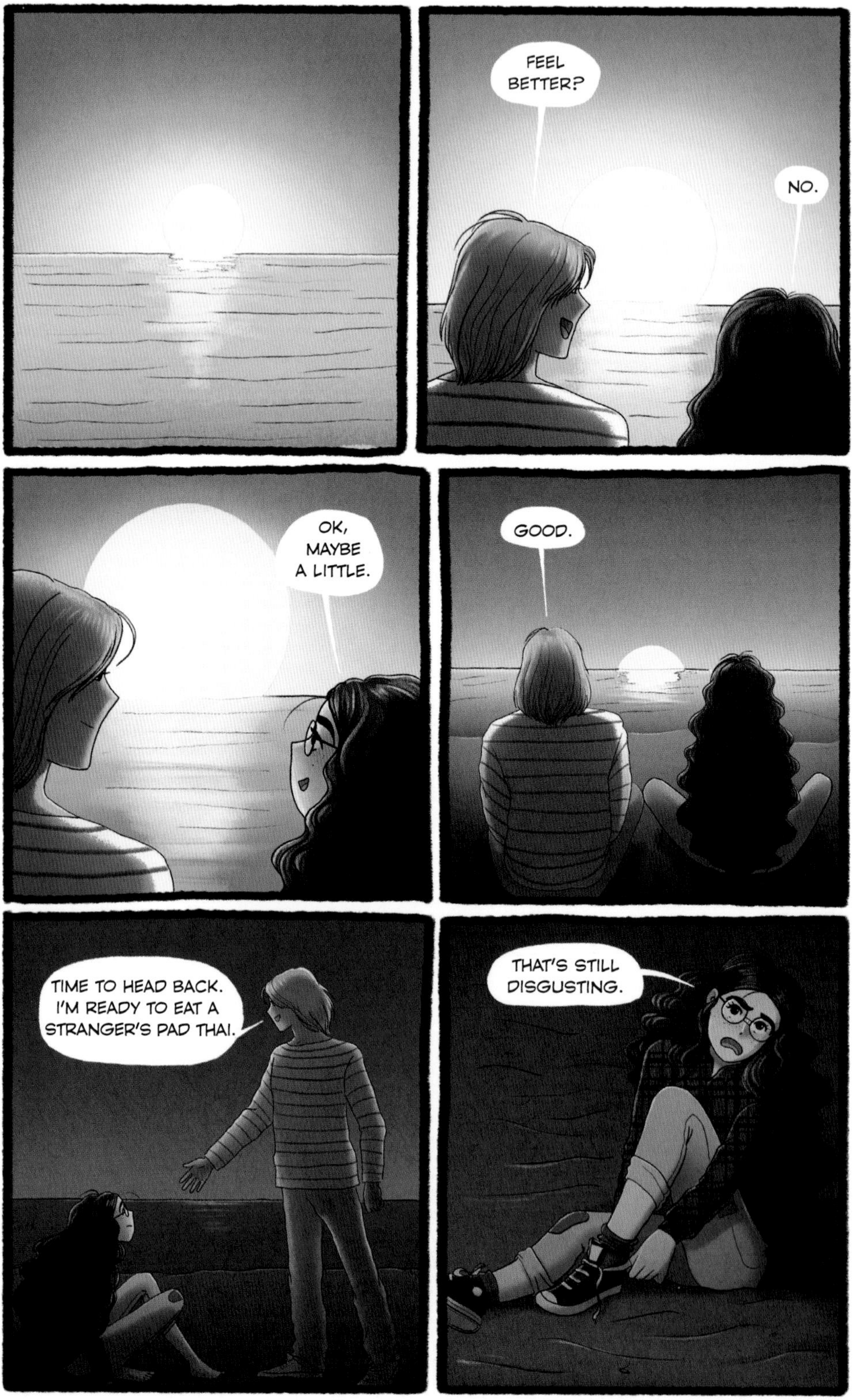
FEEL BETTER?
NO.
OK, MAYBE A LITTLE.
GOOD.
TIME TO HEAD BACK. I'M READY TO EAT A STRANGER'S PAD THAI.
THAT'S STILL DISGUSTING.

AND, UM, DON'T TAKE THIS THE WRONG WAY, BUT CAN I STAY WITH YOU—I MEAN, WHEREVER YOU'RE STAYING—TONIGHT?

SURE. NO PROBLEM.

THANKS. I DON'T WANT TO SLEEP IN THE LIBRARY AGAIN.

THE LIBRARY, HUH? AND YOU DIDN'T GET CAUGHT?

NOPE.

IMPRESSIVE.

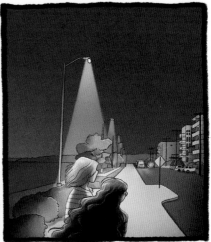

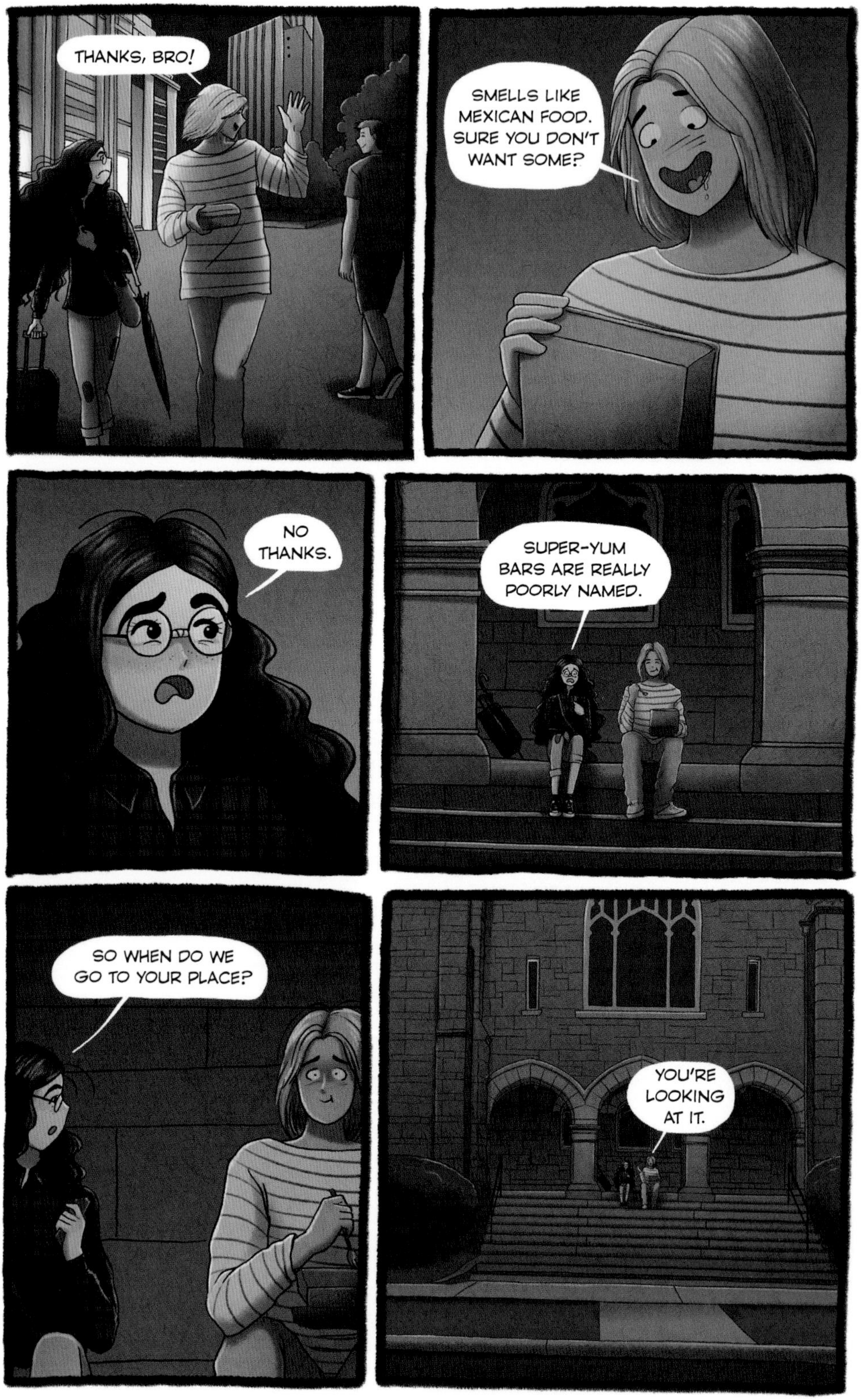
THANKS, BRO!
SMELLS LIKE MEXICAN FOOD. SURE YOU DON'T WANT SOME?
NO THANKS.
SUPER-YUM BARS ARE REALLY POORLY NAMED.
SO WHEN DO WE GO TO YOUR PLACE?
YOU'RE LOOKING AT IT.

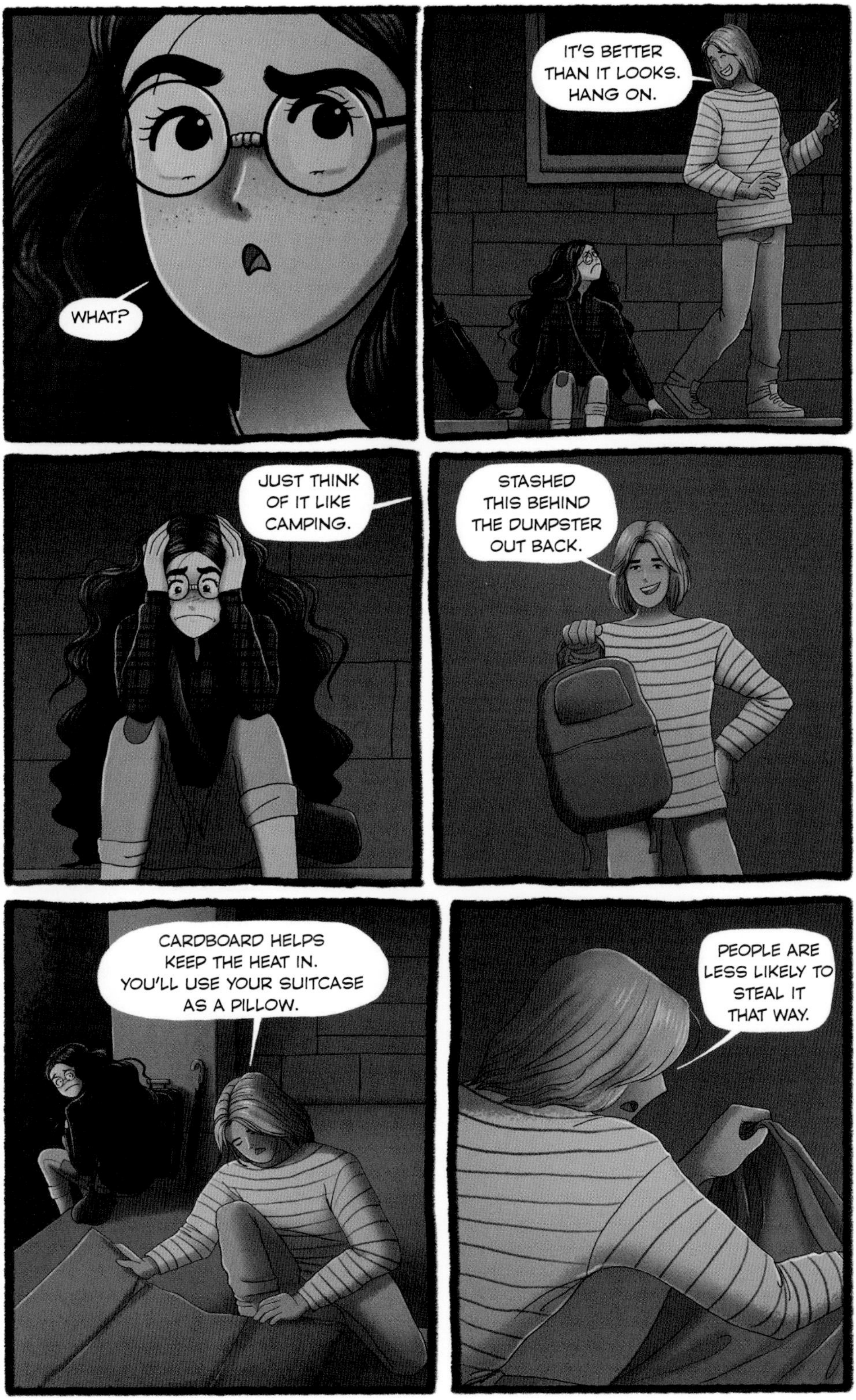
WHAT?
IT'S BETTER THAN IT LOOKS. HANG ON.
JUST THINK OF IT LIKE CAMPING.
STASHED THIS BEHIND THE DUMPSTER OUT BACK.
CARDBOARD HELPS KEEP THE HEAT IN. YOU'LL USE YOUR SUITCASE AS A PILLOW.
PEOPLE ARE LESS LIKELY TO STEAL IT THAT WAY.

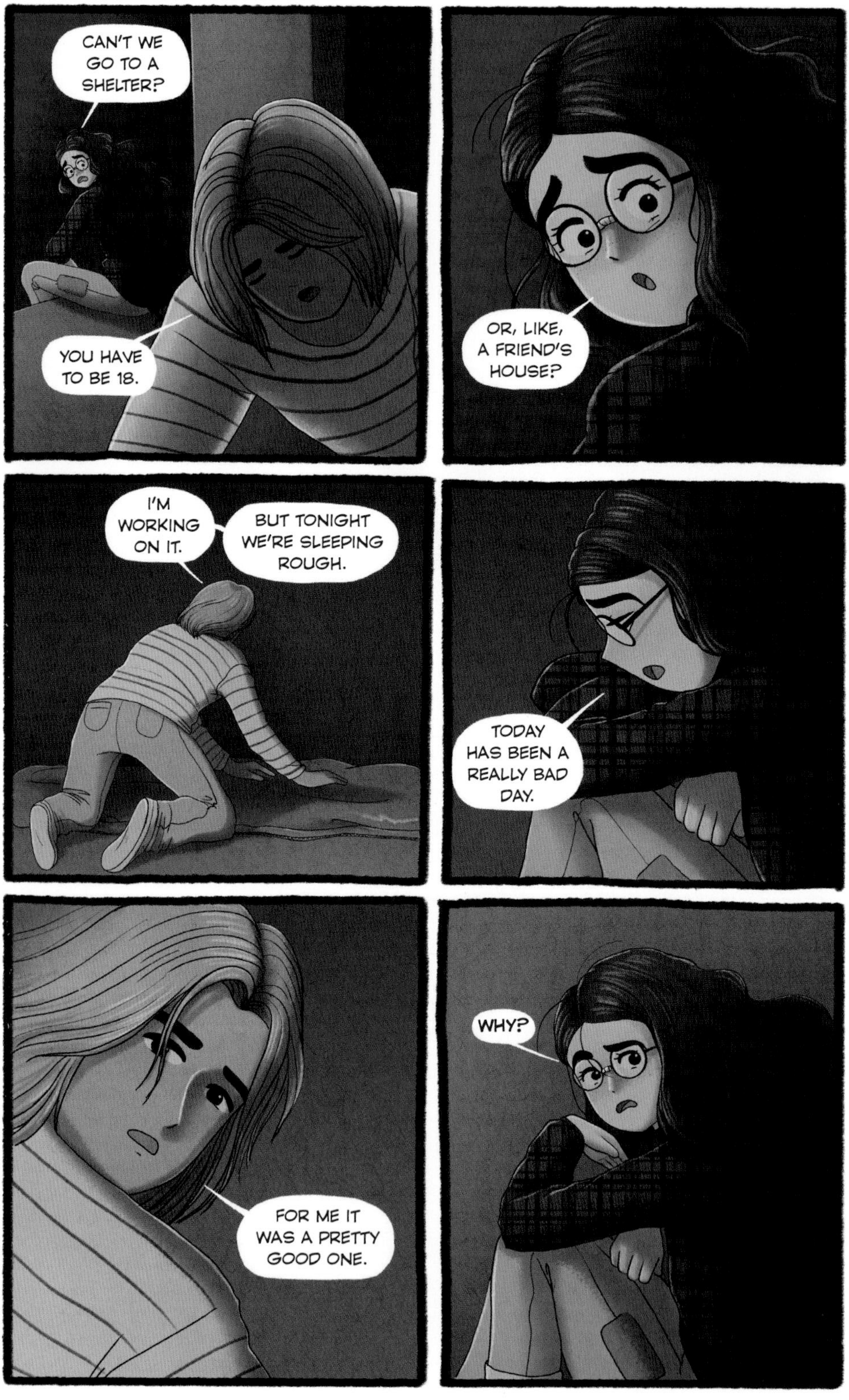
CAN'T WE GO TO A SHELTER?
YOU HAVE TO BE 18.
OR, LIKE, A FRIEND'S HOUSE?
I'M WORKING ON IT.
BUT TONIGHT WE'RE SLEEPING ROUGH.
TODAY HAS BEEN A REALLY BAD DAY.
FOR ME IT WAS A PRETTY GOOD ONE.
WHY?

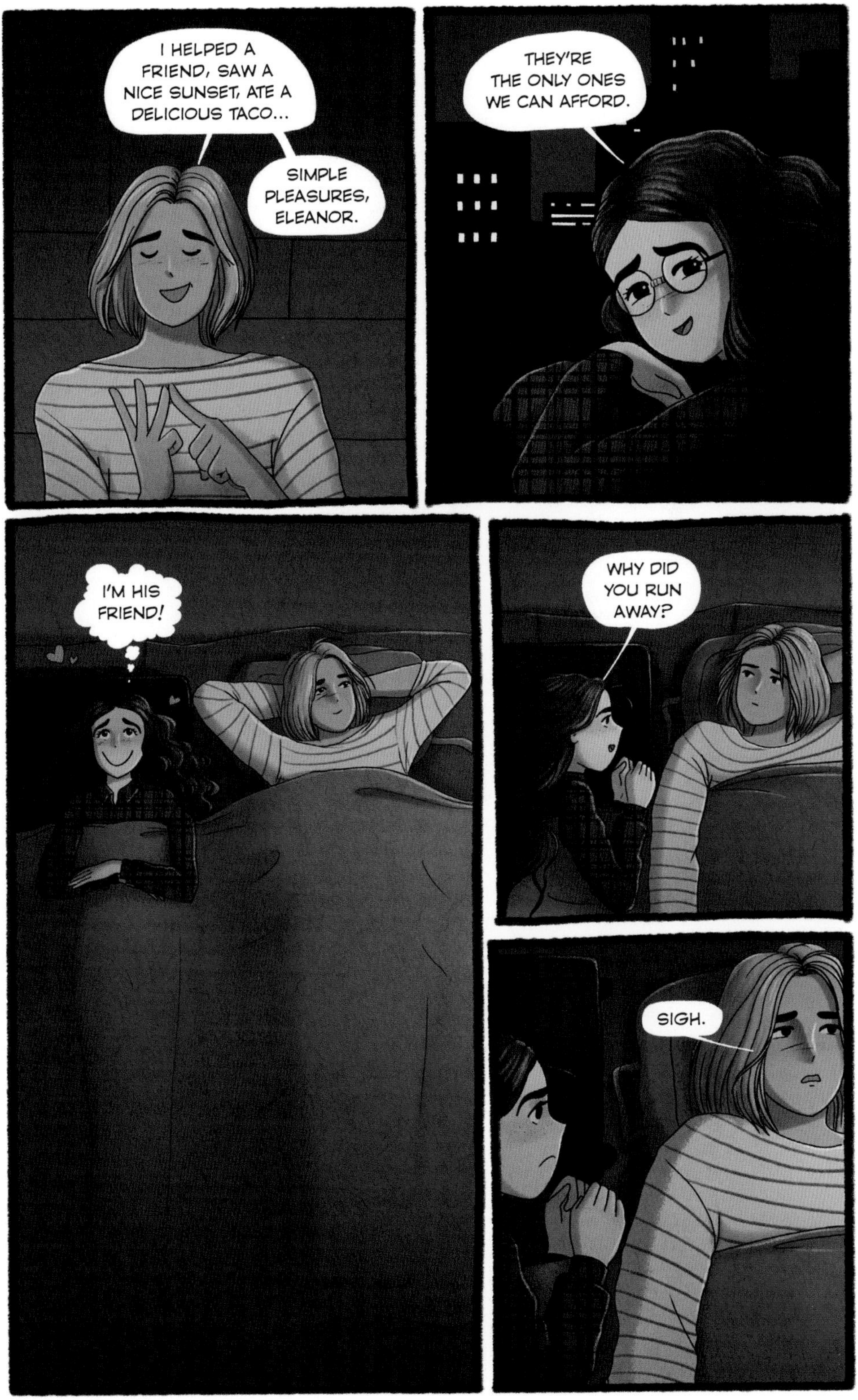
I HELPED A FRIEND, SAW A NICE SUNSET, ATE A DELICIOUS TACO...
SIMPLE PLEASURES, ELEANOR.
THEY'RE THE ONLY ONES WE CAN AFFORD.
I'M HIS FRIEND!
WHY DID YOU RUN AWAY?
SIGH.

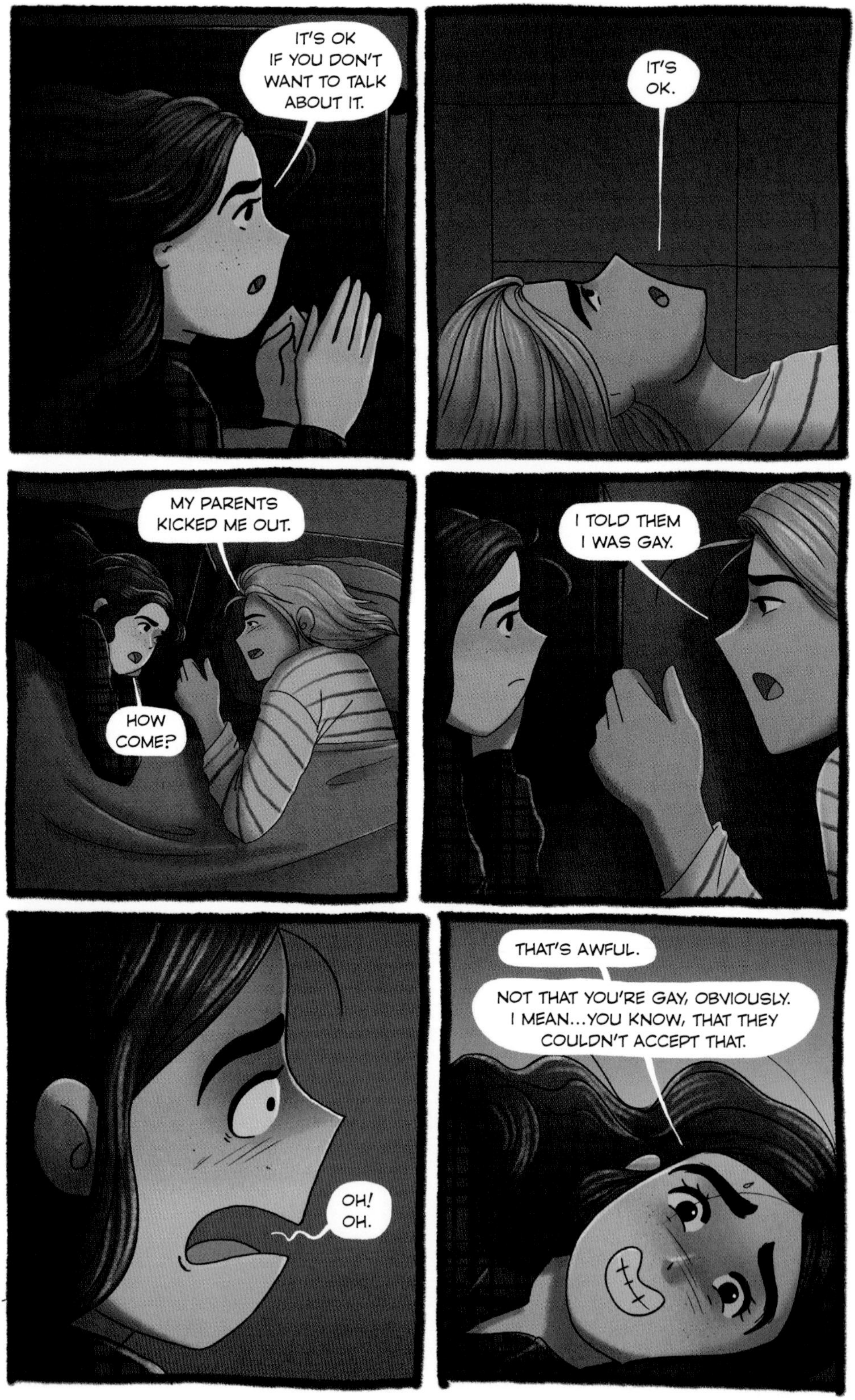
IT'S OK IF YOU DON'T WANT TO TALK ABOUT IT.
IT'S OK.
MY PARENTS KICKED ME OUT.
HOW COME?
I TOLD THEM I WAS GAY.
OH! OH.
THAT'S AWFUL.
NOT THAT YOU'RE GAY, OBVIOUSLY. I MEAN...YOU KNOW, THAT THEY COULDN'T ACCEPT THAT.

NOT GONNA LIE. IT *WAS* AWFUL.

I'M SORRY.

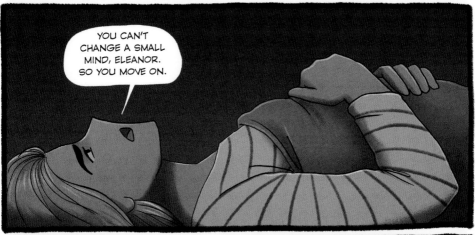

YOU CAN'T CHANGE A SMALL MIND, ELEANOR. SO YOU MOVE ON.

ANYWAY, WE SHOULD GET SOME SLEEP.

OK.

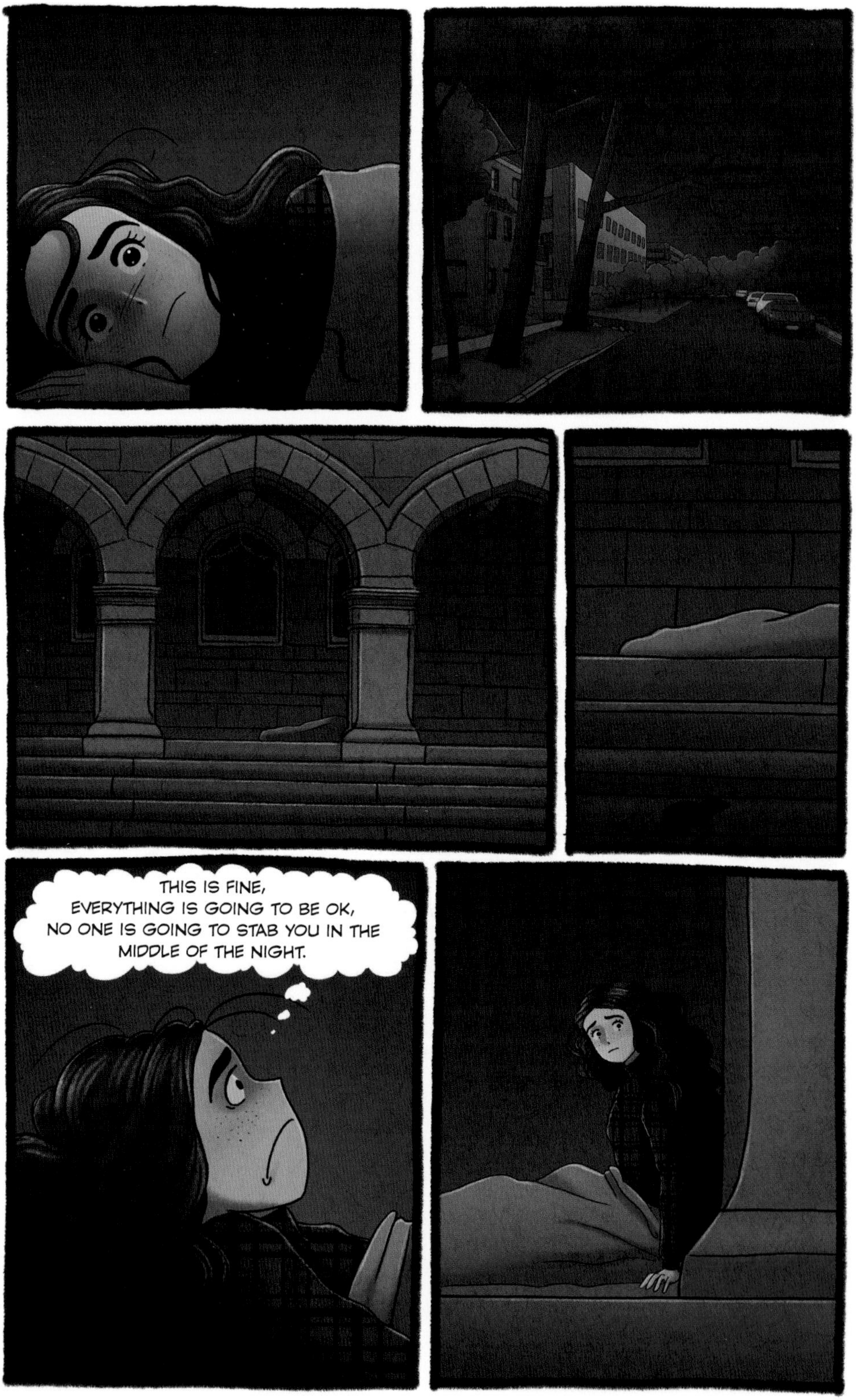
THIS IS FINE,
EVERYTHING IS GOING TO BE OK,
NO ONE IS GOING TO STAB YOU IN THE
MIDDLE OF THE NIGHT.

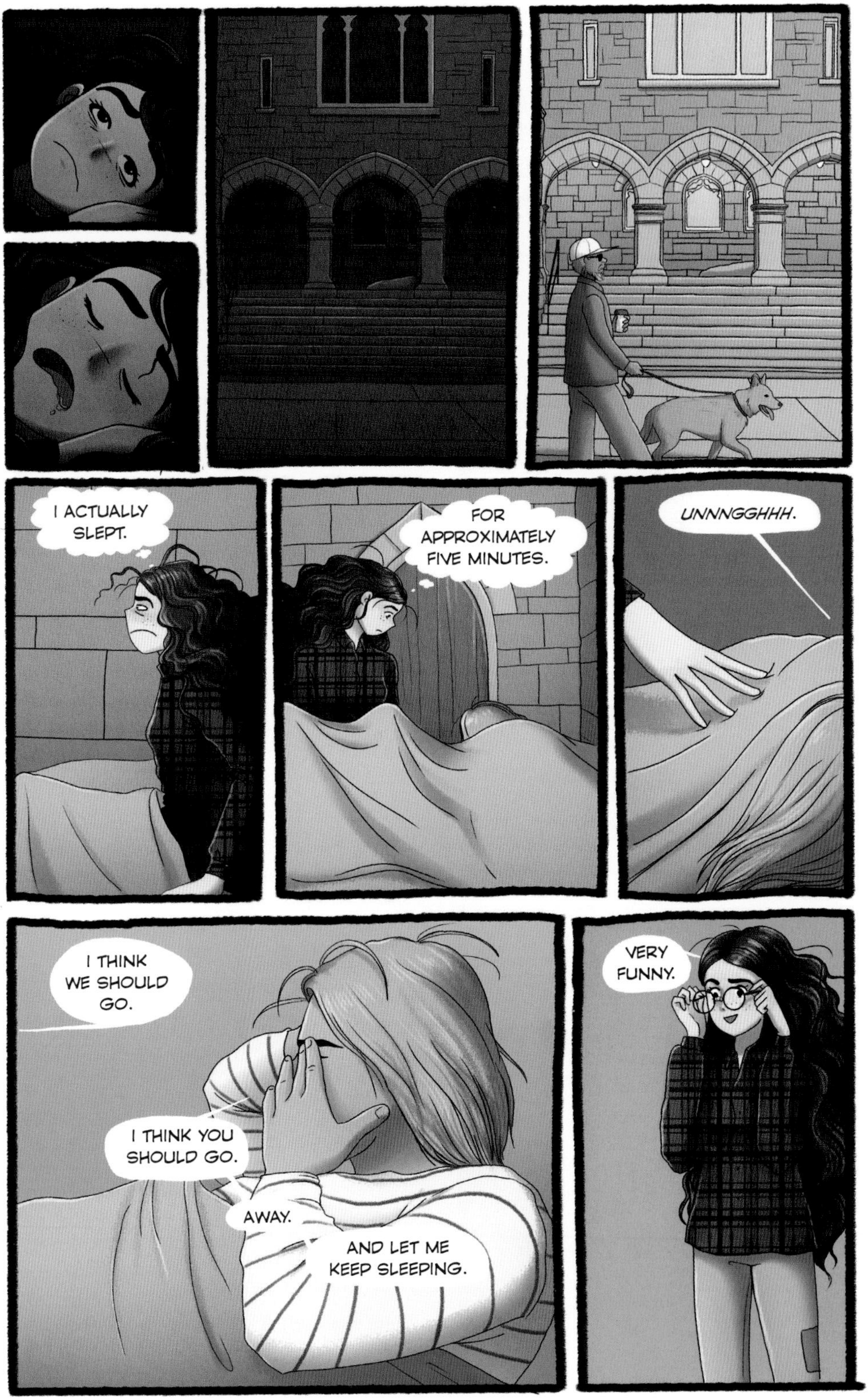
I ACTUALLY SLEPT.
FOR APPROXIMATELY FIVE MINUTES.
UNNNGGHHH.
I THINK WE SHOULD GO.
I THINK YOU SHOULD GO.
AWAY.
AND LET ME KEEP SLEEPING.
VERY FUNNY.

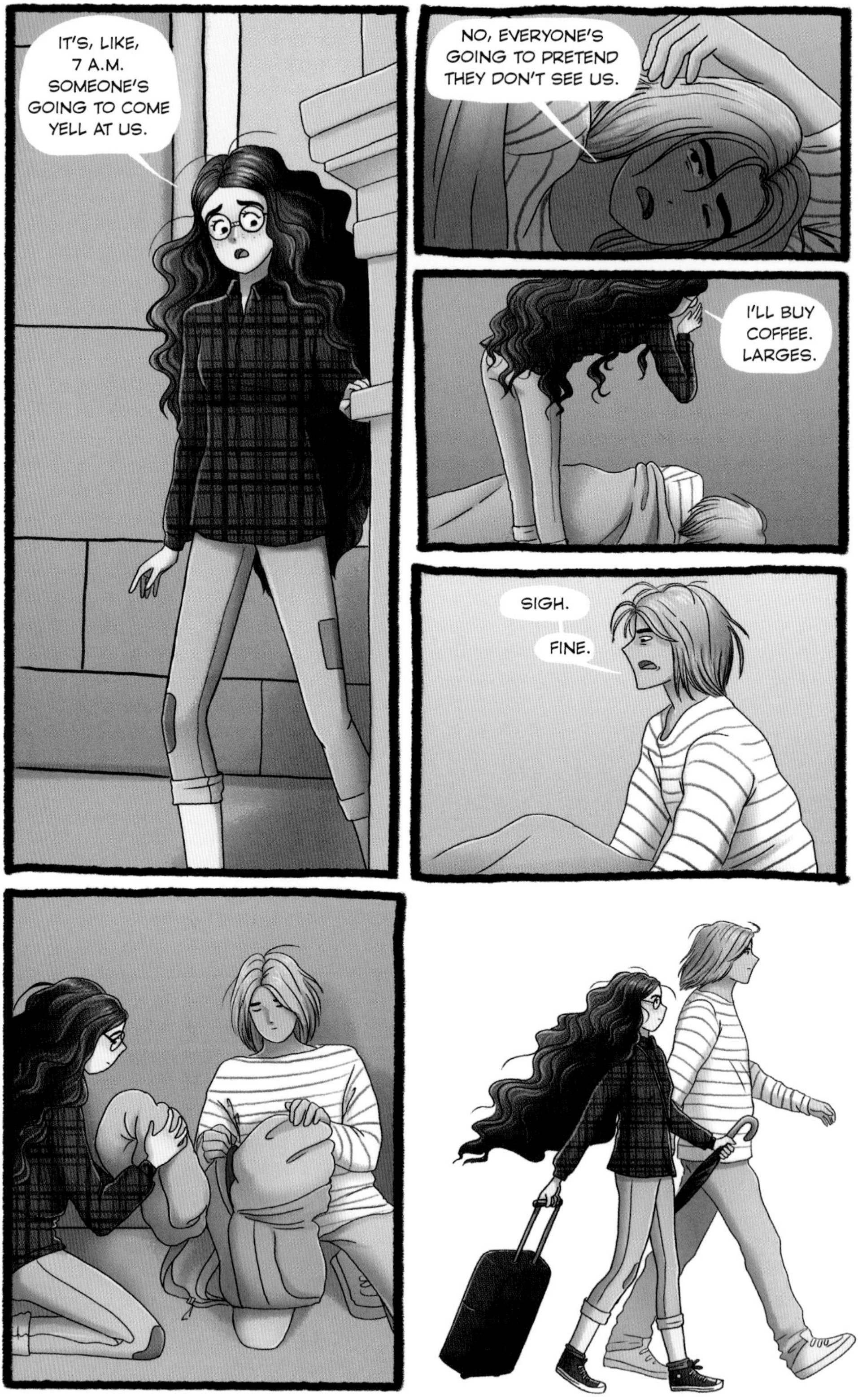
IT'S, LIKE, 7 A.M. SOMEONE'S GOING TO COME YELL AT US.
NO, EVERYONE'S GOING TO PRETEND THEY DON'T SEE US.
I'LL BUY COFFEE. LARGES.
SIGH.
FINE.

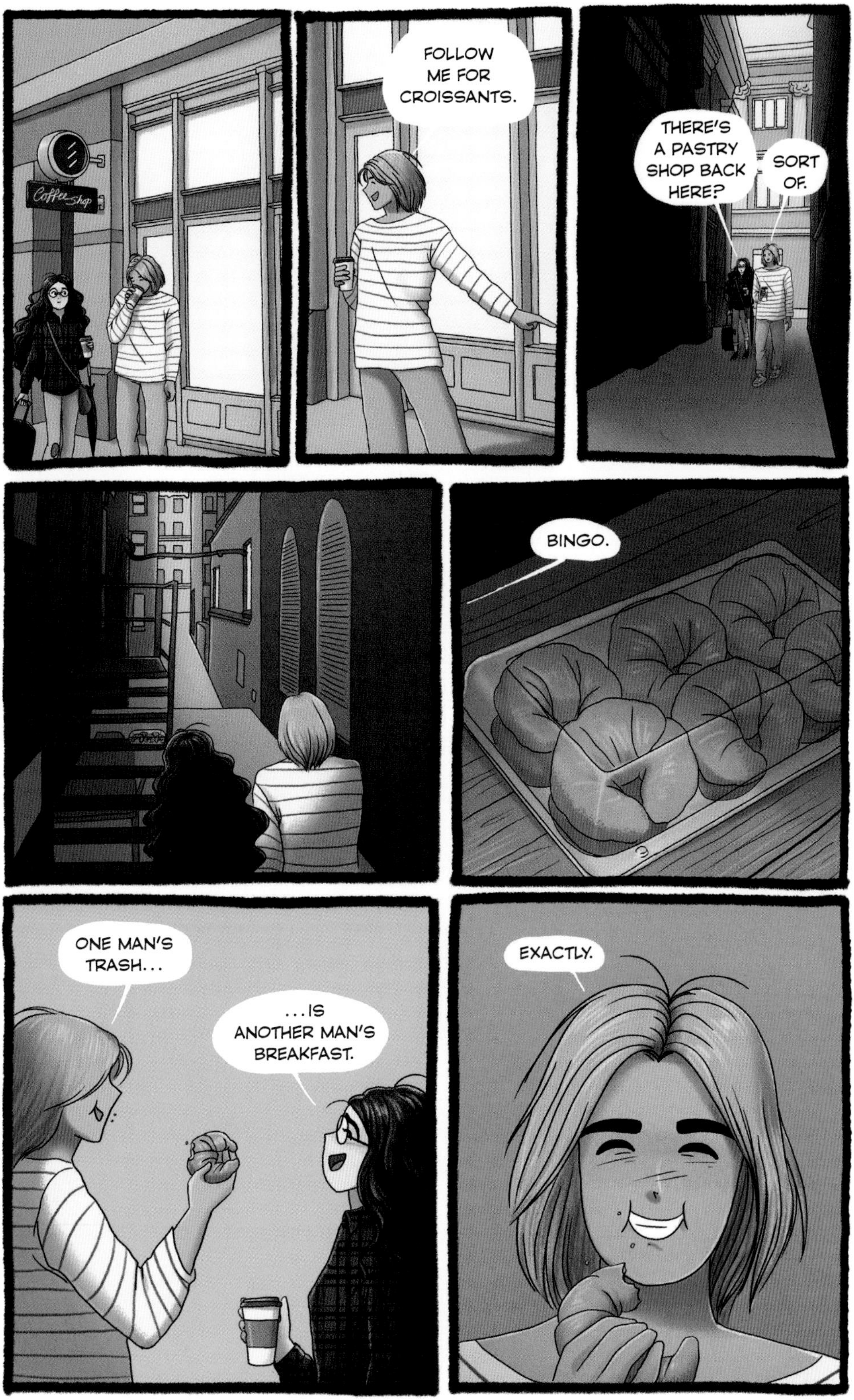
Coffee Shop
FOLLOW ME FOR CROISSANTS.
THERE'S A PASTRY SHOP BACK HERE?
SORT OF.
BINGO.
ONE MAN'S TRASH...
...IS ANOTHER MAN'S BREAKFAST.
EXACTLY.

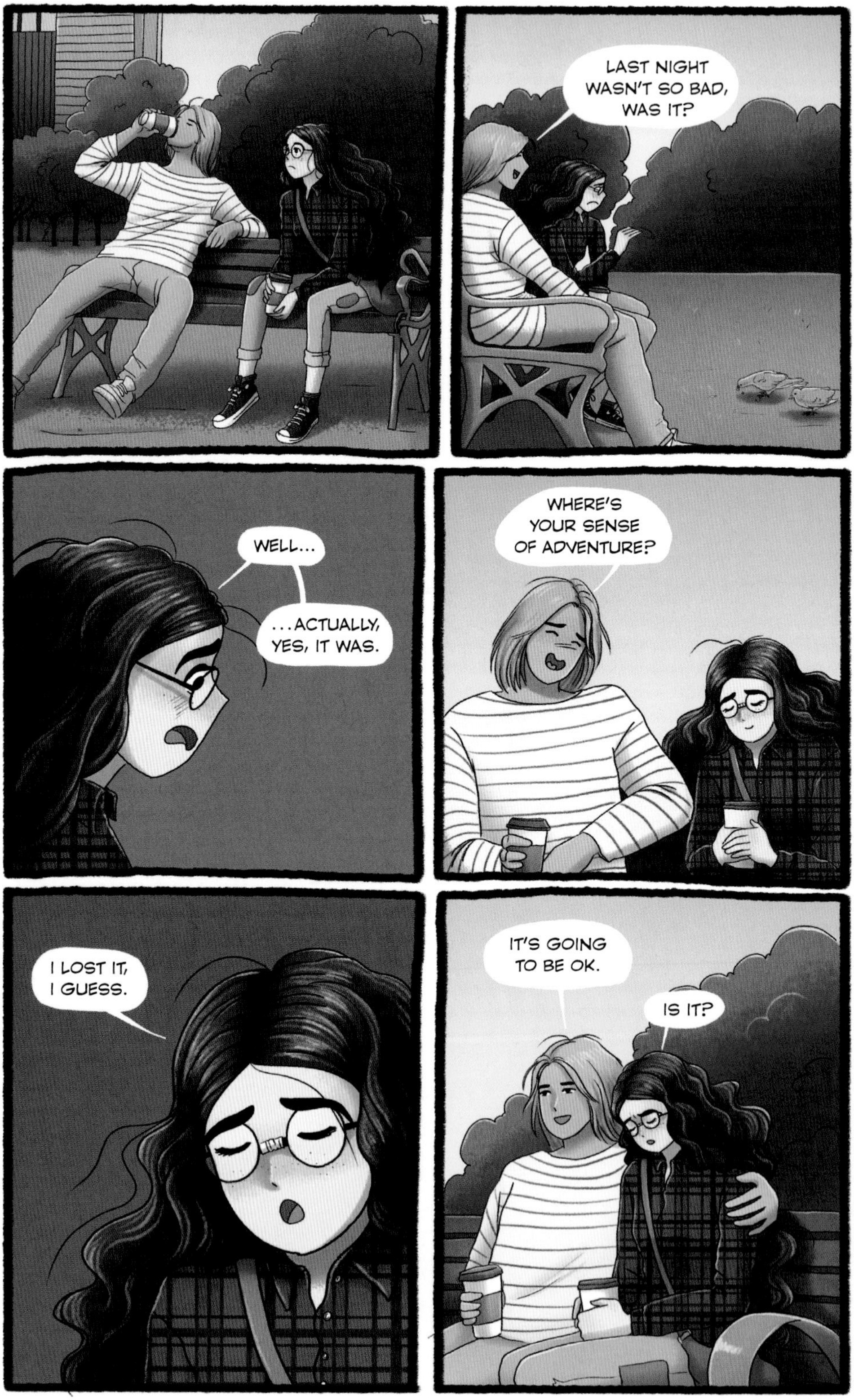
LAST NIGHT WASN'T SO BAD, WAS IT?
WELL...
...ACTUALLY, YES, IT WAS.
WHERE'S YOUR SENSE OF ADVENTURE?
I LOST IT, I GUESS.
IT'S GOING TO BE OK.
IS IT?

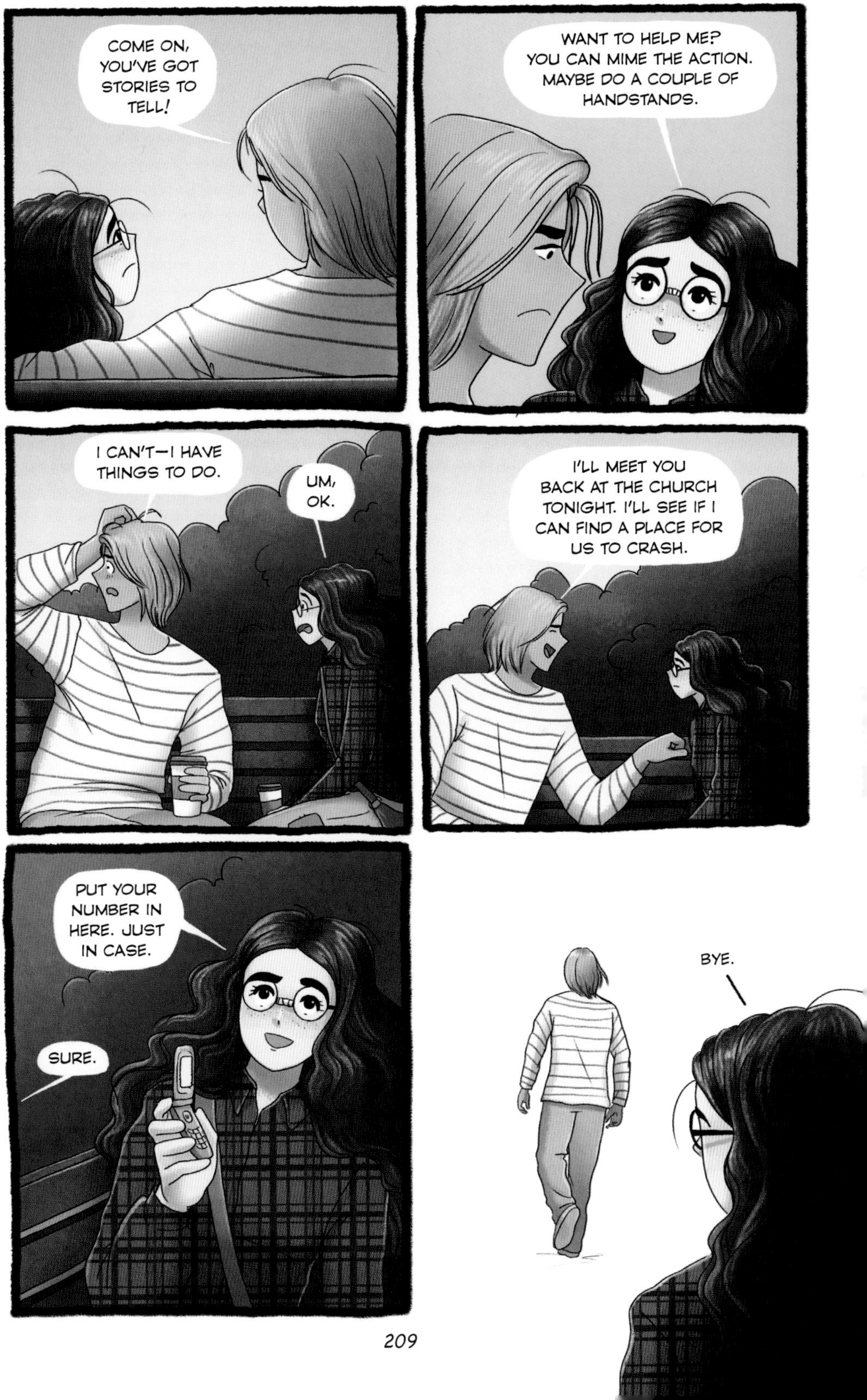
COME ON, YOU'VE GOT STORIES TO TELL!
WANT TO HELP ME? YOU CAN MIME THE ACTION. MAYBE DO A COUPLE OF HANDSTANDS.
I CAN'T—I HAVE THINGS TO DO.
UM, OK.
I'LL MEET YOU BACK AT THE CHURCH TONIGHT. I'LL SEE IF I CAN FIND A PLACE FOR US TO CRASH.
PUT YOUR NUMBER IN HERE. JUST IN CASE.
SURE.
BYE.

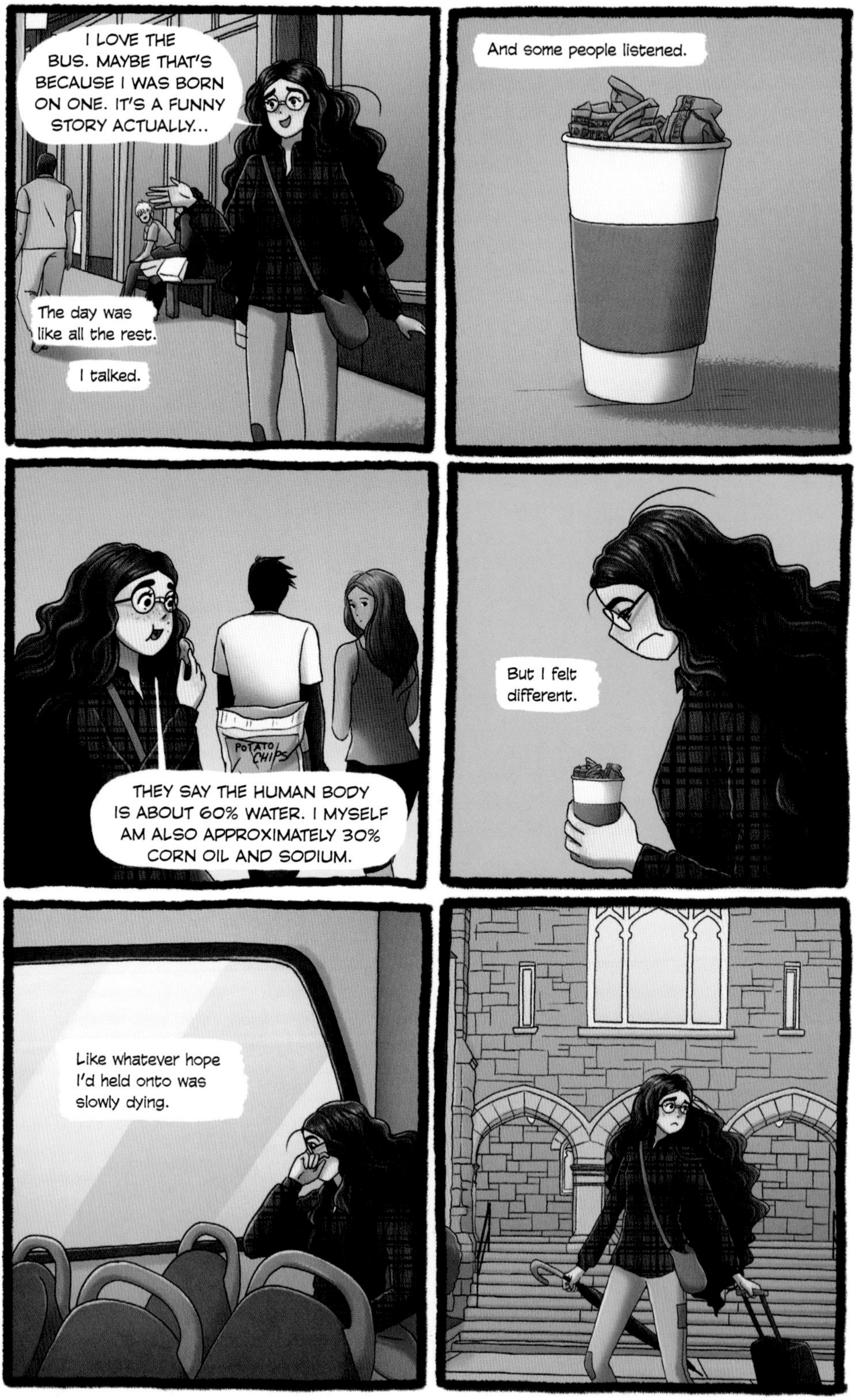
I LOVE THE BUS. MAYBE THAT'S BECAUSE I WAS BORN ON ONE. IT'S A FUNNY STORY ACTUALLY...
The day was like all the rest.
I talked.
And some people listened.
POTATO CHIPS
THEY SAY THE HUMAN BODY IS ABOUT 60% WATER. I MYSELF AM ALSO APPROXIMATELY 30% CORN OIL AND SODIUM.
But I felt different.
Like whatever hope I'd held onto was slowly dying.

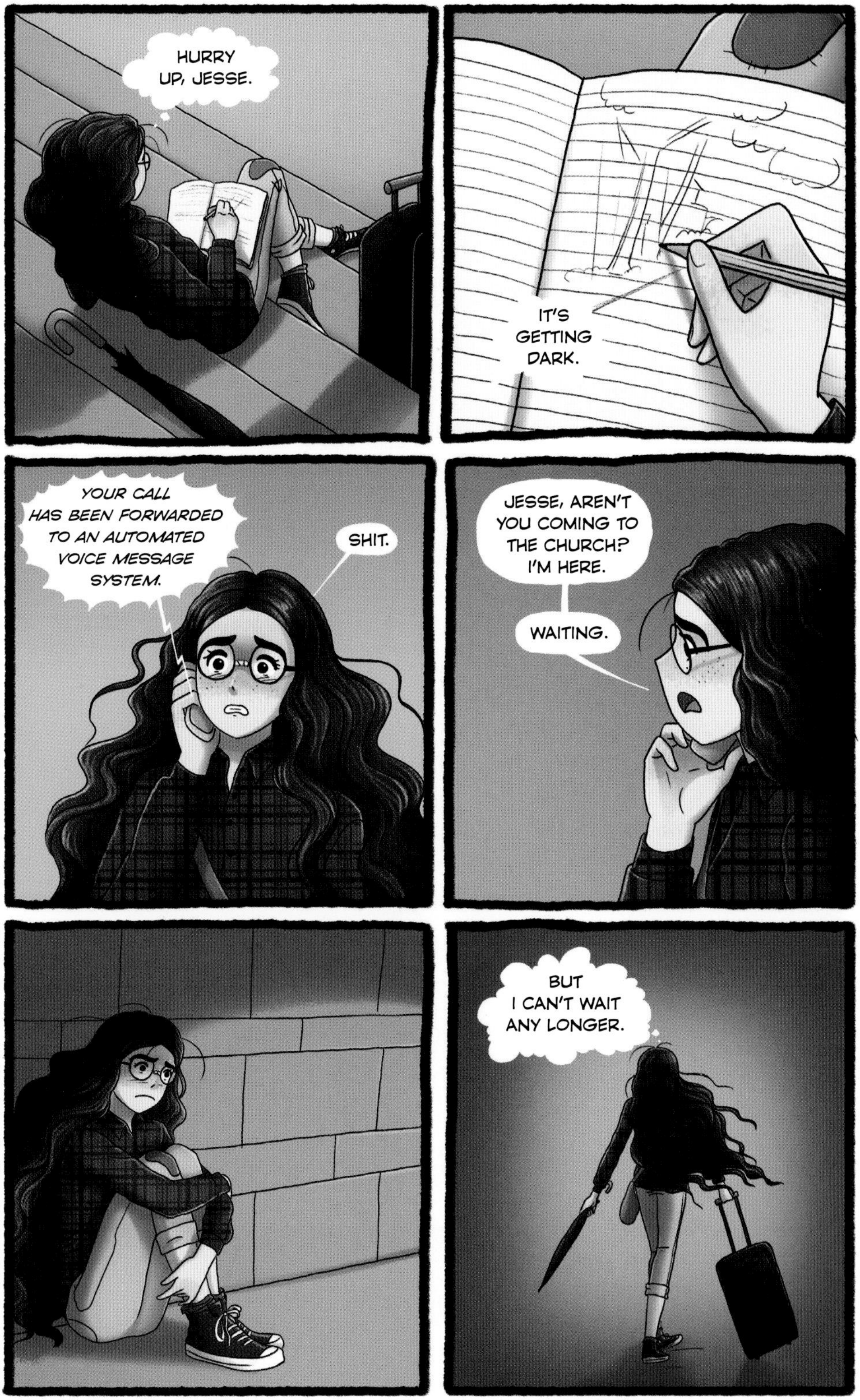
HURRY UP, JESSE.
IT'S GETTING DARK.
YOUR CALL HAS BEEN FORWARDED TO AN AUTOMATED VOICE MESSAGE SYSTEM.
SHIT.
JESSE, AREN'T YOU COMING TO THE CHURCH? I'M HERE.
WAITING.
BUT I CAN'T WAIT ANY LONGER.

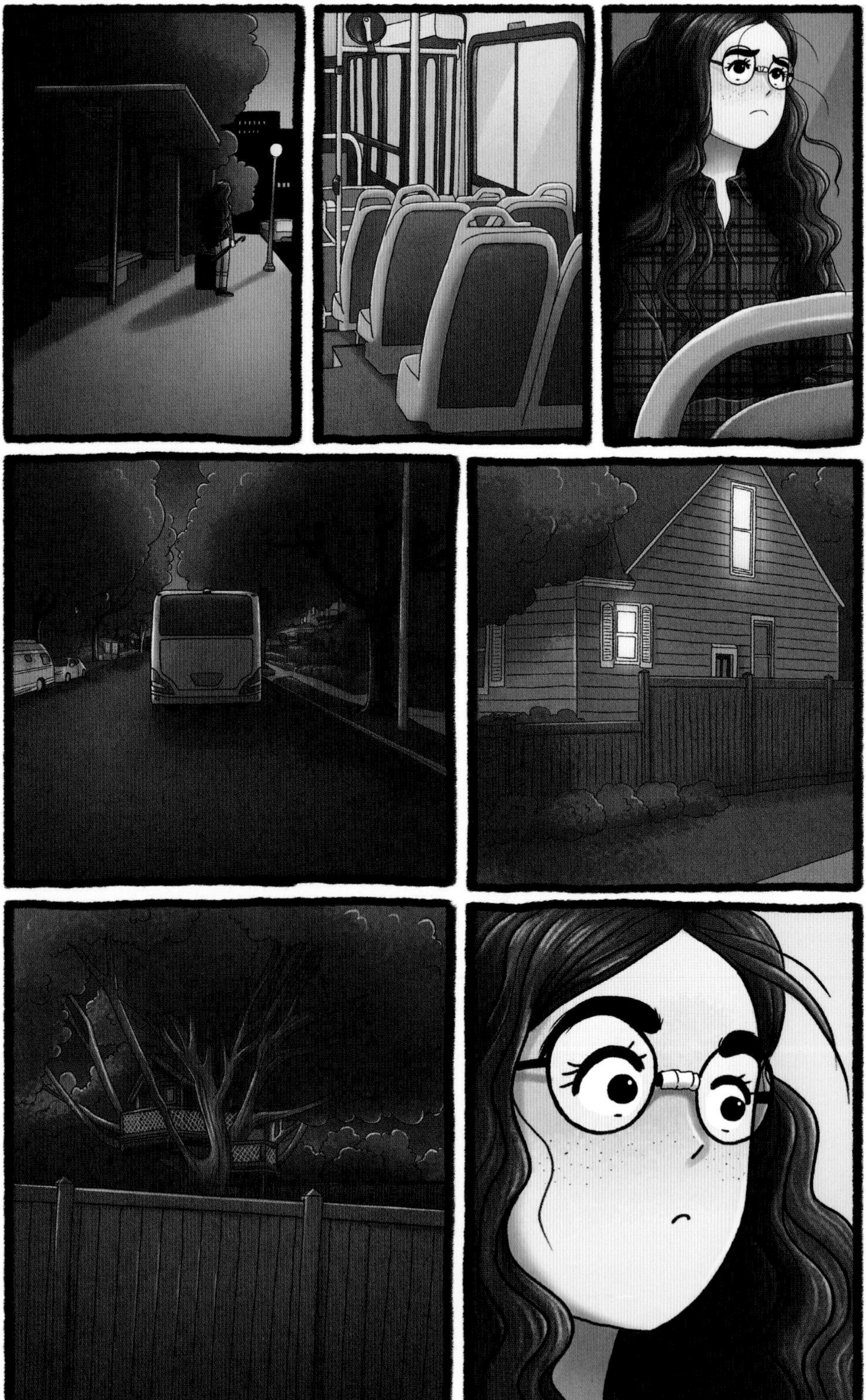

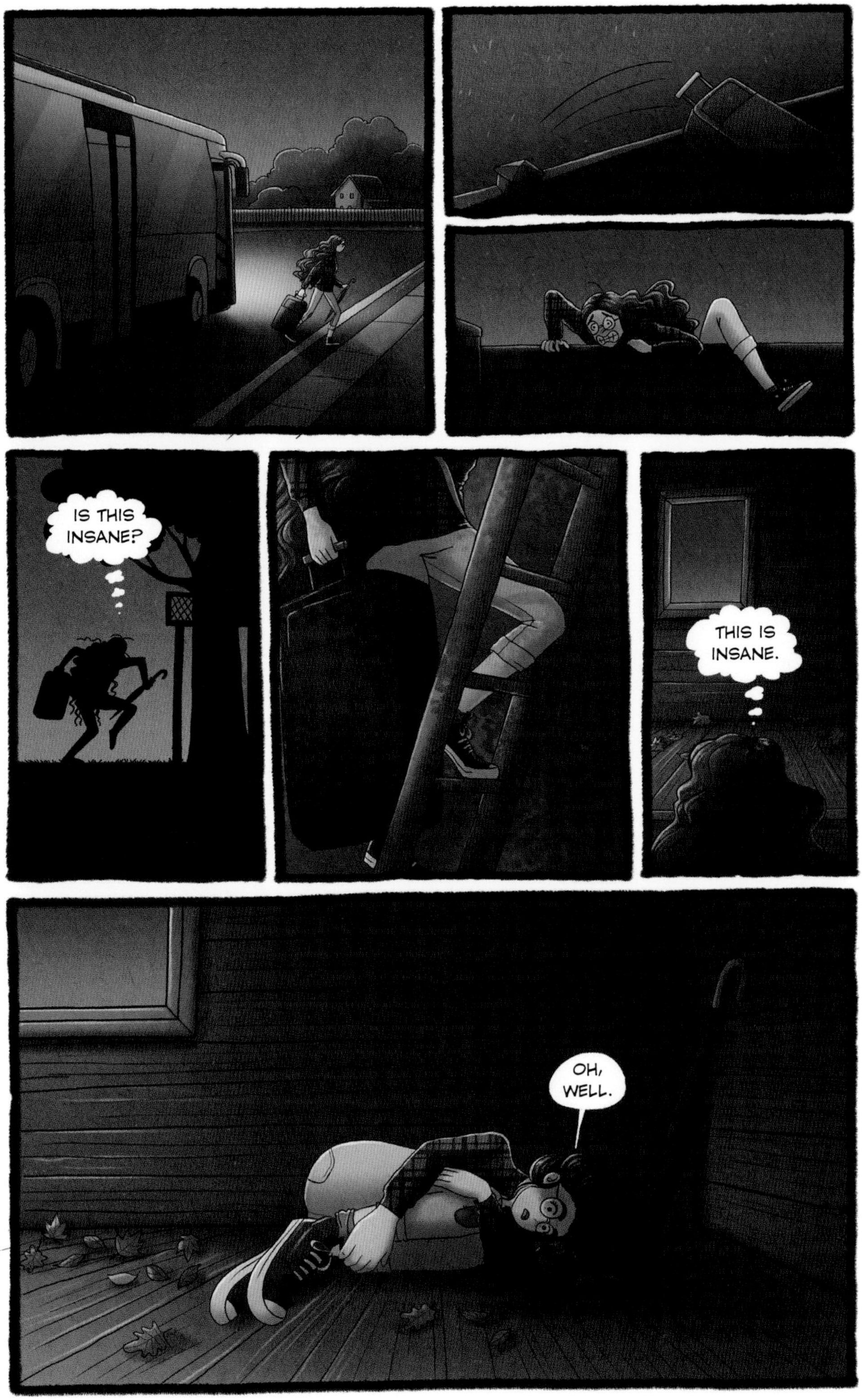
IS THIS INSANE?
THIS IS INSANE.
OH, WELL.

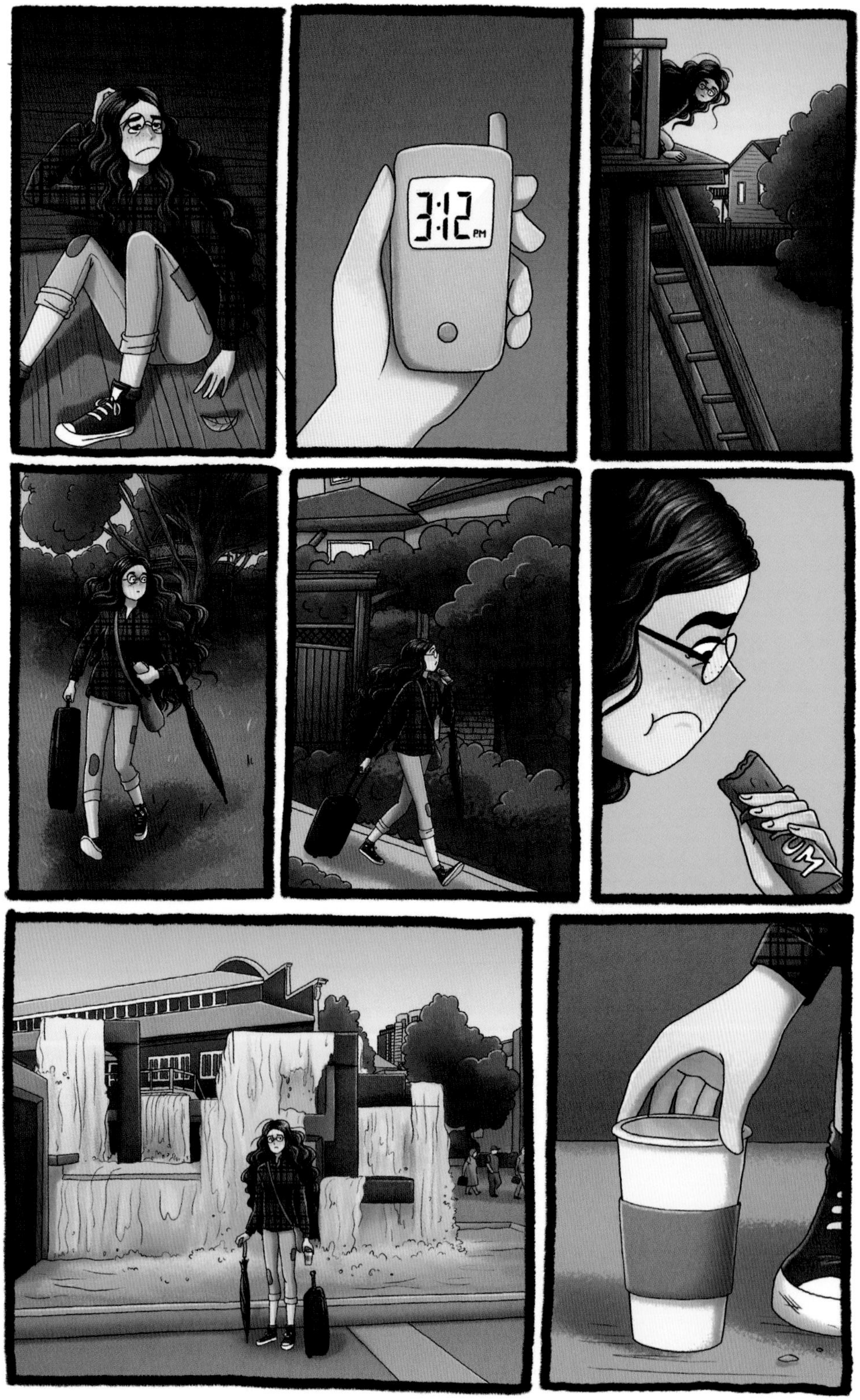
3:12 PM
YUM

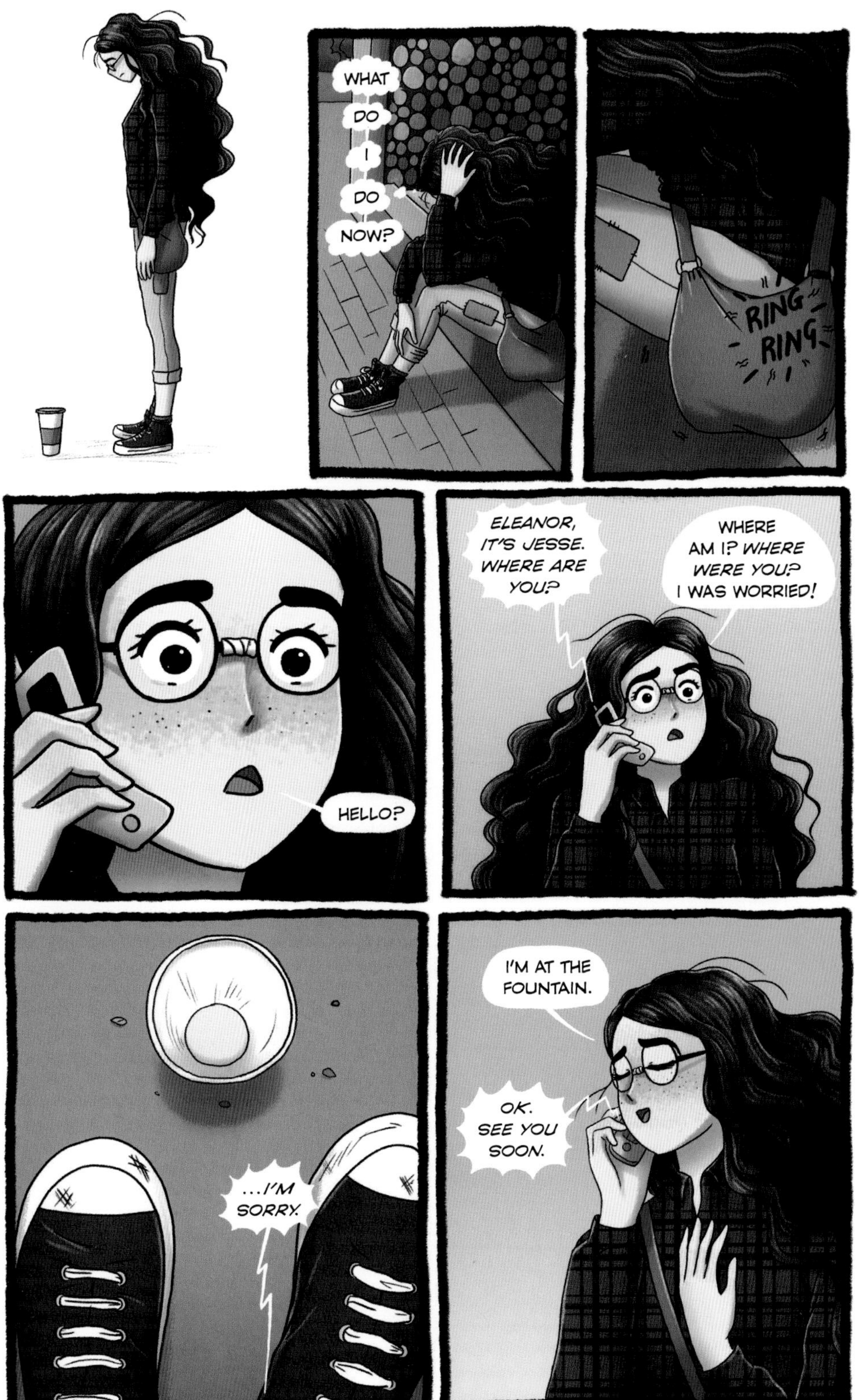
WHAT DO I DO NOW?
RING RING
HELLO?
ELEANOR, IT'S JESSE. WHERE ARE YOU?
WHERE AM I? WHERE WERE YOU? I WAS WORRIED!
...I'M SORRY.
I'M AT THE FOUNTAIN.
OK. SEE YOU SOON.

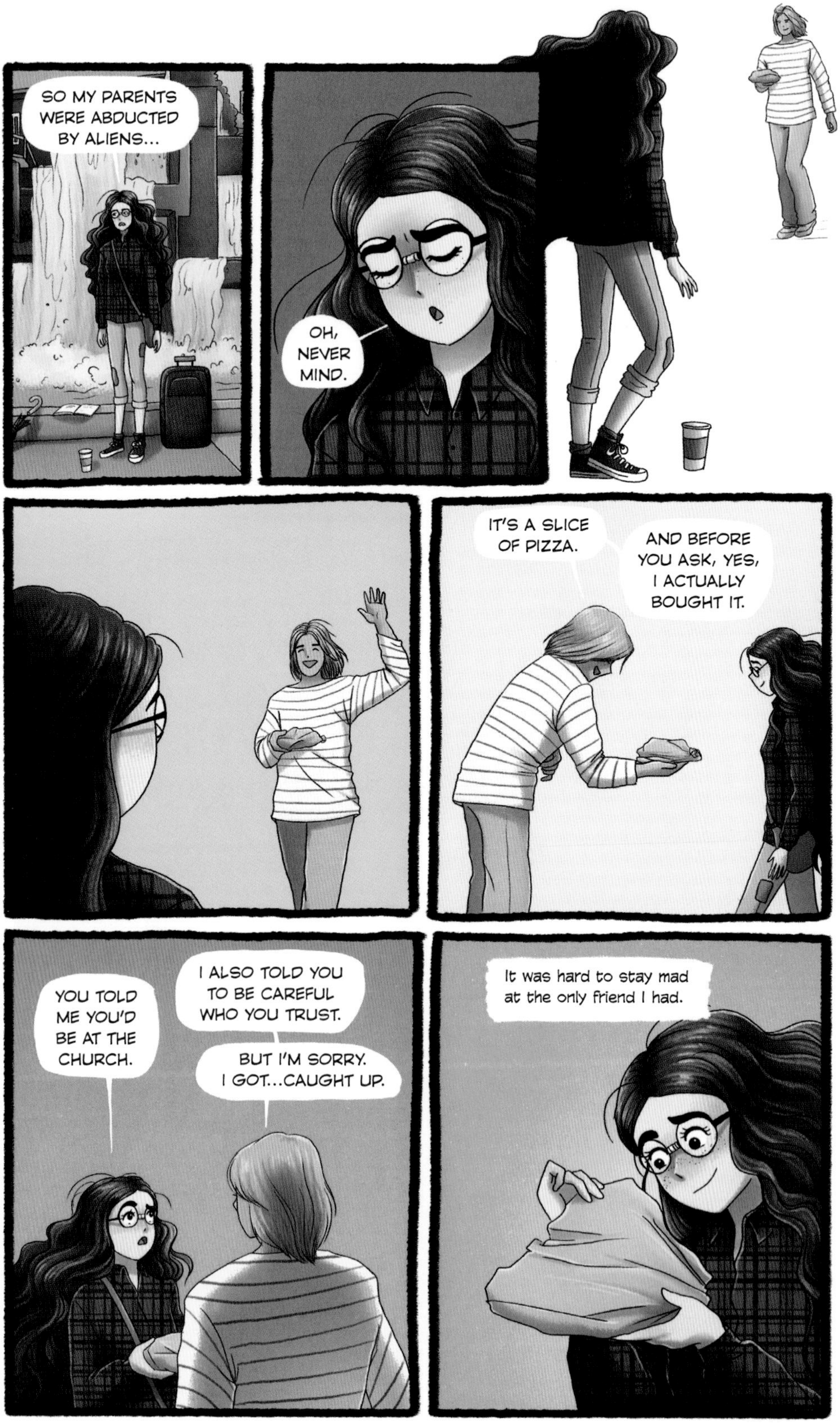
SO MY PARENTS WERE ABDUCTED BY ALIENS...
OH, NEVER MIND.
IT'S A SLICE OF PIZZA.
AND BEFORE YOU ASK, YES, I ACTUALLY BOUGHT IT.
YOU TOLD ME YOU'D BE AT THE CHURCH.
I ALSO TOLD YOU TO BE CAREFUL WHO YOU TRUST.
BUT I'M SORRY. I GOT...CAUGHT UP.
It was hard to stay mad at the only friend I had.

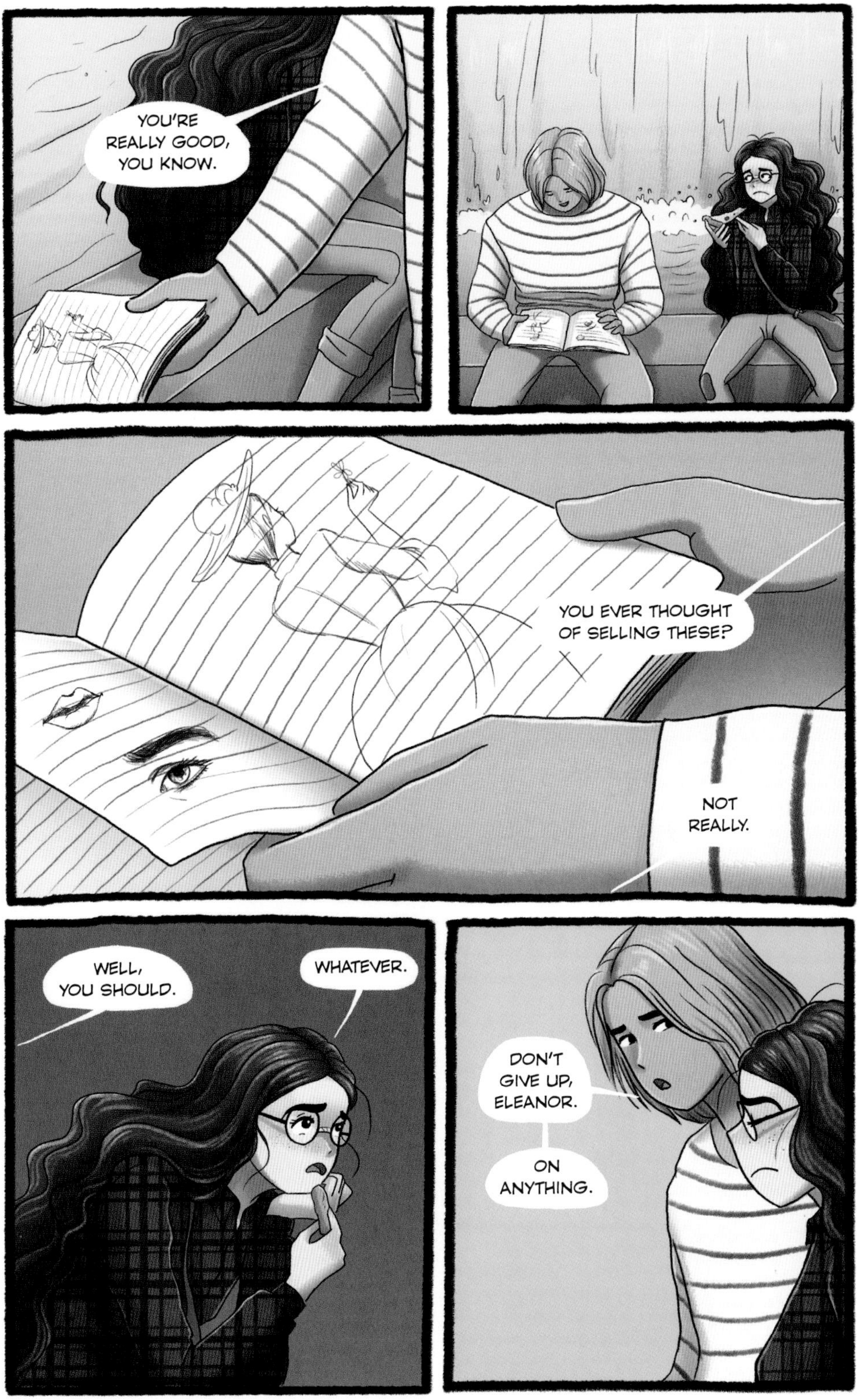
YOU'RE REALLY GOOD, YOU KNOW.
YOU EVER THOUGHT OF SELLING THESE?
NOT REALLY.
WELL, YOU SHOULD.
WHATEVER.
DON'T GIVE UP, ELEANOR.
ON ANYTHING.

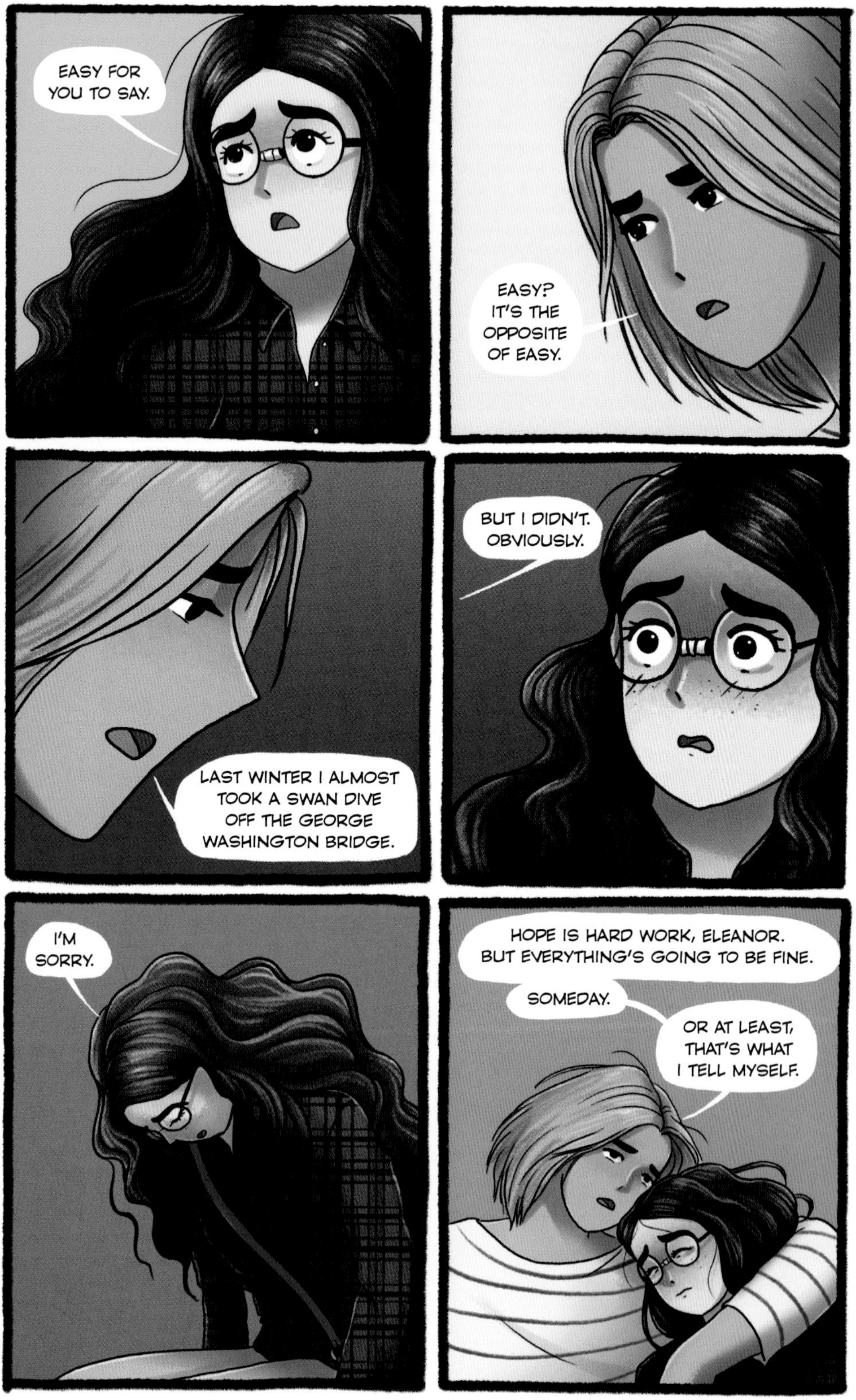
EASY FOR YOU TO SAY.
EASY? IT'S THE OPPOSITE OF EASY.
LAST WINTER I ALMOST TOOK A SWAN DIVE OFF THE GEORGE WASHINGTON BRIDGE.
BUT I DIDN'T. OBVIOUSLY.
I'M SORRY.
HOPE IS HARD WORK, ELEANOR. BUT EVERYTHING'S GOING TO BE FINE.
SOMEDAY.
OR AT LEAST, THAT'S WHAT I TELL MYSELF.

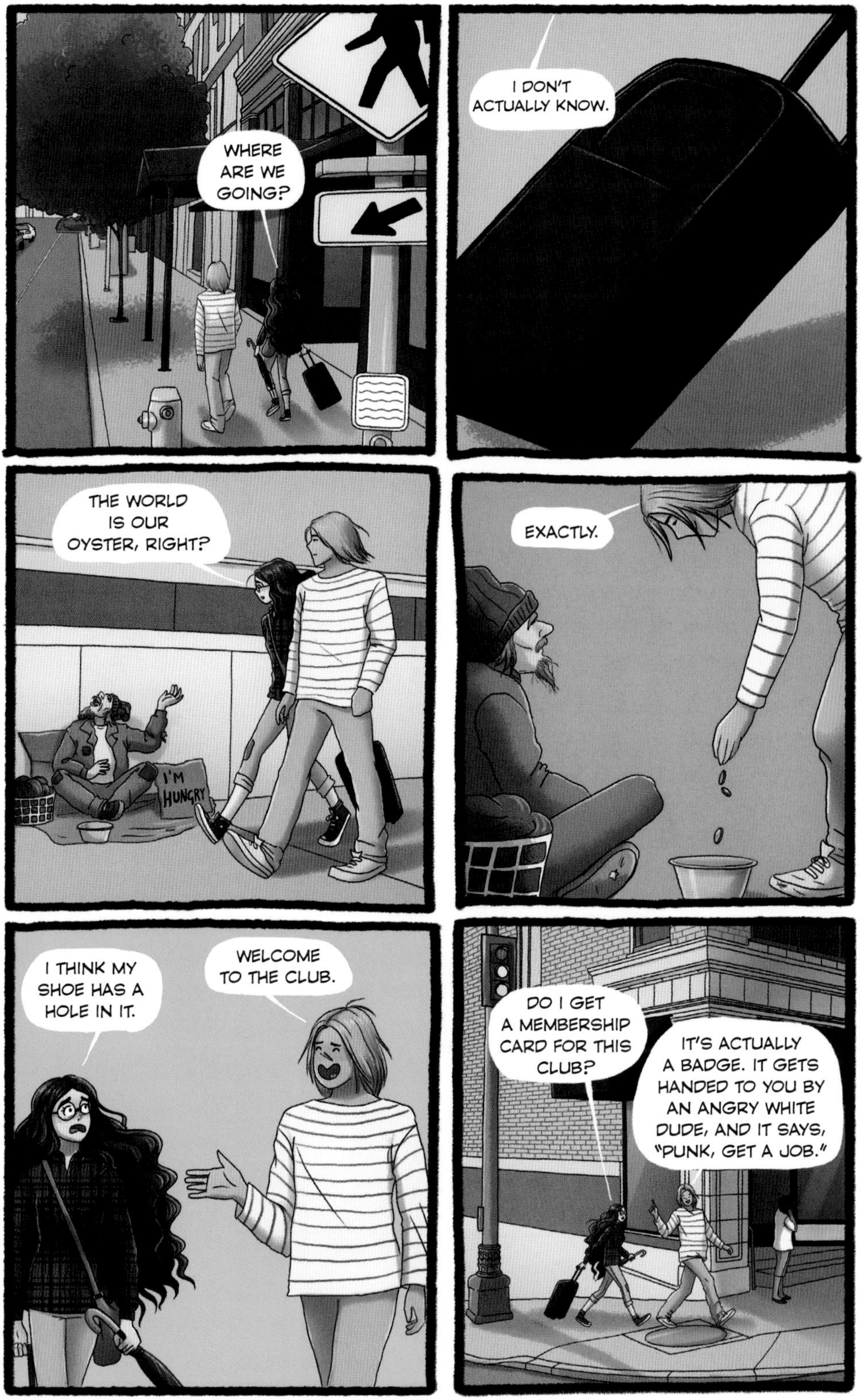
WHERE ARE WE GOING?
I DON'T ACTUALLY KNOW.
THE WORLD IS OUR OYSTER, RIGHT?
I'M HUNGRY
EXACTLY.
I THINK MY SHOE HAS A HOLE IN IT.
WELCOME TO THE CLUB.
DO I GET A MEMBERSHIP CARD FOR THIS CLUB?
IT'S ACTUALLY A BADGE. IT GETS HANDED TO YOU BY AN ANGRY WHITE DUDE, AND IT SAYS, "PUNK, GET A JOB."

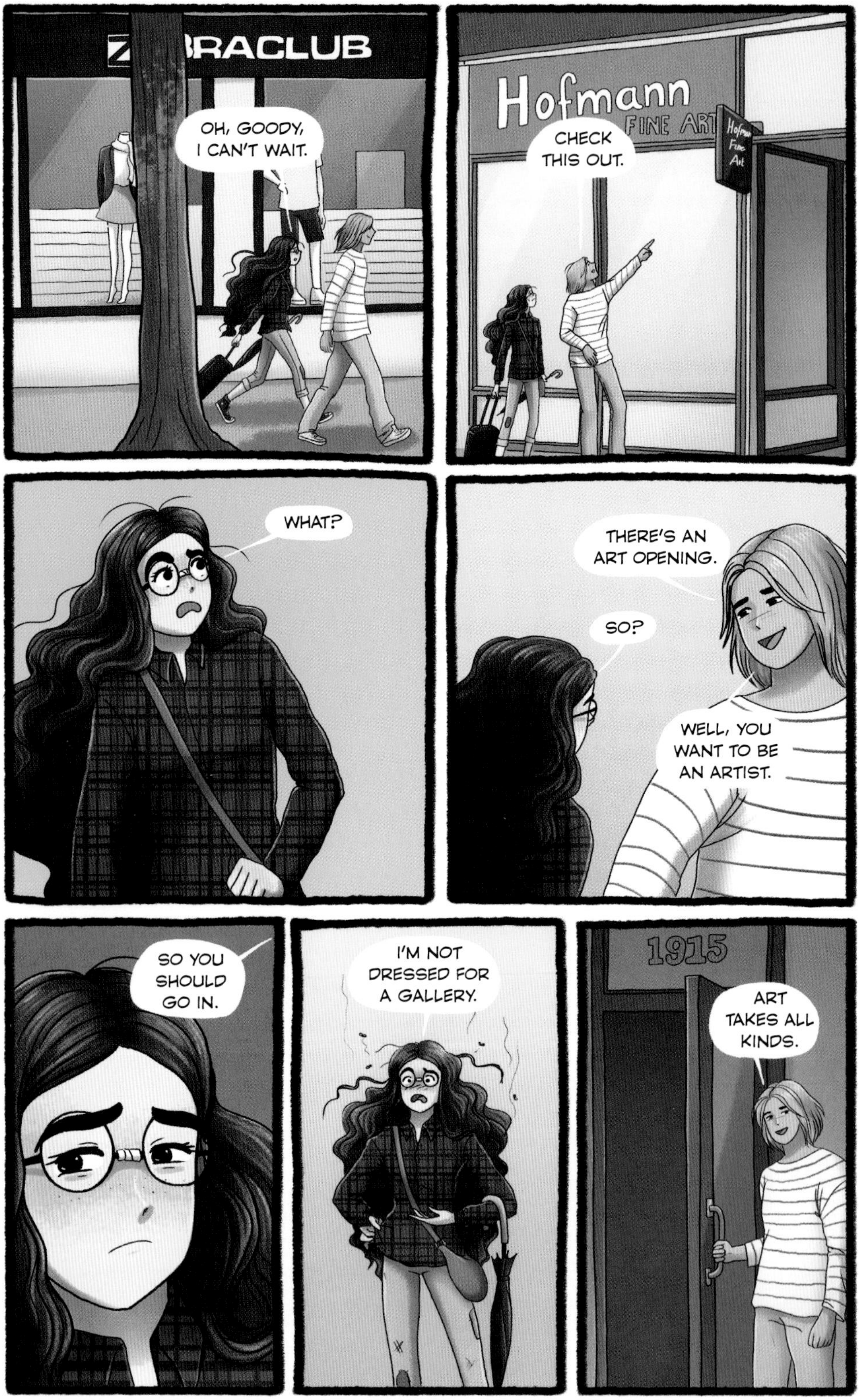

ZEBRACLUB
OH, GOODY, I CAN'T WAIT.
Hofmann FINE ART
Hofmann Fine Art
CHECK THIS OUT.
WHAT?
THERE'S AN ART OPENING.
SO?
WELL, YOU WANT TO BE AN ARTIST.
SO YOU SHOULD GO IN.
I'M NOT DRESSED FOR A GALLERY.
1915
ART TAKES ALL KINDS.

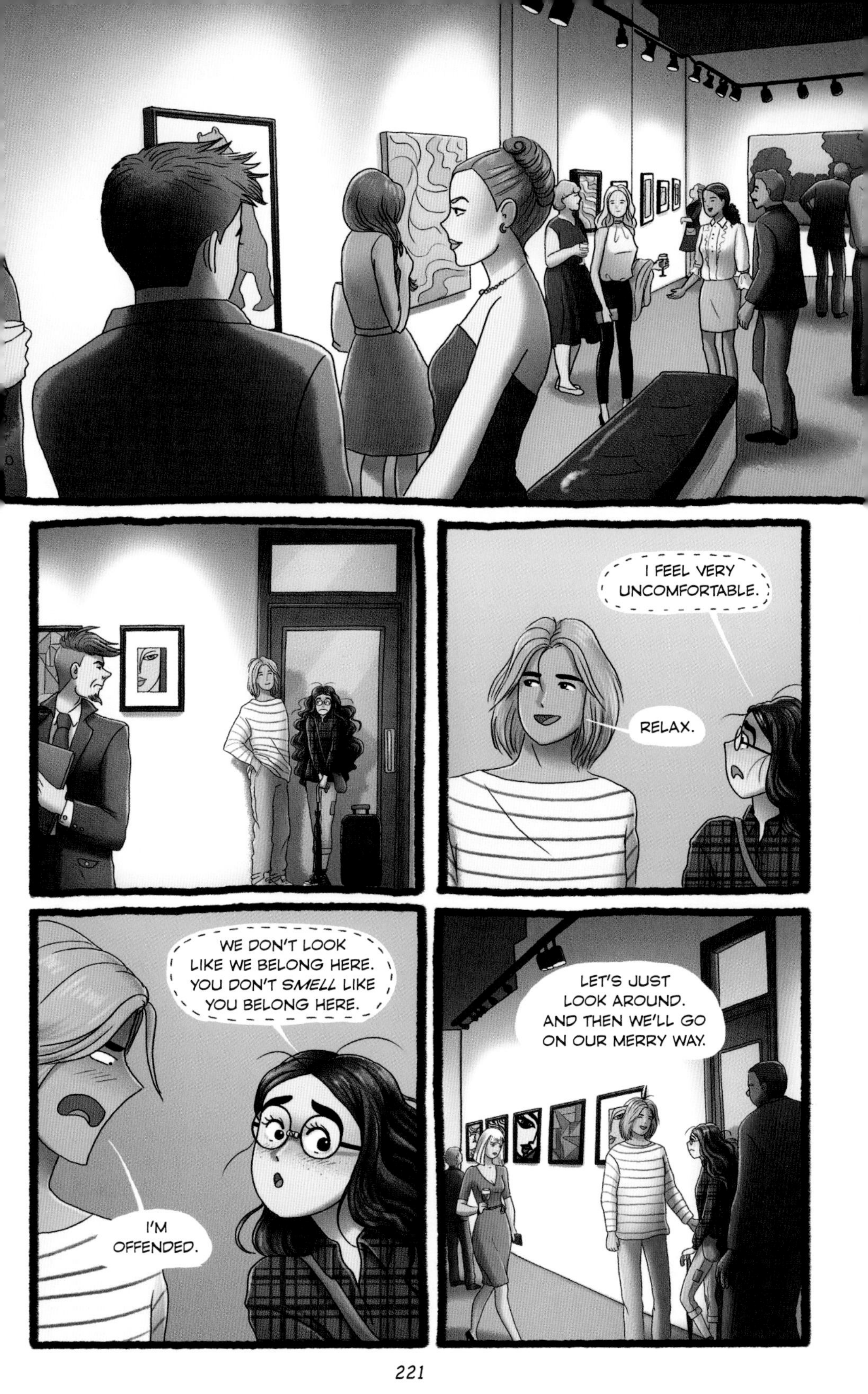
I FEEL VERY UNCOMFORTABLE.
RELAX.
WE DON'T LOOK LIKE WE BELONG HERE. YOU DON'T *SMELL* LIKE YOU BELONG HERE.
I'M OFFENDED.
LET'S JUST LOOK AROUND. AND THEN WE'LL GO ON OUR MERRY WAY.

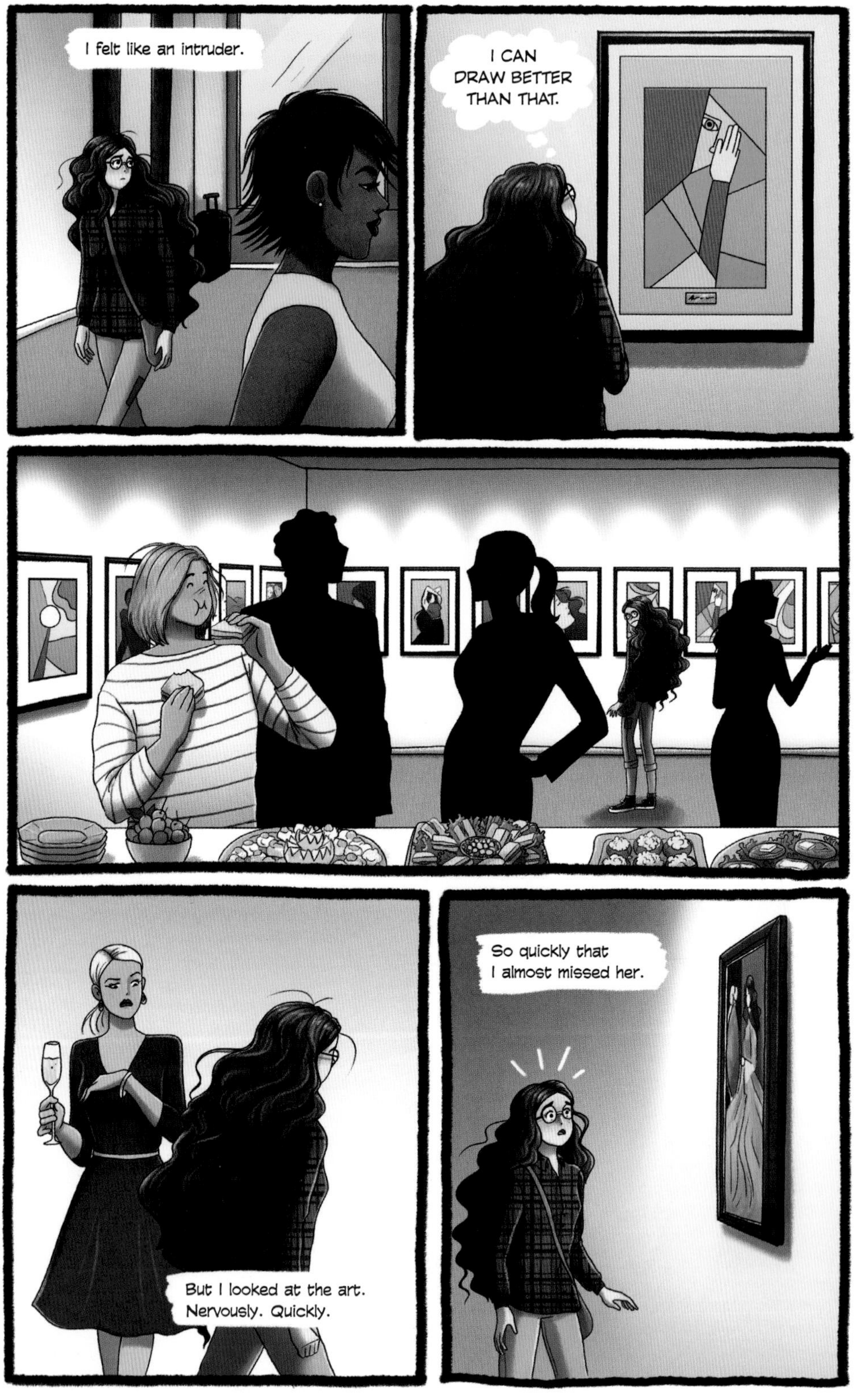
I felt like an intruder.
I CAN DRAW BETTER THAN THAT.
But I looked at the art. Nervously. Quickly.
So quickly that I almost missed her.

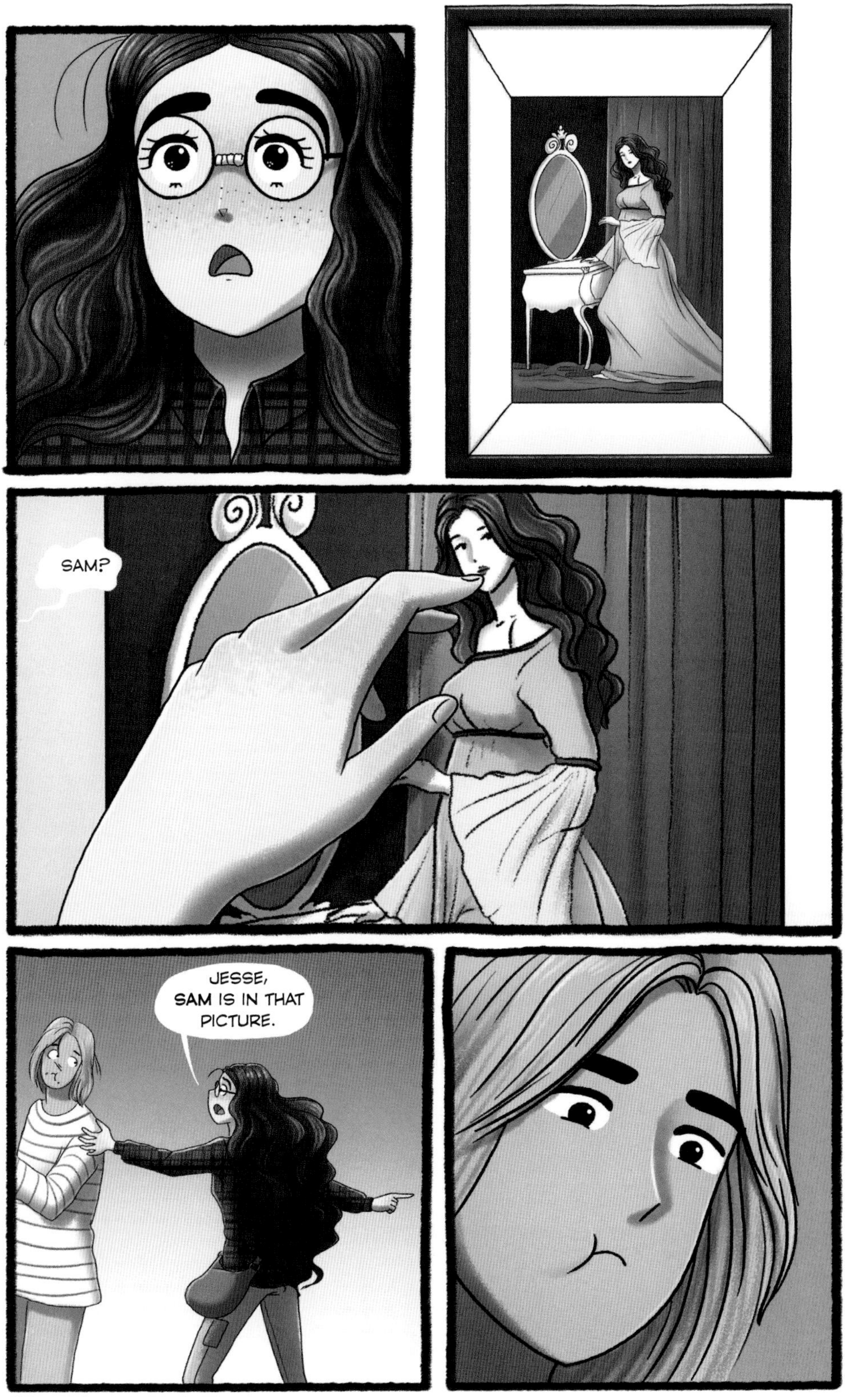
SAM?
JESSE, SAM IS IN THAT PICTURE.

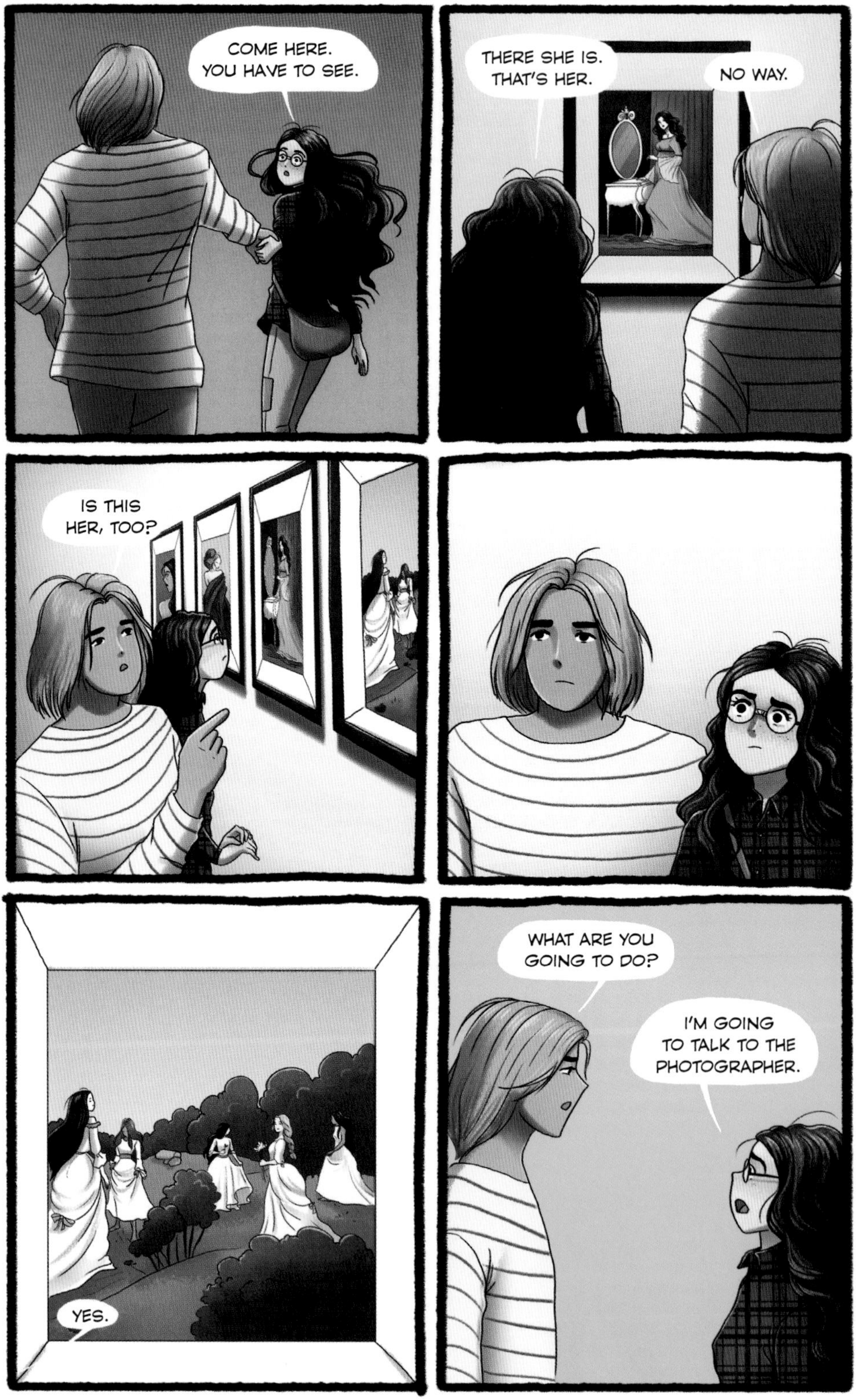
COME HERE. YOU HAVE TO SEE.
THERE SHE IS. THAT'S HER.
NO WAY.
IS THIS HER, TOO?
YES.
WHAT ARE YOU GOING TO DO?
I'M GOING TO TALK TO THE PHOTOGRAPHER.

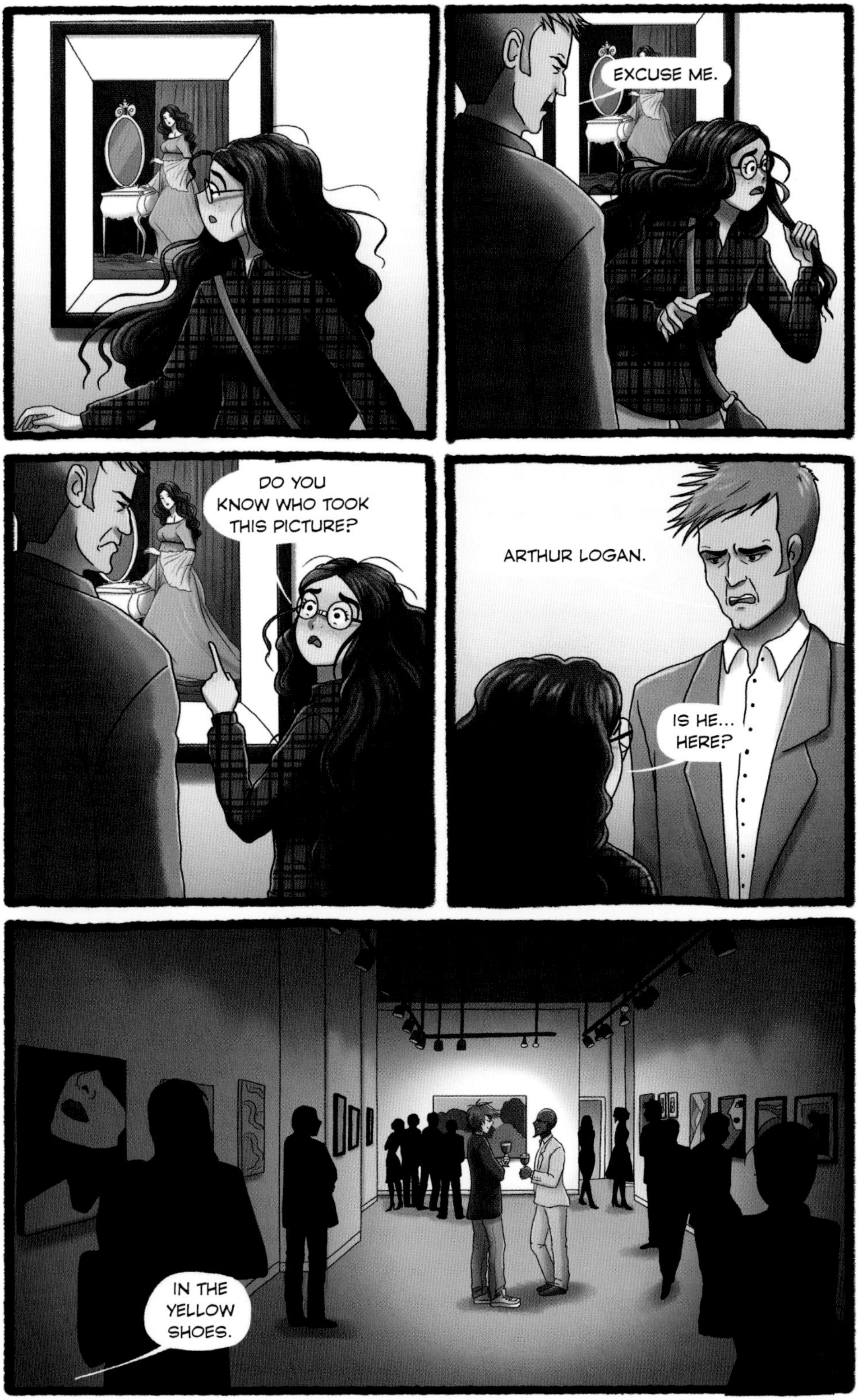
EXCUSE ME.
DO YOU KNOW WHO TOOK THIS PICTURE?
ARTHUR LOGAN.
IS HE... HERE?
IN THE YELLOW SHOES.

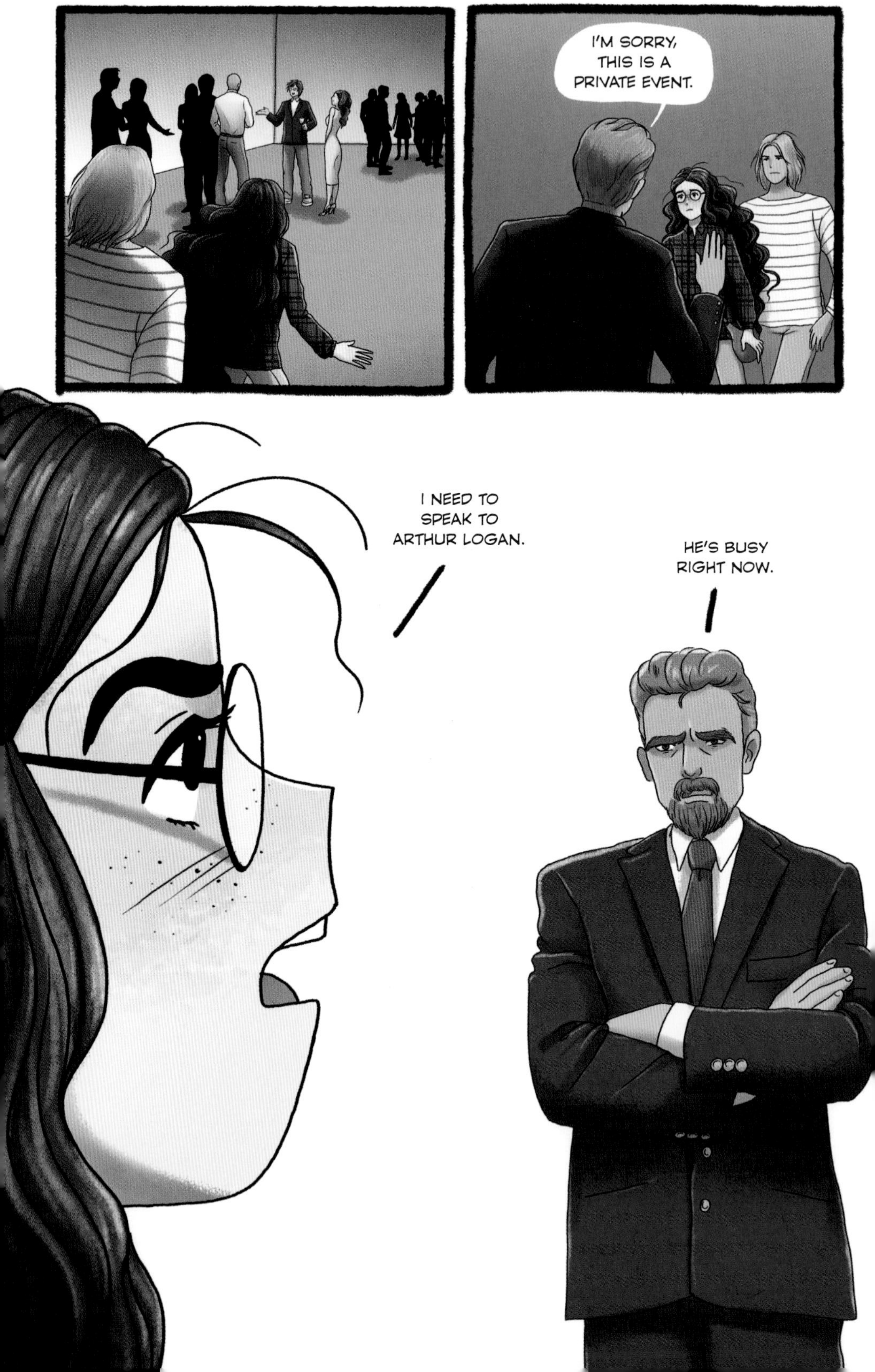
I'M SORRY, THIS IS A PRIVATE EVENT.
I NEED TO SPEAK TO ARTHUR LOGAN.
HE'S BUSY RIGHT NOW.

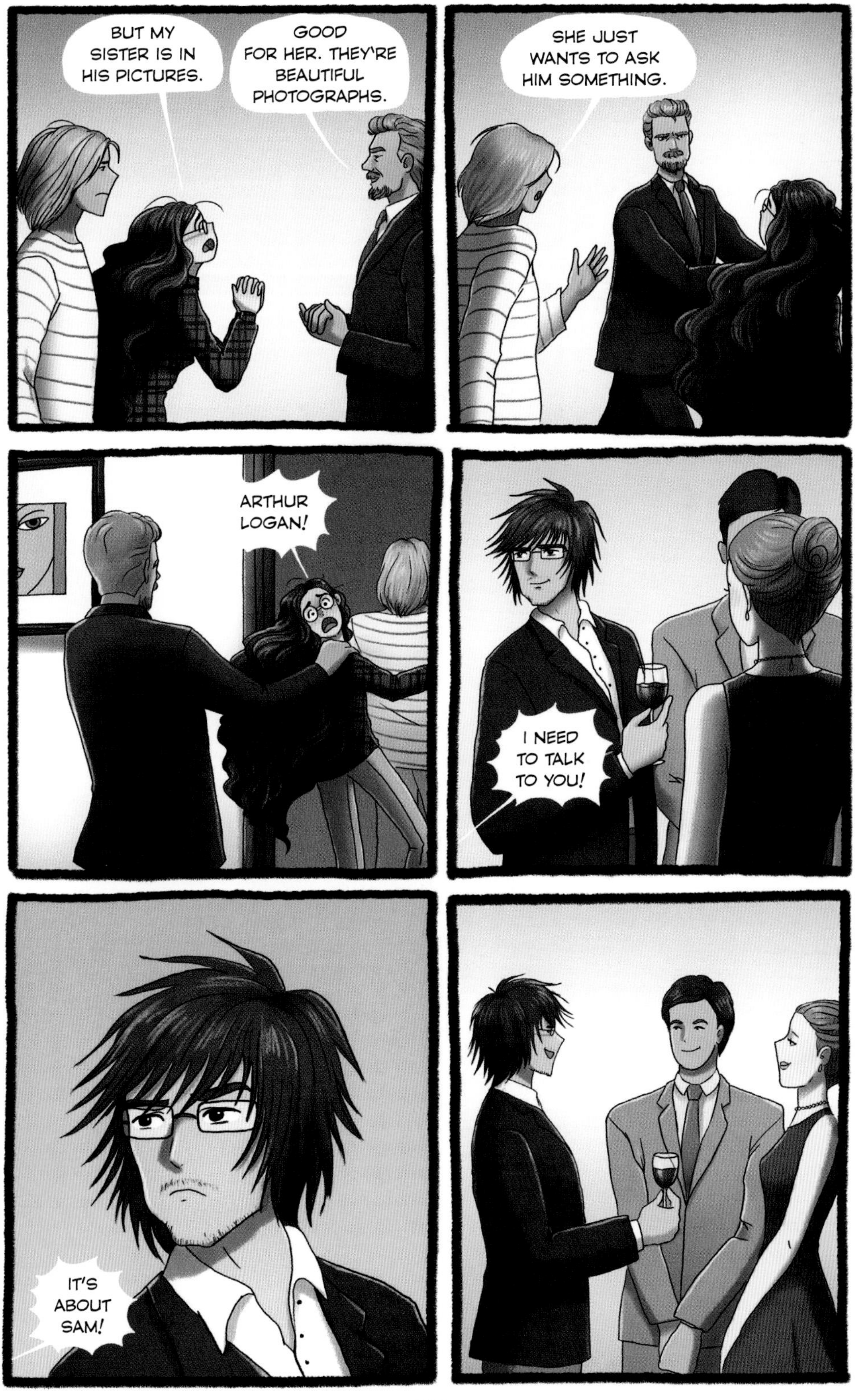
BUT MY SISTER IS IN HIS PICTURES.
GOOD FOR HER. THEY'RE BEAUTIFUL PHOTOGRAPHS.
SHE JUST WANTS TO ASK HIM SOMETHING.
ARTHUR LOGAN!
I NEED TO TALK TO YOU!
IT'S ABOUT SAM!

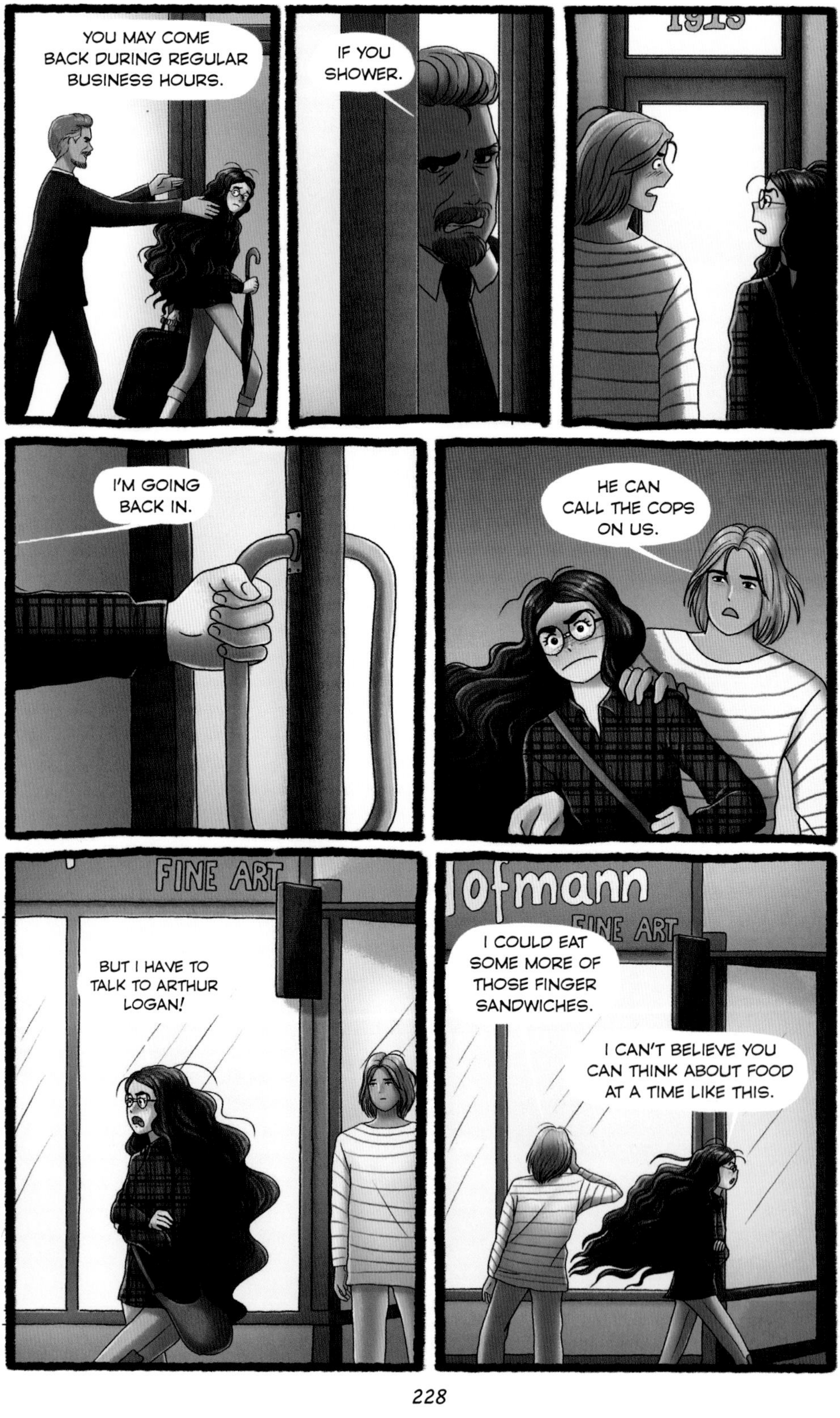
YOU MAY COME BACK DURING REGULAR BUSINESS HOURS.
IF YOU SHOWER.
1915
I'M GOING BACK IN.
HE CAN CALL THE COPS ON US.
FINE ART
BUT I HAVE TO TALK TO ARTHUR LOGAN!
ofmann
FINE ART
I COULD EAT SOME MORE OF THOSE FINGER SANDWICHES.
I CAN'T BELIEVE YOU CAN THINK ABOUT FOOD AT A TIME LIKE THIS.

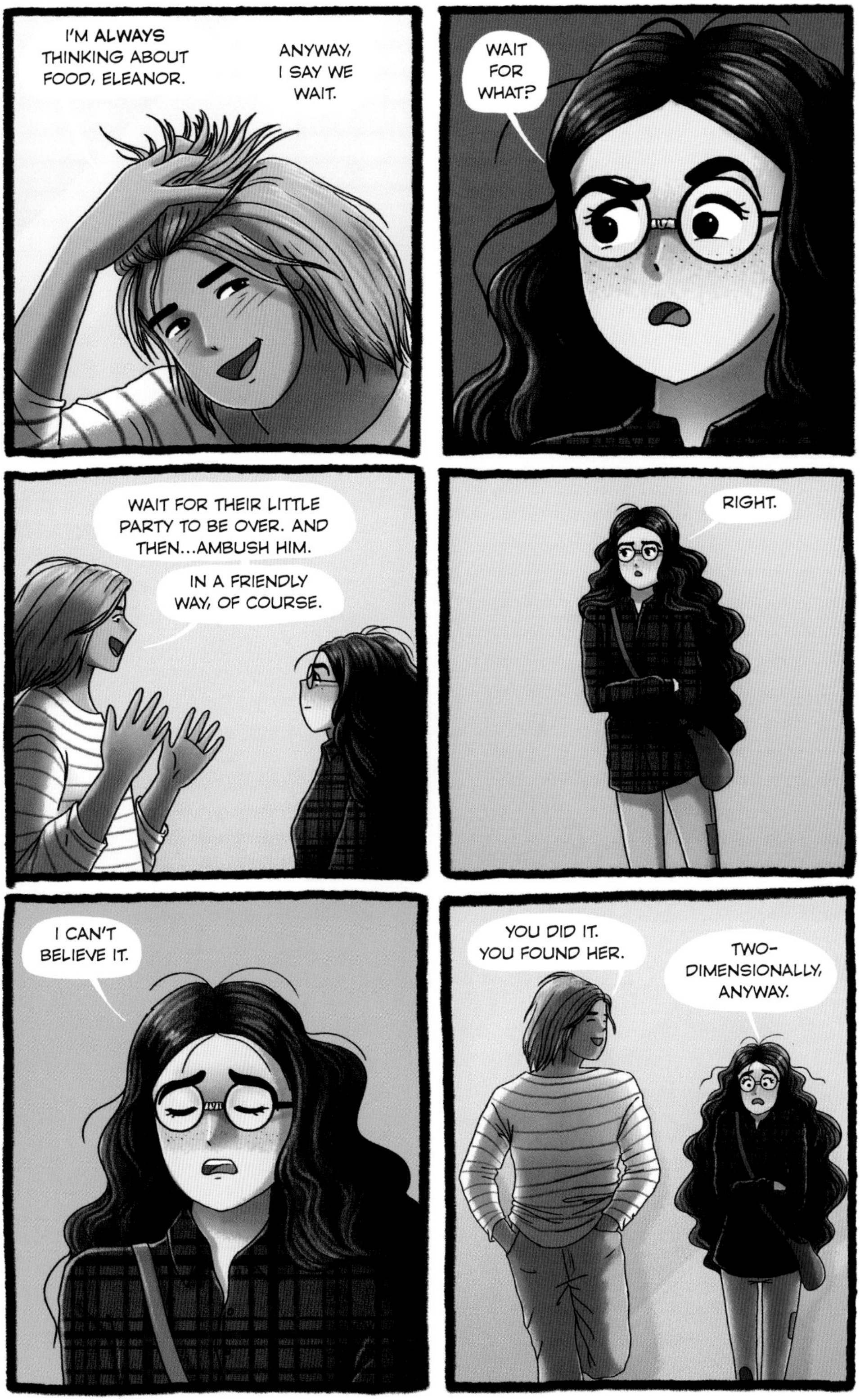
I'M ALWAYS THINKING ABOUT FOOD, ELEANOR.
ANYWAY, I SAY WE WAIT.
WAIT FOR WHAT?
WAIT FOR THEIR LITTLE PARTY TO BE OVER. AND THEN...AMBUSH HIM.
IN A FRIENDLY WAY, OF COURSE.
RIGHT.
I CAN'T BELIEVE IT.
YOU DID IT. YOU FOUND HER.
TWO-DIMENSIONALLY, ANYWAY.

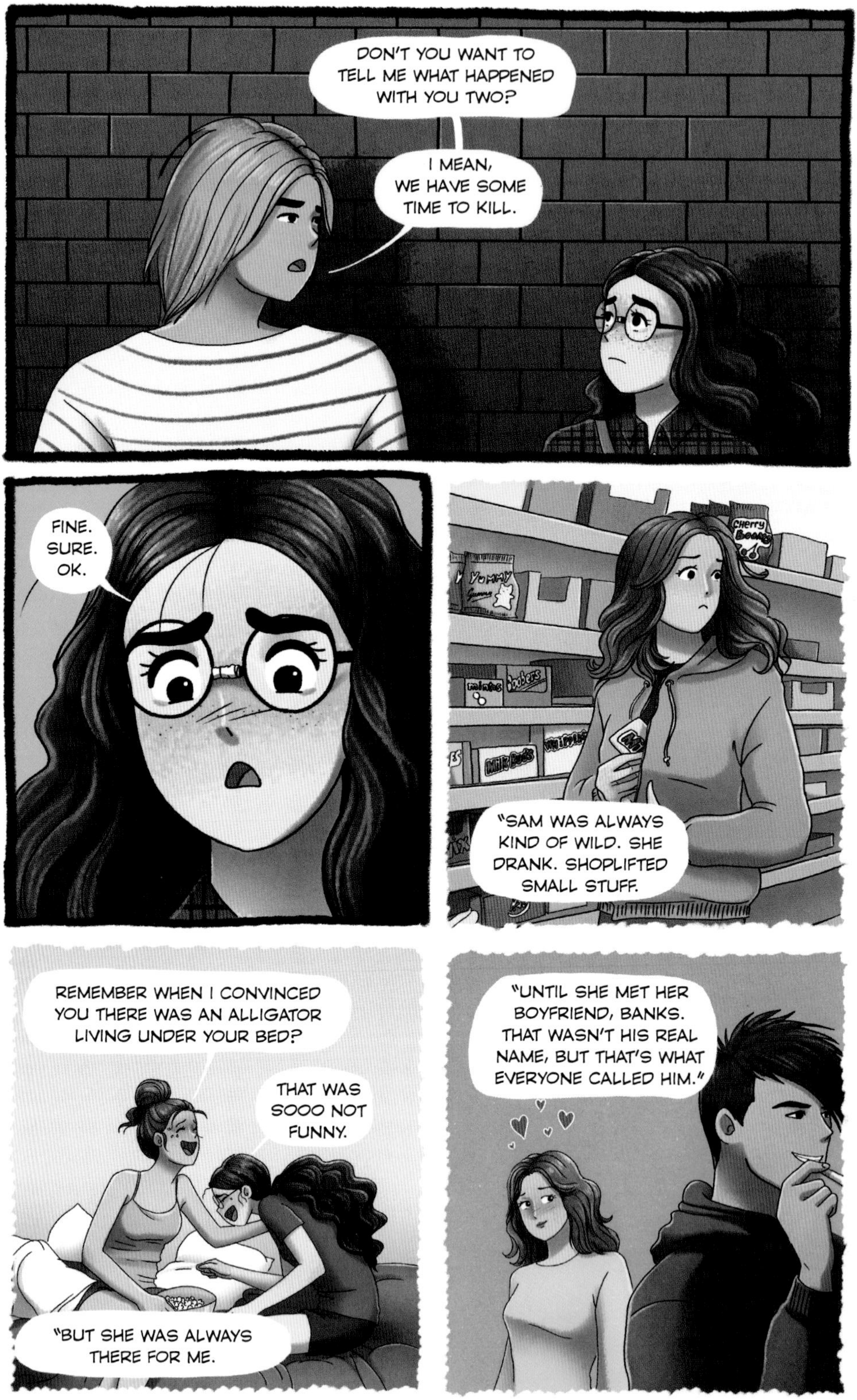
DON'T YOU WANT TO TELL ME WHAT HAPPENED WITH YOU TWO?
I MEAN, WE HAVE SOME TIME TO KILL.
FINE. SURE. OK.
"SAM WAS ALWAYS KIND OF WILD. SHE DRANK. SHOPLIFTED SMALL STUFF.
REMEMBER WHEN I CONVINCED YOU THERE WAS AN ALLIGATOR LIVING UNDER YOUR BED?
THAT WAS SOOO NOT FUNNY.
"BUT SHE WAS ALWAYS THERE FOR ME.
"UNTIL SHE MET HER BOYFRIEND, BANKS. THAT WASN'T HIS REAL NAME, BUT THAT'S WHAT EVERYONE CALLED HIM."

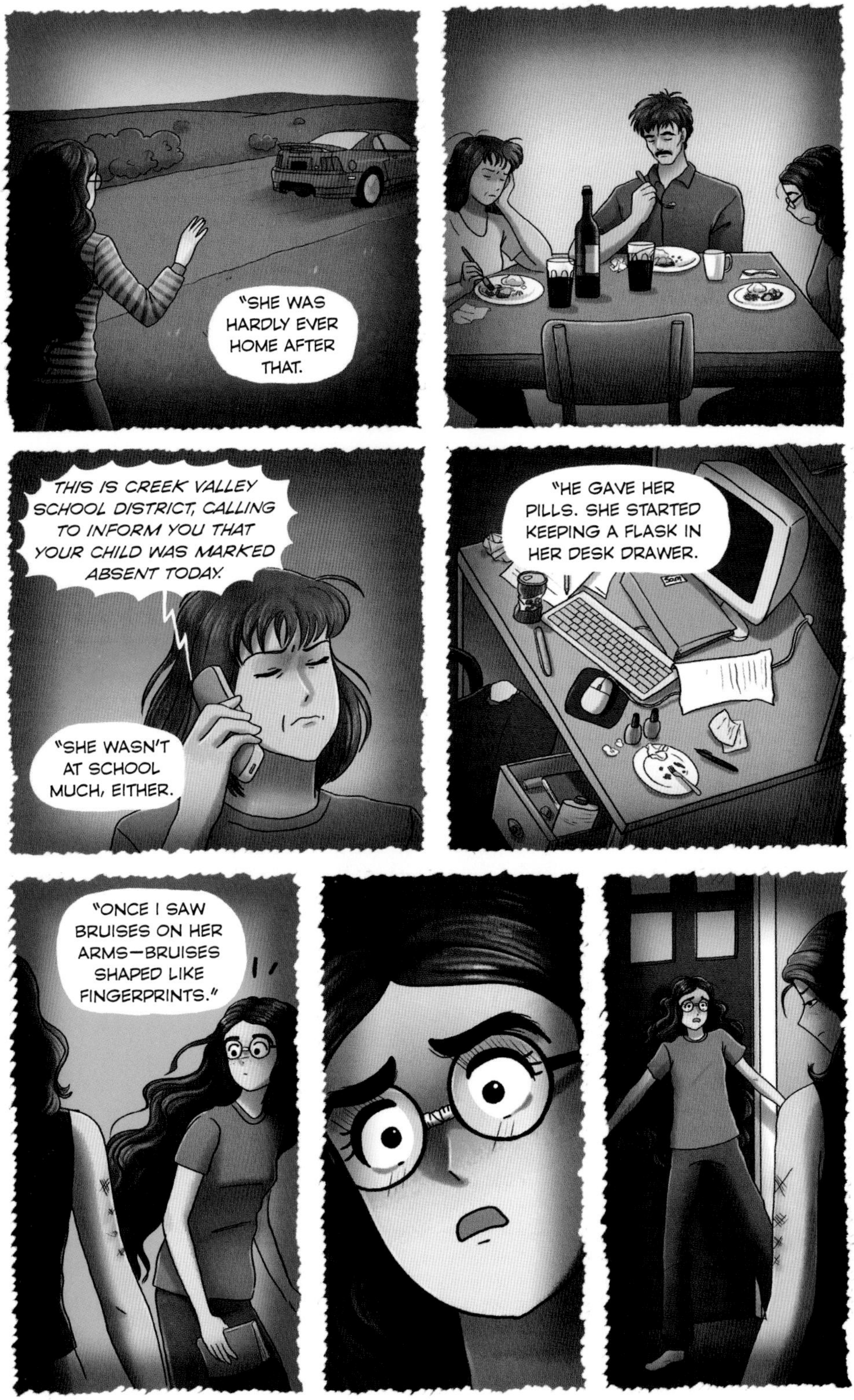
"SHE WAS HARDLY EVER HOME AFTER THAT.
THIS IS CREEK VALLEY SCHOOL DISTRICT, CALLING TO INFORM YOU THAT YOUR CHILD WAS MARKED ABSENT TODAY.
"SHE WASN'T AT SCHOOL MUCH, EITHER.
"HE GAVE HER PILLS. SHE STARTED KEEPING A FLASK IN HER DESK DRAWER.
"ONCE I SAW BRUISES ON HER ARMS—BRUISES SHAPED LIKE FINGERPRINTS."

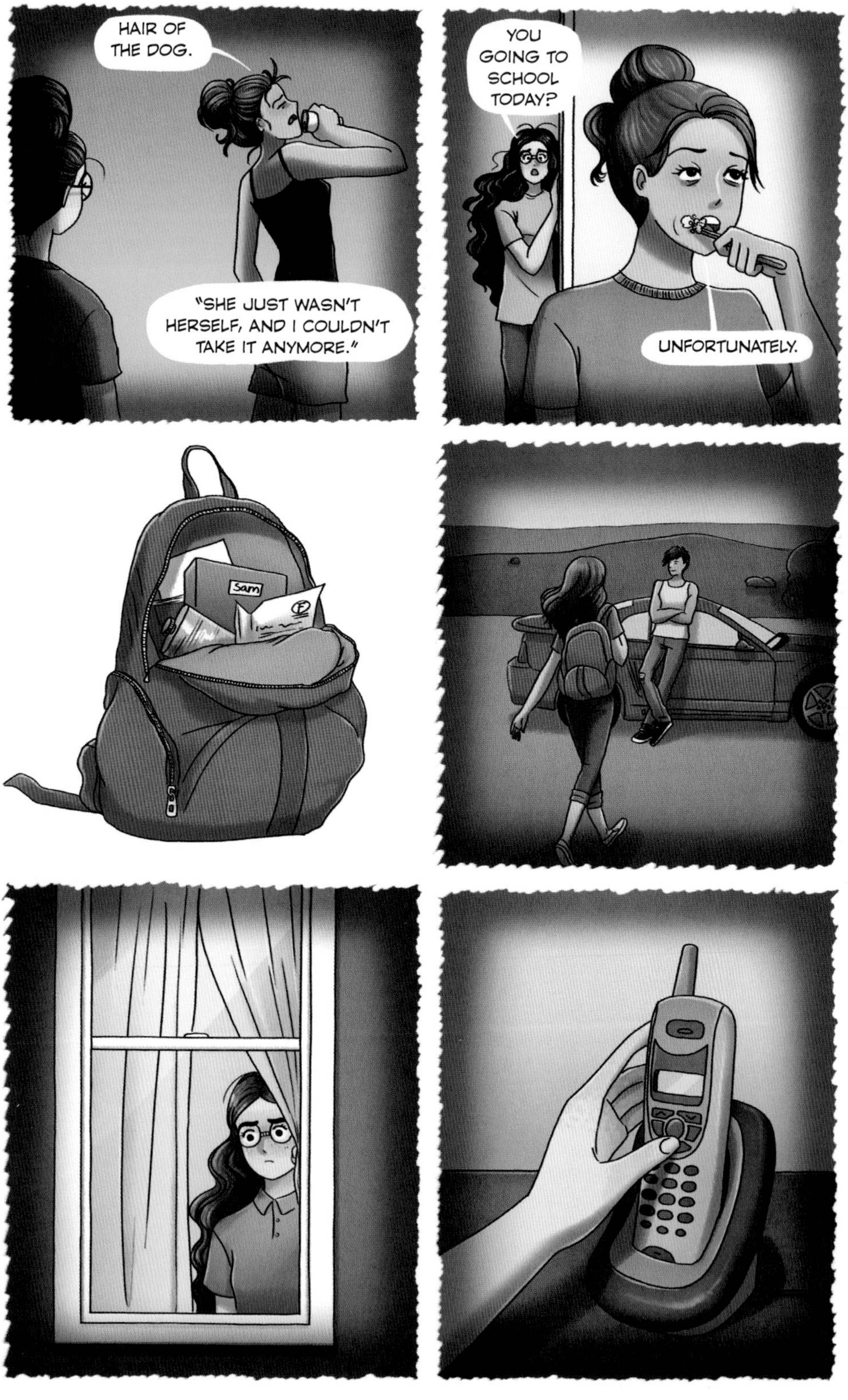
HAIR OF THE DOG.
"SHE JUST WASN'T HERSELF, AND I COULDN'T TAKE IT ANYMORE."
YOU GOING TO SCHOOL TODAY?
UNFORTUNATELY.
Sam

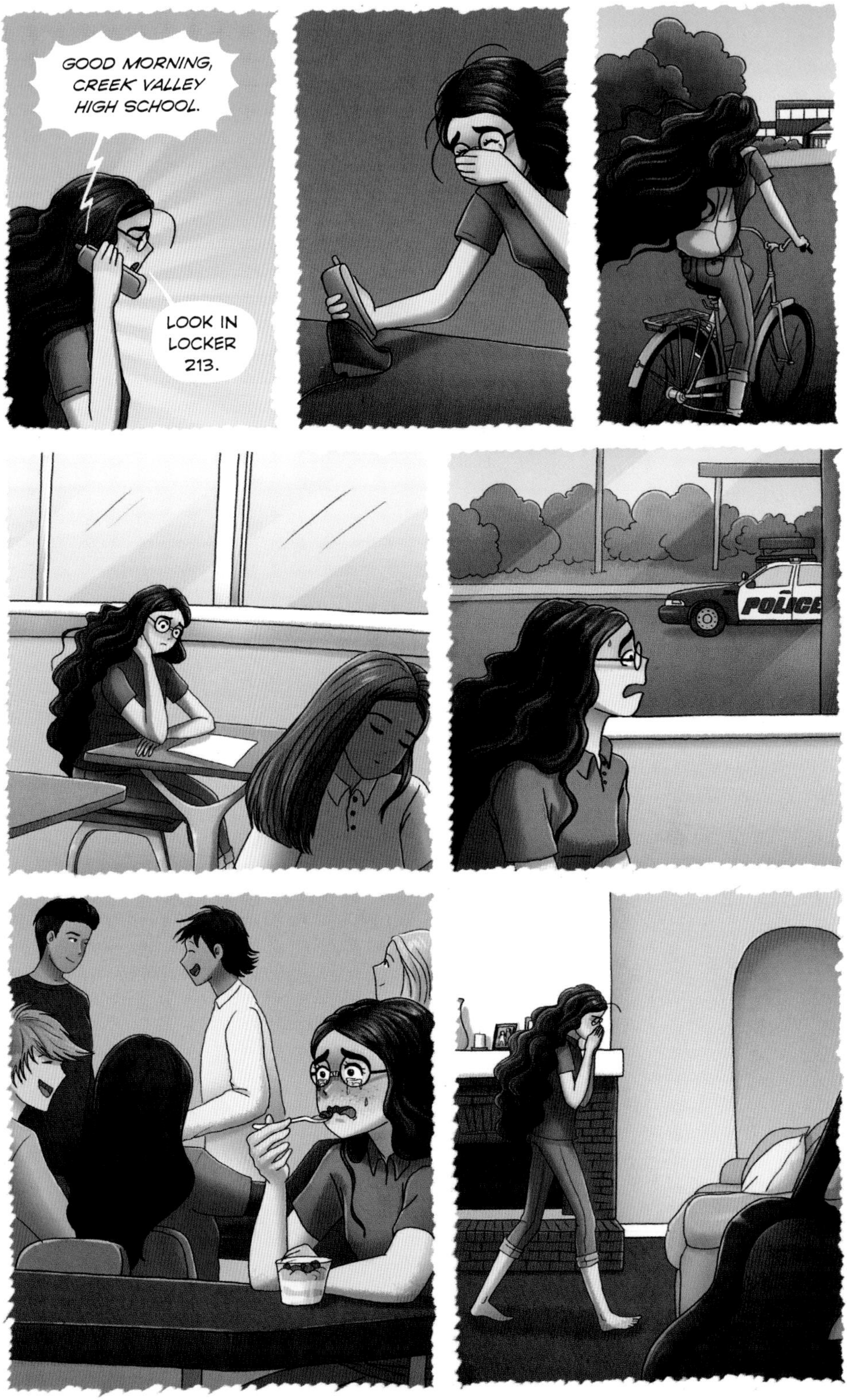
GOOD MORNING, CREEK VALLEY HIGH SCHOOL.
LOOK IN LOCKER 213.
POLICE

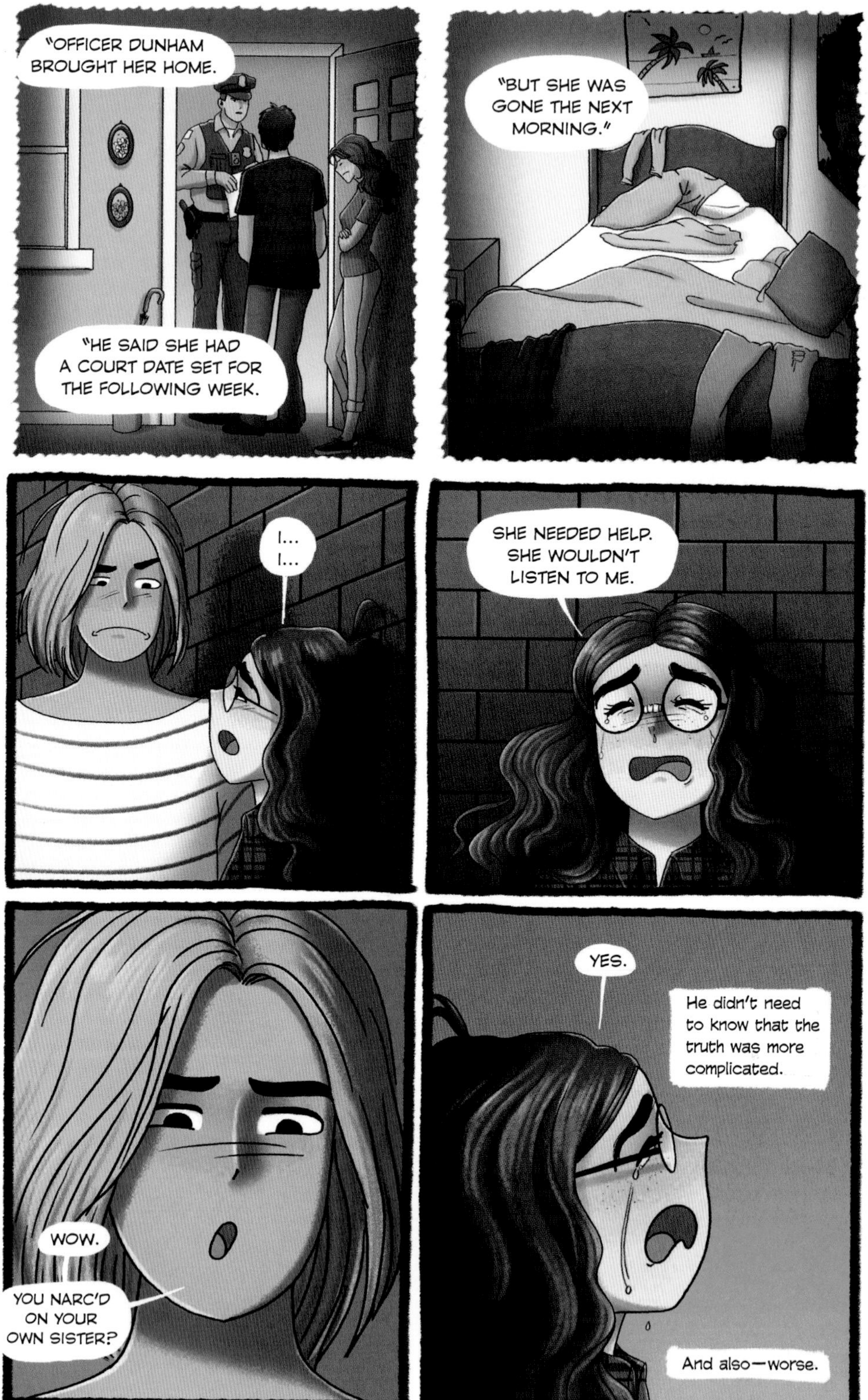
"OFFICER DUNHAM BROUGHT HER HOME.
"HE SAID SHE HAD A COURT DATE SET FOR THE FOLLOWING WEEK.
"BUT SHE WAS GONE THE NEXT MORNING."
I... I...
SHE NEEDED HELP. SHE WOULDN'T LISTEN TO ME.
WOW.
YOU NARC'D ON YOUR OWN SISTER?
YES.
He didn't need to know that the truth was more complicated.
And also—worse.

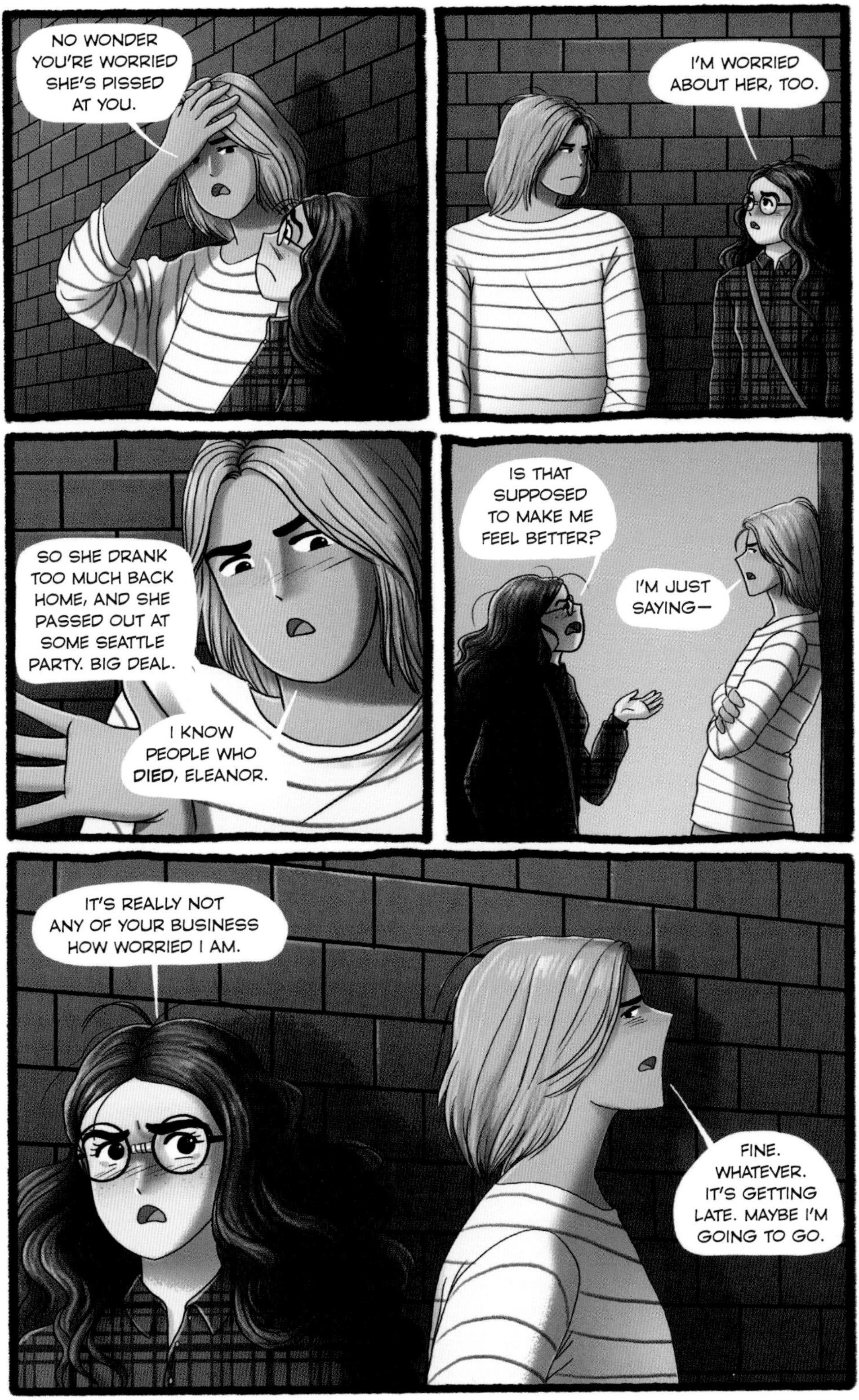
NO WONDER YOU'RE WORRIED SHE'S PISSED AT YOU.
I'M WORRIED ABOUT HER, TOO.
SO SHE DRANK TOO MUCH BACK HOME, AND SHE PASSED OUT AT SOME SEATTLE PARTY. BIG DEAL.
I KNOW PEOPLE WHO **DIED**, ELEANOR.
IS THAT SUPPOSED TO MAKE ME FEEL BETTER?
I'M JUST SAYING—
IT'S REALLY NOT ANY OF YOUR BUSINESS HOW WORRIED I AM.
FINE. WHATEVER. IT'S GETTING LATE. MAYBE I'M GOING TO GO.

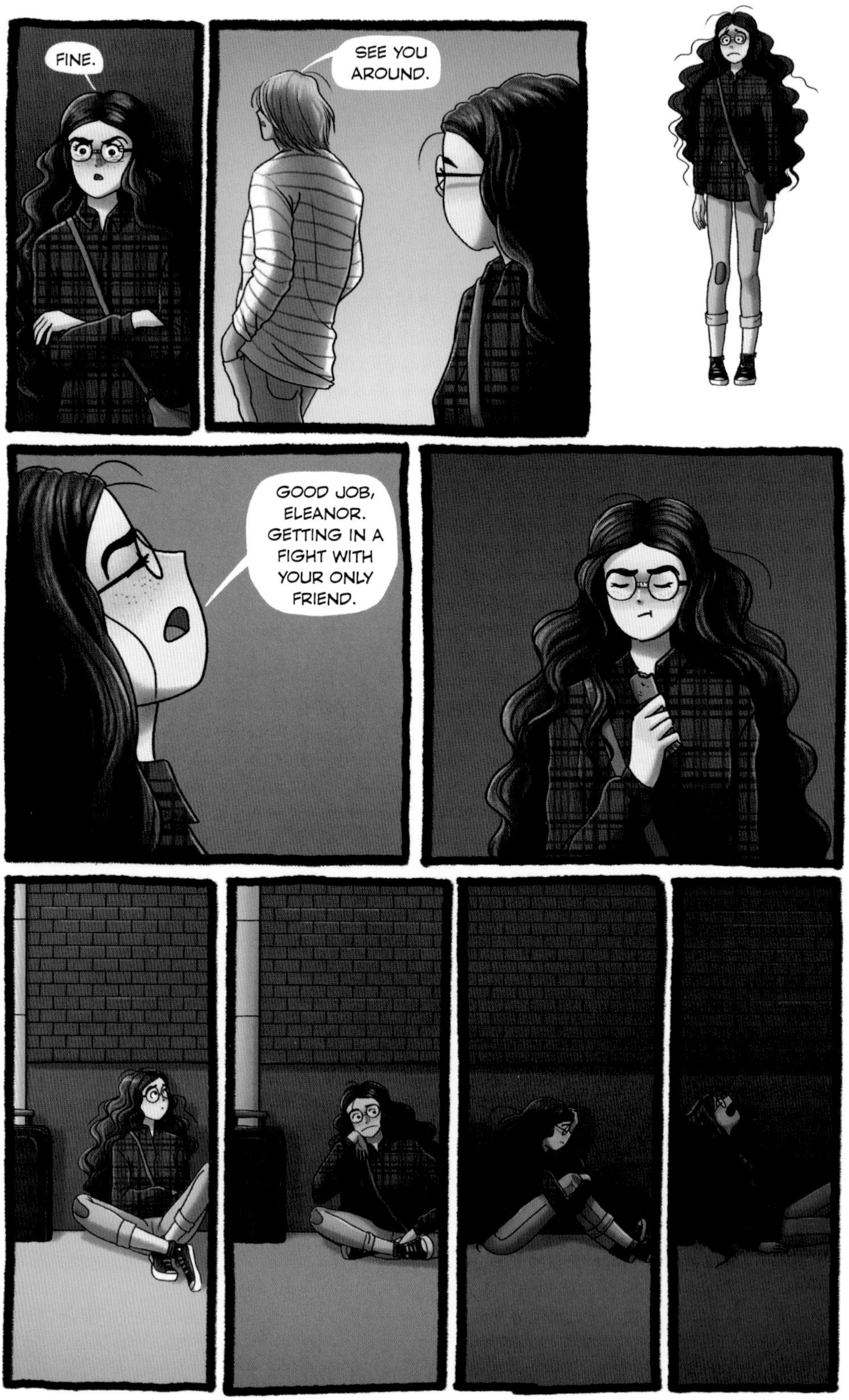
FINE.
SEE YOU AROUND.
GOOD JOB, ELEANOR. GETTING IN A FIGHT WITH YOUR ONLY FRIEND.

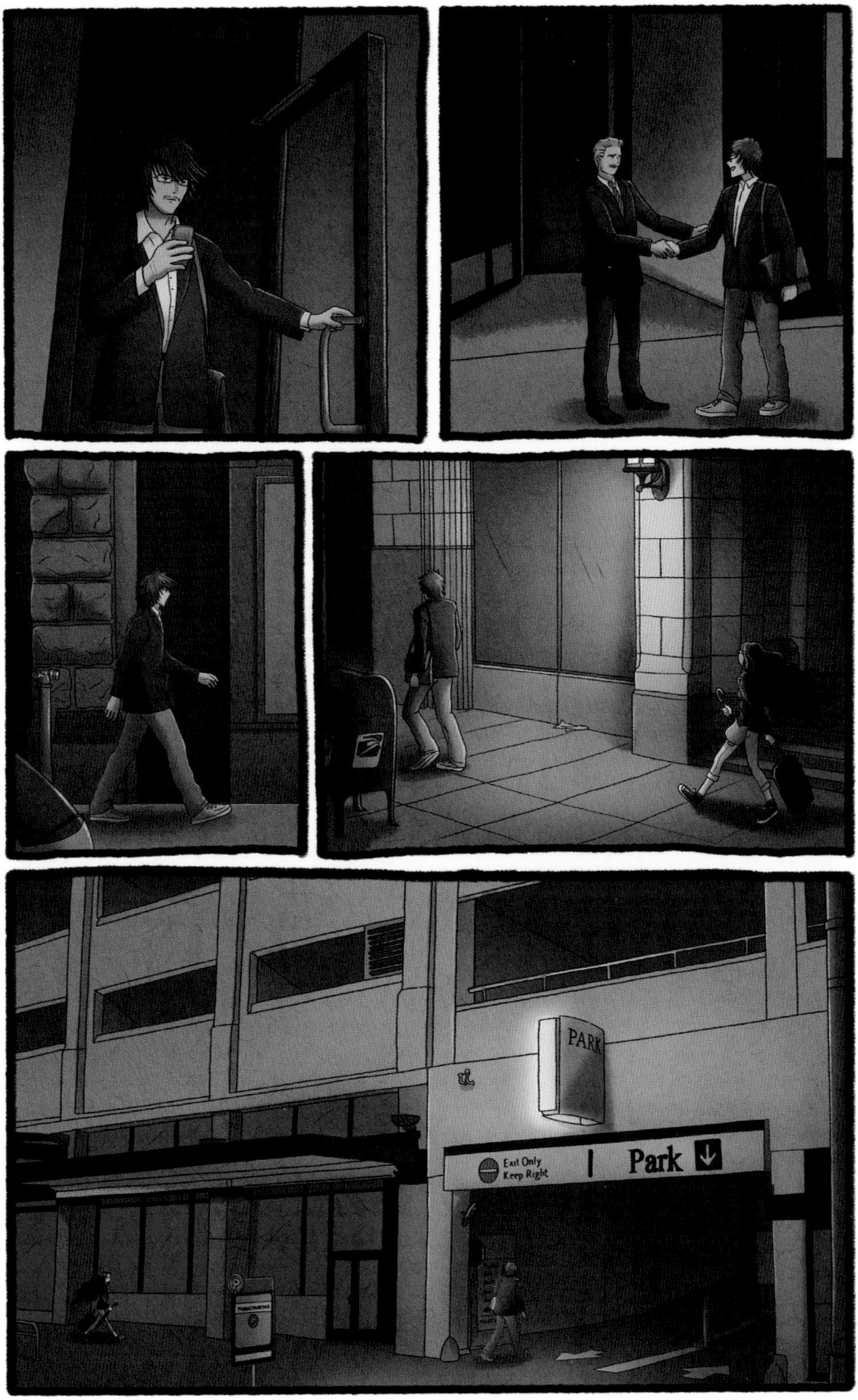
PARK
Exit Only
Keep Right
Park

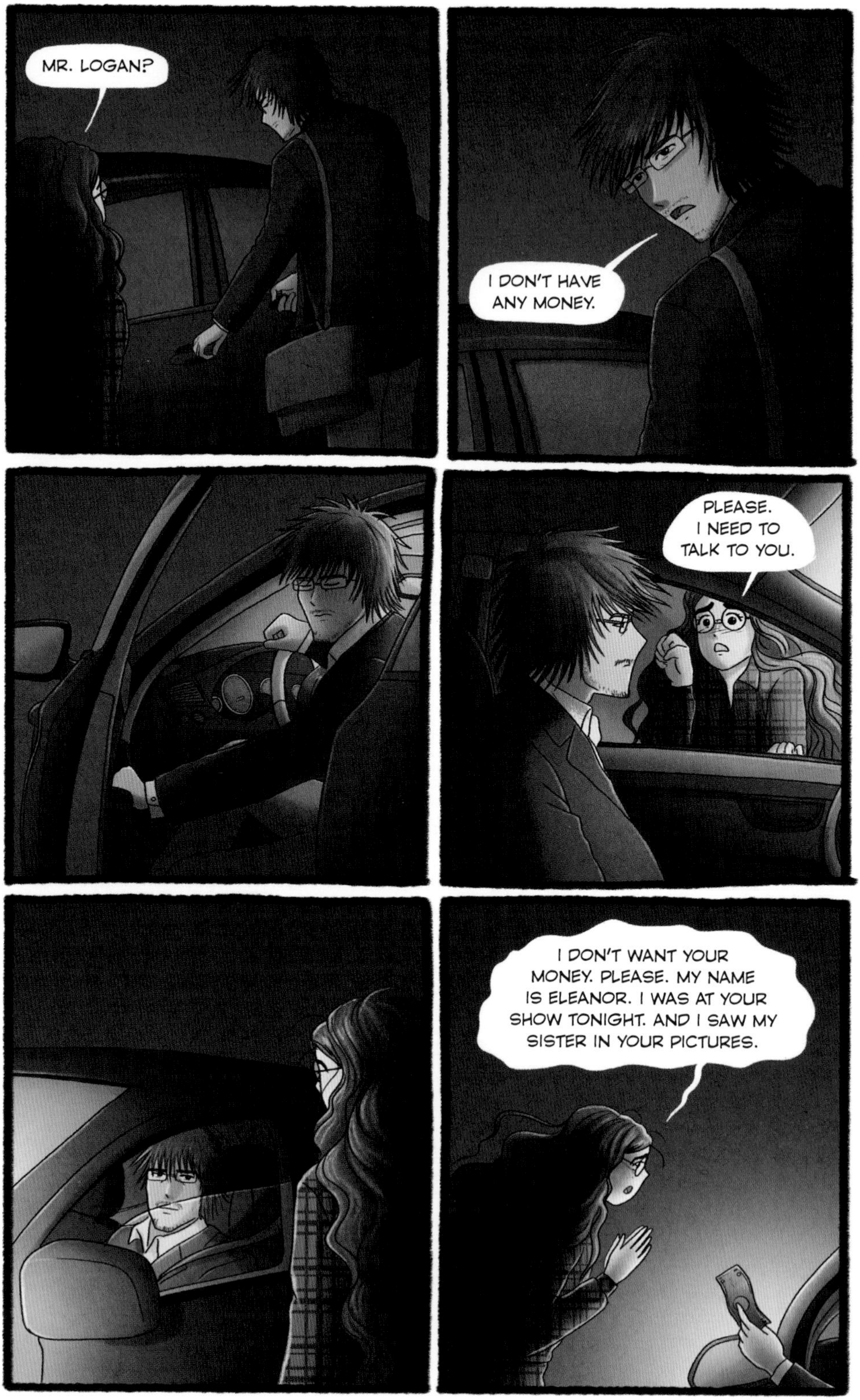
MR. LOGAN?
I DON'T HAVE ANY MONEY.
PLEASE. I NEED TO TALK TO YOU.
I DON'T WANT YOUR MONEY. PLEASE. MY NAME IS ELEANOR. I WAS AT YOUR SHOW TONIGHT. AND I SAW MY SISTER IN YOUR PICTURES.

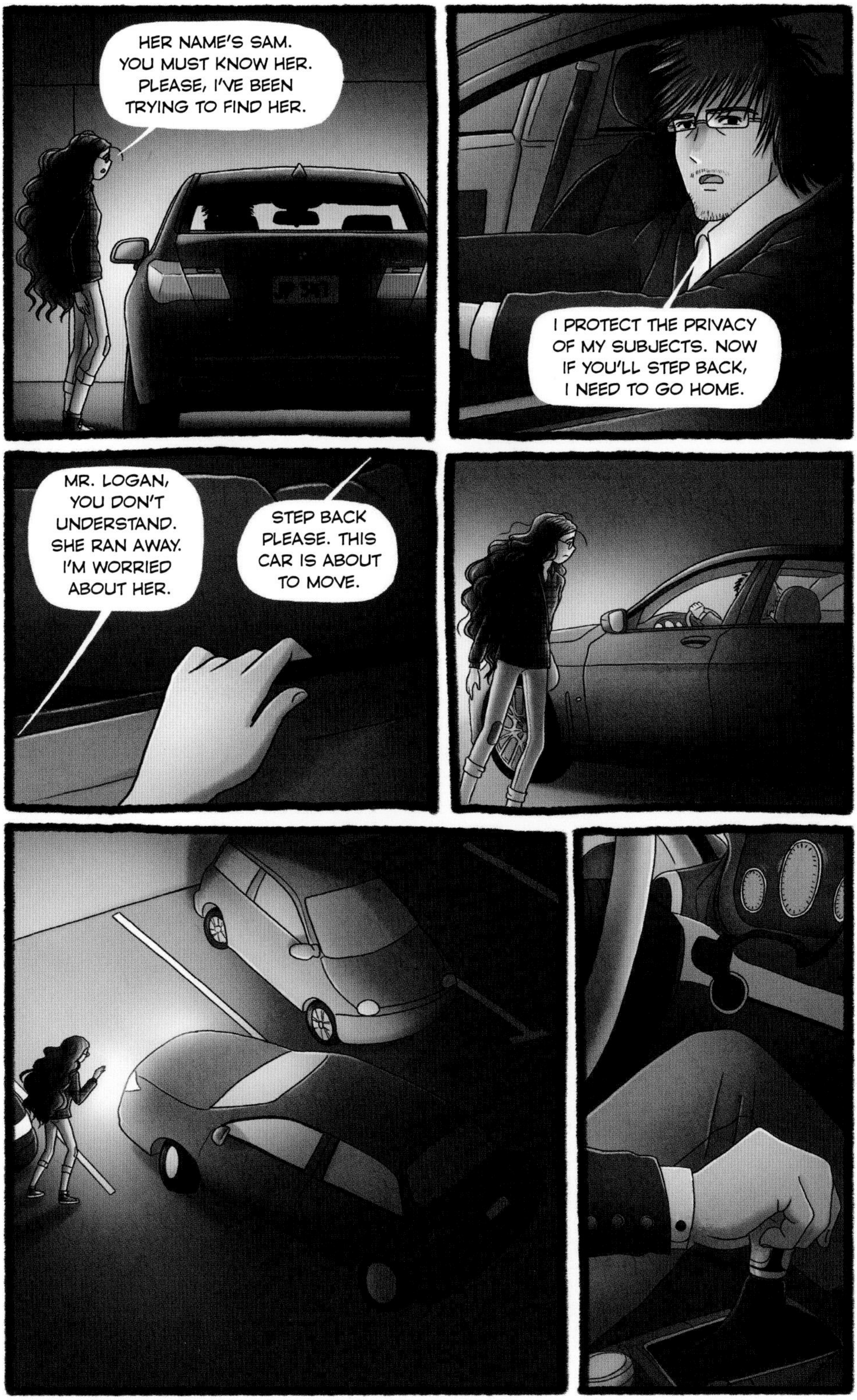
HER NAME'S SAM. YOU MUST KNOW HER. PLEASE, I'VE BEEN TRYING TO FIND HER.
I PROTECT THE PRIVACY OF MY SUBJECTS. NOW IF YOU'LL STEP BACK, I NEED TO GO HOME.
MR. LOGAN, YOU DON'T UNDERSTAND. SHE RAN AWAY. I'M WORRIED ABOUT HER.
STEP BACK PLEASE. THIS CAR IS ABOUT TO MOVE.

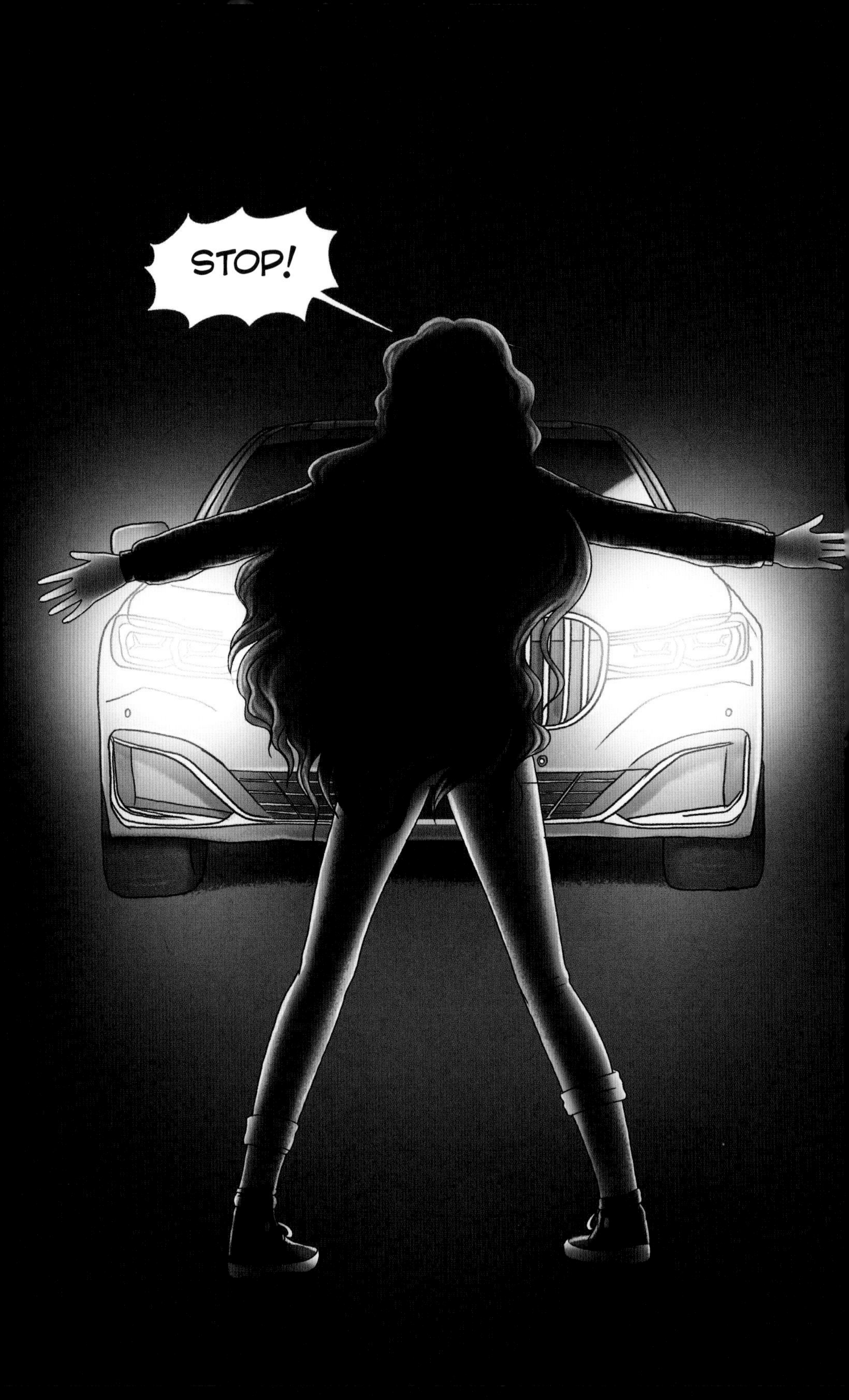
STOP!

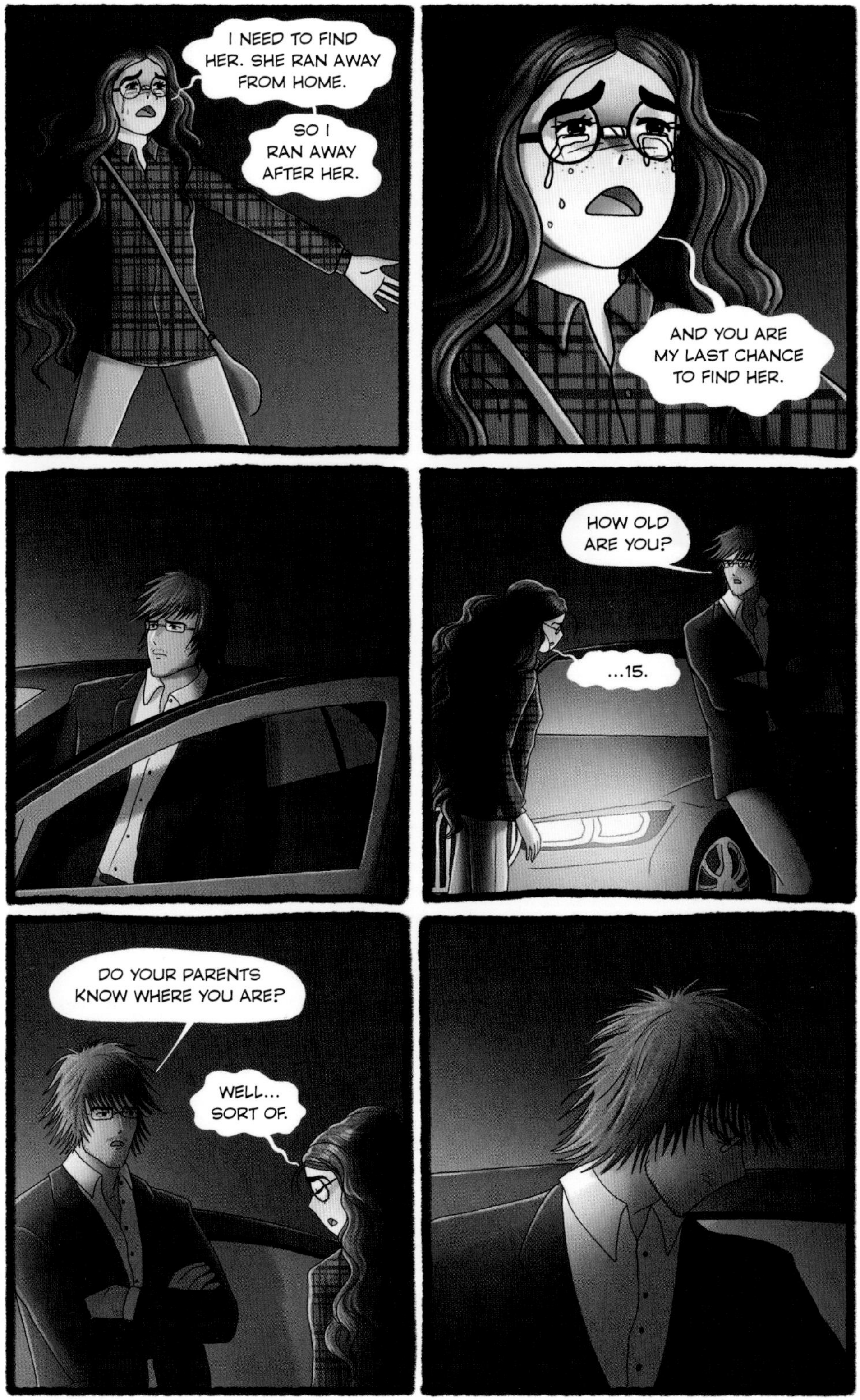
I NEED TO FIND HER. SHE RAN AWAY FROM HOME.
SO I RAN AWAY AFTER HER.
AND YOU ARE MY LAST CHANCE TO FIND HER.
HOW OLD ARE YOU?
...15.
DO YOUR PARENTS KNOW WHERE YOU ARE?
WELL... SORT OF.

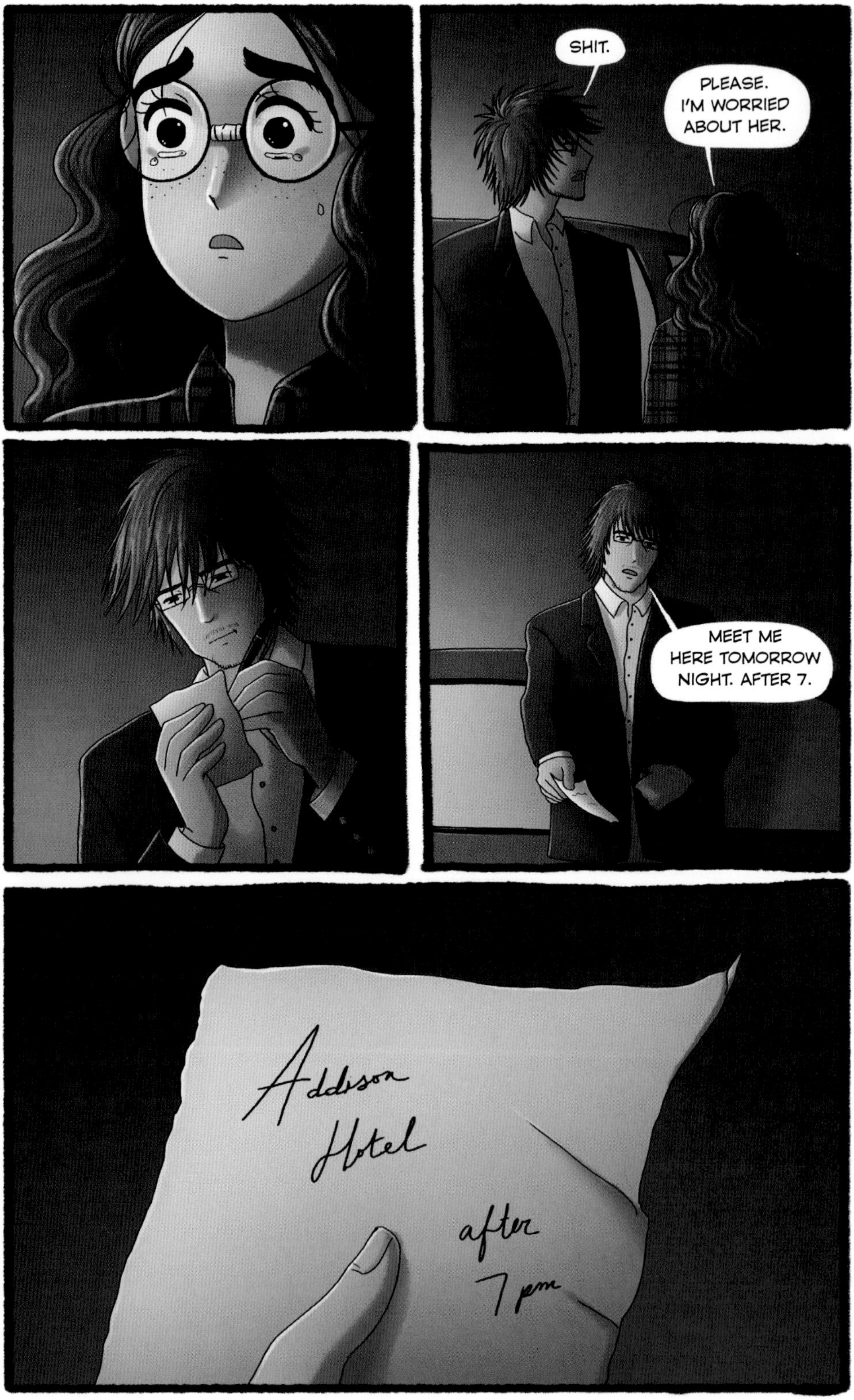
SHIT.
PLEASE. I'M WORRIED ABOUT HER.
MEET ME HERE TOMORROW NIGHT. AFTER 7.
Addison Hotel after 7pm

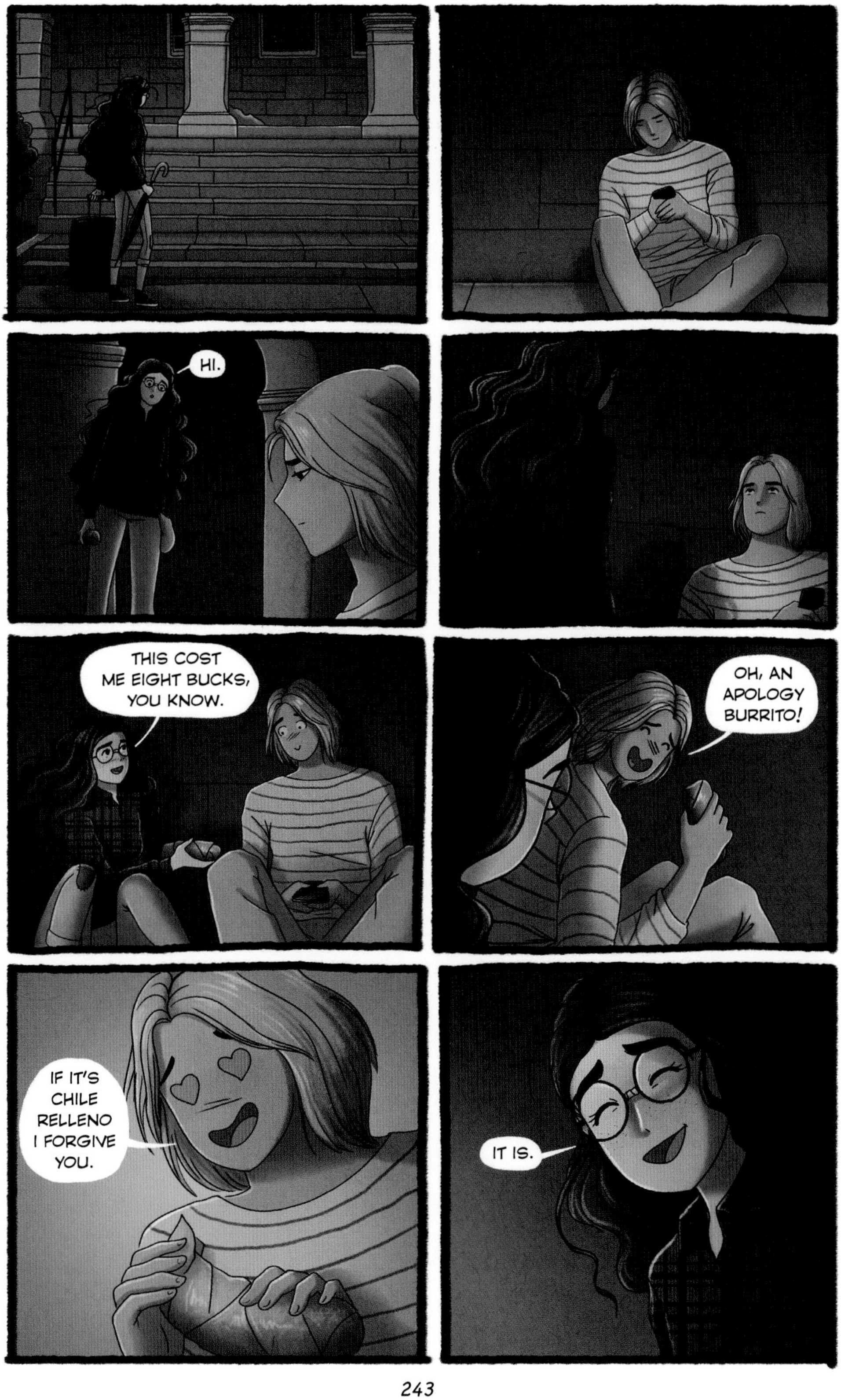
HI.
THIS COST ME EIGHT BUCKS, YOU KNOW.
OH, AN APOLOGY BURRITO!
IF IT'S CHILE RELLENO I FORGIVE YOU.
IT IS.

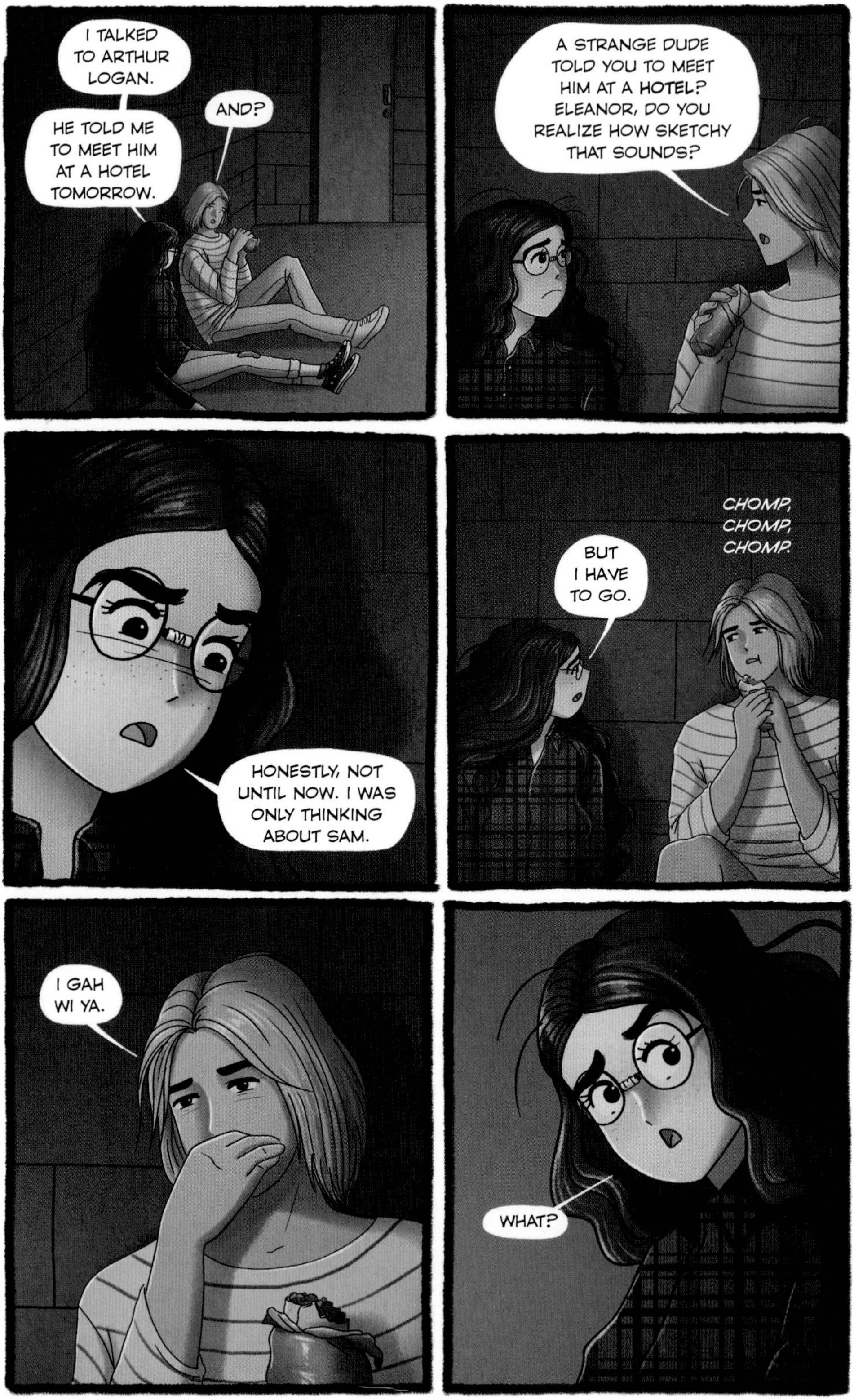
I TALKED TO ARTHUR LOGAN.
HE TOLD ME TO MEET HIM AT A HOTEL TOMORROW.
AND?
A STRANGE DUDE TOLD YOU TO MEET HIM AT A **HOTEL**? ELEANOR, DO YOU REALIZE HOW SKETCHY THAT SOUNDS?
HONESTLY, NOT UNTIL NOW. I WAS ONLY THINKING ABOUT SAM.
CHOMP, CHOMP, CHOMP.
BUT I HAVE TO GO.
I GAH WI YA.
WHAT?

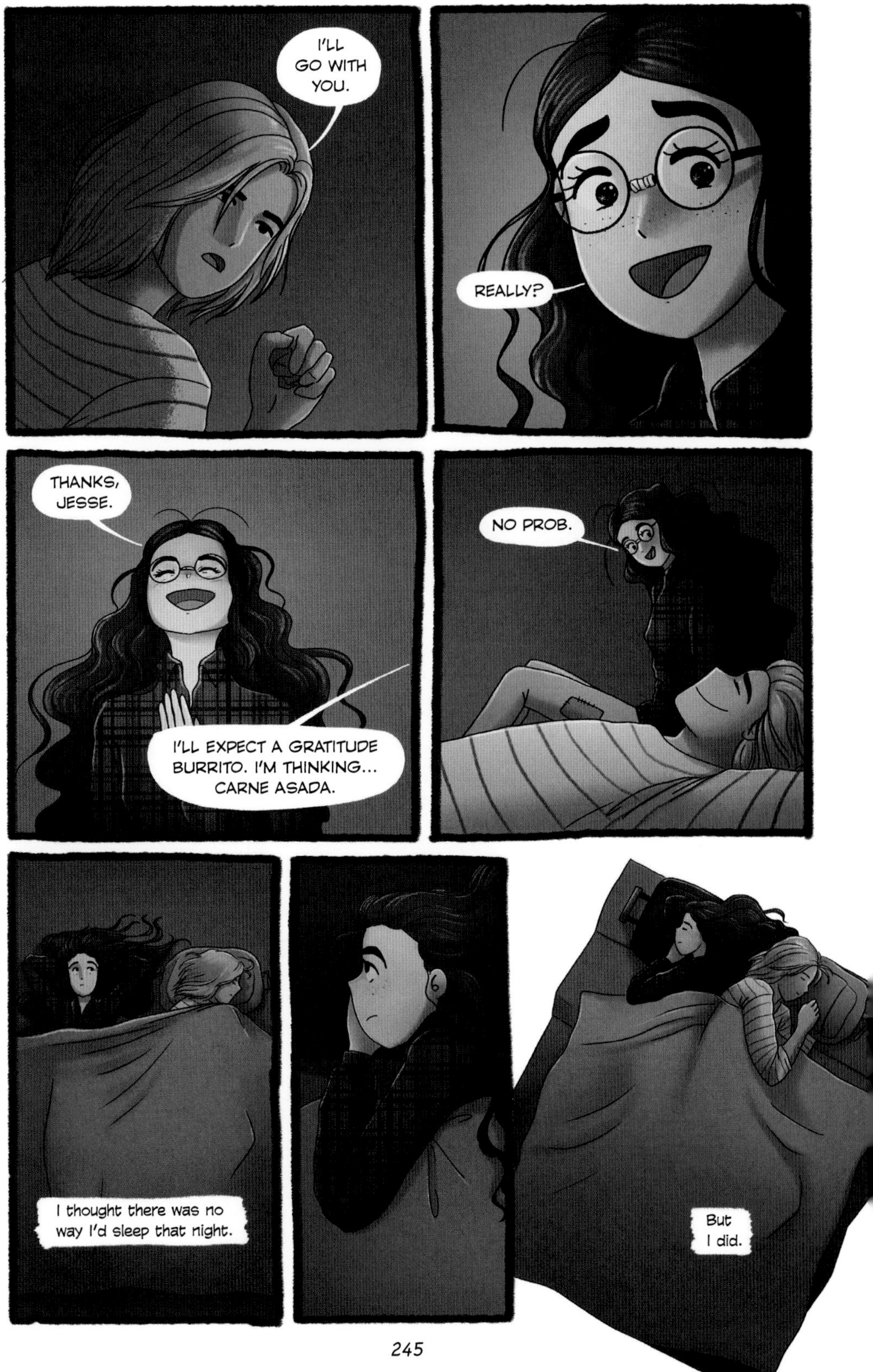
I'LL GO WITH YOU.
REALLY?
THANKS, JESSE.
I'LL EXPECT A GRATITUDE BURRITO. I'M THINKING... CARNE ASADA.
NO PROB.
I thought there was no way I'd sleep that night.
But I did.

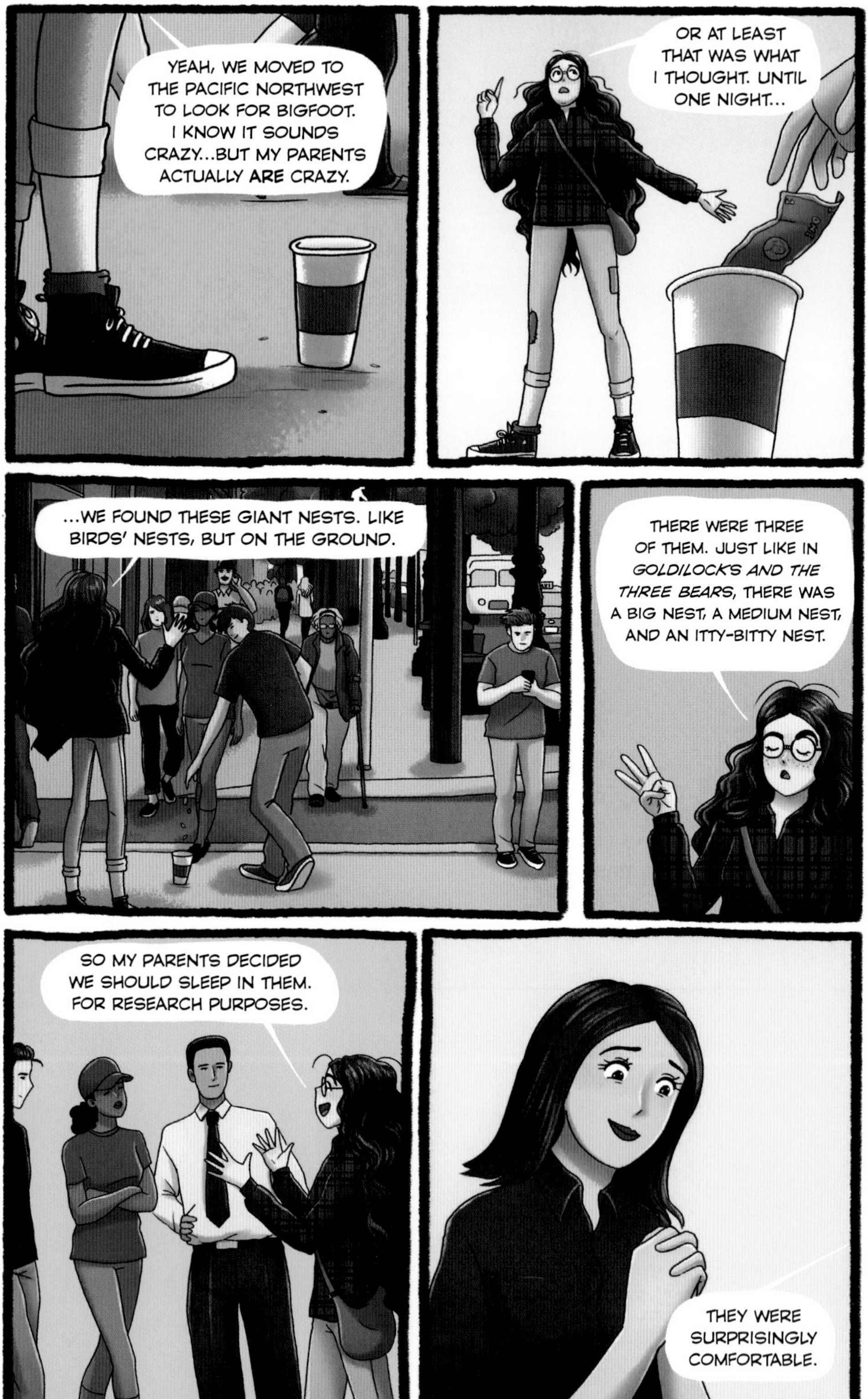
YEAH, WE MOVED TO THE PACIFIC NORTHWEST TO LOOK FOR BIGFOOT. I KNOW IT SOUNDS CRAZY...BUT MY PARENTS ACTUALLY **ARE** CRAZY.
OR AT LEAST THAT WAS WHAT I THOUGHT. UNTIL ONE NIGHT...
...WE FOUND THESE GIANT NESTS. LIKE BIRDS' NESTS, BUT ON THE GROUND.
THERE WERE THREE OF THEM. JUST LIKE IN *GOLDILOCKS AND THE THREE BEARS*, THERE WAS A BIG NEST, A MEDIUM NEST, AND AN ITTY-BITTY NEST.
SO MY PARENTS DECIDED WE SHOULD SLEEP IN THEM. FOR RESEARCH PURPOSES.
THEY WERE SURPRISINGLY COMFORTABLE.

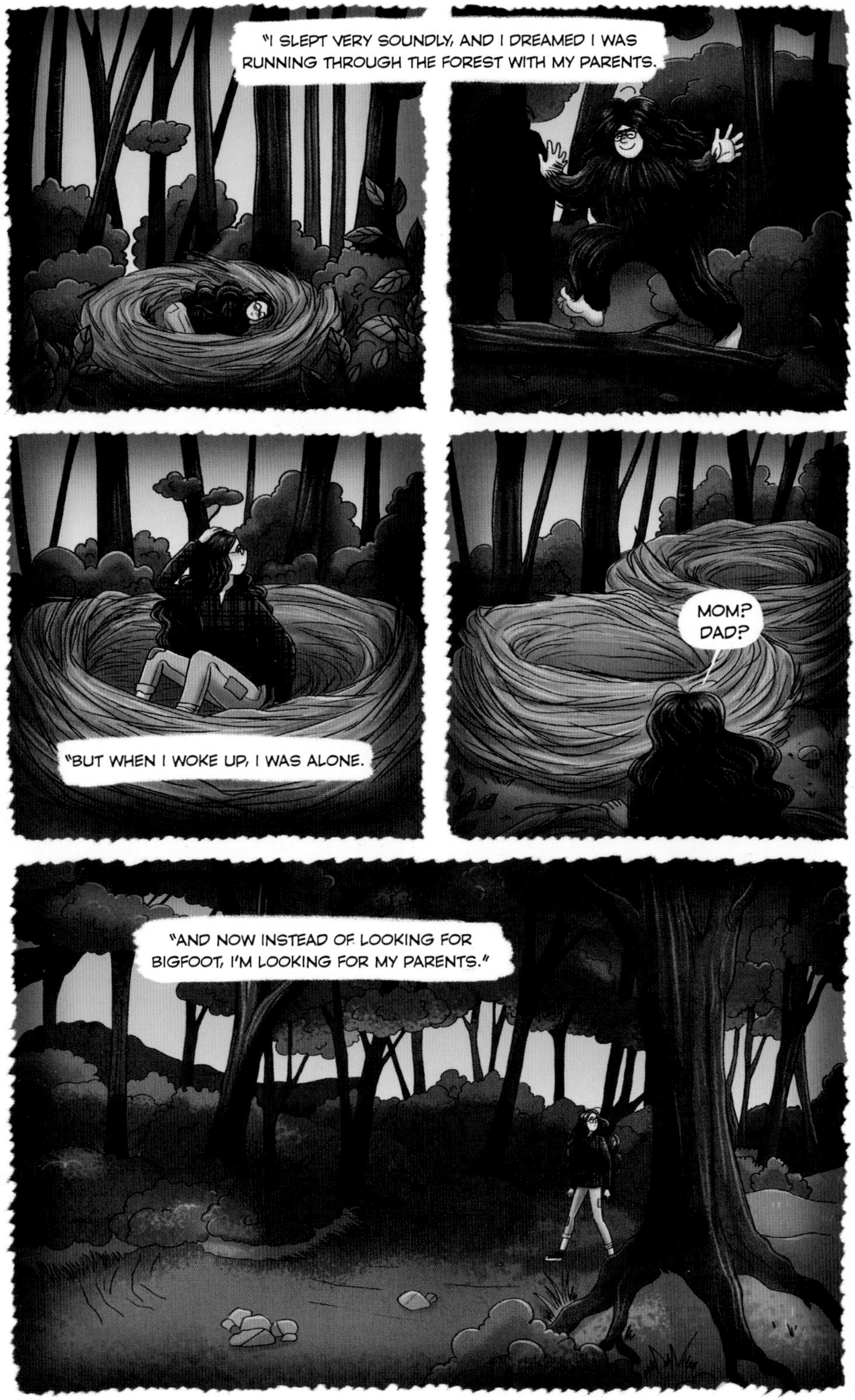
"I SLEPT VERY SOUNDLY, AND I DREAMED I WAS RUNNING THROUGH THE FOREST WITH MY PARENTS.
"BUT WHEN I WOKE UP, I WAS ALONE.
MOM? DAD?
"AND NOW INSTEAD OF LOOKING FOR BIGFOOT, I'M LOOKING FOR MY PARENTS."

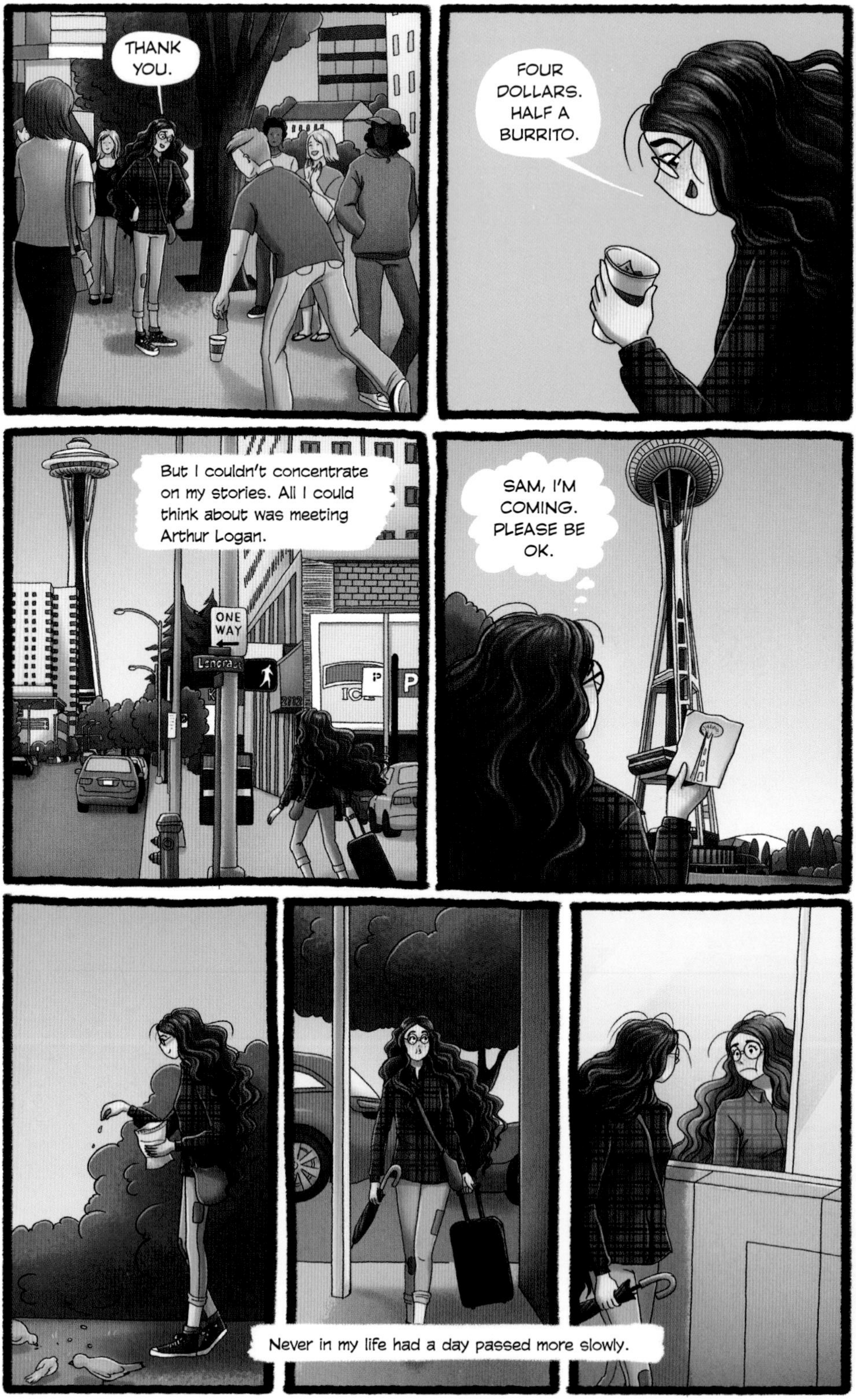
THANK YOU.
FOUR DOLLARS. HALF A BURRITO.
But I couldn't concentrate on my stories. All I could think about was meeting Arthur Logan.
ONE WAY
SAM, I'M COMING. PLEASE BE OK.
Never in my life had a day passed more slowly.

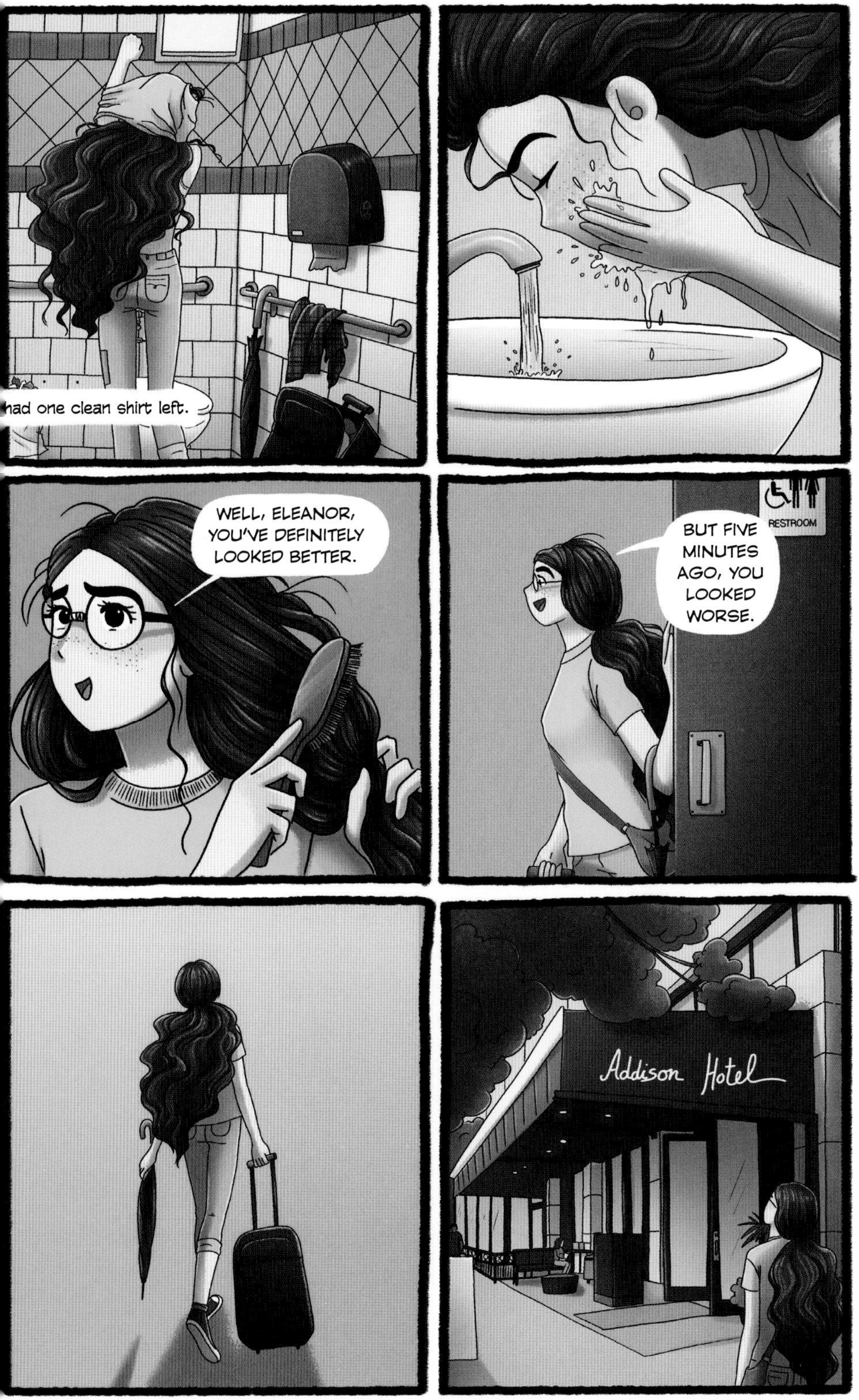
had one clean shirt left.
WELL, ELEANOR, YOU'VE DEFINITELY LOOKED BETTER.
RESTROOM
BUT FIVE MINUTES AGO, YOU LOOKED WORSE.
Addison Hotel

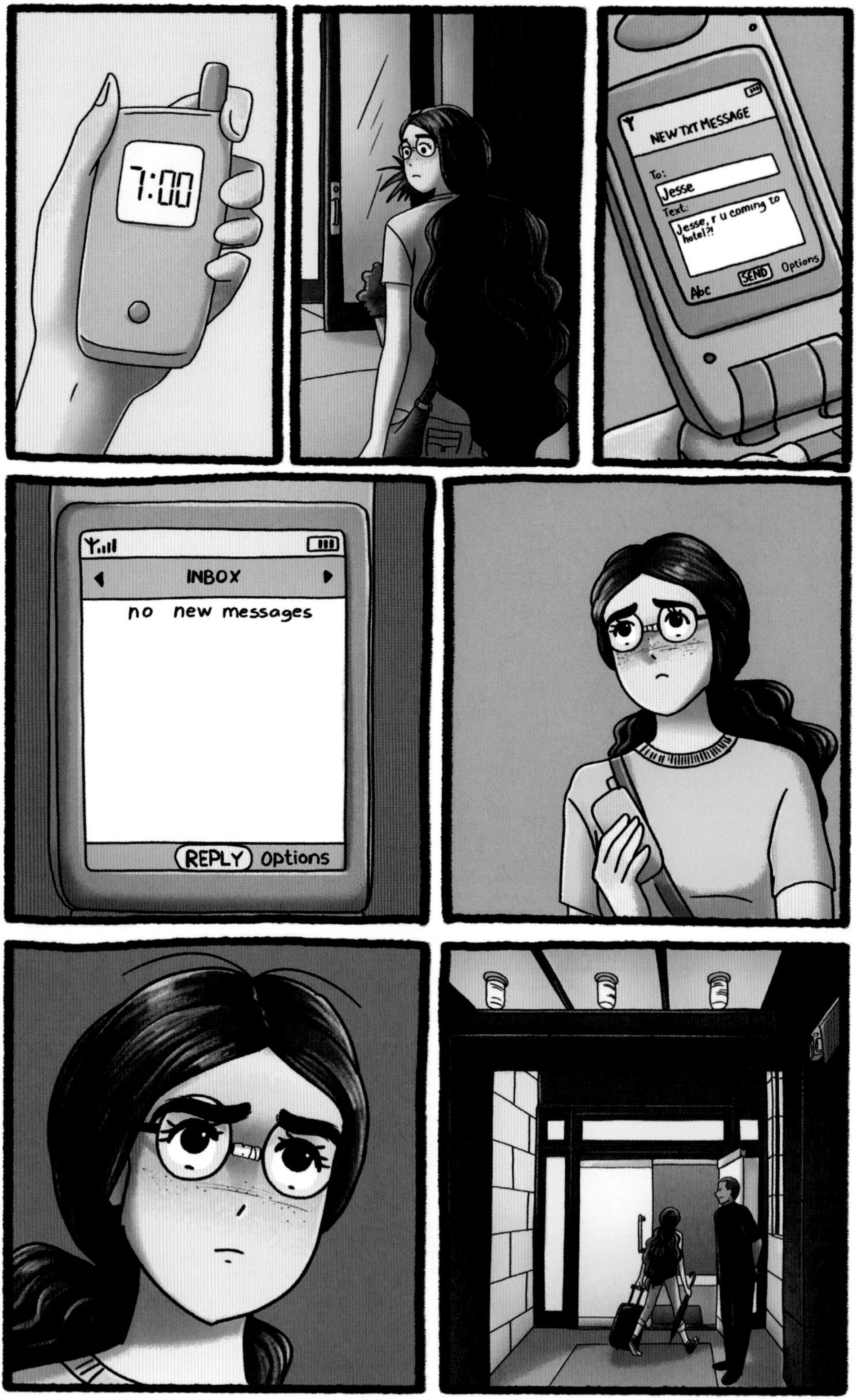
7:00
NEW TXT MESSAGE
To:
Jesse
Text:
Jesse, r u coming to hotel?!
Abc
SEND
Options
INBOX
no new messages
REPLY
Options

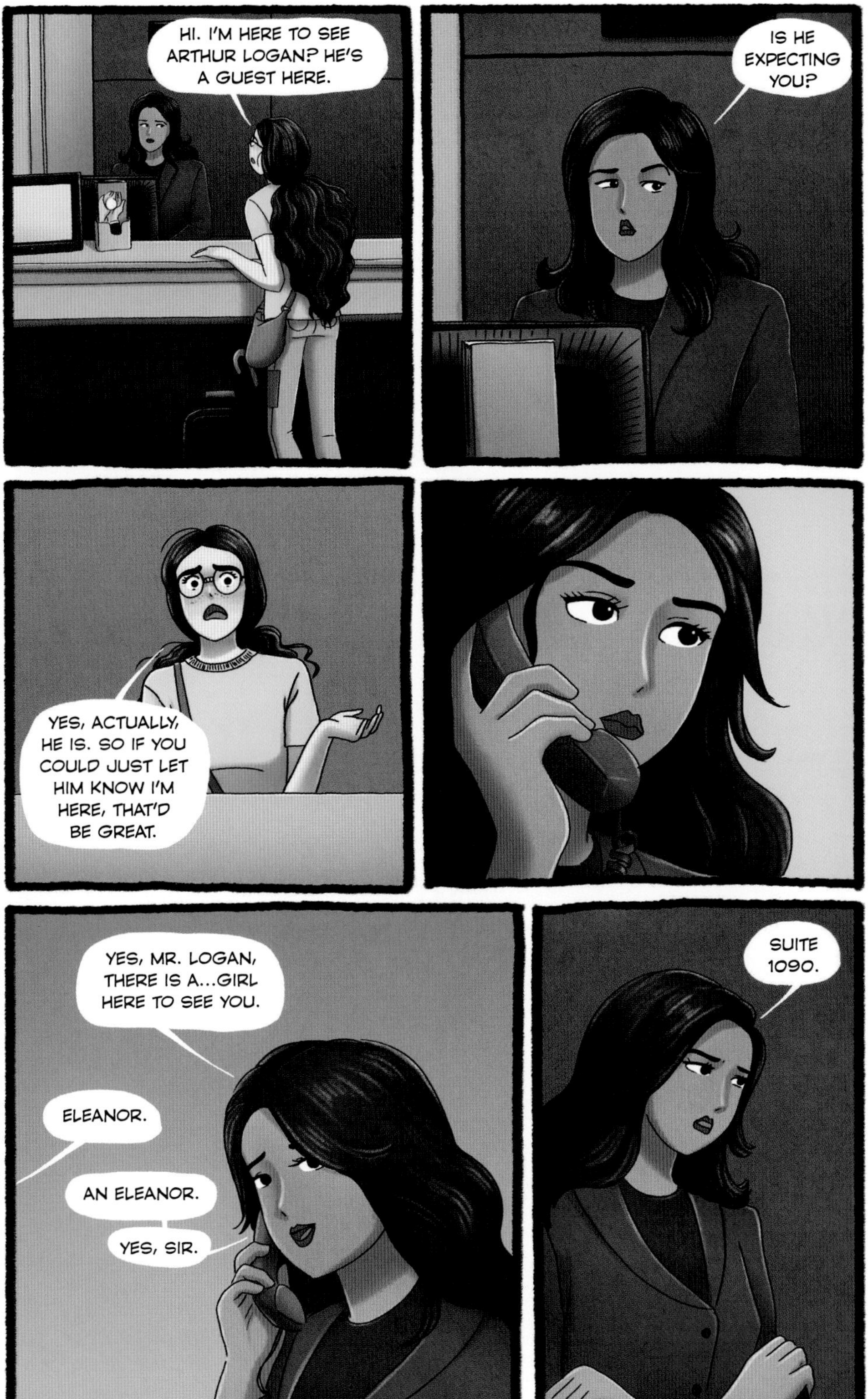
HI. I'M HERE TO SEE ARTHUR LOGAN? HE'S A GUEST HERE.
IS HE EXPECTING YOU?
YES, ACTUALLY, HE IS. SO IF YOU COULD JUST LET HIM KNOW I'M HERE, THAT'D BE GREAT.
YES, MR. LOGAN, THERE IS A...GIRL HERE TO SEE YOU.
ELEANOR.
AN ELEANOR.
YES, SIR.
SUITE 1090.

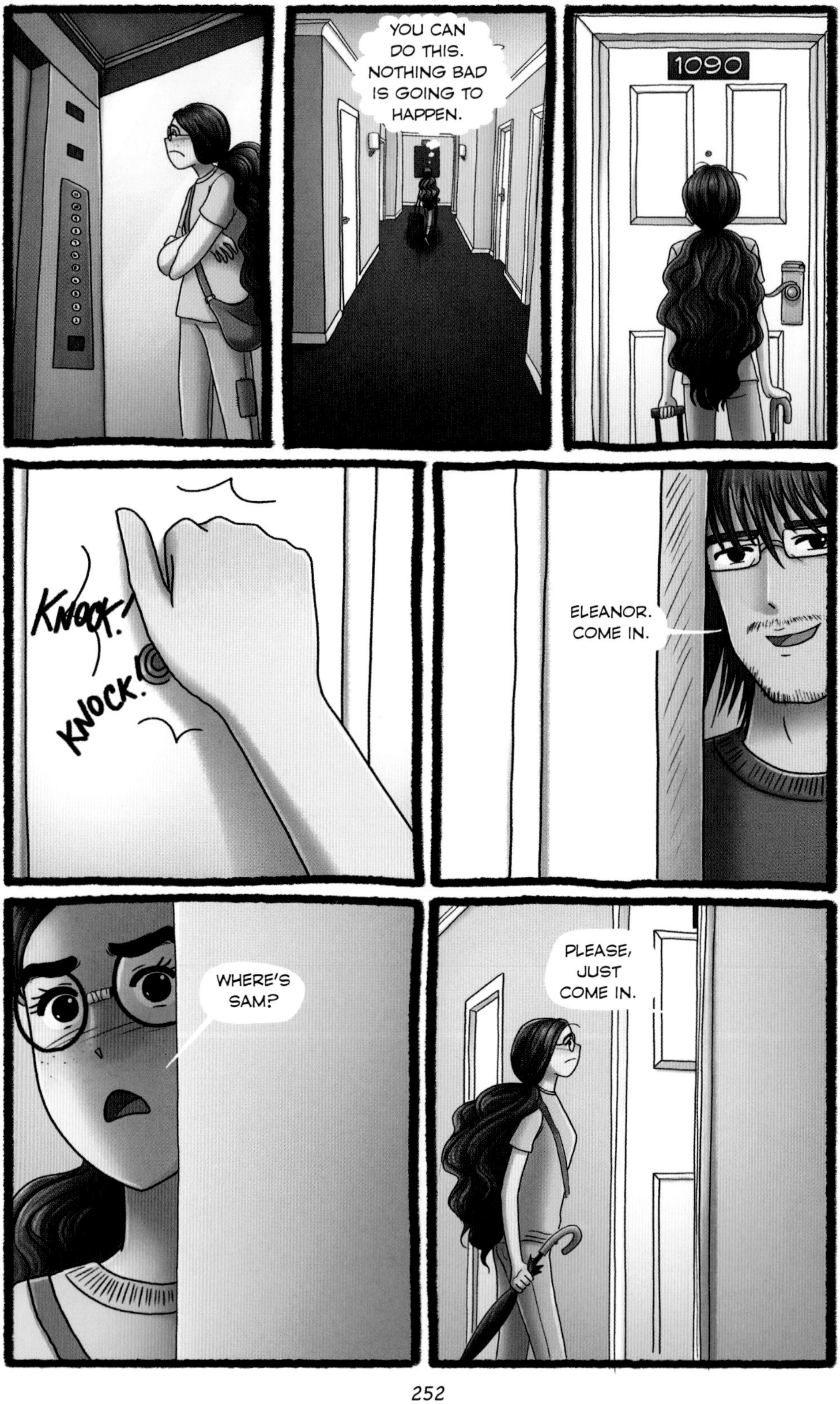
YOU CAN DO THIS. NOTHING BAD IS GOING TO HAPPEN.
1090
KNOCK!
KNOCK!
ELEANOR. COME IN.
WHERE'S SAM?
PLEASE, JUST COME IN.

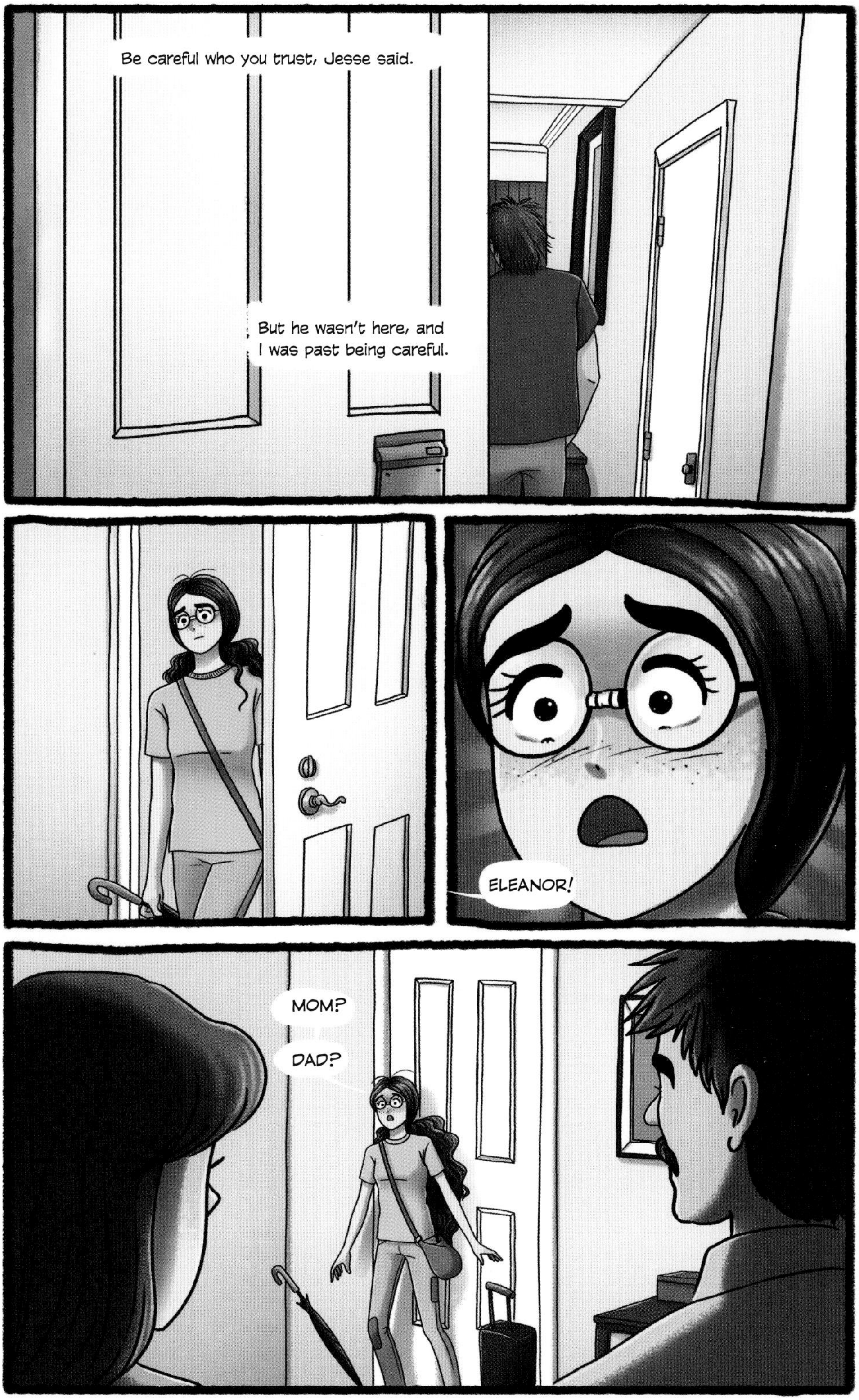
Be careful who you trust, Jesse said.
But he wasn't here, and I was past being careful.
ELEANOR!
MOM?
DAD?

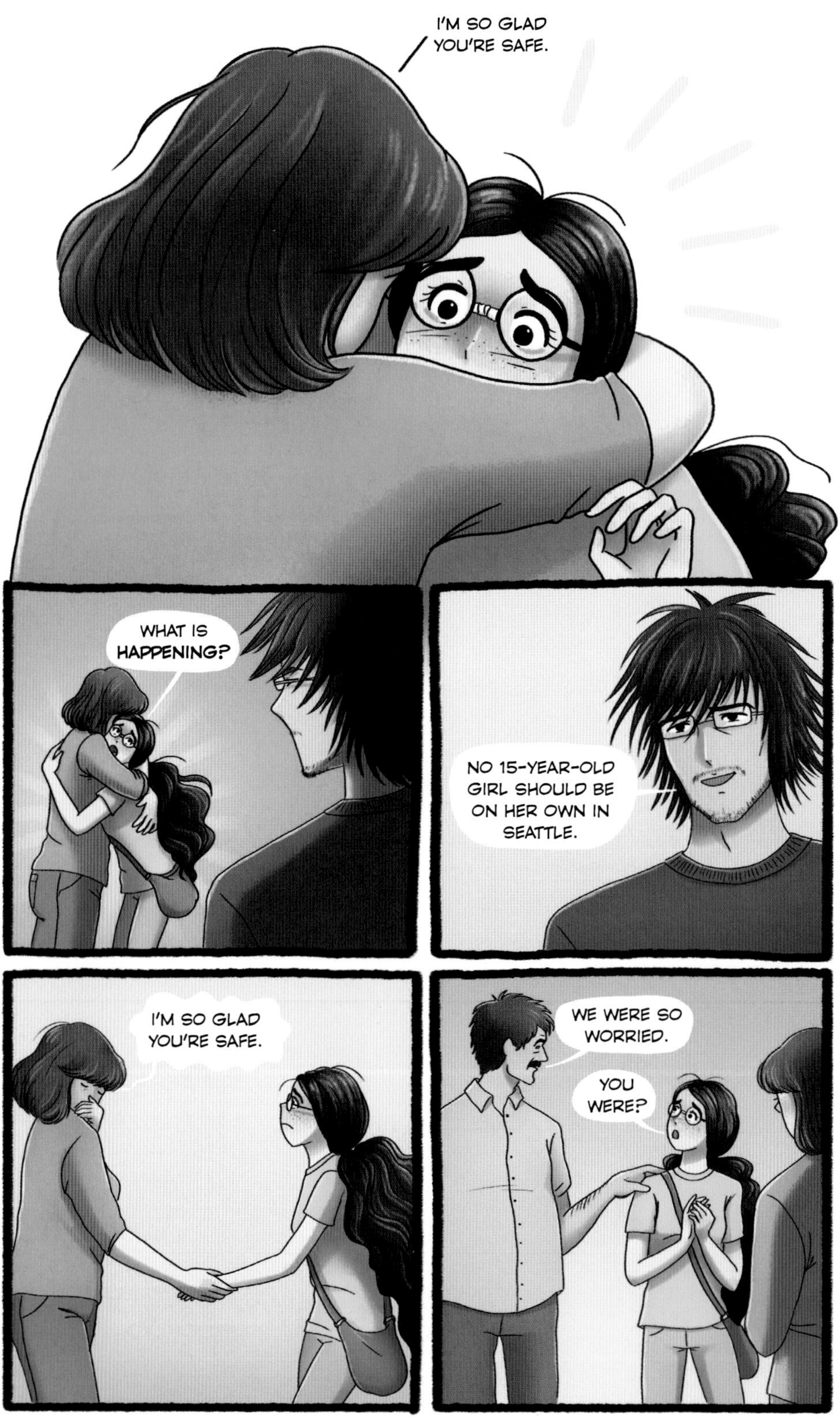

I'M SO GLAD YOU'RE SAFE.
WHAT IS HAPPENING?
NO 15-YEAR-OLD GIRL SHOULD BE ON HER OWN IN SEATTLE.
I'M SO GLAD YOU'RE SAFE.
WE WERE SO WORRIED.
YOU WERE?

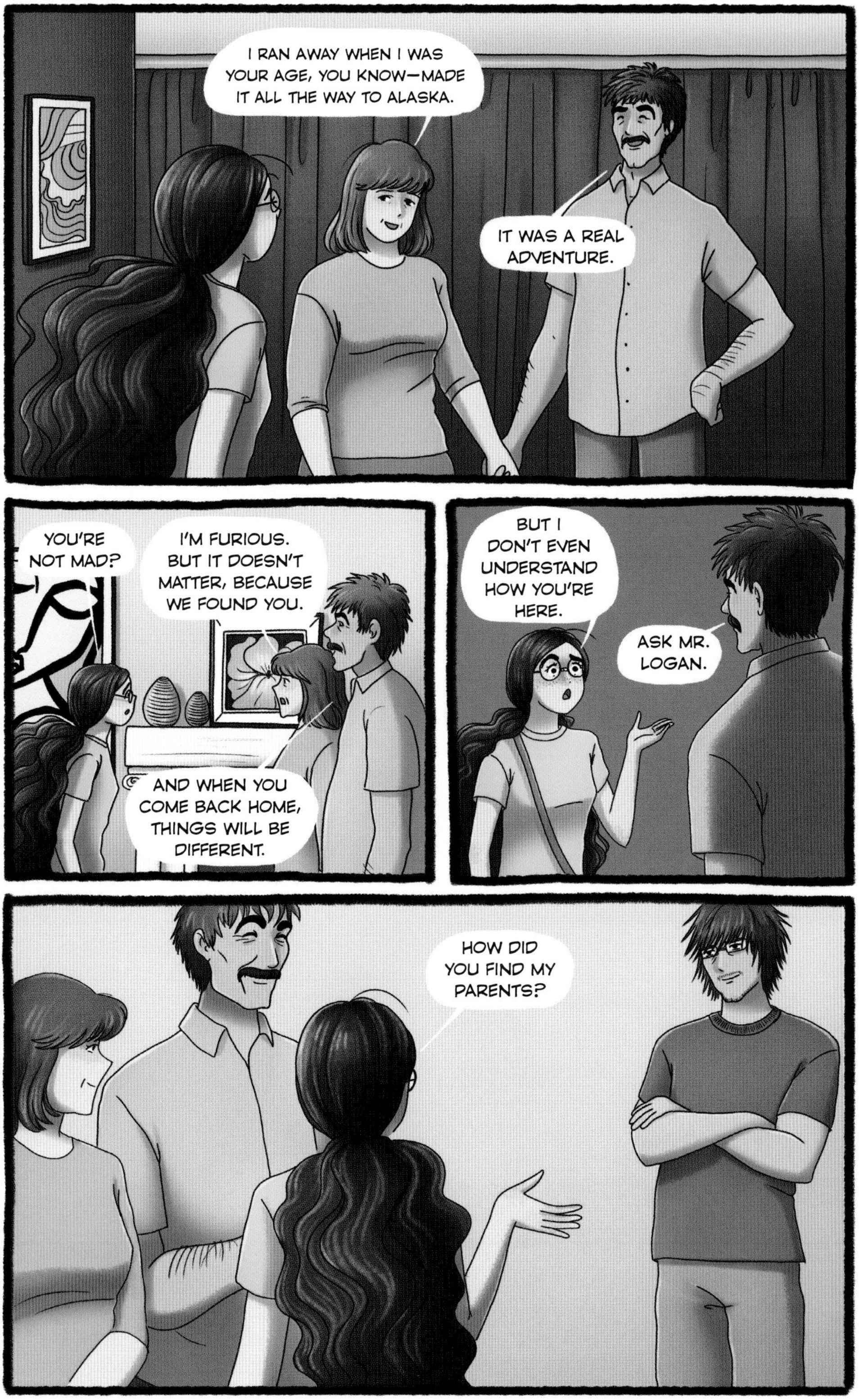
I RAN AWAY WHEN I WAS YOUR AGE, YOU KNOW—MADE IT ALL THE WAY TO ALASKA.
IT WAS A REAL ADVENTURE.
YOU'RE NOT MAD?
I'M FURIOUS. BUT IT DOESN'T MATTER, BECAUSE WE FOUND YOU.
AND WHEN YOU COME BACK HOME, THINGS WILL BE DIFFERENT.
BUT I DON'T EVEN UNDERSTAND HOW YOU'RE HERE.
ASK MR. LOGAN.
HOW DID YOU FIND MY PARENTS?

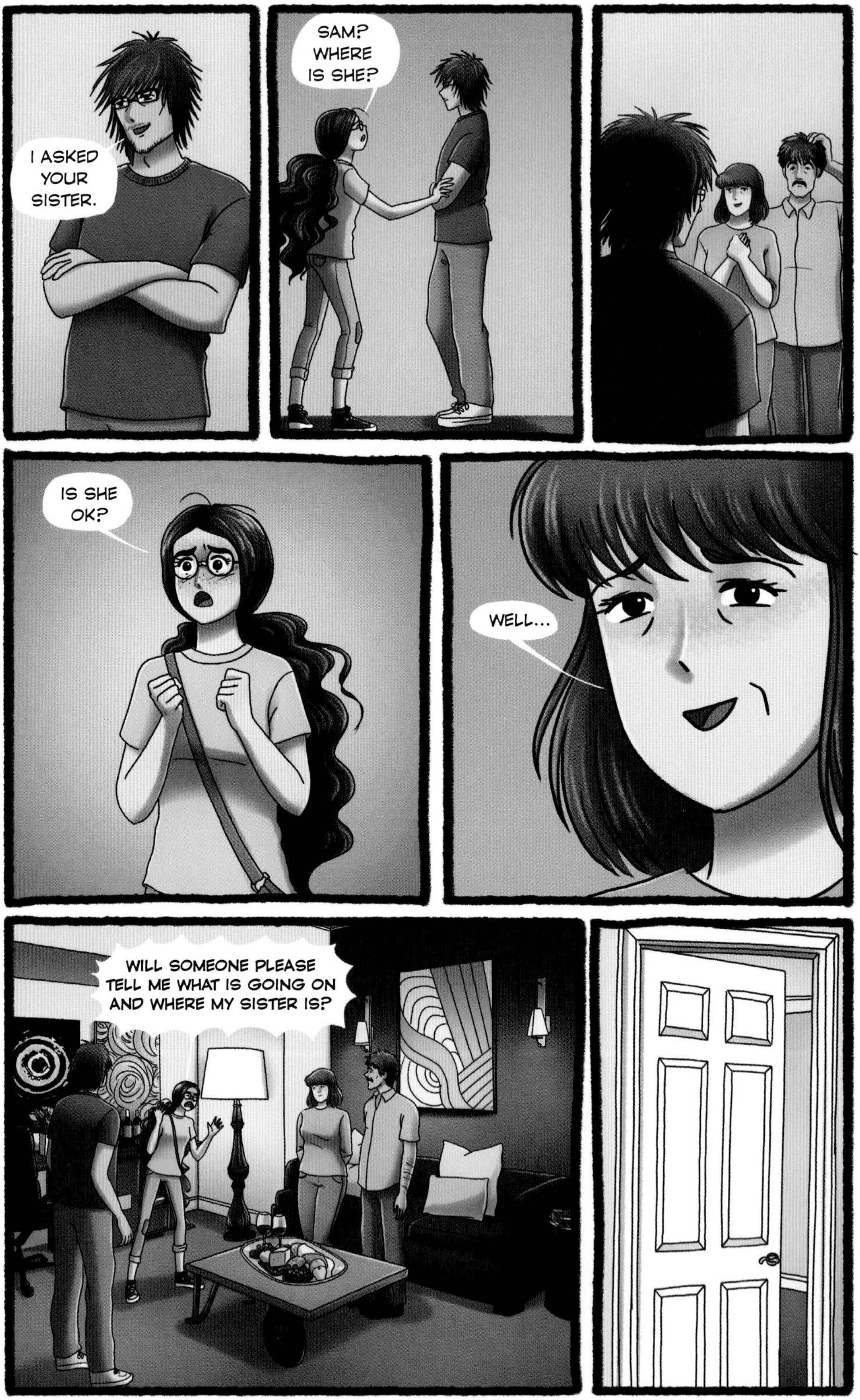
I ASKED YOUR SISTER.
SAM? WHERE IS SHE?
IS SHE OK?
WELL...
WILL SOMEONE PLEASE TELL ME WHAT IS GOING ON AND WHERE MY SISTER IS?

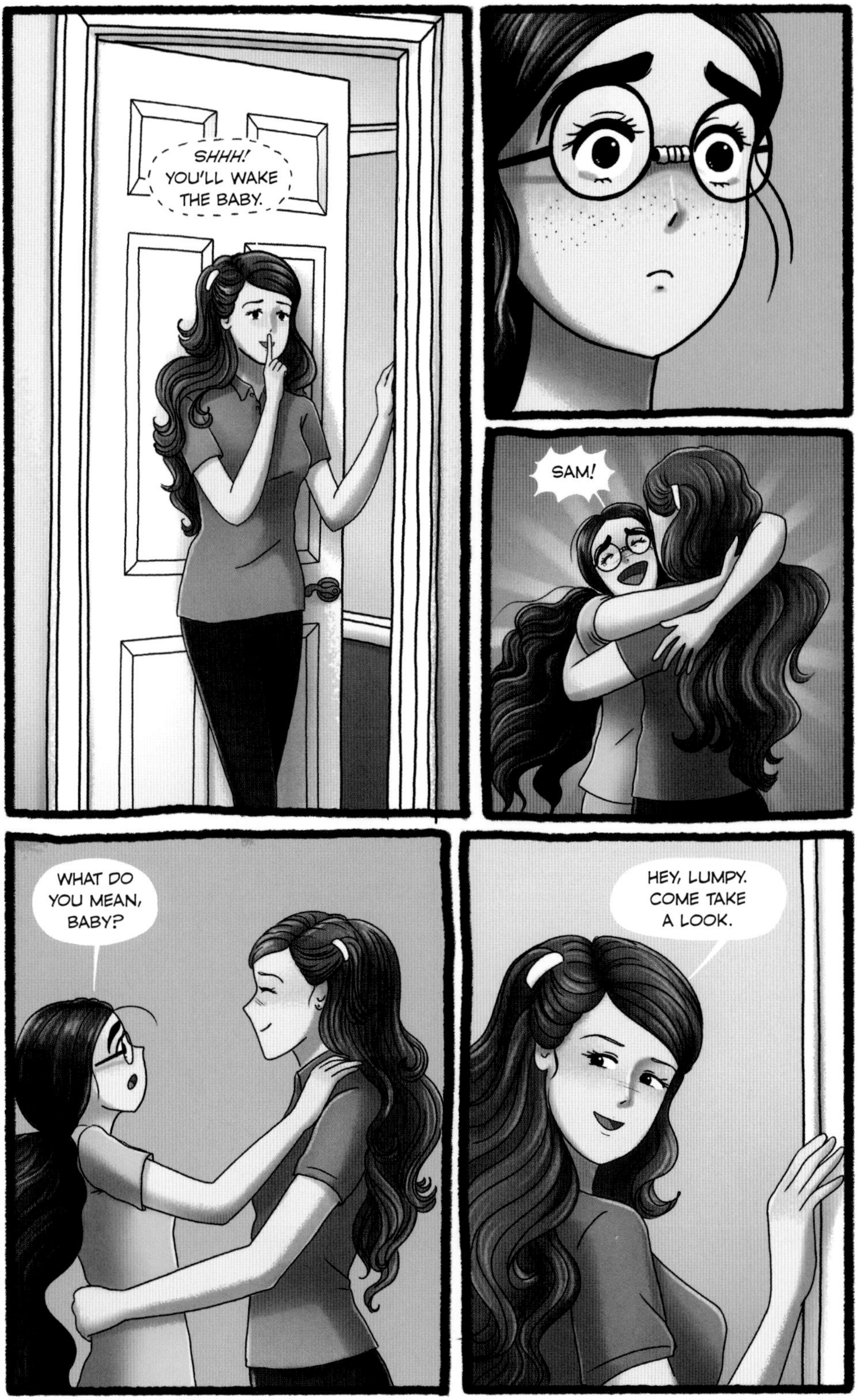
SHHH! YOU'LL WAKE THE BABY.
SAM!
WHAT DO YOU MEAN, BABY?
HEY, LUMPY. COME TAKE A LOOK.

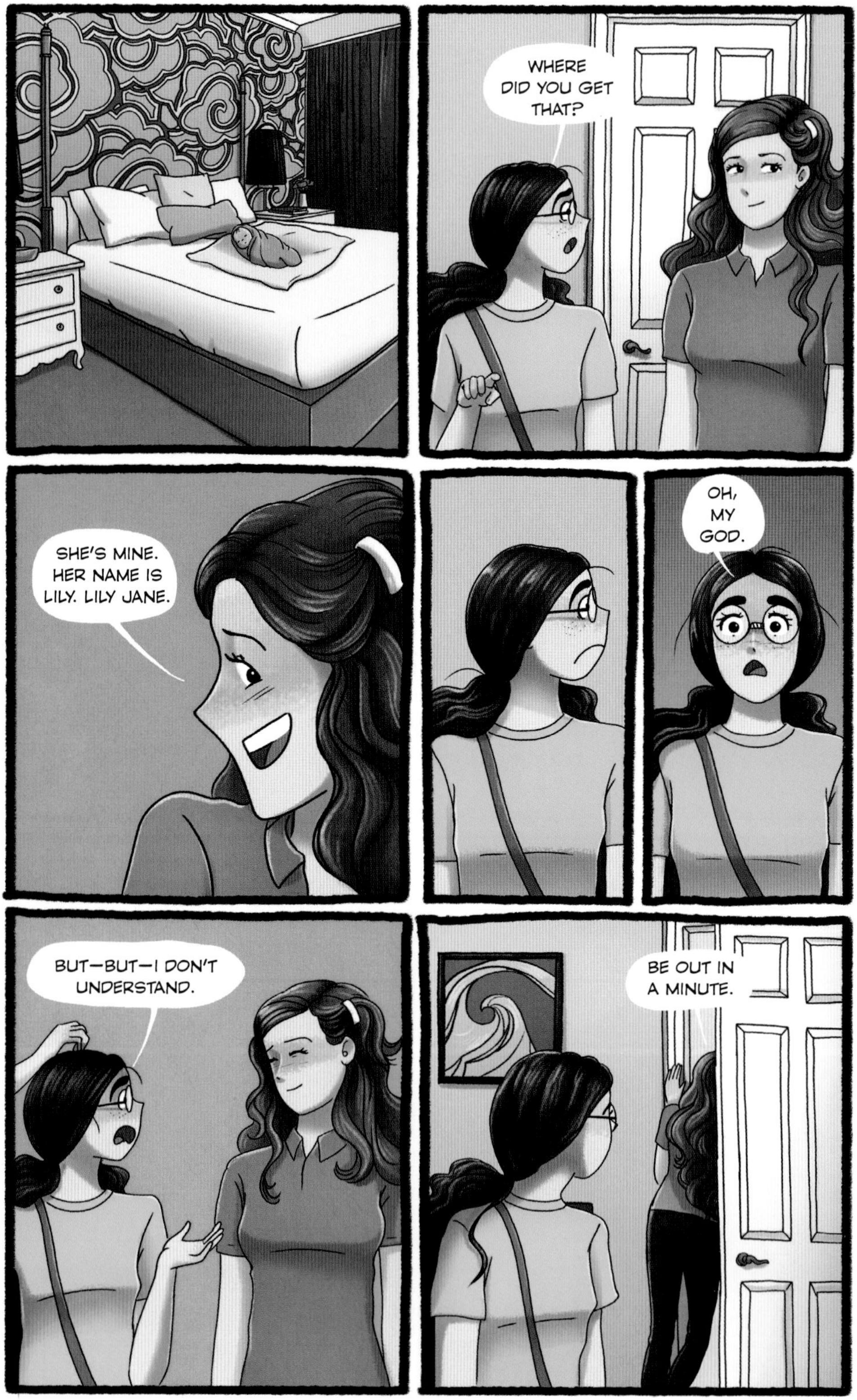
WHERE DID YOU GET THAT?
SHE'S MINE. HER NAME IS LILY. LILY JANE.
OH, MY GOD.
BUT—BUT—I DON'T UNDERSTAND.
BE OUT IN A MINUTE.

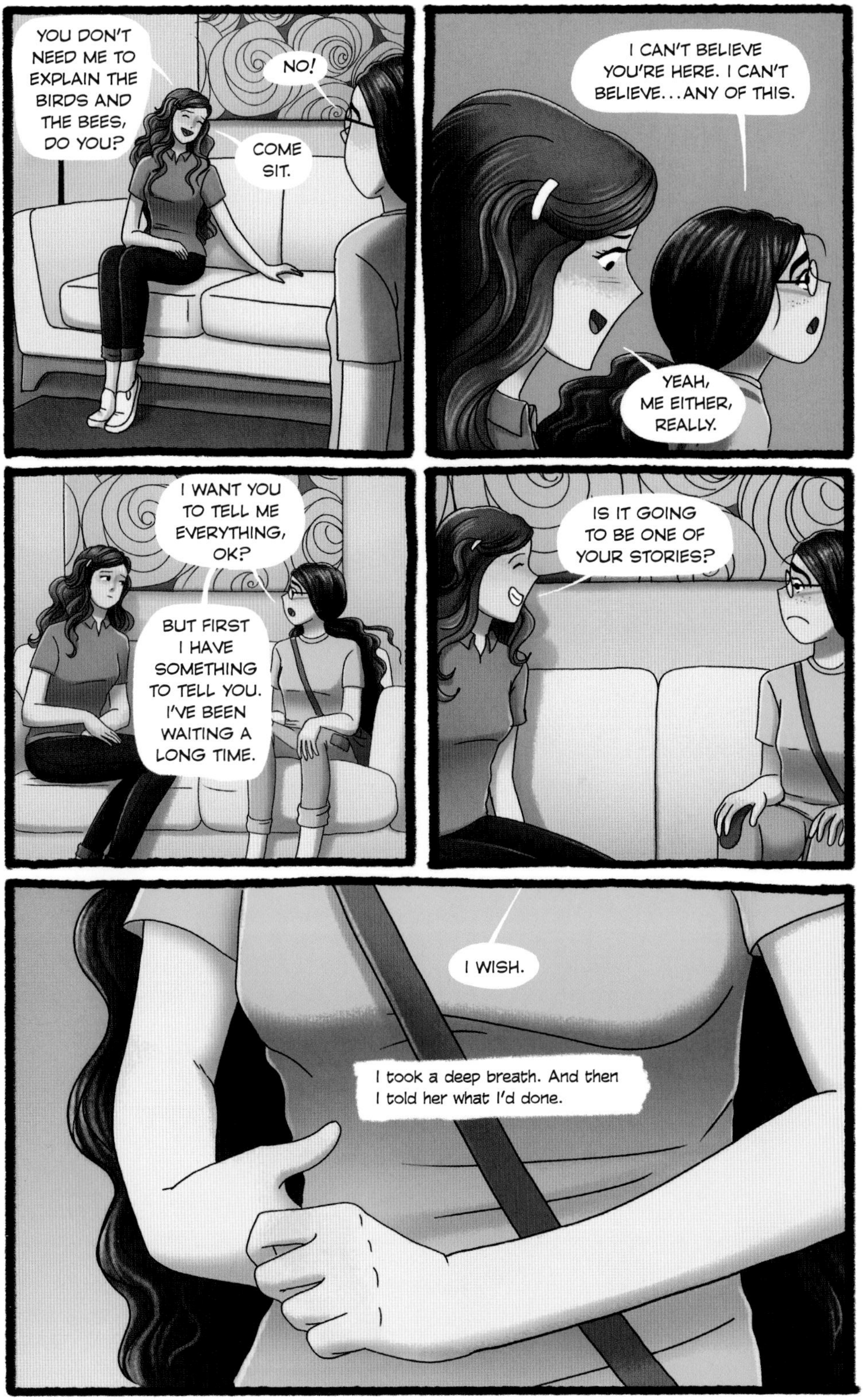

YOU DON'T NEED ME TO EXPLAIN THE BIRDS AND THE BEES, DO YOU?
NO!
COME SIT.
I CAN'T BELIEVE YOU'RE HERE. I CAN'T BELIEVE...ANY OF THIS.
YEAH, ME EITHER, REALLY.
I WANT YOU TO TELL ME EVERYTHING, OK?
BUT FIRST I HAVE SOMETHING TO TELL YOU. I'VE BEEN WAITING A LONG TIME.
IS IT GOING TO BE ONE OF YOUR STORIES?
I WISH.
I took a deep breath. And then I told her what I'd done.

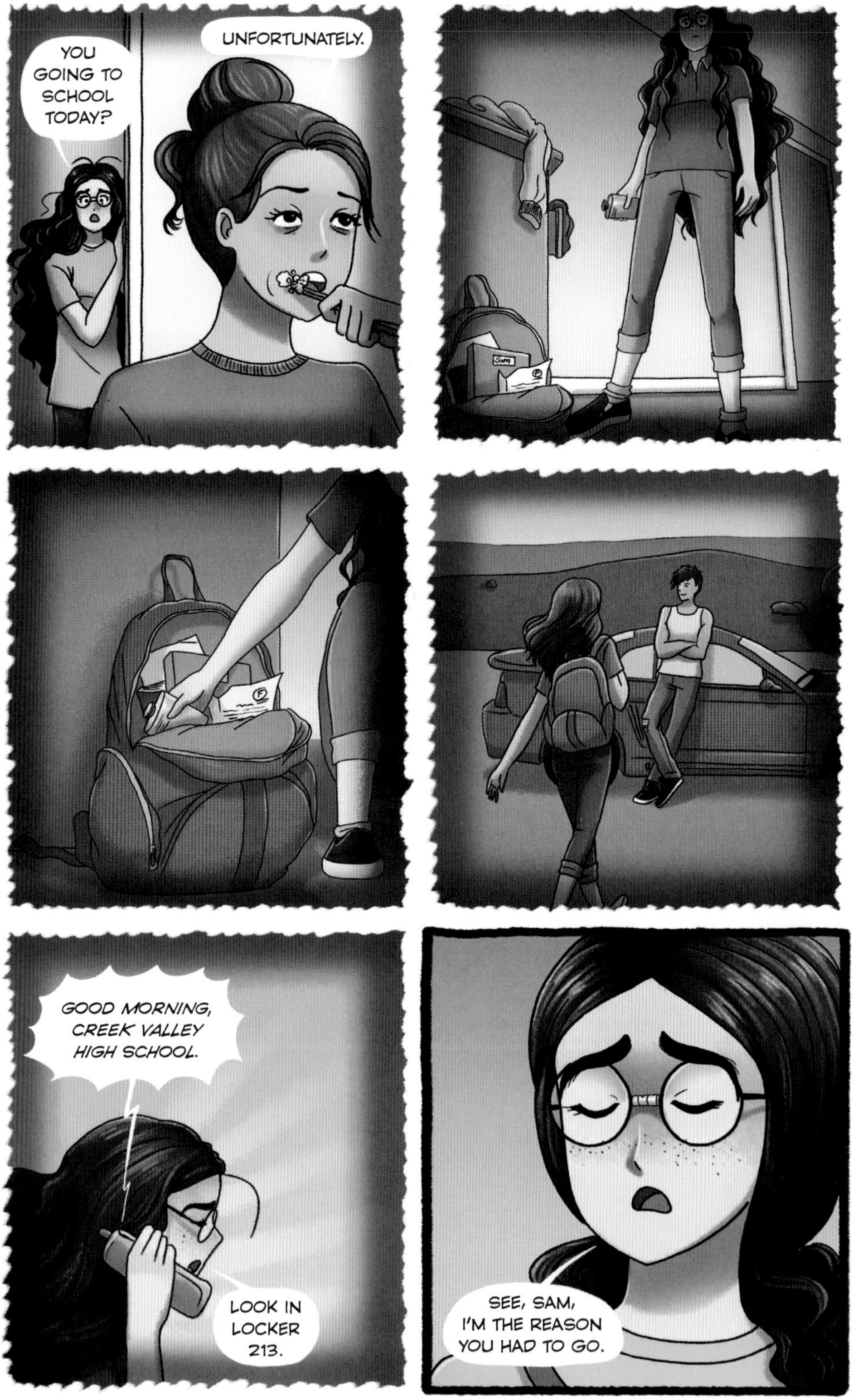
YOU GOING TO SCHOOL TODAY?
UNFORTUNATELY.
GOOD MORNING, CREEK VALLEY HIGH SCHOOL.
LOOK IN LOCKER 213.
SEE, SAM, I'M THE REASON YOU HAD TO GO.

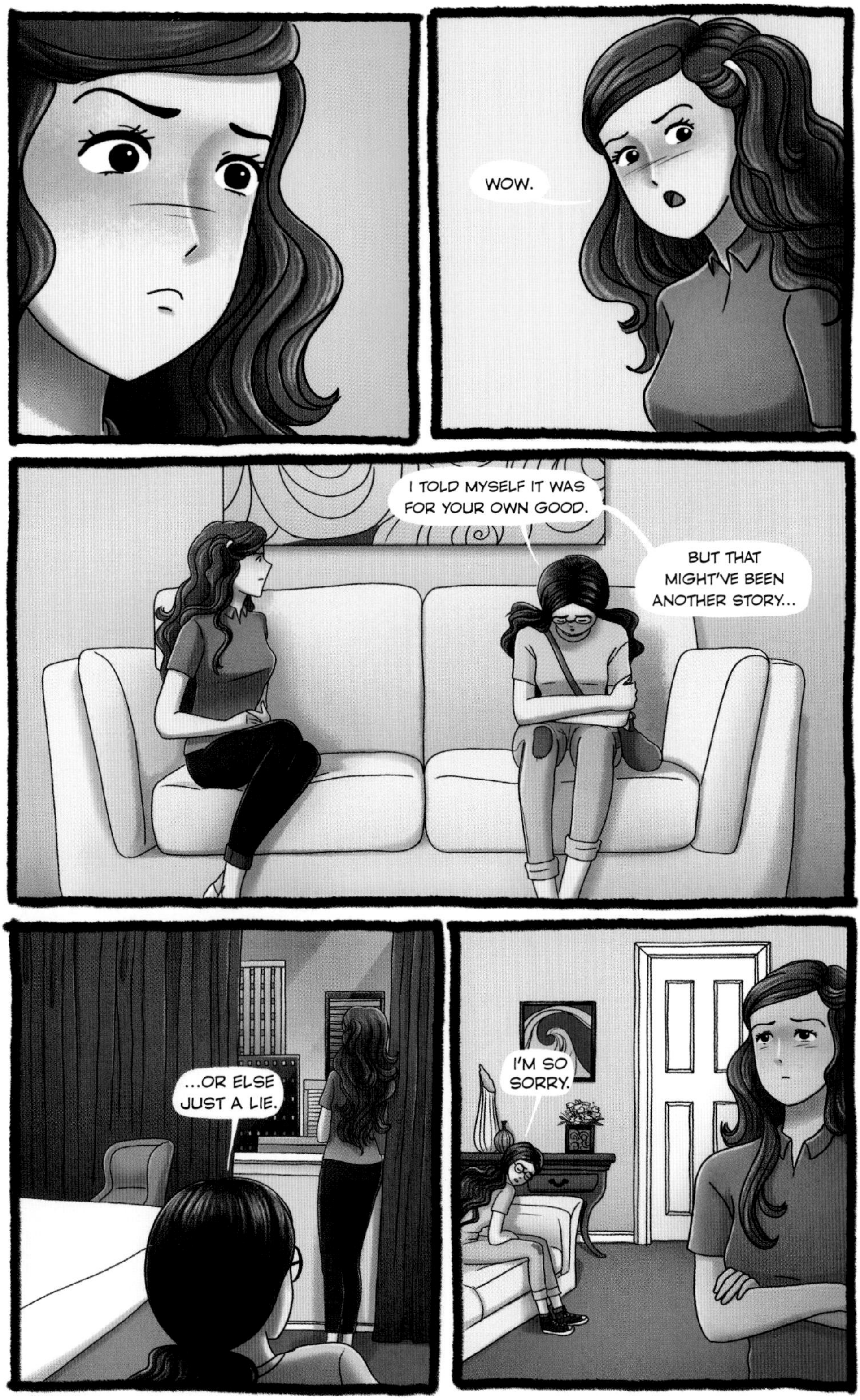
WOW.
I TOLD MYSELF IT WAS FOR YOUR OWN GOOD.
BUT THAT MIGHT'VE BEEN ANOTHER STORY...
...OR ELSE JUST A LIE.
I'M SO SORRY.

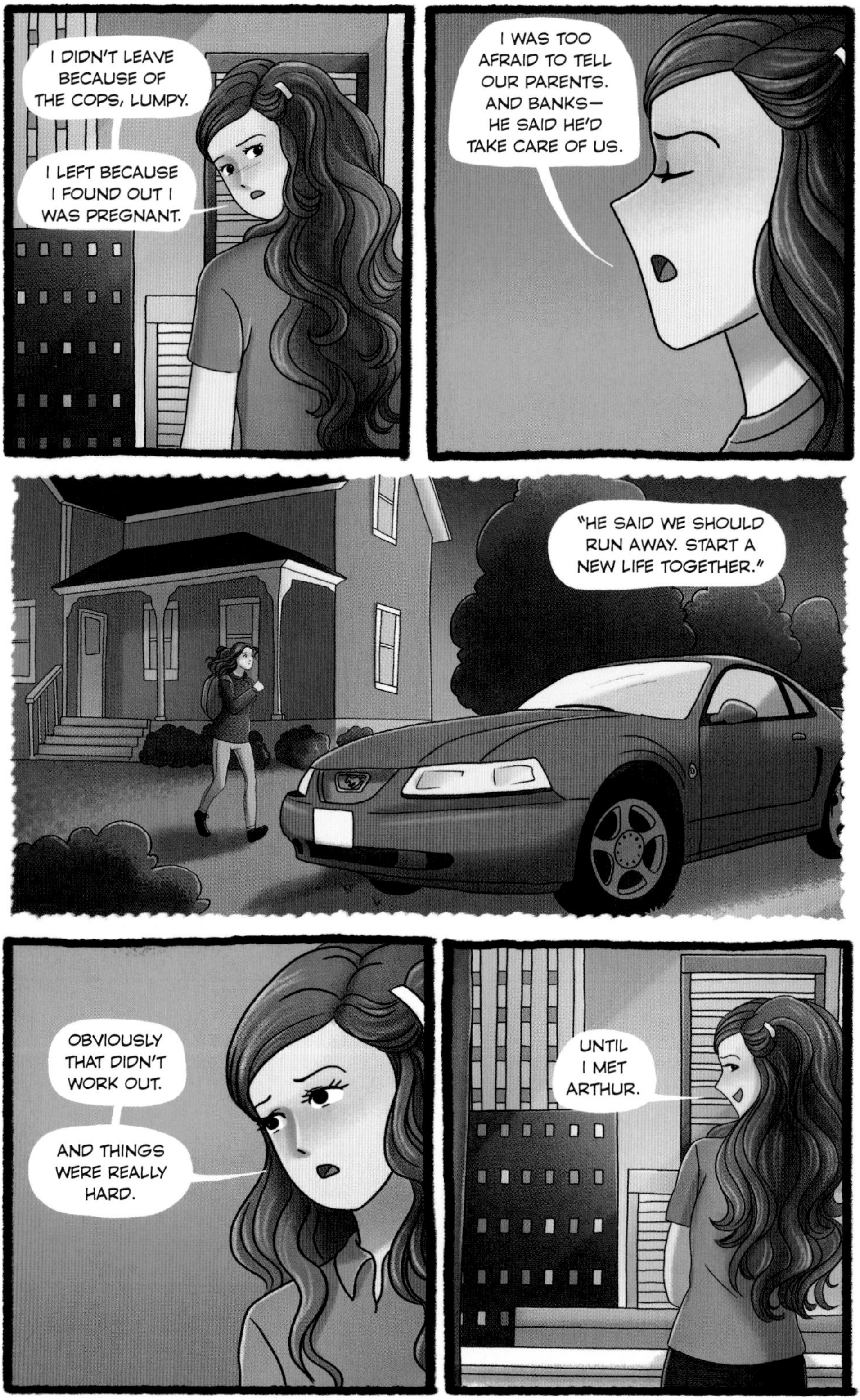
I DIDN'T LEAVE BECAUSE OF THE COPS, LUMPY.
I LEFT BECAUSE I FOUND OUT I WAS PREGNANT.
I WAS TOO AFRAID TO TELL OUR PARENTS. AND BANKS— HE SAID HE'D TAKE CARE OF US.
"HE SAID WE SHOULD RUN AWAY. START A NEW LIFE TOGETHER."
OBVIOUSLY THAT DIDN'T WORK OUT.
AND THINGS WERE REALLY HARD.
UNTIL I MET ARTHUR.

YOU'RE NOT DATING HIM, ARE YOU? HE'S, LIKE, 40!

NO. HE PAID ME TO POSE FOR HIM. ENOUGH TO AFFORD A ROOM IN A LITTLE APARTMENT. ENOUGH TO LIVE ON FOR A WHILE. MONEY FOR FOOD. DIAPERS, ONCE LILY WAS BORN.

YOU WERE PREGNANT IN THOSE PICTURES HE TOOK!

YEAH. I LOOKED PRETTY GOOD, DIDN'T I? EVEN THOUGH I HAD MORNING SICKNESS BASICALLY 24/7.

GOD, I BARFED EVERYWHERE.

OH, MY GOD, LIKE AT MEAN MR. MUSTARD'S...

YEAH. THAT WAS REALLY EMBARASSING.

I WAS SO WORRIED, SAM. WHY DIDN'T YOU CALL ME BACK? I LEFT YOU A MILLION MESSAGES.

I DIDN'T GET ANY.

WAAAH

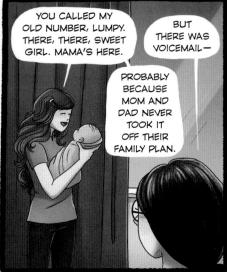

YOU CALLED MY OLD NUMBER, LUMPY. THERE, THERE, SWEET GIRL. MAMA'S HERE.

BUT THERE WAS VOICEMAIL—

PROBABLY BECAUSE MOM AND DAD NEVER TOOK IT OFF THEIR FAMILY PLAN.

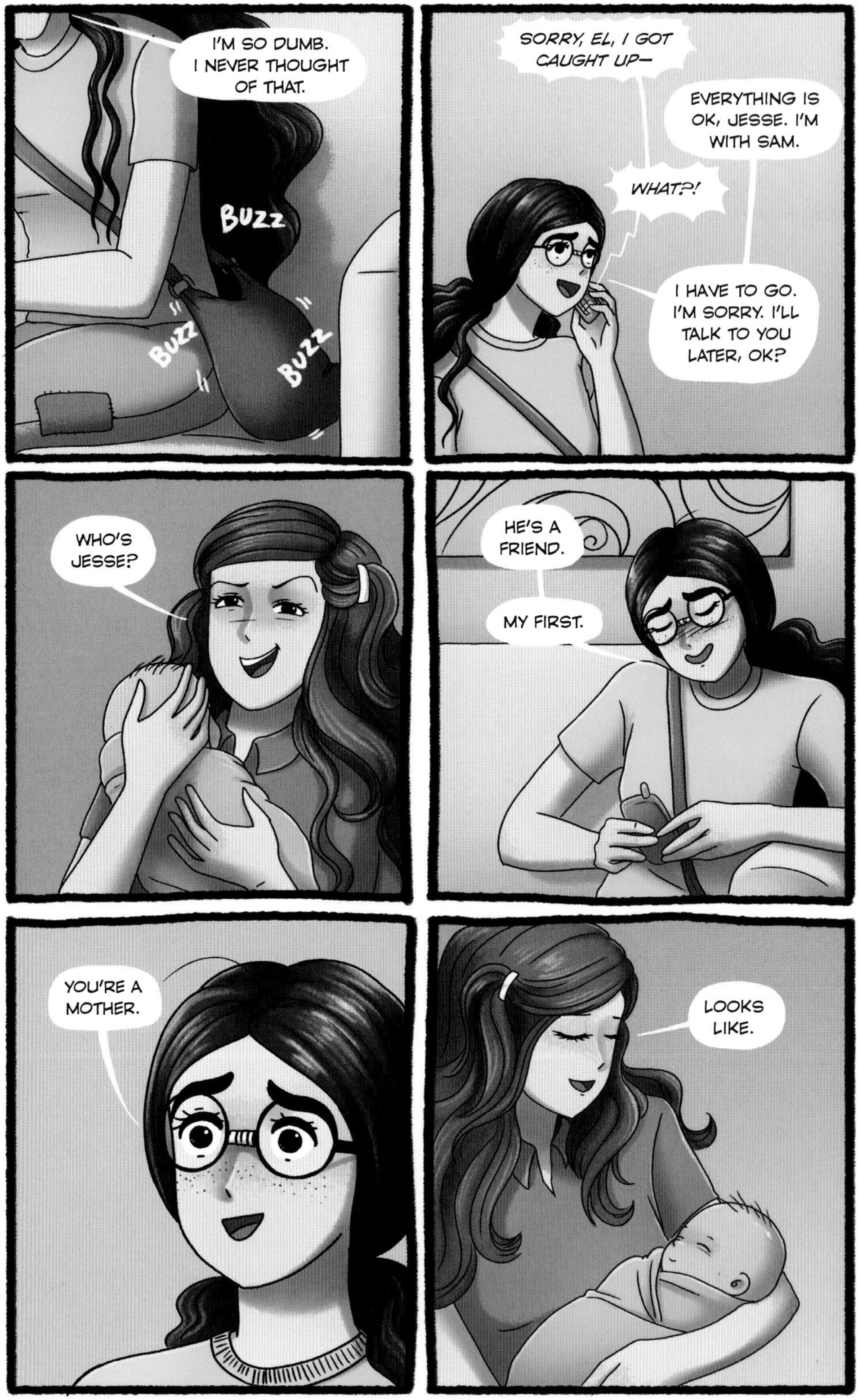
I'M SO DUMB. I NEVER THOUGHT OF THAT.
BUZZ
BUZZ
BUZZ
SORRY, EL, I GOT CAUGHT UP—
EVERYTHING IS OK, JESSE. I'M WITH SAM.
WHAT?!
I HAVE TO GO. I'M SORRY. I'LL TALK TO YOU LATER, OK?
WHO'S JESSE?
HE'S A FRIEND.
MY FIRST.
YOU'RE A MOTHER.
LOOKS LIKE.

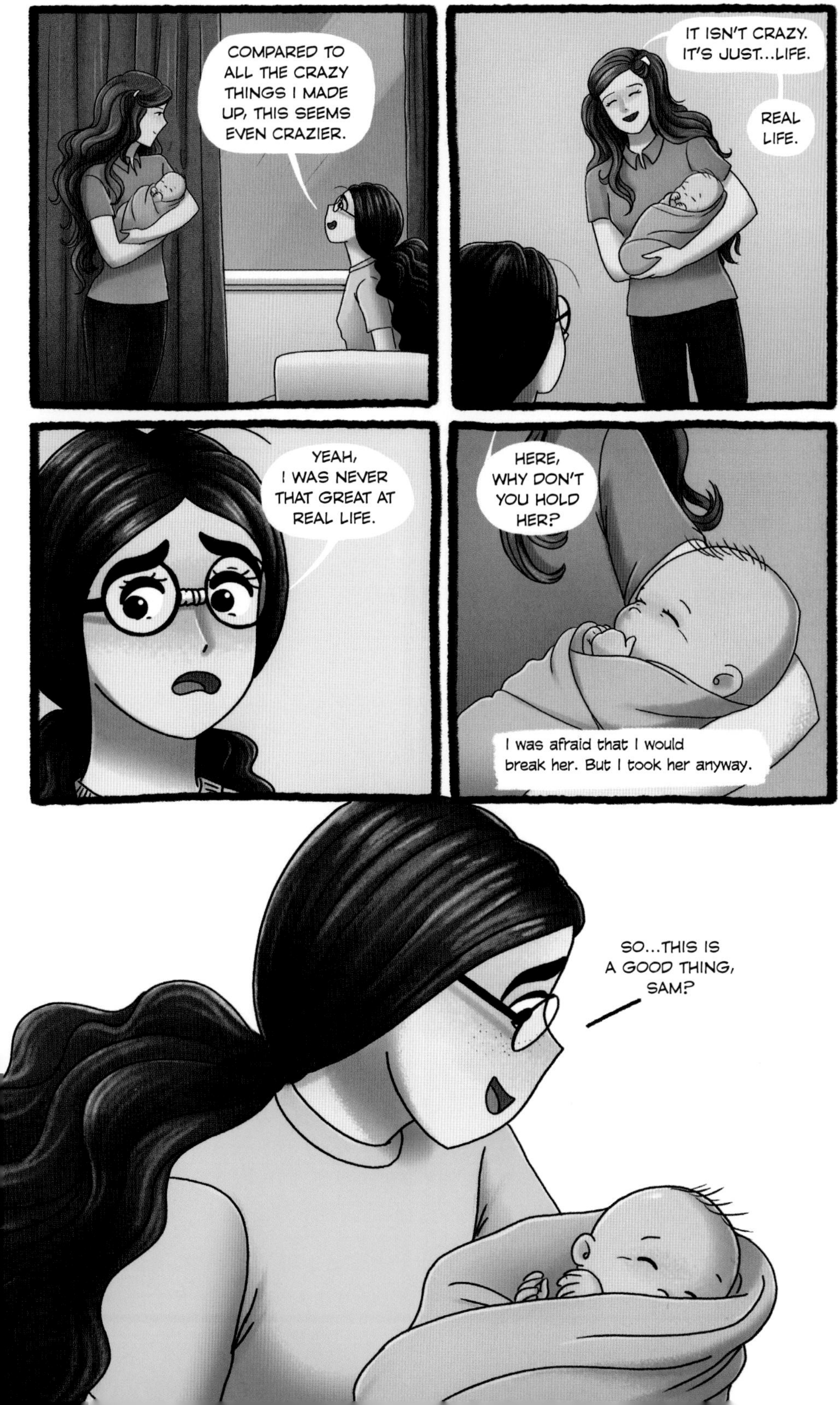
COMPARED TO ALL THE CRAZY THINGS I MADE UP, THIS SEEMS EVEN CRAZIER.
IT ISN'T CRAZY. IT'S JUST...LIFE.
REAL LIFE.
YEAH, I WAS NEVER THAT GREAT AT REAL LIFE.
HERE, WHY DON'T YOU HOLD HER?
I was afraid that I would break her. But I took her anyway.
SO...THIS IS A GOOD THING, SAM?

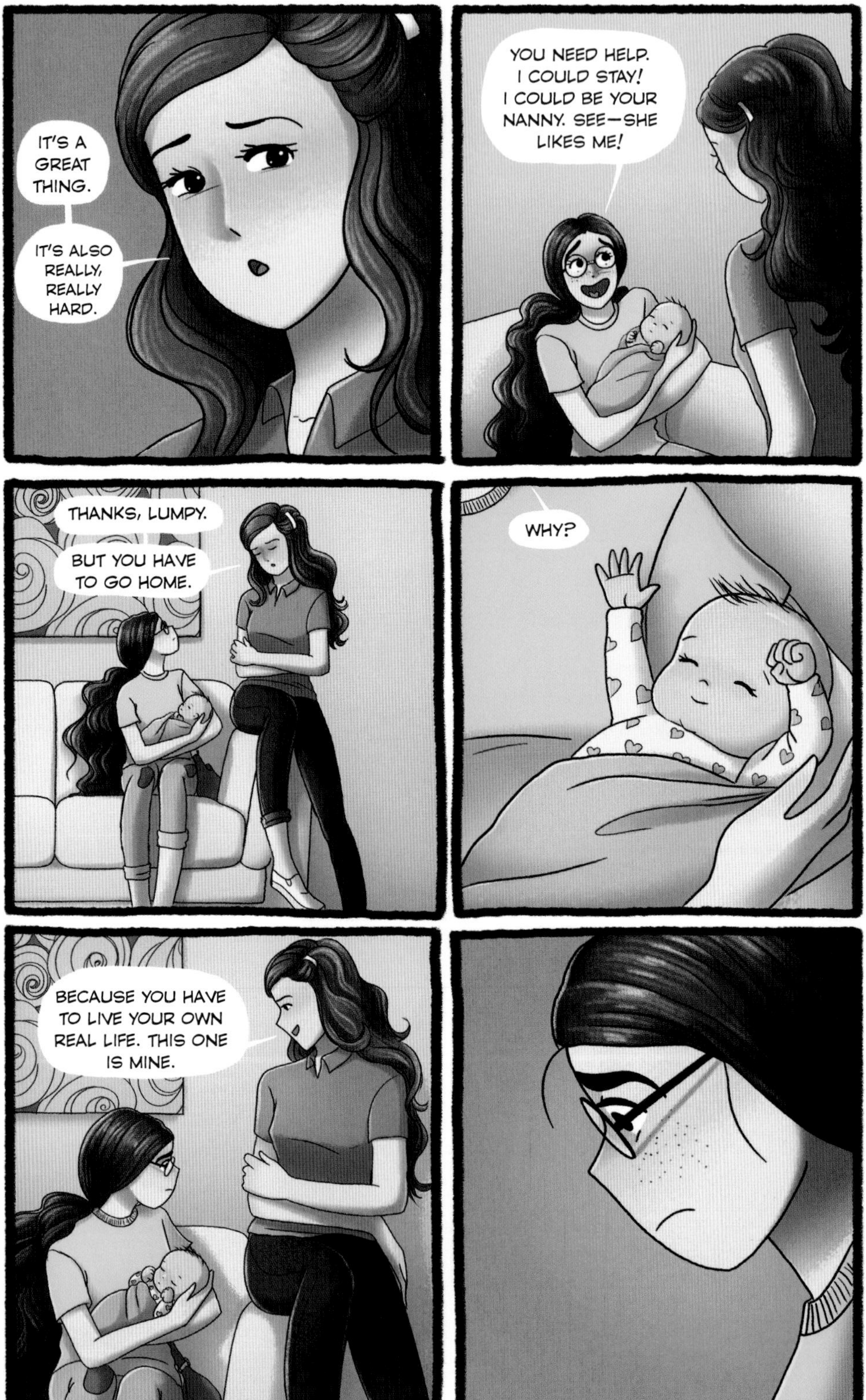
IT'S A GREAT THING.
IT'S ALSO REALLY, REALLY HARD.
YOU NEED HELP. I COULD STAY! I COULD BE YOUR NANNY. SEE—SHE LIKES ME!
THANKS, LUMPY.
BUT YOU HAVE TO GO HOME.
WHY?
BECAUSE YOU HAVE TO LIVE YOUR OWN REAL LIFE. THIS ONE IS MINE.

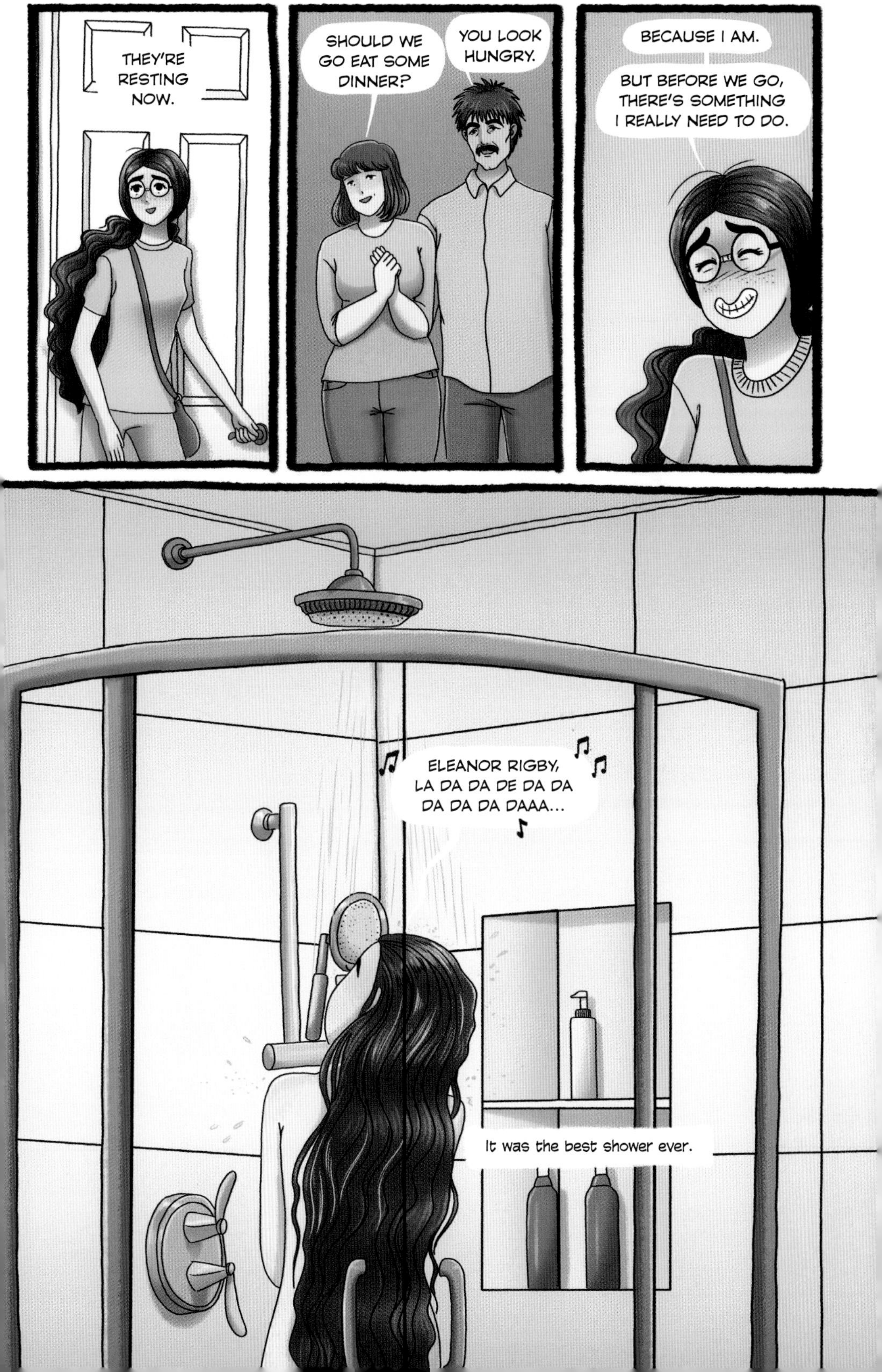
THEY'RE RESTING NOW.
SHOULD WE GO EAT SOME DINNER?
YOU LOOK HUNGRY.
BECAUSE I AM.
BUT BEFORE WE GO, THERE'S SOMETHING I REALLY NEED TO DO.
ELEANOR RIGBY, LA DA DA DE DA DA DA DA DA DAAA...
It was the best shower ever.

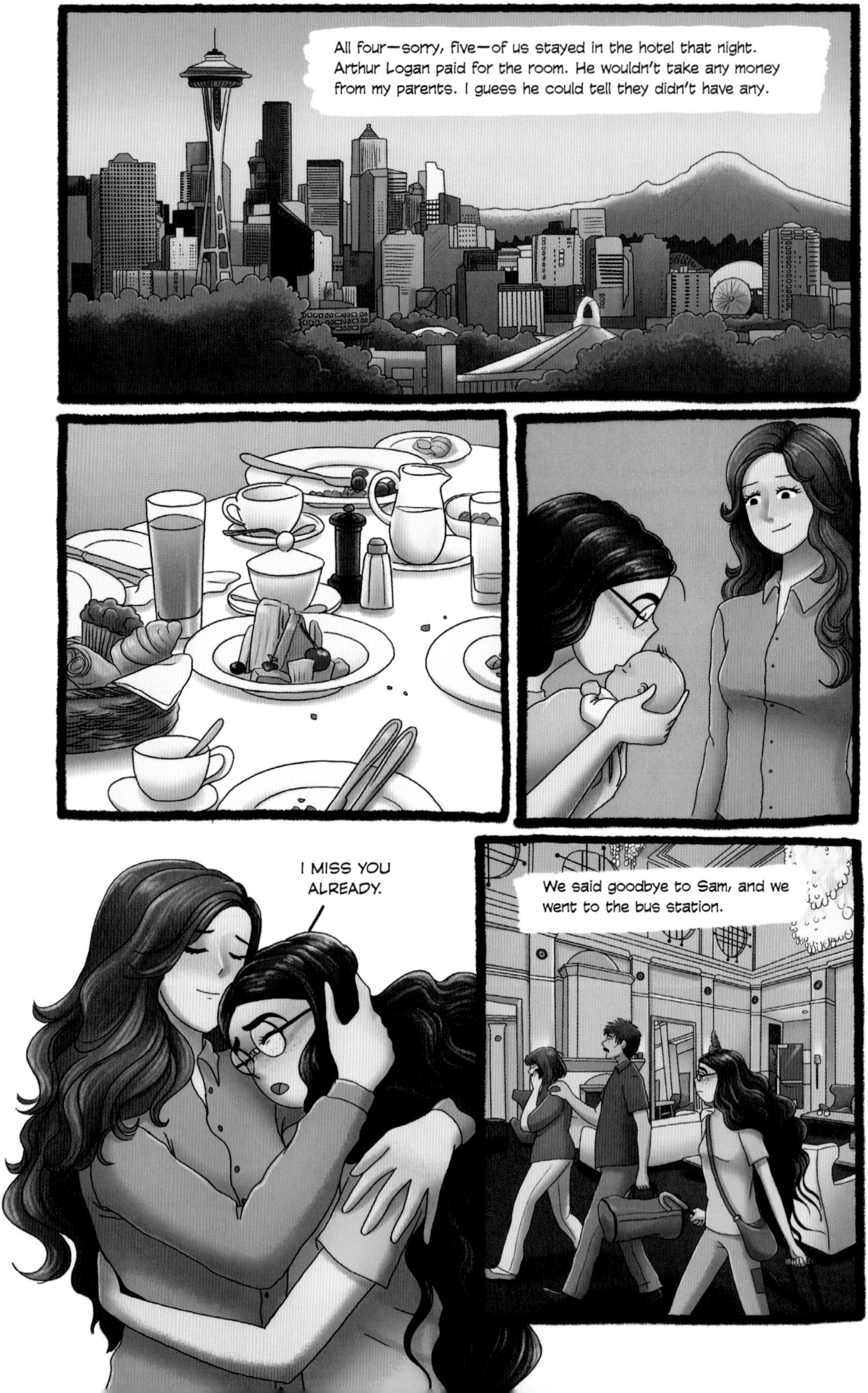
All four—sorry, five—of us stayed in the hotel that night. Arthur Logan paid for the room. He wouldn't take any money from my parents. I guess he could tell they didn't have any.
I MISS YOU ALREADY.
We said goodbye to Sam, and we went to the bus station.

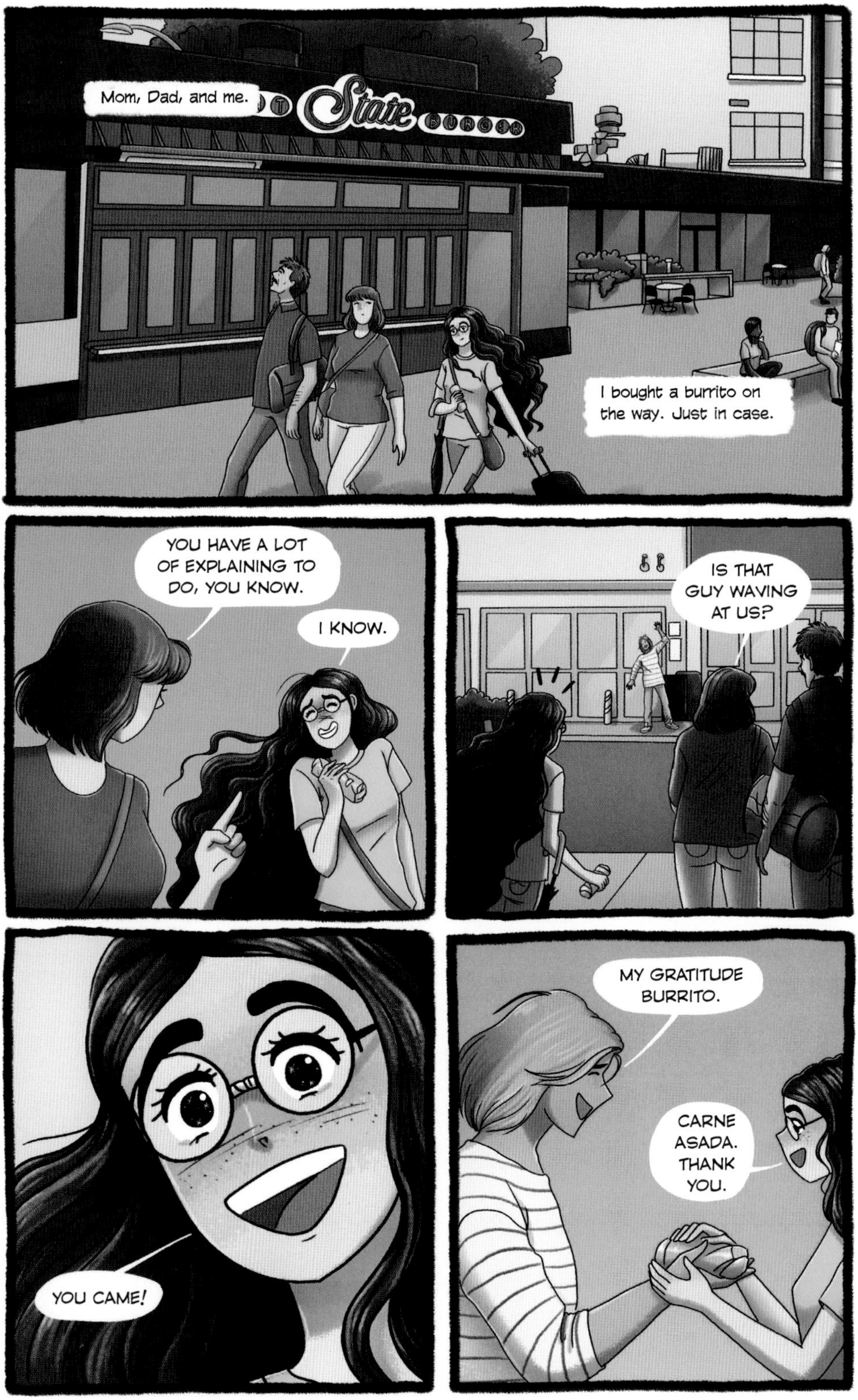
Mom, Dad, and me.
State Burger
I bought a burrito on the way. Just in case.
YOU HAVE A LOT OF EXPLAINING TO DO, YOU KNOW.
I KNOW.
IS THAT GUY WAVING AT US?
YOU CAME!
MY GRATITUDE BURRITO.
CARNE ASADA. THANK YOU.

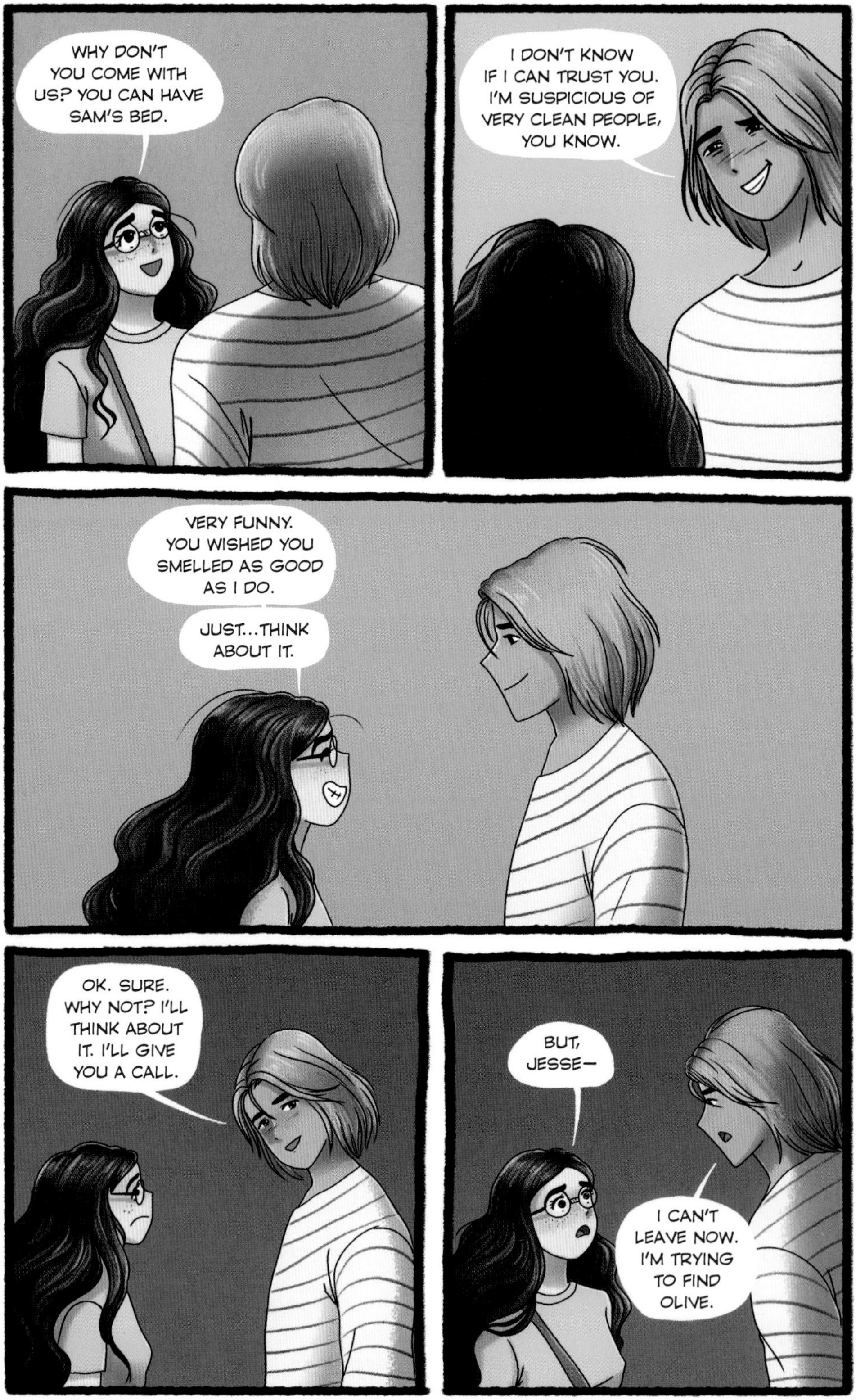
WHY DON'T YOU COME WITH US? YOU CAN HAVE SAM'S BED.
I DON'T KNOW IF I CAN TRUST YOU. I'M SUSPICIOUS OF VERY CLEAN PEOPLE, YOU KNOW.
VERY FUNNY. YOU WISHED YOU SMELLED AS GOOD AS I DO.
JUST...THINK ABOUT IT.
OK. SURE. WHY NOT? I'LL THINK ABOUT IT. I'LL GIVE YOU A CALL.
BUT, JESSE—
I CAN'T LEAVE NOW. I'M TRYING TO FIND OLIVE.

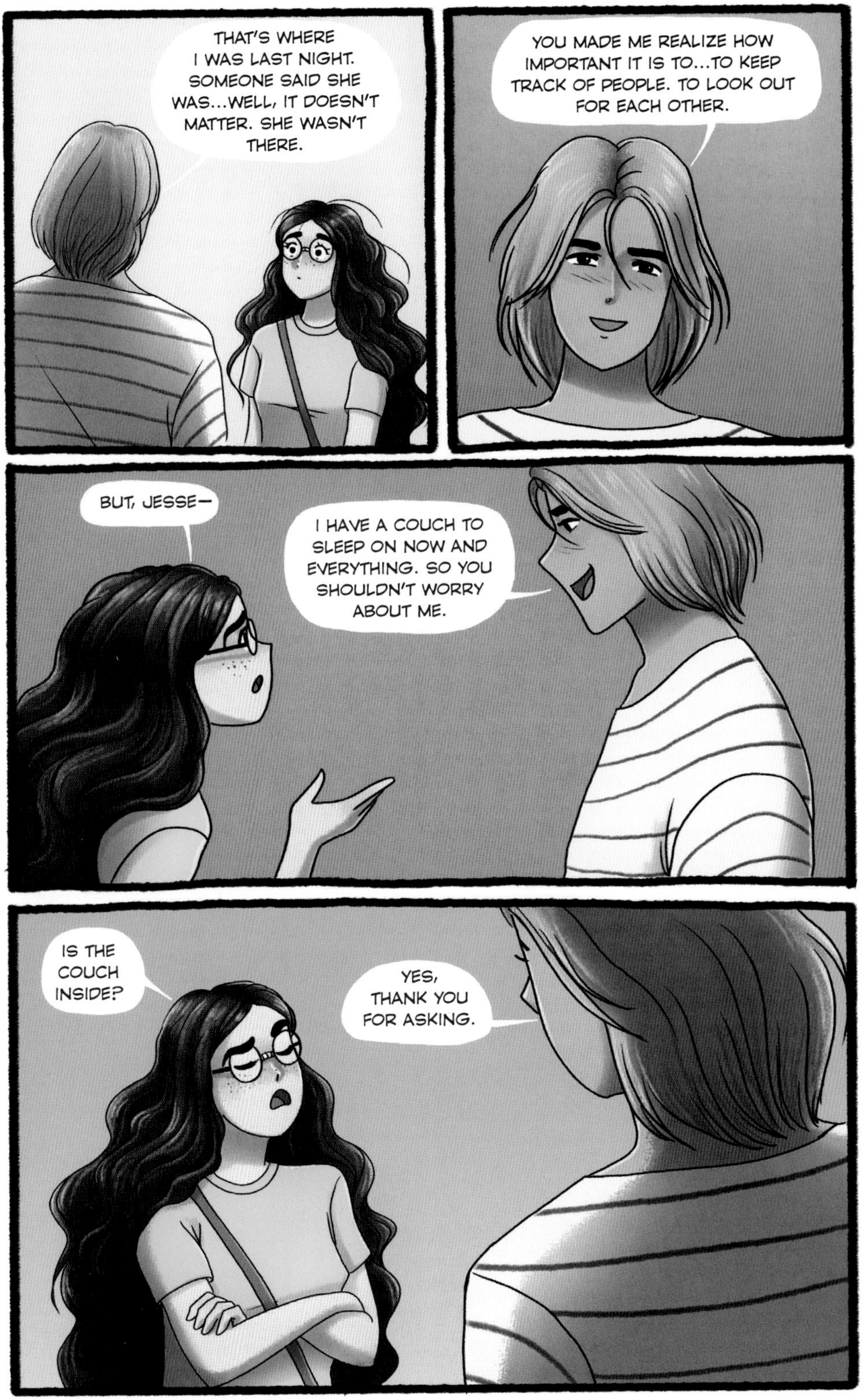
THAT'S WHERE I WAS LAST NIGHT. SOMEONE SAID SHE WAS...WELL, IT DOESN'T MATTER. SHE WASN'T THERE.
YOU MADE ME REALIZE HOW IMPORTANT IT IS TO...TO KEEP TRACK OF PEOPLE. TO LOOK OUT FOR EACH OTHER.
BUT, JESSE—
I HAVE A COUCH TO SLEEP ON NOW AND EVERYTHING. SO YOU SHOULDN'T WORRY ABOUT ME.
IS THE COUCH INSIDE?
YES, THANK YOU FOR ASKING.

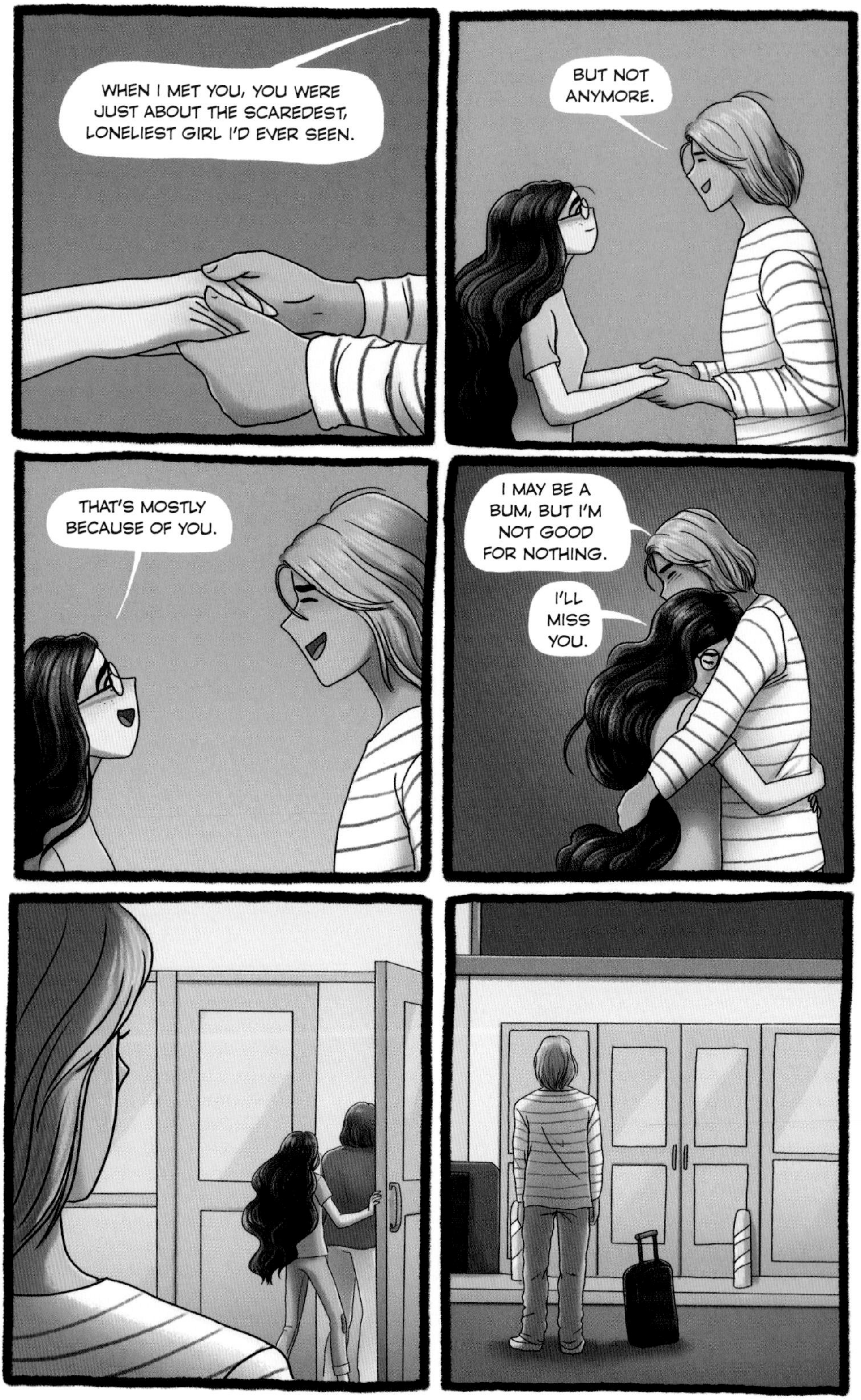
WHEN I MET YOU, YOU WERE JUST ABOUT THE SCAREDEST, LONELIEST GIRL I'D EVER SEEN.
BUT NOT ANYMORE.
THAT'S MOSTLY BECAUSE OF YOU.
I MAY BE A BUM, BUT I'M NOT GOOD FOR NOTHING.
I'LL MISS YOU.

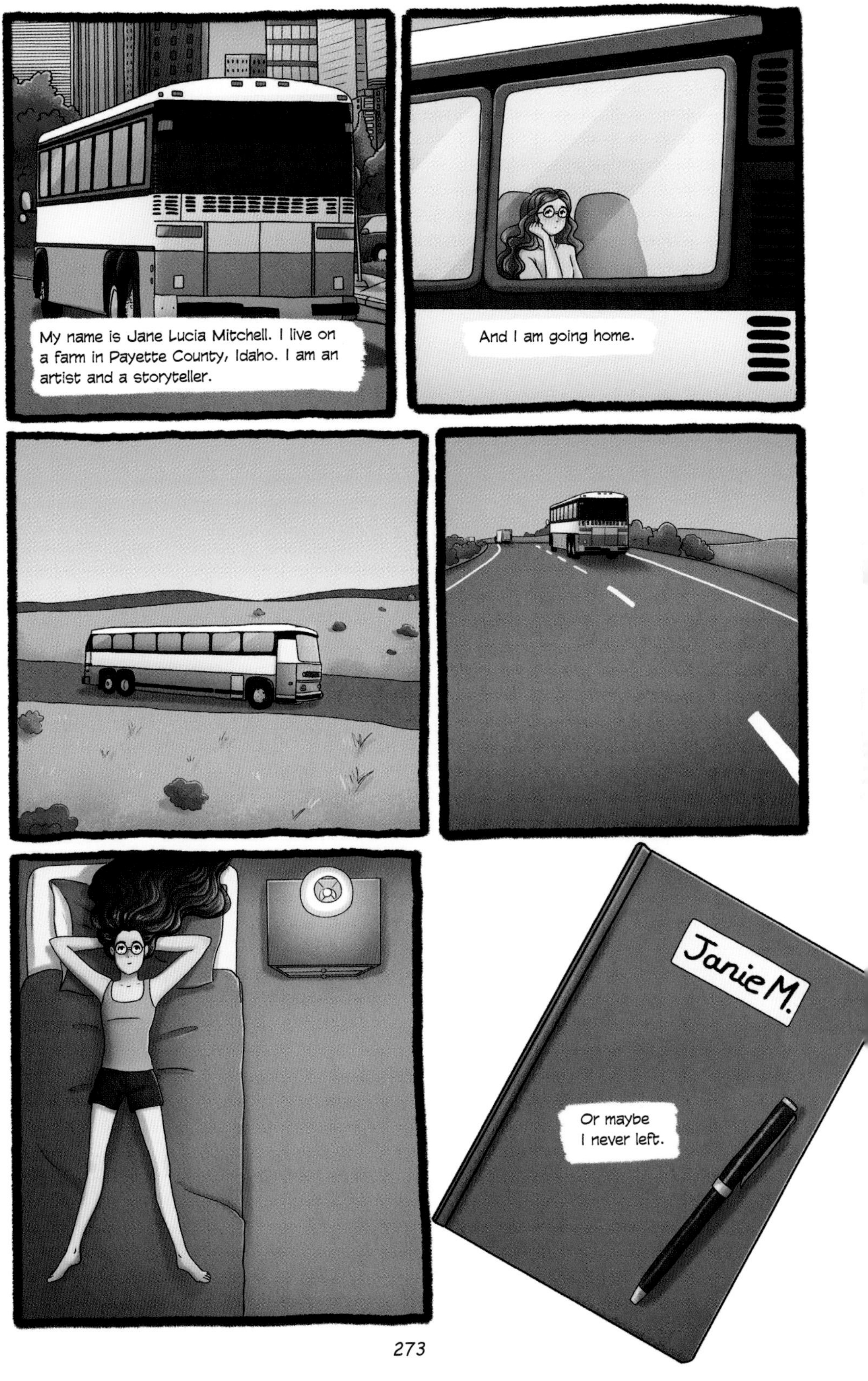
My name is Jane Lucia Mitchell. I live on a farm in Payette County, Idaho. I am an artist and a storyteller.
And I am going home.
Janie M.
Or maybe I never left.

About the Authors

For his prodigious imagination and championship of literacy in America, **James Patterson** was awarded the 2019 National Humanities Medal, and he has also received the Literarian Award for Outstanding Service to the American Literary Community from the National Book Foundation. He holds the Guinness World Record for the most #1 *New York Times* bestsellers, including *Confessions of a Murder Suspect* and the Maximum Ride and Witch & Wizard series, and his books have sold more than 400 million copies worldwide. A tireless champion of the power of books and reading, Patterson created a children's book imprint, JIMMY Patterson, whose mission is simple: "We want every kid who finishes a JIMMY Book to say, 'PLEASE GIVE ME ANOTHER BOOK.'" He has donated more than three million books to students and soldiers and funds over four hundred Teacher and Writer Education Scholarships at twenty-one colleges and universities. He also supports 40,000 school libraries and has donated millions of dollars to independent bookstores. Patterson invests proceeds from the sales of JIMMY Patterson Books in pro-reading initiatives.

Emily Raymond worked with James Patterson on *First Love* and *The Lost*, and is the ghostwriter of six young adult novels, one of which was a #1 *New York Times* bestseller. She lives with her family in Portland, Oregon.

Valeria Wicker is an Italian art school graduate passionate about all types of art. When she's not drawing, she can be found in her shop working on projects such as carving wood sculptures, restoring antique trunks, and refinishing furniture. Valeria resides in eastern Pennsylvania with her husband Mike, their five beautiful children, a bunny, and an adorable teddy-bear-like Labrador named Mia.

JIMMY Patterson Books for Young Adult Readers

Confessions

Confessions of a Murder Suspect
Confessions: The Private School Murders
Confessions: The Paris Mysteries
Confessions: The Murder of an Angel

Crazy House

Crazy House
The Fall of Crazy House

Maximum Ride

The Angel Experiment
School's Out—Forever
Saving the World and Other Extreme Sports
The Final Warning
MAX
FANG
ANGEL
Nevermore
Maximum Ride Forever
Hawk
City of the Dead

Witch & Wizard

Witch & Wizard

The Gift

The Fire

The Kiss

The Lost

Cradle and All

First Love

Homeroom Diaries

Med Head

Sophia, Princess Among Beasts

The Injustice

The Runaway's Diary

For exclusives, trailers, and other information, visit jimmypatterson.org.

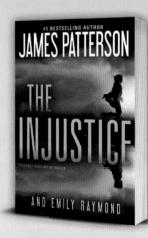

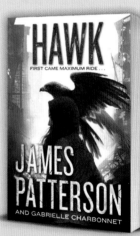